MW01028142

THE CHRONICLES OF
MALUS DARKBLADE
VOLUME ONE

THE DARK ELVES are feared throughout the Old World for their evil, savage ways, yet one member of this despicable race stands out for his treachery and cunning – Malus Darkblade. Tricked by the ancient daemon Tz'arkan, Darkblade is faced with a stark choice – recover five items of unimaginable power within one year or lose his soul!

This volume tells of Malus's quest to find the first three artefacts, pitting him against monsters, magic and even his own kin in wonderful tales of dark fantasy.

The Daemon's Curse: When he steals a map to a secret power hidden deep within the Chaos Wastes, Malus collects his warriors and sets off to seek his fortune. But Malus is outwitted by the daemon guardian of the treasure, who forces him into a terrible bargain.

Bloodstorm: Malus has only a year to find the five artefacts that the daemon Tz'arkan covets, or his soul will be forfeit. To retrieve the Idol of Kolkuth, Malus has to call on all his wits and cunning to survive a magic labyrinth and its fearsome guardian.

Reaper of Souls: Malus Darkblade must now steal the Dagger of Torxus, but the blood he spills to do so comes at a high cost, making him an outlaw even in the cruel and unprincipled society of the dark elves.

In the same series

DARKBLADE: WARPSWORD
DARKBLADE: LORD OF RUIN
by Dan Abnett & Mike Lee

More Warhammer Omnibuses from the Black Library

GOTREK & FELIX: THE FIRST OMNIBUS
by William King

(Contains the novels
Trollslayer, Skavenslayer and *Daemonslayer*)

GOTREK & FELIX: THE SECOND OMNIBUS
by William King

(Contains the novels
Dragonslayer, Beastslayer and *Vampireslayer*)

THE VAMPIRE GENEVIEVE
by Jack Yeovil

(Contains the novels
Drachenfels, Genevieve Undead, Beasts in Velvet and *Silver Nails*)

BLACKHEARTS: THE OMNIBUS
by Nathan Long

(Contains the novels
Valnir's Blood, Broken Lance and *Tainted Blood*)

VAMPIRE WARS: THE VON CARSTEIN TRILOGY
by Steven Savile

(Contains the novels
Inheritance, Dominion and *Retribution*)

THE AMBASSADOR CHRONICLES
by Graham McNeill

(Contains the novels
The Ambassador and *Ursun's Teeth*)

A WARHAMMER ANTHOLOGY

THE CHRONICLES OF
MALUS DARKBLADE
VOLUME ONE

DAN ABNETT
& MIKE LEE

A Black Library Publication

The Daemon's Curse and *Bloodstorm* copyright © 2005 Games Workshop Ltd.
Reaper of Souls copyright © 2006 Games Workshop Ltd.

This omnibus edition published in Great Britain in 2008 by
BL Publishing,
Games Workshop Ltd.,
Willow Road, Nottingham,
NG7 2WS, UK.

10 9 8 7 6 5 4 3 2

Cover illustration by Clint Langley.
Map by Nuala Kinrade.

Black Library, the Black Library logo, Black Flame, BL Publishing, Games Workshop,
the Games Workshop logo and all associated marks, names, characters, illustrations
and images from the Warhammer universe are either ®, TM and/or © Games
Workshop Ltd 2000-2008, variably registered in the UK and other countries around
the world. All rights reserved.

A CIP record for this book is available from the British Library.

ISBN 13: 978 1 84416 563 6
ISBN 10: 1 84416 563 9

Distributed in the US by Simon & Schuster
1230 Avenue of the Americas, New York, NY 10020, US.

No part of this publication may be reproduced, stored in a retrieval system, or
transmitted in any form or by any means, electronic, mechanical, photocopying,
recording or otherwise, without the prior permission of the publishers.

This is a work of fiction. All the characters and events portrayed in this book are
fictional, and any resemblance to real people or incidents is purely coincidental.

See the Black Library on the Internet at
www.blacklibrary.com

Find out more about Games Workshop
and the world of Warhammer at
www.games-workshop.com

Printed and bound in the US.

THIS IS A DARK age, a bloody age, an age of daemons
and of sorcery. It is an age of battle and death, and of the
world's ending. Amidst all of the fire, flame and fury
it is a time, too, of mighty heroes, of bold deeds
and great courage.

AT THE HEART of the Old World sprawls the Empire, the
largest and most powerful of the human realms. Known for
its engineers, sorcerers, traders and soldiers, it is
a land of great mountains, mighty rivers, dark forests
and vast cities. And from his throne in Altdorf reigns
the Emperor Karl Franz, sacred descendant of the
founder of these lands, Sigmar, and wielder
of his magical warhammer.

BUT THESE ARE far from civilised times. Across the length
and breadth of the Old World, from the knightly palaces
of Bretonnia to ice-bound Kislev in the far north, come
rumblings of war. In the towering World's Edge Mountains,
the orc tribes are gathering for another assault. Bandits and
renegades harry the wild southern lands of
the Border Princes. There are rumours of rat-things, the
skaven, emerging from the sewers and swamps across the
land. And from the northern wildernesses there is the
ever-present threat of Chaos, of daemons and beastmen
corrupted by the foul powers of the Dark Gods.
As the time of battle draws ever near,
the Empire needs heroes
like never before.

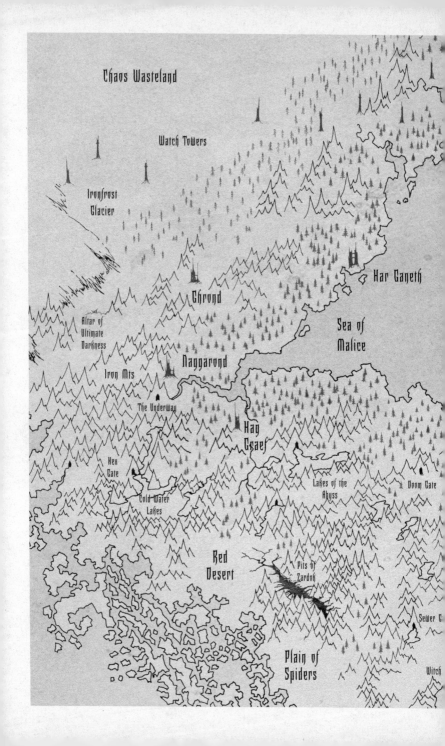

NAGGAROTH

Karond Kar

Sea of Chill

The Monoliths

Granite Hills

Hotek's Column

Black Forests

N

Clar Karond

Vaul's Anvil

Doom Glades

Sea of Serpents

Grasslands

Arnheim

CONTENTS

AUTHORS' INTRODUCTION

Contained herein are the first three novels from the tales of Malus Dark-blade. Talking to the Black Library, authors Dan Abnett and Mike Lee trawl the depths of their collective psyche to reflect on the creation and development of this infamous dark elf anti-hero.

Black Library: Where did the idea for Malus Darkblade come from and how did it develop?

Dan: You know, I'm not entirely sure. The most honest answer to that is probably a little lame. I'd just started working with the Black Library, and Malus was one of the first characters I came up with. I think, in fact, that Black Library founders Andy Jones and Marc Gascoigne suggested I looked at dark elves as a possible basis for a comic strip (Darkblade began as a comic strip for *Warhammer Monthly*). I was still very much learning the ropes in terms of both the Warhammer and Warhammer 40,000 universes, and the dark elves had an instant appeal in terms of their look and style. Put simply, to a newcomer, they seemed easy to grasp: very pure and direct. And, of course, very evil. There was no point trying to devise a story about an uncharacteristically nice or heroic dark elf. From the outset, it was going to be a tale where the central character was entirely villainous.

Mike: Well, I can't lay claim to the original idea, of course, but the development of the character stemmed from a conversation I had with

Dan Abnett and Marc Gascoigne at San Diego Comic Con back in 2005. We sat around for a bit and discussed the essential elements of Malus's personality, and what sorts of things we wanted to see from the character going forward, and then I took things from there. The one thing that Dan really emphasized about Malus was that he wasn't necessarily the smartest, the strongest, or the deadliest druchii out there. What made him special was that, no matter how bad things got or how far the odds were stacked against him, he simply *would not quit*. This was the one quality that set him apart from everyone else, and it became the touchstone for everything I did with the character going forward.

When we sat down to plan out the story arc for the first series, I wanted Malus to grow and change over the course of the books. At the beginning of the first novel he's young and reckless, staying one step ahead of his enemies by virtue of fast thinking and his family connections. Over the course of the stories, however, the rash decisions he makes come back to haunt him, sometimes in unexpected ways. Dealing with the consequences of those decisions transforms Malus from a callow young noble into a force to be reckoned with.

Black Library: Why do you think the Darkblade series has become so popular?

Dan: Two reasons, really. I think it appealed to readers in the same way it appealed to me as a writer: Malus was a bad guy, and it made a change to focus narrative attention on an evil character. Malus's cruel and wicked streak captured the nasty, bleak characteristics of Warhammer particularly well. It wasn't a safe or cosy fantasy tale, and that was Warhammer to a 'T'. The other factor was his look. Malus and Spite, as originally drawn by Kev Hopgood, were an instantly iconic duo. In the novels, Mike Lee's fabulous contributions have helped to add great depth and texture to the stories. Darkblade is very sinister, very macabre and very atmospheric.

Mike: The thing I hear most from readers is that, as awful as Malus is, before long they can't help but find themselves rooting for him! He's the quintessential anti-hero: treacherous, spiteful and vicious (even to his friends), and I think that makes a refreshing change from typical fantasy protagonists.

Black Library: In Darkblade all the characters are evil, and some are even more evil than others! As an author, what special challenge does this present?

Dan: Yes, they are all evil. The challenge was to create degrees of that, and to give the reader someone that it was possible to root for, otherwise it would all become rather nasty and unrelenting. I think Malus's sheer villainy and ruthlessness can be a huge source of fun but by involving him with a character like Tz'arkan, you almost end up feeling sorry for him.

Mike: I knew from the outset that the only way to be true to Malus's personality – and yet make him a character that readers could sympathize with – was to make his enemies even more horrible and vicious than he was! I also wanted to provide a logical context for his actions, so I put a lot of thought into how druchii society worked and why they did the things they did. Malus is a product of his culture – from a druchii standpoint, Darkblade would be their idea of an epic hero, a paragon of their own twisted virtues.

Black Library: Who is your favourite supporting character in the Darkblade series, and why?

Dan: Working with Mike on the novels, it's been possible to flesh out the original stories to a much greater depth and complexity, and add in many wonderful new characters. It's actually hard to pick a favourite. I would like to cast a special vote for Spite, though. He's stoic and faithful in his way and, hey, he's a cold one.

Mike: Why, Hauclir, of course! The funny thing is that I'd never intended him to be a major, recurring character; he wasn't originally going to survive past chapter two in *Bloodstorm*. On a whim, I decided to keep him around, and he turned into the perfect foil for Malus's grandiose schemes. He's smart, sarcastic and surprisingly down-to-earth for a druchii, and his black humour is a great counterpoint to Malus's constant brooding.

Black Library: What's the most common question you get asked about Dark-blade?

Dan: 'When can we have some more?' Soon, I hope. Not too far in the future.

Mike: Yep, the most common question is: 'When will the next book be out?'

Black Library: What do you consider to be Malus Darkblade's greatest asset, and his most debilitating weakness?

Dan: Malus's greatest assets are his ruthlessness and ambition. He simply never gives up until he gets what he wants, whatever the cost. And those qualities are most definitely his greatest weaknesses too. In the end, he's his own worst enemy.

Mike: As Dan first pointed out, Darkblade's greatest asset is that he just won't quit – he simply doesn't accept defeat. The only way to really stop him is to kill him, and that's much easier said than done.

His most debilitating weakness? Goodness. I have to pick just one? Honestly, it's probably his impetuousness. Malus tends to act first and think about the consequences later, and no matter how bad things get, he always believes he can stay one step ahead of everyone else.

Black Library: Who is the most evil, in your opinion – Malus Darkblade or Tz'arkan?

Dan: Well, Tz'arkan is a daemon, so on the cosmic scale of things, he clearly wins on points. He's a force of evil that eclipses Malus for sheer power. But he IS also a daemon, and therefore has absolutely no choice in the matter. Evil is what he is. Malus, on the other hand, is a dark elf, and though that race might be culturally, genetically and even magically predisposed to what we would call evil, his actions are always choices. Like all dark elves, he's not stupid. He must be aware that there are alternative, positive moral choices he could make. They just don't appeal to him. Tz'arkan couldn't be good even if he tried. Malus could, even though it's very unlikely, and that factor of choice, in my opinion, makes Malus the more evil of the two.

Mike: Tz'arkan of course. Malus is merciless and evil by human standards, but even he has his limits. Tz'arkan is a daemon. He's evil personified.

Black Library: How have you found the collaborative writing experience?

Dan: Excellent. I couldn't have wished for a more diligent, talented and creative writing partner than Mike. He deserves a huge amount of credit for the ideas he has invested in the series.

Mike: It's been fantastic, honestly. Dan's been closely involved in the evolution of the series, and his insights and suggestions have been a huge help to me in bringing these books to fruition. I'm hoping I'll have the opportunity to collaborate with him on future projects!

Black Library: What does the future hold for Darkblade?

Dan: The first five novels adapt and expand the original comic series, which was collected in just the first of three graphic novels. I would love to see those other stories get the novel treatment, and that's something I hope Mike and I can undertake before too long.

Mike: That's an excellent question! There's still a great deal more stories to be told about Malus and his adventures – just going by Dan's graphic novels alone we could write ten more novels at least! When we first sat down to plan out the first five books, we went into it with the idea of creating an epic story arc that went well beyond the first series of stories. As long as the fans are interested in seeing more of Malus and his cohorts, I'd say that chances are good there will be more Darkblade novels in the future.

THE BLOOD PRICE

A FOREST OF black oak masts shifted and swayed in the bitter wind blowing from the Sea of Malice, causing the druchii sailors to hunch their shoulders and curse the Dragons Below as they went about their work. Captains bellowed between the gusts and leather lashes cracked. Slaves struggled beneath the weight of crates, baskets and canvas sacks, staggering up shifting gangplanks to unload their burdens in the black holds of sleek-hulled raiding ships. The docks at Clar Karond, City of Ships, bustled like an ant hive as the corsairs of Naggaroth made ready for sea.

At the far end of the docks a captain of the city guard nosed his black warhorse into the chaotic crowds, hissing curses and laying about with his cudgel to clear a path through the bedlam. A half-dozen guardsmen walked their mounts behind his, glaring and shouting at the cursing tradesmen and the rough-voiced merchants as they made a path for the black-armoured highborn in their midst.

Malus of Hag Graef slumped forward in the saddle, bound hands clasped to the rim of the high cantle, and gritted his teeth against the savage pounding in his skull. The reins dangled loosely in his fingers as he let his borrowed horse follow its fellows through the crowd. The inside of his mouth tasted like boot leather and his bones felt like they'd been pulled out through his ears, smashed to jagged bits and poured back in again. Every sound was like a dagger thrust between his

17

eyes. As his escort ploughed their way across the dockyard he fought to keep his stomach in its proper place and swore to every god he could think of that he would never touch another drop of wine for the rest of his miserable life.

His escort shouldered its way across the traders' square and along the granite quays, passing one rakish vessel after another. Each ship crawled with dark-robed sailors working feverishly underneath the baleful gaze of their captain and his mates. Though the first day of spring was still a week away, it was a two-week journey to the Slavers' Straits in the north, and the corsair captains planned to be there the moment the narrow passages were free of ice and open to the ocean beyond. The first ships out would be the first ships to reach the rich coasts of the Old World, and to them would go the choicest spoils. A druchii slave raider had barely five months out of each year to make his fortune, and the competition for flesh and plunder was merciless and often lethal.

Down the long line of ships they went, until Malus began to wonder if the guard captain meant to drive his escort off the stone pier and into the icy waves. Finally, near the very end of the quay, the captain gave a satisfied grunt and reined in beside the gangplank of a black-hulled raider that rolled and creaked uneasily against its mooring ropes. Unlike the other ships at dock, there were no long lines of slaves labouring up to its deck. Members of the ship's crew hung like crows in the nets and rigging, studying the guardsmen with sullen interest. Standing on the dock just a few feet from the gangplank waited a solitary druchii knight, his patched cloak flapping fitfully against his armoured legs. The knight raised his pointed chin in greeting as the guard captain reined in. There was a sombre cast to his youthful features, and his black hair was drawn back in an unadorned braid. A silver steel hadrilkar gleamed about his neck, worked with the sigil of a nauglir.

'And who are you, then?' the guard captain growled into the gusting wind. His breeches and cloak were stiff with salt spray, and his plate armour was speckled with rust.

The proud knight would have bristled at the captain's tone. 'Silar Thornblood, of Hag Graef–'

'So I thought,' the captain said with a sharp nod. He jerked his thumb at Malus. 'This here is your man. His father paid good coin to see he got on board.' The captain turned to one of his men. 'Cut his bonds.'

One of the guardsmen slid from his saddle, a dagger gleaming dully in his hand. Malus held out his bound wrists with a baleful glare, but the guardsman paid the highborn no mind. The leather straps parted with an expert jerk of the blade, and then a strong hand pulled Malus firmly from the saddle. The highborn managed barely a single step before a sharp flare of pain in his thigh brought him to his knees.

The captain twisted in his saddle and reached back for a bundle of saddle bags. 'The young master made the acquaintance of most of the lower taverns last night,' he said, tugging at the binding straps. 'Cheated at dice, started a fight with a gang of sailors and damned near gave us the slip. He'd made it through the city gate and was a half-mile back to Hag Graef when we caught up to him.' The captain tugged the bags free and dropped them beside Malus with a weighty thud.

Silar's dark eyes widened in shock as the captain's words sank in. 'This is outrageous!' he snarled. 'You lowborn thugs can't treat a highborn in this fashion!'

The captain's eyes narrowed. 'I've got my orders, young sir,' he growled. 'And your master put a knife in two of my men when we tried to turn him back to Clar Karond.' He glared down at Malus. 'So here he is. Now he's your problem.'

With a nod to his men, the captain nudged his horse around and headed off down the pier without a backwards glance. Silar stared helplessly after them, one hand still gripping the hilt of his sword.

'If you're going to challenge them, be my guest,' Malus said darkly. 'But don't expect any thanks from my father if you do.'

The highborn's voice brought Silar's head around. 'Your father's thanks? What has that to do with anything? I'm your sworn man–'

Malus cut him off with a bark of laughter. 'Bought and paid for by Lurhan of Hag Graef,' he snapped.

The young knight stiffened. 'A highborn embarking on his hakseer-cruise ought to have a retinue attending him,' he replied. 'Your father wishes–'

'Do not presume to tell me what my father wishes,' Malus shot back. 'You're here because no self-respecting highborn back home would swear himself willingly to my service, and it would reflect badly upon Lurhan if I went on this cruise alone.' He shot a bitter look at the young knight. 'The Vaulkhar of Hag Graef must think of his image, after all. Now help me up, damn you!'

Silar's jaw bunched angrily at the highborn's tone, but the young knight leapt to obey. With an awkward heave and a clatter of armour he pulled his new master to his feet. The two druchii were of a similar age, both at the cusp of adulthood, though Silar stood a head taller than Malus and was broader across the shoulder. The retainer's articulated plate armour was old and plain but well cared-for, its surface burnished and gleaming, and his twin swords were unadorned and functional.

Grimacing in pain, Malus eyed the young knight up and down. 'Whose wargear is that? Your grandfather's?'

'As a matter of fact, it is,' Silar answered sharply. 'They aren't much, but they've seen their share of battles. Can my lord say the same for his?'

Malus glanced down at his own harness. The armour was expertly made but likewise devoid of ornamentation, its edges still gleaming with oil from the armourers' shop. 'Like you, my wargear was provided for,' he muttered. Silar made to reply, but the highborn cut him off with a raised hand. 'Enough, Silar. My head is pounding and my guts are tied in knots. Neither one of us wants to be here, so let's just call a truce and try to get through this damned cruise without killing each other, all right?'

'As my lord wishes,' Silar replied coldly.

'Fine,' Malus said, and as Silar turned to gather up the highborn's saddle bags the highborn quietly resolved to kill the young knight just as soon as he possibly could. *Lurhan probably told you to wait until we were well out to sea before slitting my throat,* Malus thought grimly. *Or perhaps one of my brothers promised you a bag of gold to slip some poison into my food.*

While the young knight struggled with his and his master's possessions, Malus took a few tentative steps with his right leg. The muscles were still weak and ached down to the bone, but he forced himself to remain upright.

Silar eyed the highborn's halting movements and frowned. 'Are you hurt?' he asked. 'Did the guardsmen beat you?'

'Oh, most assuredly,' Malus answered, 'but this was a going-away present from one of my siblings, I think. Someone slipped a rock adder into my wardrobe yesterday morning. Fortunately it bit both my bodyservants first before it got to me, so it had little venom left.'

'Ah. I see,' Silar replied. 'Will you need help climbing the gangway?'

'Don't be stupid,' Malus hissed, turning his back on the retainer and eyeing the long gangplank balefully. Then, setting his jaw, he started upward.

By the time Malus reached the deck of the corsair the crew had passed word of his coming back to the ship's master, who arrived to greet the highborn at the rail.

Hethan Gul was sleek as an eel in a fine black kheitan of human hide and a shirt of expensive chainmail. His robes were of thick wool, and his high boots were supple leather, too new to be stained with sea salt and tar. Rings glittered on his scarred fingers, and a single, heavy cutlass hung from a studded leather belt.

'Welcome aboard the *Manticore*,' he said smoothly, his thin lips pulling back to reveal a mouthful of gold-capped teeth. Gul bowed low, causing the weak sunlight to glint on the gold bands that secured his corsair's topknot. The long tail of hair was streaked with grey. 'We are honoured to have been chosen for your proving cruise, young lord.'

Malus paused at the rail, surveying the deck and the assembled crew. Sailors wearing faded robes and kheitans of orc or human hide climbed nimbly up the raider's ice-coated lines or busied themselves stowing the last crates of provisions into the *Manticore's* forward hold. Blackened mail covered their chests and upper arms, and their wide belts bristled with a vicious assortment of knives, cudgels and heavy, single-edged swords. Their faces were lean and weathered, scarred from long years prowling the sea lanes, and they studied the highborn with cold, predatory stares.

The ship was an old one, as far as he could tell, but the lines and fittings were new, as well as the deep, red sails furled overhead. New weapons shone in notched wooden racks set at intervals along the length of the ship, and the reaper bolt throwers fore and aft showed signs of recent installation. Likewise, the cluster of officers at Gul's shoulder wore armour and weapons as freshly minted as the highborn's own.

'Quite a lavish honour indeed,' Malus growled. 'I see my father spared no expense to refit your ship, captain.'

The corsair's golden grin widened. 'Of course, young lord. No son of Lurhan should put to sea without the best that Clar Karond can offer. But you must not call me captain,' he said. 'From the moment you set foot upon this deck, that title belongs to you. You will refer to me as Master Gul, and I will be at your service in all things.'

Malus's gaze sank to the scarred planking on the other side of the ship's rail. One more step and there was no turning back, he thought. He wouldn't be able to back out of the cruise without appearing weak, and he'd sooner die that give his family that satisfaction.

Of course, once he stepped onto the *Manticore* he'd be as good as dead anyway. Up until now, Malus's entire world had been the tall spires of Hag Graef, never far from the distant but watchful eyes of his mother Eldire. The hakseer-cruise, a right of passage for all druchii highborn, was his father's first and best chance to have him killed without fear of repercussion from his sorceress concubine.

Still, he thought, better dead and bold than dead and weak. Gritting his teeth, he stepped down onto the oaken deck.

'Excellent,' Gul murmured, nodding to himself. He turned to the assembled crew. 'Hark, sea ravens! The sea calls, and your captain heeds her summons! Malus, the young son of Lurhan commands you. May he guide us to a red tide of gold and glory!'

'Gold and glory!' the crew shouted as one. Gul turned to Malus and grinned. 'Your success is assured, young lord,' he whispered. 'Have no fear of that. I know just where to go for you to reap a fine fortune in gold and slaves.'

'Of that I have no doubt,' Malus replied, 'since a third of the plunder goes to you and the crew.' The highborn wondered who would get his share if he died on the long voyage. Would it go to Lurhan instead? It wouldn't surprise him one bit.

Gul indicated a trio of nearby corsairs with a sweep of his arm. 'Captain, your ship's officers stand ready to pay their respects.'

'Let's get on with it then,' the highborn replied, gesturing impatiently to the officers.

Each druchii stepped forward in turn and knelt before Malus. First came Shebyl, the ship's navigator, a thickset, pox-scarred corsair with bright, rodent-like eyes. Next came the ship's second officer, a square shouldered, fierce-looking raider named Amaleth. He muttered the proper words of allegiance, but his gaze was direct and challenging.

Malus was surprised to find that the last of the three was female. She was tall and fit, her skin made dusky by months of life at sea. Fine, pale battle scars cross-hatched her high cheeks. Her dark hair was pulled back in dozens of fine braids and bound up in a corsair's topknot. The worn hilts of a pair of highborn swords rested at her hip.

'Lhunara Ithil, first mate of the *Manticore*,' she said in a husky voice as she sank to one knee. 'Through wind and storm, red rain and splintered shields, I will serve thee, captain. Lead, and I will follow.'

The highborn's eyes widened at the sight of her. Perhaps this voyage wouldn't be entirely unpleasant after all. 'Perhaps I'll lead you to my cabin and keep you there,' he said with a predatory grin.

Howls and hisses of laughter rose from the assembled crew. Lhunara looked up at the highborn with a broad smile, her eyes gleaming. She rose to her feet in a fluid motion and punched Malus full in the face. The highborn's feet flew in the air and he hit the deck with a tremendous crash.

'Try it and I'll feed your guts to the gulls,' she said, still smiling.

There was a hiss of steel and Silar leapt onto the deck, sword in hand. With a startled shout, Gul leapt between the young knight and the first mate. 'Stay your hand, young lord!' he said to Silar. 'You're aboard ship now, not at a highborn court. She was well within her rights to reply as she did.'

But Silar refused to yield. 'What would you have me do, my lord?' he said to Malus.

For a moment, Malus was sorely tempted to turn Silar loose on the first mate. Lhunara was a bit older than the young knight and looked like she knew how to use those swords she carried. He could certainly vouch for the strength of her hands, he thought, wiping blood from his chin. At worst, he would be rid of Lurhan's hired man. After a moment's thought, however, he shook his head. 'Put away your sword,' he told Silar. 'I'll not go stirring up a feud among the crew.'

'Well said, captain,' Gul said quickly, bending to help Malus to his feet. Lhunara gave Silar a disdainful look before turning on her heel and striding away, snapping orders to the ship's crew as she went.

'All is in readiness,' Gul continued as he pulled the highborn to his feet. 'The crew was at work all night long to ready *Manticore* for sea. If we're to find the best pickings for you, it's crucial we cast off and make for the straits as soon as possible.' The gold-toothed corsair's unctuous expression faltered a little, and he looked over the rail at the empty pier. 'Ah, has my young lord arrived earlier than planned? Normally one's father and mother are present to commemorate the occasion. Why, it is well-known that Lurhan sent his eldest sons on their first cruises with great fanfare–'

Malus spat a stream of red over the rail. 'There will be no fanfare, Master Gul,' he snapped. 'My father has done what he must to protect his reputation, and that's as far as his regard for me extends.'

'I… see,' Gul replied thoughtfully. 'Do you wish to give the order to depart then?'

The highborn turned about and scowled at the complicated array of rope, tackle, mast and sail. 'Master Gul, I know that those upright poles are masts, and the cloth bundles up there are sails. I know I'm standing on a deck, and I assume there's an anchor around here somewhere, but I wouldn't know where to look for it. That is the sum total of my knowledge of sailing,' he said. Malus waved his hand dismissively at Gul. 'You're the ship's master. Get us out of here.'

If Gul was appalled at his captain's utter lack of skill, he gave no sign of it. If anything, his grin only broadened further. 'Of course, sir,' he said, bowing once again. Leave everything to me. You are in good hands aboard the *Manticore*.'

'Oh, I have no doubt of that,' Malus replied sourly. 'I'm going below. Wake me when we get to Bretonnia.'

SLATE-COLOURED WAVES crashed against the *Manticore's* sleek hull, spraying icy water along the deck. Near the forward citadel deck a group of corsairs huddled together in their sealskin cloaks and crouched low next to the wooden bulkhead.

The three dice clattered across the damp planks and rebounded from the bulkhead, showing a trio of sharpened bones: the horns, a losing toss. 'Damnation!' Malus hissed angrily, and the sailors covering him from the elements chuckled and hissed their amusement. Grimy hands reached down and plucked coins out of the highborn's winnings. 'Another go,' Malus grumbled. 'All this damned pitching and heaving is souring the dice.'

Some of the corsairs shifted about on their heels and grumbled. One of the men, a one-eyed druchii with half a nose, ducked his head fearfully. 'Most of us have to stand watch, dread lord…'

'Not if I say otherwise!' Malus snapped. 'We'll go until I say we stop, and that's an order!'

The corsairs looked to one another and shrugged. Coins were pressed to the deck, and Malus picked up the dice. There were definite advantages to being the captain, he thought.

The *Manticore* was riding rough seas up the neck of the Slavers' Strait, and according to the navigator they would slip into the wide ocean in less than a day. Then – as Master Gul constantly reminded Malus – his proving cruise would well and truly begin.

Once free of the harbour at Clar Karond the raiding ship had made excellent time, racing across the inland seas a day or more ahead of their rivals. Malus had spent the first few days in utter misery, too sick to eat or drink anything stronger than water. When he'd finally got his sea legs and felt hungry again, Silar had tried to serve Malus in his cabin, but the highborn refused, fearful of the possibility of poison. Instead, Malus went to the ship's cooks directly for his meals. Not long after he fell into gambling with them.

Eventually he hit upon the notion of hiring one or two of the crewmen to murder Silar. The young knight often walked the decks after dark once the highborn had dismissed him from his duties. Surely it would be simple enough to knock him in the head and toss him over the side? And the sooner the better, Malus reckoned; the farther they got from Naggaroth, the greater the odds that Lurhan's paid man would try to make his move. So far though, the highborn hadn't managed to find any useful candidates for the job. To a man, the crew preferred to keep its distance from him, despite all the games of dice he played with them. Perhaps I shouldn't keep taking so much of their coin, he mused, rolling the dice in his palm.

The knot of crouching sailors around Malus shifted suddenly, letting in a gust of freezing air and sea spray. Malus glanced up, a snarl curling his lip, and caught sight of Silar. The young knight surveyed the gamblers with a disapproving frown. 'Master Gul wishes to speak to you in his cabin, my lord,' he said coldly.

Malus growled under his breath. He was tempted to tell the unctuous ship's master to wait while he won back his silver. The highborn eyed the sad handful of coins at his side and decided to try and build a bit of goodwill with the men. He shrugged, gathering up his paltry winnings. 'You've plucked me to the bone this time, you sea birds,' he said to the corsairs. 'We'll see who the gods favour next time.'

The corsairs gathered up their coins and got back to work, grinning to themselves. Malus sighed and waved his hand at Silar. 'All right. Take me to him,' he said.

Silar led him through a narrow door in the fortress deck aft, then down to the master's cabin. A corsair stood watch outside Gul's cabin door. At the sight of Silar and Malus, the scarred druchii pushed the door open and stepped aside.

Tall, narrow windows dominated the aft bulkhead of Gul's cabin, throwing bars of weak, grey light across the broad expanse of the master's oaken table. A huge map was spread across its surface, showing Naggaroth, Ulthuan and the domain of the humans etched in fine, black lines. Gul sat on the far side of the table, sipping wine and smiling to himself as he traced the sinuous lines of prevailing currents across the map. The navigator Shebyl sat nearby, consulting a thick set of scrolls marked with astronomical charts. Lhunara stood off to one side, arms folded tightly across her chest. She studied Malus and Silar thoughtfully as they entered the cabin.

'Welcome to my humble quarters, Captain Malus,' Gul said, opening his arms expansively. 'Please, sit. Have some of this fine wine. I stole it in a raid off Ulthuan many years ago, and it only gets better with time.'

Malus picked up a goblet and poured from a crystal flagon set on a tray at the end of the table. It was the first time he'd been invited into Gul's personal quarters, and he was impressed at its luxurious appointments: a feather bed, expensive chairs of oak and dwarf hide, shelves of books and an impressive collection of trophies, from gilt skulls to jewel-encrusted ceremonial daggers and silver-inlaid armour. Whatever else Gul may be, Malus had to admit the gold-toothed corsair knew a thing or two about his trade.

'Far be it from me to turn down an offer of wine and hospitality,' he said, taking a deep drink. 'What is the occasion?'

Gul tapped the map with a calloused finger. 'We're nearly to the open sea, my captain,' he said. 'Time for you to approve the course I and the good navigator have laid out.'

Malus sampled some more of the wine. It was, indeed, quite fine. 'All right,' he said with a shrug. 'Tell me.'

'Since your father approached me last winter I've been thinking about a course that would be suitable to your, ah, level of skill,' he said. 'There is a great deal riding on this cruise, after all. You are about to enter highborn society. The wealth and fame you win on the *Manticore* will determine your initial status at court, after all.'

The highborn cast a momentary glance at Silar. 'Provided some human doesn't dash in my skull or I suffer a similar misfortune along the way.'

Gul smiled. 'Well, life is about risk, is it not?' He leaned forward over the map. 'But have no fear. I have gone to great effort to chart a route that minimizes such risk, but will still yield a handsome profit over time.'

Provided my damned retainer doesn't find some way to kill me between now and then, Malus thought. 'Show me.'

'Well, to start with, with your father's coin I was able to hire a good crew, and outfit them with proper weapons and armour,' he began. 'We've not enough men to hazard a large human city or fortress, such as your older brother Bruglir might, but there are any number of towns that would be easy pickings along the Bretonnian coast.' Gul's finger traced a long arc, dipping south of Ulthuan and then north and east to the shores of the human kingdom. 'We will avoid cities like Bordeleaux or l'Anguille and strike at the small fishing towns that stretch between them. Sweep in at midnight, kill any who resist, and cart everything else back to the ship. Nothing left but ashes by morning.' Gul traced a seemingly meandering route up the coastline, past l'Anguille and then east. 'We take a bite here and a bite there, always staying a few days ahead of the Bretonnian forces. By late summer we could be at the inlet leading to Marienburg, by which point our holds will be bursting, and it will be time to head for home. After a brief stop at Karond Kar to unload our slaves, you would arrive at Clar Karond a rich and successful young highborn.'

Gul leaned back in his chair and folded his slim hands across his chest, clearly pleased with himself.

Malus scowled down at the map. 'I see none of these small towns you speak of on this map.'

Gul chuckled. 'Rest assured they are there, young captain. I've plied this route many a time myself. Slow, perhaps, but safe and profitable. Just the sort of thing to prove your worth to the nobles back at Hag Graef. So. What do you say? Shall I tell Shebyl to chart the course?'

The highborn thought it over. Near Marienburg by late summer, he thought. Five months at sea, by the Dark Mother! He took a contemplative sip from his cup.

'No,' he said at last.

Gul's gleaming smile faltered. 'What did you say, my lord?'

'I'm here to make my reputation,' he said, 'and I won't go back to the Hag after five long months smelling like a fishmonger. We've got a good ship and good men, so let us take a prize that's worthy of our mettle.' He glanced down at the map and let his finger fall with a portentous *thump*.

The ship's master paled. 'Ulthuan?' he stammered. 'Surely you jest.'

'Did I say something amusing, Master Gul?' the highborn said darkly.

Gul managed an uneasy chuckle. 'No doubt the young captain is aware that Ulthuan is very well defended,' he began. 'Its shores are constantly patrolled, and our traitorous cousins have ships nearly as swift and deadly as our own. Not even your older brother and his fleet have dared strike there.'

Malus grinned mirthlessly. 'Then I'll truly have something to boast about when I reach home,' he said. The highborn waved dismissively at the map. 'Chart us a course to take us close around the southern tip of the Blighted Isle, then on to the west coast of Ulthuan,' he said. 'That shouldn't be too demanding, should it? We'll find a good-sized town and sack it, and make our fortunes in a single stroke.'

'But... you can't do this!' Gul sputtered. His face was white as alabaster. 'It would be suicide! I forbid this!'

'You may be the master of this ship, but for the duration of this voyage, I am the captain,' Malus snarled. 'And I know very well what my rights are regarding mutineers.' He looked at the navigator. 'Chart the course. Now.'

'I...' Shebyl began, then recoiled at the look in Malus's eyes. 'Very well, sir.'

Malus nodded. 'That's more like it.' He drained the cup. 'Good wine,' he said, setting the goblet on the table. 'Hopefully there's more where that came from.'

SILAR THORNBLOOD WAS waiting for Malus when he returned to his cabin after the evening meal. The young knight stood opposite the narrow, wooden door, his arms folded tightly across his chest.

This is it, Malus thought the moment he caught sight of his hired retainer. On reflex, his hand darted to the sword at his belt, then he realized that as far as he could tell Silar hadn't armed himself. The highborn paused in the doorway, uncertain how to proceed. We're an hour away from the straits, Malus realized, but if Silar is here to kill me he's picked a damned strange way to go about it.

Finally the highborn stepped inside the cramped room. 'What in the Dark Mother's name do you want?' he growled. 'Shouldn't you be up pacing the deck or something?'

The young knight gave Malus a hard stare. His jaw worked as he struggled to find the right words to say. Finally, he simply blurted out, 'What in the name of all the gods is wrong with you?'

Malus blinked. 'What?'

'Were you dropped on your head as a child? Kicked by a horse? Was your mother cursed?' The young knight's voice rose as a tide of pent-up frustration bubbled forth. 'Master Gul handed you a chance at easy wealth, but you'd rather die at Ulthuan instead?'

'Mind your damned tongue!' the highborn snapped. 'Another word out of you and I'll have the first mate strip the skin from your back!'

'You don't know the first thing about sailing. You waste your time gambling with the common sailors. I haven't made sense out of a single thing you've done since I met you,' Silar replied. 'And with all the advantages you've been given–'

'*Advantages?*' Malus spat. 'Is the cheese in the trap an advantage for the rat? Mother of Night! Who do you think you are, Silar Thornblood?'

The young knight let out a derisive snort. 'Merely a very poor knight from an all but extinct house,' he answered. 'My grandfather made the mistake of scheming against your father, long before you and I were born. Lurhan destroyed my grandfather and all but wiped out our house. We've no property, no patrons, no allies at the Hag. We're little better than common folk now.' He glared angrily at Malus. 'There will be no hakseer-cruise for me. No one will hand me a fortune in slaves and gold, plucked from the coasts of the human kingdoms. I have to take a paltry wage, like a tradesman, and be glad for it.'

Malus was speechless. His anger was overwhelmed by a wave of sheer incredulity. 'And here I thought you might actually be dangerous,' he muttered to himself. 'Is that what you think is going on here? Ask yourself this, then: if my future is so damned bright, why do you imagine my father had to *hire you* to be my one and only retainer?'

Silar paused. 'I thought Lurhan was just trying to humiliate me,' he said. 'A final slap in the face for the last of my grandfather's line.'

The highborn sighed. 'If he'd hired you to serve anyone but me, you'd probably be right,' Malus said. 'But I'm nothing to Lurhan. *Nothing.* I was the price he had to pay when he brought my mother back from the Black Ark of Naggor. He wanted a sorceress, and she wanted a son. He's been dreaming of killing me ever since, and now the opportunity has arrived. This isn't a glory cruise; it's a death sentence. My father has no doubt gone to a great deal of trouble to ensure that I don't return to Naggaroth alive.'

Silar's eyes widened. Before he could reply, there came a knock at the cabin door.

Both druchii frowned in consternation. Malus turned, reaching for his sword, and opened the door with his left hand.

Lhunara Ithil stood outside. 'I want to talk to you,' she said quietly, glancing surreptitiously up and down the passageway.

For a moment, Malus didn't know what to say. Finally he shrugged. 'Well, come in then,' he replied, and stepped aside. 'We'll have just enough room left over to strangle each other.'

Lhunara gave Silar a passing glance and leaned against the forward bulkhead. Malus took the bulkhead opposite. She waited to speak until the cabin door latched shut. 'How did you know about Gul's trap?' the first mate asked.

Malus scowled. 'Trap?'

Her brow furrowed quizzically. 'Lurhan paid Gul to get you killed in Bretonnia,' she said. 'Didn't you know?'

Malus gave Silar a sidelong look. 'And how did he plan to do that, exactly?'

'Gul has an arrangement with one of the coastal barons,' she said. 'Each year the baron empties out his dungeons and hands the prisoners over to us – sometimes he throws in a servant or two if it's been a lean year. We leave his towns and crops alone in return.' Lhunara shrugged. 'Gul was going to stage a raid on one of the baron's villages, and then let the baron kill you when he and his men arrived.' She shrugged. 'It was a good deal for both sides, because the baron could make a big show of killing a druchii corsair captain while Gul sailed home to claim Lurhan's reward.'

The young knight scowled at the first mate. 'That sounds like a great deal of trouble just to kill a single highborn,' he said. 'There are dozens of simpler ways to kill someone aboard ship. Accidents happen at sea all the time.'

'Accidents happen,' Malus agreed, 'but no one with any sense would believe it – even if it was true. And Lurhan must be very careful, or he risks the wrath of my mother, Eldire.' He tapped his lip thoughtfully. 'If she believes he was a party to my death, she would spare no effort to destroy him.' He gave Silar a sidelong glance. 'Previously, I suspected that someone had simply been instructed to stick a knife in my ribs once we were so far from Naggaroth that my mother could no longer watch over me with her sorcery. But this... this plan is much cleverer, actually. By arranging to have me killed on the battlefield, Lurhan places himself above suspicion. Gul reaps a fine reward in stolen loot, and no one else is the wiser.'

After a moment, Malus gazed at the first mate thoughtfully. 'Why are you here, Lhunara?'

She considered her words carefully before replying. 'I thought that if you knew what Gul was up to, he was living on borrowed time, which suits me fine.'

'You don't care much for Master Gul, then?' the highborn asked.

'I think he'd look just fine hanging off the end of my sword,' she replied matter-of-factly. 'If he hadn't made me first mate I'd likely have killed him before now.'

Malus smiled. 'I'm told there aren't many female corsairs. How did you wind up on the *Manticore*?'

She shrugged. 'I marched with the Witch King's army during the last invasion of Ulthuan,' she said. 'I got a taste of war and found that I liked it. Since there's no place for a female in a highborn's warband, it was the sea or nothing. Now, tell me: how did you know what Gul was planning?'

'I didn't,' the highborn replied.

Lhunara frowned. 'Then why–'

'I looked at the map and saw that Ulthuan was half the distance from Naggaroth than Bretonnia,' he said simply. 'That meant a shorter cruise and less time trapped on this damned ship.'

The two druchii gaped at Malus. He studied them in turn, contemplating his sudden change of fortune. The question was, did he dare trust them?

'It would seem that all of us have a vested interest in my continued survival,' he suggested.

Silar stole a glance at Lhunara, then regarded his erstwhile lord. 'And how is that, exactly?'

'I represent an opportunity for both of you,' the highborn replied. 'Alone, I believed that my chances of surviving this voyage were slim.'

'You're leading us on a raid to Ulthuan,' Lhunara said. 'I'd say your chances are still pretty poor.'

Malus raised his hand. 'Let's leave that aside for the moment. It's possible that, with help, I could return to Hag Graef a very wealthy druchii.'

'We've had this conversation before,' Silar grumbled.

'No, we haven't,' Malus replied. 'I would return home rich and powerful. And I would have need of retainers. Druchii I could trust.' He gave Lhunara a meaningful look.

'You'd take me into your service?'

'Of course,' Malus replied.

'And you'll raid Bretonnia?'

Malus shook his head. 'Certainly not. Going to Ulthuan has thrown Gul off-balance. I want him to stay that way.'

Silar shook his head. 'You'd take my oath, knowing how much your father hates my house?'

'For that reason *especially*,' Malus replied with a grin. 'Imagine how much it will vex him.'

The young knight considered this, and a baleful light came to his eyes. 'I'll swear whatever oath you desire.'

Malus turned to Lhunara. The first mate hesitated. 'I need to think on this some more,' she said.

The highborn suppressed his irritation. 'As you wish. But do not wait too long. My patience is notoriously short.'

With a nod, Lhunara went to the door. At the threshold she paused. 'One thing more,' she said. 'Gul has done this sort of thing before, helping fathers deal with troublesome sons.'

'What of it?' Malus asked.

'Well, most times these fathers don't like to leave matters to chance,' she replied. 'They'll have a fallback in case Gul can't get the job done.'

Malus frowned. 'So you're saying there could be an assassin among the crew as well.'

She shrugged. 'Something to think about,' she said, and shut the door.

Malus turned and scowled thoughtfully at Silar. 'Damnation,' he muttered.

* * *

FOR A WEEK the *Manticore* crossed the cold sea, curving south and east with the currents as they drew closer to Ulthuan. News of their destination had made its way inexorably to the ears of the crew, and their mood had turned ever more anxious and grim with each passing day. Malus tried a few games of dice with the sailors, determined to lose a bit of coin to lighten the mood, but none of the sea birds would try him. Master Gul kept to his cabin, relaying instructions to the navigator and the first mate by way of Amaleth, the second mate.

By the sixth day the fog-shrouded bulk of the Blighted Isle loomed on the eastern horizon. The sighting brought Gul to the fortress deck, and he spent several tense minutes conversing with Shebyl and Lhunara. Finally, it was decided to cleave as closely to the isle and its mists as possible, in the hopes of avoiding enemy patrols. By the end of the day the black hull of the raider was wreathed in cold mists that clung to the skin like grasping fingers, chilling the druchii to the bone.

The master's plan was a good one, but luck wasn't with the *Manticore*. On the following morning, Malus was shaken roughly awake by Silar.

'Mother of Night!' the highborn exclaimed, tangled in sheets and glaring up at his retainer. 'What in the name of the Abyss are you doing?'

The young knight's face was tense. 'The lookout's spotted a sail.'

Malus was awake at once. 'What time is it?'

'First light.'

'Have they seen us?'

'Lhunara seems to think so.'

'Damn it all,' Malus breathed. 'All right. Get me my boots.'

By the time Malus and Silar reached the fortress deck the master and his mates were already in the middle of a heated debate. Dawn was stretching pale streamers of light across the sky, outlining the vague shape of the Blighted Isle to their north. Malus went to the rail and peered into the fading darkness. There, off to the north-east, he could make out a pale triangle of sail. The enemy patrol ship had their stern to the *Manticore*, and seemed to be getting smaller with each passing second.

The highborn turned to Lhunara. 'What's happening?'

Lhunara shot him a worried look. 'The ship changed course almost as soon as we spotted it. It's possible that it's just following a standard patrol route.'

'Or it might have seen us and is running for help,' Master Gul interjected, his teeth glinting coldly.

'All right,' Malus said. 'What do we do?'

Lhunara spoke first. 'We have to catch it. We can't take the chance that it didn't see us.'

'Or we could give up this fool's errand and turn back now!' Gul urged. 'The enemy won't give chase. This is our only chance to escape.'

'Escape?' Malus growled. '*That* ship there is trying to escape,' he said, pointing off at the receding elven ship. 'And with good reason. Lhunara, can we catch it?'

The first mate nodded. 'The wind is with us. I believe we can.'

'All right then. Lower all the sails, or start rowing, or whatever it is you do,' he replied, waving in the general direction of the masts. 'And prepare the crew for battle.'

And with that, the chase was on. Red hides crackled in the wind as *Manticore* put on full sail, and boots drummed over the deck as the crew readied their weapons and counted the distance between them and their prey.

For a time, it seemed as though nothing changed between pursuer and pursued. The sun rose into the cloudy sky, and Malus could see little more than the fleeing ship's sail, an angular chip of white on the horizon. But slowly, steadily, as the hours wore on into the morning, the elven ship took shape. Malus moved forward to the citadel deck, where the bowmen and the reaper bolt thrower crews waited for action.

Then, at mid-morning, the corsair's luck turned with the wind. It shifted from north-east to north-west, blowing towards the Blighted Isle, and the fleeing patrol ship lost some of her headway. The distance shrank quickly after that, until Malus could clearly see the outline of the enemy vessel. She was low and sleek like *Manticore*, with three masts and angular sails. Her twin hulls were painted a rich blue and her ship's fittings were golden. Sunlight glinted coldly off the points of spears and silver helmets arrayed at the stern of the ship.

'Gul is an odious bastard, but he was right this time,' Lhunara said quietly, just over Malus's shoulder. The young highborn felt his heart leap into his chest, but struggled not to show it.

'How's that?'

'With every minute we draw closer to Ulthuan,' she said. 'That ship could be leading us right into a trap. Ulthuan's patrol ships frequently work in pairs. We could very easily be getting into something we have no way of getting out of.'

'Are we going to catch them?'

'As long as the wind holds and nothing drastic happens.'

Just then Malus caught a glint of light flash from the stern of the fleeing ship. A slender shape blurred through the air and plunged into the sea barely twenty yards from the corsair. A moment later another bolt splashed down, this one five yards closer.

'Something like that?' Malus asked.

Lhunara stepped beside the highborn and grinned like a wolf. 'Here's where things get interesting,' she said. The first mate gave Malus a searching look. 'We're past the point of no return now. If we live long enough to reach Ulthuan, you do have a plan for getting inside whatever village we find, right? There will be a garrison, a wall and a barred gate. You've thought of that, right?'

Before Malus had to lie to her the reaper bolt thrower crew cut in. 'Do your jawing somewhere else,' the chief bowman yelled as the weapon swung their way. 'Unless you want to get to that ship a whole lot faster than you planned.'

The two druchii ducked out of the way, and the reaper bolt thrower banged against its mount. After a moment the corsairs in the citadel let out a cheer. Malus squinted at the enemy ship. Had they hit it? He couldn't tell.

The highborn turned to Lhunara and was about to ask her what happened when there was a humming sound in the air and an elven shot struck the forward rail. The yard-long bolt smashed the wooden rail to splinters and flashed overhead, burying itself in the forward mast. Cries of pain and bitter curses filled the air as wounded corsairs lurched aft, pawing at jagged splinters that jutted from their arms, faces and chests.

Another bang resounded from the citadel, and this time Malus saw the long, black bolt punch a neat hole through the patrol ship's aft sail. The chief bowman laughed like a devil. 'We've got them now!' he cried. 'Bring up the pitch-pots!'

On the heels of the command came another crash, and this time Malus heard the disconcerting sound of steel meeting flesh. Hot blood sprayed his face, and a druchii let out a gurgling scream. A corsair less than ten paces away fell to the deck, his left arm and shoulder torn away by a glancing blow from an enemy bolt.

'Don't bunch up!' Lhunara yelled to the druchii manning the citadel. 'Spread out and duck your heads when the bolts come in! You can't fight a damned thing with a splinter in your eye!'

For ten long minutes the two ships exchanged shots as the range dwindled. The elven repeater bolt throwers laid down a withering fire: heavy blows hammered into the prow and smashed more of the railing, and bolts flashed overhead to puncture sails and split ropes like wet threads. One horrifying shot seemed to slither through a group of corsairs, ricocheting between their bodies and smashing them to a pulp before caroming off into the sea. The citadel reeked of spilt blood and entrails. Malus knelt beside Lhunara and wondered when his turn would come.

Then a pair of corsairs clambered onto the deck with buckets of pitch and a lit torch in their hands. They took one of the bolts and dipped it in the thick tar, then loaded it and set it alight. The reaper bolt thrower banged, and a streak of fire arced like a meteor through the leaden sky. Malus watched it plunge toward the enemy ship and bury itself in the aft mast. In moments the sail and rigging were ablaze.

A blood-hungry howl went up from the corsairs. Lhunara turned to Malus. 'Now we go to work,' she said. To the surviving archers the first mate called, 'Get ready!' Then she leaned over the aft rail and shouted down at the main deck. 'Hooks and lines, starboard side!' she ordered. 'Gold and glory!'

'Gold and glory!' the corsairs answered lustily, and leapt into action.

Lhunara led Malus down to the main deck, where the boarders were gathering. Druchii stood at the rail with grappling hooks and coils of heavy cable, surrounded by corsairs bearing crossbows, swords and axes. Silar was waiting for Malus there, a blade in one hand and a small crossbow in the other. Amaleth, similarly armed, stood a short way off. The second mate's expression was focused and intent.

Suddenly, Malus was very aware of the mob of armed druchii surrounding him. Any one of them could be Lurhan's hidden assassin.

Lhunara readied her weapons and looked over Malus and Silar, noticing or the first time that both were still in their plate armour. 'You'll want to watch your step,' she said pointedly, adjusting the weight of her own chainmail hauberk.

Malus tried not to think about it. 'Have you made your decision?'

Just as she was about to reply the bowstrings on the citadel hummed, and the roar of flames filled the air. Without warning the heaving flank of the elven patrol ship loomed alongside, and a sleet of deadly arrows rained down on the waiting corsairs. The druchii with the grappling hooks suffered the worst; more than half of them fell, their bodies riddled with white shafts from neck to waist. But before they died they hurled their grapples through the air, and most of them found purchase on the enemy ship, snagging the patrol craft's port hull. Crossbows snapped in response to the Ulthuan volley, and answering screams drifted across the space between the two ships as more corsairs ran forward and hauled on the cables. Moments later there was a shuddering crash as predator and prey slammed together in a lethal embrace.

'At them!' Amaleth roared, and the air rang with battle-screams as a black tide of corsairs swept onto the burning enemy ship. They leapt onto the elven ship's narrow port hull and clawed their way up and over the rail, slipping and stumbling on the bodies of the dead as they charged at the closed ranks of the Lothern Sea Guard.

Malus found himself carried along in the rush, roaring and shouting along with the rest. When he reached the rail he leapt as hard as he could, and landed on the far deck with a jarring thud. With a start, the highborn realized he hadn't yet drawn his sword. He dragged his blade from its scabbard just as the mob of corsairs surged forward again, and he was shoved toward the Lothern shield wall.

The enemy spearmen were all but completely hidden behind their tall, oval shields, and they held their weapons in an overhand grip, ready to stab downward at exposed faces and throats. Malus smashed full onto a foeman's shield, throwing off the warrior's aim enough that the answering spear thrust missed his head by inches. The highborn let out a scream and fumbled for the spear haft with his left hand. He seized the ebon shaft and pulled it towards him, then chopped at the hand holding it. The sword bit into fingers and wooden haft, and the spearman screamed in agony. Malus smashed the pommel of his sword into the warrior's face and the spearman recoiled from the blow.

Screaming incoherent curses, Malus forced his way into the spear wall, lashing wildly at the warriors to either side of him. He smashed a spearman's jaw and opened his throat with a vicious cut, then struck the helm of the second. The warrior he'd driven backwards collapsed onto the deck, and the highborn nearly fell with him. He drove his sword into the fallen warrior's neck, then lurched forwards once more to discover that the enemy formation had melted away around him. Malus saw that most of the warriors were falling back towards the ship's main mast, which had now caught fire as well. He gave chase, howling like a madman.

The first warrior he reached glanced behind him a moment before it was too late, and turned to raise his shield against the highborn's killing blow. The enemy's spear lunged at Malus, glancing off his breastplate; he feinted at the spearman's helmet and then swung low, chopping into the side of the warrior's knee. The spearman fell with a shout and the highborn literally ran over him, charging for the next enemy in line. As he ran, a hard blow rang off his shoulder blade, nearly unbalancing him, and the distraction almost cost him his life. At that exact moment the next warrior spun on his heel and thrust his spear at the highborn's midsection. The tip struck him squarely, just above the navel, and lodged in a chink in his armour. Without thinking he hacked at the spear haft with his sword and it splintered before the keen steel point could drive into his midsection. The spearman dropped the broken weapon with a curse and fumbled for the short sword at his side, but Malus kept on coming, driving the point of his blade into the warrior's left eye. Dead instantly, the body collapsed, taking Malus's sword with it. He stumbled, nearly wrenched off his feet before he could drag the weapon clear.

The next thing Malus crashed into was the ship's mast. The retreating warriors had fled even further, retreating towards the bow. Burning ash and pieces of flaming rope fell all around him as the highborn leaned against the splintered trunk and tried to catch his breath. Druchii with dripping blades rushed past him, chasing after the foe.

Bodies littered the deck all around him. A dead spearman looked up at Malus with glazed eyes, his handsome features spattered with red. Wisps of pale hair fluttered in the sea breeze. So like us, he thought, shaking his head, and yet so foul. And just like that, he realized how they were going to get inside the walls of the coastal town.

'My lord!' Silar cried, rushing to join Malus at the mast. His armour was streaked with gore; somewhere in the brief fight he'd lost his cross-bow, but his sword was stained with crimson. 'Lhunara says the enemy captain is dead and the ship is ours. What do we do now?'

'Get some sailors and start collecting the bodies of the spearmen,' Malus gasped. 'We need to take them to the *Manticore*.'

For a moment it looked as though the young knight might argue, but instead he turned and shouted to a nearby group of druchii. Malus inspected the bodies carefully, looking for those whose gear was most intact. The corsairs seized a half-dozen of the bodies and began drag-ging them back to the ship. Malus and Silar chose two more and followed as quickly as they could. Around them, other druchii were looting the corpses of their Ulthuan cousins, taking anything of value they could carry.

Just as Malus got to the ship's rail, a horn wailed from the *Manticore's* fortress deck. Shouts went up from the corsairs on the deck of the burning patrol ship, but the highborn paid them no heed. 'Get this body across, then come back for another,' Malus told Silar, then turned and ran back into the thickening smoke. Silar shouted something in reply, but it was drowned out amid the clamour.

Malus searched the remaining bodies more carefully, hoping to find one of the ship's mates or perhaps her captain. His eyes stung from the smoke; by now, all three masts were blazing torches, and flaming debris had spread the blaze to parts of the deck as well. Moving quickly, he checked a dozen more corpses, but none suited his needs. Then came a rending crash as part of the main mast toppled onto the deck nearby, and the highborn reckoned he'd run out of time.

Suddenly he realized that Silar was nowhere to be seen. The corsairs were gone as well. He was the only druchii left aboard the ship.

Fighting a surge of panic he turned and ran for the rail, plunging through billows of choking smoke. Coughing and cursing, he emerged from the haze and saw the *Manticore* – now almost a yard apart from the patrol ship and getting further by the moment. Someone had ordered the cables cut, and the burning ship was drifting away!

'Mother of Night!' Malus cried. He thought of the heavy armour enclosing him and the grey sea waiting below, but still he clenched his teeth and ran for the rail as fast as he could. At the last moment he leapt, hurling himself through space – and immediately saw that he wasn't going to make it.

The highborn hit the hull of the ship with a clatter of steel, and one flailing hand grasped the base of the rail. Icy water washed up over his legs, almost to his hips. He could feel the strength in his fingers failing and roared in desperation – then a hand closed about his wrist and he felt himself being drawn upward.

Silar Thornblood heaved Malus onto the deck, amid a throng of cheering corsairs. The retainer knelt beside the highborn. 'Didn't you hear the horn?' he said. 'I tried to tell you not to go back–'

'What in the name of the Dark Mother is going on?' Malus gasped.

'We've spotted another enemy ship,' Silar replied. 'South of us, but closing fast. They must have seen the fire on the horizon. Master Gul and Lhunara are going to make for the Blighted Isle and try to lose the pursuer in the mists.'

The highborn clambered to his feet and headed for the fortress deck. He found Lhunara and Gul standing by the aft rail, studying the enemy warship on the horizon. It was a big one, Malus saw at once, easily as large as *Manticore*, or larger.

'Why are we running?' he snapped. 'We've wrecked one ship today already.'

Lhunara shot Malus an irritated look. 'They've got the wind at their backs, a large crew and probably more bolt throwers than we do. The fight would be too much in their favour. No, we'll shake them off in the mists around the Blighted Isle. They won't dare follow us in there.'

'She's right,' Gul said emphatically. 'Now do you see the folly of your plan? We should turn around at once.'

Malus stared thoughtfully at the ship's master, wondering if perhaps the order to cut the cables had been more calculated than he'd imagined. You almost had me there, he thought. Another minute and I would have been lost. He nodded slowly. 'We'll shake them off in the mists, right enough,' he said, 'but tonight we make for the coast of Ulthuan.'

Even Lhunara looked worried at the thought. 'That patrol ship will spread the alarm for miles in every direction.'

Malus nodded. 'But they'll be expecting us to flee now, won't they? They'll circle around to the western side of the Blighted Isle and try to catch us as we come out of the mist. So we'll go the other way, and hit them where they least expect us.'

'That's madness!' Gul exclaimed. 'You're taking too many damned chances with my ship, and I won't have it!'

Malus stepped close to Gul. 'I should be more concerned about the chances you're taking with me, Master Gul. Sooner or later they'll come back to bite you.'

The ship's master paled slightly and turned away. Behind Gul's back, Malus gave Lhunara a conspiratorial look. She nodded, and the highborn smiled. He was gaining the upper hand.

As he turned to go, the first mate said. 'What's that on your shoulder?'

Malus frowned. 'How should I know? I don't have eyes in the back of my head.'

Lhunara stepped forward. The highborn felt a sharp tug and heard a scrape of steel. At once, he remembered the blow he'd taken on the patrol ship as he'd run towards the main mast.

The first mate held something out to him. It was a druchii crossbow bolt.

'I guess wearing all that plate was a good idea after all,' she said.

STREAMERS OF SILVER cloud wreathed a solitary moon, painting the rocky headland in patterns of shadow. The druchii raiders kept to the darkness beneath the trees that ran alongside the curving coastal road. Just ahead, around the bend of a rocky outcrop, lay their objective.

Malus pulled the cloak of Ulthuan wool tighter about his shoulders. The ship's crew had washed out as much of the blood as possible, and they had to hope that the darkness would conceal the rest. In his right hand he held a looted spear, and the Sea Guard's heavy shield hung from a strap on his left arm. Beneath the cloak he wore a hauberk of druchii chainmail, similar in size and bulk to Ulthuan scale armour. The silver helm was too big, and kept wanting to slide down over his eyes. He had hoped that the spearman's long, blond scalp would have given him the extra padding he needed, but it still wasn't enough.

There were nearly a hundred corsairs in the raiding party – slightly more than two-thirds of the *Manticore's* surviving crew. Malus had been forced to leave Master Gul, Amaleth, and the navigator Shebyl back on the ship with a skeleton crew; if the treacherous ship's master wanted to abandon him, he'd be leaving most of his corsairs behind as well. The highborn hoped that would be enough to give the bastard pause.

Gul had put the raiding party ashore just before midnight, five miles further north. After recovering his boats, the ship's master was supposed to take the *Manticore* farther out to sea to avoid detection, then swing back to a point two miles south of the town to pick up the raiders and their plunder. By Malus's reckoning they had less than two hours left to make the attack and reach the pickup point.

Lhunara, Silar and four other corsairs were also disguised in Ulthuan cloaks and wargear. The rest of the attackers wore dark cloaks and unadorned helms; in the darkness, they could pass for Lothern Sea Guard so long as no one looked too closely. Malus turned to the first mate. 'Are you sure the rest of the raiding party knows what to do?'

She scowled at him from beneath the brim of her dented helm. 'It's not exactly complicated,' she replied. 'They've done this sort of thing before, you know.'

'Fine,' Malus growled. 'Lead on.'

The disguised druchii stepped out onto the road, and Lhunara took a few moments to make sure the 'spearmen' were arrayed in proper marching order before heading off. Malus walked alongside her, his spear resting against his shoulder.

'I can't believe we're doing this,' she muttered.

'Neither can I,' Malus said.

'This was your idea!'

The highborn chuckled under his breath. 'Well, yes. I just wasn't sure I'd live long enough to get this far.'

Just past the outcrop of rock the druchii found themselves at the north end of a broad, shallow cove, edged with forests of dark green pine. The coast road ran on for another hundred yards or so, and ended before the high gate of the elven town. As Malus watched, the moon slipped from behind the clouds, and the pearly light gleamed off the white stone of the town's high wall and its tall, graceful buildings. He suppressed a shudder at the sight of the place: it was decadent and debased, with its gleaming white stone and jewel-like lamps. The highborn could almost smell the weakness of its inhabitants, and felt the sudden urge to put it all to the torch.

Globes of turquoise-coloured light shone at regular intervals along the top of the town wall, and Malus saw solitary figures pacing along its length. Lhunara muttered a curse. 'They've been alerted,' she murmured. 'I warned you about this.'

'So what does that mean, exactly?'

'At this hour, about a third of the town watch will be on the walls and guarding the gates. The rest will be sleeping nearby in full armour.'

'How many warriors will there be?'

She shrugged. 'For a town this size? Maybe a hundred.'

Malus grunted. 'Is that all? We can take them.'

'If we can get inside the walls!' Lhunara hissed.

'Well, then, you'd best be convincing, hadn't you?'

They marched along the road in plain view, their helmeted heads bowed as if in weariness. Malus could feel the eyes of the sentries upon him as they came up to the gate.

'Who goes there?' spoke a cold, quiet voice from above. The language of Ulthuan was a debased relative of druhir, but close enough that Malus could make out most of what the sentry was saying.

'A shore patrol from the *White Lion*,' Lhunara answered, her husky voice thick with feigned weariness. 'The captain put us ashore north of here to look for signs of the druchii raiders. Have any of you seen anything?'

'None,' the sentry replied. 'You say you're from the *White Lion*? I don't know that ship.'

'This isn't our normal patrol route,' the first mate replied without skipping a beat. 'We'd been out hunting pirates west of the Blighted Isle and were heading back to port at Lothern when we got word there was a raider in the area.' Lhunara shifted from foot to foot. 'May we enter, cousin? We'd like a place to rest our feet and get some food if we could. We've got another five leagues to march before the dawn.'

The sentry didn't reply right away. Malus kept his gaze focused on the paving stones at his feet and tried to appear tired and bedraggled. Finally the warrior spoke. 'Very well. Come inside.'

A ripple of tension ran through the raiders as quiet orders were passed beyond the gate, and the sound of heavy bolts being drawn back. The highborn turned and surreptitiously glanced back at the outcropping a hundred yards distant. He hoped the raiders were paying attention, and were fast on their feet.

The tall gates swung open. Malus waited until Lhunara started to move, then fell in line beside her. His hand tightened on the haft of his spear.

There were two warriors on each of the gates, their spears laid aside as they wrestled the portals open. Beyond them the road continued through an open square – where almost two score soldiers slept or tended their weapons in a temporary bivouac.

Malus felt his blood run cold. 'Blessed Mother of Night,' he cursed under his breath.

One of the warriors on the gate next to him raised his head at the sound. 'Did you say something, cousin?' he asked.

The highborn glanced up at the warrior, trying to think of a quick lie – and met the spearman's gaze. Too late, he saw the look of shock on the warrior's face as the warrior noticed the highborn's dark eyes, and knew that their ruse was finished.

'At them!' he yelled, smashing the rim of his oval shield into the spearman's face. The elf staggered backwards with a cry, blood spurting from his broken nose, and the highborn buried his spear in the soldier's throat.

Shouts of alarm rang through the air all around the druchii. Lhunara threw off her cloak and helm and attacked the spearmen to her left with a feral shriek. Silar dropped spear and shield and drew his long sword, readying himself as the first of the soldiers camped in the square charged at them.

The second spearman to Malus's right turned and dashed for his weapon. The highborn reversed his grip on the spear and hurled it at the warrior, striking the elf between the shoulder blades. 'Stay beneath the arch!' he warned the corsairs. They just had to hold the gate open long enough for their reinforcements to arrive, but with seven against forty, he didn't think they were going to last very long.

Malus raced up to join Silar just as the enemy spearmen attacked. The young knight knocked a thrusting spear aside and caught his attacker full in the face with a backhanded cut. Another elf warrior charged forwards and stabbed two-handed with his spear, driving the keen point through the mail covering Silar's left shoulder. Malus stepped in with a snarl and severed the spearman's left arm at the elbow, hurling him back in a spray of steaming blood. As Silar pulled the spear free, the highborn stepped past him and caught another spear-thrust against his looted shield. The enemy warrior, in his haste, had forgotten his own shield, and Malus made him pay for the error. His blade slipped beneath the edge of the spearman's scale hauberk and plunged deep into the warrior's guts.

Screams and shouts of pain sounded all around Malus. More and more soldiers were joining the battle, and he was forced to give ground in the face of a thicket of stabbing spears. Two of the corsairs lay dead beneath the gate arch, and another bled from a wound in his chest. Malus caught a trio of spearmen swinging wide to his right, and real-ized they were trying to reach the gate. They could use the oak barrier to push the druchii outside.

Cursing, Malus turned to rush at them – and then a spear-thrust from his left glanced off his stolen helmet and knocked the rim down over his eyes. Yelling, he raised his shield to ward off another blow and fumbled with the unfamiliar helm, trying to shift it around and hold onto his sword at the same time. There was a searing pain in his left leg as a spear point sank into his thigh. Furious and blind, he knocked the weapon loose with the rim of his shield. Then a huge impact on his back knocked him off his feet and a triumphant roar echoed in his ears.

Malus covered himself with his shield as he hit the ground, and the bone-jarring impact sent the helmet flying. Heavy footfalls shook the ground all around him; the highborn looked about frantically and realized that the bulk of the raiders had finally arrived. Screaming cor-sairs raced out of the night and swept in a black tide over the startled defenders, driving them past the gate arch and back into the square. Within seconds the battle was receding into the distance as the surviv-ing spearmen retreated deeper into the town.

Safe for the moment, Malus cast aside his shield and tried to check on the wound in his leg. Blood had already soaked through his robes and was dripping freely on the ground. Silar stood nearby, stuffing a bloodstained rag into the hole in his armour. Seeing the highborn's wound, the young knight forgot what he was doing and joined Malus. 'How bad is it?' Silar asked.

Malus grimaced. 'Damned if I know,' he said. 'It hurts like the blazes, but I think I can stand.'

'It's bleeding freely, my lord. Best let me bandage it first,' Silar replied, and began tearing strips from one of a dead spearman's cloak.

By the time Silar had knotted the field dressing tight the battle in the town was over. Lhunara came jogging back to the gate, her sword dripping red and her face spattered with gore. 'I was wondering what happened to the two of you,' she said.

'Never mind us,' Malus growled. 'What of the battle?'

The first mate grinned. 'The town is ours,' she said. 'The garrison is finished, and we're searching the houses for captives. Looks like the women and children fled earlier in the day, though. Probably hiding somewhere up in the hills. Lots of plunder, though, so we won't be leaving empty-handed.'

Malus nodded as Silar helped him to his feet. It wasn't a total victory, but not a total loss, either. 'Take everything you can, but be quick. We're running short on time.'

It was just over an hour before the raiders were ready to move again, with three looted wagons laden with plunder and a coffle of thirty slaves. Losses among the raiders had been light, and despite the precariousness of their situation the corsairs were jubilant as they set off down the southern coast road. Malus rode in the lead wagon, cursing the wound in his leg. He could walk, but there was no way he could keep up the pace to get to the rendezvous in time. The druchii gave their captive cousins a taste of the lash to hurry them along.

They raced down the curving road, trading caution for speed and trusting to the fickle luck of the gods to see them through. It was just past the hour of the wolf when Lhunara gave the signal to leave the road and make for the narrow strip of beach to their right. Malus focused his tired eyes and peered into the darkness offshore. If the *Manticore* was out there, she was invisible in the night.

Exhausted, the coffle of slaves collapsed onto the sand. Lhunara barked another set of orders and the corsairs got to work posting lookouts and unloading the wagons. Silar came up alongside the highborn and searched the dark horizon as well. 'You don't think he left us, do you?' the young knight asked, giving voice to Malus's fears.

'Gul's chances of making it back to Clar Karond with such a small crew would be very slim,' Malus said. 'Even I know that.' Still, he thought, it could be done. He wished he'd insisted on having the navigator accompany the raiding party, but it was likely that even the crew would have balked at such a reckless notion.

'They could have run into that other patrol ship,' Silar mused. 'Or hit a squall and had their masts carried off.'

'Mother of Night!' Malus hissed. 'Are you always this gloomy?'

'I prefer to say I'm no stranger to misfortune,' the young knight replied.

'More's the pity,' Malus said. Then a glimmer of movement caught his eye. 'There!' he said, pointing out to sea.

The first of *Manticore's* longboats heaved into view, its rowers straining mightily against the oars. A ragged cheer went up from the corsairs until a hissed warning from Lhunara put their minds back on business.

Within minutes all four of the corsair's longboats were being dragged ashore, and *Manticore* herself had hove into view less than a mile from the beach, outlined like a ghost ship in the moonlight. Amaleth jogged up the strand, eyeing the raiders' haul. 'Sailors and plunder first,' the second mate suggested to Malus. 'Then the rest of the crew and the slaves.' He noticed the bloodstained bandage on the highborn's leg. 'Will you head back with the loot?'

And look weak in front of the men, Malus thought? Oh, no. That would only encourage Lurhan's hidden assassin. The highborn shook his head. 'Get the boats loaded as quickly as you can,' he said. 'I'll go with the second wave.'

The second mate nodded. 'Of course, sir,' he said with a faintly mocking smile. Before Malus could reply, Amaleth had turned and was running back to the boats.

They loaded the plunder aboard double-quick, and less than ten minutes later the longboats were rowing back to *Manticore*, burdened with loot and a third of the surviving raiders. Once there, however, it seemed to take hours to unload their cargo. Before long Malus was looking worriedly to the east, expecting to see the first rays of dawn at any moment. 'What's taking them so long?' Malus muttered.

Just then there was a commotion from farther down the south road. One of the lookouts came charging onto the beach and delivered a breathless report to Lhunara. The first mate sent the corsair back the way he came and hurried over to Malus, her expression grim.

'There's a column of troops coming up fast along the coast road,' she said. 'Looks like Sea Guard.'

'By the Dark Mother!' Malus swore. 'How did they get here so fast?'

Beside him, Silar pointed out to sea. 'That's how,' the young knight said.

It was the warship that had chased *Manticore* into the mists near the Blighted Isle, her white sails billowing like wings in the moonlight. She was bearing down fast upon the druchii corsair, eager for revenge. The hunters had now become the hunted.

'Can our boats make it back to us in time?' he asked Lhunara.

'It doesn't look like it,' she said, her voice hollow. Malus turned to the first mate and saw she was staring at the distant *Manticore*. The corsair ship was taking her boats aboard. Gul was abandoning the rest of the raiding party to its fate.

In an awful flash of intuition Malus saw the trap that Gul had sprung on him. The ship's master had delayed the offloading at the ship as long as he could to increase the chance they would be found. It was possible he'd even taken steps earlier to make the corsair easier to discover. And the timing had worked out to perfection. Gul now had a hold full of treasure and just enough sailors to make it back home and claim Lurhan's reward.

Lhunara looked up at Malus, a stricken expression on her face. 'The Sea Guard will be here any minute,' she said. 'What do we do now?'

Malus straightened in his seat and took stock of their situation. Around fifty corsairs waited on the sand, surrounding thirty increasingly defiant slaves. Bile rose in Malus's throat. He shook his head. There was only one thing left to do.

'We die,' the highborn said.

TEN MINUTES LATER came the soft jingle of harness and the drumming of swift feet along the coast road, and the relief column of Sea Guard troops came swarming down onto the beach, weapons at the ready. The sight that awaited them left many of the young warriors reeling in shock.

The white sands were black with blood in the fading moonlight. Dark-robed bodies lay everywhere, their limbs strangely contorted in death. Bloodstained figures in the simple garb of fisherman sat or staggered about the scene of carnage, many with slave manacles still dangling from their wrists. Many wielded gory knives as they stalked among the dead.

In moments the leader of the column arrived at the beach, and he, too, was stunned by the brutality of what had happened. He pulled his winged helm from his head, his face pale with shock. 'For pity's sake, help them,' he commanded his troops, and the spearmen put down their weapons and moved to help the survivors.

The lieutenant bit back a wave of despair as he surveyed the awful scene. His gaze fell upon another villager, sitting alone against the side of a wagon's wheel. He approached the hunched figure, kneeling respectfully at his side.

'We came as soon as we could, cousin,' the lieutenant said. 'What you did here was... very brave.'

The figure sighed. 'I know,' he replied in a dead voice. 'But we had no choice.' Before the lieutenant could reply Malus drew a dagger from within his sleeve and stabbed the sorrowful elf in the eye.

As one, the 'villagers' leapt at the surprised spearmen, slashing and stabbing with their knives. Other corsairs leapt from the sands and attacked the elves from behind. In moments the slaughter was complete.

Lhunara pulled off the villager's tunic she'd worn over her armour. Breathless, she staggered over to Malus. 'The Lord of Murder favoured us,' she gasped. 'But what now?'

The highborn levered himself painfully to his feet and pulled off his own disguise. 'All is not yet lost.' He gestured out to sea. '*Manticore* wasn't as fleet-footed at Master Gul hoped.'

Delayed by taking on her boats and with only a minimal crew to work her sails, the corsair had been quickly overtaken by the elven warship, and now they were grappled together in a brutal boarding action.

'These Sea Guard must have come ashore a few miles to the south,' Malus said. Their boats are likely waiting for them on the beach. If we can reach them in time we can still rescue *Manticore* and get ourselves out of this mess.'

Lhunara thought it over and nodded. 'We'll load everyone into the wagons and ride the horses to death if we must,' she said with a fierce grin, and turned to shout orders to the corsairs.

As the raiders clambered aboard the wagons Malus surveyed the bloodstained sands one last time. Killing the slaves had been the only way, he realized, but the loss still ate at him. 'Worth their weight in silver,' he muttered, shaking his head in disgust. 'I'll likely not see such wealth again.'

MANTICORE WALLOWED IN the cold swells of the Sea of Malice as she limped the last few leagues back to port. It had been a long voyage back; the raider had suffered considerable punishment at the hands of the vengeful elves, and by the time Malus and the raiding party had managed to sneak onto the enemy warship's deck, Gul's troops had already been decimated. But the enemy captain had been overconfident, believing his troops had finished the raiders trapped on the beach, and had never expected a sudden attack from shore. By the time he realized his mistake it had been far too late. The battle ended swiftly after that. Malus ordered the warship set ablaze and the *Manticore* made good her escape, and rewarded the crew with the plunder he'd taken from the village in Ulthuan, in a single stroke he'd won the allegiance of the crew away from Hathan Gul.

Master Gul had abased himself at Malus's feet when the fighting was done. His apologies were voluminous, and his pleas for mercy were most sincere. The highborn gave the treacherous slug every opportunity to convey the depth of his regret, slicing off only a small part of Gul's body each day. The ship's master was still alive when Malus offered him to the sea witches as they passed the tower of Karond Kar.

Standing at the prow of the crippled ship, Malus fished into the small coin pouch at his belt. His fingers closed on a handful of rough objects and he held them up to the sunlight. 'All that plunder, and this is all the gold I have to my name,' he said, showing Silar and Lhunara a handful of Gul's teeth.

The young knight shook his head and turned his gaze back to the docks of Clar Karond, just a few miles off the bow. Lhunara chuckled. 'Melt them down and have them made into a set of dice,' she suggested.

'Perhaps I will,' the highborn mused.

'What happens once we reach port?' Silar asked. 'We're more than three months early, and you've nothing to show for your cruise.'

The highborn shrugged. 'I could have come back dragging Teclis by the hair and it wouldn't have mattered,' he said. 'I'll return to Hag Graef and start plying the flesh houses again. Who knows? I might even start breeding nauglir.' He regarded Silar thoughtfully. 'I misjudged you, Silar. A poor knight you may be, and too honest for your own damned good, but you served me well. I'll release you from your oath here and now if you wish. You needn't accompany me back to that den of vipers at the Hag.'

Silar chuckled. 'And miss the look on your father's face? No, my lord. I'll accompany you.'

Malus nodded, then turned to Lhunara. 'You, on the other hand, never gave me any oath. Gul is dead, and Amaleth was killed in the battle off Ulthuan. By law, *Manticore* is your ship now.'

'True enough,' the first mate said, 'but I'm done with sailing the seas. If you're still serious about taking me into your retinue, then I'll give you my oath.' She smiled. 'But I expect to be well rewarded for my service.'

'You may wind up with more than you bargained for,' the highborn answered sardonically.

'Speaking of bargains,' Silar interjected. 'There's still the matter of who shot you on board that patrol ship off the Blighted Isle.'

Malus frowned. 'Ah, yes. Lurhan's hidden assassin. That was Amaleth, I expect. I saw him with a crossbow just before the battle.'

'It was him, right enough,' Lhunara said. 'I paid a couple of corsairs to shadow him during the battle.' Her expression soured. 'They weren't supposed to let him take a shot at you without my permission, though.'

'Your *permission*?' The highborn's eyes went wide with shock. 'You knew Amaleth was Lurhan's assassin the whole time?'

'Of course. I kept him alive as insurance, just in case you had any treachery of your own in mind,' Lhunara replied. 'What, did you imagine I would take you at your word?'

For a moment, Malus was speechless, torn between murderous out-rage and grudging admiration. Silar leaned against the rail and chuckled softly, staring out to sea.

'We'll be the death of you yet, my lord,' the young knight said.

THE DAEMON'S CURSE

Chapter One
BLOOD AND COIN

THE SHADOWBLADE RODE the Sea of Malice with a winter gale at her back, her indigo-dyed sails of human hide stretched to their limit and the slate-grey sea hissing along her sharply-raked hull. Her druchii crew knew their trade well, gliding effortlessly along the pitching deck like hungry shades at the sibilant orders of their captain.

They wore heavy robes and thick leather kheitans to keep out the icy wind, and their dark eyes glittered like onyx between the folds of dark woollen scarves. They were racing before the storm with a full load of cargo chained below, but the craggy southern coastline and the mouth of the river leading to Clar Karond lay only a few miles off the bow. The wind howled hungrily in the black rigging, singing an eerie counterpoint to the muffled cries rising from the hold, and the sailors laughed in quiet, sepulchral tones, thinking back to the revels of the night before.

Malus Darkblade stood at the corsair's prow, one gauntleted hand resting on the ship's rail as he watched the sharp towers of the sea gate rise before him. A heavy cloak of nauglir hide hung from his narrow shoulders and wisps of black hair spilled from the confines of a voluminous hood to twist and dance in the wind. The cold clawed at his face and he bared his teeth at its touch. The highborn elf pulled a carefully folded token from his belt and held it to his lips, breathing in its heady perfume. It smelled of blood and brine, setting his senses on edge.

51

This is the smell of victory, he thought, his lips twisting into a mirthless smile.

The raiding cruise had been a gamble from the outset, and he'd pushed his luck every step of the way. With only one small ship, an equally small crew and a late start hindering his efforts, it wasn't enough to merely succeed; nothing short of a rousing triumph would impress his reluctant allies back at Hag Graef. So they had lingered along Bretonnia's western coast weeks after their peers had set course for home.

The captain had complained bitterly about the turning weather and the damnable Ulthuan Seaguard until Malus had put a knife to his throat and threatened to take command of the *Shadowblade* himself. When a gale blew up in the dead of night off the shores of Couronne all had seemed lost, and six sailors had vanished into the black waves while fighting to keep the wind and the sea from dashing the corsair against the rocks. But by dawn their luck had turned along with the wind; the Bretonnian coastal patrols had fared far worse than they, having been cast up on the rocks or blown down the long inlet towards the free city of Marienburg.

In swift succession, the raiders struck three villages along the coast and sacked the battered fort at Montblanc in four days of pillage and slaughter before escaping out to sea with a hold full of slaves and two chests brimming with gold and silver coin.

He would see to it that his backers were well paid for their efforts; to risk the ire of his family by borrowing the funds he needed for the voyage from other sources had been a risky gambit. After being stalemated for so long, it was tempting to let the money flow through his hands like spilled blood, hiring assassins, tormentors and vauvalka to revenge himself on his brothers and sisters. Part of him yearned for an orgy of revenge, of torture and death and agonies that lingered beyond death. The need was sharp, like steel on the tongue, and sent a shiver of anticipation along his spine.

The darkness awaits, brothers and sisters, he thought, his eyes alight with menace. You've kept me from it for far too long.

The darkly-stained deck creaked slightly and heeled to starboard as the corsair settled onto a course for the narrow river mouth leading to the City of Ships. Closer now, Malus could make out the tall, craggy towers of the sea gate rising on both banks of the narrow approach; a heavy iron chain stretched between them, just beneath the surface of the swift-running water. Cold mists, shifting and swirling in the wind, clung to the rocky shore and the flanks of the towers.

From high in the corsair's rigging, a sailor blew a hunting horn, its long, eerie wail echoing across the surface of the water. There came no reply, but Malus's skin prickled as he studied the thin arrow slits of the citadels, knowing that predatory eyes were studying him in turn.

The highborn's ears caught a subtle change in the sound of the corsair's hissing wake, as a faint hum like a chorus of mournful spirits rose from the water near the hull. He peered over the rail and his sharp eyes caught sleek, dark shapes darting swiftly just beneath the surface of the water. They passed in and out of view, vanishing into the icy depths as silently as ghosts, only to reappear again in the blink of an eye. As he watched, one of the figures rolled onto its back and regarded him with wide, almond-shaped eyes.

Malus caught a glimpse of pale, almost luminous skin, a smooth belly and small, round breasts. An eerily druchii-like face broke the surface with barely a ripple, water gleaming on high, sharp cheekbones and blue-tinged lips. *Aaaahhh*, it seemed to sigh, a thin, wavering sound, then back it sank into the depths, its lithe body surrounded by sinuous strands of indigo-coloured hair.

'Shall I catch a fish for you, my lord?'

The highborn turned to find four cloaked figures standing just beyond sword's reach – proper hithuan for lieutenants and favoured retainers. The dual hilts of highborn swords rode high on their hips and fine silver steel mail glinted in the weak afternoon light over black, grey or indigo kheitans. All of the druchii had their hoods up against the punishing, icy wind, save one.

She was taller than her companions, her long, black hair woven in a multitude of long, thin braids and bound back into a corsair's topknot. Fine, white scars crisscrossed her oval face, from her high cheekbones to her pointed chin, and the tip of her right ear had been sliced away in a battle long ago. Three livid red cuts, fresh from the night's revels, ran in parallel lines down her long, pale neck, disappearing beneath the gleaming curve of a silver steel hadrilkar, etched with the nauglir sigil of Malus's house. As ever, there was a glint of mockery in Lhunara Ithil's appraising stare. 'Will you have her for your plate, your rack or your bed?' she asked.

'Must I choose?'

The retainers laughed, a sound like bones rattling in a crypt. One of the hooded highborn, a druchii with sharp features and a shaven head save for a corsair topknot, arched a thin eyebrow. 'Do my lord's tastes run to beasts, now?' he hissed, drawing more cold chuckles from his companions.

The druchii woman shot her companion a sarcastic look. 'Listen to Dolthaic. He sounds jealous. Or hopeful.'

Dolthaic snarled, lashing out at the woman with the back of a mailed gauntlet that the tall raider batted easily aside.

Malus laughed along with the cruel mirth. The years of inaction had soured the spirits of his small warband to the point where he'd begun to wonder which of them would try to assassinate him first. A season of blood and pillage had changed all that, sating their appetites for a time and promising a chance for more. 'Arleth Vann, how fares the cargo?' he asked.

'Well indeed, my lord,' spoke the third retainer, his sibilant whisper barely audible above the keening wind. The druchii's head was bald as an egg and his face and neck were cadaver-thin, like a man rendered down to corded muscle and bone by a long and merciless fever. His eyes were a pale yellow-gold, like those of a wolf. 'We had a small amount of spoilage on the return crossing, but no more than expected. Enough to keep the cook busy and give the survivors some meat in their stew to see them through the march to the Hag.'

The fourth retainer pulled back his hood and spat a thin stream of greenish juice over the rail. He was the very image of a druchii noble, with fine-boned features, a mane of lustrous black hair and a face that looked merciless even in repose. Like Malus, he wore a cloak made of nauglir hide, and his kheitan was expensive dwarf skin, tough but supple. The silver steel hadrilkar around his neck looked dull and tawdry against the fine craftsmanship of the noble's attire.

'That's still good coin lost needlessly,' Vanhir said, his rich and melodious voice at odds with his stern demeanor. 'If we'd made port at Clar Karond your backers would already have their investments repaid, and us besides,' he said, showing white teeth filed to fashionable points. 'The slave lords will not be pleased at the breach of custom.'

'The Hanil Khar is two days from now. I have no time to waste haggling with traders and flattering the whipmasters at the Tower of Slaves,' Malus hissed. 'I intend to stand in the Court of Thorns at the Hag, in the presence of my father and my *illustrious* siblings,' he said, the words dripping with venom, 'and present the drachau with a worthy tribute gift.' And show the court that I am a power to reckon with after all, he thought. 'We march for Hag Graef as soon as the cargo is ready to travel.'

Dolthaic frowned. 'But what of the gale? It will be a hard march to the Hag in the teeth of a winter storm–'

'We'll march through snow, ice and the Outer Darkness if we must!' Malus snapped. 'I will stand in the City of Shadow in two days' time or every one of you will answer for it.'

The retainers growled an acknowledgment. Vanhir studied Malus with narrowed eyes. 'And what then, after you've made your grand entrance and showered the drachau with gifts? Back to the blood pits and the gambling dens?'

Dolthaic grinned like a wolf. 'After four months at sea I've got a thirst or two I wouldn't mind quenching.'

'I shall indulge myself for a time,' Malus said carefully. 'I have an image to maintain, after all. Then I shall begin putting my new fortune to good use. There's much to be done.'

They were close enough to hear the booming of the waves against the shoreline. The citadels of the sea gate loomed high above the *Shadowblade*, barely a mile ahead and to either side of the corsair's rakish bow. The gusting wind carried the sounds of a struggle aft. Malus looked back and saw three druchii warriors wrestling with a manacled human slave. As the highborn watched, the slave smashed his forehead into the face of one of his captors. There was a crunch of cartilage as blood sprayed from the warrior's nose. The druchii staggered a half-step back with a bubbling snarl and raised a short-handled mace.

'No!' Malus cried, his sharp, commanding voice carrying easily over the wind. 'Remember my oath!' The druchii warrior, blood streaming down his face and staining his bared teeth, caught the highborn's eye and lowered his weapon. Malus beckoned to the struggling guards. 'Bring him here.'

The slave wrenched his body violently, trying to tear free of his captors' grip. The mace-wielding druchii gave the human a shove, pushing him off his feet, and the other two warriors lunged forward, dragging the man across the deck. Malus's four retainers slid aside to let them pass, eyeing the slave with cold, predatory interest.

The warriors forced the slave to his knees; even then, he rose nearly to Malus's shoulders. He was powerfully built, with broad shoulders and lean, muscular arms beneath a torn, stained gambeson. He wore dark woollen breeches over ragged boots, and his hands were crusted with scabs and blue with cold. The man was young, possibly a yeoman or a Bretonnian squire, and bore more than one battle-scar on his face. He fixed Malus with a hateful glare and began bleating something in his guttural tongue. The highborn gave the human a disgusted look and nodded to the two warriors. 'Remove his chains,' he told them, then turned to Arleth Vann. 'Shut the beast up.'

The retainer glided across the deck, swift as a snake, and grabbed the slave with a claw-like grip at the point where his neck met his right shoulder. A steel-clad thumb dug into the nerve juncture there, and the slave's heated words vanished in a sharp hiss, his whole body going taut with agony. There was a soft rattle of metal, and the two druchii warriors retreated, holding a set of manacles between them.

Malus smiled. 'Good. Now tell him what I have to say.' He stepped before the slave, staring down into his pain-filled eyes. 'Are you the one called Mathieu?'

Arleth Vann translated, almost whispering the thickly-accented Bretonnian into the man's ear. Grunting with pain, the slave nodded.

'Good. I have a rather amusing story to tell you, Mathieu. Yesterday, I stood at the entrance to the slaves' hold and announced that, as a gesture of charity, I would release one of your number, unharmed, before we made port in Naggaroth. Do you remember?'

A tumult of emotions blazed behind the slave's eyes: hope, fear and sadness, all tangled together. Again, he nodded.

'Excellent. I recall you all talked among yourselves, and in the end you chose a young girl. Slender and red-haired. Green eyes like eastern jade and sweet, pale skin. You know of whom I speak?'

Tears welled in the slave's eyes. He struggled vainly to speak, despite Arleth Vann's terrible grip.

'Of course you do.' Malus smiled. 'She was your betrothed, after all. Yes, she told me this, Mathieu. She fell to her knees before me and begged for you to be set free in her place. Because she *loved* you.' He chuckled softly, thinking back to the scene. 'I confess, I was astonished. She said I could do anything I wanted with her, so long as you went free. *Anything.*' He leaned close to the slave, close enough to smell the fear-sweat staining his filthy clothes. 'So I put her to the test.'

'Clar Karond was only a day away, and the crew deserved a reward for their labours, so I gave her to them. She entertained them for hours, even with their unsophisticated ways. Such screams… surely you heard them. They were exquisite.'

Malus paused for a moment as Arleth Vann struggled for the right translation, though by this point the slave's eyes had glazed over, fixed on some distant point only he could see. His muscular body trembled.

'After the crew was spent, they returned her to me and I let my lieutenants take their turn.' Off to the side, Lhunara grinned and whispered something to Dolthaic, who smiled hungrily in return. 'Again, she did not disappoint. *Such* pleasures, Mathieu. Such sweet skin. The blood sparkled across it like tiny rubies.' He held out the token in his cupped hand, unfolding it gently and reverently. 'You were a very lucky man, Mathieu. She was a gift fit for a prince. Here. I saved you her face. Would you like one last kiss before you go?'

With a shriek of perfect anguish the slave surged to his feet, but Arleth Vann lashed out with his other hand and sank his fingertips into the nerve juncture beneath the thick muscle of the human's upper right arm. The slave staggered, unmanned by blinding pain. His eyes were wide, and Malus could see the darkness there, spreading into the human's mind like a stain. The slave let out a despairing wail.

'Wait, Mathieu. Listen. You haven't heard the really amusing part yet. By the time the crew was done with her she was begging, *pleading* to be set free instead of you. She cursed your name and renounced her love for you again and again. But of course, I had my oath to consider – I said I would let a slave go unharmed, you see, and that hardly applied to her any more. So in the end her love won out, and oh, how she hated it!' Malus threw back his head and laughed. 'Enjoy your freedom, Mathieu.'

All at once Arleth Vann changed his grip on the man, seizing him by the neck and the belt of his breeches, and with surprising strength the lithe druchii picked the large man off the deck and threw him over the side. He hit the water with a loud, flat slap and disappeared into the freezing depths. The druchii slid along the rail, watching intently. The wind whistled and howled. The sighing of the mere-witches had fallen silent.

When the man surfaced, gasping for air, he was no longer alone. Two of the sea creatures clung to him, wrapping their thin, pale arms around his chest. Ebon talons sank deep, drawing blooms of crimson across the white fabric of the man's gambeson. Thick indigo strands – not rich hair, but ropy, saw-edged tentacles – wrapped around his wrist and throat, sloughing off long strips of skin as they wound tight around their victim. Mathieu choked out a single, gulping scream before one of the mere-witches covered his open mouth with her own. Then they sank beneath the surface and were lost in the *Shadowblade's* wake.

A rattling, ringing sound filled the air ahead – the citadels were lowering the great chain barring entrance to the river. Tendrils of icy sea mist, drawn by the corsair's passage, rolled in on either side of the river mouth, whirling and tangling in the ship's wake.

High atop the tower to the left, Malus could see lithe figures in dark robes and billowing scarves appearing at a small cupola to observe the corsair's progress. They offered no sign of greeting, no gesture of welcome, merely watched in stony silence. As the ship cleared the river chain, one of the figures raised a horn to his lips and blew a long, wailing note, warning the City of Ships of the bloody-handed reavers heading their way.

Malus Darkblade turned back to his retainers, a slow, heartless smile spreading across his face.

'It's good to be home.'

Chapter Two
PROCESSION OF CHAINS

THE WIND SHIFTED, blowing from the north-west, and the cold one's nostrils flared as it caught the scent of horseflesh. Without warning the one-ton warbeast snapped at the harbour lord's warhorse, its powerful, blocky jaws clashing shut with a bone-jarring crunch. The horse shrieked in terror, rearing and dancing away from the nauglir and drawing a stream of curses from the harbour lord himself. Malus pretended not to notice, drawing Spite up short with a jerk of the reins and a good-natured kick to his flanks as he opened the letter the harbour lord had delivered to him.

The *Shadowblade* rode uneasily at its moorings as the leading edge of the winter storm reached up the Darkwine River and lashed Clar Karond with gusts of sleet and freezing rain. The black masts of scores of druchii corsairs crowded the skies along the waterfront, bristling like a forest of black spears – fully two-thirds of Naggaroth's nimble fleet anchored at the City of Ships during the long winter months, when the straits to the Sea of Chill were frozen solid.

The city lay in a broad valley bounded by the forbidding crags of the Nightsreach Mountains. Dry docks, warehouses and slave quarters dominated the eastern shore of the river and the city proper with its walls, tall manors and narrow streets rose to the west. The highborn citizens of the city kept their own docks on the western shore as well, and Malus had paid the harbour lord a substantial sum, in silver and young flesh, for the privilege of temporarily claiming one of the highborn docks as his own.

Three bridges of stone and dark iron connected the two halves of Clar Karond, and it was well known that highborn in the city paid bands of thugs to extort 'tolls' from travellers crossing in either direction. Any other day Malus would have relished such a confrontation, but not with almost two hundred human slaves in tow.

It was a fortune in flesh and blood that stumbled and shuffled down the *Shadowblade's* gangway, hobbled by chains that bound them at the wrist and ankle and linked them in two long coffles of a hundred slaves each. Malus's small warband of a dozen nobles mounted on cold ones and a company of spear-armed mercenaries surrounded the shivering slaves on the granite quay.

A handful of taskmasters kept the humans in line with the flickering tongues of long whips, while the troops turned their gaze outwards, watching the three narrow approaches leading to the quay and the narrow windows of the surrounding buildings. Nearly four hours had passed while the ship's hands had offloaded the volatile nauglir, the slaves and finally the warband's baggage. Night was drawing on, and every passing minute set Malus further on edge. The sooner he was out of the city and on the road to Hag Graef, the better.

The letter had been waiting for Malus when the *Shadowblade* arrived, delivered by the harbour lord, Vorhan, when he'd come to collect his bribe. The highborn turned the little packet over in his gloved hands, absently checking for hidden needles or razor edges. It was fine, heavy stock, sealed with a blob of wax and a sigil that was faintly familiar. Frowning, Malus pulled a thin-bladed dagger from his boot and sliced the package open. Inside was a single sheet of paper. Malus stifled an impatient snarl and held the paper close to his face, trying to make out the barely-legible handwriting.

To the Esteemed and Terrible Lord Malus, honoured son of the Dread Vaulkhar Lurhan Fellblade, greetings:

I pray this message finds you flush with victory and your appetites whetted after a season of blood and plunder off foreign shores. Though we have not met before, cousin, your name is well-known to me. Recently I've come to possess certain family secrets that I daresay would be of great value to a clever and capable lord such as yourself.

I await your pleasure at the Court of Thorns, dread lord. Great power lies for the taking if your heart is cold and your hand is sure.

Fuerlan, scion of Naggor

The highborn's eyes narrowed angrily when he reached the letter's signature. With a hiss of disgust he crumpled the paper in his fist.

'Word from the Hag, my lord?'

Malus looked over to see Lhunara nudging her cold one alongside his. Like him, she had added an articulated breastplate of silvered steel over her coat of mail, and her swords were buckled to her high-canted saddle for an easy draw.

Her nauglir, Render, was a giant beast, fully a third again as long as Malus's Spite and half a ton heavier. Much of the creature's weight lay on thickly muscled rear legs; when coupled with a long, powerful tail, a cold one was capable of swift sprints and even long leaps at its rider's command. Its slightly smaller forelimbs came into play when walking or trotting for long distances, and to pin larger prey to the ground while the cold one's massive jaws and razor-edged fangs sliced flesh and pulverised bone.

Render's thick, scaled hide was a dark greenish-grey, with a ridge of larger, broader steel-grey scales running from its blunt, squarish snout to the tip of its tail. A pair of heavy reins ran from a ring on the saddle and clipped to steel rings that pierced the cold one's cheeks; though impressive-looking, they offered little real control over the huge creature. Nauglir were powerful and nearly impervious to injury, but they were also typically slow-witted.

Riders steered their mounts with sharp kicks from their knobby spurs and occasionally the butt of their lances, and used the reins more as a handhold than anything else. Lhunara held her lance upright, couched atop her right stirrup, dark green pennons crackling in the stiff wind.

'Just the croaking of a toad,' Malus growled, swaying in the saddle as Spite shied a bit from the presence of the larger cold one. 'That lickspittle Fuerlan has kissed every boot in the Hag, and now he's set his sights on mine.'

Lhunara frowned, throwing a knobby scar at the corner of her eye into sharp relief. 'Fuerlan?'

'The hostage from Naggor. My cousin,' Malus sneered, 'as he was so careful to mention.' A thought occurred to him and he turned to the seething harbour lord. 'Lord Vorhan, when did this letter arrive?'

'Two days ago, dread lord,' Vorhan said, his words clipped and carefully neutral. 'Delivered by special messenger, direct from the Hag.'

Lhunara raised an eyebrow at the answer. 'A toad, but a well-informed one,' the retainer mused.

'Indeed,' Malus said. 'How long until we are ready to depart?'

'The slaves and the rest of the baggage have been unloaded,' Lhunara replied. 'Vanhir is still in the city, gathering provisions.'

Malus let out a curse. 'Sating his appetites for courva and soft flesh, more like it. He can catch up with us on the road, and I'll have a strip of his hide for every hour he's late.' He stood in the stirrups. '*Sa'an'ishar!*' He cried, his voice pitched to carry across the quay. 'Make ready to march.'

Without a word, Lhunara heeled her nauglir about and sent it loping towards the rear of the slave coffles. Practiced over weeks of raids and marches, the warband shook itself out into marching order quickly and professionally, with the company of spearmen splitting into two files and marching along the flanks of the shuffling slaves. Half the cold one cavalry formed a rearguard under Lhunara, while Malus took the other half at the head of the column. 'Up, Spite!' Malus called, prodding his mount in the direction of the Slavers' Road. As the great beast stalked forward, the highborn reached back behind the saddle and lifted a black repeating crossbow from its carry hook.

The harbour lord's horse stamped and tossed its head, but this time its rider brought it under control with an angry hiss and a sharp twist of the reins. 'Does my dread lord require anything more?' he asked, fingering his long moustache. 'Casks of spirits for the cold nights? A butcher, perhaps? You'll lose a few of your stock before you reach the slave pits, I warrant.'

'My provisions are attended to,' Malus replied, cranking the complicated mechanism that drew back the crossbow's powerful bowstring and levering a steel-tipped bolt into the track. 'And my raiders are well-skilled at separating flesh from bone. You will, however, have the honour of escorting us across the city to the Skull Gate.'

The harbour lord's eyes widened. He was a young druchii for such a high-ranking position, which spoke of his cunning and ambition. Judging by the cut of his robes, his fine, red-dyed kheitan and the jewels glinting from the pommels of his swords, he'd already grown wealthy lining his purse with bribes from the river trade. 'Escort you, dread lord? But that's not my responsibility...'

'I know,' Malus said, laying the loaded crossbow across his lap. 'But I insist. Without a guide, I and my valuable stock might come to mischief, and that would be... tragic.'

'Of course, dread lord, of course,' Vorhan stammered, his lean face turning slightly pale. Reluctantly, he kicked and cursed his skittish horse along in the nauglir's wake.

The streets of Clar Karond were made to kill the unwary. Like all druchii cities, high-walled houses loomed over narrow, twisting streets lost in shadow. Narrow windows – crossbow slits, in fact – looked down on passers-by. Each home was a citadel unto itself, fortified against trespassers in the streets, and against the neighbouring families to either side. Many streets and alleys led nowhere, coming to an end in cul-de-sacs riddled with murder-holes, or leading down into the poisonous sewers beneath the city. It was a place where strangers trod lightly, and Malus fought to keep from betraying his unease as the column worked its way slowly along the Slavers' Road.

The awnings of the houses kept much of the sleet and rain at bay, but the wind howled like a daemon down the narrow streets, driving many of the denizens of the city to seek their pleasures indoors. There was barely enough room for three men to walk abreast, packing the column tightly together. Lord Vorhan was between the spearmen guarding the slave files and the menacing phalanx of the nauglir leading the way; every now and then Malus stared back at the harbour lord, scrutinising his face for any telltale sign of treachery. Such a thing was to be expected when so much wealth was at stake.

Their best chance was to escape the confines of the city before the gates were shut at nightfall. If the column was trapped inside the city overnight, Malus had no idea where they could find a large enough place to encamp and keep watch on their stock. They would be at the mercy of every gang and cutthroat in the city, fighting in an environment where their cavalry would be at a disadvantage. Malus didn't care much for those odds.

Despite the risks, they had made good time, crossing most of the western half of the city in just over an hour. With Lord Vorhan at their side they'd made good time, avoiding costly detours. The sun was very low in the sky, creating a deep twilight in the shadow of the tall buildings. Pale green witchlight, streaming from the high windows, gleamed on the pointed helmets of the infantry and along the glittering edges of their spears. But the Skull Gate was close – Malus had begun to catch brief glimpses of the spiked ramparts in gaps between the buildings and their peaked roofs.

He gritted his teeth. If there was to be an ambush, it would have to be soon. Twisting in his saddle, he reviewed the order of the column, but the line was so long he couldn't see more than a third of the way along it until the rest was lost out of sight around a turn. There had been no sign of Vanhir and the provisions at all; he could have joined up with Lhunara's rearguard or could be stretched out in a stupor in one of the city's flesh houses for Malus knew.

Malus admitted to himself he'd been too clever by half when he'd accepted the highborn's oath of service rather than tearing out his guts. Lingering humiliation and a means to blackmail another highborn family had seemed like a cunning idea at the time. Now he vexes me at every turn, Malus thought balefully.

Lord Vorhan straightened in the saddle, mistaking the intent of the highborn's glare. 'Not long now, dread lord,' he called. 'Just around the corner up ahead.'

'Indeed?' Malus said. He raised his hand, and the column staggered to a halt. 'The vanguard will proceed,' he ordered, loud enough so his assembled retainers could hear. 'And you–' he pointed to Vorhan– 'will accompany us.'

Without waiting for a response, Malus spurred his mount forward.

The road continued for another thirty yards and turned abruptly right. The vanguard came around the corner in two columns, lances held high. Malus led the way, his hand resting lightly on the crossbow's grip. Around the turn, the road opened into a small square, the first Malus had seen since leaving the quay. Directly ahead lay the city gates, still open. A detachment of guards stood in the relative shelter of its high arch.

There was no one on the square. Malus surveyed the scene warily. The tall windows were shut tight against the building storm, and a thin coating of ice on the cobblestones revealed that no large body of men had passed through the square recently. The Dark Mother smiles on me today, Malus thought. He signalled to one of his riders to head back and call the column forward.

Lord Vorhan edged his horse forward. The harbour lord cleared his throat. 'The gate captain will expect a token of… courtesy… in order to keep the gate open long enough for the column to depart. I would be happy to facilitate the transaction of course–'

'If there's a bribe to be paid you'll pay it yourself,' Malus snapped. 'As a *courtesy* to me, you understand.'

Lord Vorhan bit back his reply, but there was no mistaking the hatred gleaming in his eyes. You may prove to be trouble next season, Lord Vorhan, Malus thought. I believe your career is going to come to a tragic and sudden end.

Perhaps reading the intent in Malus's gaze, the harbour lord blanched and looked away.

'On, Spite,' Malus commanded, giving the beast a kick. As one, the vanguard moved forward.

If the gate commander entertained any thoughts of enriching himself, the sight of a troop of highborn cavalry and the grim look of the young noble at its head quickly persuaded him otherwise. At the captain's urging, the guardsmen stepped out into the sleet and rain to give the cold ones a wide berth as they entered the echoing tunnel between the inner and outer gates.

The Skull Gate opened onto a road at the far end of the valley, passing through rock-strewn fields for a quarter of a mile before disappearing into a forest of black pine and hackthorn. From experience, Malus knew the road ran through the woods for another few miles before opening onto farmers' fields and pasture land. There, a branch of the road turned north and west, beginning the weeklong march to Hag Graef. Once out from under the ominous weight of the gatehouse, Malus nudged Spite out of the column and onto the roadside to watch the rest of the warband pass. He idly fingered the hilt of the skinning knife at his belt, hoping to see Lord Vanhir and the pack train trailing in the rearguard's wake.

Lhunara's cavalry troop was almost clear of the outer gate when Malus heard a furious bellow from one of the cold ones in the vanguard, now almost a hundred yards away. Suddenly, Spite jerked as two sharp blows struck the cold one's shoulder with a meaty *thunk*.

Malus was struck on the shoulder plate of his armour by a small, sharp blow. The missile ricocheted, buzzing within an inch of his nose. *Crossbows!* His mind raced as he twisted in the saddle, trying to look in every direction at once.

Pandemonium reigned all along the column. Slaves shrieked and wailed as more projectiles buzzed through the air. The taskmasters bent to their whips and cudgels with a will, battering the stock back into line, while infantry officers on either side of the road sang out orders to their men. More bellows of rage echoed from the vanguard – the cold ones likely smelled fresh blood. There were two black-fletched bolts jutting from Spite's right shoulder, the small wounds leaking a thin stream of ichor. The beast's scaly hide had clearly stopped much of their impact.

There! Malus caught sight of a small knot of figures crouching among the boulders along the right side of the road, firing bolts at the column in ragged volleys. They wore dun and grey robes that blended perfectly with the rocky terrain.

With a smooth motion, Malus stowed his crossbow behind the saddle and drew his sword from its scabbard with a ringing hiss. 'Lhunara! Crossbows to the right!' He pointed towards the attackers with the tip of his sword.

The druchii retainer caught sight of the attackers and her face twisted into a mask of savage glee. '*Sa'an'ishar!*' She called to her rearguard. 'Ambushers to the right. Open order... *charge!*'

The air rang with the bloodcurdling war-screams of the cold one knights as they kicked their scaly steeds into a lumbering run across the rocky field. Lances still pointed skyward, they fanned out into a loose formation, dodging around large boulders and leaping small ones in their path. Malus hung back, looking along the length of the column.

The taskmasters had forced the slaves face down on the icy ground, and the twin files of spearmen had grounded their shields, facing outwards away from the road. A bonus for their captain, Malus noted. There were shouts and roars coming from the direction of the vanguard. More crossbowmen somewhere up there, he decided. The knights in the vanguard will take care of them. With that, he slapped Spite's flank with the flat of his sword and the huge predator leapt after Lhunara's knights with a hunting roar, sensing prey in the rocks ahead.

There was a score of the robed crossbowmen lurking in the rocks, and they stood their ground to fire a volley into the face of the thunderous charge. The light bolts sprouted from the snouts and shoulders of the oncoming nauglir, but the huge warbeasts had their blood up and nothing could stem their headlong rush. The knights, skilled riders all, waited until the last moment to level their pennoned lances, and drove their steel points home with a rending sound of torn flesh and splintered bone.

Lhunara, in the lead, bore down on a cluster of crossbowmen, trying to load their weapons for one last volley. Too late, they realised their mistake. Their leader let out a wild scream and grabbed for his sword as Lhunara's lance struck him full in the chest. Eighteen inches of hardened steel punched through cloth and light mail as though it were paper, splitting the druchii's sternum and ribs with a brittle crunch. The lance tip and the first two feet of a blood-soaked pennon burst from the man's back and struck another crouching ambusher in the side of the head. The druchii's skull burst like a melon, showering his fellows with a spray of blood, bone and brain matter.

The weight of the two bodies dragged the lance downwards and Lhunara let the weapon fall, drawing her two curved highborn swords as Render bit another shrieking crossbowman in two.

Malus caught sight of another small knot of crossbowmen slipping behind the cover of a large boulder, heading in the direction of the city walls. Gripping his sword tightly, he guided the cold one right at the cottage-sized stone. At the last moment he crouched low in the saddle, dragged back on the reins and shouted 'Up, Spite, up!'

The nauglir gathered its powerful hindquarters and jumped, landing for a heart-stopping moment atop the boulder before leaping down the other side. Malus caught a momentary glimpse of a cluster of pale, terrified faces staring up at him and picked one as his target, rising in the stirrups and holding his curved sword high.

Spite landed on two of the men with an earth-shaking crash, and Malus brought his sword down in the same motion, striking the druchii full in the face and splitting the man from crown to groin. Hot, sticky blood sprayed across the highborn's face and the stink of spilled entrails filled the air. Spite slipped and slid over a slick mush of mud, flesh and pulped intestines. A severed head bounced like a ball across the icy ground, leaving splotches of bright crimson in its wake.

A thrown spear hit Malus full in the chest, striking sparks as it glanced from his heavy breastplate. Two surviving ambushers were running flat out for the city walls and Spite needed no prompting to charge after them. The cold one covered the distance in three bounding strides, clamping his jaws on one of the men and shaking his scaled head like a huge terrier. The druchii literally flew apart, arms and legs cartwheeling off in every direction. The man's lower torso hit the city wall with a gelid slap before sliding to the earth.

The second druchii veered sharply to the right, howling in wide-eyed terror. Without thinking, Malus vaulted from the saddle and sprinted after him, a lusty howl on his blood-spattered lips. They ran for nearly twenty yards across the rocky field before the druchii turned at bay.

Malus saw the man suddenly whirl, and without thinking, swept his sword in front of him, knocking the thrown dagger aside even before his mind had fully registered it. He lunged in, quick as an adder, but the man met Malus's sword with his own. Silvered steel rasped and rang as Malus blocked a low cut aimed for his thigh and then answered with a backhanded slash that nearly opened the druchii's throat. Malus pressed his advantage, hammering at his opponent's guard with heavy blows aimed at shoulder, neck and head. Suddenly the man ducked and lunged forward, his sword aimed for the highborn's throat. Malus twisted sideways at the last second and felt the flat of the cold blade slide along the surface of his neck.

The druchii looked down and screamed, registering the length of cold steel jutting from his thigh. Bright red arterial blood spouted from the wound in time with his beating heart.

Malus pulled his sword free and the druchii crumpled to the earth. With a snarl he drew back his blade for the killing blow – and a mighty impact sent him tumbling through the air. His trajectory was cut short by a large rock, and for a moment the world went black.

When he could see and breathe again, Malus saw Spite chewing the wounded druchii to bits. The nauglir's eyes rolled wildly in their armoured sockets and the warbeast shook its heavy head as though wracked with pain. Suddenly the cold one threw back its head and let out a wild roar, revealing rows of crimson-stained teeth as long as daggers. The nauglir spun in a circle, snapping at the air, then its nostrils flared and it charged off towards the road, bellowing in rage.

Malus felt his body go cold. He staggered to his feet. Something was wrong. Terribly wrong. He staggered around the rock he'd struck and looked toward the road.

The cold ones had gone wild.

The huge beasts were lost in a frenzy of bloodlust, bucking and snapping at the scent hanging in the air. Every one of the dozen cold ones had thrown off their riders and turned their jaws on every living thing they could find. The knights themselves were safe – they coated their skin with the poisonous slime of the nauglir so the fierce beasts would think them pack mates – but every other man and woman within reach was fair game.

The spearmen had tried to make a stand against the berserk animals, but their shield wall shattered like glass under the impact of the raging beasts. Dozens of mercenaries were crushed or torn apart, their armour useless against the nauglirs' powerful teeth and claws. The broken hafts of spears jutted from their heaving flanks, but the beasts were oblivious to pain or injury.

Then the cold ones fell in amongst the coffled slaves and the orgy of slaughter truly began.

'No!' Malus screamed as the roadway turned into a churning abattoir in the space of a dozen heartbeats. The slaves' cries mingled into a single, shattering wail of terror as the cold ones tore them to pieces, biting through bone and manacle with equal ease.

The highborn raced towards the carnage, dimly registering his retainers doing the same. His eye caught the black fletchings of the crossbow bolts jutting from Spite's shoulder. Poison, he thought. Something to drive the nauglir wild. The ambush had never been meant to make off with the slaves, but to eliminate them.

Malus ducked the lashing tail of a nauglir and darted to Spite's blood-streaked side. The cold one had its snout buried in the torso of a dead slave. With a quick leap, the highborn grabbed the hafts of both crossbow bolts and pulled them free with a wet pop. Spite shuddered and turned on Malus, and for a thrilling moment the highborn feared that the slime no longer protected him. Then the huge creature bolted for the field to the left of the road and began to pace in circles, sniffing at the air. After a moment he settled onto his haunches, flanks heaving, his energy spent. The highborn raised the bolts in one blood-stained hand and shouted angrily, 'The bolts have poisoned the cold ones! Pull them out, quickly!'

Around him the other knights began attending to their mounts, pulling at the bolts sticking from their hides. Malus staggered into the field after Spite, stopping when he reached the nauglir's side before turning to face the devastation behind him.

For a hundred yards, the roadway was a red mass of churned meat. Bits of pale bone or glittering chain shone in the misty rain. The armoured forms of dead spearmen littered the ground, their bodies twisted into unnatural shapes. The cries of wounded men filled the air.

Two years of scheming, three months of hard raiding and a prince's ransom in flesh swept away in just a few minutes. Someone had ruined him in a single stroke, and it had been expertly done.

The rattle of armour and weapons carried across the field from the direction of the city gate. A contingent of the city guard made their way towards him, spears ready. Lord Vorhan walked his horse alongside the troops, his expression inscrutable. He reined in and studied the scene a mere ten yards away.

'A terrible turn of fate, dread lord,' he said darkly, shaking his head at the carnage. He looked at Malus. 'Perhaps your luck will turn next season.'

The highborn considered the harbour lord. 'Perhaps,' he said evenly, then plucked the crossbow from his saddle and shot Lord Vorhan in the face.

Chapter Three
GAZING INTO DARKNESS

LIGHT FROM BEYOND the living world seeped through the great crystal skylight of the audience chamber, bathing the inner court with a boreal display of shifting, unsettled light. High upon a circular dais in the centre of the vaulted room, the drachau of Hag Graef, merciless fist of the Witch King, loomed like a nightmare before his subjects.

He wore the ancient, sorcerous armour of his station, an intricate harness of blackened ithilmar plates, sharpened, fluted edges and cunningly-forged hooks. Fiery light and bitter steam seethed from the seams in the armour and the eyes of the daemon-mask carved into his ornate helm, and when the drachau moved, the joints of the armour cried like the souls of the damned. Three freshly-severed heads hung from trophy hooks at the drachau's waist, and the heavy, curved sword in his left hand steamed with clotted gore. His right hand was enclosed in an armoured gauntlet tipped with barbed talons and carved with thousands of tiny, glowing sigils. In that clawed, vicelike grip a highborn noble writhed in his own blood and filth, his eyes gleaming with fear and pain between the drachau's armoured fingers.

The noble saw only darkness, agonising and absolute, but he uttered not a single sound. The pale faces of the court shone like ghosts in the chamber's unsteady light, bearing witness to the highborn's brush with ancient night and waiting for their own turn to come.

This was the culmination of the Hanil Khar, the presentation of tribute and the renewal of the oath of fealty to the drachau, and through him, in turn, the Witch King. The inner court was packed with the true highborn of the city – prominent nobles rich in gold, slaves or battle honours, with hoary lineages and titles. The families clustered in discrete groups, maintaining a wary distance from rivals and even allies – assassination attempts were a matter of course during public gatherings, especially on such ceremonial days. Every family member was further insulated by a circle of favoured retainers, leaving each high-ranking druchii lost in his own solitary thoughts.

Malus watched the highborn suffer on the steps before the dais and wished that he were the one wearing the dreadful gauntlet. The need to lash out, to slice into skin and muscle and spill sweet blood was so intense it set his teeth on edge. He could feel the eyes of his former allies upon him, those nobles who'd invested in his scheme and risked the wrath of his siblings – to say nothing of his dreaded father. They were watching him like wolves, waiting in the shadows for the right moment to sink their teeth into his throat. And they could do it. They knew exactly how weak he was.

He'd broken with ancient tradition, going outside his own family for the funds and alliances to embark on his late-season raid. Worst of all, he'd returned empty-handed. Now there was a large debt to be paid, and his father could easily disavow any obligation in the matter. The Vaulkhar hadn't yet, but only because the druchii lords hadn't yet pressed the issue. Of course. they would when they sensed the time was right. He had little support to draw on; the survivors of the mercenary spearmen had left his service as soon as they'd reached the Hag, and Malus had been forced to pay them in full or risk a blood feud he could ill afford. That left him no more than a score of retainers and twice that many household servants.

He'd only brought three retainers with him to court: Lhunara, Dolthaic and Arleth Vann. The retainers stood in a tight semicircle behind him with their hands on their swords. It was a token guard at best, but against the massed strength of his debtors his entire complement of warriors wouldn't have been enough. Better to keep them guessing at his display of bravado than confirm their suspicions with a phalanx of bodyguards.

The children of the Vaulkhar were arrayed in order of age and ostensible power, though gauging the relative strengths of a highborn family was a murky business in the best of times. There was a conspicuous gap between the tall, armoured figure of Lurhan Fellblade and his second-oldest child, Isilvar.

Bruglir the Reaver, eldest son of the great warlord, was still at sea with his raiding fleet, filling his holds with plunder and the choicest slaves from Ulthuan and the Old World. He would not return until the first of the spring thaw, spending most of the year at sea. It was a feat that only a handful of corsair lords could accomplish, and his favour with the Vaulkhar was such that Lurhan made it plain that none of his siblings was fit to take Bruglir's place, regardless of circumstance. It also had the effect of focusing the resentment of Lurhan's other children, chiefly on Bruglir, a fact that had not escaped Malus.

There were no fat druchii – like their debased cousins, the elves of Ulthuan, the peoples of Naggaroth were typically lithe and muscular, hard and swift as whipcord. Isilvar was *fleshy*. His skin had the greenish pallor of the libertine, pouchy and swollen from too many years of potent spirits and mind-altering powders. He wore his black hair braided with dozens of tiny hooks and barbs, and his long, drooping moustache hung like two thin tusks past the line of his pointed chin. His long-fingered hands, with their sharpened, black-lacquered nails, were constantly in motion; even when folded before him, the fingers riffled and danced like the white legs of a cave spider. Isilvar had made no raids past his own hakseer-cruise; indeed, he often disdained to carry a sword in public, relying on a large contingent of lavishly-appointed retainers for protection.

At some point in the past he and his elder brother had reached an agreement of sorts – Bruglir reaped a harvest of flesh and coin from the spineless kingdoms beyond Naggaroth, and Isilvar oversaw its investment at the Hag and elsewhere across the Land of Chill. This kept Bruglir at sea spilling blood and gave Isilvar all the gold and slaves to sate his prodigious appetites.

At the heart of this strange arrangement were Isilvar's relentless cravings, or so the rumours went – his apartments in the Vaulkhar's tower were said to be a charnel house, rivalling the Temple of Khaine elsewhere in the city. So long as he could bathe in the blood of the tormented each and every day, he was loyal to his brother the provider. Isilvar was surrounded by a score of heavily armed and armoured druchii, each of them resplendent in plate armour lacquered in shades of ruby and emerald. They formed a horseshoe-shaped formation around him, taking care not to deny their lord an unobstructed view of the excruciations occurring on the dais. Isilvar watched the agonies of the highborn with rapt attention, his eyes fever-bright. His long hands, spotted with drops of old blood, spasmed greedily at each of the supplicant's convulsions.

If Isilvar wore his hunger like a rich, stained robe, Lurhan's third child wore a mask of cold, perfect marble, revealing nothing of her inner thoughts. It was said that Lurhan's long-dead wife had been a creature of stunning, lethal beauty – stories recounted duels fought over a single, passing caress offered at court, or rivals torn apart by eager young nobles who lived and died at her whim.

Her daughter Yasmir was said to be her living image. Tall and effort-lessly poised, lithe and muscular as one of Khaine's blood-draped brides, Lurhan's eldest daughter wore a gown of indigo-coloured silk beneath a drape of delicate, yellowed finger bones bound together with fine silver wire. Her thick, lustrous black hair was pulled back from the perfect oval of her face. She had large, violet eyes, the mark of an ancient bloodline stretching back to drowned Nagarythe; they added an exotic air to her otherwise classical features.

A pair of long, bone-handled daggers hung from a narrow girdle of nauglir hide, and it was well-known that she could use them as well, or better, than any man with a sword. She was closely guarded by a dozen retainers, each one a rich and powerful son of one of the city's highborn families.

Yasmir was a living, breathing treasure to them – a wealth of power, influence and beauty, seemingly ripe for the taking. Malus knew better. *They* were *her* baubles, to be toyed with and expended to suit her needs. And for the few months he was at the Hag, Yasmir and Bruglir were inseparable, taking up residence in his spartan quarters in the Vaulkhar's tower. So long as she held her brother's undivided atten-tion, no other man would dare press a challenge of marriage for her.

Other druchii tended to fade into the background when in the pres-ence of Yasmir's glimmering beauty, but none more so than her younger sister. Nagaira was more the child of her brooding father: her skin was duskier, her frame smaller and her figure fuller and less ath-letic. She had Lurhan's black eyes and strong nose, and her thin lips were often compressed in a fine, determined line.

Unlike her sister, Nagaira preferred robes of indigo and deep red over a lightweight kheitan worked with the cold one sigil of the Vaulkhar's house. She wore her black hair in a thick braid that hung only to her waist; it was streaked with strands of glistening grey and white, the telltale sign of one who trafficked in dark lore. Rumours of her secret pursuits had circulated through the court for many years, but if she were troubled by the hint of scandal she took no steps to miti-gate it. Like her siblings, she was well-attended, though her retainers were less a show of strength or vanity than a nod towards function and propriety.

The ten druchii that surrounded her were a motley crew, a mix of priests, rogues and mercenary swords, but she chose her tools well and knew how to use them when she put her mind to it.

But if Nagaira was the shadow to Yasmir's cold radiance, Lurhan's youngest true child was a patch of deepest night. Urial stood straight and tall, nearly of a height with his father, but the heavy black robes masked the withered right arm and bent leg that had marred him from birth. The druchii had no place in their houses for cripples; the malformed were slain at birth or the males given as a sacrifice to the Temple of Khaine.

The infant Urial had been cast into the Lord of Murder's cauldron, and if the stories were true, the ancient brass split with a thunderclap that knocked the priestesses senseless. It was not unheard of for a sacrifice to survive the seething cauldron; such children were seen as marked by the Lord of Murder and taken in by the Temple to be trained in the arts of assassination. But Urial's body was too deformed to make him a holy warrior. He had been raised in the temple as an acolyte, though what he learned there was a mystery oft-speculated.

After fifteen years the maidens returned him to the Vaulkhar's household without explanation, and since then he had occupied a tower all to himself, attended to by a handful of anonymous retainers. Half a dozen of them stood in a tight cluster behind their lord, wearing night-masks of polished steel fashioned in the shape of skulls. Like their lord, they wore black robes over fine hauberks of blackened mail and carried great, curved swords in scabbards of leather and bone strapped across their backs. They were still as statues.

Malus noted that they made no sound when they moved. He couldn't say for certain that they even breathed. Urial's skin was so pale it was almost blue, his features too gaunt to be handsome, and his long hair was almost entirely white. It was well-known that the only thing that aroused the druchii's passions, besides his studies and the ceremonies of the temple, was his sister Yasmir, but it was just as well known that she loathed the sight of him. For many years Malus had expected Yasmir to take her stories of Urial's clumsy advances to Bruglir, who would tear his malformed brother apart in a jealous rage – it had happened to other misguided suitors before. Yet despite Bruglir's famous temper, the eldest son of the Vaulkhar had never raised a hand to his youngest true brother.

Urial the Forsaken, Malus thought, cast aside by your father and vomited up from Khaine's own cauldron. You make no raids, you hold no influence at court and your retainers are faceless and few. And yet the drachau favours you. What gifts do you place at his feet?

As if sensing his stare, Urial's head turned slightly in his direction. Eyes the colour of molten brass, bright but devoid of feeling, locked with his own. A chill ran though Malus, and he was unnerved to discover he could not meet Urial's stare. *The man has dragon's eyes,* he cursed inwardly.

That left him. The bastard child born of a witch. Even Urial held more of his father's favour, or at least a surfeit of fear. Malus was simply a burden Lurhan had to bear, or so the highborn had come to believe. It was the only explanation he could think of for why he hadn't been strangled at birth. His half-brothers and sisters seemed to sense it as well; they were all much older than he and could have murdered him at any time. Instead, they were content to monopolise the household's wealth and leave him to wither on the vine.

One of them had laid the trap at Clar Karond. Of that Malus was certain.

He'd been a fool to think that they would be too busy with other intrigues to take an interest in his sudden absence. But how did they know he would land at the City of Ships? The question had tormented him on the long journey home. Custom – and commerce – required every corsair to make port at the Slave Tower of Karond Kar and auction his cargo to the slave lords who resided there.

Avoiding the tower and sailing directly to Clar Karond had been another rash and unorthodox act, and yet his enemies had been waiting for him. There was even that damned letter, he thought with disgust. Karond Kar was hundreds of leagues to the north-east, one of the most distant and isolated citadels in Naggaroth. Could a messenger have outrun the *Shadowblade*, riding horses to death along the coastal road as the corsair crossed first the Sea of Chill and then the Sea of Malice? Was such a thing possible?

If he did learn who was responsible, what could he *do* about it?

Whatever I must, he answered himself. He still had his swords and a handful of loyal highborn. It would be enough. Let the wolves come, he thought. I will prepare a feast for them.

'Malus, of the House of Lurhan the Vaulkhar!'

The voice ground through the air, reverberating in his bones. Shaped by the power of the drachau's armour, the voice sank into him like a slow, dull knife, reaching for his heart. At the dais, the vassal lord collapsed from his ordeal, his feet slipping in the congealing blood staining the marble steps, and tumbled bonelessly to the audience chamber's floor. His retainers moved quickly to drag him from the drachau's presence, back to the outer court where the lesser ranks waited.

A poor showing, there at the end, Malus noted. That will go hard on him in the year to come. He straightened and shrugged out of his cloak, handing it to Dolthaic. Like Nagaira, he wore only a lightweight kheitan of human hide over black woollen robes. 'Here I am, Terrible One,' he said, providing the ritual response. 'Your servant awaits your bidding.'

'Come before me, and present me with your gifts.'

Eyes turned his way. He could feel their hungry scrutiny. Was he predator or prey? Malus squared his shoulders and approached the dais. Knots of highborn and their retainers stood aside to allow his passage. For a brief moment he found himself face-to-face with Lord Korthan, one of the cabal of ambitious lords he'd convinced to invest in his raid. The druchii fixed him with a glare of pure hate, and Malus returned the stare defiantly as he slipped past.

The pool of blood at the base of the dais was starting to dry, sticking to his heels as he walked through it and ascended the steps to stand before the drachau. The drachau held the power of life and death over every druchii in Hag Graef; one or more lost their head at the end of every Hanil Khar. Some died for crimes, others for insulting the drachau with paltry gifts. Some died simply because the drachau wished to demonstrate his power.

Three steps below the dais Malus stopped, placing his neck within easy reach of the huge, curved sword.

'Another year has passed in exile, another debt of blood for the usurpers in Ulthuan,' the drachau intoned.

'We do not forgive, and we do not forget,' Malus answered.

'We are the people of ice and darkness, sustained by our hate. We live for the Witch King, and to set the ancient wrongs aright.'

'Through fire, blood and ruin.'

The drachau loomed over him, his eyes hidden behind the red glare seething from his visor. 'The loyal vassal offers tribute to his lord. What gifts do you lay at my feet, loyal one?' The drachau's hand tightened fractionally on the hilt of his sword.

Malus met the drachau's fiery stare with one of his own. A thought occurred to him: does he know of my failure? Will he seek to embarrass me before the court? He fought down a surge of murderous rage.

'Great and Terrible One, all that I have is yours: my sword, my household, my hatred. They are all that I possess.' And you would do well to fear them, his defiant stare implied.

For a moment, the armoured figure was silent. This close, Malus could hear the drachau's breath, rumbling like a bellows through the breathing slits in his helmet. 'Every year the answer is the same,' the drachau rumbled threateningly. 'Other lords lay gold and flesh and wondrous relics at my feet. They serve the city and the Witch King and bring torment upon our foes. Naggaroth has no place for the weak or the craven, Malus Darkblade.'

A subtle tremor reverberated through the crowd. Malus stiffened at the age-old slight. 'Then strike me down, Terrible One,' he snarled. 'Water your silvered steel with my blood. But the severed hand cannot strike at the enemy or uphold the laws of the kingdom. It cannot serve the state.'

'Except as an example to others.'

'My lord and master does not lack for those, I think. But devotion is a precious thing, and the wise lord does not squander it. We druchii drink deep of the world. We stand at the edge of the outer darkness and revel in it as no one else will. We spill oceans of blood and harvest kingdoms of souls to suit our wishes, but we do not waste things that are of use to us.'

The drachau considered Malus in silence. For the first time in his life the highborn sensed he rode on a razor's edge, teetering towards the abyss. Then, abruptly, the druchii overlord extended the great, taloned gauntlet. 'I accept your pledge of fealty, Malus, son of Lurhan. But it is not enough to be loyal; the slave must also fear his master, and know to respect the touch of the lash. Since your gifts are meagre, your taste of suffering must be that much greater.'

Malus gritted his teeth. With an effort of will he forced himself to take another step towards the drachau. You've spared my life but named me prey before the entire court, he seethed inwardly. Well then, let's show them what manner of beast I am.

'Do your will, Terrible One,' he said, going so far as to place his head into the drachau's grip. 'The darkness awaits.'

And I will learn from it, Malus thought, his mind boiling with hate. I will sup from it. I will fill my veins with blackest poison and sow my muscles with hate, and in time you will squirm and foul yourself and cry for mercy before me.

CONSCIOUSNESS FLOWED BACK like the tide, filling in the corners and crevices of his mind. He was walking, his stride numb and halting. His robes were soaked in sweat and piss and blood. The taste of blood was in his mouth, and his tongue was swollen where he had bitten into it. Crowds of people passed by on either side on him, their pale faces blurred and floating at the edges of his perception.

There were shadows in his mind, receding stealthily from his consciousness. Dark, cold, taloned things, ancient beyond understanding. They tantalised him and unnerved him. If he concentrated too much on the memories he felt his tenuous hold on his body start to fray.

Abruptly he stopped. He sensed figures very close by, surrounding him on three sides. They did not touch him, offering no hand to steady him. Malus took a deep breath, and the world drew back into focus. 'Did I scream?' he whispered.

'You made not a sound,' Lhunara murmured in his ear, her breath close and warm. 'Nor did you stumble.'

Malus straightened and faced the doors leading to the outer court. Distantly, he could hear Urial's voice addressing the drachau in turn.

'How long?' Malus asked.

Lhunara paused. 'The longest I've ever witnessed. I heard Isilvar tell one of his men that he thought you were going to die from it.'

The highborn managed a wolfish grin. 'Then I am pleased to disappoint once again.'

His steps stronger and more purposeful, Malus strode toward the great doors of blackened oak, which opened before him without the slightest sound. Beyond, the multitudes of low-ranking nobles and their households waited. Their turn to face the drachau would come, but the touch of the gauntlet was not for them. Instead they inflicted their own forms of self-mortification, slicing and piercing their flesh to show their fealty.

The air was electric with the smell of so much blood. Among the lower ranks there was more of a festival atmosphere in the outer court, with servants carrying trays of food and wine or suffering at the whim of their masters. Laughter, sighs of pleasure and sharp cries of pain rose like grace notes over the general buzz of conversation.

A long processional, flanked by the city guard, was cleared through the crowds so the highborn could come and go without hindrance. Druchii nobles thronged along the aisle, watching the haunted faces of the departing highborn and whispering in one another's ears. Malus surveyed the assembled faces with disdain, forcing his body to function as he walked the length of the processional.

At the end of the line another, smaller group of druchii waited. After a moment, Malus noticed that one of the three nobles in particular was eyeing him with considerable interest. He forced his brutalised mind to try and recognise the face, but no name came to mind.

The noble was of average height and somewhat scrawny, as if the gangly time of his youth had never fully given way once he finally reached adulthood. His head was shaved except for a corsair's topknot, and rings of silver glittered from his pointed ears. His narrow chin was shadowed with a thin goatee, and his dark eyes were wide with excitement and glittering with hidden knowledge.

Who does this fool think he is? Malus frowned. The druchii's robes and kheitan were of some quality, but had a rustic cut, the leather reaching nearly to the man's knees. The dark red hide was worked with the sigil of a mountain peak. Malus stopped cold.

Fuerlan. Of course.

'Well met, my lord,' Fuerlan said unctuously, bowing low. Before Malus could respond, the Naggorite rushed up to him, ignoring any pretence of propriety. His two men, evidently local knights with no other prospects, or possibly mercenaries, followed reluctantly in their master's wake. Lhunara hissed threateningly, but Malus stayed her with a slight wave of the hand.

'Did my lord receive the letter?' Fuerlan asked quietly. 'I went to no small expense to deliver it to Clar Karond ahead of your arrival.'

Malus studied the Naggorite hostage carefully. His presence at court was meant to ensure the peace between Hag Graef and Naggor, a recent development after decades of bitter and bloody feuds. As such, the fool enjoyed a degree of protection few others at court did. Caution warred with black rage in Malus's heart. 'Oh, yes. I received it,' he said coldly.

'Excellent!' Fuerlan leaned closer, his voice taking on a conspiratorial tone. 'There is much for us to discuss, dread lord. As you know, I've been among the court and your kinfolk for some time, and–' he attempted a self-effacing smile– 'I flatter myself that I have some skill at the art of intrigue. I have learned of some things, some *very interesting things*, that I think you would find of import.' Fuerlan laid a hand on the highborn's arm. 'There is much we could both profit from if we were to form an alliance of equals– *urk!*'

Malus's left hand closed around Fuerlan's throat in a blur of deadly motion. The Naggorite paled, his eyes bulging. One of his retainers rushed forward with a shout, reaching for Malus's wrist, but Lhunara's sword sang through the air, severing the knight's head in a fountain of gore. Fuerlan's second retainer staggered back, raising his hand in surrender and then fading quickly into the crowd.

'Oh, yes, Fuerlan, you and I have some things to discuss,' Malus hissed, tightening his grip. Fuerlan's face was now turning a pale shade of red, his hands scrabbling futilely at the highborn's iron grip.

'After I've flayed the skin from your scabby chest and flensed the muscles away with fine, sharp knives, after I've spread your ribs and shown you your shrivelled organs. After I've reshaped that pitiful face with my hooks and barbs and worn it before you like a mask, *then* you will tell me how you knew when and where I would return to Naggaroth. You will tell me who gave you that information and why. You will tell me everything. And then you will pray through ragged lips that I forbear showing you just how deep the darkness in me truly goes.'

No one knows, Malus thought savagely. But oh, I will show them.

Chapter Four
MIDNIGHT PACTS

MALUS DARKBLADE RECLINED in a carved chair of black ashwood, a leg thrown over one of the chair's curving arms, and studied the twitching, pulpy shape hanging from hooks in the centre of the small room. Each convulsion set the iron chains softly clinking, a soothing sound after the heated exertions of the previous hours. Sensing their master's urges were spent, the half-dozen slaves slipped quietly from the shadows around the perimeter of the room and stood a respectful distance from their lord.

'Bathe him in unguents and stitch him shut, then feed him wine and hushalta and return him to his quarters,' Malus said, his voice hoarse from shouting. The weakness and fugue he'd felt after the drachau's ordeal was gone, replaced by a dark, oily calm. In the past the horrors of the ordeal always faded swiftly, arising only later in nightmares or moments of great passion; this time had been different somehow. He had outdone himself with Fuerlan. Such an exquisite tapestry of pain, such horror, such *darkness*... he'd learned many things, gained many important insights that he'd never known before. And Fuerlan had, too. Malus could see it in his eyes. Whether the glimpse into the abyss had provided wisdom or madness only time would tell, but that mattered little to him.

He'd learned all he needed to know. That, and much more besides.

Footsteps echoed across the floor behind him. A tall druchii wearing a polished steel breastplate and greaves stepped to Malus's side. He was a young man, handsome and unscarred, wearing the hadrilkar of Malus's house. His eyes were troubled as he considered the artful ruin of Fuerlan's body. 'That was unwise,' he said, offering Malus a goblet of steaming wine.

Malus accepted the goblet gratefully. His hands and arms were painted crimson up to the elbows, and streaks of gore glistened against the hard muscles of his bare chest. 'I was careful, Silar. He'll live, more or less.' He smiled darkly around a mouthful of wine. 'Nothing in the treaty says I can't be... *entertained*... by my guests from time to time.'

'He isn't your guest, Malus. Fuerlan belongs to the drachau, who wants the feud with Naggor ended. Trifling with that is dangerous, especially now.'

Malus gave Silar a sharp look. Most retainers would never dare speak so frankly to their master – it was a good way to wind up hanging from a set of chains like Fuerlan, or worse. But Silar Thornblood was a druchii of considerable skills and bafflingly little ambition, and so Malus afforded him a little more latitude than most. 'Why are you in your armour?'

'We caught an assassin in the tower while you were at court.'

The highborn's eyes narrowed. 'Where?'

'In your quarters.' Silar shifted uncomfortably, glancing at the floor. 'We still don't know how he got in. The... precautions... your half-sister placed on your bedchamber warned us of his presence, but he still managed to kill two men before we could corner him.'

'You took him alive?'

Now Silar looked even more uncomfortable. 'No, my lord. He hurled himself into the bedchamber's fireplace when we pressed him hard. Naturally, I take full responsibility.'

Malus waved his hand dismissively. 'He's dead, I'm not. It sounds as though he was exceptionally skilled.'

Silar caught his master's eye, reading the implication in the highborn's words. 'He was from the temple. I'm certain of it.'

There were no deadlier assassins in Naggaroth than the acolytes of the Temple of Khaine. Malus took a thoughtful sip of wine. 'My former backers have deeper connections – and purses – than I imagined. Unless...'

'Unless?'

Malus pursed his lips, considering. 'Fuerlan, much to my surprise, turned out to have quite a few interesting things to say. Some of it might even be true. And if so...' All at once, the vague notion of a plan began to take shape in his mind.

Do I dare? Then – there was an assassin from the temple in my quarters. What have I to lose at this point? To hesitate is to die!

The highborn drained the goblet in great, thirsty gulps and sprang from the chair. 'Get me two guards,' he commanded, handing the cup back to Silar. 'I'm going to see Nagaira.'

Silar's eyes widened as Malus swept purposefully across the room, already belting his robe in place. 'Don't you wish to clean yourself up a bit first?' the retainer asked.

Malus laughed coldly. 'Conspiracies thrive on spilt blood, Silar. It tends to focus one's mind on the business at hand.'

THE CITY OF Hag Graef lay at the bottom of a narrow valley, like a nauglir crouched over its prey. Its broad streets, conducive for the heavy industry that was the city's main source of wealth, radiated out from the huge Plaza of Conquest that lay at the foot of the drachau's fortress. The fortress, a mighty collection of spires, courtyards and deadly cul-de-sacs bound by an inner and outer perimeter of high walls, contained not only the households of several high-ranking druchii lords and ladies, but also the city's convent of witches and the cold one stables of the city guard.

The apartments of the Vaulkhar and his children occupied an entire set of spires on the eastern quarter of the huge castle, overlooking the three mountain entrances to the East Foundry and the broad avenue of crushed cinders leading north to the caverns of the Underworld.

Many of the towers belonging to Lurhan's children were connected by narrow bridges, allowing the highborn to come and go without troubling themselves with a long descent to the public levels of the castle and then back up again. Such was the theory; in practice the children of the Vaulkhar saw the bridges as an invitation to murder and avoided them scrupulously.

Except for tonight. Malus moved swiftly along the delicate-looking stone bridge connecting his spire with Nagaira's, his cloak billowing like a spread of ebon wings in the gusting wind. The auroras seeping from the Chaos Wastelands in the far north had subsided, leaving tattered clouds scudding fast across the face of a single moon. Arleth Vann moved several yards ahead of him, Lhunara several yards behind. Lhunara held a crossbow ready and scanned the nearest overlooking spires, while Arleth Vann tested his footing on the bridge with each heavy tread.

It took ten long minutes for the three druchii to work their way across the vaulting reach. At the far end there was a recessed door lit from above by a flickering globe of witchlight. Arleth Vann paused, and Malus was surprised to find a sentry waiting for them, sheltered in the doorway's small niche. He was one of Nagaira's pet rogues, and watched the trio with hooded eyes as he played at cleaning his fingernails with a wicked-looking stiletto.

'If you've murder in mind, red-hand, you'll find no welcome here,' the rogue drawled with a sly grin. Yet there was nothing frivolous about the set of his shoulders, or the careful, precise movements of his knife.

'If I'd meant you murder, Dalvar, I'd have had Lhunara put your eye out from back at the other end of the span,' Malus hissed. 'Now get that door open, you half-penny thug. I've a mind to speak to my beloved sister before I freeze to death.'

'Beloved *half*-sister,' Dalvar corrected, pointing with his knife for emphasis. 'And it's not within my power, bloody fingers or no. You'll wait here on my mistress's pleasure.'

'Suppose I have Arleth Vann cut you into pieces and we feed you to the night-hawks?'

'It won't get the door open any faster.'

'No, but it will be a pleasant diversion in the meantime.'

'About as pleasant as a knife in the eye, I suspect.'

Both sides grudgingly conceded the other's point and then settled down to wait.

Nagaira kept Malus out on the bridge long enough for the cold to have settled deep into his bones. It was an effort of will to keep his teeth from chattering or his limbs from shivering. Dalvar continued to work on his nails, seemingly oblivious to the conditions. Finally, there was a dull thud of bolts being drawn back, and the door opened a finger's width. Dalvar leaned back and shared a few whispered words with whoever was on the other side, then bowed deeply to Malus. The stiletto had magically disappeared. 'My mistress will see you now, dread lord,' he said with a grin. 'Pray accompany me, but leave any thoughts of ill intent at the threshold…'

'Against Nagaira, or you?'

'…for there are spirits within these walls who would take such things amiss,' Dalvar finished, his eyes dancing with black mirth.

The retainer led the trio inside, past a bowing servant and down a short passage into a small guard chamber. Four guards in full armour sat at a small, circular table, eating a late meal of bread and pickled eels and eyeing Malus with casual menace. Globes of witchfire flickered from sconces on the walls and racks of spears and crossbows sat ready to repel an assault from the bridge or the levels below. A flight of stairs curved both upwards and downwards along the curving outer wall of the room, and a stout oak door stood in the wall opposite the passage.

Malus knew the way as well as, or better than, Dalvar. The highborn pushed past the retainer, who offered a token protest, then turned right and leapt lightly up the tower's curving stair. Up and up he climbed, and with each step he felt the light touch of invisible forces caressing his face and lingering along his gore-stained hands. They flowed in and out of him on the tide of his breath, touching his heart with icy fingers. He'd made light of Dalvar's warning, but he knew all too well that it was no idle boast. Nagaira did not suffer uninvited guests lightly.

The stairs finally ended at a small, dark landing. Icy wind whistled through a number of arrow-slits set into the thick stone walls. Two retainers in glittering mail and thick robes glistening with frost stood to either side of a pair of tall oak doors. They regarded him coldly from behind golden caedlin worked in the shape of snarling manticore faces. Their gauntleted hands rested easily on the pommels of unsheathed great swords, but they made no move to hinder Malus as he pushed the double doors wide and rushed into Nagaira's sanctum like a rising wind.

It was the law of the Witch King that magic was forbidden to the druchii, save for a select group of women who dedicated their lives to him and spent their days in convents in the cities and citadels across Naggaroth. The Dark Brides of Malekith, or the hags as they were commonly known, served their local overlord as needed, but ultimately they answered to none other than the Witch King himself. Any other druchii – especially a male – who was caught pursuing the dark arts was bound in red-hot chains and delivered to the Witch King's fortress at Naggarond and was never seen again.

Naturally, there were exceptions. Minor hedge-sorcerers, practitioners of curses and the secretive shade-casters, all of whom took the coin of the lowborn in exchange for their meagre services. The priestesses and blood-witches of the Temple of Khaine and the hierophants of the Temple of Slaanesh kept sorcerous traditions that were old when lost Nagarythe was young, rites that not even Malekith dared trifle with. And then there was Balneth Bale, the self-styled Witch King of Naggor, who had encouraged the studies of his sister, Eldire, and kept them secret in hopes of profiting from them himself. Instead he'd received a bloody rebuke by Malekith in the form of Vaulkhar Lurhan and the army of Hag Graef, who defeated Naggor's army and made Bale and his people a vassal city to the Hag.

By the same token, it was an open secret that Nagaira, the second daughter of the fearsome Lurhan, was a scholar of the dark paths. Not necessarily a practitioner, but someone who studied the ancient ways and the arcane lore for her own personal ends. No one had ever seen her cast a spell or bind a spirit to her will, nor had anyone ever successfully claimed to have been a victim of her enchantments. Thus she kept herself poised on the razor's edge, dabbling in forbidden knowledge that lent her power and influence without allowing it to be her undoing.

That said, Malus suspected that Nagaira's sanctum contained the sorts of arcane tomes, debased scrolls, potions, idols and artefacts that any sorcerer would sell the remainder of his tattered soul to possess. It was also, the highborn noted, thankfully warm. A small circular hearth rose in the centre of the room, giving off hissing flames of green and blue that turned the curved walls into a swirling chiaroscuro of dancing, threatening shadows. A sinuous, scaly creature with tightly-furled leather wings darted into the shadows at his sudden entrance and hissed threateningly from behind an overflowing bookshelf.

As far as Malus knew, he was the only member of the family Nagaira had ever permitted to enter the room.

His half-sister looked up from a low divan set near the fire. A short table had been pulled up to the divan; sitting atop it was a huge, dust-covered book propped on a small lectern and a curious tripod of copper wire supporting half of a human head. The head had been sheared cleanly through just below the nose, and the grisly trophy rested in the tripod with the open brainpan pointing towards the ceiling.

Nagaira had pulled back the left sleeve of her woollen robe, exposing her sleek, pale forearm which was covered in an intricate tattoo of tightly woven loops and spirals, stretching from her fingertips to her elbow. As Malus watched, she took a fine, brass-handled brush and dipped it carefully in the gaping brainpan. She shot a glance at Malus. He wasn't sure if it was a trick of the shifting light, but her eyes appeared to be a vivid, pale blue. Nagaira looked pointedly at her brother's hands. 'Are those your idea of tattoos?' she asked, using the brush to touch up one of the lines on her arm. 'If so, I think my brush-work is much better than yours.'

'I grew cold waiting on the bridge outside, so I warmed my hands around Dalvar's beating heart,' Malus snarled.

'Liar,' she said with a sly grin. 'That man's blood runs colder than the Sea of Chill. Why else would I take him into my household?' Finished, she licked the tip of the brush with a dainty pink tongue and set the instrument in a felt-lined box. She reclined gracefully on the divan, ostentatiously admiring her work. 'I'm very displeased with you, Malus,' she said lightly. 'Running off on your little raid without warning me. While you were gone that worm Urial tried to practise his charms on me, as though that would make Yasmir jealous. I had to fend off his disgusting advances for months on end.' At the mention of her brother's name Nagaira's face darkened. The lines on her arm seemed to sharpen, then shift, like coiling snakes. Malus found he couldn't take his eyes off them, even though the sight set his heart to hammering and sent cold spasms through his guts.

'I... I'm certain you disappointed him at every turn,' he stammered, then grit his teeth against the show of weakness.

'I told him I was saving my heart for another,' she said, her voice smooth and cold as polished steel. 'It made him very angry, I think. He seems to think he's entitled to salve his frustrations with me, the twisted little creature.' Nagaira lowered her arm and glared at Malus. 'You could at least have the decency to sound jealous.'

With an effort, Malus crossed the room and settled on the divan next to her. 'I had to sneak away, dear sister. You and Bruglir and the rest left me no choice. Surely you didn't expect me to sit in my tower and wait for some noble to put his knife in me?'

Nagaira sighed. 'It's the law of the wolves, Malus. The biggest wolf cub gets the most milk, and so on down the line. Bruglir gets the biggest share, and the rest of us have to fight for what's left. I get barely enough wealth to survive on, and naturally I make sure Urial gets as little of the cut as possible.' She shrugged, but her cold eyes were intent. 'Unfortunately, the temple takes care of their own, even the forsaken ones like him. If you are to blame anyone, blame him for taking your rightful share.'

Malus considered his sister for a moment, contemplating his next move. Beneath her diffident façade, he could sense an insatiable curiosity. What he didn't know was how still and deep her malice towards him ran. If she were truly displeased about his absence, there was every possibility he wasn't getting out of her sanctum alive. 'As it happens,' he said, 'I have more than just my pathetic allotment of gold to hold against dear, twisted Urial.'

'Oh?' Nagaira said, arching one slender eyebrow. Her eyes had darkened to a stormy grey. Faint lines and spirals coiled in their depths.

'Do you know Fuerlan? The hostage from Naggor? A craven little sack of skin with an exaggerated sense of his own worth?'

'I hear that's a common failing in Naggorites, you know. A weakness in the blood, perhaps,' she said, her smile full of sweet poison.

Malus ignored the jibe. 'Fuerlan and I had a long, energetic conversation this evening,' he said. 'He'd been entertaining the delusion of making an alliance with me.'

'An alliance? Against whom?'

'Does it matter? He was most eager, though. He sent a letter by special messenger to meet me when I got off the boat at Clar Karond.'

Nagaira frowned. 'Clar Karond? But how?'

'How did he know I hadn't disembarked at the slave tower? How else? No rider could have made the journey from Karond Kar faster than my ship. So that leaves–'

'Sorcery,' she said.

'Just so,' Malus answered. 'That same sorcerous knowledge enabled someone to arrange a cunning little ambush for me on the Slavers' Road.' He leaned close to Nagaira, his voice dropping to a silken whisper. 'And now I hear that my beloved sister has been using my name to spite the one magic-wielder in Hag Graef who isn't locked up in the local convent.' His hand shot out, closing around Nagaira's pale throat. 'So now I'*m* the one who is most displeased.'

Nagaira's breath caught in her throat at the touch of his sticky, clammy grip – but then she smiled, and began to laugh. The sound was rich and smoky, mocking and seductive. 'Clever, clever little brother,' she breathed. 'But why would Urial the Forsaken entertain the likes of Fuerlan?'

'The little toad grovelled to get an audience, no doubt,' Malus said, 'just as he's grovelled before each of you, in turn. I'm sure Urial agreed to see him to find if he'd learned anything of interest about you or the others.' The highborn tightened his grip minutely, feeling the hot pulse of blood in his half-sister's throat. 'Fuerlan, it seems, was given to believe that Urial possessed a magical relic of some kind, supposedly a source of terrible power.'

'A relic? Where would Fuerlan hear such a thing?'

Malus pulled Nagaira close, his thin lips mere inches from her own. 'Why, from you, sweet sister. I didn't believe it myself at first, but Fuerlan went to great pains to convince me.'

For a moment, she was silent. Her breath was warm and fragrant against his skin. Then she smiled. 'I confess. I hoped Urial would eat the little hostage's heart, and then even the temple couldn't protect him. The drachau would have had him unravelled one nerve at a time, and I would have savoured every moment.' She frowned. 'Sadly, it appears that the Forsaken is repulsive, but not a fool.'

'Indeed.' Malus let his lips brush her cheek. Her breath caught in her throat, and for an instant his mind was full of worms, writhing, spiralling shapes of darkness that wove in and out of his brain, leaving long tunnels that filled with inky shadows in their wake. He shuddered and leaned back against the divan, his hand jerking back from her as though stung. Nagaira regarded him with depthless black eyes.

'Is it true, then?' Malus asked. 'Does Urial have such a relic?'

Nagaira smiled. She, too, leaned back, increasing the distance between them. She tapped a tattooed finger thoughtfully against her lower lip. 'So I have been led to believe,' she said. 'My spies tell me that Urial has been seeking it for some time now, and acquired it recently at great expense after numerous failed expeditions. Why do you ask?'

Malus took a deep breath. 'Because I find myself wanting in power and surrounded by enemies. If the relic is useful to him, why not me?'

'Urial is a sorcerer, Malus, and you are not.'

'Great power finds a way to make itself felt, sister. Sorcerer or no, I can bend it to my will.'

Nagaira laughed, and it seemed the shadows on the walls danced in time to the sound. 'You are a fool, Malus Darkblade,' she said at last. 'But I confess that fools sometimes succeed where other mortals fail.'

'So what of this relic?'

'It is not, in fact, a source of power – at least, not in any sense you would understand. It is a key that, legend has it, will open an ancient temple hidden deep within the Chaos Wastes. The power you want for lies within that temple.'

'What is it?'

Nagaira shook her head. 'No one knows for certain. It was locked away in the days when Malekith fought alongside foul Aenarion in the First War against Chaos,' she said, 'many thousands upon thousands of years ago. It's possible that the temple no longer even exists, or lies at the bottom of a boiling acid sea.'

Something in Malus quickened, like a spark on dry tinder. 'But if the temple and its treasure were beyond reach, the magic of the key would be affected, would it not?'

The druchii woman smiled approvingly. 'Indeed. You are more canny than I thought, brother dear.'

'So the temple and its treasure still lie within reach,' Malus said. 'It could lie within *my* reach, if I had a way to steal the key from Urial and seek the place out myself.'

'You wish to pit yourself against the forsaken one in his lair? Your foolishness borders on the suicidal.'

'Urial doesn't spend his every waking hour in his tower. In fact, the temple has rites of its own to observe in the wake of the Hanil Khar. He will be in the city every night for the next few nights, will he not?'

'True,' Nagaira agreed. 'But that leaves his servants, his guards and most importantly, his web of protective wards and traps.'

Malus leaned forward and rested his fingertip lightly in the hollow of her throat. 'I'm sure you have ways of getting past his many enchantments.'

Nagaira chuckled. 'And why should I help you?'

'To hurt Urial, of course. And to share in the power once I've brought it out of the Wastes.'

She smiled. 'Of course.'

'Now can you get me and a small group of my retainers into the tower?'

Nagaira's eyes roamed the crowded bookshelves and tables around the room, as if taking a mental inventory. 'I can get a small group inside the tower,' she said after a moment's thought. 'But I will have to accompany you as well. I expect some traps will require more than a protective amulet to slip past.'

Malus thought it over. He didn't like the idea, but he didn't see that he had any choice. At least with her along he could be certain she would do everything in her power to ensure they got out alive. 'Very well.'

'And we share in whatever power you bring out of the Wastes?'

'Of course,' he said, the lie sliding smoothly off his tongue.

His half-sister smiled, reclining languidly on the divan. 'Then linger with me here a while, dear brother,' she said. 'It's been so long since we've seen one another, and you and I have much to catch up on.'

Chapter Five
STRATAGEMS

THE ICE-COLD WATER was a shock to his skin, enough to make Malus catch his breath as he scrubbed the dried blood from his chest and arms, but not quite enough to banish the crawling sensation of worms coiling through his flesh. He fought to keep his gorge down against the squirming sensation filling his mouth and caressing his tongue.

'I do not like this,' Silar Thornblood said. 'It's reckless.' The tall druchii stood by his lord's side, his long face grimmer than usual. 'How do we know she can be trusted?'

Unable to stand it any more, Malus plunged his face into the freezing, pink-tinged water. The searing cold banished the lingering memories of his sister's embrace, if only for a moment. He came up for air gasping, unsettled, but for a moment the master of his own skin. 'She *can't* be trusted,' he said, wiping his face on a towel offered by Silar. 'But for the moment she and I have a common objective – stealing Urial's precious relic and seizing the power it protects. Nagaira can be counted on to ensure her own interests are met, and no more.'

The highborn's bedchamber was a crowded place in the wake of the evening's assassination attempt and the sudden meeting with his sister. Along with Silar, Lhunara and Arleth Vann paced or brooded at different points around the small, dimly-lit chamber, clearly unhappy with the outcome of the night's events. The druchii woman stood at one of the chamber's narrow windows, watching the night begin to fade in a slow ebb from black to grey.

Hag Graef was called the City of Shadows for a reason – surrounded by steep mountainsides, the bottom of the valley felt the direct touch of sunlight for only a couple of hours each day, and even then only on rare, cloud-free days in the summer. For much of the year Hag Graef was wrapped in a perpetual twilight. Far below in the city proper, she could see the faint, flickering gleam of witchfire globes, guttering like stars amid the currents of caustic night fog roiling in the streets.

'Silar is right,' she said thoughtfully. 'You are being too hasty, my lord. There are too many unknowns, too many things that can go wrong… We do not even know where this temple is. Somewhere in the Chaos Wastes? We could be gone for years – if we ever come back at all.'

'Nagaira claims that the relic will point to the location of the temple,' Malus said, 'and I would rather be raiding the Wastes than waiting here for the next temple assassin to take my head.'

'But surely we can wait for a few more days at least? Spend some coin and see what we can learn about Urial's tower to make a better plan–'

'We don't have a few days. We have to strike while Urial is out of his lair. We think he'll be at the temple for the next several nights, but the only night we can count on for certain is tonight. Isn't that right, Arleth?'

Arleth Vann stirred from the shadows in the far corner of the room. With his heavy black cloak pulled about him and the top of the broad cowl hanging down over his face, he was nearly invisible in the darkness. 'Yes,' he said reluctantly. 'Every supplicant in the city must attend the veneration ceremonies tonight, which last from sunset to sunrise.'

Malus caught Lhunara eyeing Arleth speculatively. Many in the warband suspected that the retainer had been involved with the temple at some point in his past. Arleth had good reason not to discuss his life before coming to Hag Graef, and Malus kept what he knew to himself. It was a worthwhile trade to gain a retainer of Arleth's particular skills.

'So you see, we've little time to prepare,' the highborn interjected, 'and my enemies are moving against me. If things get too far out of hand it's possible that Lurhan will exile me – or worse – rather than risk drawing the entire family into a blood feud. I do not have the resources, the *power*, to fight off these threats. It will be difficult enough just to equip this expedition, much less fight a house war against an alliance of petty nobles.' Malus pulled on a sleeping robe and went to the polished ashwood table near the foot of the bed. He picked up a jug of looted Bretonnian wine and filled the goblet standing alongside it. 'If this… relic… is half as fearsome as Nagaira seems to think it is, things will be very different here upon our return.'

'Do you truly plan to share it with her?' Silar asked.

'Only if I must,' Malus admitted, sipping his wine. 'And only until I'm certain I can master it myself. If I think I can wield it without her... well, the Wastes are a dangerous place, aren't they?'

Lhunara nodded to herself, spinning a web of stratagems and contingencies in her mind. 'How many men will she take with her?'

'Six, including that throat-cutter Dalvar. I'll be bringing six as well, including you and Vanhir. Silar, Dolthaic and Arleth Vann will remain here with the rest of the warband to keep watch over what little property I have left. I don't doubt Urial will retaliate in some fashion once he learns of the theft.'

'Don't take Vanhir,' Silar growled. 'He'll betray you if he can.'

'I agree,' Lhunara said, 'especially after your retribution on the road from Clar Karond. He hates you now more than ever.'

'Precisely why I want him where I can keep my eye on him,' Malus replied. 'He will keep his oath to the letter, to the last minute of the very last day. That's more than a month away. If we're still in the Wastes by then, it might be easier just to kill him, but until then he's one more sword I can use to achieve my ends.'

Lhunara folded her arms and turned back to the window, clearly unhappy with the idea. 'Do we take the nauglir, then?'

'Yes,' Malus said. 'I'll take teeth and claws over a horse's hooves any day. Besides, they can carry more gear and move further each day than a pack train of horses.'

'They'll also need to eat a lot more,' Lhunara pointed out.

Malus chuckled. 'Where we're going, I don't think we'll lack for bodies to feed to the cold ones. Dolthaic will have them saddled and ready in the stables as soon as we emerge from Urial's tower. I don't plan on staying here one more minute than I must once the deed is done.'

'I'm more interested in hearing how you're going to get in and out of Urial's tower,' Silar said.

Malus poured a second cupful of wine. 'No one knows for certain how many servants Urial has, nor how many retainers. He gets many of them from the temple, and they all wear those heavy robes and masks. He could have twenty or two hundred. Worse, Nagaira is certain his lair will be heavily guarded by magical wards and bound spirits. Even monsters, perhaps.'

The highborn glanced at Arleth Vann. The two locked eyes for a moment, then the retainer shrugged. 'It is possible,' Arleth Vann said. 'None but the priestesses know how far Urial has progressed in the mysteries of Khaine. He could be capable of a great many terrible things. It is even possible that his lair may no longer be... entirely of this realm.'

Lhunara took a step towards the cowled retainer. 'What does that mean?'

Arleth Vann's head bowed. Malus could see the tension in the line of his muscular shoulders and the stillness of his frame. 'Go, on, Arleth,' the highborn prodded.

'I can't say for certain. I don't even understand it fully, myself. But… there are places in the great temples, deep places where only the most holy may go, that bear witness to ancient rites and observances. Only the finest sacrifices are made there; there is no word spoken in that place that is not an offering to the Lord of Murder. It is a place where the highest priests go to look upon the visage of Khaine and his realm of slaughter. They thin the weave between worlds, until sometimes it becomes difficult to tell what is of this realm and what is not.'

Lhunara frowned. 'Now you're speaking in riddles.'

No, Lhunara, he isn't, Malus thought. But it's for the best that you don't understand, else I might have a mutiny on my hands. Considering the implications was like a cold knife twisting in his gut. 'Are you saying that his sanctum could be such a place?'

Arleth Vann looked up at the highborn's voice. The face beneath the hood was guarded, except for the eyes. They were bleak. 'It is possible,' he said. 'Nothing is certain with one such as him. He is bound by no law, in this world or the next.'

'From what you're both describing, this sounds like a fool's errand,' Lhunara snarled.

'Not so,' Malus said. 'Nagaira knows of a hidden way into the tower from the burrows—'

'The *burrows?*'

'Enough, woman! She will lead us into the burrows from an entrance elsewhere in the fortress, and then up into Urial's storerooms. She says she has talismans that will allow us to pass unnoticed through his wards and calm his unnatural sentries. Since she will be with us the entire time I have no doubt that she is certain of their power.'

'And if she's wrong, my lord?'

'Once inside,' he continued, ignoring her question, 'we will kill any servants or guards we encounter on the way to Urial's sanctum. If the Dark Mother smiles on us, that won't be necessary. Ideally, we will be able to slip in and out with no one the wiser. Nevertheless, once we get inside the sanctum we will have to move very quickly. Now, Nagaira does not know exactly what this relic looks like—'

Lhunara started to speak, her eyes going wide, but Malus silenced her with a sharp glare.

'But she is certain she will know it when she sees it. We will search the sanctum, locate the relic and depart the same way we arrived. With luck, we should not be inside the tower more than half an hour at most. Once we are back in the burrows we should be able to reach the stables within minutes, and be out of the Hag and on the Spear Road within the hour. By the time Urial returns and finds the relic gone we will be leagues away.'

'Leaving us to bear the brunt of his wrath,' Silar said, his voice full of dread.

Lhunara shook her head. 'I do not like this, my lord. It stinks too much of misadventure. If one thing goes wrong the whole plan could unravel, and then where would we be?'

'Not much worse off than we are now, Lhunara,' Malus replied coldly. 'The temple has been promised my head, and if my suspicions are correct, Urial was responsible for the ambush on the Slavers' Road. No, I will not sit here and wait for the kiss of the axe. Urial owes me a debt of ruin, and I mean to collect it tonight. If I die in the attempt, then I will do it with a blade in my hand and blood in my teeth! Now go,' Malus said, draining his cup once more. 'Rest yourselves. We meet at Nagaira's tower tonight after the rising of the fog.'

As one, the retainers bowed and moved to the door. Silar was the last to depart. 'Do not tarry long in the Wastes, my lord,' he said with a rueful grin. 'There may be nothing left of us upon your return.'

'I know, noble Silar,' Malus answered. 'But fear not. I have a long, long memory and a pitiless heart. Whatever evil Urial wreaks on you I will repay him a hundredfold.'

Silar paused at the doorway, considering the highborn's words. Then, reassured, he left to see to his duties.

Chapter Six
FORSAKEN HALLS

THE NIGHT BROUGHT heavy clouds and a cold wind whistling through the spires of Hag Graef. More than a hundred feet above the castle courtyards, a heavily cloaked figure leaned slightly from a recessed doorway and studied the two bright moons gleaming over the eastern horizon.

After a moment, a patch of iron-grey cloud slid across the face of the moons, plunging the fortress into abyssal darkness. Without a sound the cloaked figure leapt from the doorway and glided like a spectre across the narrow stone bridge. Seven similarly cloaked figures followed, seemingly heedless of the vast gulf yawning beneath them. By the time the moons had shed their gauzy shroud the procession had disappeared into the tower at the other end of the span.

Once inside Nagaira's tower, Malus pulled back his woollen cowl and scrutinised the small group waiting for him in the passage just beyond the doorway. Tonight, he and his retainers were dressed for war: beneath the heavy, dark cloaks each druchii wore an articulated breastplate and a mail skirt over his dark leather kheitan. Pauldrons protected their shoulders, lending them a bulkier, more imposing silhouette, while their arms and legs were sheathed in articulated vambraces and greaves. Each piece of armour rested on a layer of felt to muffle the rattle of joints and plates and to help insulate the body from the cold steel. Malus and two of his retainers carried

94

repeating crossbows under their cloaks along with their customary swords.

Nagaira's warriors were similarly equipped, surrounding their mistress like baleful crows. Several carried short throwing spears of a type Malus had never seen before, while others carried small repeating crossbows. They eyed the heavily-armed interlopers with clear suspicion – all but Dalvar, who spun one of his stilettos on an armoured fingertip and grinned mockingly at the newcomers.

Like Malus, Nagaira wore plate armour over her kheitan and robes and carried two swords at her hip. The bookish diffidence was gone, and Malus was surprised to see how much she resembled her fearsome father. She held out a gauntleted hand draped with seven leather thongs; from each thong hung a glittering object of silver and crystal the size of a druchii thumb.

'Wear these somewhere against your skin,' Nagaira said, her voice sharp and commanding. 'Once we are inside the tower, touch nothing unless I say so.'

Malus took the talismans without a word, picked one for himself and passed the rest on to his companions. On close inspection, each talisman was a small silver fist clutching a ball of crystal. The irregular crystal had somehow been fractured in such a way as to create a complex spiral within the centre of the stone. The silver hand was etched with dozens of tiny runes that defied easy identification. When he tried to focus on one, Malus's eyes began to blink and water as though someone had blown a handful of sand into them. He gave up trying after a moment and slipped the thong around his neck, then carefully tucked the talisman under the lip of his breastplate. It dug into his chest just underneath the armour plate and felt like a piece of trapped ice.

Nagaira watched carefully to make sure that each of the druchii followed her instructions. Once she was satisfied, she said, 'The entrance to the burrows is fairly close by. Once we're in the tunnels, stick close and keep your weapons ready. There are wild nauglir roaming down there, and worse. It won't take long to reach the tunnels underneath Urial's tower, but we may have to do some digging once we get there.'

The last part brought Malus up short. 'We *might* have to do some digging? You don't know anyone who's used this approach before?'

Nagaira shrugged. 'I don't know for certain that the entrance even exists. In theory, it should.'

'In *theory*?'

'You would rather storm the ground floor entrance, or climb the tower wall in full view of half the fortress?'

Dalvar's mocking grin widened. Malus dreamed of peeling the skin from his shrieking face. 'Lead on,' he hissed.

With a smug half-bow, Nagaira turned on her heel and led the raiding party down the long stairs to the ground floor of the tower. Like all the spires in the drachau's fortress, the tower could only be entered through a single pair of reinforced double doors that opened onto a short corridor leading deeper into the castle complex. When they reached the doors, Malus was surprised to find four of Nagaira's retainers in full armour, holding naked swords in their hands. Nagaira caught the expression on the highborn's face and gave a wolfish grin.

'I can't guarantee that Urial doesn't have agents of his own in my household,' she said, pulling her cowl over her head. 'So Kaltyr and his men are going to ensure that no one leaves the tower until dawn.' With that, she led the party out into the castle proper.

Over hundreds of years, the drachau's fortress – also referred to as the Hag by residents of the city – had grown almost like a living thing. Dwarf slaves were expensive and relatively rare, so many years could pass between opportunities for needed repairs and additions.

When a part of the castle fell into ruin, other sections were built over and around the wreckage, creating a madman's labyrinth of chaotic passageways, abandoned towers and walled-off courtyards. What had begun as a relatively small citadel with a single octagonal wall now covered more than a square mile of land and possessed four concentric defensive walls, each one built to enclose a new wave of expansion. It was said that no one person knew the fortress in its totality; new servants were often sent on errands into the sprawling grounds and not found again for days, if at all.

Nagaira led the cowled procession quickly and assuredly through a series of courtyards and execution grounds, swiftly leaving the more-populated precincts of the fortress behind for a region that showed signs of progressive abandonment. The farther they went, the more desolate and decrepit the surroundings appeared. They crossed over cracked, vine-covered flagstones and under leaning piles of rock that used to be walls or spires. At one point they were forced to climb over a pile of broken stone that was all that remained of a span linking two old towers. Small creatures scuttled through the shadows around them. At one point, traversing a larger, overgrown courtyard, something large hissed a warning at them from a pile of vine-covered rubbish. The druchii levelled their crossbows, but Nagaira waved impatiently for them to continue.

After a time, the raiders reached a section of the fortress that had clearly been abandoned for many decades. Crossing through a doorway stained with mould, Malus found himself in a large, rectangular space dominated by what appeared to be a huge hearth. After a moment he realised that he was standing in an old forge – the bellows and other wooden tools had long since rotted away.

Suddenly there was a flare of blue-green light; one of Nagaira's retainers handed her a shuttered lantern burning with pale witchfire. She held it aloft and turned in a quick circle, gaining her bearings. 'There,' she said, pointing to a corner of the room. 'Shift the rubbish aside. You'll find a trap door.'

For a moment, no one moved. Nagaira and her rogues eyed Malus and his band.

'Tired already?' Malus sneered, impatient at the petty contest of wills. 'Very well. Virhan, Eirus – open the trapdoor.' The men moved at once, throwing black looks at their erstwhile allies. Aided by Nagaira's lantern, the two retainers quickly located a pair of iron rings set into the floor. After several minutes' effort, they managed to heave one of the doors open with a shriek of rusted hinges. Below was a nearly perfect circular tunnel that sank like a well deep into the earth.

According to legend, the burrows had been made several hundred years after the Hag was first built. One winter the earth trembled beneath the castle from sundown to sunrise each night. Flagstones heaved and sank and towers swayed beneath the moon. Nobles and slaves brave enough to venture into the castle cellars claimed to have heard a slow, deep groaning reverberating through soil and stone, and sometimes clouds of noxious fumes seeped through cracks in the ground and poisoned the unwary.

The strange episode ended as abruptly as it had begun on the first day of spring; later that summer a work crew rebuilding a collapsed tower discovered the first of the tunnels. Nearly perfectly round and bored through solid rock, the passages ran for miles, turning back on themselves again and again as though formed by a monstrous worm. No one ever found the creature – or creatures – that had formed the tunnels, though over the centuries a multitude of vermin had made the labyrinth their home.

There were small, crescent-shaped iron rungs bolted to one side of the tunnel wall. 'Remember: stay close,' she said, then stepped to the edge of the hole and started descending the rungs, holding the lantern below her as she went. Dalvar stepped quickly up behind her, but Malus froze him in his tracks with a forbidding look and went next instead, crossbow held ready.

After about twenty feet the passage began to curve back towards the surface, until finally the rungs came to an end and Malus could stand upright. He stood beside Nagaira as they waited for the rest of the band to make their way down. The only sounds in the echoing space were the scuffing of boot heels on iron and the distant echo of dripping water. At one point he stole a glance at his half-sister, but he could see nothing of her expression in the shadowy depths of her cowl – only the tip of her chin and a flash of her pale throat. The edges of her spiral tattoo now crept up the side of her neck – in the unsteady light it seemed to pulse and shift with a life all its own.

As the raiding party sorted itself out, Malus organised his retainers with subtle nods and gestures to intermingle themselves with Nagaira's men. If the two sides couldn't extricate themselves from one another very easily, they couldn't sacrifice the other at the first sign of trouble.

It was clear to Malus that the burrows were not made by a thinking being – or at least, not a sane one. They were rarely level, plunging and ascending, curving, intersecting and re-intersecting themselves again and again to no evident purpose. Progress was slow, though Nagaira seemed to know exactly where she was going. If there were clues or markers that pointed the way, Malus could not fathom them. A slow tide of unease began to eat at the edges of his steely resolve, but he fought it back with a surge of black hatred. I will prevail, he thought angrily. So long as I have my sword and my wits about me I will not fail.

The raiding party worked their way through the tunnels in silence, their nerves taut and their senses sharp. The air was musty and damp, and a gelid slime covered many of the curved walls. Frequently their booted feet crunched over piles of old, brittle bones. Malus bared his teeth at every sound, wondering what creatures might be drawn to investigate the noise.

There were numerous points where the burrows rose towards the surface and encountered the foundations of the fortress above. Sometimes the tunnel passed through an abandoned cellar or dungeon – in such cases Malus saw the remains of crates, tables and ironwork crushed flat along the burrower's passage. They crossed through several such chambers, each one as deserted as the one before, and the highborn began to relax a little. That was when they nearly stumbled into a deadly trap.

The raiding party had stumbled onto yet another large chamber – it was so wide Malus thought at first that the burrow had intersected a natural cavern, until he noticed the fitted paving stones underneath his boots. The flare of Nagaira's witchlight could not reach the walls or ceiling of the huge space. The parts of the floor Malus could see were strewn with refuse almost ankle deep. He saw bits of bone and old clothes, rusted tools, leather goods and scraps of what might have been withered flesh, plus many more less recognisable items.

Nagaira led the party deeper into the chamber, stepping carefully through the piled debris. She paused to get her bearings, which was when Malus heard the rustling. It was very quiet, almost like the patter of many small feet, but there was something very strange about the sound that the highborn couldn't place. He raised his hand in warning. 'No one move,' he whispered. 'There's something here.'

The druchii paused, their heads turning this way and that as they strained to detect the slightest movement in the darkness surrounding them. The rustling came again – a rapid patter of tiny feet somewhere ahead of them. A pile of refuse was knocked over, scattering what sounded like bits of crockery and loose rock across the chamber. Small feet but a large body, Malus thought. And it's trying to circle behind us. Then the pattering sounds came again – but from the other side of the group. More than one, the highborn realised. But how many?

Now the druchii were shifting uneasily, the wary looks on their ghostly faces suggesting that they were thinking along much the same lines as Malus. Lhunara edged slightly closer to the highborn, her twin swords held ready.

Malus heard the rustling again, much louder and quicker this time – only it came from *directly overhead*.

Nagaira let out a cry, and her globe of witchlight suddenly flared like a bonfire, driving back the darkness. Malus's eyes narrowed against the glare, and he saw that they were standing in an expansive cellar nearly twenty yards to a side, piled with the rotting remains of casks, crates and shelves. Pale, hairy cave spiders the size of ponies scuttled amongst the refuse or reared up aggressively at the sudden burst of light. Their eyes were the colour of fresh blood, and dark fangs as long as daggers dripped with venom as the scent of fresh meat drove them wild with hunger.

Shouts of alarm went up from the druchii, and Malus tried to look in every direction at once as he struggled to get a sense of how many spiders there were. Five? Six? They were moving too fast, and there were too many pools of shadow to keep track of them all. The highborn raised his crossbow and sighted on the nearest one – but the shot went wild as Lhunara knocked him forwards and out of the path of the spider who pounced from the chamber's high ceiling.

Malus rolled onto his back as the rest of the spider pack charged the druchii. Lhunara had gone down beneath the body of the falling spider, and the highborn watched as the creature's mandibles jabbed again and again at the retainer's armoured form, looking for a weak spot to inject its load of venom. He dropped the crossbow and drew his sword just as the point of one of Lhunara's blade's punched through the back of the spider's thorax. The second sword flashed in a short arc, severing one of the creature's fangs in a spurt of greenish poison. The spider seemed to constrict into a ball, its legs closing around its prey, but Malus leapt forward, severing three of the limbs with a single, sweeping cut. Lhunara's swords flickered again in the witchlight, and the body of the spider, now missing the rest of its limbs, fell off to one side.

The highborn reached down and grabbed his retainer by her forearm, pulling her roughly to her feet. 'Are you wounded?'

'No,' Lhunara said, shaking her head. Blobs of venom ran down the front of her breastplate. 'It was close, though.'

Malus looked about wildly, searching for the other spiders. Once the druchii had recovered from their initial surprise, they had reacted with customary savagery. Two of the spiders had fallen prey to the short spears of Nagaira's warriors, pierced through and through in their headlong charge. Two others had been surrounded and hacked to pieces, their soft bodies no match for steel blades. The fifth spider lay at Nagaira's feet, slowly dissolving into a steaming pile of mush as Malus's half-sister stoppered a now-empty flask and returned it to a pouch at her belt.

The encounter had lasted less than a minute, and none of the druchii had been injured, but had it not been for Nagaira's flare, things might have turned out very differently indeed. She turned away from the dissolving spider and sought the tunnel leading out of the chamber. 'That way,' she said, pointing across the room, and set off as though nothing untoward had happened.

Malus retrieved his crossbow and reloaded it. 'Everyone stick close,' he said to the assembled druchii. 'And don't forget to look up.'

THEY WALKED ON for nearly an hour more, cautiously traversing several more dark and abandoned cellars and storerooms. Finally, at the opening to one such chamber Nagaira stopped, her hand raised in warning. 'We are here,' she said quietly.

Malus drew back his hood and shrugged the cloak over both shoulders. The rest of the raiders did the same, exchanging stealth for visibility and ease of movement. Swords hissed from their scabbards.

Nagaira extended her hand, palm out, towards the opening, moving in a widening circle as if getting the sense of the shape of an invisible structure. Slowly, as if pushing against a strong wind, she crossed the threshold into the room. Malus turned back to the raiders. 'Remember, touch nothing. Kill silently, and leave no witnesses behind.' Then he stepped across the threshold.

The highborn fought down a gasp at the shock of cold – and the sense of profound unease – that washed over him as he stepped through the portal. It was like pushing through a caul of living flesh, a barrier that yielded to his will yet somehow seemed alive and aware.

When he came to his senses, he was standing in a room that must have once been a cellar. Like the other chambers, there was a path of crushed furniture and masonry outlining the course of the maddened burrower, but otherwise the room was bare. A spiral stair wound around the perimeter of the room, ending at a small landing and a door of dark iron.

There was something wrong about the room. Malus couldn't quite place it at first. Then, as the next druchii stepped into the room with an audible cry of surprise, he realised – there were no echoes in the stone room. The sound was simply swallowed up, as if they stood at the verge of an endless abyss. When he studied the walls, formed of huge stone blocks, he could not shake the sense that they were somehow porous – as if he could poke through them with his finger into something just beyond. He could not shake the sensation, no matter how solid the stones appeared to his eyes.

One by one the raiders crossed into the room; each one was affected in the same fashion. Only Nagaira seemed untouched. 'We are through the tower's first set of wards,' she whispered as she began to climb the stairs, I expect there will be one or two others as we near Urial's sanctum. Beyond each threshold things will be more… unsettled… than the one before.'

Nagaira reached the iron door. Centuries of disuse had turned the door handle and hinges to barely recognisable lumps of rust. The druchii pulled a small vial from a pouch at her belt and scattered droplets of a silvery liquid across the door's surface. Where they struck, stains of crimson bloomed, spreading rapidly like great wounds across the pitted metal. There was a brittle tinkling sound, and all at once the door collapsed in a darkening pile of rust.

As she was returning the vial to her pouch, Malus moved nimbly past his sister and took the lead on the stair that rose beyond the doorway. Nagaira's head came up, a sharp rebuke on her lips, but Malus shook his head. 'We can't afford to have you walk into an ambush,' he said gravely. 'Better you keep to the centre of the group.' And leave me to issue the commands, Malus thought smugly. 'Dalvar, look to your mistress.'

Before she or Dalvar could reply, Malus turned and crept up the stairs. The climb lasted more than a minute, passing several landings along the way – if Nagaira was any indication, he expected Urial's sanctum to be at the top of his spire – until the stairway ended in another door. This one was in far better condition than its companion in the lower cellar.

Just as he was reaching for the door's iron ring, it swung open from the other side.

A human slave, his emaciated face covered in scars and open sores, saw Malus and opened his mouth to scream. The highborn moved without thinking, raising his crossbow and firing a bolt point-blank through the startled 'O' of the man's scabbed lips.

There was a crunch as the steel head of the bolt punched through the man's spine and part of his skull, and he collapsed without a sound. There was a gasp just beyond the dead slave, and Malus caught a glimpse of a female slave raising a trembling hand to the spatters of blood and brain covering her face. Without hesitation Malus worked the steel lever that drew back the crossbow's powerful string and loaded another bolt into the track. Just as the slave overcame her shock and turned to run, a scream bubbling from her lips, Malus took aim and buried a black-fletched bolt between her shoulder blades. The highborn was readying another shot even as he leapt past her fallen body into the space beyond the door.

He was in a small, dimly lit chamber, with a stone floor incised with carvings of skulls and intricate, sharp-edged runes. What illumination there was seemed to seep from the walls themselves – a dark, crimson glow like banked embers that plucked at the corners of his eyes and seemed to ebb and flow like the surge of blood in some great heart. Silhouetted in the bloody light were smooth-featured faces shaped of some silvery metal inset into the walls. Some snarled, others leered, still others exuded a soulless calm. Their eyes were nothing more than black pits, yet Malus could feel the weight of their stares against his skin. The feeling sent a chill down his spine and set his teeth on edge.

There were three sets of double doors, all closed, and another flight of stairs leading higher up the spire. Malus suspected that they were at the ground floor of the tower, but he was disturbed to discover that his sense of direction had failed him. He could not tell where he was in relation to the rest of the fortress, something he'd never experienced before.

Nagaira stepped over the bodies of the slaves and dashed across the room. 'Did they see you?'

Malus frowned. 'Who?'

'The faces! Did they see you kill the slaves?'

'Did they see me? How should I know, woman?' Damned sorcery! He'd already had his fill of the place.

Nagaira eyed the silvery faces warily. Her eyes shifted from one to the other, almost as though she were following something that moved behind the wall, peering out at them through the black eye sockets. 'We must be very careful how we spill blood in this place,' she whispered. 'The wards here are very potent. If we draw attention to ourselves the tower's guardians may see through my protective talismans.'

Malus hissed in aggravation. Two of the raiding party were rolling the bodies of the slaves down the spiral staircase, but there was no way to know how quickly they would be missed. An alarm could be raised at any time. *I wonder if Urial would feel such a thing, all the way over at the temple?* He bit back a curse. *No time to worry about that now.* Malus reloaded his crossbow and hurried for the stairs.

The stairs curved upwards into darkness. Malus pressed his back to the inside wall of the staircase and moved stealthily ahead, his ears straining for the sounds of movement. The stone at his back was warm, like a living body. He could feel it seeping through his cloak and the back plate of his armour. The highborn continued his ascent, past two landings with dark, ironbound doors.

Between the second and third landings Malus heard a door open and the sound of footsteps descending the stairs. He shifted the crossbow to his left hand and froze, raising his right hand to warn the column. Moments later, a slave came around the bend of the staircase, hurrying on some errand. Quick as a snake, Malus grabbed the slave's right sleeve and pulled, dragging the human off his feet. The slave's body tumbled down the stairs past him, bouncing off the stones. The highborn heard the sounds of steel against flesh, and then silence. After a moment, Malus pressed on.

The staircase ended at the third landing. Malus saw that the doorway here was more ornate than the ones he'd seen before, carved with numerous sigils and inset with three of the silvery faces along the arch. He felt their empty gaze upon him as he took the door's iron ring in his hand and pulled it open. The space beyond was even more dimly lit than the landing itself. Holding the crossbow ready, he eased through the doorway – and passed through another protective ward.

This time the magic caul was even harder to push through. When it parted, the transition was so sudden he stumbled forward several steps and felt the surface of the floor give slightly under his weight. The air was close and humid, but the moisture didn't settle on his skin. The stench of rotting blood hung in the dimness. Distantly, he thought he could hear screams, but when he tried to focus on them he could not make out where they were coming from. The walls of a narrow corridor closed around him, yet he felt as though he stood on the edge of a great plain. His mind warred with the conflicting sensations, and he swayed on his feet.

Nagaira stepped through next. Malus noticed that her small strides made a thick, squishing sound, as though she stepped over rain-soaked ground. She seemed unaffected by the forces at work around her. Her lantern was shuttered, yet Malus could see her face quite clearly in the gloom, as if she stood apart from the darkness around her. The other druchii staggered through the doorway, and the highborn found he could see them clearly as well.

'Hurry now!' Nagaira commanded the dazed retainers. 'We are nearly there.' She once again resumed the lead, heading off down the passage, and Malus found he hadn't the presence of mind to protest. He felt a flash of anger – and surprisingly, his mind became clearer. Very well, he thought. Let hatred be my guide.

Malus focused on Nagaira's back as she led them through the gloom. He had a sense of walls and doorways, of turning corners and ascending steps, but they were only vague sensations, dimly felt. With every step he focused on his age-old hatreds, on all the different ways he dreamt that his family would suffer for the insults they'd done to him. With every step he dreamt of the glory that was his due. I will be Vaulkhar. Not Bruglir. Not Isilvar. I will destroy them all and pluck the scourge from my father's stiffening fingers, and then this city will learn to fear me as they have no other!

He saw Nagaira float through an archway made of bleached, blood-streaked skulls. Malus followed her into a small, octagonal room formed of huge blocks of basalt. Another set of double doors stood at the opposite end of the room, the pointed arch crowned with a trio of snarling, silvery faces. The screams were louder here, punctuated by a chorus of ringing tones, like the sound of steel striking bone. The floor was awash in congealing gore, sticking to the soles of his boots.

Nagaira crossed the room and grasped the door's iron ring. She turned to say something to him. Suddenly the air shook with ululating howls as three misshapen figures emerged from the inky depths of the very walls.

Chapter Seven
FLIGHT FROM THE TOWER

THE MONSTERS WERE scabrous, bloody things, with lashing, segmented tails and an odd number of clawed, disjointed legs. They hurled themselves at the invaders, their bulbous, blind heads splitting wide to reveal rows of jagged, saw-edged teeth.

The druchii cried out as one, and at that moment the room seemed to snap into focus. Crossbows thumped, and black fletching sprouted from the chests of two of the twisted creatures. Malus raised his crossbow and shot one-handed, burying a bolt in the third monster's misshapen skull before the beasts were among them. The highborn dropped the crossbow and drew his sword just as the creature he'd shot leapt at him.

Jagged teeth slicked with poisonous slime snapped shut mere inches from his head as Malus ducked to one side and drove the point of his sword into the monster's flank. Black ichor bubbled from the wound, and the beast let out a discordant howl as it flashed past. Its stinger-tipped tail smashed into his left pauldron, half-spinning him around. A gob of venom struck the armour and began to sizzle, filling his nostrils with an acrid stench.

The creature landed, gathered itself and spun – but Malus leapt at it, slashing for its head. The beast shied to one side, and the keen sword sliced through one of the monster's forelegs instead. Again the tail flicked out at him, but the creature's aim was off; the black stinger, long as a dagger, blurred past the highborn's face.

105

Howling, the monster began to circle to his right, dragging the stump of its foreleg across the gore-stained floor. Steeling himself, Malus feinted with a thrust to the beast's head. The tail flicked out and the highborn pivoted, letting it slide past, and then severed it with a backhanded stroke of his sword. Ichor pumped from the gaping wound, and the creature roared and gibbered with rage.

Pressing his advantage, Malus rushed at the beast, and in an eye blink the blind head ducked low and closed its jaws on Malus's armoured calf. For the moment the curved plates held. Malus shouted a vicious oath and brought his sword down on the monster's thick neck. The blow sliced halfway through the thickly-muscled trunk, and he felt the beast's jaws slacken their grip. Another blow and the creature's headless body was thrashing in a spreading pool of black ichor. Another stroke cracked the monster's jaw and he shook the head loose from his leg with a savage kick.

Reeling a little, Malus took in his surroundings. One of the raiders had pinned a monster to the floor with one of his short spears and two other druchii were methodically hacking the creature apart. Lhunara stood over the second beast, wiping her ichor-stained sword on the monster's hide. One of Nagaira's men leaned against one of the walls, pressing his palm to a wound in his side.

The highborn turned to Nagaira. 'What now?'

'Urial's sanctum lies just beyond,' she replied, still holding the door's iron ring. Malus realised with a start that she hadn't moved so much as an inch during the whole struggle, and the sorcerous creatures had somehow ignored her. 'There is one last ward,' she continued. 'Things beyond will be… unnatural. Perhaps it is best that I go on alone.'

'No,' he said, surprised to find his voice had grown hoarse. Had he been shouting? 'If you go, dear sister, then so do I. The others may remain here.'

Nagaira's face showed a momentary flash of anger, then she quickly composed herself. With a mocking flourish, she pulled the double doors wide. Beyond was nothing but darkness.

'After you,' she said coldly. 'We can't afford for me to be injured, after all.'

The sense of disorientation was returning as the druchii's anger began to wane. Malus's fist tightened on the hilt of his sword. 'Do not tarry, sister,' he said through clenched teeth, and then rushed through the doorway.

THE PAIN WAS like nothing he had ever felt before.

There was no sensation of resistance; he crossed the threshold and felt himself tear from within. Malus fell to his knees with an angry cry, and blood pooled from the spongy floor around his greaves.

The pain went on and on. Trembling, he clenched his fists, focusing on them – and saw a drop of crimson splash on his right knuckle. He brought his hand to his face, and it came away slick and red. Blood was weeping from his skin, soaking through the robes beneath his kheitan.

The chamber was suffused with reddish light. Pillars of bloody skulls stretched from floor to ceiling, framing more than half-a-dozen alcoves around the irregularly-shaped room. Directly ahead of him, Malus could see an altar formed from severed heads. As he watched, he saw mouths gape and mumble, trying to form words of fear or exaltation. Upon the altar rested a huge tome bound in pale leather. Its pages, made from fine human parchment, curled and rustled in a nonexistent wind.

He could not see the walls of the chamber. Malus knew, even as his mind rebelled against it, that space had no meaning in the place where he now stood. His guts clenched, and he vomited blood and bile.

A hand twisted in his hair. Nagaira pulled him roughly to his feet. 'I warned you, brother,' she said, her voice reverberating in his ears like the clashing of cymbals. 'We stand at the edge of a whirlwind that hungers for the living. Only those anointed by the god of slaughter can survive here unscathed.' As she spoke, a single, red tear ran down her pale cheek. 'Do not touch the book upon the altar. Do not even look at it. We must pass beyond into the alcoves yonder. The thing we seek lies there.'

Malus shook his head free with a snarl and lurched past the altar. There were three alcoves in a tight cluster just beyond, each one with a shelf populated by a collection of arcane items. On instinct, he staggered to the one in the centre. There, resting on a tripod of iron, sat an ancient, misshapen skull. The yellowed bone was covered in hundreds of tiny, incised runes and bound with a mesh of silver wire. Even in his wretched state, Malus could sense the power radiating from this artefact – the empty eye sockets seemed to regard him with malevolent awareness. Next to the tripod rested a small book, a quill and a bottle of ink.

'Take it,' Nagaira commanded, her voice strained.

Malus took a pained breath, tasting blood in his mouth, and took the skull in his trembling hands. As he was about to turn away, the highborn impulsively snatched the book as well, tucking the volume into his belt. Nagaira, her face a mask of crimson, had already retreated back to the doorway. 'Hurry!' she said. He noticed that she was pressing something small into one of the pouches at her belt. What had she stolen while his back was turned?

Nagaira leapt through the doorway as he approached, and Malus followed, directly on her heels.

He emerged into the octagonal chamber to cries of alarm from Lhunara and his other retainers. Before he could say a word, however, the air was rent with a chorus of thin, unearthly wails that emanated from the doorway behind him.

Malus spun, his sword ready, but the doorway was empty. Instead, just above his head, he saw three misty shapes streaming from the eyes and mouth of each of the silver masks. As he watched, the mists took the shape of small, thin-limbed figures with long, almost skeletal fingers. Their faces were druchii-like, but their eyes were solid black.

'Blessed Mother of Darkness,' Nagaira whispered, her voice full of fear. 'The maelithii! Run!'

At the sound of their name, the maelithii howled like the souls of the damned, showing mouths full of glittering black fangs. The very air reverberated like a struck gong. An alarm, Malus thought wildly. One of us triggered it. Was it you, Nagaira? Your greed may be our undoing! He swung his sword at one of the spirits. The blade passed harmlessly through it, but a shock of freezing cold shot up his sword arm, as though he'd plunged it into an icy river. The maelithii hissed hungrily at him, and Malus turned on his heel and ran. Nagaira was already moving, fleet as a deer, and the rest of the raiding party bolted after them.

It was all Malus could do to stay focused on Nagaira's retreating form as she plunged through the gloom. A quick look over his shoulder revealed that they had either left the maelithii behind or the spirits had abandoned their pursuit. Hardly daring to trust his luck, the highborn plunged on, feeling sensation return to his numbed arm.

They reached the second ward in minutes. Nagaira stopped at the threshold and put out a warning hand to Malus as he approached. 'Send another through,' she said. 'I don't care who.'

Malus turned to the first retainer who caught up to them, one of his own druchii named Aricar. 'Go!' he commanded, pointing at the doorway, and without hesitation the warrior dove through.

The maelithii pounced on Aricar just on the other side of the door. It was the masks, Malus realised. The spirits could travel from mask to mask throughout the tower.

Aricar staggered as the spirits sank their obsidian teeth into his face and neck. He spun, hands lashing at empty air, but Malus could see the skin around where the spirits bit turn bluish-grey, like a corpse left out in the snow.

'Now!' Nagaira shouted. 'While they're feeding! Run!'

Without hesitation, the highborn plunged across the threshold. At once, it felt as though a crushing weight slipped from his shoulders. Aricar had fallen to his knees, his eyes wide. His breath came in choking, misty gasps through cracked, blue-black lips. Malus pushed past the dying man, thinking of all the silver masks lining the walls at the bottom of the tower. He hoped there were only the three maelithii.

Malus bolted down the curving staircase, hearing shouts echoing from below. Four silver-masked retainers came around the turn, swords in hand. The highborn barrelled into them with an angry cry, hacking left and right with his sword.

Urial's retainers were as swift as nighthawks. With preternatural agility they halted their charge up the stairs and gave way slightly in the face of Malus's charge. They weren't retreating, however – merely opening the distance enough to bring their swords to bear on the highborn. Malus lashed viciously at the retainer to his left, aiming savage blows at his head and neck, but the man blocked one blow with a ringing stroke of his sword and ducked the other, then struck like a viper at one of the articulated lames in the highborn's breastplate. At the last second Malus twisted his whole body, causing the retainer's sword to glance along his breastplate instead of digging in and sinking into his stomach.

There was a glint of silver to his right, followed by the sharp scratch of what felt like a red-hot claw just above his temple. His sudden motion had saved his life from more than one blow, as the retainer to his right had been aiming for his forehead.

Blessed Mother, they're fast, Malus thought. Whatever else his faults may be, Urial knows how to choose his men. The highborn feinted at the retainer to his left, jabbing at the man's eyes – and then Lhunara was beside him, her twin blades flickering like lightning at the man to Malus's right. No longer forced to deal with both men at once, the highborn grinned savagely and bent himself to the destruction of the man on his left.

The narrow staircase rang with the sounds of clashing blades. The silver-masked warrior was a master with the sword, blocking the highborn's every attack with fluid speed and power. Despite Malus's slight advantage of fighting from a higher step and raining blows on the retainer's head, neck and shoulders, the warrior had a countermove for the highborn's every tactic. Well, he thought, as Surhan, his childhood swordmaster had often said: when they're better at the game than you are, change the rules.

Malus let out a roar and brought a vicious blow down towards the top of the retainer's head. The warrior easily blocked the blow – and Malus kicked him hard in the face. The silver mask crumpled beneath the blow and the man staggered backwards. Pressing his advantage, Malus lunged forwards and sliced open the retainer's sword arm from wrist to elbow. A stream of bright red blood sprayed across the stones of the stairwell, but the retainer made no sound.

Another body went tumbling down the stairwell – Lhunara's foe collapsed, blood pouring over his hand as he clutched futilely at his slashed throat. She advanced a step towards the next man in the group, and in passing lashed out with her left-hand sword. Malus's opponent saw the blow at the last moment and twisted away from the sword, catching only a glancing blow against the side of his head, but it was a fatal distraction. Malus brought his sword down on the opposite side of the man's neck, shearing deep and severing the retainer's spine. He collapsed in a heap, his sword tumbling end-to-end down the stairs.

The retainer behind the dead man had to dodge to the side to avoid the falling corpse, and Malus took advantage of the moment, stabbing his sword at the man's eyes. The warrior dodged the blow with a jerk of his head and chopped viciously at Malus's knee. The blade slammed into the armoured joint of his greave, and a thrill of fear raced along the highborn's spine as he thought the metal might fail. But the joint held, and Malus brought his sword down on the retainer's sword wrist, shearing neatly through the limb. Blood sprayed across Malus's legs and feet, but the retainer didn't give up the fight.

To Malus's surprise, the retainer grabbed for his lost sword with his other hand, all but oblivious to the terrible wound he'd received. Moving swiftly, the highborn stepped on the flat of the retainer's blade and thrust his own sword into the warrior's neck. Steel grated on bone and the warrior collapsed, sliding down the stairs in a welter of his own blood. Lhunara was drawing her right-hand sword from the chest of her second foe, and for the moment the way ahead was clear. Raising his sword, Malus rushed down the stairs.

At the next landing a knot of slaves leapt from his path, wailing in fear. He sped past, but just as he turned the next curve he slowed abruptly. Ahead, just out of sight around the turn, he could hear the thin keening of the maelithii – not just three of them but, judging by the sound, a whole pack.

The highborn's mind raced as Nagaira and the rest of the retainers caught up with him. The wailing of the spirits and the cries of the slaves at the landing above made for a discordant chorus. Malus gritted his teeth in irritation. He was half-tempted to send one of the men back upstairs to start cutting throats so he could hear himself think–

Malus straightened. He turned back to the assembled raiders, seeking out Lhunara's scarred face. 'Take two men and bring me those slaves,' he ordered. She gave him a sharp nod and took two of his men back up the stairs. Within moments the wailing of the humans changed pitch, turning from fear into near-hysterical terror.

Rough hands pushed the humans down past the group of raiders. The lead slave, a scrawny human with wide, stupid eyes, tried to recoil from Malus as the highborn reached for him, but the druchii was much too fast. He took the slave by the shoulder, plunged his sword into the human's chest, then hurled the body down the stairs. The

wounded man plunged out of sight, and the keening chorus below
went silent.

'That's it!' Malus said with a feral grin. 'Cut their throats and hurl
them down the stairs! Quickly!'

In moments the bodies of the rest of the slaves tumbled down the
stairs. 'Now run!' Malus cried, rushing after them.

The corpses made a bloody pile at the bottom of the stairs, their
blood freezing into a black sheet of ice as almost a dozen maelithii
swarmed over their rapidly-cooling forms. Malus leapt off the stairs
into the room and bolted for the first set of double doors.

'What are you doing?' Nagaira cried. 'The burrows–'

'The burrows be damned!' Malus snarled, dragging the doors open.
Beyond lay a short corridor that, to his relief, led into the drachau's
fortress. Praying the maelithii could not travel out of Urial's tower, he
bolted down the passage.

The far end of the corridor opened onto a small courtyard. A light
snow was falling, blowing in fine drifts across the cobblestones. Malus
paused, gasping in the freezing air. A pair of druchii highborn conversing at the other end of the courtyard reached for their swords as the
raiding party came to a halt outside Urial's spire, but one look at the
raiders' stained armour and frenzied expressions convinced them that
this was something they wanted no part of. They faded quickly into the
shadows as Nagaira and Dalvar appeared, bringing up the rear.

Malus gave his half-sister a baleful look. 'You stupid witch!' he
snarled. 'What did you take from the sanctum?'

'I took what I pleased, brother,' she shot back. 'Is that not the right
of the plunderer? If anything triggered Urial's trap, it was most likely
your theft of the skull!'

'Does it matter at this point?' Lhunara cried. 'Urial could be here at
any time, with a troop of the drachau's guard with him. We need to get
to the stables and get out of here before someone orders the gates
closed.'

'She's right,' Nagaira said. 'If you move quickly you may just escape–'

'Me?' Malus said. 'What about you?'

'I have to get back to my tower,' Nagaira replied. 'Urial will waste no
time uncovering who attacked his sanctum and made off with his
prize. He'll call upon all the forces at his command to try and recover
the skull. If I stay behind I can call on forces of my own to conceal your
trail and at least slow any pursuit.' She eyed her men. 'Dalvar, you will
take the rest of the men with Malus. See to it that he reaches the temple. Do you understand?'

'Of course, mistress,' Dalvar replied, clearly unhappy with the order.

Malus's mind whirled. Things had gotten completely out of hand.
Was Nagaira abandoning him to Urial's wrath? His brother would find

Aricar's body, and that would lead him to Malus. Nothing as yet pointed towards Nagaira's involvement in the raid. Malus considered his options. Did it matter?

Let her go, the highborn thought. I still have the skull. 'Go then,' he spat. 'I will reach the temple and return when I can. Then we'll meet again.' By then I'll have thought of a hundred ways to make you pay for this, he promised.

If Nagaira sensed the hatred in his voice, she gave no sign of it. 'Until then, Malus. I will be waiting.' Then she turned and raced off towards her tower, quickly disappearing from sight.

Malus straightened wearily, his bloody cheeks stiff from the cold. In the distance he could hear shouts and the blowing of the horn from the Hag's city gate. Someone was coming through in a hurry. He sheathed his sword and resettled his cloak around his shoulders. 'To the stables,' he ordered, pulling his cloak over his head. 'I want to be a league from the Hag before Urial realises who trespassed in his tower.'

Chapter Eight
RIDERS ON THE ROAD

THE AIR REEKED of scorched iron and the seared flesh of slaves. The caustic night fog of Hag Graef swirled and eddied in the roads and alleys, a thick greenish-yellow pall that oozed down into the valley from the chimney vents of the forges on the mountain slopes above. Silver steel, the precious, semi-magical metal prized by the druchii, was difficult and expensive to make, and thousands of slaves died every year around the great crucibles, their throats and lungs ravaged by the poisonous fumes.

Malus wore a nightmask of black iron worked in the shape of a snarling nauglir, his cloak pulled close around his head to keep the fog from his neck and scalp. His cold one, Spite, loped along the Spear Road at a steady, ground-eating pace. Occasionally he would toss his head and snap at the stinging clouds of mist that attacked his nostrils and eyes.

They had slipped from the drachau's fortress without incident, swinging into the saddles and setting off as soon as they reached the stables. Malus knew that the drachau would take no personal interest in a family feud – the highborn were encouraged to fight amongst themselves, ensuring that the strongest and smartest survived to fight for the Witch King. Yet it was possible that Urial had enough influence at court to order the gates of the city closed against him. Trapped within the city, he could much more easily be located and retaliated against. Urial could conceivably turn him over to the Temple of Khaine, ensuring an agonising death for his half-brother and gaining increased favour from the priestesses besides.

Speed was of the essence. Right now, Malus imagined Urial restoring order and having the entire tower searched while he rushed to his sanctum to ensure that his most precious relics were safe. When he realised the skull was missing, Urial would spare no effort to keep the thieves from escaping.

How long, Malus wondered? How long until his brother realised what had happened? How quickly will he react?

The city's north gate, also known as Spear Gate, was just ahead. Normally reserved solely for military traffic heading north to the watchtowers near the Chaos Wastes, it was the closest way out of the city. Malus turned in his saddle to look back along his small column of riders. The druchii who'd been stung by one of Urial's guard beasts, a man named Atalvyr, was getting steadily worse as the creature's poison ravaged his body. They'd stuck a cloth in the wound and lashed Atalvyr to his saddle. He hoped the guard-captain at the gate wouldn't inspect the warriors too closely and wonder why they were leaving for the frontier with a wounded man in the column.

Snow was still falling from the leaden sky, turning to mist as it descended through the currents of warm night fog. The city wall gained definition as they approached, resolving itself from a looming, dark grey band into a smooth, black barrier some thirty feet high and crowned with spiked merlons all along its length. The north gatehouse was well lit with witchfire globes, gleaming like the eyes of a huge, patient predator. The maw-like opening of the great gate was shut against the darkness outside.

Malus was nearly beneath the gatehouse's massive overhang when a muffled voice from above cried, 'Halt! Who goes there?'

The highborn reined in Spite, raising a hand to halt the column. 'I am Malus, son of Lurhan the Vaulkhar!' Malus shouted up at the invisible sentry.

For a moment, there was no reply. Then: 'The gate is closed for the night, dread lord. What is your business?'

Malus gritted his teeth in aggravation. 'My father has ordered me to lead a party of men north to the Tower of Ghrond, and to go with all haste.'

This time the silence stretched uncomfortably long. They're trying to make heads or tails of the situation, Malus thought. On the one hand, it meant they have no specific orders concerning him. On the other hand, the longer they dithered, the greater the chance that such orders could arrive. He straightened in the saddle. 'Will you make me wait here until dawn?' he cried. 'Open the gate, damn you!'

The echoes of his shout were still reverberating from the walls when there was a rattle of metal at one of the gatehouse's doors, and a guard captain in full armour stepped into view. Spite hissed menacingly and took a half-step towards the man before Malus jerked the nauglir's head aside with a pull of the reins. 'Stand,' Malus ordered, and the cold one settled onto its haunches. The highborn slid smoothly from the saddle, throwing a glance over his shoulder to Lhunara, who was second in the column. Her expression was inscrutable behind her nightmask, but her hands hovered close to the crossbow hooked to her saddle.

Malus walked over to the guard captain, pulling aside his iron mask so that his impatience was clearly evident. 'I've had men skinned alive for making me wait this long,' he said with an air of casual malevolence.

The guard captain was no callow recruit, however; his pale, scarred face regarded Malus impassively. 'We don't open the gate after nightfall, dread lord,' he said calmly. 'Orders from your father the Vaulkhar. It's been that way since the start of the feud with Naggor.'

The highborn's eyes narrowed appraisingly. You could have told me that from behind a firing slit, he thought. What are you really after, captain? 'I'm certain Lurhan is well aware of the standing orders, captain. I'd also say that if anyone can make exceptions to those orders, it would be him.' He lowered his voice. 'Is there anything I can offer you as proof?'

The captain inclined his head thoughtfully, studying the gatehouse overhang. They were both outside the line of sight of the guards above. 'Well,' he said, running his tongue along carefully filed front teeth. 'If you could show me some written orders, dread lord... or some other proof of authority...'

Malus smiled mirthlessly. 'Of course.' I ought to ram my dagger through your eye, he thought brutally, but that wouldn't get the gate open.

Just then a high-pitched, querulous piping floated through the snowy air overhead. Malus looked up in time to see a long, almost snake-like shape furl broad, leathery wings and arrow through one of the gatehouse's narrow windows. He caught a glimpse of long, indigo coloured jesses dangling from the reptile's taloned feet. The guard captain frowned. 'That's a message from the Hag,' he said. 'Perhaps that's word from your father there, dread lord.'

My father? No, the highborn thought. Malus reached into a pouch at his belt. 'Here is proof of my authority, captain.' He pressed a ruby the size of a bird's egg into the man's palm. It was one of the last pieces of treasure left from his summer raid.

The guard captain held the gem up to his eye and his face went slack with wonder. 'That'll do,' he breathed, tucking it into his coin purse.

'Of course, you'll need proof of authority to get back into the city upon your return as well.'

The highborn laughed at the sheer audacity of the man. On one hand, he had to admire such implacable avarice. On the other hand, extorting money from above one's station demanded a brutal reprisal. 'Don't worry, captain,' he said. 'I've an excellent memory. When I return to the Hag I'll make certain you're amply attended to. You have my oath on it.'

The guard captain smiled. 'Excellent. I'm always at your service, dread lord. If you'd kindly mount up, I'll have the gate open in a moment.' The druchii spun smartly on his heel and stepped back inside the gatehouse, closing the ironbound door behind him.

Malus fought the urge not to run back to Spite. One man is ordering the gate opened, he thought. Another is reading the letter from Urial and deciding what to do. Which one will trump the other? 'Make ready!' Malus hissed to the column as he swung into the saddle.

From within the gatehouse came a rattle of enormous chains. Slowly, slowly, the enormous iron gates began to pull back, revealing the tunnel leading to the outer portal. At once, Malus kicked Spite into motion, waving the column to follow. We could get trapped inside, he thought, gritting his teeth. They could shut the inner gate, trap us between the two portals and rain fire down on us if they wish.

He made a snap decision: if he couldn't see the outer gate starting to move he'd wheel the column about and race into the city. We'll climb the wall at another point if we have to, he raged inwardly. I will not be caged here like a rabbit!

Spite's leathery feet slapped along the cobblestones, eager perhaps for the open country and relief from the biting fog. The gate swung ponderously on its ancient hinges; it was just wide enough to allow a nauglir to pass. Malus spurred his mount forward, his eyes straining to pierce the gloom beyond. Was that a shaft of grey light? Yes!

'Ha!' Malus cried, jabbing sharply with his spurs. Spite lurched into a run. The sounds of heavy footfalls reverberated through the narrow passage beneath the gatehouse, an echoing rumble like sullen thunder. Malus could see a bar of wan moonlight just ahead and bared his teeth triumphantly. Too late, brother, the highborn thought. Spite leapt through the yawning gates with a rumbling growl, his clawed feet slipping on the snow-covered road.

There was a shout from above and a sharp thump as a bolt as long as Spite's tail punched into the frozen ground a hand span to their left. There was a whickering sound and another shaft blurred past the cold one's scaly snout, causing the nauglir to snap its jaws and shy to the side.

The druchii in the tower had evidently reached a compromise: let the riders out onto the killing field before the gate and present a pile of corpses to Urial when he arrived. Corpses thoroughly picked clean of valuables, of course.

'Faster!' Malus cried, applying the spurs. Another bolt went wide, ricocheting off the hard surface of the road and skimming its icy surface like a steel-headed viper. The highborn stole a look over his shoulder: most of the warband was already clear. Two of the riders were looking back over their shoulders as well, aiming their crossbows one-handed and firing bolts at the narrow embrasures mostly for Spite's sake.

Already the walls of the city were losing focus, their edges going grey behind gusts of snow as the highborn sped farther down the Spear Road. There was another thump from the gatehouse, and Malus watched the black diamond shape of a heavy bolt swell in his vision. But the gunner on the wall had misjudged the range, and the bolt fell short, striking a rider a yard behind the highborn.

The armour-piercing point punched through the rider's breastplate with a loud crack and plunged on into the back of his nauglir's thick skull. Rider and mount tumbled end for end, kicking up a spray of blood-tinged snow, then fetched up in a broken heap in the middle of the road. Malus steeled himself for another shot, but when he glanced warily back at the gatehouse he saw that Hag Graef was just a ghostly smudge, grey against the winter night.

Malus gave a wild, vicious laugh, hoping the guards at the gatehouse could hear him. That was your best chance to catch me, brother, he thought. Now, every league will carry me further from your grasp. Soon there will be nothing more for you to do than wait in your twisted spire and dread my return. 'Run, Spite!' the highborn called to his mount. 'Tireless beast of the deep earth! Carry me north, where the tools of vengeance await!'

THEY'D COVERED HALF a dozen leagues in the darkness and the snow before Atalvyr toppled from his saddle.

The first indication Malus had of a problem was the change in the sound of the loping nauglir. The steady run of a dozen cold ones was not quiet; even on the snowy road they moved with a low rumble of heavy-footed thunder. Suddenly, the rumble slackened. Looking back, Malus could not at first discern why the column had stopped.

He reined Spite around and headed back down the road until he found Dalvar and the rest of Nagaira's men clustered around their fallen comrade. Atalvyr's cold one had wandered off the road and rested on its haunches in a snowy field nearby. Lhunara had kept the rest of the warband mounted, eyes scanning the road and the surrounding countryside. Malus slid from the saddle, seething with impatience. The snow had slackened as they'd moved north, and he was counting on it to cover their tracks as much as possible. 'What's this?' he said to Dalvar.

Dalvar looked up from Atalvyr's writhing form. 'That damned poison! He had some kind of spasm and snapped his lashings, then fell from the saddle. I thought the venom would have run its course by now, but it's getting worse.'

The wind shifted, and the highborn's nose wrinkled. 'He's putrefying,' Malus snapped. 'The venom is eating him from within. Cut his throat and have done – we've many more miles to go before dawn.'

Nagaira's men studied Malus coldly. Dalvar slowly shook his head. 'I have some potions in my saddlebag. Let me see if I can slow the poison's work, get him back in the saddle–'

'And what then? Ride another few leagues before he collapses again? Speed is our only ally now – we must make it past the watchtowers before Urial can organise a pursuit.'

Dalvar stood, folding his arms. 'Would you squander a fighting man for a few minutes' riding time? We'll need every sword we can muster in the Wastes. Surely you know that.'

Malus ground his teeth, fighting the urge to strike the man's head from his shoulders. A move against Dalvar would bring out the knives from every quarter. When the dust settled, his warband would be cut in half, no matter the outcome. 'Ten minutes,' he said, then headed back to Spite.

He heard the leathery tread of a nauglir sidling up behind him. Malus looked back to see Lhunara and Vanhir pacing him back along the road. 'He's going to be a problem,' Lhunara murmured, the wind whipping long strands of dark hair about her pale face.

'They're *all* a problem,' Malus replied sourly. 'I trusted Nagaira to keep her thugs in line once we'd left the Hag – her greed for the power hidden in the temple would have ensured her cooperation, at least to a point. Dalvar is another matter. If we move against him, no matter how subtly, the rest will turn on us. And I expect he's right; we'll need every sword we can muster where we're going.'

'Has my lord never hunted in the Wastes?' Vanhir's tone was utterly cold, his formerly melodious voice now flat and portentous as a dirge.

Malus glared over his shoulder at the highborn knight, but the warrior was watching the forest opposite their side of the road. Vanhir had suffered every night on the weeklong march from Clar Karond to the Hag; he'd lost enough skin to make Malus a fine pair of boots, all told. Since then the knight's hatred had crystallised into a cold hardness that Malus couldn't quite fathom. It was as if Vanhir had reached a decision about something, and was only just biding his time. Was the knight ready to cast aside his famous honour for the sweet wine of treachery?

'I have not,' Malus said evenly. 'I took a turn with the garrison at Ghrond, during my father's misguided attempts to get me killed in some border raid. But no, I have never travelled into the Wastes. Have you?'

Vanhir turned to regard his erstwhile master. His dark eyes were like polished basalt. 'Oh, yes, dread lord. The best hunting can be found there, just a week's ride or so from the frontier. My family made its wealth ambushing nomadic raiders along the steppes.' He straightened in the saddle and shot Malus a challenging look. 'It is not a place for the brash or the foolish, or warriors of poor mettle.'

Before Malus knew it, his sword was naked in his hand and he'd crossed half the distance to Vanhir when Lhunara let out a sharp hiss. 'Horse's hooves! Someone's riding fast up the road from the Hag!'

Malus restrained himself with an effort of will. He cocked his head, straining to hear over the restless wind, but heard nothing. But the highborn knew better than to doubt Lhunara's keen senses. He leapt into the saddle, blade still in hand. 'Off the road! Quickly!'

The three druchii spurred their mounts back to the rest of the warband. Malus quickly sized up the terrain. They were in the foothills north and west of the Dragonspines, a place of dense woods and treacherous marshes. Off the road to the left were stagnant pools and stands of tall thorngrass, leading back to dense woods and underbrush on the other side of a shallow pond. 'That way!' he pointed with his sword. 'Into the tree line across the pond!'

Dalvar was kneeling by the fallen warrior, whose convulsions had eased but who still seemed incapable of moving. 'What about him?'

'Put his sword in his hand and leave him, or stay behind and die at his side!'

For a moment, Dalvar looked ready to protest, but the sound of distant hoof beats galvanised him into action. He drew the man's sword and pressed it into the druchii's palm, then scrambled into the saddle and joined the warband as they dashed across the fen.

The cold ones handled the terrain with ease, something a horse would have been hard-pressed to emulate. They nosed into the thick undergrowth, panicking small animals in their path and brushing aside thickets of brambles without slowing their stride. Once out of sight, the druchii dismounted, and Malus led them back to the edge of the trees. 'Crossbows ready,' he ordered as they settled down behind fallen logs and thick underbrush. 'No one fires unless I give the word.'

Malus took cover behind a broad oak tree. Dalvar settled into a crouch beside him. 'Another minute and he'd have been ready to move,' the retainer growled.

'Then it's fortunate for us that our pursuit came early and Atalvyr could still serve us as bait.'

Before Dalvar could reply, a group of riders swept into view riding tall black warhorses. They wore heavy black cloaks with full hoods, and held long, ebon-hafted spears in their hands. One of the riders surveyed the area surrounding the fallen druchii, and Malus saw moonlight glint on a silver steel nightmask. Urial's men all right, Malus noted. They must have left right on our heels to have caught up with us so quickly. He counted only five riders, however, which surprised him. Possibly an advance force, hurriedly dispatched ahead of a larger hunting party? He and his men would make short work of these riders, and hide the bodies in the fen.

Until he noticed that something wasn't quite right about the men and their mounts. Steam curled from the horses' muscular flanks, and they pranced and pawed at the earth as though fresh from the stables, not at the end of leagues of hard riding. And there was something strange about the riders themselves – the way their masked faces turned first one way and then another, like hounds searching for a scent.

Suddenly the air shook with a deep-throated roar as Atalvyr's cold one rose from its haunches and crept up onto the road. The slow-witted beast had finally caught the horses' scent; nauglir loved the taste of horseflesh.

Malus's concern deepened when none of the horses panicked at the nauglir's hunting roar. The riders reined their mounts around to face the approaching cold one, moving as though driven by a single mind. Malus felt the cold touch of dread run a talon down his spine.

The cold one leapt, and the riders spurred their mounts to meet it. At the last minute they split to either side of the beast, but one horse was not as fast as its mates and the nauglir knocked it to the ground with its powerful shoulder, then locked its jaws around the animal's neck. The horse screamed – not a cry of fear or pain, however, but of rage. Its rider rolled easily out of the saddle and sprang to his feet, readying his spear.

The other riders struck at both of the cold one's flanks, driving their spears deep into the beast's side. The nauglir roared and lashed its tail, catching one rider full in the chest. There was a splintering sound and the rider flew backwards out of the saddle, landing in a misshapen heap almost fifteen feet away.

'That's one!' Dalvar hissed triumphantly.

'No,' Malus said. 'Look.'

The broken, twisted shape was still moving. As they watched, the man pushed himself to his knees, then climbed to his feet. One arm hung limp, and the man's ribcage was clearly smashed – yet he stood, and drew his sword, and rejoined the fight.

Even the horse the cold one had bitten had scrambled back up and bolted away from the creature, blood pouring from its neck.

The cold one thrashed and spun in a wide circle, trying to attack all its tormentors at once. Its flanks bristled with long spears, and a huge pool of crimson melted the snow beneath its scaly body. The first dismounted rider was edging closer, his spear levelled at the nauglir's right eye, waiting for the right moment to strike. Sensing his opportunity, he leapt forward – right into the creature's gaping jaws.

The beast had not been as oblivious to the man's approach as it had appeared. It moved like a striking snake, taking man, spear and all into its fanged mouth up to the rider's waist. It bit down with a shattering crunch, spraying blood in a wide fan, and shook the man in its teeth like some great terrier with a rat.

The other riders paused, seemingly considering their next move – then suddenly the cold one let out a strangled cry. It shook its head fiercely once more, then swayed on its feet. Suddenly Malus saw the creature's skin start to bulge slightly, just behind the eyes, and then with a sharp cracking sound, a silver steel spearhead punched through the nauglir's skull from the inside out. Blood and brain matter stained the sharp point. The beast gave a shudder, then collapsed.

'Blessed Mother of Night,' Dalvar said, his voice strained. 'What are those things?'

'They are… murder given form,' Malus said, struggling to believe what he'd seen with his own eyes. 'Urial must be very, very angry.' Or possibly afraid, he thought with a start. If so, the treasure that awaits must be very great indeed.

While they watched, the remaining three riders dismounted and drew their swords. One began cutting into the nauglir's side, while the others started hacking the beast's skull apart to free their companion. Within a few moments' time the spearman staggered free, his entrails spilling from his ravaged belly and catching on the beast's jagged teeth.

The third swordsman pulled the nauglir's steaming heart from its chest and held it up to the sky. The other four lurched over to him, and one by one pressed the great organ to their bodies, sluicing gouts of sticky blood across their chests. The two wounded riders seemed to gain strength from their enemy's lifeblood; their wounds did not heal, but neither were they any longer a hindrance. Suddenly moonlight glinted on a spinning blur of metal and a dagger sprouted from the throat of one of the riders. Atalvyr let out a fevered howl of challenge, holding his sword before him as he swayed on unsteady feet.

The riders turned to face the warrior as if noticing him for the first time. The stricken rider reached up and slowly pulled the needle-bladed knife from his throat.

As one, they advanced.

Malus considered the odds and bit back a curse. 'That's it. I've seen enough. We're getting out of here, as quickly as we can.'

'But our crossbows–' Dalvar began.

'Don't be a fool, Dalvar. It wouldn't make any difference.' The highborn's hand went to the cold lump of metal and stone beneath the lip of his breastplate. 'The only reason we're still alive right now is because of your mistress's talismans, but I'll wager that if these hounds get much closer they'll be able to sense the skull no matter what, and then we'll be finished.'

There was a clash of steel back by the road. Malus turned away. Dalvar watched, his eyes widening. 'Where are we going to go?'

'Back through these woods, for a start, and then up into the hills. These... killers... are going to be searching the Spear Road for us, all the way to the Tower of Ghrond and possibly beyond. We must find another way across the frontier and into the Wastes.'

Dalvar's eyes widened. 'Back into the hills? But they're full of Shades!'

'That's what I'm counting on. If anyone can get us through the mountains unseen, it is they.'

The retainer's face twisted in fear. 'You're mad! The things they do to trespassers–'

'I would rather try my luck with a foe that dies when I pierce his heart!' Malus snarled. 'If we stay here, we die.'

The highborn pulled back deeper into the woods, and one by one, the rest of the warband followed. The screams of the man they'd left behind echoed through the snowy trees long after he was lost to sight.

Chapter Nine
FELL SHADOWS

SPITE LOWERED ON his haunches and leapt again, rear legs clawing for purchase on the frozen, leafy ground. The talons of his left hind leg caught on a thin sapling. For a moment the green wood held, then splintered under the huge beast's weight. The cold one started to slide again and Malus threw himself against Spite's hindquarters, pushing for all he was worth. The weary nauglir leapt as though stung, whipping about and snapping at the highborn in irritation.

Dagger-like teeth clashed shut less than a foot from Malus's face, spraying him with thick tendrils of poisonous slime. Malus snarled and punched the cold one full on the nose, and the beast whipped back around with a roar, stomping further up the slope. The highborn wiped his face and thanked the Dark Mother that they'd at least managed to climb a little further up the hill.

It had been two days since the terrible encounter on the Spear Road, and Malus doubted that they'd covered more than ten miles in the rugged, densely-wooded terrain of the Dragonspine foothills. Each night the warband made camp wherever they happened to be when the weak sunlight faded from the cloudy sky. Each time they built a small fire and roasted some of their precious store of meat, and each time they laid out a generous portion on a plate in a place of honour, hoping that one of the hill-druchii would accept the invitation and enter the camp. So far, the Shades had kept to themselves.

Malus was certain they were out there. The legends said that when the druchii came to Naggaroth, some two thousand men, women and children turned their backs on the great Black Arks and the nascent great cities, travelling instead into the mountainous wilderness to live according to their own laws.

No one knew how many had survived those first few years in the pitiless Land of Chill, but it was well known that the Autarii – the Shades – claimed much of the mountain country north of Hag Graef as their own, and did not suffer intruders lightly. At various times he'd felt his scalp prickle with the undeniable sensation that they were being watched, but not even the nauglir smelled any threats nearby. For whatever reason, the hill-folk were keeping their distance.

Privately, Malus hoped that the Autarii would take their invitation soon. After only two days in the hills he'd begun to seriously consider heading back for the road and taking his chances with Urial's riders. Hour after hour of steep slopes, frozen ground and treacherous under-brush had sapped the warband's strength.

The nauglir were hungry and irritable because Malus had been forced to ration their meat. Each beast could easily consume a full-grown deer or a human body each day, and the highborn was very leery of sending out hunting parties when the risk of ambush was so great. The warband bore the conditions stoically, though more than once Malus had caught sight of Dalvar whispering quietly among Nagaira's other retainers. It could be nothing, but he couldn't afford to take that chance. The question, Malus thought, is what could he do about it?

Spite paused, and Malus suddenly realised that they had reached the top of the slope. He reached out and tugged on the beast's thickly mus-cled tail. 'Stand,' he commanded, a little breathlessly, and the cold one eagerly complied, snowflakes steaming off its scaly hide.

Malus clambered up alongside the cold one and saw that the trees were considerably thinner on the reverse slope, affording a good view of the next hill over and the small vale in between. In the far distance, he could see the dark, broken teeth of the Shieldwall, the huge east-west mountain range that marked the beginning of the frontier. Leagues and leagues away, Malus thought tiredly. It'll take a thousand years to get there at this pace.

The crackle of brush behind him brought Malus's head around. Dal-var clambered up alongside him using a roughly carved cedar stick for support. The druchii's normally smug face was flushed and worn. 'It will be dark soon,' the retainer said, leaning a little on his makeshift staff. 'The men are exhausted, dread lord, and the nauglir besides. If we make camp now, we might have a little light left over to hunt for some fresh meat.'

Malus shook his head. 'No hunting, Dalvar. I'll not lose men to Autarii crossbows.' He indicated the vale below. 'There is some clear ground down there, and what looks to be a stream. We'll set up camp there.'

Dalvar surveyed the vale wearily. 'We'll get weaker every day at this pace. Soon the Autarii won't need to pick us off one by one – they'll just send their striplings in to round us up with willow switches.'

'City living has made you soft,' Malus said with a snort. 'Right now the Shades are testing us, gauging our strength. Each day sees us a few miles deeper into their domain. As long as we keep our force together and afford them no opportunity for easy ambushes, the Shades will have to choose a different tactic – and accepting our invitation is the simplest and easiest option available. They know we're interested in talking with them,' Malus said confidently. 'Sooner or later they're bound to become curious.'

It was well known that, like any druchii, the Autarii had a mercenary streak. Shades served wealthy warlords as hired scouts and skirmishers, and when the Witch King rode to war, entire tribes of Shades marched in the vanguard and claimed their share of the plunder.

'Or they could simply wait until we're too weak from hunger to fight back and take us all captive. Your man Vanhir says that the Autarii bargain only when they have no other choice.'

You've been talking to Vanhir, have you? How disquieting, the highborn mused. I'll have to have a talk with Lhunara about that. 'If they ambush us as a group, we can fight them off – possibly even kill one or more of them. They're excellent woodsmen, but they lack good armour and we have the nauglir on our side. The cold ones will warn us if they catch the scent of a large ambush party. No, I think we still hold a slight advantage here if we stay disciplined.'

Dalvar gave Malus a long look that was frankly doubtful, if not outright challenging. 'Then I suppose we'll see what the night brings,' he said, then turned and made his way carefully back down the slope.

Malus watched him go. 'Tread carefully, Dalvar,' he said. 'The footing here is more dangerous than it appears.'

'Thank you for the warning, dread lord,' the rogue replied over his shoulder. 'You'd do well to remember that yourself.'

You're going to have to die, Dalvar, Malus thought. And it is going to have to happen soon, unless I can find a way to discredit you in the eyes of your men. But how?

'Up,' Malus commanded, slapping Spite's flank. 'It's downhill from here, and then you can rest.'

The nauglir lurched forward, muscles bunching in its shoulders and hips as it negotiated its way down the slope. Malus had to jog to keep pace, until suddenly the cold one let out a barking roar and broke into a run. 'Spite! Stand!' he called, but the nauglir sped on, head low and tail stiff as a spear. He's hunting, Malus realised. What's he got wind of? A deer?

Then, farther upslope, he heard the other nauglir take up the roar as well, and Malus suddenly realised he was in the path of a multi-tonne stampede. Thinking quickly, the highborn cut to the left and slightly back upslope, knowing that there weren't any trees or boulders large enough to protect him from an out-of-control cold one. He could only get out of the way as much as possible and hope for the best.

The hillside shook with dozens of pounding feet. The nauglir, being pack animals at heart, thundered down the slope in a single, lumbering mass, kicking up a huge cloud of powdery snow as they went. In their wake scrambled their owners, clambering down the hill and shouting ineffectual commands at the galloping beasts. Under other circumstances it might even have been amusing, but suddenly Malus felt very vulnerable indeed.

A deer wouldn't have set them off like this, he reasoned. Not the entire pack. They only responded like that when they were hungry and there was blood in the air. Someone's baited them, he thought. There's probably a fresh deer kill in the copse of trees, its body opened to the cold air.

Malus felt his guts turn to ice. He saw that the nauglir were already halfway across the small meadow at the bottom of the hill, galloping for a small copse at the far end. The druchii were in hot pursuit, running lightly across the snowy field.

The warrior in the lead suddenly stumbled and fell. A heartbeat later the druchii behind him collapsed. Then the third warrior in line spun in a half circle, and this time Malus caught the blurred flight of the blunted crossbow bolt that struck the man in the centre of the forehead and dropped him to the snow. The ambushers were firing from the dense tree line on the opposite side of a winding streambed, and Malus's men had nowhere to hide.

There was a faint scuffling sound behind him. Malus whirled, his sword springing from its scabbard, and caught the knobbed end of the Autarii's club right between the eyes.

SOMEONE WAS FORCING a thin, bitter liquid down his throat. Malus gagged and spat, jerking his head violently away from the wooden tube that was being pushed between his lips. The motion set a flare of agony blooming behind his eyes and his stomach roiled. A calloused hand grabbed him by the jaw and despite the awful sickness he jerked his head once more and snapped at the offending hand, sinking his teeth deep into the flesh between forefinger and thumb. He tasted blood and his stomach finally betrayed him. The hand pulled free as he retched a thin stream of bile, and then the blackness behind his eyelids exploded with white fire as a fist smashed into his cheek.

The next thing he felt was a blade against his cheek. It was cold, rough and sharp, and he cried out in fury as it was slowly drawn against his skin, slicing easily through into the flesh beneath. The white-hot pain sharpened his senses into full awareness. He blinked his eyes as warm blood leaked down his face and when he could focus he saw the silhouette of a short, lean-limbed druchii standing before him.

The Shade's sharply-angled features were covered in spiral tattoos of indigo and red, giving him a snarling, daemonic expression even when in repose. When he leered at Malus, his face was the very image of otherworldly hate. The man wore layers of loose robes and soft, leather boots, and an assortment of daggers protruded from a wide belt at his waist. He was backlit by a roaring fire that illuminated a small clearing surrounded by a circle of trees. More of the Shades crouched or paced around the roaring flames, most wearing cloaks of mottled greens and browns that blended artfully with the shadows of the forest. Each druchii in Malus's warband was tied to one of the surrounding trees, as he was himself.

It was difficult to focus, despite the pain. It was full dark, with both moons shining in an unusually clear sky. Malus tried to think. How long was I out? Hours? Days? He tried to concentrate, tried to summon up the fires of his anger. 'Misbegotten runt,' he snarled. 'Is this how you treat an embassy from the great Vaulkhar of Hag Graef?'

The Shade cocked his head at the highborn's outburst, then with a smile he brought the knife to his lips and licked the blood from its edge. His eyebrows rose appreciatively, and he turned to his compatriots, speaking in such thickly-accented druhir that Malus couldn't understand a single word of. The men around the fire laughed, and the highborn didn't like the sound.

'Have a care, my lord. The short one likes the way you taste.'

With an effort, Malus forced himself to turn his head towards the sound of the voice. Vanhir was bound to the tree immediately next to Malus, his face a mass of purple bruises. He spoke with effort through swollen lips. 'The blood and flesh of highborn warriors is a delicacy to the hill clans, so I wouldn't mention your father quite so forcefully if I were you.'

'You're mad!' Malus exclaimed. 'They wouldn't eat their own kin–'

Vanhir managed a pained laugh. 'We *aren't* their kin,' he said. 'We're city folk, and prisoners besides. We're just meat to them, fat and soft, like those Bretonnians were to us.'

There was a rattle and clink of metal near the fire. Malus looked and saw one of the Shades unfolding a roll of soft leather sewn with a number of different-sized pockets. A bone or wood handle protruded from each pocket. As the highborn watched, the short Autarii drew forth a pair of flensing knives and a well-polished bone saw.

'If you're lucky and they've eaten recently, they might settle for just a hand or a forearm,' Vanhir said. 'They're very good at taking only what they need and keeping the victim alive for later.'

The short Autarii spoke, and several of his fellows went to work. One shook out a length of rope and looped it over a sturdy branch hanging near the fire. Another Shade took the end of the rope and walked over to Malus, looping the cord around the highborn's ankles in a few swift, practiced strokes. Two others untied the bonds that held Malus to the tree, leaving his hands bound tightly behind his back.

'You wouldn't dare!' Malus roared. 'Touch me again with your filthy knives and by the Mother of Eternal Night I will call a curse down on you that will blight these hills for a thousand years!'

The short Autarii made a disgusted sound and barked a short command. Two of the Shades hauled on the rope and Malus was hoisted upside down, his body swinging perilously close to the fire. Rough hands stopped his pendular motion, and another Shade set a large brass bowl underneath his head.

Malus watched the short Autarii pull a sickle-shaped knife from the leather cloth. His body was trembling like a plucked wire, seething with white-hot rage. 'Kill me and the Vaulkhar of the Hag will hunt you and your kind to extinction.'

The Shade stepped close and smiled, showing a mouth full of jagged teeth. 'You are nothing but smoke, high man,' the Shade whispered. 'In a moment – puff! You will be gone, as though you had never been. Your Vaulkhar will never know what became of you.'

The knife was cold as ice against Malus's throat.

Chapter Ten
TRIALS AND TORMENTS

SUDDENLY THERE WAS a shout from the other side of the roaring fire, and the Shade paused. A harsh voice barked commands in rustic druhir, and the short Autarii answered in rapid-fire retorts that Malus couldn't follow.

Without warning, the highborn was dropped to the ground, landing painfully on his shoulder and neck. Malus rolled onto his back, craning his head around to try to see what was going on.

There were a number of Shades standing at the edge of the firelight, led by a broad-shouldered Autarii with tattoos on both his face and hands. The other Shades who had been slinking about the fire backed away from these new Autarii, treating them with a mixture of deference and fear.

The heavily-tattooed Shade surveyed the bound druchii and rattled off a long query to his shorter cousin, who spat a quick reply. The newcomer asked another question, and this time got a longer response. The Shade rubbed his chin with a tattooed hand.

They're haggling over us, Malus realised. And the prospective buyer doesn't much care for the price.

The bigger Shade turned as if to say something to his fellows – and abruptly tackled the shorter Autarii. The two men rolled back and forth over the damp earth, and firelight glinted from the knives that had appeared in their hands. I see some things are still the same between us and the hill-folk, Malus noted.

There was the sound of steel against flesh, and the bigger Shade snarled in pain, but then Malus saw a tattooed hand shoot up and plunge its knife down with a meaty smack. The larger Autarii stabbed again and again, and the shorter man let out a single, bubbling cry before the struggling finally ceased.

The victor staggered to his feet, blood oozing from a cut to his arm. One look at the remaining Shades set them to work cutting Malus's retainers from their trees.

A pair of rough hands hauled the highborn to his feet, and a knife slashed through the bonds at his ankles. The broad-shouldered Autarii spared him a single, appraising stare, then nodded in satisfaction and began looting the body of his dead foe. Before Malus could speak, he was spun around and propelled forward with a hard shove, towards the deep shadows beyond the fire.

Malus staggered a few steps, then regained his balance. Suddenly he spun, and in a few swift strides he reached the spot where his former captor lay. The highborn bent as close as he could to the Shade's tattooed face; he was pleased to see the fading glow of life still there. 'Savour your feast of blood and cold steel, runt,' he hissed. 'I warned you what would happen if you trifled with me.'

There were angry shouts behind Malus, and the burly Shade reached up with a broad, scarred hand and shoved the highborn backwards with surprising ease. Malus crashed into two strong bodies. Hands grabbed his arms and a dark sack smelling of sweat and vomit was thrown over his head and tied loosely around his neck.

HE MARCHED FOR hours in stifling blackness with a rough hand clasping each of his arms, keeping him upright no matter how many roots he stumbled over.

Over time his head cleared, and Malus strained to hear every sound emanating around him. He could hear the footfalls and curses of his warband, strung out in a line behind him. From the quiet conversations around him, he suspected that he'd been taken by a large group of Autarii, easily twice the size of his small band. From the relaxed way they talked, they were somewhere within their home territory, and thus had no fear of being attacked. He was further shocked to hear the somnolent groan of a nauglir far to the rear of the column; how the Shades had managed to handle the volatile cold ones was a mystery to him.

Time ceased to have meaning. The Shades seemed tireless, never pausing in their swift, ground-eating march. Malus concentrated on making his legs work, putting one foot in front of the other, until finally his whole world boiled down to a cycle of simple, rhythmic motion. Thus, he was surprised when his senses registered the smell of wood smoke and new voices penetrating the darkness of his hood.

Without warning, his minders came to a halt, and there was a brief exchange between them and their broad-shouldered leader. Just as abruptly the men were moving again, this time leading him off to the side and away from the rest of the group. They walked for several yards, and then a hand at the base of his neck bent him in an awkward bow and he was hurled unceremoniously forward. His foot hit something soft and he sprawled headlong, landing in what felt like a pile of furs or blankets.

There was another curt exchange of words behind him, and then the sounds of movement. Strong hands grasped him and turned him over, and then nimble fingers plucked at the ties around the hood. The vile sack was pulled away, and Malus greedily gulped at the smoke-tinged air.

His eyes, already accustomed to blackness, quickly took in his surroundings. He lay on his back amid a pile of furs, in what looked like a tent with a curved roof. There was a banked fire nearby, reflecting a wan, orange light against bent wood poles with rawhide lashings. There were three figures crouched over him, their hands gliding over his face and body. Fingertips brushed his head, lingering briefly at the swollen lump on his forehead, then floating over his patrician nose and down across his lips. Their touch was feather-light, unnaturally gentle. Then someone stoked the embers of the fire, and as the fire bloomed back into life Malus saw why.

Three druchii women crouched over him, each one dressed in a simple tunic of doeskin. Their heads were bald and tattooed with identical glyphs on their foreheads. Collars of beaten iron rested around their necks. Their ears were gone; nothing but lumps of gnawed scar tissue remained. The tips of long, ropy scars peeked from beneath the top and bottom of their collars, showing how their vocal chords had been crudely cut. The faces of the slaves hovered above him in the wavering light, their expressions seemingly rapt. Pools of darkness swallowed up the light in the holes where their eyes had once been.

'You lie in the tent of Urhan Calhan Beg,' croaked an old, implacable voice somewhere near the firelight. 'You are to be treated as a guest, but first you must make the guest-oath.'

The blind slaves reached down as one and pulled Malus upright. He fought, but could not quite suppress, a shudder of loathing. To cripple a person – a druchii – in such a way, to rob them of their essential strength and then deny them the release of death was cruel beyond belief.

Once he was sitting up, Malus caught sight of the crone sitting by the fire. She was ancient, her alabaster features grown lustreless and still, like cold marble. The old woman moved slowly and carefully, as if each motion threatened to crumble her into dust. She reached out a long-fingered hand and fetched an object from a low shelf next to her.

The crone whispered a command and one of the blind slaves moved silently and surely to take the object from the crone's hand and hold it before Malus. It was a statue, shaped from a dark rock that swallowed the light and was as cold as death itself. The carving was of a woman, sharp and slender as a blade, with cruel, cold features and deep-sunken eyes. The age of the thing surrounded it like a mantle of frost. It could have been carved in lost Nagarythe, thousands of years past.

'Swear upon the Dark Mother that you will make no attempt to escape from this camp, nor do any harm to your caretakers while you are a guest here.'

Malus considered for a moment, then nodded. 'Before the Mother of Night, I swear it,' he said, and pressed his lips to the ancient stone.

The crone nodded solemnly as the slave returned the statue to her frail hands. 'Undo his bonds.'

Two of the slaves undid the ropes around his wrists. Malus stretched his shoulders and tried to massage the feeling back into his hands. 'Where are my men?' he asked.

The crone shrugged.

'Was it the Urhan who brought me here?'

'No. That was his second son, Nuall. I expect you are intended as an offering to appease his father's wrath.'

'His wrath? Why?'

'Enough questions,' the crone hissed. 'You are hungry. Eat.'

While he and the crone were talking the slaves had retreated to the other side of the tent. Now they returned, bearing a platter of bread and cheese and a goblet of spiced wine. The highborn ate swiftly and methodically, taking only small sips of the wine. The crone watched in funereal silence.

By the time Malus was done, a man's face appeared at the entrance to the tent. 'Come,' the Autarii said, beckoning to him. The highborn bowed respectfully to the impassive crone and stepped carefully into the night.

Once outside, Malus discovered that the night was all but gone; the sky above was paling with the touch of false dawn. Through the dimness, the highborn could see that he stood at the end of a narrow, wooded canyon that ended in a sheer wall of rock. Numerous other domed tents crouched amid the tall trees, surrounding a large, permanent structure of cedar logs and piled stone built out from the sheer cliff face – the longhouse of the Urhan. The Autarii headed for the building and Malus squared his shoulders and followed.

The air in the longhouse was raucous and smoky. Two large fireplaces dominated the long walls of the building, and a blue haze of pipe-smoke curled and eddied among the cedar rafters of the ceiling. Piles of furs and floor pillows were thrown over a thick carpet of rushes, and the Autarii lounged about the single great room like a pack of wild dogs.

At the far end of the longhouse the Urhan Calhan Beg presided over his clan, sitting in the building's single chair on a raised dais while attended by three female slaves. The druchii women had been blinded and rendered mute like the others in the Urhan's tent. Malus watched as one of the slaves carefully served Beg a goblet of wine; he noted that the wretched creature was missing both of her thumbs.

Calhan Beg was an old, grey wolf of a man. He was lean and wiry and bore a multitude of scars from a lifetime spent battling man and beast alike. Half of his left ear had been gnawed away at some point, and a sword had cut a deep notch from the top of his prominent nose. Intricate tattoos covered face, neck, hands and forearms, speaking volumes of his deeds as warrior and chieftain. Beg had a long, drooping grey moustache and piercing blue eyes as cold and hard as sapphires. At present that pitiless stare was fixed on the man standing at the foot of the dais – his second son Nuall.

Malus's guide picked his way across the crowded floor and the highborn passed in his wake, carefully ignoring the looks of challenge aimed his way. When Nuall caught sight of them, he indicated Malus with a sweep of his arm.

'And here is another mighty gift to you, father – a highborn prisoner, son of the Vaulkhar of Hag Graef. He will fetch you a great ransom from his decadent kin.'

The Urhan shot Malus a cold look of contempt before refocusing his ire back on his son. 'Did I tell you to go fetch me slaves and hostages, Nuall? Is this my tribute day, that you seek to shower me with gifts?'

Several of the Shades in the hall laughed derisively. Nuall's jaw clenched. 'No, father.'

'No, indeed. I sent you to reclaim our family's honour and return to me the treasure of our household. But where is it? Where is the medallion?'

'It… I know where it is, father, but we couldn't reach it! The river–'

'Be silent, whelp!' the Urhan roared. 'Enough of your witless puling! You think to excuse your failure with gifts, as though I'm some tent-wife? You're no fit son, not like your brother,' Beg growled. 'Perhaps I'll have a dress made for you and see if I can get you married off to some blind old Autarii in need of a bed warmer.'

The assembled crowd howled with laughter, and Nuall's face went chalk-white with rage. His trembling hand went to the long knife at his hip, yet his father made no attempt to protect himself, frankly challenging Nuall with his stare. After a moment's hesitation the younger

man snarled and spun on his heel, staggering clumsily through the
crowd of jeering clansmen and slamming the door of the longhouse in
his wake.

Beg watched his son's retreat with evident disdain. 'All muscle and
no guts,' he grumbled, drinking deeply from his cup. 'Now I'll have to
watch for vipers in my boots or stray arrows on the hunt, or some other
such callow thing.' He eyed Malus balefully. 'No doubt you found that
entertaining.'

Malus took his time before responding, considering the situation
carefully. 'All fathers want for strong sons,' he said at length. 'In that, we
are not so very different, great Urhan.'

'You have children?'

The highborn shook his head. 'No, I am a son with something to
prove to his father.'

Beg cocked his head to one side and studied Malus closely for the
first time. 'So you're one of Lurhan's sons, eh? Not his eldest, and not
that twisted thing he gave to the temple. The middle son, perhaps?'

Malus smiled coldly. 'No, great Urhan. Lurhan's late wife had no part
in my making.'

At that, Beg's eyes narrowed. 'Then you're that witch's whelp. The
one they call Darkblade.'

'My name is Malus, great Urhan,' the highborn replied. 'Dark blades
are flawed things, objects of scorn. That's a name only my enemies use.'

'Well, then, Malus, what ransom will your father pay for you?'

The highborn laughed. 'About half as much as you'd pay if he had
Nuall as his prisoner.'

The Autarii laughed, and even Beg managed a sour smile. 'Then that
bodes ill for you, my friend. I have no use for a guest who cannot
enrich me in some way.'

'Ah,' Malus raised a cautionary finger, 'that is a very different matter
entirely, great Urhan. I believe my stay here can profit you very well
indeed.' He folded his arms. 'I believe you mentioned that you'd lost a
certain precious heirloom, is that not so? A medallion?'

The Urhan straightened in his chair. 'I did. What of it?'

Malus shrugged. 'I came into the hills looking for a guide who
could show me a path to the frontier. You are keen to reclaim your
family's honour. It seems that we both have something to offer one
another.'

Beg snarled impatiently. 'Cut to the heart of it, city-dweller. What do
you propose?'

'I will retrieve this medallion for you, great Urhan, if you will free me
and my men and guide us through the hill passes to the frontier.'

The Urhan laughed coldly. 'Suppose I just start cutting pieces off you
until you'll fetch the moons from the sky if I wish it?'

Malus smiled. 'In the first place, I've sworn the guest-oath before the crone in your very tent. Raise a hand to me now and you tempt the Dark Mother's wrath. In the second place, I've seen how you practise your art, great Urhan, and it isn't the sort of thing one fully recovers from. I expect I'll need to be at my best if I am to reclaim your family's honour. Or–' the highborn indicated the assembled Shades– 'perhaps you should ask your clanmates for help instead.'

Beg shifted uncomfortably in his chair.

That's what I thought, the highborn mused. You don't want anyone else getting their hands on your lost medallion, lest they crown themselves Urhan in your stead.

Malus spread his hands, acting the conciliator. 'All I ask is a simple service, something you and your clan are justly famous for. In return, you regain your family's precious honour. It is an arrangement clearly to your benefit.'

The Urhan rubbed his chin thoughtfully, but Malus could see in his eyes that the Autarii chieftain had already made up his mind. 'So be it,' Beg declared. 'But on one condition.'

'Very well. But I will name a condition in return.'

'You have until dawn tomorrow to recover the medallion and bring it to me. If you have not returned by then I'll hunt you through the hills like a stag.'

Malus nodded. 'Done. In return I want my warband out of your slave pens. Since we're allies now they are your guests just as much as I, and bound by the same oaths.'

Beg grinned. 'Clever. Very well, they go free. But no weapons.'

Malus affected an elaborate shrug. 'I can hardly blame the great Urhan if he fears for his safety with ten armed highborn in his camp.'

The great longhouse fell silent. The Urhan's eyes narrowed in irritation. Then Beg threw back his head and laughed. 'By the Dark Mother, you're a reckless one!' he cried. 'I can see why your father wants no part of you.'

Malus smiled mirthlessly. 'My father's loss is your gain, great Urhan. Now tell me of this medallion, and where I might find it.'

YET IT WAS not so simple as that. The Urhan insisted on breaking bread and sharing wine with his new 'ally', and made a show of having the highborn's warband brought into the hall and given places of honour. More of the Autarii made their way to the hall in the meantime, and it was clear that word of Malus's deal with the Urhan was racing like wildfire through the camp. It wasn't long before Malus caught sight of Nuall, surrounded by a half-dozen men, muttering darkly to one another at the far side of the great hall. The old wolf is laying out an unspoken challenge to Nuall, Malus reckoned, struggling to conceal his irritation.

The meal stretched for more than an hour. Finally, Nuall seemed to reach a decision of sorts, and he and his men slipped out of the hall. Not long afterward, the Urhan clapped his hands, and an Autarii stepped from behind the dais and presented Malus with his weapons and sword belt. As the highborn quickly buckled his sword belt in place, the Urhan leaned back in his chair and spoke.

'Understand, friend Malus, that this is no simple trinket that I ask you to retrieve. It is the Ancri Dam, a potent talisman that my ancestors claim was given to them by the Dark Mother when they migrated to these hills. It is a symbol of our divine right to rule this clan, and has been passed down from father to son for generations. As the eldest son reaches manhood the medallion becomes his, to show that he is to be the next Urhan. So did the medallion pass from me to my eldest son Ruhir.'

The Urhan's face darkened. 'Then, a week past, Ruhir went hunting as was his wont, and went missing in a storm. We went searching for him, and eventually we found one of his boots by the shore of a nearby river. This river is home to many black willows, and one in particular has an evil reputation. We call it the Willow Hag, and it has claimed many lives.'

'Including Ruhir's,' Malus said.

'Even so.'

Malus's mind raced. *Your thick-witted second son can't fetch a medallion from the roots of a willow tree? What else aren't you telling me, Beg?* Malus waited for the Urhan to continue, but after a few moments it became clear that his tale was done.

'Well, since the sun is now well on its course to mid-morning, perhaps I should be about my appointed task. And since forty pounds of silver steel isn't the wisest thing to wear by the banks of a treacherous river–' he rapped a knuckle on his enamelled plate armour. 'I'll leave my harness in the care of my warband. Now, how shall I find this Willow Hag?'

Beg studied him carefully, his expression inscrutable. 'Walk out of my hall and turn west. Cross the hills until you come to a swift-flowing river, then walk upstream until you find a great riverbend. The Willow Hag waits there.'

Malus nodded. 'That seems simple enough. I shall return with the Ancri Dam before sunrise, Urhan Beg. Then we will discuss my journey north.'

With that the highborn stepped from the dais and crossed quickly to his warriors. Lhunara, Dalvar and even Vanhir rose at his approach. 'Get this armour off,' he said quietly, unbuckling his recently secured sword belt.

Lhunara's nimble hands worked at the buckles of his armour, while Dalvar leaned in close. 'He means to betray you, dread lord.'

'I can see that, Dalvar,' Malus hissed. 'He's using me as a goad to push Nuall into more forceful action. I expect his stupid son will wait until I've recovered the amulet and then try to kill me for it.'

'What do we do?' Lhunara asked, as she pulled his breastplate free.

'For now, nothing. We still need the Autarii to get us to the frontier. But–' As the armour was pulled away and Malus still had his back to the dais, he ran his thumb along the outside of one of his sword scabbards. A thin blade of dark iron popped out of a hidden sheath. With a deft movement, he slipped the tiny weapon into Dalvar's hand. 'If I don't return by dawn, make your escape any way that you can. Get to the nauglir and try to make it back to the road. Though, if possible, leave that piece of iron in the Urhan's skull before you go.'

Dalvar pocketed the blade. 'You have my oath on it,' he said darkly.

Lhunara watched the exchange with hooded eyes. She glanced meaningfully at Malus. 'I hope you know what you're doing.'

The highborn gave her a wolfish grin. 'Right or wrong, Lhunara, I always know what I'm doing.'

The retainer watched her lord and master stride confidently from the hall, throwing a hard stare at any man with the temerity to meet his gaze. 'Somehow that doesn't reassure me one bit,' she muttered.

Chapter Eleven
RIDDLES OF BONE

MALUS LEANED AGAINST the rough bark of a thorn oak and once again gauged the light seeping through the overcast sky. It was late afternoon. By his estimation he'd covered barely three miles from the Autarii camp and he hadn't even seen the river yet, much less the Willow Hag.

Birds called shrilly across the hilltops, and back the way Malus had come he saw a black-furred stag creep stealthily among the trees. Without a large pack of nauglir and a rattling column of knights frightening the wildlife out of their path, the highborn found that the undergrowth teemed with creatures large and small. Hunting cats yowled in the shadows, hoping to frighten their prey into the open, and hawks swooped low over the brush. Winged serpents sunned themselves in high branches, their leathery wings spread like fans to soak up the feeble warmth.

Malus had learned early on to stay close to the trees, moving in short hops from bole to bole. Almost two hours after he'd left camp he'd begun to hear the sounds of something heavy pushing its way stealthily through the brush to his right. When he stopped, it would stop. The highborn found himself wishing for his crossbow as he pressed on, listening as the sounds of his pursuer grew slowly but steadily closer to his own path.

Finally, Malus reached the bottom of one of the hills and discovered a small clearing just ahead. His first urge was to dash across the welcome patch of light brush, but his pursuer was close behind him now, and instinct prompted him to choose a different tack. Drawing his sword, the highborn leapt nimbly into the low branches of a hackthorn. Quietly as he could, he scrambled more than a dozen feet up, settling carefully on a large branch that was still covered in a mantle of reddish leaves.

He sat there, controlling his breathing, for several long minutes. Then, without warning, the brush beneath him parted. A huge, hump-backed shape crept into view. It was a boar, a huge, black-skinned animal with a scarred, bristly hide and two cruel, dagger-like tusks. It stood beneath the tree for several heartbeats, sniffing the air and seeming to listen for Malus. Then, looking left and right, the great beast moved cautiously into the clearing.

Malus leaned his head back against the trunk of the hackthorn, cursing his skittish nerves. A boar, he thought, fighting the urge to laugh. Treed by a pig!

Suddenly there was a rushing sound in the air and the entire tree swayed like a sapling. Malus fell from his branch and only just stopped his plunge with a desperate grab for a nearby limb as a dark shadow swept before the sun. There was a heavy thud in the clearing and then the air was filled with shrill squeals and grunts. Eyes wide, Malus climbed back onto his branch and watched the scene below.

The boar was squirming in the talons of a huge wyvern, its long, reptilian head clamped around the animal's thick neck. Blood scattered across the grass, then there was a crunch of bone as the boar's neck snapped. Its limbs drummed a brief tattoo, then went still.

As Malus watched, the wyvern raised its head and surveyed the clearing, its gaze lighting briefly on the highborn in the tree. It was in the branches above me the entire time, he thought, waiting for its next meal to stumble through the clearing. He smiled weakly at the huge predator. 'I'm too lean and full of gristle,' he said to the beast. 'Be content with the great ham in your talons and don't waste your time on a morsel like me.'

The wyvern studied Malus for a moment longer, its expression flat and devoid of mercy. Then it bunched its shoulders and leapt into the air, carrying the boar effortlessly beneath it. The highborn listened to the flapping wings receding in the distance, but it was some time before his hands were steady enough to hazard the climb down and resume his hunt for the river.

Once again, he'd underestimated the difficulty of traversing the steep slopes and rough terrain of the foothills, even without the heavy weight of his armour. Malus was starting to think the Shades didn't bother walking along the ground – they just climbed the trees and swung from limb to limb like Lustrian gibbons. The notion was beginning to sound pretty appealing.

At this rate it will take me most of the night just to get back to camp, Malus thought angrily. Providing of course I don't get lost in the darkness. Or killed by Nuall and his men.

Malus pushed away from the tree trunk and resumed his climb up the steep hillside. One way or another, Nuall is going to die, he vowed to himself. If this fool's errand gets the better of me, I'll be damned if that idiot is going to profit from it!

The climb to the top seemed to take an eternity as he struggled for footing on the slick, icy soil and worked around tangles of brambles and thick underbrush. When Malus finally reached the top, however, he was rewarded with the sight of a fairly wide valley, curving away slightly to the north-east, and a rushing black ribbon of water running along its base. The river bend that Beg described was nowhere in sight. About a mile to the river, Malus calculated. Another couple of hours at least, and the light is fading fast. The prospect of digging around the roots of a willow tree in freezing water and at night didn't appeal to him in the least. The sun, however, wasn't going to linger at my convenience.

Gritting his teeth, he began his descent.

As it happened, Malus made better time than he expected, reaching the river in less than an hour by virtue of losing his balance and tumbling, head over heels, down the bramble-choked hill. His face and hands were raw and bleeding, and the stumps of broken thorns still jutted from his cheeks and chin. What light remained needed to be used for covering ground, not tending trivial hurts.

Unfortunately, the undergrowth only thickened as he drew closer to the river, weaving into tangles so dense that for a time Malus feared he wouldn't get to the riverbank at all. When he did at last find a break, he soon saw that there was no stretch of bare shoreline he could walk along between river and brush. The highborn stood for a moment, watching the river go by, and reached an abrupt decision. Slipping one of his scabbarded swords from his belt, he tested the depth of the water at its edge. Satisfied it wasn't too deep, Malus stepped into the swift-flowing water up to his knees and started to work his way carefully upstream.

Malus's boots were nauglir hide, expensive and well made, and for a short time the freezing cold water didn't have a significant effect. The strong current was something different entirely, but he was certain that he was still making better time than he would fighting through the thick scrub on land.

An hour passed. Then another. The sky began to grow dark. He was getting very tired from fighting the current, and his calves and feet were numb. Malus rounded another bend in the river, and there, about a half-mile ahead, the river took another sharp turn around a narrow bend. Rising up from that narrow talon of land was a broad, black stain against the iron-grey sky. It was a huge, old black willow, rising high above its stunted cousins along the riverbank. Even from this distance, Malus could see the twisted mass of cable-like roots that spread like a tangled net down into the icy water. Battened on the flesh of the dead, the highborn thought grimly. Someone should have taken an axe to the thing years ago.

With his objective in sight, Malus forced himself to pause and consider the terrain – though, after a moment's study it was clear that there was very little to see. The thick brush along the riverbank obscured the land beyond; Malus could see the tops of trees, but nothing of what lay beneath. The good news, however, was that unless Nuall had a lookout high in one of those very trees he couldn't see Malus, either. It would almost be worthwhile to leave the same way I got here, he thought, but for the fact I'm half frozen to death as it is. Nevertheless, the highborn sank a little lower in the current, suppressing a sharp hiss as the freezing water stung his thighs. Moving slowly, so as not to generate any more noise than the river itself, Malus worked his way towards the great tree.

Night came on swiftly as he approached. The Willow Hag seemed to stand out against the blackness of night, swathed in its own inky aura of malevolence. There was a smell on the wind – the stink of fleshy rot, wafting from the tree. Then the wind picked up, and Malus realised that the tree's branches weren't stirring in the breeze. It seemed to crouch motionlessly over the riverbend, waiting like a predator for its next meal.

The sound of rushing water increased the closer Malus came to the tree, and in the wan moonlight he could see thin traces of foam marking whorls and eddies of churned water on the downstream side of the tree.

The swift water was being forced through the tangled roots in such a way as to create strange crosscurrents. Malus reckoned there would also be a sharp undertow on the upstream side. No wonder this Hag eats men, he thought. After a moment's consideration, he decided that he would first try to penetrate the tangle of roots on the downstream side. Better to fight something pushing him away from the tree than let himself get dragged inside.

Malus soon discovered that the water grew deeper the closer he got to the tree, until he was forcing himself to wade in water that rose above his waist. The current lashed at him from first one direction, then another, trying to spin him around. He forced himself ever closer to the great tree until finally he could throw himself forward and grab one of the thick willow roots. His hands closed around a root as thick as a ship's cable, its springy core sheathed in a slick, almost viscous skin. The highborn fought a shudder of revulsion. It felt just like rotting flesh, he thought. Icy rotten flesh, at that.

Using the slimy roots for leverage, Malus began to probe his way deeper into the mass of roots. Almost at once, his sword scabbards became entangled in the convoluted mass. This is an invitation to disaster, Malus thought. Reluctantly, he undid his sword belt and tied it securely around a thick root near the edge of the mass, then pressed ahead.

Soon he was up to his neck in freezing water, crouching low under overhanging roots that pressed him closer and closer to the water's surface. He'd penetrated perhaps an eighth of the way into the root complex and he was entirely swallowed up in the malignant labyrinth. As he proceeded deeper, he was surprised to find a pale green luminescence emanating from the larger roots, glowing like grave-mould and providing a faint illumination. So far there were no signs of bones, but Malus figured he still had a way to go.

A few minutes and as many feet later, he came to a place where his way was blocked by a thick root broader than his leg. The only way ahead was to swim beneath it, and for the first time the idea gave him pause. The dank air beneath the tree smelled like a crypt, and a palpable aura of dread hung over Malus's head like a funeral shroud. I didn't come this far to drown beneath some damned old tree, he thought angrily. At the same time, he wasn't about to leave his warband to be mutilated at the hands of Beg and his savages.

No one steals my property from me, he thought grimly. With a sharp intake of breath, he slipped beneath the water and pushed his way under the great root, trusting that there would be another pocket of air on the other side.

There was – but the space was much tighter than he'd imagined, barely enough to hold his head. He gasped at the agonising cold, only dimly aware that the narrow space was brightly lit by the greenish mould. Malus filled his lungs and dived again, pushing himself ahead.

He came up – and his head struck a springy net of roots. Further, he thought. With an effort, he pushed himself lower and farther on, running his hand along the tangled mass above him.

Two feet. Three feet. Still nothing. His lungs began to burn. Do I turn back? He fought the first stirrings of panic.

Four feet. Five feet. No end in sight. The burning in his chest became an ache. It was hard to resist the urge to press his face against the ceiling of roots, hoping to find a mouthful of air.

Six feet – and the ceiling of roots began to curve sharply downwards. It was all he could do to keep from opening his mouth and gasping for air that didn't exist. Mother of Night, Malus thought, help me!

Malus turned around, struggling to keep his bearings in the darkness, when suddenly his ears filled with a slow, torturous groan. The entire mass of roots around him shifted – and the current shifted with it. The powerful force he'd been pushing against abruptly pulled him downwards and deeper towards the centre of the tree.

He tumbled in the vortex, striking roots that were tough as iron. His hands and feet caught in loops and sharp bends and were just as roughly yanked free. There was a buzzing in his ears, and the last breath in his lungs burst from his mouth and nose in a thin stream. Succumbing to panic, his eyes snapped open in the tumult – the pain was sharp and numbing, causing him to blink fiercely – and he caught a glimpse of greenish luminescence ahead of him. He struck another root, and this time he grasped it with a drowning man's iron grip. With all his failing strength he worked his way hand over hand towards the grave-glow, his eyes squeezed shut with the effort.

Malus's head burst through the surface of the churning water with a whooping gasp for air. It reeked of the sickly sweet taste of decay, but the highborn drank it down all the same. For a moment it felt as though he couldn't possibly inhale enough.

And then a pair of cold, rotting hands closed about his throat.

The highborn's eyes snapped open in shock. The glow came not from grave-mould, but from the figure of a woman. Rotting skin sagged like melted wax from her bones, which themselves were stained dark with age, like the bark of the tree.

Much of her hair was gone, and beneath her shrivelled cheeks her lips had rotted completely away, leaving only a death's-head snarl. Her eyes were empty sockets, but Malus could still see the burn scars around the edges, and the remnants of a rusted iron collar around her withered neck.

Silent and hateful, the Willow Hag pushed him downwards, until the raging water was roaring in his ears. She was not strong, but she had leverage and she was tireless as death. Malus beat at her rotting arms, feeling the bones flex like willow roots. His strength was failing fast, and her bony fingers closed inexorably tighter around his neck.

Desperate, Malus pulled at the hands until he could draw a thin stream of breath. 'Hateful wight, release me!' he gasped. 'I am a druchii of Hag Graef, not a Shade like those who blinded you! Let me live, and I'll give you another chieftain's son to pour your hate upon!'

For a terrifying second, nothing happened. Then there was another groaning sound, and Malus felt his surroundings shift once again. The churning water grew still. With eerie slowness, the fingers loosened their grip on his throat. As soon as he was free, Malus pushed away, putting as much space between himself and the wight as possible.

He was in a hollow of sorts, possibly directly under the tree itself. Walls, ceiling and floor were shaped by an impenetrable web of strong, layered roots. Skeletons, dozens of them, were enmeshed there, held together by tatters of clothing.

The stench of rot hung like a haze in the air, coating the inside of his nostrils and throat. At the same time this realisation struck home, Malus's backwards-reaching hand sank into a soft, pulpy mush. Gelid body fluids oozed around his splayed fingers. The highborn turned and found his hand buried in the rotting goo of a dead Autarii's stomach. Well met, Ruhir, Malus thought, pulling his hand free of the mess with a frown of disgust. Beg's son was splayed on a rack of tree roots like the Hag's other victims; beneath the mangled throat hung a silver medallion worked with the image of a rearing stag.

Malus turned back to the Hag, his mind working furiously. Clearly the wight was the hate-filled spirit of an Autarii slave who'd escaped her captors, only to stumble blindly into the river and die beneath the tree. Studying the rotting form, he saw by the ragged kheitan she wore that she'd once been a noble. In the uncertain light, it appeared that the tree's roots pierced the body in dozens of places; indeed, it was difficult to tell where the tree ended and the Hag began.

'Hear me, fell spirit,' Malus said hoarsely. 'Even now, another chieftain's son waits nearby to murder me when I emerge from your chambers. He means to make slaves of my warriors, just as he enslaved you. I mean to see him dead, and it would please me to deliver him into your hands. If you allow me to leave here with the medallion around this corpse's neck, I'll give him and his men to you. That's seven lives for the price of one, and sweeter prey besides. I give you my oath as a highborn.'

The wight regarded him silently for long moments. Dark water lapped gently at the tree roots, and insects crawled and chattered through Ruhir's decaying corpse. Then, suddenly, the hollow shifted again, elongating and contracting, pushing Malus inexorably closer to the Hag.

She stood less than a foot away when the movement finally stopped. Cold air wafted down from above. Malus looked up to see that a channel had opened through the roots at a slight angle, opening to the dark sky a dozen feet or so above. With a creak of old sinew and leather the wight pointed silently upwards.

Malus bowed his head to the Hag. 'Your wish is my command,' he said with a cruel smile.

SHIVERING IN THE cold wind, Malus looped his sword belt over an overhanging branch that stretched out over the river on the upstream side.

With a grunt of effort, he pulled the limb back until he could reach it, then hung the Ancri Dam from it and carefully returned it back to its original place.

The black willow's overhanging branches and long, black tendrils created a curtain of foliage that encompassed a space larger than a campaign tent. Plenty of room to manoeuvre, he thought. Next, he concealed his swords amid a cluster of roots close to the water's edge. Once all was in place, he turned and ran inland, bursting through the curtain of foliage into full view.

'Nuall!' he shouted, having no difficulty sounding tired and hurt. 'Show yourself! I know you're out here! I have a bargain for you!' Malus walked a few yards from the tree and sank to his knees.

Wind whispered in the bushes and shook the branches of the trees. Malus peered warily into the darkness. Then, without warning, seven Shades coalesced out of the shadows, surrounding him with bared blades. Nuall grinned at the shocked look on the highborn's face. '*I'll* make *you* a bargain,' the chieftain's son replied. 'Give me the medallion and I'll kill you quickly.'

'I don't *have* the medallion, you fool,' Malus said contemptuously. 'Your father neglected to mention that the Hag was haunted. I'm lucky to have gotten away with my life.'

Nuall took a step forward, extending the point of his sword until it was scant inches from Malus's eye. 'Well, your luck just ran out.'

'Wait!' Malus cried, holding up a warding hand. 'I saw the medallion. I know where it is. Let me live and I'll take you to it. You can have the Ancri Dam and my warband besides. I've had enough of your damned hills.'

The chieftain's son thought it over, clearly struggling with the competing urge to please his father and sate his bloodlust. Finally he nodded. 'Very well.'

'I want your oath, Nuall!'

'All right, my oath on it! Now show me the medallion!'

Malus rose painfully to his feet. Surrounded by the Shades, he turned and walked back to the tree. The Autarii hesitated when they reached the curtain of black tendrils, but when the highborn passed through without harm they quickly followed suit.

He led them up to the base of the old tree. Nuall looked around. 'All right, now what?'

'The medallion is hanging from a limb on the opposite side. We'll have to work our way over across the tops of the roots–'

'You're mad, highborn!' Nuall exclaimed.

'Or you're a coward,' Malus answered. Before Nuall could respond, the highborn stepped onto the tangled mass of roots. 'It's slick, but not impossible to cross. Now, are you coming?'

Nuall gave him a glare of pure murder, then set his jaw stubbornly and followed Malus onto the roots. As he did, he turned and pointed at three of his men. 'You go around the other way and meet us.'

Reluctantly, the Autarii obeyed. Malus turned and walked carefully along the roots, working his way around the wide bole of the tree. Nuall followed closely, growing bolder with every step. Finally, Malus pointed to the medallion, turning gently on its chain out over the river.

'There it is,' he said. 'If two stout men can climb onto the branch enough to bend it back towards the tree, a third man could grab the medallion.'

Nuall nodded. 'A good plan.' Just then, the retainers who'd made the journey on the opposite tack around the tree stepped carefully into view. Nuall pointed at them. 'Two of you get up on that branch and start bending it towards us. You–' he pointed at Malus– 'grab the medallion and hand it to me.'

Malus nodded, trying to look fearful. 'If you insist.'

The two Autarii climbed nimbly up the bole of the willow and began edging their way along the limb. Slowly but surely the branch dipped, bending closer and closer to the trunk. Malus crouched, as though to steady himself. His right hand felt between the roots beside him and closed on the hilt of one of his swords.

The medallion inched towards him. Malus stretched out his left hand, while the other loosened the sword in its scabbard. *Just a little bit more…*

'Ha!' Nuall cried, lunging forward without warning and closing his fist around the medallion. 'Kill the highborn!'

Just as I expected, you oath breaking bastard, Malus thought scornfully, and leapt a heartbeat after Nuall. He grabbed Nuall's wrist and heaved downwards, drawing his sword in the same motion. The chieftain's son let out a yell, and the branch cracked like a thunderclap, spilling one of the Shades into the river. Nuall overbalanced and fell in as well, dragging Malus with him.

All around them, the Willow Hag groaned hungrily, and the undertow at once became a ravenous vortex. Malus pressed back against the roots, held momentarily in place by the force of the undertow rushing through a gap just beneath his boot heels.

The Shade disappeared beneath the surface with a startled gasp. Nuall thrashed about, groping for the shifting tree roots. He held the Ancri Dam in a white-knuckled grip. 'Release me!' he roared, threatening to pull Malus away from the roots and into the undertow.

'As you wish, fool,' Malus snarled. His sword flickered in the moonlight, slicing through Nuall's forearm just below the highborn's own clutching hand.

The chieftain's son screamed, bright blood pumping from the severed limb. Broken ends of bone gleamed pale white in the moonlight.

Malus repositioned himself carefully, digging his boots into the network of roots for support.

'Your brother is waiting below, Nuall,' he said coldly, 'along with a serving girl eager to take you into her arms!'

Nuall screamed as Malus brought his blade down on the Autarii's other wrist. Blood bloomed darkly beneath the water, and then the chieftain's son was gone.

Suddenly there was a sharp blow along the top of Malus's head, tracing a line of fire along his scalp. The highborn cried out in pain as hot blood poured down the side of his head. The second Autarii still clung from the overhanging branch directly above Malus, swinging down at him with a short, broad sword. Much of the man's body was protected by the dark wood, an advantage the Shade was trying to use to its fullest effect. Of the other Autarii, nothing could be seen, though the Hag's roots were writhing hungrily like a bed of snakes.

Malus pushed against the roots beneath him and hacked upwards, getting a shower of wood chips for his efforts. He struck again, and this time the Shade took the opportunity to slash at his forearm, leaving a deep cut just behind the highborn's sword wrist. Malus thrust at the Shade's leering face, but the distance was too great, and the tip faltered well short of its target. The Autarii lashed downwards again with a stroke that left a shallow cut on the back of the highborn's sword hand.

The highborn let out a roar and slashed his long blade in a backhanded arc that buried the blade in the tree branch – and widened the crack made earlier. With a grinding crash the limb broke away, plunging the terrified Shade into the river. Autarii and limb hit the water with a flat slap, but only the limb surfaced again, spinning lazily along the surface of the river.

With a supreme effort, Malus pulled himself up onto the mass of writhing roots. His left hand still clenched Nuall's severed forearm; its hand still held the medallion in a death grip.

Unwilling to let go of his sword and lose it in the roiling mass of roots, Malus sank his teeth into Nuall's stiff fingers and pried each one away from his prize. The medallion fell away, and the highborn hurriedly tossed the severed limb into the whirlpool at the base of the tree. Immediately, the palpitating tendrils fell still. Malus rolled onto his back and managed a breathless laugh. 'Such an appetite,' he said to the tree stretching above him. 'That's the kind of epic hate I can truly admire.'

He lay there in the cold for some time, catching his breath and contemplating a nap. Just a short one, he thought. The roots aren't so bad. Just a short nap, to get my strength back. But finally a tiny, strident voice in the back of his mind pushed itself to the fore and warned him that if he paused to rest for much longer he would never get up again.

Groaning, Malus pushed himself upright, then clambered carefully to his feet. He buckled on his sword belt and fumbled the medallion over his blood-caked head. The cut on his scalp ached and burned, and he focused on the pain, drawing strength from it. The wisdom of the Dark Mother, he thought, his mind turning back to the catechisms of his childhood. In pain, there is life. In darkness, endless strength. Look upon the night and learn these lessons well.

Malus worked his way carefully around the tree. There was a cold wind blowing down into the valley, and the branches of the Willow Hag rustled and whispered above him.

Wait, Malus thought. This tree doesn't shift in the wind–

The highborn turned just as the Shade leapt onto him from one of the willow's broad branches, and the knife stroke meant for Malus's heart tore a ragged furrow along his back instead. Both men went down, howling for one another's blood.

Malus snarled like a wolf and drove the pommel of his sword into the Autarii's face, crushing the man's left cheekbone like brittle wood. He pushed away from the Shade and hacked down with his sword in the same motion, but the man threw up his left hand to protect his exposed throat.

The sword rang like a struck chime as it hit the soft flesh between the man's middle fingers and split his hand down to the wrist. Runnels of bright blood poured down the Shade's forearm, but incredibly the berserk Autarii clenched his fist and twisted his hand, pinning the sword in his grip. The man rolled onto his back and stabbed wildly with his knife, scoring another bloody line across Malus's cheek. Another quick stab sank the point of the Shade's knife two inches deep in the highborn's shoulder. Roaring, Malus grabbed the Shade's knife wrist and leapt atop him, trying to pull his sword free for the killing stroke.

There was a rumbling beneath the Shade, and the ground began to sink around the combatants. Sensing what was happening, Malus let go of his sword and grabbed the Autarii by the throat, pressing him down into the earth's embrace. Then the ground parted, and both men were plunging down a chute of pulsating roots.

The plunge stopped as swiftly as it began. The chute had narrowed, and the Shade was at the bottom, wedged headfirst down the hole. Without warning the chute constricted and the Shade began to scream and thrash, his feet beating desperately against the glistening roots. The walls of the chute closed in around Malus as well, pushing the two men apart. The screams rose to a crescendo amid the creaking of pliant wood. There was a sound like a melon dropped onto cobblestones and the Shade spasmed, then went still.

More creaks and groans filled the chute, and the walls continued to constrict. Malus felt a surge of anger, but it guttered like a candle in a gale. He was all but spent. With his last burst of strength he grabbed at the hilt of his sword and drew it firmly into his grip.

It took a few moments to realise that he was being pushed steadily upwards. Malus glanced down and saw the soles of the Shade's boots disappearing amid the tangled roots. Soon his head was in the open air again, and he weakly managed to push himself the rest of the way out of the hole.

His ravaged body cried out for rest, but he was wary of that siren song now. The highborn forced himself to his feet, facing the old, black tree. Wearily he raised his sword in salute. 'You keep your oaths better than the living, hateful wight,' he said. 'If it lies within my power, I'll see you're well fed for years to come.'

Malus carefully sheathed his stained sword and staggered into the night. The branches of the Willow Hag rustled faintly in a nonexistent breeze, and then settled down to savour its fleshy feast.

In pain there is life. In darkness, endless strength. Or, as Malus's childhood sword master was fond of saying: as long as you're hurting, you're still living.

Malus had stopped hurting some time ago. He wasn't exactly sure when. He crawled like an animal up the slopes, over the brambles and around the many trees, and then tumbled down the opposite sides. Sometimes the climb took longer than usual – he'd be climbing and then realise that for a while he hadn't been moving at all, just staring down at his bloodstained hands.

When he finally hit level ground the change was so profound it left him stunned for quite some time. It was only when he noticed that he could see the blue tinge to his hands that he realised false dawn was colouring the sky overhead. Malus looked up and saw the round shapes of tents not far away, and the longhouse beyond. He took a deep, shuddering breath and forced himself to stand. There were the shadows of men lingering at the corners of his vision – sentries, his exhausted mind supposed, trailing along behind him but unwilling – or afraid – to lend him aid.

The next thing he knew, he was pushing the longhouse doors open. Inside, the Autarii were sprawled about on their pillows, and the Urhan passed out in his chair. Malus's retinue sat in a tight knot near the hearth, their eyes wide upon seeing their lord's return. The warmth of the room touched the highborn's frozen skin, and now his body awoke in a grinding onslaught of pain.

Malus let out a roar that was born of triumph and agony intertwined, and the Autarii leapt to their feet with steel in hand, believing themselves under attack. The highborn laughed wickedly at their distress, then fixed his eyes on the astonished face of Urhan Beg.

Slowly, painfully, Malus pulled the Ancri Dam from around his neck and tossed it at the Urhan's feet.

'A gift from the Willow Hag,' Malus said, 'plucked from the gold and pieces of jewellery scattered upon her cold breast. There is a king's ransom down there among her roots, but this was all I escaped with. Much good may it do you.'

Pandemonium erupted in the great hall, but Malus was already falling, down into oblivion's waiting arms.

Chapter Twelve
THE WIGHTHALLOWS

THE OLD, WEATHERED skull had the chill of the grave about it, even in the fire-lit warmth of the Autarii tent. The delicate silver wire felt like a thread of pure ice beneath Malus's slender finger as he traced its convoluted path. During his first, tortured glimpse of the relic he'd believed that the wire was meant to hold the skull and the lower jaw together, but now he could see that this wasn't so. It was one continuous loop that turned and twisted upon itself again and again, enclosing the bone within a weave that had a pattern and a purpose to it that was maddening in its complexity.

The skull itself felt like cold, unyielding stone – it leeched the heat from his hand, leaving it numb and aching even as the rest of him sweltered in the tent's hot, smoky air. Worst of all were the skull's empty eye sockets. The black pits swallowed up the firelight and revealed nothing of their depths, yet for all that Malus could feel the cold weight of the skull's penetrating stare. It was as if some remnant of the owner's malignant intelligence still haunted the empty braincase and studied him with cold, reptilian interest.

Damned sorcerous thing, Malus thought. I'd just as soon take a mallet to it. He knew next to nothing about sorcery, and what Malus didn't know, he didn't trust. Not for the first time he wished he'd forced Nagaira to come along and take charge of the relic. She would have had its riddles unravelled in a moment, leaving him to focus on getting to the temple and reaping its hidden treasures.

Malus sat propped against a pile of floor pillows near the tent's fire
pit, with a weight of furs and wool blankets lying over his lower body.
The cuts to his hand, forearm and scalp had been neatly stitched, and
the healing skin itched fiercely despite the soothing ointment covering
the wounds. A wooden tray dusted with crumbs and an empty water
flagon lay on its side close by, next to the highborn's swords and his
saddlebags. The journal of Urial the Forsaken lay in Malus's lap, the
parchment pages opened to the book's final entry.

There was the sound of rustling leather, and Malus glanced over to
see Lhunara stooping through the entryway of the tent. She let out a
grunt of surprise at the sight of him. 'Awake at last!' she said, clearly
relieved. 'We were starting to fear you'd sleep through the winter, my
lord.'

Malus frowned. He knew from the aches in his muscles and joints
that he'd been lying asleep for some time. 'How long?'

'Nearly four days, my lord.' She shuffled across the tent and began
adding fresh sticks to the fire. 'The first day was the worst – you were
like ice, and nothing we did would warm you up. The Autarii who were
guarding the camp said you looked like a vengeful spirit when you
came staggering down out of the hills. Even the Shades in the longhouse thought you were a ghost come back to haunt them. That's what
they're calling you now: *An Raksha.*'

The highborn chuckled. 'The Wight, eh? If only they knew.' Unconsciously, his free hand went to his throat, where he could still feel the
long bruises left by the Willow Hag's implacable grip. 'Is it morning or
night?'

'Night, and late at that. I've just got back from checking the men
keeping watch on the nauglir. Dalvar and Vanhir are drinking with
Urhan Beg in the longhouse.

Nothing good can come of that, Malus thought. 'Whose tent is this?'

Lhunara shrugged. 'Yours now, my lord. It was Nuall's, but Beg
ordered his things moved into Ruhir's old tent, since he's now the
eldest surviving son. Not that anyone has seen Nuall in the last four
days or so.' The retainer gave Malus a pointed look. 'The Urhan wants
to talk to you as soon as you've awakened.'

'Yes, I imagine he does,' Malus said, ignoring the implication in Lhunara's tone. 'I expect he wants to fulfil his part of the bargain and be
rid of us just as quickly as he can.'

Lhunara poked at the embers with a short length of kindling, then
indicated the skull with the stick's smoking end. 'Has it given up any
secrets yet?'

'No,' the highborn said reluctantly, reaching for his saddlebags. 'And
there's very little that makes sense in Urial's journal.' Malus pulled a
thick scarf from the saddlebag, wound it tightly around the relic and

carefully placed it back in the bag. 'Unless I'm much mistaken, I don't think Urial knew much more about the skull than we did.'

'Why do you say that, my lord?'

Malus leaned back against the pillows, concealing a sigh of relief. He was startled at how weak he felt after the ordeal in the hills. A small part of his mind reeled at the thought of how close he'd come to dying. No, he thought fiercely. It proves that if my will is strong, nothing can stop me.

He picked up the journal, flipping back through the delicate sheets of human parchment. 'Urial's notes make reference to a number of sources – *The Saga of Crimson, The Ten Tomes of Khresh,* and others – but very few direct observations about the skull itself. No insights about the runes or the silver wire. Either he was already familiar with the runes and what they said, and knew what the wire did, or–'

'Or they weren't relevant to the mystery of the temple and its contents, which leaves us with nothing to go on.'

Malus suppressed a smile. You're almost too clever sometimes, Lhunara, he thought. Good thing for me you have nowhere else to go.

'That's true. But,' he said, raising a long finger, 'the journal does mention a few possible clues.' The highborn searched the entries carefully. 'Here we are. There's a note here that reads "Kul Hadar in the North", and describes "a wooded valley, haunted by beasts, in the shadow of a mountain cleft by the axe of a god". Then–' he flipped through a few more pages– 'there's a reference here to "the key to the Gate of Infinity, and the temple beyond"'.

Lhunara frowned. 'And this Kul Hadar is the name of the valley?'

'Or the temple perhaps,' Malus said. 'I'm not sure.'

The retainer poked at the fire some more, considering her next words carefully. 'I thought Nagaira said the skull would lead us to the temple.'

'She did.'

'And yet...'

'And yet it's doing nothing of the sort,' Malus replied. 'It's possible that Nagaira didn't know as much about the skull as she let on.'

Lhunara nodded slowly, her face carefully neutral. 'Perhaps so, my lord. That being the case, is it wise to continue at this point? As weak as you are–'

'Weak? *Weak?*' Malus flung the furs and blankets aside. Anger burned along muscle and sinew in his chilled limbs, propelling him to his feet. He leapt at Lhunara, one hand snatching a half-burned stick from the fire while the other closed about his retainer's throat. 'I should put a red coal under your tongue for such insolence! Do not presume to judge my strength, Lhunara. I will find this temple and reap whatever treasures it holds and *nothing* will stand in my way – least of all you.'

Lhunara had gone rigid at Malus's touch. She met her lord's eyes with a cold, black stare of her own. 'No one questions your terrible will, my lord,' she said with preternatural calm. She eyed the red-hot ember hanging scant inches from her face. 'Shall I quench the hot coal with my tongue?'

With an effort, Malus reined in his temper. He dropped the stick back in the fire. 'And how would you give orders to the men afterwards?' The highborn gave her a rude shove that sent her sprawling. 'Go to the Urhan and tell him I am coming,' he said. 'And don't question my strength ever again.'

'Yes, my lord,' Lhunara replied, her face carefully neutral. She rose smoothly to her feet and slipped gracefully from the tent.

Malus waited for the space of two more deep breaths and then collapsed onto the blankets. His arms and legs quivered in the wake of the sudden burst of energy. His mind roiled with a tumult of thoughts. It was bad enough that he'd taken such a gamble with Lhunara – she could have handled him like a kitten if her anger had gotten the better of her, as his had. Worse, it was foolish to make an enemy of one's own lieutenant on an expedition as risky as this one.

But worst of all was the suspicion that now festered like poison in the back of his mind. If Nagaira knew less about the skull than she'd let on, perhaps she had other reasons for remaining back at the Hag. Had she made a cat's paw out of him?

The notion did little to improve his humour, but the anger soon quelled his rebelling muscles and returned a little fire to his veins. Slowly and deliberately the highborn rose to his feet and started to dress.

As DRAINED AS he was, Malus still felt more at ease with his armour on and his swords belted in place. It was indeed well past midnight, and one moon shone full and bright in a sky crowded with tatters of high-flying cloud. The pale light glimmered on a carpet of freshly-fallen snow. He drank in the cold air gratefully, a little surprised at how pleasant it felt. Not so cold as the Willow Hag's embrace, Malus thought ruefully as he made his way to the longhouse.

The great hall was practically empty; a light dusting of ash from the fireplaces lay on the tumbled floor pillows and rugs. Dalvar, Vanhir and a half-dozen older Shades sat near the Urhan's dais, passing a wineskin between one another and smoking from pale clay pipes. Neither of Malus's men appeared drunk, though it was clear that several of the Shades were deep in their cups. Urhan Beg had evidently declined the wine, and instead reclined in his great carved chair, brooding over a pipe of his own. Lhunara was nowhere to be seen.

Vanhir rose silently to his feet as the highborn approached the dais, his expression calculating. Dalvar finished off a long swig from the skin and raised it in salute. 'My lord An Raksha walks the world of the living once more,' he said with a roguish grin. The other Autarii chuckled respectfully. The Urhan made no reply.

'My thanks, great Urhan, for your hospitality,' Malus said, 'and your generosity to my men. I trust they haven't been seduced from their duties by your fine wine and warm hearth.'

The Urhan shrugged. 'It's no affair of mine if they have.'

'As it happens, my turn at watching the nauglir is almost at hand,' Vanhir said smoothly, then offered Malus a short bow. 'With your leave, my lord, I will depart.'

Malus nodded severely, but the knight made no reaction, instead bowing to the Urhan and striding quietly from the hall.

'And you, Dalvar?' the highborn inquired.

Nagaira's man shrugged expansively. 'The morning watch is mine, dread lord, but there's plenty more night left for sleeping. In the meantime, I'm learning what I can at the feet of these old ghosts.'

And what are they learning from you, I wonder? Malus thought. Since his realisation about Nagaira, his mind had started to boil with suspicions. The sooner they were in the Wastes the better. Fighting for one's life left little time for treachery.

'What brings you walking in the snows so late at night, city-dweller?' Beg asked, his gaze hard and appraising.

The highborn bowed to Urhan Beg. 'My lieutenant informed me that you wished to speak with me as soon as I awoke, great Urhan. I did not wish to keep you waiting.'

'Your *lieutenant*,' Beg sneered. 'A woman bearing swords and armour in peacetime? It's unseemly.'

Malus shrugged. 'The brides of Khaine bear arms all year long, and no one faults them. Lhunara Ithil went to war and found she liked the taste of it. What's more, she is very, very good at it. I would be a fool to overlook such skills simply because Naggaroth is not at war now. Regardless, as you so clearly pointed out, my retainers are no affair of yours. Now what did you wish to speak to me about?'

Beg leaned forward in his chair, his hand going to the medallion at his neck. 'The Ancri Dam is a powerful relic,' the chieftain said, rubbing the polished ithilmar thoughtfully. 'With it, I know when a man lies to me. I haven't seen my son Nuall for almost four days, not since you left to visit the Willow Hag. Did you see him that night?'

Malus considered Beg carefully. He could be bluffing, Malus thought. Do I take that risk? 'Yes. I saw him,' the highborn said after a moment's thought. 'He waited until I left the tree and tried to steal the medallion from me.'

Several of the Autarii shook their heads at the news. They didn't seem much surprised. The Urhan eyed Malus balefully. 'Did you kill him?'

'No, I didn't.'

'Did you hurt him?'

Malus smiled, holding up his stitched arm. 'I gave as good as I got, great Urhan. But there were seven of them.'

'Then what happened to Nuall and his men?'

'I can't say for certain,' Malus replied. 'I had the medallion, they tried to take it from me, and I escaped. Beyond that, I don't know.'

For a long time the Urhan said not a word, staring into the highborn's dark eyes as though he could pore through them like a book. Eventually he gave a snort of disgust and leaned back in his chair. 'Stupid boy,' he muttered, half to himself. 'What's the point of having the medallion if there's no one to pass it on to?'

You should have thought of that before you set him against me, Malus thought, suppressing a smile.

One of the Shades spoke up as he reached for the wineskin. 'What about the story Janghir told, about those dark horsemen near Seven Tree Hill?'

'Horsemen!' Beg spat. 'Who brings horses into these hills?'

Malus saw Dalvar stiffen. He shot a surreptitious glance at Malus, who kept his face impassive. Dark riders, Beg, filled with Khaine's wrath, the highborn thought. Horses and men who do not suffer from wounds, fatigue or fear. Deathless, patient and relentless...

'I can appreciate your concern for your son, great Urhan,' Malus said. 'And I do not wish to distract you from the search for Nuall and his men. So let us be on our way and create no further distractions for you or your clan.' The highborn drew himself to his full height and folded his arms imperiously. 'I require a guide to the frontier, one who can lead me past the druchii watchtowers and to the edge of the Chaos Wastes.'

'Why not take the Spear Road?'

'I don't recall personal questions being included as part of our bargain, Urhan Beg. It's enough for you to know that I need to get to the frontier quickly and quietly.'

'What part of the Wastes are you trying to reach?'

Malus squared his jaw. 'There is a mountain in the Wastes that looks as though it were split by the axe of a god. Somewhere near the foot of that mountain is Kul Hadar.'

The assembled Shades stirred uneasily, throwing dire looks at one another. Beg gave Malus a bemused look, his eyebrows furrowing in concern. 'You're looking for Kul Hadar? Why?'

'*Questions*, Urhan Beg. Can you get me to that part of the frontier or not?'

The Urhan thought it over for some time, while the Autarii passed the wineskin between them and muttered under their breath. 'Yes, this can be done,' he said carefully. 'In fact, it can be done very quickly, if your heart is up to the task.'

'Now I ask *you* to speak plainly, Urhan Beg. What do you mean?'

Beg tapped the stem of his pipe against his stained lower teeth. 'There is a path through the hills,' he said. 'A… a path that's not entirely of this world. At certain times, it is possible to walk that path from one end to another and cover a hundred leagues in a single night. I did it myself once, many years ago. But it is not for the faint of spirit.'

Malus smiled. 'Believe me, we have no small experience with such places. I'm certain we are up to the journey.'

The Urhan looked Malus in the eye, and for the first time he smiled. 'On your head be it, then. As it happens, the moons and the season are in a very favourable alignment, so the road should be easy to follow. Gather your men, Darkblade; we will leave an hour before sundown.'

'And in the meantime?'

Beg leaned back in his chair, his eyes glittering in the firelight. 'In the meantime take what joy of the sunlit world you can.'

BY LATE AFTERNOON Malus had roused his warband and set them to making preparations for travel. Despite Urhan Beg's ominous warnings, he was eager to be moving once more.

Malus uncorked the glazed earthenware jug and poured another dollop of viscous fluid onto the silken cloth in his hand. For an instant, the poisonous slime was shockingly cold against his bare skin, but within moments the affected area had gone numb from the effects of the toxin. Over time, most cold one knights lost all feeling in their skin – in some cases, even the ability to smell and taste – after years of exposure to the nauglir's slime. But those were concerns for the future. Today, Malus needed the use of his nauglir, Spite, and so he paid the necessary price.

Lhunara waited patiently in the dark confines of the tent, holding the backplate of the highborn's armour as Malus shrugged into his robes and kheitan. 'Any sign of Beg?' Malus asked.

'None, my lord. The crone in his tent says she has not seen him since last night. I don't think he's anywhere in the camp.'

Malus pulled the laces on the kheitan tight, then picked up his breastplate and fitted it into place. With the ease of long practice, Lhunara fitted the snug backplate around the highborn's shoulders and waist, and then began to buckle the two halves together. Malus grunted thoughtfully as Lhunara drew the straps tight. 'Possibly out looking for his son, or planning some other sort of mischief. Inform the men to keep their crossbows ready once we set out.'

'Yes, my lord.'

The highborn paused. 'How long until Vanhir's oath runs its course?'

'Three more weeks,' the retainer answered. 'Do you suspect something?'

'I always suspect something, Lhunara. He's been talking a lot to Dalvar, and Dalvar has been talking to the Urhan. His oath doesn't allow him to act directly against me, but that wouldn't stop him from sharing what he knows about me with anyone who will listen.'

Lhunara picked up the highborn's left vambrace and slipped it over his arm, sliding it up to Malus's shoulder like a jointed steel sleeve. 'You never should have accepted his oath,' she said darkly. 'Far better to have taken his life and been done with it.'

Malus shrugged, a gesture mostly lost beneath the weight of his armour. 'He comes from a powerful household. I thought it would be useful to have something to hold over them. And at the time, binding him to me seemed like the most humiliating punishment I could imagine. It was a fair wager, and his pit fighter lost.'

'His nauglir lost,' Lhunara corrected. 'You were wagering on the cold one fights after the gladiatorial games.'

Malus frowned. 'Were we? No matter – he bet against me and lost. And since then he's observed the particulars of his oath with ruthless, hateful punctiliousness. I greatly admire him for that, truth be told.'

'Do you still intend to kill him?'

'Oh, yes. Possibly even today. Keep a close eye on him and Dalvar. If Beg tries any treachery and either of them tries to help the Urhan, make certain you kill them both.'

THE AFTERNOON SKY had turned leaden, and drifts of snow whirled about in the cold air. The cold ones were saddled and drawn up in line, under the wary eyes of their riders – five days in a corral had left them snappish and sullen despite regular meals of venison and boar. It was already getting dark beneath the snow-covered limbs of the forest, and Malus was growing increasingly impatient. Sensing his master's mood, Spite clawed restlessly at the frozen earth and rumbled deep in his throat.

Malus paced down the length of the column, making a show of inspecting the warband as a way of concealing his unease. Lhunara sat in her saddle at the end of the line, her crossbow in her lap, her eyes searching the shadows to either side of the column.

Dalvar and his mount were in the centre of the column. Malus came upon Nagaira's man as he was checking the girth-straps on his saddle. 'I believe you still have something of mine,' the highborn asked, holding out his hand.

The rogue grinned up at Malus, and the small iron knife seemed to magically appear in his palm. 'Are you certain you don't want me to hold onto it?' Dalvar asked. 'We still have Urhan Beg to deal with.'

'Do you think he'll try to turn on us?'

Dalvar shrugged. 'Of course. Don't you?'

Malus plucked the blade from Dalvar's hand. 'You've been spending time in his hall. What do you think?'

'I think he believes you've killed his son. Even if you didn't, you embarrassed him by recovering that medallion of his when Nuall couldn't.' The druchii pulled the last strap tight and turned to face Malus. 'Frankly, he's *obligated* to betray you. They're rustics, but they aren't that much different from us. If he doesn't get the better of you at this point his clan will think him weak. That wouldn't bode well for his future.'

Malus studied the retainer carefully. 'And how do you suppose he's going to do this?'

Dalvar shook his head. 'I don't know. I've tried to get a sense of the man in the last few days, but he's a canny one. If you want my advice, my lord, you'll keep him close at hand once we've started on this path he's been so ominous about.' The druchii straightened and glanced past Malus's shoulder. 'There's the old wolf now.'

Malus turned to see Beg and two of his men standing in the shadow of a snow-covered cedar, speaking quietly among themselves. The highborn looked back at his men. '*Sa'an'ishar!*' Malus called. 'Mount up!'

As the druchii swung into their saddles, the highborn approached Urhan Beg. The Autarii chieftain eyed him with undisguised malice.

'My men are ready, great Urhan,' Malus said. On closer inspection, the highborn saw that the old Shade's boots and breeches were damp. *You've been searching by the river,* Malus thought.

'Ready? That remains to be seen,' sneered Beg. 'But we'll find out soon enough. Stay close – we've much ground to cover before nightfall.' With that, the three Autarii set off at a silent, ground-eating pace, slipping through the camp and heading north. Malus was forced to jog back to Spite and mount quickly before the scouts were lost to sight.

'Forward!' Malus ordered, grabbing up the reins. He caught sight of the scouts' retreating backs and put the spurs to his nauglir's flanks.

Let the game begin, he thought.

It was not long at all before Malus and his warband were forced to dismount, prodding their recalcitrant mounts up steep and overgrown slopes as they had in days past. After the first hour, however, Malus began to note that the wildlife in the area was much more subdued – if not entirely nonexistent.

With each mile northwards, the sounds of the woods grew quieter, and fewer birds darted between the black-boled trees. The growing stillness conveyed a sense of menace that set the highborn's nerves on edge. He could tell the rest of the warband felt it too, from the way they eyed every deep shadow they passed. Some of the men had taken to carrying their crossbows at the ready, as if expecting an ambush at any moment.

After less than two hours, the light started to fade in the western sky. Strangely, the going became somewhat easier; the trees and undergrowth had grown sparse and taken on a grey, sickly cast. Malus began to notice a chill in the air – not the dry cold of the winter wind, but a kind of clammy stillness that ran along the ground beneath the trees and sank deep into one's bones.

Soon the landscape was painted in hues of inconstant, otherworldly light, as the auroras of the Chaos Wastes lit the northern horizon. Against this unsettling display, Malus could see that the hills ahead were giving way to larger, broader mountains – the old, granite bones of the earth, stripped bare by millennia of wind and snow. The highborn focused his eyes on the dark-robed figures several yards ahead and drove Spite onwards, wondering how much further they had yet to go.

As it happened, when Malus led Spite over the next hilltop, he found the Autarii waiting for him halfway down a long, fairly gentle slope leading to a broad valley. The slope was dotted with dozens of moss-covered boulders and tussocks of low grass. Everything was silhouetted in shifting, pale-green light, making the wisps of fog in the valley below seem to glow with a life of their own.

Beg and his men waited near one of the boulders. Malus hoisted himself into the saddle and urged Spite in their direction. He relaxed minutely, more comfortable in the open terrain than he had been in the overgrown hills behind him.

The Urhan's eyes were hidden in shadow as Malus approached, but the highborn could feel the weight of his stare all the same. 'We've come to the beginning of the path,' the chieftain said. 'We will walk along with you for a way, but the rest of the journey is for you alone.'

'What is this place?' Malus asked, shifting in the saddle.

'It is called the Wighthallows,' Beg answered. 'It is a place where the dead do not rest easy. Does this frighten you, city-dweller?'

Malus glared at the man. 'I've faced one wight already, Urhan. I can face another.'

Beg chuckled. 'We shall see.'

The Shades turned and made their way downslope. Malus paused to make certain the rest of the column had crested the hill and had closed the distance behind him, then sent Spite padding along after the Autarii.

As the column proceeded, Malus noticed that the boulders and the scattered tussocks grew more numerous closer to the bottom of the slope. The boulders themselves were oddly shaped, with a mix of rounded and sharp edges that seemed maddeningly familiar.

Suddenly there was a strange, metallic crunch and Spite's gait stumbled a bit. Malus glanced down and saw that the cold one had stepped on one of the tussocks. The gleam of bare metal winked in the ghostly light. Malus realised with a start that he was looking at a crumpled steel breastplate, covered in a thin layer of dirt and grass.

They had come upon the edge of a great battlefield.

Ahead, the Autarii had all but disappeared into the lambent mist. Malus fought down a rising sense of unease and pressed on.

The fog hungrily swallowed rider and beast, restricting vision and muffling all sound. Spite balked at the change in atmosphere, but Malus nudged him on. Shapes came and went in the mist. Two great obelisks appeared to either side of Malus, carved in the looping sigils of old Ulthuan. Faintly, Malus could hear Spite's talons clicking along bare stone. Were they on a roadway?

More shapes appeared, clustered on either side of the path. Malus took them for more boulders at first, but upon second glance he realised they were elven chariots, their wheels rotted away and their armoured flanks dented and rent. He caught sight of helmets, rusted swords and spearheads, their hafts long gone to dust.

The highborn looked about for any sign of the Autarii. He felt a vague sense of dislocation. It's the fog, he thought. Or was it?

He could just see the shapes of the scouts ahead. Malus kicked Spite into a trot, expecting to catch up with them in moments, but the fog had apparently distorted his sense of distance. It felt like long minutes before he caught up with Beg and his men. 'What happened here?' Malus asked. His voice sounded strange and indistinct, even to his own ears.

'One of old Aenarion's generals built a road here during the First War,' Beg replied, his voice sounding as though it were coming from a long way off. 'It winds through these valleys for many, many leagues – in the daylight you can just see the black stones of the roadway poking up from the earth. Legend says it was built for a siege against a city of daemons, far to the north, but no one knows for certain. If such a place ever existed, it's long gone now.

'The general took his mighty army north and met with tragedy. Some stories say he was betrayed – a rare few even go so far as to accuse your great Witch King of the deed – while others claim the general was simply a fool. Regardless, the great march turned into a bloody, bitter retreat, fraught with sorcery and slaughter. Every mile of this road is soaked in blood, the stories go. The stones of the road are mortared with bone.'

Malus felt a chill sweep across his skin. The wind moaned faintly in the darkness – or was that the sound of a distant horn?

'It is said that such was the power of the daemon host that they fixed the moons in their courses and fought beneath a mantle of perpetual night. The echoes of that power – and the restless spirits of the dead – linger here even now. When the proper season comes around and the moons are in the right phase, that long night resumes once more.'

The fog appeared to be thinning now; it lingered like a pall at the edges of his vision, but at the same time Malus could see more of his surroundings. Piles of armour, splintered shields and notched swords, ruined chariots with the barding of their horses resting in their rotted traces. A banner pole leaned at a drunken angle amid a tangle of breastplates, helmets and mail. The standard was heavy with dried gore, hanging listlessly in the mist. Malus could taste the dread in the air. It had a coppery tang, like spilled blood.

They travelled on. Malus began to notice more details as they went: the elaborate carvings of chariots and armour stood out in sharp relief. Polished ithilmar glowed with a pale, bluish light. He began to see the bones of skeletons amid the piles of armour. Once he passed an upturned helm still holding the skull of the man who wore it. The jaws gaped wide in a silent scream of anguish or rage.

There was a light up ahead. A bluish radiance suffused the mist, growing in intensity as they drew nearer. The sides of the road were crowded with chariots and wagons – the detritus of an army on the retreat. Their sides were raked and torn, hewn and hacked by tooth, claw and blade. The bodies of the dead were everywhere, still clutching their weapons in skeletal hands.

The air trembled. Malus felt the vibration against his skin. It shook with the din of battle, but no sound reached his ears. The highborn reached for his sword, taking some comfort in the familiar solidity of its hilt. He could feel the presence of others around him – horses and men, moving past him, away from the nightmare they'd found in the far north.

The air quivered with silent screams.

Suddenly there were robed figures on either side of him. The Shades had stopped and he hadn't realised it. Their gaze was focused on the road ahead. As Malus reined in his mount, he saw the horror they beheld.

An army of the dead stood astride the road, gleaming with the unearthly glow of the grave. Enamelled armour shone in the pale, blue light, hanging on the skeletal frames of soldiers and horsemen. Some held spears and swords, while others held up grasping, claw-like hands. Points of cold blue light gleamed from the pits of their eyes, and their jaws gaped in silent cries of despair.

At their head stood a great prince, his armour enamelled in silver and gold. In his right hand he held a fearsome-looking sword, its length etched with runes of power. His left hand held a torn standard. Its ragged hem dripped with fresh blood.

'Who disturbs our rest?' The undead prince cried. His voice was a thin, keening whisper, like the sound of wind whistling over stone.

Chapter Thirteen
FIELDS OF DESPAIR

THE GHOSTLY PRINCE's helmeted head turned to regard Malus, the weight of his burning gaze falling on the highborn like the blow of a sword. He reeled from the wight's baleful stare, feeling his heart turn to ice. Around him he could dimly sense his warband pulling up, the druchii hauling back on their reins in shock and fear. One of the men let out a wail of terror, and the ranks of the dead lunged a half-step forward at the sound, as if hungry to set themselves against a foe who would bleed and die beneath their blades.

Before Malus could master his own tongue and make a reply to the fearful apparitions, Beg took a measured breath and spoke in a loud, strained voice. 'We are but travellers on the road, mighty prince! Forgive us our trespass, and we will honour you with obeisance… and sacrifice.'

Sacrifice! Malus's mind raced. Now the Urhan's scheme was all too clear.

The prince took another step towards the terrified warband with a creak and rattle of harness and ancient steel. 'Sacrifice!' The wight whispered hungrily. 'Who will stand atop my cold, stone bier and warm my bones with a libation of hot blood?'

With a cry of desperate rage Malus tore his eyes from the prince's paralysing stare and ripped his sword from its scabbard. Before Beg could reply, the highborn rose in his saddle and raised his blade high.

'Ride!' he called to his men. 'Ride for death and ruin, warriors of the Hag! RIDE!' The highborn clapped his spurs to Spite's flanks and the nauglir charged at the ghostly horde with a thunderous roar. A heart-beat later the unearthly air rang with the war-howls of Hag Graef as the cold one knights bared their steel and charged the fearsome host at the command of their lord.

The air filled with the shrieks of the damned as the spectral host charged to meet its foes. Malus lost sight of the banner-wielding prince amid a mob of howling wights as the two forces met with a great, rend-ing crash. The charging cold ones ploughed into the elf army in a rough wedge, shattering ancient bodies and flinging bits of armour and bone in a gruesome shower back upon the ranks of their fellows.

Swords flickered and scythed through the frenzied ranks of the dead, shearing through limbs, torsos and skulls. Withered flesh and sinew parted in white clouds of rot; bleached bone was ground to powder beneath the stamping tread of the cold ones. A mortal host would have reeled in shock from the sheer ferocity of the warband's charge, but the howling dead swept around the druchii like a flood. Every warrior torn asunder was instantly replaced by another, all of them hammering at the armoured warriors with blades, spears, axes and claws.

'Forward!' Malus roared into the din, his blade hacking left and right at the frenzied horde. Spite tossed his head and snapped at his attack-ers, biting rotting corpses in two and scattering their remains in a wide arc. The highborn spurred the beast forward and the cold one charged into another knot of shrieking wights, bearing down on them with a sound like splintering wood.

The nauglir let out a furious bellow as one or more of the foe's weapons bit deep into his scaly hide. A corroded spear point glanced off Malus's left pauldron and scored a bloody track across the back of his neck. Hands scrabbled at the smooth armour enclosing his arms and legs, struggling to pull him from the saddle. With a roar he brought his sword down and smashed through wrists and forearms; rusty mail burst in glittering clouds of split links.

And then the prince was upon Malus, his gleaming blade flickering at him like the tongue of a viper.

Malus twisted in the saddle and brought his sword around in a des-perate block that caused the prince's thrust to glance across the highborn's armoured thigh. The highborn chopped down at the prince's sword arm, but the wight blocked the stroke with supernatural speed. The enchanted ithilmar blade licked out again and Malus cried out as its point sliced a line of icy pain across his cheek. Blood trickled down his face and steamed from the frozen edges of the wound.

Malus could hear other screams around him now as the impetus of the warband's charge was spent and the warriors were surrounded by the tide of hungry dead. He leaned forward, slashing at the prince's eyes, but the wight no longer feared the thought of blindness. Instead of flinching back, the skeletal warrior ducked low enough to take the blow on his helm and slashed at the highborn's calf. The enchanted blade carved a neat line through the steel plate, and Malus gasped as his lower leg went numb.

Think, the highborn's mind raged. You can't best him sword to sword! Think of something quickly or you're dead!

The highborn cried out in defiance and slashed again at the prince's face. The wight leaned back fractionally, just beyond the limit of Malus's stroke, then leapt forward, swinging his blade in a brutal arc for the knee joint of the highborn's armour.

But Malus's attack was only a feint; anticipating the prince's blow, he jerked his boot from its stirrup and caught the wight's sword wrist with his heel. With a blood curdling howl, Malus brought his sword down on the crown of the prince's helm, splitting the ithilmar armour in two.

The prince reeled back, his skull wreathed in leaping blue flames and his skeletal jaw gaping in fury.

Malus snarled in reply and hauled on his reins, dragging Spite hard to the left. The nauglir's thickly muscled tail whipped around like a battering ram and smashed into the prince's chest. The wight's body exploded in a cloud of dust and shattered armour, his rune-carved sword spinning end-over-end through the air.

The highborn had barely a heartbeat to savour his triumph before a wight drove his spear deep into Spite's shoulder and the cold one jerked sharply away from the blow. The sudden change in motion caught Malus by surprise. For a dizzying second his numbed leg flailed for the empty stirrup, then clawing hands seized his shoulders and dragged him from the saddle. He landed on his back on the stones of the roadway with a frenzied mob of wights standing over him.

Blows rained down on his armour like a clatter of hail. A spear point found a gap in his left vambrace and gouged deep, causing Malus to hiss in pain. The blow of an axe smashed against his left knee; the armour held, but the joint beneath was wrenched by the impact. The tip of a notched sword sliced across his forehead, spilling a curtain of blood down the sides of his temples.

Malus roared like a man possessed, smashing his sword at the legs of his foes. Armoured foes toppled onto him, their cold hands clawing for his face and throat. Spite roared, and the crowd around him was knocked momentarily back as the cold one smashed them aside with a sweep of his armoured head.

The highborn threw his foes off him with a convulsive heave, shattering the skull of one determined wight with a short, chopping stroke of his sword. He leapt to his feet, propelled by battle-frenzy even as his mind fought a rising tide of panic. Without warning, his wrenched knee gave way and he fell forward against Spite's bloody flank. His free hand closed on one of his saddlebags for support, but the worn leather parted beneath his weight.

He fell, and a blazing skull tumbled into his grasp.

Malus's hand closed reflexively on the wire-wrapped relic despite the sizzling lines of blue fire that arced and snapped along its length. The skull's hollow eye sockets, formerly black pits of shadow, now seethed with globes of fiery light. When the relic settled into the highborn's hand a jolt shot through him, shooting down his arm and causing his heart to clench painfully. His whole body jerked – and words came bubbling up his throat and boiling from his mouth.

He couldn't understand what he was saying – he couldn't even hear the words, just a savage buzzing sound that sawed at the air. But he could *feel* the phrases tumbling from his mouth, taking shapes that were jagged and hard. He tasted blood in his mouth and felt the skin of his lips split from the pressure. With a terrible moan, the wights fled from him, falling back upon one another and clapping their shrivelled hands to their skulls.

As the wights fell back, the sizzling energy of the skull began to wane, but Malus lurched to his feet and willed the fire to blaze brightly again, focusing his anger at the incandescent relic. The terrible words twisted and writhed in his brain like a living thing, resisting his command. Burn brightly, wretched thing, Malus raged. Burn or I'll break you to pieces!

At that, the words surged through him again like a torrent, savaging his throat with their sharp edges and searing heat. The wights retreated still further, fleeing the sound of his voice. The din of the battle subsided, stunned into silence by the highborn's raging tongue.

Malus threw himself back into the saddle. His chest ached. It was as if a hot coal had been put in the place where his heart had been, and his lungs were shrivelling in the heat. The highborn held the relic high and swept his merciless gaze across the horde of the damned. Malus stood in the saddle and roared at the wights. 'Our blood is not for the likes of you! Raise a hand against us and I will scourge the spirit from your worthless bones and hurl you into the Outer Dark! Flee before my wrath, wretched sons of Aenarion! The Dark Mother waits, and if you press me I shall offer your souls up to her!'

The wights howled in fear and pain, their clawed hands raised in supplication. Malus looked back along the roadway and caught sight of the Shades, who'd dared to linger and watch the city-dwellers' demise. The highborn locked eyes with Urhan Beg and savoured the expression of terror on the chieftain's face.

Malus pointed his sword at the three Autarii. 'Slake your thirst on them, foul wights – they who thought to cheat you of your due.'

Beg screamed, and the heads of the malevolent wights turned at the sound. Then the air was rent with eerie howls as the Autarii turned to run and the skeletal warriors took up the chase.

The fire was ebbing again. Malus sought to stoke it once more, but found his fury wanting. His insides felt twisted and torn. Blood leaked from the corner of his mouth and spattered on his thigh. His sword drooped in his hand.

Around him, the druchii of his warband drooped wearily in their saddles or leaned against the heaving flanks of their mounts. The gore that streaked their faces and stained their armour was their own. Two knights lay near the corpses of their cold ones, one pierced with spears and hacked by swords and the other lying in bloody, twisted pieces, his guts shrivelled and blackened with frost.

Spite shuddered beneath him. The nauglir sported a score of wounds from head to tail. None of those who had survived had escaped unscathed.

The druchii looked to their leader, their faces gaunt and pale. Around them stretched a panorama of shattered bones and crumpled armour, broken spears and splintered shields. All of them, even Lhunara, looked upon their lord with an expression of utter fear.

A scream tore through the murky air, then another. The voices of the damned howled in reply.

Malus sheathed his sword and grasped Spite's reins. 'We ride,' he growled, each word a brilliant spike of pain. 'Leave the dead to their feast.'

With that, he turned his cold one north and set off along the road, bones crunching beneath Spite's feet.

MALUS AWOKE TO the hollow moaning of the wind. Slowly, achingly, he opened his eyes. He lay on his back beneath an iron-grey sky, his arms spread wide. The wind rustled through the tall grass in which he lay.

Something large stirred behind him. The highborn rose to one elbow, his whole body leaden and throbbing. Only a few feet away, Spite shifted on his haunches, regarding his master with one blood-red eye. The cold one's flanks were streaked with grave-dust and splashes of ichor.

He lay on a grassy hill, facing a line of weathered mountains perhaps a mile away. Malus could see the mouth of a valley winding between two craggy peaks. Was that the end of the Wighthallows? The highborn frowned, trying to think. How did we come to be here? Memories eluded him, slipping away like shadows into the recesses of his mind. It seemed as though he'd ridden for an eternity, always in darkness, hounded by the voices of the dead. When dawn finally came he remembered falling from the saddle and a deeper darkness rushing up to meet him.

Malus tried to stand and bit back a hiss of pain as he put his weight on his wrenched knee. Like Spite, his dark armour was nearly white with grave-dust, darkened in places with splotches of old blood. There were cuts on his face, neck and forehead, and his cheeks were stiff with dried blood. The wound in his arm throbbed painfully, aggravated by a bent piece of metal forced into his skin by the wight's spear point. The cut in his right calf ached, but he was grateful to be able to feel the pain.

The skull was still in his left hand. His fingers were locked in a death-grip around the braincase. Its shadowed eye sockets seemed to be taking stock of him.

After a moment, the highborn noticed other furtive sounds of movement amid the waving grasses. Groans and whispers carried on the wind. A cold one let out a pained cry as someone pulled the point of an enemy weapon free and threw it across the hill, the thin steel ringing as it spun through the air.

Lhunara limped into view, the wind twisting loose strands of her braided hair. Her face was a mask of dust and blood, and the dark lines of fresh cuts marked her cheek and chin. Her eyes were haunted and sunken, ringed with dark circles of fatigue. She held a waterskin in one hand and a naked sword in the other, her gaze sweeping the surroundings with the practiced ease of a long-time veteran. She walked over to Malus and settled on her haunches, wincing at the loud popping of her knees. 'Are you hurt, my lord?' the retainer asked, a little out of breath.

'My damned knee–' the words came out in a horrid croak, dissolving into a string of wracking coughs. The inside of his mouth and throat felt scabby and dry, and his lips were cracked and stiff. Lhunara passed him the waterskin and he drank greedily in spite of the pain it caused. 'My damned knee,' he said in a hoarse whisper. 'That's the worst of it, I think.'

The retainer took the waterskin back and stoppered it. There was a wariness to her movements that Malus hadn't seen her use around him before. She eyed the relic. 'Still holding on to that?'

Malus looked down at the skull. With an effort, he forced his hand open. The metal creaked, and the relic fell onto the grass. At once, his knuckles began to throb and ache.

Lhunara seemed to relax a little. 'How did you do that, back there in the valley? What were the words you spoke?'

The highborn shook his head. 'I don't know. It… it was the skull. It put the words in my head somehow.' Unbidden, his sister's words echoed in his head: *It is not, in fact, a source of power – at least, not in any sense you would understand.* 'I don't know why.'

'Well, it saved us. I suppose that's all that matters,' Lhunara said. 'But we lost Hularc and Savann to the wights. That just leaves Vanhir and myself out of the six you brought from your household. The remainder are your sister's men.' She lowered her voice. 'And there's talk of turning back.'

Malus sat up, his hurts forgotten. 'Turn back? We've barely begun.'

Lhunara shook her head. 'I'd be wary about saying such things, my lord. That ride last night shook the men to their core. If you push them too hard, they'll break, and we can't afford to lose anyone.' She looked wearily to the south, at the mountains they'd only just departed. 'Like you said, we've barely begun.'

The highborn bit back his anger. Part of him wanted the names of the men who questioned his authority, but Lhunara was right. What could he do? He needed every sword he could muster. All he could do was lead them, and deal with a mutiny when it finally reared its head. 'Dalvar and Vanhir charged along with the rest, back in the valley?'

Lhunara nodded. 'They did.'

Malus grunted. The news puzzled him. 'They weren't going to get a better opportunity for treachery than that,' he muttered. 'Strange.'

Lhunara shrugged. 'You're assuming Dalvar is plotting against you. Why should he? I'd think it more likely he'd wait until you'd discovered the temple, then slip the knife between your ribs.'

'Unless he knows that we aren't going to reach the temple, and his orders are simply to ensure my demise.'

The retainer eyed him sharply. 'Why do you say that?'

Because I'm starting to think my sister tricked me, Malus started to say, then thought better of it. 'Never mind. I'm being overly suspicious,' he answered instead.

With an effort, he climbed slowly to his feet. Every part of him hurt in some way, like the day after a great battle. Malus limped over to Spite and slipped the skull into his other surviving saddlebag. As he did, he peered over the cold one's back and saw miles of rolling plains, covered in a rippling sea of brown grass.

Beyond them lay a band of dark green forest, and past that, rising high on the northern horizon, the dark, triangular bulk of a great mountain, its peak wreathed in snow and cloud. A sharp cleft, like the mark of an enormous axe, split the mountain at a shallow angle, stretching two-thirds of its length from tip to broad base. The highborn leaned against his saddle, trying to gauge the distance. It seems so close, he thought. A few days, perhaps? Then we'll see just how much Nagaira really knew.

Malus rested his forehead against the leather saddle for a moment, gathering his strength. Then, with a deep breath, he climbed painfully into the saddle. Spite barked in aggravation, but obediently rose to his haunches. 'Tell the men to mount up,' the highborn said, studying the sky. 'The day is nearly half-done. I want to cover a few more miles before dark.'

Lhunara stared at him. 'But, my lord, the men are tired and injured–'

'We aren't camping here,' Malus interjected. 'Better to reach the edge of those woods, where we can gather some wood for a fire.' And give the men something else to think about instead of plotting a mutiny, he thought. Bad morale was like an infection. It couldn't be allowed to sit and fester.

The retainer started to protest, but quickly regained her self-discipline. 'Yes, my lord,' she replied, and started barking orders to the rest of the warband.

As the warband checked their mounts and got back into their saddles, Malus kneed Spite around until he could face the mountain directly. He surveyed the plains and the dark woods carefully. So this is the Chaos Waste, he thought. Not so greatly different from home. I had expected much worse.

The wind shifted and moaned across the plains, stirring the sea of dead grass. He could not see what would cause such a hollow, funereal sound.

THEY WERE NO closer to the distant line of trees by the time night fell. The cloud cover remained heavy, but the auroras leaking from the northern horizon played across the underside of the clouds somehow in an eerie display of blue, green and yellow light. The shifting colours set a riot of shadows dancing among the windblown grasses, playing tricks on the eyes as the members of the warband kept watch for nocturnal predators. As long as there was enough light to ride by, Malus urged the column on. From time to time he caught himself nodding, his chin drooping to his chest. Fatigue and hunger were starting to take their toll.

There was a sound from up ahead. Malus tensed, his ears straining to hear over the incessant wind. Just when he thought he'd imagined it, he heard the sound again, like a faint scream of rage or pain. The highborn reached back and unhooked the crossbow from his saddle.

Moments later he heard the sound again. Definitely an angry cry, like a druchii war-scream. It was coming their way, but all he could see were dancing shadows and rippling waves of grass silhouetted against the dark horizon. He raised a gauntleted hand, waving his warband forward.

The warriors fanned out to either side of him, their weary faces tense. 'Arm yourselves,' Malus said. 'Something's coming.'

Lhunara pulled alongside him. 'What–'

Then the scream came again. This time it was joined by two others. The sound brought the nauglirs' heads up.

Malus worked the arming mechanism on his crossbow. He was halfway done when the monsters burst from the grasses into the warband's midst.

They looked like great Lustrian lions, but their sleek flanks were soaked in crimson and their faces were broad and almost human. The cold ones roared a challenge and the cats responded with their eerie scream, like a man with a hot iron against his skin. Crossbows thumped and black fletchings sprouted from the lions' flanks, but it only enraged them further. One of the beasts gathered itself and leapt at Spite, crashing into the nauglir's shoulder and knocking the great beast onto its side. Malus tried to leap from the saddle as the lion's wide jaws clamped around the cold one's neck, but his left foot got caught in its stirrup and the nauglir rolled atop his leg.

The lion's face was less than a foot away, its strange green eyes studying Malus even as the creature's jaws clamped down on Spite's scaly hide. The highborn frantically tried to kick his way loose with his one free leg, to no avail. Only the armour encasing his trapped leg had prevented it from being crushed; if the nauglir rolled again, however, nothing would save him.

Malus frantically worked to reload his crossbow as Spite thrashed and snapped at the lion. The cold one's jaws closed on the lion's ribs, and the lion lashed out with its claws, raking deep furrows across the nauglir's shoulder just scant inches from the highborn's free leg. He could feel the cold one twisting, trying to roll onto his back. Suddenly the crossbow's string locked into place with an authoritative clack, and a bolt popped into the track. Malus braced himself with his free foot and fired the bolt point-blank into the lion's eye.

The lion leapt from the nauglir with a strangled cry, its head snapping around in pain. The huge creature spun in a circle, howling in torment, then its legs collapsed beneath it and it fell in a twitching heap.

Spite rolled to his feet, hissing angrily at the creature's corpse, and Malus jerked his trapped leg free from the stirrup. He looked frantically about as he reloaded the crossbow, but the other lions had disappeared. 'Where did they go?' he shouted to no one in particular.

Dalvar's voice answered. 'They ran on past us!'

Malus leapt to his feet, crossbow at the ready. 'But why...' He looked to the north, and suddenly he understood.

The darkness he'd taken to be the horizon swept over them like a thrown blanket, and suddenly the howling wind rose to a terrible roar. Hot rain lashed at his face, running down his neck. He could barely see more than two feet in front of him. 'Circle up!' he shouted over the wind. 'Cold ones on the outside, men inside! Quickly!'

By the time he'd grabbed Spite's reins he could see the dark bulks of other cold ones looming around him. It was a manoeuvre that every knight was taught before he went on campaign as a way to shield themself in a blizzard. Within minutes the great beasts were arranged in a circle and the druchii slumped down against their flanks, shielded somewhat from the worst of the wind.

It was only after Malus had huddled against Spite's heaving flanks that he noticed the cold one was covered in red. Rivulets of crimson ran down his sides and pooled in the grass.

The highborn held out his hand, listening to the rain spatter on his palm. He brought it to his lips.

It was raining blood.

Malus tried to peer through the dark rain, dimly seeing his men huddled in their cloaks against the sides of their mounts. They looked exhausted beyond measure. If they were aware of the strange nature of the storm, they gave no sign of it.

The highborn pulled his own cloak around his shoulders, drawing its hood over his head. Drops of blood drummed against the cloth.

We're well and truly in the wasteland, he thought grimly, and drifted off into a fitful sleep.

Chapter Fourteen
HUNTERS AND THE HUNTED

THE DAMNED PLAINS seemed to go on forever.

They rode from sunrise until well after dark, navigating by the lunatic glow of the northern lights and stopping only after they were too tired to go any further. Yet when they awoke the next day they seemed no closer to the dark mountain and its surrounding forest.

The warband rode beneath a sky of swirling cloud, forever shrouding the light of the sun. Night and day were merely different degrees of grey and black, shading from one to the other in a subtle, stealthy pattern that robbed the mind of any sense of time. Storms came and went, often blowing up without warning and passing just as swiftly. They no longer paused to wait them out, instead just huddling in their cloaks and spurred their mounts forward toward the elusive forest and the hope of shelter.

Food was also becoming a concern. They were down to iron rations now; rock-hard biscuits and thin strips of dried meat, enough for one meal per druchii per day. They saw very few animals during the day – mostly dark shapes like vultures, soaring low over the hilltops in the distance. Once, one of the birds strayed too close to the column and Lhunara shot it out of the air with her crossbow. But when the hungry druchii cut the bird open they found its guts riddled and squirming with pale worms.

There were howls and hunting cries at night. Some sounded like the lions they'd encountered in the past, while others were like nothing the druchii had ever heard before. In camp the nauglir would rise off their haunches and bellow a challenge when one of the creatures came too close – jolting everyone from fitful attempts at sleep and sending them scrambling for their weapons. Finally, Malus had ordered the cold ones' saddles removed and left them free to hunt every night.

The huge beasts had to eat regularly or even their legendary stamina would start to fail, and the highborn couldn't imagine anything on the plains that could fight off an entire pack of hunting nauglir. From what he could tell, however, it didn't look as though they were having much better luck than the druchii. They were becoming increasingly short-tempered, sometimes snapping at their riders when approached with saddle and reins. Unless something changed soon, their aggressive behaviour would become a much more serious problem.

The druchii took to sleeping in their saddles during the day, weaving drunkenly with their mounts' rolling gait. Malus pushed them as hard as he dared, both to reach the forest as quickly as possible and to keep the warband too tired to contemplate rebellion in the meantime.

To the best of Malus's reckoning, it was their fifth day on the plain when they stumbled upon the tribesmen. Spite had been acting tense for close to an hour, sniffing the air and growling deep in his chest, but the highborn had been too tired and hungry to consider the cause. Then he began to hear a faint clatter every time the wind shifted from the north. Finally his fatigued mind recognised the sound for what it was – steel clashing on steel. The sound of battle.

After a quarter of a mile the plain began to slope gently upwards, rising to a low ridgeline another half a mile ahead. The closer they came to the ridge, the louder the sound grew, punctuated now by screams and bloodthirsty shouts. The other members of the warband had heard it as well by this point, and several had their crossbows loaded and ready.

As they ascended the ridge, Malus raised his hand and signalled for the knights to form into line. Just as they crested the top, a small part of his mind observed that they might have been better off sending a couple of scouts ahead to see what was happening before committing the entire force. The highborn cursed quietly to himself; exhaustion and hunger were getting the better of his judgement.

The battle was effectively finished by the time the druchii edged over the ridgeline; more than a quarter of a mile away the victors were surrounding the remnants of their foe and systematically slaughtering them. Bands of horsemen galloped about in the plain below, hemming in smaller groups of riders and bringing them down with thrown spears and axes.

Dozens of bodies, both horses and men, littered the churned earth. The warriors were human, from what Malus could tell, wearing furs and mismatched pieces of armour. They rode stout, shaggy ponies that seemed to make up what they lacked in size with nimbleness and stamina. Near the centre of the swirling mass, Malus made out what appeared to be the remnants of a camp.

The highborn brought Spite to a shuddering halt. The nauglir pawed at the earth, excited by the presence of so much horseflesh within reach. 'Vanhir!' Malus called as he wrestled with the reins.

Obediently the knight swung out of line and wrestled his cold one over to Malus. 'My lord?'

Malus indicated the battle on the plain with the point of his chin. 'What do you make of that mess?'

'Feral humans,' the knight said at once. 'Nomadic tribesmen by the looks of their ponies. We're close to their tribal lands, and I would guess this is a raiding party on their way back to winter quarters.'

Malus frowned. 'Who are they fighting?'

'One another,' Vanhir said disdainfully. 'A falling-out over plunder, I expect. They are close enough to their home range that some must have felt it safe to start cutting others out of their share.'

Not so different from us, then, Malus thought. He tried to estimate the number of tribesmen on the field – at least thirty, victors and vanquished combined. 'Greater numbers, but poor armour,' the highborn mused. 'Do you think they've seen us yet?'

Just then one of the cold ones reared onto his haunches, its patience exhausted, and let out a hunting roar that the rest of the nauglir took up as well. By the time the druchii had their mounts under control the plain was covered in rearing ponies and shouting, gesticulating nomads.

'You were saying, my lord?'

'Never mind,' Malus hissed. 'What will they do now?

Vanhir seemed shocked that the highborn would ask such a question. 'Why, they'll attack, my lord,' he said. 'The nomads worship the Lord of Skulls. You see – here they come now!'

Sure enough, the tribesmen had gotten over their initial surprise, and now the raiders – all of them, apparently united against a common foe – had formed into a loose mob and were trotting their way. They waved bloody axes over their heads and shouted ululating war cries as they rode.

'Very well. Back in line, Vanhir,' Malus ordered, then stood in the stirrups. '*Sa'an'ishar!* Crossbows ready!' he commanded. 'Two volleys on my order, then prepare to charge!'

Malus reached back and grabbed his own weapon just as the nomads urged their ponies into a canter. They were nearly at the base of the ridge. At this distance, he could see that their faces were painted with a white paste that gave them the look of skulls. Thick heads of braided hair flapped wildly in the wind. Each rider, the highborn saw, had a clutch of severed heads tied by the hair to their saddles. 'Make ready!' he cried, lifting the crossbow to his shoulder.

His eyes scanned the front ranks of the oncoming mob, looking for their chieftain. He settled on a huge nomad riding a shaggy black pony and carrying a massive battle-axe in one broad hand. The man's head had been shaved bald and tattooed with crude, red sigils, and his face had more in common with a wolf than a man. As Malus watched, the nomad bared pointed teeth and let out a howl, and the horde spurred to a gallop.

'Fire!' Malus cried, and the crossbow thumped in his hand. The wolf-headed nomad reeled in the saddle as a black-fletched bolt punched into his chest. He clung to the saddle for the space of two heartbeats, then the great axe fell from nerveless fingers and he pitched backwards onto the ground.

The highborn was already working the reloading mechanism with swift, sure movements, honed by years of hard practice. A half dozen tribesmen had fallen, shot from the saddle or thrown from dying ponies and trampled by their fellows. The raiders were halfway up the slope now, streamers of blood trailing from their axes. Malus's cross-bow clicked into firing position and he chose another target.

'Ready!' he cried, hearing answering yells from his men. Malus picked a rider at random who was hefting a short throwing spear. 'Fire!' The crossbow thumped and the bolt took the man in the throat, punching cleanly through and severing his spine; there was a bloom of red around the nomad's skull and he toppled bonelessly to the earth.

Malus hooked the crossbow onto the saddle and drew his sword. The humans were almost upon them. Blades rasped from their scabbards along the druchii line.

'Charge!'

The nauglir leapt forward with a frenzied roar. For a moment it was all Malus could do to stay in the saddle as Spite leapt hungrily at the closest pony. The animal shrieked in terror and tried to swerve away, but the cold one caught the pony by the throat and bit through in a fountain of hot blood. The rider was thrown forward by the impact, sprawling across the back of Spite's neck, and Malus buried his sword in the nomad's skull. Another raider swept past on the right and struck the highborn a resounding blow across his breastplate, knocking Malus flat against the back of the saddle and sending his sword spinning through the air. Grabbing the saddle, he spurred the cold one savagely away from his impromptu meal and fumbled his second sword from its scabbard as he pulled himself painfully upright.

Another rider galloped at Malus from the left. The highborn hauled left on the reins, pulling Spite's head into the nomad's path, and the cold one snatched the man from the saddle. The raider screamed in rage and found the strength to hack weakly at the cold one's snout before Spite bit through the man's torso and sent limbs and head tumbling to the ground.

By now the raiders had swept past the druchii and were reining around at the top of the ridge. A dozen nomad bodies littered the slope, and one of the druchii lay in a crumpled heap – his famished nauglir had pounced on the first pony it reached and rolled downslope with its prey, crushing the rider to a pulp. Less than half the raiders were left, but the wild-eyed tribesmen showed no signs of abandoning the fight. Malus brought Spite around and spurred him back up the slope, and the nomads rushed to meet him.

Once again, Spite lunged for the nearest pony, but this time the nomad was an expert rider and mad with battle-lust to boot. At the last moment he jumped his pony over the cold one's head, and Malus found himself staring wide-eyed at the animal's bunched legs and broad chest as the beast hurtled at him like a falling boulder. Before he could react, Spite caught the hurtling pony's hindquarters in his jaws and suddenly riders, mounts and all were tumbling end-over-end back down the slope.

The nomad's pony struck Malus a glancing blow and sent him flying from the saddle. He landed hard nearly a dozen yards away in a shower of dirt and grass, but the blow had very likely saved his life. Spite and the dying pony crashed past, the animal shrieking wildly in terror and pain. The raider fetched up close by, stunned senseless by the fall, and Malus leapt upon him while he was helpless, severing his head with a stroke of his sword.

By the time Malus staggered back to his feet, the battle was over. Riderless ponies shrieked and galloped in every direction, some pursued by out-of-control nauglir as their riders cursed and wrestled with their reins. A dismounted nomad lurched down the slope at one of the druchii, his left arm hanging uselessly at his side. Malus watched Dalvar pluck a knife from his belt and send it in a glittering arc to bury itself in the back of the raider's skull.

Lhunara caught sight of Malus and trotted over, Vanhir following in her wake. Her own bone-weariness had vanished in the thrill of the charge, and the wolfish grin on her face was the first he'd seen in days. 'A pleasant afternoon's diversion, my lord!' she called.

'Any prisoners?' Malus asked.

Vanhir shook his head. 'The tribesmen aren't the sort one captures,' he said. 'They'll fight with their teeth and the splintered stumps of their arms if that's all they have.'

'Orders, my lord?' asked Lhunara.

Malus snatched a handful of brown grass and started cleaning the blood from his sword as he surveyed the battlefield. 'Dismount the warband and let the nauglir eat their fill. The men can plunder the camp while the cold ones gorge themselves. There are bound to be valuables among the tents, and the men have earned a reward. Then we'll take all the food we can find and be gone from here before night-fall.'

Vanhir frowned. 'If we let the cold ones stuff themselves they'll become sluggish–'

'When the nauglir get hungry enough they turn on the weaker members of the pack – in this case, that's us.' Malus said. 'This was a gift,' he said, taking in the battlefield with a sweep of his sword. 'I want to take as much advantage of this as possible, because who knows when we'll have so much meat on hand again?'

The knight considered this and shrugged. 'As you wish,' he said, and turned his mount back upslope. Lhunara watched him go.

'He looks disappointed.'

Malus shrugged. 'He might well be. With their bellies full and their pouches heavy with gold the men will have less reason for slitting my throat tonight.'

'True enough,' she said, then looked down at the highborn with a wry smile. 'Of course, there's always tomorrow.' The retainer then turned her own mount around and headed off to issue Malus's orders.

THE CITY SEEMED to appear from nowhere. One moment there was nothing but arid plains and a steel-grey horizon, and then they were crossing a low ridge and the ruins were rising into the sky from the plain to the north less than half a mile away. The druchii sat in their saddles on the reverse slope and tried to make sense of the thing. We couldn't see it before because of the dust, Malus thought. Nothing else makes sense. But then, this *is* the Wastes.

Malus fidgeted with the scarf pulled over his nose as another gust of wind sent a billow of dust and sand into their faces. It had been days since they'd left the nomad camp behind, and the terrain had gone from grassland to cracked earth and clouds of dirt. The gusts of wind were hot and stank of sulphur, like breaths of air from an open furnace, even though the heavy grey clouds overhead threatened snow. The mountain, at least, appeared closer now. At least Malus believed it did. He was no longer certain.

'Well, Vanhir, what do you make of that?'

Vanhir sat to Malus's right, holding his scarf to his face. 'I don't know what it is, my lord,' he said, shaking his head. 'We never roamed this far north when my household hunted the humans.' He paused, studying the toppled walls and broken towers in the distance. 'It appears deserted – at least, I don't see any signs of activity. Perhaps it's the daemon city Urhan Beg spoke of outside the Wighthallows?'

'If the place is deserted, I don't care who built it,' Lhunara said irritably. She sat her mount to Malus's left, her hood pulled up over her head and her nightmask protecting her face. 'I'd fight a daemon if it meant getting out of this damned dust storm for an hour or two!'

Malus considered his options. The ruined city did appear deserted, but such an impression could easily be deceiving. It looked to be the size of Hag Graef, and a hundred raiders could shelter there with no one the wiser. Still... 'If someone built a city in this place, there must be a well in there somewhere,' he said. 'And we're running low on water.'

The highborn bit back a curse, trying to force his exhausted mind to function. He wished he had enough men to risk a patrol, but their numbers were so few now that risking one or two druchii was tantamount to risking the whole party. 'Let's go,' he said, collecting Spite's reins. 'Like Lhunara said, at least we can get out of the dust for a while.'

It took nearly half an hour to cross the dusty plain and reach the broken walls of the city – as ever, distance and time in the Wastes were deceiving. As they drew near, Malus and the druchii saw that the piles of stone – a dark, veined marble all at odds with the barren nature of the plain – were deeply weathered.

Statues that might have stood for thousands of years had been eroded down to vague man-shapes, and only faint shadows remained of the carvings over the high, vaulted gate. Drifts of sand piled in small dunes along the empty streets, and many of the buildings they could see were little more than piles of rubble.

Malus's hackles rose as they rode down the short passage between the inner and outer gates, but the narrow murder holes overhead were long choked shut with sand and dust. Beyond, they emerged into a refuse-strewn courtyard. Weak light gleamed along the cobblestones – they were a dark green, polished to a kind of translucence that gave them the look of ornamental glass.

The highborn pointed towards a cluster of spires near the centre of the city. 'That must be the citadel,' he said. 'That will be the most likely place to find a well or cistern.'

Spite growled, his broad nostrils flaring as he tasted the air. Malus studied the shadowy alleys between the buildings and the gaping doorways, but he could discern no imminent threat. *Too long out on those cursed open plains*, he thought. *The narrow city streets make me feel like I'm threading a needle.*

The small column worked its way through the ruins. The warband was tense; they'd seen enough unexpected danger to become wary of everything they encountered. But their only companion in the city seemed to be the relentless wind, stirring up a pall of choking dust wherever they went.

Navigating the city proved surprisingly difficult. They had gone barely a hundred yards down one narrow street when they found their way blocked by a channel almost thirty feet deep and more than fifty feet wide that ran from left to right as far as the eye could see in either direction.

The sides of the channel were smooth and vertical, and the road they were travelling on met a cross street that paralleled the rim of the channel. Some kind of defensive construction, perhaps, Malus thought? A ditch to delay the progress of invaders? He frowned, unable to see the sense of it. He turned the column to the right and began searching for a way across the gap. After another hundred yards, the druchii found a narrow bridge spanning the gap, though as far as Malus could tell the span would be a poor spot to defend in the middle of an attack.

He led the column over the decaying structure, and his roving eye caught sight of carvings along both sides of the bridge. The marble was carved with the sinuous image of sea dragons, their graceful arcs lending the appearance that they were leaping from one end of the ditch to the other.

Not a ditch, Malus suddenly realised. A *canal*.

The column encountered two more such canals as it worked its way deeper into the city. In the last dried-up watercourse they found the remains of a ship, leaning drunkenly to port with its splintered masts hanging over the far side of the canal. How long ago had this city sat at the edge of a great sea? Malus shook his head in wonder.

Farther into the centre of the city the buildings were in better condition. The streets were narrow and winding, reminding Malus somewhat of distant Clar Karond, and the sheer bulk of the structures seemed to lend them more resilience against the constant wind. There were statues of leaping sea dragons and mosaics of coloured stone depicting underwater scenes – or so the highborn supposed, given all the depictions of fish and eels. One mosaic in particular held his eye: it showed a city beneath the water, its broad streets travelled by fish and serpents and other creatures the highborn couldn't easily identify. The image disturbed him, but he couldn't explain why.

The buildings themselves were expertly constructed, of the same dark, veined marble they'd seen around the city gate. The sheer expense of the construction was staggering, to say nothing of the effort that must have been required to quarry so much high-quality stone and carry it to the site. The structures were made almost exclusively of stone – Malus saw very little wood of any kind, which hinted at a degree of craftsmanship that rivalled that of the dwarfs. Yet no dwarf had lent a hand to the construction of this place – the buildings lacked the broad, squat solidity of their structures. Of course, Hag Graef was built by dwarf slaves to druchii specifications, the highborn mused.

Could not the same thing have happened here? Logically, it was possible, but some instinct told Malus that it wasn't the case. Someone else had built this city by the sea. Perhaps it had been the craftsmen of old Aenarion, but if so, the secrets of their trade had died with them many millennia ago.

It took almost three hours before the column found its way to a large square that lay in the shadow of the city's central fortress. Like the city gates, the entrance to the citadel lay wide open, its defenders long since departed. The castle, with its tall, narrow spires, reminded Malus somewhat of the Hag. Or of a forest of coral rising from the seabed, the highborn realised, somewhat uncomfortably.

The citadel as a whole was in better condition than the rest of the city. The riders emerged into another sand-choked courtyard, but the high walls mitigated the wind somewhat, and Malus recognised an intact barracks and forge set against the inside of one of the outer walls. 'Stand,' Malus commanded, and slid gratefully from the saddle. Spite remained tense, his powerful shoulders hunched and his nostrils flaring with each breath. 'Vanhir,' Malus said as the rest of the warband reined in. 'Take a man and stand watch over the mounts. The rest of us will see if we can find some water.'

They draped water skins over their shoulders and combed the courtyard for more than an hour, searching the barracks and forge and discovering kitchens, stables and storehouses, but no sign of a well.

The silence of the place began to weigh on Malus. Every so often he would catch himself staring up at the narrow windows of the citadel's central keep. The hackles rose on the back of his neck and he was certain that he was being watched. Their steps echoed in the empty buildings; not even rats stirred at their approach.

Finally there was no place left to search but the keep itself. They returned to the cold ones and gathered three lanterns then the five druchii made their way inside.

Past the open doorway the drifts of sand rapidly gave way to a floor of slate tile that echoed with every step. Malus led the way, lantern held high. They walked through a succession of great halls filled with piles of dust and broken statuary. Mounds of old bones lay in some corners, hinting that the citadel had been home to some predator in the past. Pale witchlight from the lanterns picked out mosaics of more underwater scenes lining many of the walls in the great rooms. Once again, Malus saw depictions of undersea cities, this time peopled with vague figures that bore the heads and arms of men but the bodies of fish or serpents. Several mosaics featured rakish sailing ships battling what appeared to be huge kraken. Shining figures in pale green armour hurled lances of fire into the monsters' eyes, even as the kraken wrapped their thorny tentacles around mast and hull.

Every now and then the highborn thought he heard furtive sounds among their echoing footsteps – the shuffle of feet or tentative steps from the deep shadows of a side passage or a branching chamber. Beyond their globe of lantern light, the search party moved through an echoing abyss, its boundaries only dimly and infrequently glimpsed. Lhunara seemed to sense it, too – she walked at the rear of the party with a naked blade in hand, her face a mask of concentration.

Finally they crossed another great hall that might have once been an audience chamber – no throne remained on the dais at the end, if ever there had been one. Beyond they found a series of empty rooms and a flight of stone steps leading down into deeper darkness.

Malus stood at the top of the stairs and took a deep breath, holding his lantern high. Among the heavy pall of dust and mildew the air had a cool, damp feel to it. He turned to pass the news to the rest of the party, but the words died in his throat. They were deep in the citadel, surrounded by stone and echoing blackness, and a part of him feared to speak. He didn't know what else might hear and come looking for the source.

The highborn led the way downwards, sword in hand. The stairs descended into a cavern-like cellar, with columns of veined marble supporting vaulted stone arches. Carvings of sea dragons spiralled sinuously up the columns, and the close-set flagstones were more pieces of dark, polished glass. In the flickering witchlight the floor gleamed like a seascape in the moonlight. Try as he might, Malus couldn't catch sight of any walls – the chamber stretched off in every direction – but he could smell the water now. The moisture hung in the air of the chamber. 'Spread out,' the highborn said quietly. 'And watch where you put your feet.'

Within minutes, there was the sound of shifting stone, then Lhunara whispered, 'Here! I've found it!'

Malus and the other druchii converged on the retainer, who stood by a broad, circular opening in the rock floor. She had pulled aside a stone cover carved with a sea shell design to reveal the water's still surface, only a few inches below the lip. Another of the retainers was taking a tentative sip under Lhunara's insistent eye as Malus approached. The druchii warrior nodded tentatively to Lhunara, who in turn addressed her lord. 'It appears to be safe to drink.'

'Good,' Malus replied tersely, shrugging his water skins off his shoulder. 'Let us fill the skins and be gone. I don't like the feel of this place.'

The water party bent to the task. Malus fought the urge to turn in slow circles and peer warily into the gloom. It wouldn't achieve anything except to make the others nervous, so he forced himself to be still and wait.

As tense as he was, the highborn still didn't hear Dalvar slip silently up beside him. 'My lord?' Dalvar murmured. 'I found something that I think you need to see.'

'What?' Malus asked, but by the time he'd turned around the retainer was already slipping away into the darkness, heading deeper into the chamber. Frowning, the highborn hurried after him, lantern held high.

He followed Dalvar for the space of several heartbeats, drawing farther and farther away from the cistern. Then, abruptly, the retainer came to a halt. 'Watch your step my lord,' Dalvar said quietly. 'The footing is uncertain here.'

Malus stepped to the edge of what appeared to be a large sinkhole. At some point, possibly hundreds of years in the past, a large section of the floor had collapsed into a cavern beneath it. Peering down, the highborn could see piles of glassy rubble and tall stalagmites pushing up from the cavern floor nearly fifteen feet below.

The highborn studied the area with wary eyes. 'I don't see what's so important,' he said.

'That's not what I wanted to show you, my lord,' Dalvar said, nearly whispering in Malus's ear. 'This is.'

The point of the dagger slipped effortlessly into the skin beneath the highborn's right ear. It was an assassin's blade, razor sharp – Malus barely felt the tiny pinprick, but the message it sent was clear: *Don't move. It won't do you any good.*

'It is said that in the city of Har Ganeth, assassination can be seen as a gesture of respect – even admiration,' Dalvar whispered. 'It's also an expression of art. The act itself is not as important as the manner in which it is executed. Of course, such art can only be appreciated by a single spectator, and if the execution is successful, it is the very last experience the spectator ever has. It is sublime, you see?'

Malus said nothing. His sword was in his hand, but Dalvar stood very close, effectively trapping the blade.

'Consider the tableau set before you, my lord. A single twitch of my arm, and the dagger will penetrate into your brain. Death will be instantaneous – and almost painless, if that matters to you. Best of all, the heart will stop, so there will be little or no blood from the wound; a smudge of dirt from my thumb would render it invisible. You then collapse onto the rocks below, and I tell the others you were tired and careless and fell over the edge.'

'Lhunara will kill you,' Malus said.

'Perhaps. Perhaps not. She is loyal, but pragmatic. Each warrior who dies is one less sword to help fight our way back home. Either way, that's my risk to take, not yours. You will be past caring.' The dagger pressed fractionally deeper into the highborn's neck. 'Now, do you appreciate how precarious your life is at this moment?'

'Oh, yes,' Malus replied. He was surprised at how calm he felt.

'Excellent,' Dalvar replied – and the dagger was suddenly gone. 'Now you will hopefully appreciate the fact that I have no interest in taking advantage of this opportunity.'

Malus turned slowly to face Dalvar. The sword trembled in his grip. 'You have an interesting – and possibly fatal – way of making a point,' he said.

The retainer shrugged. 'I could think of no better way to allay your suspicions, my lord. If I had any interest in killing you, I could have done so just then with minimal risk.'

Malus gritted his teeth. It was an infuriating notion, but also an accurate one. 'All right. What is your interest then?'

'Survival,' Dalvar said simply. 'Not to put too fine a point on it, my lord, but I believe you have been deceived. And Nagaira has sacrificed me and my men to lend that deception extra weight.'

The highborn's eyes narrowed suspiciously. 'How do you know this?'

Dalvar shrugged. 'I don't know for certain. But several assurances my mistress made to you – and me, incidentally – haven't proven true, have they? The skull isn't leading us anywhere, and Urial had those riders on our trail almost as soon as we'd left the Hag.'

'So what does she gain from all this?'

'She hurts both you and Urial in one stroke. You've taken one of Urial's most prized possessions and carried it far beyond his reach on a dubious expedition into the Chaos Wastes. Even if you survive, your half-brother will bend all his energies towards destroying you, and you have no allies within or without the Hag who will aid you. This, incidentally, also keeps Urial too busy to continue harassing Nagaira. She was very angry with you for sneaking away on your raiding cruise this summer and abandoning her to his attentions.'

'Urial has to know she helped me invade his tower.'

Dalvar shrugged. 'Perhaps. But you have the skull, and she doesn't. Also, he lusts after her.'

'And she would sacrifice her closest lieutenant and five retainers just for the sake of a deception?'

'As I said, she was *very* angry.'

Malus took a deep breath and composed himself. 'All right, what do you want?'

'Want? I don't want anything. I'm offering you my service.'

The highborn blinked. 'What would I want with a rogue like you?'

Dalvar's mocking grin reappeared. 'Come now, my lord. Your chief lieutenant is a woman, you've got a knight in your service you won on a bet, and if the rumours are true you're sheltering a former assassin who fled Khaine's temple. You've as much use of rogues as the next highborn – and you're not so careless with their lives.'

Malus considered this. 'All right. What can you tell me about Vanhir, then? What treachery is he planning?'

'Treachery? None, my lord.'

'You expect me to believe that, Dalvar?' Malus snapped.

'Of course,' the retainer replied. 'I think you've misjudged that man, my lord.'

'Really? How so?'

'He's not about to betray you, my lord. Vanhir is a proud and honourable man – hasty and impetuous, perhaps, but proud and honourable nevertheless. He's not the sort to slip a knife in your back or slit your throat when you sleep. No, he'll fulfil his oath and return to the Hag, and then dedicate the rest of his life to destroying you, one small cut at a time. And he'll make certain you know he's the one that's doing it the whole time. In that, I suspect the two of you are much alike.'

Malus thought it over carefully, and was pained to admit that the rogue had a point. 'What about your men?'

Dalvar spread his hands. 'They belong to me now, not her. They'll do as I say.'

The highborn nodded. 'Very well. But remember this: as you so cleverly pointed out, *I* have the skull, and I mean to claim the power behind it, no matter how many of you have to die in the process. I'll walk out of the Wastes alone if that's what it takes. Do you understand me?'

Dalvar bowed deeply. 'I live and die at your command, my lord.'

'My lord?' Lhunara's voice echoed across the cavernous space, tinged with mild concern. 'We've filled the water skins. Is everything all right?'

'All is well,' Malus answered, meeting Dalvar's eye. 'We've got everything we need. Let's head back up.'

Malus led the way back up the stairs, alternately seething and calmly considering his next move. His suspicions about his sister seemed to have been confirmed, and the thought galled him to the core. But she'd overplayed her hand. Her retainers belonged to him now, and soon, so would the power in the temple.

His footsteps quickened through the dark and empty halls and he grinned savagely in the blackness. If anything, his position was even stronger than before.

The party was just short of the citadel door when the ambushers struck.

Chapter Fifteen
KUL HADAR

THE CITADEL'S LARGE feasting chamber was separated from the keep's entry hall by a long passageway that essentially took one huge room and separated a third of its length into a separate space opposite the keep's tall double doors. As Malus and the water party cut across this passage, the highborn could see grey sunshine slanting through the open doorway and painting a faint square of light on the sand-strewn floor. The dead light of the Wastes had never looked so welcoming before.

He and Dalvar had just stepped into the entryway when the darkness around them erupted in howls and bestial roars, and broad, bare feet slapped across the slate tiles. Malus caught a glimpse of a huge, horned, muscular form rearing up in the lantern light, then a heavy club smashed into his left vambrace and threw the lantern from his hands. The highborn retreated, raising his sword as the lantern shattered on the tiles, scattering burning oil across the floor.

Malus's attacker let out another inhuman roar and rushed at the highborn with his club held high. The weak light of the burning oil gleamed on a broad, heavily muscled chest fringed with black, wiry hair and powerful, furred legs that terminated in large hooves. The monster was close to seven feet tall and looked far stronger than any druchii, and moved with the speed of a plains lion.

As fast as the monster was though, the highborn was faster still. As the man-beast charged, Malus leapt forwards as well, ducking beneath the monster's thick arms and stabbing his sword deep into its belly. The sword pierced the monster's thick wall of abdominal muscle and the power of its charge forced the blade through its body, grating against its spine as it punched out through the creature's back.

The man-beast bellowed in shock and anger, doubling up around the druchii sword, but its left hand reached over and caught Malus by the hair. It flung him backwards against the nearby wall; the highborn's head struck the stone and sparks exploded across his vision. Then came the creature's club, smashing against his thick breastplate, and Malus thought he'd been kicked in the chest by a god.

Malus bounced off the stone wall and fell to the ground, gasping for air. The armour plate was the only thing that had saved him, and even then he could tell that the tough, flexible steel was deeply dented just to the left of his heart. The club smashed down again, this time striking the wall and part of his shoulder, and the joint flared with a sharp spike of pain. Malus cried out in pain and anger, fumbling a long dagger from a sheath in his boot. When the man-beast lifted his club once more, Malus leapt from the ground and grappled the huge creature, stabbing again and again into the monster's chest and throat.

The monster roared, its mouth right above the highborn's left ear. Malus could smell the thing's fetid breath, and was battered by the tips of thick tusks or horns as the creature tossed its head in pain. Hot, bitter blood washed down the monster's chest, and its bellows turned to a choking rattle.

Once again, the monster's broad, callused hand grabbed Malus by the hair and neck and tried to pull him free, but the highborn snarled in pain and held on, driving the knife again and again into the man-beast's body. The heavy club tumbled to the floor, but the highborn's triumph was short-lived as the beast smashed its right fist into the side of his head, once, twice and then a third time that sent him sprawling across the floor.

Stunned and disoriented, Malus scrambled to regain his feet. There were shouts and screams echoing in the empty room, and the beasts seemed to be everywhere. A fur-covered figure crashed into him, bearing him down, and the highborn sank his teeth into the thing's torn and bloody throat before he realised that it was in its death throes. A moment later, the man-beast died, and Malus rolled the creature off himself. His sword was still buried to the hilt in its abdomen.

The ambush was as brief as it was brutal. As Malus recovered his senses he saw another monster topple onto the still-burning oil, but the dagger protruding from the creature's eye spared the beast the agony of burning alive. Two other creatures sped in front of the flickering light, arms and legs flashing as they ran for the open doorway. 'Stop!' Malus roared as they ran headlong into the courtyard, and the highborn staggered to his feet in pursuit.

A nauglir bellowed a challenge just as Malus reached the doorway. The beastmen – for there was no better term to describe them – stood frozen in place just a few feet from the doors as seven cold ones stalked their way. The cold ones were fanning out in a rough semicircle to surround and pin their prey against the wall of the tower.

'Stand!' Malus commanded, his voice crackling with authority. All seven of the war-beasts paused, their training briefly overcoming instinct.

The beastmen turned at the sound of his voice and fell to their knees, bleating words in a language Malus had never heard before. In the grey light of day, the highborn saw that the creatures were both powerfully built and covered with black fur except across their biceps and chest. Their legs ended in glossy black hooves, and their fingers were tipped in thick, claw-like nails. The beastmen had heads like great rams, with black eyes and heavy, curved horns that sprouted from their foreheads and hung down to their chests. One wore a bracelet of crude, beaten gold around his right wrist, while the other had a necklace of bone and assorted feathers hanging around his thick neck. As far as Malus could tell, the twisted creatures were pleading for their lives.

Vanhir and one of Dalvar's men came from the gatehouse at a dead run, crossbows in their hands. The side of Malus's face throbbed, and blood dripped on his neck from deep gouges in his cheek and ear. The rest of the water party stumbled out into the light, many covered in blood themselves.

'How many attackers?' Malus asked.

Dalvar shook his head, pressing a hand to a cut on his cheek. Lhunara wiped her hair from her eyes. 'Five, all told. Those two ran as soon as they realised they were the only ones left.'

Malus turned to Vanhir. 'What are they?' he said, pointing to the two creatures.

The retainer shrugged. 'Beastmen.' As the highborn's expression paled with rage, Vanhir quickly added, 'The Autarii say they live in loose tribes in the farther reaches of the Wastes, where the mystical energies warp their bodies into blasphemous shapes. They sometimes raid our watchtowers along the frontier, but the Shades slay any that trespass in the hills.'

'Can you speak their language?'

'Certainly not, my lord,' Vanhir replied, offended by the very idea. 'I don't think even the Autarii understand them.'

'Then they aren't of much use to me besides sport,' Malus growled. 'Why do you suppose they are here?'

'I'm a knight of the Hag, my lord, not some damned oracle,' Vanhir said archly. 'If I had to guess, I would suppose they were fugitives of some kind. These beasts typically travel in bands hundreds strong – for one reason or another, these are far away from their litter mates.'

Malus rubbed his chin thoughtfully, wincing as the motion set his torn ear to aching. 'They're from farther north, you said?'

Vanhir nodded. 'Farther north than here, at least.'

The highborn eyed the beastmen speculatively, then strode quickly over to Spite's side. He fumbled through his saddlebag and produced the wire-wrapped skull. Malus returned to the two creatures and showed the relic to them both. 'Kul Hadar?' Malus asked. 'Kul Hadar?'

One of the beastmen let out a cry of surprise. '*Hadar! Hadar!*' it grunted, pointing at the skull, then gobbled out a long string of gibberish.

Malus smiled. 'That's better.' He turned to his men. 'It appears we have a guide,' he said, pointing to the babbling creature. 'That one lives. The other one will entertain us tonight.'

The druchii smiled, their eyes glittering at the prospect of an evening's flirtation with darkness. One night's revelry would be good for morale – tomorrow, Malus felt, they would be at the edge of the forest that skirted the mountain.

And then Kul Hadar, he thought, smiling with anticipation.

'Are you certain?' Malus asked, feeling a fist close about his heart.

The druchii looked from Dalvar to Malus, clearly nervous at earning the highborn's undivided attention. 'Y-yes, my lord. The nomads wore furs, but these riders had on black cloaks and rode proper horses.'

Malus stepped to the closest gatehouse window. The sun had only just cleared the horizon, and already hot gusts of dusty wind blew against his face. From this height he could see a long way past the broken walls and across the desolate plain. 'How far would you say?'

The retainer shrugged helplessly. 'Half a day, my lord? Less than five miles, I think. I only caught a glimpse as the sunlight silhouetted them along one of the ridgelines. The way distances are warped here. Who can say for certain?'

'Urial's riders must have followed us through the Wighthallows,' Dalvar said, his face paling. 'You don't suppose they *fought* their way through the wights?'

'Perhaps,' Malus growled. 'Or perhaps they're close enough to being dead themselves that the wights couldn't tell the difference. It doesn't matter. We're leaving. Now.' The highborn headed swiftly for the stairs.

Out in the courtyard the warband was saddling the cold ones for the day's travel. For the first time in days the warriors were talking easily among themselves, their humour improved by the entertainment of the previous night.

The beastman hung from an improvised rack they'd built with steel bars taken from the old forge. The creature's prodigious endurance had prolonged the revels well into the early morning hours, until, drunk with torture and running short of time, the warband had adopted much cruder tactics to bring the celebrations to an end. The beastman now resembled nothing so much as a badly butchered slab of meat, its blood staining the sand around the rack. The surviving beastman didn't seem overly troubled by the death of its companion; it had watched the revels with some curiosity once he'd been persuaded that he wasn't about to be the next victim.

Now it stood among the druchii as they loaded the animals, running its hands along its arms and chest with a troubled look on its face. It had taken a large amount of the nauglir slime to cover his scent so the cold ones would accept him. Malus hoped they hadn't accidentally poisoned their guide. Lhunara and Dalvar alike tried to tie the beast-man's hands, but Malus had prevented them despite their heated objections. He wanted the creature to think they were potential allies, not captors.

If the beastman thought it had a chance of being released when they reached Kul Hadar, it would be more inclined to cooperate and get the whole thing over with. Plus, the highborn hoped it sent a signal to the creature: *It doesn't matter to us if you try to run. You can't escape us, no matter what you try.*

They were almost ready. Malus considered the dead beastman. It would be easy enough to pull the corpse down and conceal it in one of the buildings. After a moment's thought he shrugged in resignation. Let the riders find the body and traces that they'd been here. With luck they would search the rest of the city for them and waste precious time while the druchii escaped. 'Sa'an'ishar!' he cried. 'Mount up! We leave in five minutes!'

The warband immediately bent themselves to finishing their last-minute tasks. Malus gathered Spite's saddle and headed for his mount. Lhunara was waiting for him, her expression troubled. 'What's happened, my lord?'

'Urial's riders,' he said with a grunt as he threw the heavy saddle over Spite's back. 'The sentry thinks he saw them on the plains, about half a day's ride away. I want to put as much distance between them and us as possible.'

The retainer muttered a curse under her breath. She eyed the beast-man warily. 'Do you think you can trust it?'

'I think after what it saw last night it knows that it'll be next unless it gives me exactly what I want.'

'That was a wise decision last night, my lord. The men seem much improved.' Lhunara glanced sidelong at him as Malus tightened the saddle's girth strap. 'Or does this have something to do with the conversation you had with Dalvar underneath the keep?'

Malus grinned. 'Clever girl. A bit of both, I think. Dalvar and I have come to an understanding of sorts. He and his men have sworn themselves to me.'

'To you? What of Nagaira?'

'They've seen enough to believe that my dear sister has washed her hands of them. Thus, they no longer consider themselves in her employ.'

'Your sister will not be pleased.'

'At this point I am beyond caring what my dear sister thinks.' Malus stood and leaned close to her. 'It's possible that this is all an elaborate scheme to punish both Urial and myself. She's sent me out here with my brother's precious relic in the hopes that I'll be lost forever.'

Lhunara looked grim. 'So far I'd say she's succeeding. So why continue this fool's errand? Why not head back for the Hag?'

'Because Urial is there, and my former allies, *and* their contract with the temple,' Malus hissed. 'Nagaira has thought this through carefully. If I stay here in the Wastes, I die. If I return empty-handed, I die. The only way out is through the temple. I must succeed, or I'm finished.'

'You're assuming there even is a temple! All you have to go on is what your sister told you!'

'Not so,' Malus said. He pointed to the beastman. 'That thing knows where Kul Hadar is. And that's where we're going.'

Lhunara opened her mouth to protest, but she knew the implacable look in Malus's eye all too well. 'As you wish, my lord,' she said with a sigh. 'I only hope the rest of us survive to celebrate your triumph.'

The bleak look on Lhunara's face elicited a sharp laugh from Malus. 'Fear not, terrible one,' he said, not unkindly. 'If I want you to die I'll kill you myself. Now mount up and let's be gone.'

THEY REACHED THE outskirts of the city within the hour, navigating ponderously over piles of fallen stone and shifting mounds of sand. There was no northern gate, as it happened – the warband was forced to seek out a large enough section of collapsed wall and clamber their way over the rubble. The dark mountain loomed in the distance, shrouded by drifts of wind-borne dust.

Malus turned to the beastman, who rode on Lhunara's nauglir just behind the retainer's saddle. The highborn wasn't certain who appeared more uncomfortable with the arrangement – the cold one, Lhunara, or their erstwhile guide. 'Kul Hadar?' Malus inquired.

The guide pointed a clawed finger – off to the northwest, seemingly away from the cleft peak. '*Hadar,*' the creature grunted, then added more in his guttural speech.

Malus gazed from the mountain to the direction indicated by the beastman. It made no sense. But this is the Wastes, he thought. Besides, what's the point of having a guide if you don't follow his directions? 'All right,' the highborn said to the creature. 'But remember your pack-mate back in the keep. That's what happens to those who aren't any more use to me.'

From the look in the beastman's eye, the creature may not have understood the words, but the meaning was clear enough. '*Hadar!*' the beastman replied, more forcefully this time, pointing to the north-west.

Malus tugged on the reins and pointed Spite away from the mountain. 'This makes as much sense as anything, I suppose,' he muttered, and spurred the nauglir into a trot.

THEY REACHED THE forest by nightfall.

For the entire day the mountain rose from their left, never receding but at the same time growing no closer. The warband rode through desolate plains of shifting dust and grit, passing the occasional withered tree or empty lakebed.

As the sun sank low in the west, the terrain began to slope slightly upward and the vegetation became more abundant. The hot, sulphurous wind tapered off, and before they knew it the druchii were riding across rolling hills thick with underbrush and scraggly, black-leafed trees. Unseen animals hissed and chattered in their wake, and once a creature with broad, leathery wings burst from the scrub and soared away to the north, screaming its agitation at the intruders.

Malus was starting to look for possible campsites when Spite crested a tall hill and he found himself staring at the outskirts of the elusive forest. Beyond rose the great mountain, its deep wound standing out as a line of abyssal blackness against the steel-grey of its flanks. For a moment, Malus couldn't believe his own eyes. When had their course begun curving back towards the peak? Try as he might, he could not remember. No matter, he thought. We're here.

Lhunara sidled her cold one up alongside Spite. 'Do we camp here, my lord?'

The daylight was almost spent, but the northern auroras were already boiling across the sky in the most vivid display Malus had ever seen. Streaks and great loops of blue and red and violet arced across the underside of the clouds, casting unsteady shadows among the tall trees. 'We'll press on a bit longer,' the highborn decided at length. 'Urial's riders have no need for sleep, I suspect. I want to cover as much ground as possible while there's light to see by.'

Somewhere deep in the woods, a creature gave out a long, gruff howl. The cold ones shifted uneasily, and Malus could feel Spite gathering his wind for a response until he quieted the beast with a jab of the spurs. He looked to the beastman. 'Kul Hadar?'

The beastman sat with its shoulders hunched, apparently unnerved by the strange howl. Reluctantly, it pointed straight ahead, into the shadowy wood.

'All right, then,' Malus said, raising his hand to motion the warband forward and then reaching back for his crossbow.

There were a number of well-worn paths through the wood, wide enough for even cold one riders to traverse them in single file with ease. The tall oaks and cedars blocked much of the light from the auroras with their spreading branches, but colonies of green and blue fungus climbed the boles of many of the trees and gave off a faint luminescence that revealed enough of the path to navigate by. The small column moved slowly amid a preternatural stillness. No night animals disturbed the silence with their cries, an observation that set Malus's nerves on edge.

They had been riding beneath the trees for more than an hour when they heard the howl again. Once again, it was off to the west, but it seemed somewhat closer than before. Whatever made the long, hungry cry had to be huge, the highborn thought, as loud and as lengthy as the sound was. Something as big as a cold one, or possibly bigger, he thought.

Then another howl came – also from the west, but this time from a different source. It sounded a bit farther away than its predecessor, but still too close for comfort. Now another barking cry – from the east – and Malus grew concerned. A pack, he thought. And they sound like they're hunting. Spite shifted uneasily beneath him, and one of the other cold ones let out a low groan. Malus spurred his mount into a trot, his eyes straining to pick out the path ahead. Perhaps if we can just escape their path…

For a few minutes nothing broke the forest silence save the heavy *pad-pad-pad* of Spite's tread, but then another howl broke the stillness, and less than a mile to the west came a splintering crack, like a tree broken by the passage of something swift and powerful. It was answered by another howl to the east, and then another. Four of them, Malus thought. And they have our scent!

They couldn't go any faster in the darkness. The trees hung too close and the light was too poor. Malus could hear huge forms crashing through the forest on either side of the path behind them – ponderous steps of two-, four- and even three-legged gaits. And then… silence.

Malus halted the column, his senses straining to penetrate the thick shadows all around. There was nothing save the heavy breathing of the cold ones. The highborn turned to look back at Lhunara. The retainer's face was tense, but the beastman behind her looked almost mad with fear.

We can't outrun them, Malus thought. Perhaps we can stand our ground and drive them off. He reined Spite around and began to nose his way back down the length of the column. 'Crossbows ready,' he said to each of the druchii he passed.

The warrior at the end of the column was the same druchii who had stood watch in the gatehouse the night before. Malus edged alongside him. 'See anything?'

The druchii peered back the way they'd come, his face pale. 'No,' he whispered. 'But I can hear them. They're shifting about back there in the darkness behind the trees.'

Now Malus could hear them, too – huge shapes pacing slowly and carefully in the shadows, perhaps fifty yards back along the path. He strained his eyes to penetrate the gloom, but to no avail. The glow generated by the fungus only deepened the shadows beyond the trees, and whatever the creatures were, they were cautious and cunning.

'They're sizing us up,' Malus said, half to himself. 'Trying to decide if we're prey.' Malus straightened in his saddle, and after a moment's thought, put his crossbow away and drew his sword. 'Time to snarl back,' the highborn said to the druchii beside him. 'Keep your crossbow ready. I'm going to try to shake them up a bit.'

The druchii nodded, his eyes wide. Malus took a deep breath and spurred his mount forward. Spite, sensing the presence of the unseen creatures, let out a loud, rumbling growl.

Branches snapped and heavy footfalls echoed from the darkness ahead. Malus walked Spite forward, feeling the nauglir grow increasingly tense. The beast's tail began to lash angrily, and the highborn caught sight of something large nosing through the thick brush almost directly ahead of him. Malus edged Spite closer to the thing. Predictably, the nauglir let out a long, furious bellow at it, a cry that was quickly taken up by the rest of the cold ones in the column. You see? Malus thought. We are not some timid deer for you to slay. Best you seek less deadly prey.

Just then Malus caught sight of a flash of movement off to his right. He turned sharply, but all he could see was a glimpse of something large slipping swiftly through the brush past him, heading for the rest of the party. They're much stealthier than they led me to believe, Malus thought with amazement. That means the one in front of me is just a distraction!

At that moment the creature facing Malus let out a wild shriek and charged forward like a rampaging boar, the sounds answered by thunderous cries further up the path.

Brush and saplings exploded in the monster's path as it charged the highborn, and Malus could feel the air curdle at its approach. Monstrous as it was, the creature exuded an aura of palpable *wrongness* that even Spite's senses picked up on, causing the cold one to shy backwards with a startled howl. Then the monster burst onto the path, and even the highborn cried out in fear and disgust at the abomination that reared before him.

It was huge, easily as large as Spite, its body little more than a lump of cancerous flesh and muscle supported by four trunk-like legs. Long, narrow arms terminating in scythes of exposed bone lashed at Malus, severing tree limbs and tearing huge gouges from tree trunks in their path. There were no eyes nor even a face that Malus could recognise, only a round, lamprey-like mouth at the end of a thick, muscular trunk. Rings of barbed teeth pulsated in ranks down the monster's throat as its sphincter-like oesophagus dilated and expelled a maddened roar at the highborn and his mount.

'Dark Mother preserve us!' Malus exclaimed in horror as he hauled on Spite's reins. The twisted monstrosity rushed at Malus as Spite wheeled around and struck it with his powerful tail. The blow staggered the monster, knocking it into a huge oak that splintered under its weight. Scything limbs lashed at the cold one, but Malus was already putting the spurs to Spite's flanks, heading back up the path as fast as he dared.

More of the twisted creatures had burst from the woods onto the path. Malus could hear the hysterical screams of the druchii he'd spoken to only moments before. One of the monsters had leapt upon the man's cold one, pinning it to the ground with its four clawed legs and slashing it to a bloody ruin with its scythe-like arms. Malus could see the druchii's still-kicking legs as the monster forced the armoured warrior down its fanged throat.

With a furious cry Malus spurred his mount harder, directly at the hideous monster. I can play that game as well, he thought wildly. At the last moment he hauled on the reins and cried 'Up!' Spite leapt onto the monster, taloned feet slashing and scrabbling for purchase. The monster seemed to distend beneath the cold one's weight, flattening out as though it possessed no skeleton at all. Ichor sprayed from grotesque wounds as the nauglir's thick talons ripped away gobbets of putrid flesh, but it was like clawing apart a midden heap.

Malus slashed with his sword, his gorge rising at the stench of rot in the air, and the creature howled and gobbled with rage, slashing wildly with its arms. Finally, Spite's talons gained purchase and the cold one leapt over the monster, just as its packmate came lumbering up from behind. Malus sped along up the path, daring only a single backward glance to see the mortally-wounded monster pushed aside by its packmate so it could continue the chase.

The warband was in full flight, trying to break out of the trap. Malus could see the lashing tails of the running nauglir up ahead, past loping, gelid bodies bristling with bony scythes and talons. The highborn ducked low in the saddle, sword raised, and let Spite shoulder the monsters out of his path. The cold one crashed into – and in some cases through – the monsters' glutinous bodies, showering Malus with evil-smelling fluids, but in moments they had broken free of the pack and were pulling away. Howls of rage and hunger shook the dark trees and seemed to fill the air from every direction.

As surprisingly fast as the monsters were, they were far from nimble, while the cold ones negotiated the twisting paths with ease. In minutes the warband had pulled away from its pursuers, but the monsters seemed tireless, never slacking their pace. Malus worked his way swiftly up to the head of the column. Lhunara rode with a stained sword in each hand, her eyes wild with a mix of terror and battle-lust. The high-born saw that the beastman was gone. 'What happened to the guide?' Malus yelled.

'It leapt for the trees as soon as the ambush started. I couldn't stop it!'

Malus uttered a blistering curse. 'Keep your eyes peeled for branches off the path!' he cried. 'Those things can't keep up with us – if we can turn off we will, otherwise we'll see if they tire and give up.'

But the minutes stretched, and the monsters refused to give up the chase. The nauglir were racing tirelessly along, but Malus knew that even the rugged cold ones had their limits. Why are they still chasing us, the highborn thought? They can't catch us. It should be obvious by now.

Just then Malus was startled by a wash of chaotic light overhead. The path was plunging down into a mountain hollow, the trees receding substantially on either side of a dark, narrow stream. More room to manoeuvre, at least, Malus thought. If I can direct the entire warband as a single unit, we might have a chance against these things.

Malus's mind raced, devising tactics as he waved the column into a ragged line and continued to race up the hollow. They'd covered almost a hundred yards when howls and battle-cries erupted from the woods on either side of them, and a horde of beastmen came charging out of the shadows beneath the trees, waving axes and clubs in the air.

Hounds to the hunter, Malus realised, his heart growing cold. Those creatures were driving us down the path to their masters.

In the darkness and chaos there was no way to know how many beast-men there were, but it was clear that the druchii were far outnumbered and pressed from every side. In the thick of battle, Malus made the only decision he could. He raised his blade. 'Forward!' he cried.

The cold ones put their heads down and charged deeper into the hollow. The beastmen closed in behind them and took up the chase, and the wall of foes ahead rushed at the druchii in a ragged line. The charging knights met the beastmen with a crunch of bone and the whickering ring of steel against flesh.

A beastman disappeared beneath Spite's taloned feet with a hoarse scream. Malus slashed at another howling rams-head nearly as tall as himself, severing the horned head from its thickly muscled neck. Blood splashed across his armour, but Malus welcomed its bitter taste after the horrid ichor of the Chaos-spawned monsters in the forest. A heavy blow rang against the left side of his breastplate, and Malus slashed at the head of another beastman, hacking away part of one curving horn. Another foe leapt at him from the right, swinging an axe that missed his thigh and bit into the cantle of his saddle instead. The highborn responded with a backhanded slash across his attacker's eyes. The foe dropped his axe and reeled backwards, his hands reaching for his ruined face.

Malus spurred Spite forward, bowling over the beastmen in front of him and breaking bones with the nauglir's lashing tail. A clawed hand grabbed for the reins and Malus severed it at the wrist. An axe blade glanced from his armoured thigh and a club smashed into his back-plate, knocking him forward against the saddle. Then Spite leapt free of the press and charged farther up the hollow, momentarily leaving the beastmen behind.

A quick glance showed that the rest of the warband had fought their way clear as well, staggering up the hollow in a rough line alongside him. Skill, experience and heavy armour had won through, but the enemy was far from finished. Malus pointed to a scattering of boulders up ahead. 'Form a line there and ready your crossbows!' he ordered. The druchii raised their swords in acknowledgement and spurred ahead for the rocks.

They had gained perhaps thirty yards on the beastmen. Malus glanced back over his shoulder and saw that there were close to a hundred left, loping along in a disordered mob and howling at the sky. Worse, he could see the pack of scythe-armed monstrosities shambling up the hollow in their wake. He thought they could break the beastmen with a few sharp volleys and another charge, but even the cold ones were frightened of the misshapen creatures. Still, if we hurl the beastmen back upon their hounds, it might buy us some manoeuvring room, he thought. Though even then, our prospects look grim.

Malus reached the rocks beside his warriors. 'Make ready to fire,' he said. 'Three volleys, and then we charge. We'll try to break the animals and slip past their monsters in the confusion.'

Just then a horn wailed from the bottom of the hollow, a deep, banshee-like howl that echoed through the trees. Malus stood in his saddle and saw another dark knot of beastmen break from the trees to the west, waving torches over their heads. Another fifty, perhaps, he thought grimly. We're going to pay dearly for this one.

Then, to Malus's surprise, he saw the newcomers hurl large sacks or bladders at the backs of the shambling monsters. Torches followed, and suddenly the pack was wreathed in leaping blue flames. An angry shout went up from the beastmen farther up the hollow and confusion reigned as the torch-wielding beastmen charged up the hollow at them.

Several of the druchii cheered in relief. Lhunara turned to Malus. 'What in the Outer Darkness is happening?'

Malus shook his head. 'I have no idea, but I'll thank the Dark Mother for her gift.' Below, the two mobs of beastmen had crashed together, and sounds of battle filled the air. The highborn turned to his warriors. 'Check your crossbows and make certain they're fully loaded! We'll advance at a walk and fire into the melee!'

Lhunara frowned. 'Who do we aim at?'

'Who cares? They could all be foes. We'll kill as many as we can and worry about the rest when the time comes.' Malus sheathed his sword and reached for his crossbow. 'Ready… advance!'

The cold ones made their way slowly back down the hollow. The druchii raised their crossbows, choosing targets. 'Fire at will!' Malus ordered, and the slaughter began.

Crossbows thumped and bolts hissed through the air. In the darkness and the swirling melee, it was difficult to see the effects of their fire. The druchii reloaded and fired again. At the third salvo, the ranks of beastmen seemed to waver. Then suddenly a ripple of cold curdled the air around the creatures, and Malus felt the hairs on his neck stand on end. Sorcery! the highborn thought. Battle cries turned to wails of despair, and a large knot of beastmen threw down their weapons and ran – heading straight for Malus and his warband.

'Fire at will!' Malus ordered. He sighted on a running beastman and put a bolt in the centre of his chest. The druchii worked their weapons with quick, brutal efficiency, loading, firing and loading again. They'd killed nearly a score of the beastmen when they realised the peril in front of them and scattered, running for the safety of the trees to the east and west.

Malus sighted on a running beastman and fired, punching a bolt into the creature's back. 'Cease fire!' he ordered as the beastman crashed to the ground. Farther down the hollow, the torch-wielding beastmen had finished off the last of their opponents and were now advancing uphill. In their lead, Malus could see a huge beastman bearing a massive staff and wearing a heavy robe draped over his sloping shoulders.

The highborn studied the advancing mob carefully. They seemed wary, but not overtly hostile. On impulse, he put his crossbow away. 'I think they're coming to talk,' he said to Lhunara. 'Hold the men here. If something goes wrong, come and get me.'

'Yes, my lord,' Lhunara said, but the choked expression on her face spoke eloquently of her real opinion of Malus's plan. The highborn put the spurs to his mount and trotted across the corpse-strewn ground to meet the newcomers.

The beastman sorcerer grunted a command to his fellows as Malus approached, then he and one other continued their advance. The pair worked their way among the fallen beastmen until they stood approximately ten yards ahead of the torch-wielding mob.

Malus stopped within easy hailing distance and showed his empty hands. 'Well met, stranger,' he called, realising, too late, that the beastman probably didn't understand a word he was saying. 'It appears my enemy is your enemy. Do you have a name?'

At that, the second beastman stepped from behind the sorcerer, and Malus was shocked to see that it was his former prisoner. The beastman raised itself up to his full height and pointed dramatically at the towering sorcerer.

Malus's eyes went wide. He'd been wrong all along. Kul Hadar wasn't the name of a place at all.

The sorcerer tossed his horned head and smiled. 'Hail, druchii,' the sorcerer rumbled in guttural druhir. 'I am Kul Hadar.'

Chapter Sixteen
BONDS OF BLOOD

Malus's mind was a-boil as the warband followed the beastman pack through the forest. Kul Hadar, the great sorcerer, had offered little in the way of information at the battlefield in the hollow, saying the time for talk would come once they had returned to his camp nearby. The very idea had set the highborn's teeth on edge, but he was hardly in a position to refuse. The sorcerer's warband had suffered few losses in the battle, and they seemed more than ready for another fight, and Malus had no way to counter Kul Hadar's magical prowess. If the beastman lord lost patience with the druchii, Malus did not relish the thought of open battle.

Kul Hadar's beastmen set quickly to looting the bodies of the dead, and then with swift efficiency began butchering the healthiest and fattest of the corpses. Within an hour, the pack was ready to move, and quickly set off west. On the way out of the hollow, Kul Hadar made a point of leading the warband through the spot where he and his pack had fought the enemy beastmen. In the centre of the piled corpses, Malus saw a ring of pale, withered bodies, their once-muscular forms withered by the sweep of an unseen power that reduced flesh and bone to brittle ash. The bodies collapsed into dust at the heavy tread of the cold ones. The highborn took note and remembered the wave of chill that had curdled the air and broken the enemy ranks. Kul Hadar was giving him a message.

The pack moved overland, disdaining the clear paths, and the nauglir were forced to pick their way slowly through the wild terrain. Their former guide now walked alongside them, pointing out the way with infuriating smugness. Time and again Malus found himself hoping that the creature would wander too close to Spite and lose an arm for his clumsiness, but the opportunity never arose.

After almost an hour the pack turned north, and the warband found itself climbing the mountain's steep slope. The air was cold, but no wind stirred the dark trees. There was a sound – almost like a humming – in the air, so deep as to be almost undetectable. Spite felt it, and occasionally shook his head to try to free himself from the sound. If their beastman guide noticed it, he gave no sign.

Two more hours of hard travel saw them perhaps a quarter of the way up the wooded mountainside. A horn sounded mournfully up ahead, accompanied by faint cries – Malus suspected that they had reached the sentries guarding the beastman camp. Ten minutes later the warband reached a sprawling encampment of crude shelters formed from limbs and pine branches, arranged around the mouth of a large cave that gaped from the mountainside. Malus could just see the back of Kul Hadar disappearing into the cave when their guide grunted and barked, pointing them off to the right.

The guide led them to a reasonably clear area near the edge of the camp, and with gestures and grunts conveyed to them that they were to remain there. Near the centre of camp someone had got a fire going, and a chorus of voices were raised in an eerie, barking chant.

'Stand,' Malus commanded, and slid wearily from the saddle. Every part of him from the neck down ached, and he was covered in dried blood and less savoury fluids. The rest of the warband followed suit, silent and stoic as ever. 'Dalvar,' the highborn called, 'if these beasts have camped here there must be a spring somewhere nearby. Go see if you can find it. I smell like a dung heap.'

'Indeed, my lord? I hadn't noticed,' the rogue said with a mocking grin, then quickly slipped from sight. Malus threw a half-hearted glare at the retreating man, then started fumbling at the buckles of his armour.

'Are you certain that's wise?' Lhunara asked, checking her mount for injuries a few yards away.

'I've had this cursed harness on for three days,' Malus growled. 'If the beastmen wanted to kill us they'd have done it three hours ago. At this rate, the stink might do the work anyway.' His pauldrons clattered to the ground, then his vambraces, then a moment later his breast and backplates. The highborn straightened with a sigh, savouring the cold air on the sweat-soaked sleeves of his robes. He ran a hand through matted and crusty hair and scrubbed bits of gore from his cheeks. Not a bad look for social occasions or the odd negotiation, he mused, but I wouldn't recommend it for days on end. 'What's our situation, Lhunara?' he asked as he tried to untangle his hair.

'One dead. Minor wounds for everyone else. The nauglir are in good shape, but they're getting thin again. A pity we couldn't have fed them back at the hollow.'

'Kul Hadar probably wouldn't have cared, but I didn't think to ask.'

'Ammunition is running low for the crossbows, as well as food and water. Also, we appear to be camped in the middle of an entire mob of beastmen.'

'I'd noticed that last part myself,' Malus answered darkly.

'What, then, are we doing here, my lord?'

'We're here to see Kul Hadar,' the highborn replied. 'It appears that when Urial wrote to take the skull to "Kul Hadar in the north", he was referring to the beastman sorcerer. How he knew of Hadar is a mystery. Perhaps Hadar himself can enlighten me, or perhaps not.'

'Well, what are we going to do now?'

'I'm going to talk to Hadar, of course,' Malus snapped. 'Obviously he's interested in negotiations of some kind, or he wouldn't have brought us to his camp. I suspect he's after the skull, but we'll see. In the meantime, rest the men and the mounts. I expect we'll know something before long.'

As it happened, Kul Hadar kept them waiting for another three hours, while the flames in the centre of the camp grew into a bonfire and the smell of roasted meat filled the air. Dalvar found the spring quickly enough, and Malus took the opportunity to get himself and his warband cleaned and fed. By the time the beastman guide came and beckoned for Malus to follow, Vanhir and Dalvar were standing watch over the camp while the rest of the warband – druchii and nauglir alike – slept on the rocky ground. Once again buckled into his armour, Malus trooped up the slope to the cave.

Pale, greenish light flickered fitfully at the cave entrance. The highborn expected to find more colonies of glowing fungus, but was surprised to find the stone walls bare of life. Just beyond the cave entrance was a small chamber carpeted with rubbish and stinking of rotted meat. Bitter smoke hung near the cave ceiling, and the hulking shapes of beastmen slouched near the walls, eating noisily or swilling wine from huge leather skins. They eyed Malus with barely veiled hostility as the guide led him through the chamber and down a rough, twisting passageway.

The green light came from deeper in the complex of caves. The illumination grew stronger the deeper they went. Finally, the passage opened into another, larger cave. As Malus crossed the threshold, he felt a wave of coldness pass through his body, as though he'd stepped through a ghostly wall of ice. He looked down and saw that the floor was covered in crude symbols etched with pale chalk. The sorcerer's wards, he thought.

The shaman sat on a broad ledge at the far end of the cave, his large staff close to hand. The sorcerer's dark eyes were studying him with intense curiosity. Something's surprised him, Malus realised. Could it be Nagaira's talisman? Perhaps his magic doesn't work so well against it.

Unlike the previous cave, this chamber was surprisingly clean. Symbols were etched into the walls and ceiling of the space, and several collections of jars, pots, bones and feathers were arranged on rocky shelves around the cave. The chamber was lit with a powerful greenish light emanating from what looked like an enormous, faceted crystal growing from the floor of the cave.

Kul Hadar dismissed the guide with a broad, clawed hand. Up close, the beastman sorcerer was a fearsome sight. He was large and powerfully built even for a beastman – had he stood, his horned head would have scraped the cave's seven-foot ceiling. Necklaces of bone and feathers hung from his thick neck, as well as a number of brass medallions etched with crude sigils. Malus was shocked to realise that they looked strikingly similar to the runes carved on the surface of Urial's relic.

The sorcerer's black eyes studied him dispassionately, his long snout and huge, glossy ram's horns lending him an aura of otherworldly menace. Power reverberated through the air, vibrating against Malus's bones.

'Hu'ghul says you have come to the Wastes seeking me by name, and bearing a skull in your hand,' Kul Hadar said.

Malus considered the beastman's words for a moment. It was disconcerting to hear intelligible druhir rumbling from that bestial snout. More sorcery, Malus thought? Perhaps. Finally, he nodded. 'That is so.'

The highborn caught the slightest tremor in the beastman's powerful frame, and there was no mistaking the fevered gleam in his black eyes. Ah, Malus thought. Interesting.

'And how did a lord such as yourself learn the name of Hadar?' the shaman inquired, his eyes narrowing suspiciously.

Malus affected a shrug. 'I took the skull and some papers from a druchii sorcerer,' he replied. 'The papers spoke of many things I did not understand, but they also mentioned you.'

Hadar considered this. 'And what do you want of me, druchii?'

'I want the power locked in the temple – the same as you.'

The shaman studied him for several heartbeats, then chuckled deep in his chest. 'I have been the Kul – the shaman-lord – of my herd for many years, druchii. I took this mountain for my own and studied the temple when other lords took their herds to pillage the soft kingdoms of men. I know the way past the Gate of Infinity, and the Skull of Ehrenlish is the key. Long have I searched the Wastes for it, making pacts with many dark powers for clues to its whereabouts. At last, I learned of its resting place in an ancient city by the sea, but when I reached the ruins, a band of druchii rogues had got there before me and spirited the relic away.' The shaman's gaze glittered with thwarted ambition. 'But now the Ruinous Powers have brought you – and the relic – back into my grasp.' Hadar chuckled again, savouring some private amusement. 'The gods are fickle beings, Lord Malus. I will help you past the gate, druchii, but my aid does not come without a price.'

And now we get to the heart of the matter, Malus thought. If the skull was all you needed, we wouldn't be speaking to one another right now – you'd be roasting me on that fire outside. 'What do you wish?'

Hadar leaned forward, propping his elbows on his furred knees. 'At first, my herd obeyed my will and served me faithfully as I struggled against the magical defences of the temple. Aside from the great power contained within, the inner sanctum of the temple is heaped with treasure, or so the legends tell it. For a time, the promise of wealth was enough. But as the years went by without glorious raids or the sweet taste of foemen's flesh, my herd drew restless. They began to think me weak and foolish.'

Malus nodded, permitting himself a thin smile. 'I know too well what you speak of, Kul Hadar.'

'When I learned at last of the skull's resting place, I gathered my champions and journeyed to the lost city, but while I was gone, my lieutenant, Machuk, rose up and claimed the herd for his own. When I returned, empty handed, he hunted me through the forest like an animal. The hunting party you fought in the woods was one of several searching the mountain for me.' The shaman indicated the sigils carved into the walls of the chamber. 'My magics and the power of the warpstone here have been enough to conceal myself and my band, but it is only a matter of time before we are found.'

The highborn nodded thoughtfully, folding his arms. He could guess where the conversation was headed. 'You want me to help you regain control of your herd.'

The shaman grunted in acknowledgement. 'Yes. Your numbers are few, but you wear hard shells and have weapons that kill from far away, as well as fearsome beasts that carry you into battle. Machuk has ways of defeating my magics, but he has no defence against you. If we strike swiftly, we can kill him and his champions, and I can regain my control of the herd. More importantly–' Hadar pointed out, raising a clawed finger for emphasis– 'I can regain access to the sacred grove at the heart of the herd's camp. I will need the power contained there to unlock the secrets of the Skull of Ehrenlish and learn how to open the Gate of Infinity.'

At which point you'll throw me to your herd and claim the temple's power for yourself, Malus reasoned. Of course, I am no stranger to treachery myself.

'Very well, Kul Hadar. We have an agreement. I and my warriors will gain you access to the grove, and you will reveal to me the secrets of the skull. And then?'

The shaman smiled, a slow revelation of cruel teeth. 'Why then, the power in the temple will be ours.'

'THIS IS MADNESS,' Lhunara said, leaning against the flank of her nauglir with arms folded and a defiant look in her eye. The rest of the warband had circled the nauglir and now clustered around to hear the news from their lord.

A chorus of guttural shouts went up from the bonfire near the centre of the camp. Evidently Hadar had passed word of his newfound alliance down to his champions. With all the noise, Malus could feel confident that they weren't being overheard.

'The plan is not without risk,' he conceded, 'but we need Hadar to unlock the gate, and he won't turn on us until he's pacified his rebellious herd. They aren't simply going to bow their heads the minute we've killed this Machuk and go on as though the rebellion never happened. Until Hadar has cemented his authority he will still need us, and there are ways we can keep the herd restive until we've learned what we need to know about the skull.'

Vanhir shook his head. 'We're not dealing with other druchii, my lord. It's not as though we can play one lord off against another with promises of succession, or stoke buried feuds to keep this herd at one another's throats.'

'No, but we can keep them angry at Hadar, enough that he remains uncertain of his authority,' Malus replied. 'From what he told me, the herd has resented him for years. They won't be happy returning to his rule, no matter how many warriors he has on hand.'

'But this time he can promise them the treasures of the temple,' Dalvar pointed out.

'He's promised them that in the past. They won't be convinced until he's shown them the treasure – and by that point we'll have learned what we need to know and beaten him to it.'

'And how exactly are we going to do that?' Lhunara inquired. 'None of us are sorcerers.'

'The skull is not leaving my possession,' Malus replied. 'I'll be there every moment Hadar is examining it. What he learns, I'll learn. I've already discovered that his protective wards don't work against me, thanks to Nagaira's talisman–' Malus tapped his breastplate over the spot where the magical orb rested, '–so it's possible I can kill him the moment I've learned what I need. Then we can escape.'

'With a horde of vengeful beastmen howling for our skins,' Vanhir muttered.

'Once I have the power within the temple, they'll have ample reason to howl, believe me.'

'My lord, do you actually know what this great power is?' Lhunara asked. 'Does anyone know?'

Malus fought a surge of anger. 'It's a power that two great sorcerers have spent years of effort and substantial wealth to acquire,' he said coldly. 'What more do we need to know? Great power finds a way to make itself felt, Lhunara. It will obey me as much as it would Urial or Hadar, and I will not hesitate to use it on my enemies. And besides that–' the highborn spread his arms to encompass the warband, 'think of the riches the temple holds. Wealth beyond your dreams. Enough to make each of you a lord in your own right. Think of that. When we make it inside you can take as much as your nauglir can carry. You have my oath on it.'

The gleam of naked avarice thawed the masks of uncertainty on many of the druchii's faces, Vanhir and Dalvar in particular. Lhunara gave a loud snort. 'Gold's not much use to a corpse,' she growled. 'But it's not as though this is open to a vote. You've decided, and that's that, and the Dark Mother be with us all. When do we ride?'

'We ride out tomorrow night, and strike at dawn,' Malus said. 'Until then, sharpen your blades and mend your armour. There's hard fighting ahead.'

Chapter Seventeen
SWORDS AT DAWN

THE SENTRY WALKED a predictable path, shuffling almost invisibly through the undergrowth from east to west and back again. Sloppy, Malus thought. He should be sitting somewhere with a good field of view and using those long ears of his instead of moving. It was clear that the herd felt it had little to fear from Kul Hadar or anyone else on the mountainside.

The druchii crouched low as the sentry approached. It was nearly dawn, and the attackers had been working their way through the woods for hours surrounding the herd's permanent camp. Already they had intercepted and killed a handful of Hadar's former followers; hunters returning with food for the following night and small packs of scouts hunting for Hadar and his exiles. Now it was the sentry's turn, and after that, the real fighting would begin.

The attacking force was split into three smaller, mixed groups of druchii and beastmen. This allowed the force to move more stealthily and cover more of the camp's perimeter, and provided each column with two or three druchii crossbows to silence unexpected threats. Malus, Vanhir and one of Dalvar's men marched with fifteen of Hadar's champions, led by a massive beast named Yaghan. Unlike the other beastmen Malus had seen, Yaghan and his warriors were all clad in knee-length coats of heavy bronze scales and greaves, and each wielded a huge, double-bitted axe. Surprisingly, for all their size and bulk, the champions moved silently and nimbly through the woods.

Hadar had pulled aside Yaghan shortly before leaving the exile camp and grunted a series of orders at the beastman. The champion followed Malus's hand signals and relayed orders to the rest of the champions without hesitation, but never without a burning glare of resentment in its small eyes.

The sentry's movements made little more than a faint rustle among the ferns and bushes beneath the tall trees – someone less alert might have mistaken the sound for the furtive movements of a fox. Malus kept himself still and watched the spaces between the trees carefully. Within a moment he caught a glimpse of the beastman's silhouette as he crossed from the shadow of one tree to the next. He was exactly where the highborn thought he would be. Malus raised the crossbow to his shoulder and waited.

The highborn listened to the scuff of hooves along the forest floor, following the invisible presence of the sentry with his eyes. The beastman crossed Malus's field of vision, almost to a large bramble bush some five yards away. The sentry took another few steps and stopped. For a moment, there was only silence. Then Malus heard the beastman sniff the air suspiciously.

Suddenly the bramble bush thrashed and shook, and Spite lunged at the beastman. In less time than it took to draw a breath, the nauglir snapped up the sentry and bit through his torso with a muffled crunch of bone. An arm and a head thumped softly across the ground and the cold one settled back on its haunches.

Malus grinned. 'All right. That's the last of them,' he whispered to his men. 'Get to your mounts. We're moving forward.'

The two druchii nodded and slipped silently forward to where their own nauglir waited. Malus turned to Yaghan and waved him ahead. The beastman glared at him and motioned its champions forward with a nod of its horned skull. We can only hope you'll come to a glorious and messy end here in the next few minutes, Malus thought coldly. Otherwise, you might be trouble later.

The attackers worked their way forward through the woods, drawn by the light of the bonfires now burning low in the centre of the camp. The habit of the herd was to eat and drink heavily towards the end of the night and sleep it off during the day. Already Malus could hear groans and low growls as tired, drunk beastmen staggered off to their tents or one of the caves that pocked this part of the mountainside.

According to Hadar, Machuk's tent was surrounded by those of his own champions farther up the slope, near the opening of the great cleft that Hadar called the sacred grove. That was where the attackers would find him just at dawn, and it was the job of the druchii to pave the way for Yaghan and his champions to reach the tents and take the usurper's head in Hadar's name.

Malus reached Spite, running his hand across the cold one's armoured flank. He checked first to make certain the nauglir had finished eating – forcing a cold one to give up his meal was begging for disaster. 'Up, Spite,' Malus whispered, prodding the cold one behind the foreleg with the pommel of his dagger. The nauglir rose to his feet and padded quietly forward.

The edge of the forest was a mere fifteen yards away. Already Malus could see the pale light of dawn brightening the dark sky over the mountain. Faintly, he could hear the shuffling movements of the other cold ones off to his right – they formed a loose line nearly five yards across, but the plan was to tighten up considerably once they'd broken cover. The shock value of the cold ones alone would be enough to keep most of the beastmen back, at least at the beginning, but any organised resistance had to be hit quickly and with maximum force before the enemy could regroup.

Malus climbed into the saddle and looked to the notch in the mountainside. Hadar had said that the first light of dawn would send a shaft of light down the cleft and would serve as the signal for the attack. The highborn twisted his left hand in the reins and slowly, quietly, drew his sword. Much depended on the outcome of the next few minutes. If his plan worked, he would have the upper hand on Hadar. If not…

Darkness faded in thin shades of grey, and a thin shaft of light shone down into the camp. Malus raised his sword and let out a long, ululating scream that was echoed along the line of trees. The highborn put his spurs to Spite's flanks, and the attack began.

The cold ones burst from the forest growth in an explosion of leaves and branches, stretching themselves into a run up the steep slope of the mountainside. Instinctively the knights marked one another's positions and nudged their mounts closer together, until the riders were less than a sword's length apart. Honed sword blades gleamed in the weak light, and a howl of shock and dismay went up from the camp. Malus grinned like a wolf at the prospects of spilled blood and slaughter.

True to Hadar's prediction, many lone beastmen scattered out of the way of the thundering knights, their eyes wide with surprise. Halfway up the slope, however, Malus caught sight of a large knot of warriors racing around the corner of a large tent, weapons held ready. Many looked to be deep in their cups, but they were nevertheless ready for a fight. The highborn levelled his sword at the mob of beastmen and the knights put the spurs to their mounts, going to a full gallop as they rushed to meet their foe.

The beastmen remained resolute until nearly the last moment, when the thundering menace of the charge caused several of the warriors in the front ranks to waver. They turned to their fellows and tried to push through their ranks, spreading more confusion and fear. The mob surged one way and then the other, trying to rally itself with shouts and angry barks, but by then it was too late. The seven knights struck the disordered mass like a hammer on glass.

Lhunara spurred Render to leap headlong into the mob, her two curved swords held high and her face a terrible mask of death. The swords flickered and sang as they sheared through muscle and bone, and beastmen reeled away in an arc before her, dead and dying from gruesome wounds in head, throat and chest. Beside her, Vanhir slew the panicked beastmen with swift, economical strokes, knocking weapons aside and shattering skulls with rhythmic precision. The knights swayed in their saddles as though riding the deck of a storm-tossed ship, fighting their foes as the cold ones beneath them twisted and lashed out at the tempting flesh surrounding them. Bones shattered beneath their powerful paws and bodies were flung into the air with every toss of their armoured heads.

Malus swept his sword in a vicious arc that hacked a beastman's skull open, spraying its fellows with blood and brain matter. Two other warriors were flung through the air by the impact of Spite's rush, and a third lost an arm and much of its shoulder to the nauglir's powerful jaws. A beastman struck the cold one a jarring blow on his left shoulder with a heavy, knotted club.

As the warrior drew back for another blow, Malus darted forward and jammed the point of his sword through the beastman's eye. The huge warrior fell backwards, almost dragging the blade from the highborn's grip, but Malus pulled the sword free with a convulsive wrench, the steel point ringing on bone. 'Forward!' Malus cried to his knights. 'Forward. Press on!' He dug his spurs into Spite's flanks and the cold one leapt ahead, scattering maimed and retreating beastmen left and right.

Hadar wanted to use the druchii cavalry as shock troops, brushing aside any early resistance so Yaghan and his champions would have a clear path to Machuk. Malus had no intention of giving Yaghan or any other beastman the opportunity to slay the usurper. That not only meant brushing aside the enemy as quickly as possible, but also required the druchii to beat the charging beastmen to Machuk's tent and defeat the herd's best troops in the space of a few minutes.

The beastmen scattered, howling in despair. Spite snapped at one retreating warrior and neatly snipped the horned head from the beastman's neck; the body continued to run a dozen paces more before collapsing. The knights broke from the press and carried on up the slope, bloody swords held ready.

Another small group of beastmen tried to block the druchii's path, rushing from behind the shadow of another large tent to take the riders in the flank. But the charge was ill-timed, appearing too soon, and Malus simply angled Spite into the mass, aiming the cold one for the largest brute in the crowd. The nauglir smashed his blunt head into the beast's chest and tossed him through the side of the nearby tent, while Malus leaned out from his saddle and slashed open the throat of another warrior with a swipe of his blade. He hauled on the reins and Spite cut to the left, trampling two more warriors before closing back into line with the other knights.

The usurper's tents were just up ahead – a large, round tent surrounded by a constellation of smaller ones, all made from thick animal hide and wood frames. Machuk and his champions waited there. The rush of the druchii cavalry left little doubt as to their ultimate objective, and the usurper had used his time to assemble his best warriors and arrange them in something resembling a formation.

Malus noted that the lead warriors hefted large swords and battle-axes, just like Yaghan and his men, and the beastmen looked like they knew how to use them. This is going to be grim work, Malus thought. If only I had the time for a few good crossbow volleys first – but that would give Yaghan the time he needs to climb the slope and join the fight, and I can't allow that.

Malus raised his sword and sought out the usurper Machuk among the ranks of beastmen. Hadar's former lieutenant was, if anything, even larger than the shaman, and unlike Hadar, Machuk wore heavy armour like Yaghan, and carried a large sword in his hands. He'll carve me like a roast with that cleaver, Malus thought. I'd best be quick and close if I'm going to beat him.

He pointed his sword at the beastman and howled a challenge, one the usurper angrily accepted. The highborn drew a long, needle-pointed dagger from his belt and let go of the reins just as the knights' charge crashed home.

Machuk's huge sword was fearsome but slow, a near-irresistible force that took time to get into motion. It was a matter of heartbeats at most, but fights were decided in such tiny, crucial increments. Using his knees, Malus swerved Spite to the left at the very last moment, just as the usurper drew back his sword, and the highborn leapt from the saddle, blades out, right for Machuk's chest.

The din of impact was incredible. The champions held their ground, and the sound of the cold ones smashing against their line was a thunderous crash of flesh and steel. Blood sprayed in the air from friend and foe alike. Malus barrelled into Machuk, throwing his sword arm around the usurper's neck and stabbing at the beastman's throat with his keen dagger. The needle point danced across the thick bronze scales covering Machuk's neck and shoulder, and the huge beastman bellowed in rage, fanged mouth inches from the druchii's own neck.

Dark Mother preserve me, Malus thought. That didn't go according to plan.

The highborn clutched Machuk in a deadly embrace, his feet dangling nearly a foot from the ground as he pinned the beastman's left arm against his chest. Machuk thrashed and heaved with his trapped arm and the highborn's body bucked in the air, his feet going parallel to the ground. Malus held onto the beastman's neck for dear life, still trying to find a weak point with his knife. The point struck a leather and bronze collar guarding the usurper's neck and the tip broke off against a metal boss.

Machuk let go of his great sword with his left hand, grabbed Malus by the neck and slammed his thick, horned skull into the highborn's forehead.

The next thing Malus knew he was crashing to the ground. He landed on his back against the packed earth and skidded several feet, half-blind with pain. It felt like his skull had cracked like a boiled egg. Dimly, he heard a roar, and knew that Machuk was almost upon him, sword held high. Move. *Move!* his mind railed.

On instinct, he rolled to the right, and the beastman's huge sword struck him a glancing blow across his pauldron; the shoulder guard crumpled under the blow and a spike of searing pain shot across Malus's chest. He roared in shock and anger, and the highborn's vision returned as the red rage of battle-lust consumed him.

Malus rolled again – this time forwards, towards the towering figure of the beastman. Once again he placed himself within the powerful arc of the usurper's massive sword, and the highborn found himself staring up at Machuk's armoured calves and a gap of bare thigh between greave and scale coat. He lunged with his sword and the point bit deep in the beastman's right thigh, severing flesh and muscle and spilling a stream of thick, dark blood.

A less-experienced fighter would have retreated from such an attack, but Machuk was a hardened veteran. He roared his fury at the highborn and brought his left foot down on Malus's chest, pinning him in place. Then the great sword raised skyward and plunged like a thunderbolt.

The only thing that saved Malus was that he was so much smaller than the beastman and presented a poor target in his current position. Machuk struck at Malus's waist, and at the last moment the druchii rolled as far onto his hip as he could. Fully a third of the sword buried itself into the ground, but the blade struck the articulated steel plates covering his hip and bit through them. The blade's edge felt like ice beneath his skin; then the sensation was lost in the shock of the blow and the hot surge of blood and pain.

Malus snarled like a maddened beast, dropped his sword and scrabbled for the pommel of the knife jutting from his right boot. With a convulsive heave he bent far enough forward to snag the small knife and pull it free. As Machuk brought his sword up for another devastating blow, Malus drove the dagger into the back of the beastman's left knee, sawing the blade left and right through the cable-like hamstring.

Machuk screamed in fury and toppled onto Malus, his left knee smashing into the highborn's face. Blood spurted from the druchii's nose and lips, and for a moment he knew nothing but the ringing in his head and a world of red-shot blackness. The beastman's knee was still in his face, and the highborn blindly stabbed upwards with the small knife, plunging it again and again into Machuk's groin. The beastman screamed, now a tortured wail of agony, and fell forward, taking his weight off Malus. The highborn rolled away, blinking in an attempt to restore his vision.

When his sight cleared a moment later, there were two of Machuk's champions standing over him as they tried to reach their stricken lord. One bent down and grabbed a fistful of Malus's hair, pulling his head back and exposing his neck as he raised his ponderous axe one-handed. Suddenly there was a flash of light and a dagger sprouted from the beastman's eye. The champion froze, his expression one of mild surprise, and then he toppled to the side.

The second champion had pushed past and was trying to help Machuk to his feet. Malus snarled in rage and lurched to his feet. His left hip blazed in pain and his leg collapsed beneath him, causing him to fall heavily against the beastman. Before the champion could react, Malus drove his small knife into the beastman's exposed neck, sawing forward to sever the thick veins in a torrent of hot, bright blood. The champion let out a choking gasp and fell to one side, and Malus threw himself onto Machuk's back.

The usurper's wounds were mortal. Arterial blood pumped steadily from the cut to his thigh, and a huge pool of blood and fluids spread from the stab wounds in his groin. Still, Machuk was struggling to regain his feet, his thick arms trembling with effort. He didn't seem to notice the highborn's extra weight at all.

Malus caught sight of Machuck's sword off to the side, and snagged its pommel with his fingertips. He pulled the blade to him and raised its ponderous weight above his head. 'Well fought, Machuk,' he croaked through swollen lips, and brought the sword down with all his remaining strength. The heavy blade cut into the side of Machuk's neck and buried itself in his spine. The usurper gave a gasp from compressed lungs and collapsed face-first onto the blood-soaked ground. With a savage cry Malus pulled the sword free and struck once again, and Machuk's bloody head rolled across the grass.

There was a roar of fury from farther down the slope. Yaghan and his men had arrived, and the champion glared at Malus with undisguised rage. The highborn gave the champion a bloodied, bestial smile. Too late, Yaghan, he thought. Too late. He tangled his fingers in the tuft of fur atop Machuk's forehead and lifted the dripping trophy high.

'Glory to the Dark Mother and the Hag!' Malus cried, and heard his companions take up the shout in the melee around him.

A cry of despair went up from the surviving champions as they realised their leader was dead. Malus sensed rather than saw their ranks waver around him, and then a booming voice echoed across the field. Kul Hadar had appeared, striding up the slope with his staff held high. The highborn couldn't understand a word the creature was saying, but the intent was clear: The king is dead. Long live the king.

The sounds of fighting dwindled abruptly, punctuated by sharp cries from the druchii as they fought to rein in their battle-frenzied mounts. Malus thrust Machuk's sword point-first into the ground and used it to push himself painfully to his feet. He could feel blood seeping down his left leg and pooling in his boot, and his left arm was already swelling and growing stiff. He spat blood onto the ground and took slow, methodical steps towards Kul Hadar.

The shaman was turning slowly on the spot, levelling his fierce gaze at each and every member of the herd he could see. He continued to address the beastmen in low, sonorous tones, clearly laying down the new law of the herd in the wake of Machuk's demise.

Malus stood beside the shaman, raising the usurper's severed head for all to see despite the quaking of his wounded arm. The gathering herd took in the scene with various expressions, ranging from delight to dismay to weary resignation. Their stares alternated between Hadar, Machuk's head, and Malus himself. The highborn kept his gaze neutral, but his bloodied expression was none the less fierce for it.

At length Hadar turned to Malus. The shaman's bestial visage made it hard to discern his expression, but the highborn assumed that Hadar was trying to appear studiously grave for the benefit of the herd. 'This was not the plan, druchii,' the shaman hissed. 'Machuk was to be killed by my champion Yaghan! You knew this!'

Malus met the shaman's gaze calmly. 'Resistance was lighter than expected, great Hadar. I and my men reached Machuk first, and he wasn't in a mood to wait.' He offered the usurper's head to the shaman. 'The end result is the same, is it not? He is dead, and you rule the herd once more.' Though you rule by virtue of me and my men, and your herd knows it, he thought. And that gives me leverage to keep your own treacherous knives at bay.

Hadar ground his teeth in evident frustration, but within a moment he had mastered himself and took the severed head from Malus's hand. He raised it high before the herd and howled, and the assembled beastmen dropped to their knees, pressing their foreheads to the ground. He then handed it to Yaghan, and began barking orders to his champions.

As the battle-lust faded, Malus became more and more aware of his surroundings. Fully half of Machuk's champions lay on the blood-soaked ground, hacked and hewn or crushed by powerful blows. Two nauglir and their riders also lay amid the bodies of the foe, the armoured druchii and their mounts split apart by the champions' heavy swords and axes. The sun was still not fully risen – in all, perhaps five or six minutes had passed from the moment the druchii's charge began.

Malus turned and sought out Lhunara and Vanhir. They both stood nearby, splashed with blood and bits of flesh, but otherwise uninjured. The sight of them made the highborn feel a peculiar sense of relief. 'Lhunara, gather the men and take the nauglir back down the slope,' he said, the words slurred somewhat by his swollen lips. 'It would be impolitic if they started feasting on the fallen warriors here in the middle of camp. Take Spite as well – I don't know that I can walk so well at the moment.'

Lhunara frowned with concern, starting to realise that much of the blood covering the highborn's armour was in fact his. 'We should tend to your injuries, my lord–'

'Do as I say, woman,' he said, though the command had little heat behind it. At the moment, all he wanted to do was find somewhere to sit and rest, but there was still much to be done. As the retainers gathered their mounts and headed down the mountain slope, the highborn turned to find Kul Hadar waiting nearby. There was an expectant look on the shaman's face.

Malus summoned up a conciliatory smile. 'My congratulations on your victory, great Hadar,' he said, wincing in pain as he limped closer to the beastman. 'I expect you will need some time to sort things out with the herd before we may begin to plumb the secrets of the skull.'

But the highborn was surprised when the shaman bared his teeth and barked a guttural laugh. 'All that needs saying has been said, druchii,' Hadar replied. 'The herd belongs to me once more, and the moment I have waited decades for is at hand. We will not linger a moment longer, lord Malus. No, the time is now. We will go into the sacred grove and attain the key to the Gate of Infinity.'

Chapter Eighteen
TREACHERY

MALUS FORCED HIS mind to concentrate despite the fatigue and the waves of pain that dogged him with every halting step. The climb up the steep mountain slope was torturous, even using Machuk's sword as a makeshift cane. The highborn had recovered the skull from his saddlebag and carried it tucked beneath his left arm. Lhunara and Dalvar had tried to patch his wounds as best they could, but there was little they could do as long as he was buckled into his armour.

Now he and Hadar walked alone, striding purposefully toward the great cleft that split the mountainside. Yaghan and four of his champions walked a respectful distance behind the pair, laughing and boasting of their exploits in their guttural tongue.

He hadn't expected Hadar to move so quickly in the wake of the battle. Was it a matter of greed, or was he intent on catching Malus off-balance? Likely both, the druchii reasoned. He seeks to regain the initiative while I'm tired and injured. A sensible enough tactic, he thought, but it won't avail him much. When Malus had recovered the skull, he'd asked Vanhir for a strip of courva from his dwindling store. He'd chewed the piece of root mechanically, his eyes narrowing at the shockingly bitter taste. His mind was clearing though, moment by moment, growing ever sharper as the stimulant took hold. He forced himself to look around and take in his surroundings, anything to stimulate his numbed mind.

They were high enough up the slope that he had a panoramic view of the forest stretching off to the left and right around the base of the mountain. Malus could also see another, smaller mountain rising farther to the right, and in between a heavily wooded valley, still wreathed in mist. He nodded towards the valley. 'Is that–'

'Yes. The Temple of Tz'arkan lies there,' Hadar said. 'A road of skulls winds through the valley, and at the end lies the Gate of Infinity. Beyond the gate, in a space not entirely our own, lies the great temple.'

Malus stifled a groan. Damn sorcerers and their mind-twisting creations! 'When was the temple built?'

'Millennia ago,' Hadar grunted. 'During the days when your people fought the children of the Ruinous Powers, or possibly even before. Five great sorcerers, mighty servants of the Dark Gods, conspired to bind a great power into their service. They plotted and schemed for more than a hundred years, so the story goes, and in the end they bound the power behind the walls of the great temple and bent it to their will. With it, they became conquerors, cutting a great swathe across the war-torn world.'

Malus grinned hungrily, his heart quickening with anticipation. Soon, that great power would be his. *And to think I merely sought this place to slake my thirst for revenge,* he thought. *What else could I achieve with this power in my grasp?* He saw himself sitting in the Court of Thorns, encased in the drachau's armour and wearing the Claw of Night, steam rising behind the boiling red glow of his eyes as all the highborn of the city bent their knee and submitted themselves to his tortures.

The highborn saw a great army on the march with him at its head, crossing the waves to blighted Ulthuan and dashing their great cities into ruin. He saw himself in dark Naggarond, fortress of the Witch King, seated on a throne of dragon bone…

'Over time, however, fortune deserted each sorcerer in turn. They were betrayed by their companions, or their own lieutenants, or grew overconfident and were bested on the battlefield. One by one they were destroyed, but the power in the temple remained. When the last sorcerer fell, the Temple of Tz'arkan was forgotten, its secrets guarded by the most terrible of magical wards.' Hadar glanced at Malus, and once again offered him a cruel, fanged smile. 'Until now.'

They had reached the mouth of the great cleft. Up close, it was much broader than Malus expected, and widened even further as it went. Soil had settled into the crevice over the aeons and given life to dark green grass and tall, glossy-leaved trees. There was a deep humming in the air, much as Malus had felt in the exile camp, only much stronger and more intense. The trees rustled quietly at their approach, though the highborn noted that there wasn't so much as a breath of wind.

Hadar paused at the entrance to the cleft and planted his staff. 'This is our sacred grove,' the shaman said in a reverent voice. 'Here lies the source of all our power. Walk softly here, druchii. Until this day no living thing not of our race has entered here and survived.' The shaman bowed his horned head and rumbled something that sounded like a prayer, and then he pressed on.

There was a faint path of sorts that wound among the trees. Hadar followed it with the ease of long familiarity, and Malus was left to limp painfully in his wake. As they climbed up the cleft, Malus noticed that the great trees were covered in black, shiny vines that sprouted hundreds of needle-like thorns. Clusters of bones lay at the foot of each tree, some weathered by the elements and others fresh and glistening with bits of fat and gristle. Malus eyed the wood with much greater respect than before.

They walked along the path for several long minutes until Malus spied the first of the glowing crystals. The greenish rock sprouted from the ground just like the one in Hadar's cave, and Malus sensed that the formations were the source of the powerful vibrations he felt along his bones. 'What gives these stones such power, great Hadar?'

'They are gifts from the Dark Gods,' Hadar said proudly. 'The herds can hear their powerful song for leagues across the earth, and we seek them out for the power they give us. The stones make us very strong; when we feel their song in our bones we can work great magics, far more potent than your pitiful sorceries. When we stretch forth our hand, the earth and sky bend to our will!'

The shaman swept his hand in a broad arc, taking in the whole of the mountain cleft. 'A tribe is considered mighty indeed if its grove boasts three of the great stones. Here, on the mountain blessed by the God of the Axe, we have nearly a dozen. When I first led my herd here they celebrated for a fortnight, chanting my name to the dark sky. They believed I was favoured of the gods, to have led us to such power.' Hadar chuckled deep in his throat. 'The conquests, the slaughter, the terrible destruction I could have wrought. I could have bent the other herds to my will and ruled as no other of my kind had ruled for thousands of years. But I did not.' The shaman turned his horned head and fixed Malus with one dark eye. 'I did not, because I knew I stood at the threshold of a greater power still.'

The farther they went, the more crystals Malus saw, their luminescence increasing until he could feel it against his bare skin like the warm glow of the sun. The highborn also began to notice crude stone obelisks carved with spiky runes and sigils arranged around the crystal formations, and long poles hung with the rotting figures of beastman sacrifices. Old bones rattled in a nonexistent wind, and the smell of leather and rot hung in the air.

A few minutes later they reached a circle of standing stones, leaning precariously together on the steep slope. Outside the circle was a great bronze gong with a striker leaning beside it. Within the circle lay a stone floor made from slate tiles, its centre stained from years of spilled blood. Long lines of runes ran the length of each of the stones, laid atop the faint lines of carvings that were far older still. Malus sensed that Hadar's herd was not the first to claim this cleft and its power for their own.

Hadar stepped to the gong and picked up the striker. He struck the metal disk three times, slowly and purposefully, then he inclined his head to a point above the standing stones. Malus followed his gaze and saw that the far end of the cleft was surprisingly near, narrowing to a dark opening that appeared to be the mouth of a cave. The echoes bounced along the walls of the cleft and then faded to silence. The dark trees rustled, then fell still.

Moments later Malus caught a glimpse of movement within the cleft. A line of robed and cowled beastmen emerged from the darkness, bearing ceremonial staves and censers of beaten brass, jars of powders and tall coloured bottles of strange liquids. They descended without a sound, seeming to glide effortlessly down the steep slope toward the standing stones. Hadar bowed his head reverently at their approach.

Malus leaned heavily on Machuk's sword, suddenly uneasy. What good were powders and potions when the knowledge they sought was bound up in an ancient skull? 'What do we do now?' he asked.

Kul Hadar glanced sidelong at him, a flash of annoyance in his dark eyes. 'Now we call upon the shade of Ehrenlish, you fool.'

The highborn's brows narrowed in consternation. 'His shade?'

The shaman turned, his lips pulling back in a sneer. 'How did you come so far, knowing so little?' The shaman pointed gravely at the skull in Malus's hands. 'That is the skull of Ehrenlish, the greatest of the five sorcerers who mastered the power of the temple. He, last of his cabal, sensed that soon he would suffer the same fate as his fellows, and sought to cheat death by sorcerously binding his soul to his very bones.'

The shaman chuckled. 'But in the end the fool had crafted himself a most horrible prison. His head was struck from his neck by a rival and his body ground to dust. The great sorcerer then became a trophy to be passed from one hand to another for hundreds of years, his dreams of glory long forgotten.' Hadar took a step forward. 'But the secret to unlocking the gate remains bound within those old bones, and we will make Ehrenlish tell it to us.'

The highborn's mind raced, struggling with the implications. 'How then will you draw out the ghost and make him speak?' he asked numbly.

Kul Hadar smiled, his outstretched hand clenching into a gnarled fist. 'Why, we will give him your mouth to speak with, druchii.'

Bolts of green fire leapt from the shaman's hand. Malus instinctively threw himself to one side, the hair on his neck standing on end as the magical energies sizzled through the space where he'd been standing. Terror and rage seethed through his veins, banishing pain and weariness, and Malus scrambled back down the slope, lurching from one crystal formation to the next. Another volley of magical bolts slammed into the ground in his wake, burning dark holes into the grassy soil. Sorcerous thunder boomed and rattled down the cleft.

Malus ducked close to a crystal outcropping. A green bolt struck it in a shower of sparks, and shouting erupted among Hadar and the robed priests. Think, Malus, think! The highborn's brain worked furiously, trying to think of a way out. He felt a warm lump beneath the edge of his breastplate. Nagaira's talisman. Perhaps that's been throwing off Hadar's aim.

He paused for a moment to catch his breath, listening to the robed priests rushing down the slope after him. Malus considered his options, and none of them were good. The bastard has been planning this all along, he thought ruefully. No wonder he accepted my change of plans so easily. He knew it wouldn't matter once he'd got me up here.

The highborn planted Machuk's great sword in the ground. He pulled out his trusty boot knife with one hand, while the other fished out his sister's talisman. A plan fell into place. Good thing Lhunara isn't here to see this, he thought wildly. She'd tell me this was suicide – as though that weren't perfectly obvious.

Malus leapt from behind the crystal, drawing back his knife hand. He sought out Kul Hadar and hurled the dagger just as the shaman unleashed another storm of magical bolts. The sizzling energies struck the knife and knocked it aside with a bright spark and a clap of thunder. Well, so much for that, the highborn thought.

The priests rushed at him from left and right, their hands reaching for his arms. Malus ducked beneath the first one's clutches and rammed his fist into the beast's gut. The robed beastman doubled over, tumbling into the path of his compatriot, and the two went down in a tangle of limbs. Thank the Dark Mother they aren't all like Machuk, Malus thought. He turned back and snatched up the great sword, swinging it in a vicious arc that kept the remaining priests at bay as he backed swiftly down the slope.

Then the air turned bright green and sizzling energies struck Malus's chest. He went rigid as the sorcerous fire coursed along his limbs. The highborn's lips drew back in a silent scream of agony. The talisman hanging from his neck turned a bright red as it tried to hold off Kul

Hadar's power, until the crystal orb shattered in a bright flash of light and a sharp crack.

Malus was hurled off his feet, tumbling a long way down the steep slope before sliding to a stop. The great sword was still in his bloodied hand as he rolled painfully to his feet. Thanks for the boost, the high-born thought wildly, and broke into a lurching run.

He rounded the first turn in the path and almost ran into Yaghan and his champions running the other way. Yaghan saw Malus and roared out a command, and the other warriors immediately moved to surround the highborn. Snarling, Malus leapt at Yaghan, swinging the heavy blade at the beastman's chest, but the champion blocked the blow easily with the broad head of his axe. Another beastman lunged in and clouted Malus on the side of the head with the pommel of his own great sword, and the highborn swayed on his feet, blinking at the stars crowding his vision.

The beastman to the right, emboldened by his friends, rushed at the stunned druchii, but Malus wasn't as disoriented as he had let on. When the champion got close, he drove the point of his sword into the arch of the beastman's foot. When the champion's rush faltered in a bellow of pain, the highborn pulled the sword free and brought it up into the beastman's chin. Blood and teeth flew and the beastman fell backwards with a scream, lashing out wildly with his sword.

Malus ducked the blow easily and slashed at the champion with his heavy sword, tearing open the beastman's abdomen and spilling his steaming entrails onto the ground. The champion collapsed to the grass, clutching vainly at his intestines as Malus broke from the circle, edging around Yaghan so he could reach the downhill path.

He'd taken two steps when something powerful crashed into the centre of his back and knocked him headlong. The point of the great sword lodged in the ground and was wrenched from his grip as he hit the path face first. Pain bloomed from his nose and chin and blood spilled down over his lips, but Malus was already trying to get his legs underneath him and spring back upright.

Another massive blow smashed into his side, flipping him easily onto his back. One of Yaghan's champions stood over him, bellowing a throaty laugh as it wielded a massive club as though it were nothing more than a willow switch. The beastman brought the gnarled length of wood crashing down on the highborn's chest and the armour flexed beneath the blow. Malus felt his ribs bend, and all the air rushed from his lungs.

Leering fiercely, the champion planted a chipped hoof squarely in the centre of the highborn's breastplate and set the knotty end of his club on Malus's forehead. The beastman leaned forward, putting all his weight on the club, and Malus gritted his teeth against the slowly spreading bloom of pain. Drawing back his right leg almost to his chest, the highborn lashed out as hard as he could, driving the heel of his boot into the beastman's groin twice in rapid succession. The champion howled and its knees buckled, and Malus rolled swiftly to the side as the beastman crashed to the ground.

Malus scrambled to his feet and turned back just long enough to kick the downed champion in the face before dashing once more for the path. The moment of spite cost him, however. A broad hand closed on the back of the highborn's neck, and suddenly he found himself being propelled at a dead run towards the black-boled trees on the opposite side of the path. His arms flailed wildly, vainly seeking a target, until his foot struck a half-buried stone and he stumbled forwards, fetching up against the bole of a vine-covered tree. Instantly the dark tendrils slithered like snakes, writhing down the glossy bark to wrap themselves around his throat. The needle-like thorns sank deep into his flesh, and immediately his skin burned with the touch of some insidious toxin. His throat swelled from within even as the vine tightened around him, closing off the passage of both air and blood.

The highborn fumbled for a knife to cut himself free, but already his vision was narrowing. There was a buzzing in his ears. His fingers closed on the pommel of his belt knife and he gripped at it spasmodically, but the weapon refused to come free of its sheath.

There were dark figures floating towards him, hands outstretched. Beyond them he could see a huge, horned figure, green fire playing between his hands, and the coarse, braying laughter of Yaghan and his champions. Malus felt the priests' hands on him, and the vine tightened even more possessively, refusing to give up its meal. With one last burst of strength, the highborn tugged his dagger free, but he could no longer see where to cut.

Malus thrust the knife into the belly of one of the priests just as darkness rose up to embrace him.

Chapter Nineteen
THE GATE OF INFINITY

WHEN MALUS AWOKE he hung within the circle of stones, bound aloft by hissing loops of sorcerous fire.

The energies held him immobile and suffused his body with dull agony. His every muscle was tensed, as if unconsciously fighting the forces working on it. His throat was no longer swollen. He'd been arranged so that the Skull of Ehrenlish rested in the palms of his hands, clasped together at his waist. His head was forced slightly back, giving him a glimpse of the sky – from what he could tell, very little time had passed since he'd succumbed to the terrible vines. He could sense the priests forming a circle around him, murmuring a chant in low, guttural tones. The Dark Mother grant there's one less of them than there was before, he thought fiercely.

Then he felt a shadow fall over him, and Malus saw the towering form of Kul Hadar, taking his place at the head of the priests' ritual circle. The shaman had set aside his great staff, raising both hands to the sky. A low growl began deep in the beastman's throat, swelling to a powerful rumble that took the shape of guttural words. Power crackled from the shaman's lips, and Malus could make out the name Ehrenlish.

The skull quivered in Malus's grasp. Though he couldn't see the relic, he could sense that it was beginning to glow with a light of its own as the shaman called the ghost of the sorcerer forth.

The relic grew warm in his hands. There was a buzzing in the air, like an angry swarm of bees. Was it a physical sound, or a vibration trembling along his bones? Suddenly there was a jolt that shook his entire body, then another. A burning, tingling energy seethed against his belly and tried to push its way inside him. The shaman was forcing the spirit of Ehrenlish into his body. It was similar to the sensation he'd felt in the Wighthallows, only slower and more purposeful, like a dagger sinking inch by inch into his flesh. He gritted his teeth in rage and mustered his will against this unwanted invasion, but he was powerless to stop the inexorable violation of his body.

Dark power seeped slowly into his abdomen, staining his guts with the taint of psychic corruption. His stomach rebelled at the cold, gelid touch, but his body could not expel it no matter how hard he tried. Malus shrieked in impotent rage, and the shade of Ehrenlish crept like a spider along his bones.

The spirit soaked into him on a tide of madness and hate. Visions filled the highborn's mind – visions of otherworldly planes that clawed at his sanity and froze his soul. His heart writhed with worms and his veins filled with corruption. The sorcerer leaked inexorably into his skull, twisting and writhing like a serpent and probing into the dark recesses where all his secrets lay.

Then Hadar shouted a command, and Ehrenlish recoiled as though struck by a physical blow. Words clawed their way through Malus's mouth, savage, hateful curses for the animal that dared to command a champion of the Ruinous Powers. Malus raged and wailed in the remote corners of his mind as the battle between sorcerers was joined. Kul Hadar bent his will against Ehrenlish, and every blow reverberated through the highborn's body in waves of brilliant pain.

The struggle stretched for an eternity, with neither side yielding to the other. Ehrenlish roared his defiance with Malus's mouth, and the skies above roiled and thundered in response. The shade spat streams of curses that curdled the air, but each time Hadar lashed back, Malus could sense the fear in Ehrenlish's spirit.

He'd sensed that terror before, back in the Wighthallows, when the skull had fallen into his grasp, though at the time he hadn't know what the savage jolt had really meant. For all the shade's power, it also feared the darkness that waited beyond the confines of its magical prison. Ehrenlish had been an ancient and terrible force long before he had gathered his cabal to bind the power within the temple to his will. He had made many dark and fearsome pacts with things far more ancient and terrible than he, and they still waited for the reckoning that was their due. If Hadar pressed too hard, Ehrenlish would give anything to stave off his dissolution.

Malus wondered if his body would give out before the sorcerer's will finally broke.

Hadar lashed at Ehrenlish with blasphemous words of power, and the shade responded in kind. Malus felt his throat tearing beneath the force of the fearsome curses. Heat shimmered in the air over the standing stones, and Malus could see the strain evident on the beastman's face. But years of obsession lent Hadar a fevered will that seemed to match Ehrenlish blow for blow, and the highborn could sense the sorcerer beginning to weaken.

His fingers and toes were beginning to burn. Malus could feel the heat flowing from his extremities as his body tried to cope with the awesome energies coursing through it. He was being consumed like a candle, burnt from both ends, as the two sorcerers raged on, oblivious to his fate.

Malus heard screams in the air. Screams? At first he thought it was his own maddened thoughts deceiving him, but after a moment, he realised that Hadar's voice had faltered, and the cries of pain warred with Ehrenlish's shouted blasphemies.

A shadow fell across the standing stones – no, not *across* it, but *into* it, rushing up amid the priests from the lower slope. Hadar reared back, shouting in rage, and then one of Urial's riders stepped into the ritual circle, reaching for the skull in Malus's hand.

The world shook and the sky split with a cataclysmic crash of thunder, and Ehrenlish shrieked as the pent-up energies of the ritual exploded in a storm of ravening green fire.

In pain there is life. In darkness, endless strength.

The old catechism echoed from some dark part of Malus's mind. He lay in blackness. His body felt shattered like a pot in a kiln, smoking fragments scattered beyond his reach. And yet, in the darkness, a mote of the highborn's will still lingered. And slowly, bit by bit, gathering strength and speed, Malus knit himself back together.

When his vision returned, Malus found himself lying on his side, fetched up against one of the standing stones. The skull of Ehrenlish lay nearby, the bone blackened and the silver wire partly melted from a blast of intense heat. Many of the stones had been blown apart, jagged shards scything like knives through the bodies of the priests, who lay burned and ravaged all around the circle. Surprisingly, Kul Hadar still stood, his massive form wreathed in smoke. He was stunned and reeling from the blast, but his sorceries had somehow protected him from the worst of its force.

Malus couldn't think of a single reason why he'd survived, but at the moment he had far more pressing things on his mind.

It had been a desperate gamble, brandishing Nagaira's talisman. The moment it was broken he suspected Urial's hunters would be able to sense the location of the skull and then race to claim it. Malus's faith in his half-brother's single-minded hate had been borne out once again. Urial had made his minions well.

Malus had got the violent diversion he wanted. Now he just had to escape it in one piece.

The rider who'd single-mindedly breached the circle had somehow survived – the pale, ravaged figure was pulling its shattered body across the slate tiles towards Malus on the burnt stumps of its forearms. Its clothing and much of its skin had burned away in the blast, but the eyeless, blackened skull was focused on Malus with unerring, murderous intent.

Malus tried to stand, his limbs weak and pitifully uncoordinated. His feet writhed weakly on the steaming tiles as the revenant crept closer. Malus could hear the seared flesh of the rider's arms sizzling on the hot slate. With a savage cry the highborn pushed his armoured body across the stone, burning his own bare hands in the process, and snatched up the blackened skull as he forced himself out of the ritual circle. The more he moved, the more strength returned to his body; after crawling only a few feet across the bare earth, he found that he could stagger painfully to his feet.

Surprisingly, he found that the wounds on his hip and arm didn't pain him nearly as much as they had before. He suspected it was Ehrenlish's doing – the shade's fear of dissolution was so great it might have reflexively repaired the worst of his injuries to ensure his continued survival during the forced possession.

There was a battle raging in the grove. As Malus's senses returned he realised that the beastman herd had reacted violently to the arrival of the riders and their invasion of the sacred grove. Yaghan and his champions had pursued the riders into the cleft and now their great weapons and fearsome stamina posed a real challenge for the revenants. The riders had been stunned by the magical blast, and now the beastmen had them surrounded.

Dark horses reared and lashed out with bloody hooves, and their dismounted riders wove a deadly web of steel with spear and sword, but for each beastman that fell, a rider took a grievous wound in return. Already two horses thrashed impotently on the ground, their legs sheared away, and one of the riders had fallen once and for all when his head was severed from his neck.

Malus watched a rider surrounded by beastmen plunge his sword through one of the huge warriors, but the mortally wounded beastman only rocked back on its heels and gripped the rider's skull in its massive hands. The beastman squeezed, and blood began to spurt sluggishly between its fingers as it slowly crushed the revenant's skull.

The highborn heard a furious bellow and a savage peal of thunder to his right, and glanced over to see Kul Hadar savaging the crippled rider in the circle with bolts of searing green fire. Arcs of seething energy cut into the revenant like blazing knives, carving the figure into a dozen smoking pieces and scoring red-hot lines into the slate beneath. The berserk fury of the beastmen at the invasion of their grove had eclipsed all pretence of reason, handing Malus an opportunity that he knew would not last for long. The problem was the path down the cleft was packed with a mob of furious beastmen and sorcerous riders.

Malus closed his eyes and took a deep breath, summoning what little strength he had left. His hand fumbled for the sword at his hip. Drawing the blade, he hurled himself forward, running headlong down the slope. He raced past the oblivious beastmen and plunged full-tilt into the midst of the bloodthirsty trees that lined one side of the twisting path.

The hungry wood exploded into sinuous motion as he hurtled between the trees. He leapt every root that reared up in his path. Once he lost his footing and threw himself into a long, bouncing tumble, eventually leaping back onto his feet. As long as he kept moving, part of his mind desperately reasoned, the vines could not move fast enough to get a grip on him. At one point he burst from the trees and across a curving part of the path, running between a crowd of surprised beastmen before disappearing into the trees on the other side.

Thorns lashed at his face and hands, their poison burning across his skin, but to one who'd coated himself in poison for most of his adult life, the force of the toxin had little effect so long as it wasn't concentrated around his throat. His wild plunge seemed to last for hours, but only minutes passed before Malus burst from the hungry forest at the base of the cleft.

The highborn shoved his way through the crowd of beastmen gathered below the path and ran on down the slope, casting about wildly for his warriors. 'Warriors of the Hag!' he cried, his voice sounding high and wild. 'Mount up!'

Malus heard Spite's familiar bellow at the very bottom of the slope. In moments he had reached his warband, every one armed and mounted. Their faces went white with shock as they saw the ravaged, lurching form of their lord. Without a word, the highborn threw himself into the saddle.

'My lord!' Lhunara cried. 'What happened? We saw the riders – they swept past us as though we didn't exist and charged up the slope with the whole herd baying at their tail.' Her face went pale when she saw the look on Malus's face. 'What did Hadar do to you?'

Malus leaned drunkenly in his saddle. His body began to tremble, then quake, and he bent double over Spite's neck. The retainers watched him with deep concern as racking gasps welled up from deep inside his chest.

Then the highborn threw back his head and laughed with the mad glee of the damned. 'Hadar has given me the key to the gate!' the highborn cried. 'The great fool! He'd have been wiser to have cut my throat than give me such a glimpse into Ehrenlish's soul!' He dropped the skull in his saddlebag and grabbed up his reins. 'Quickly now! We must ride for the valley while we can. Once Urial's riders are finished, Kul Hadar will come at us with everything he has!'

Just then a great, angry shout echoed down from the mountain cleft, and Malus knew at once that his diversion was finished as Hadar realised that the highborn had escaped. 'Forward!' Malus cried hungrily, and put his spurs to Spite's flank. With a wild cry the warband leapt after their lord, thinking him mad but also sensing that their long hunt was nearly at an end.

MALUS EXPECTED TO find a well-worn path leading from the camp through the forest to the road of skulls that wound up the valley. As it happened he was mistaken, and it was an error that nearly cost him his life.

The warband skirted the edge of the camp, riding along the tree-line looking for a path. After nearly half a mile the slope of the mountain bulged outwards, creating a high ridge too steep for the nauglir to climb, and the forest at that point was extremely thick with brambles and close-set trees.

With a curse, Malus turned the warband around and raced back the way they'd come, looking for less dense woodland to work through. On the way back he saw the beastmen coming on at a run – the entire herd, some three hundred strong, led by Yaghan and the surviving champions. They were all howling for blood, incensed at the defilement of their sacred grove. Malus hauled on the reins and cut left, driving Spite into the first relatively passable stretch of woodland he saw.

Even then, it was slow and difficult going. Spite bucked and plunged through the undergrowth, and Malus bent low over the cold one's neck, pressing his face against the scales of the nauglir's back. The rest of the warband followed in his wake, plunging blindly ahead without a clue as to where they were going. After a time Malus began curving the cold one's path back to the left, resuming a general course back towards the valley.

By this time, however, the woods were full of howls and hunting cries as the herd plunged headlong into the forest to cut the druchii off from their intended goal. The shouts seemed to echo all around the beleaguered warband, and Malus watched along either of Spite's flanks, fearing they might be surrounded at any moment.

Fortunately, the thick woods had a similar effect even on the woods-wise beastmen – in their rage they plunged into the thick undergrowth and quickly became scattered, hunting beneath the trees singly or in small packs. More than once Malus and Spite burst through the tangled foliage into the midst of a group of beastmen; those caught in the nauglir's path were crushed beneath the cold one's feet or smashed from their feet by the beast's head or shoulders. Any the cold one missed felt the edge of the highborn's sword, leaving a trail of bloody bodies and stunned survivors in its wake.

Malus came upon the skull road without warning. One moment Spite was thrashing through brambles and brush and the next he was hurtling past a tall marble obelisk that passed within inches of the highborn's left leg. The transition from dense growth to a broad, open avenue was disorienting, even for Spite, who briefly checked his head-long pace to gain his bearings.

The road leading up the valley had been quarried from pale stone. Each smooth surface had the carved relief of a skull on it. Some were animal skulls, others elf, and still others were miniatures of mythical beasts such as dragons, manticores and chimera.

There were thousands of them stretching in an unmarred white trail through a tunnel of dark greens and greys. No living thing grew up in the thin spaces between the stones – in fact, the lowest overhanging branches were all of a uniform height, creating a tunnel-like effect through the forest. It was as if the sorcery that laid down the stones consumed any living thing that lingered too close to its surface.

Although thousands of years old, the stones looked as if they'd been laid only the day before. Every half mile an obelisk of black marble reared up on either side of the road, carved with the faces of daemons and inscribed with columns of runes that drew the eye and tormented the soul.

Once in the open, the warband thundered down the road, the forest around them erupting with howls and cries as the hunters reacted to the distinct sound of heavy footfalls on the paving stones. Malus kept the knights riding as fast as the nauglir would carry them, plunging ever deeper into the mountain valley.

The sounds of pursuit dwindled behind them. The riders raced their mounts for a mile, then two. Malus was beginning to believe the worst was behind them when he rode Spite around a bend in the road and there, just ahead, stood a score of armoured beastmen arrayed in loose order before an arch of irregular, veined marble. Beyond that stone portal the air seethed with madness and destruction, the death of worlds given tangible form. They had reached the Gate of Infinity at last.

* * *

LESS THAN A hundred yards separated the druchii from the beastman contingent. Whether they had been dispatched hours ago as a precaution by Kul Hadar, or they had been part of the pursuit and had simply made for the one place they knew the warband would head for, Malus could not tell. They waited resolutely with their backs to the silent, otherworldly storm, and Malus saw at once that the deadly barrier presented a hazard to the onrushing knights. He raised his hand, ordering the warriors to slow to a walk.

If they charged full-tilt at the beastmen and met with little resistance, there was a real risk that the running nauglir would careen headlong into the storm before they could check themselves. Malus didn't like to think what would happen to anyone unfortunate enough to cross that unearthly barrier. 'Crossbows!' he ordered.

Still at a walk, the riders readied their weapons. 'Fire at will!' Malus said, and shot one of the beastmen in the front rank. The four retainers fired a volley, and another four beastmen fell. By the time the druchii had reloaded the two sides were less than fifty yards apart, and the beastman leading the contingent had grasped the plight it and his warriors were in. Rather than stand by and be shot at, the pack leader let out a howl and the beastmen charged down the road at the druchii.

'One more volley!' Malus cried, and the five crossbows fired as one. Three more beastmen fell, and then the druchii drew their swords and kicked their mounts into a trot. When they were less than twenty yards from their foes, the knights spurred their mounts into a run, and moments later the two sides crashed together.

These beastmen might not have been among Yaghan's chosen warriors, but they still knew a thing or two about dealing with cavalry. The last of Dalvar's retainers was dashed to the ground as two beastmen buried their axes in his nauglir's chest. Before the warrior could gain his feet another beastman stepped up and crushed his skull with a two-handed warhammer.

The warriors facing Malus tried to sidestep Spite's snapping jaws and slash at the cold one's face. One beastman misjudged and had his head crushed like an egg in the cold one's jaws. The other swung his broadsword two-handed and opened a long, ragged gash in the cold one's neck. Ichor sprayed across the beastman's chest and face, momentarily blinding it. Malus leaned over in the saddle and thrust his sword through the warrior's throat.

Beside Malus, Vanhir was sorely pressed from both sides by three of the beastmen. His cold one was already backing away from the warriors, shaking his snout and blowing blood from his nostrils from a deep slash above his mouth.

Malus gave Spite his head and let the cold one pounce on one of the beastmen, while he aimed a vicious blow at the back of another warrior's head. Spite crushed his victim under his clawed feet, while Malus sliced open the back of his target's neck, causing the beast-man to bleat in shock and panic. Vanhir chopped off the right arm of the third warrior, and within minutes the surviving beastmen were in full retreat, running down the long road as fast as their feet would carry them.

'Ready your crossbows and form up before the gate,' Malus commanded, mindful of the chorus of howls and roars echoing down the long, wooded tunnel back the way they'd come. The highborn led Spite up the road toward the stone gateway. The cold one got to within ten yards of the gate and the raging energies beyond, and refused to take another step. 'I cannot say I blame you,' Malus muttered, and slid from the saddle.

Lhunara, Vanhir and Dalvar, all that remained of the eleven knights who'd ridden with him from the Hag, reined in their mounts alongside Spite and brought their crossbows to bear down the length of the road. From the wild cacophony echoing down the leafy passage it sounded like all the daemons of the outer darkness were hot upon the druchii's heels.

Malus reached into his saddlebag and drew out the Skull of Ehrenlish. The blackened relic seemed to glare at him with tangible loathing. Once, the feeling might have unsettled him; now, however, he had the measure of the spirit trapped within.

The highborn turned and regarded the raging energies beyond the portal. The very air seemed alternately gelid and charged with rapacious energies; violet and green lightning raged through billowing clouds of red and purple. From one heartbeat to the next the vista beyond the portal warped and shimmered. One moment Malus beheld vast, desert plains red as blood, another moment and it seemed he looked out on a vast, starry sky lit by hundreds of ancient suns. Another flash, and he beheld a flat, endless plain baking under a pitiless, red sun. Vast armies raged across that blood-soaked plain, fighting a war without end. Another flash, and he looked upon a land beneath a moonless sky. Under cold stars a ruined city of cyclopean towers waited for sleeping gods to rise and drown the universe in blood.

Malus watched the mad jumble of images and knew, deep in his bones, that he looked upon lands not of this world. He looked upon planes where even gods feared to tread, and he knew that if he stepped into that raging storm he would be lost for all eternity, like a handful of sand tossed into a stormy sea.

The highborn clutched the Skull of Ehrenlish. He could feel the energies of the relic reverberating through his hands as the shade was brought before the terrible ward it had once helped create.

What you can make, damned spirit, you can also unmake, Malus thought savagely. Steeling himself, he began to walk slowly and purposely through the dreadful gate.

Chapter Twenty
THE TEMPLE OF TZ'ARKAN

Y OU SPOKE THROUGH my body once before, when you feared you would be lost in the land of the dead, Malus thought as he stepped beneath the rough arch of the portal. That peril is nothing compared to the one you face now. Come forth, Ehrenlish! Open the gate or perish in the storm!

The highborn felt a tingle of nascent power wash over his body as he stepped up to the gateway. For all its rough-hewn appearance, he could sense that there were arcane mechanisms inlaid in the stone, waiting for the proper hand to summon them into use again. Malus held the blackened skull before him as he inched closer to the swirling vortex that raged beyond the arch.

Do you think me weak, Ehrenlish? Do you think I will not step into the fire? Then you are a fool. I will burn and you with me! A druchii seeks death in the face of failure. Open the gate or die with me!

There was a buzzing in the air. Malus could feel the skull begin to tremble in his hands. This close to the storm, the highborn could feel its warping pull against his skin, as though it were reaching out for him. Faces came and went in the shifting, nebulous clouds – cruel, twisted visages that leered hungrily through the archway. Whether they hungered more for the soul in the highborn's body or the shade bound in the wire-wrapped skull, Malus could not say.

Blue fire began to lick across the surface of the relic, blowing fiercely over the curves of the skull as though it were being forced into the heat of a forge. Malus could feel the lines of silver wire turn hot in his hands. The end approaches, ancient shade! Are you ready to face those who wait beyond?

The back of the skull touched the raging energy beyond the gate, and the black, empty eye sockets blazed with furious life.

Ehrenlish drove spikes of fire into Malus's brain, forcing himself into the highborn's skull like a spearhead and thrashing angrily in the tortured paths of his brain. The highborn's body went taut and his head arched back as it had in the stone circle of Kul Hadar. His mouth opened in a frozen scream, but jagged, blistering curses spewed forth instead.

Malus felt Ehrenlish's spirit clench like a knotted fist inside his skull and felt his body begin to bend backwards, away from the otherworldly storm. *NO!* he raged, grappling with Ehrenlish in a contest of terrible wills. You think to master this body, foul spirit? Fool! You cannot master me. I am Malus of Hag Graef, and I bend to no one. Do as I command, sorcerer, or meet your doom!

For a moment, the highborn's body trembled, caught between opposing forces. Then, inch by painful inch, Malus's frame began to straighten again. The stream of raging curses slurred into a wordless growl of determination as Malus forced himself to take a tiny, half-step forward and pressed the skull deeper into the vortex.

An agonised shrieking filled the air. The storm penetrated the skull, lashing at Ehrenlish and by extension into Malus. The spirit of the sorcerer gibbered and wailed at the touch of the storm, and Malus's mind shrank from the impossible vistas that unfolded in his mind. Skies of liquid fire and seas of boiling skin. Terrible creatures with bones of ice and eyes that had beheld the first night of the world. And beyond them more terrible spirits still, ancient beings of incalculable wisdom and cruelty who stirred from their meditations and gazed across the immense gulf of the storm at the two beings struggling fitfully at its edge.

And then the words burst from Malus's bloody lips. Buzzing, shrieking words of power and intent that tried to wake the arcane mechanism of the portal and hold the great storm at bay. The skull jerked in the highborn's hand and he felt more than heard the crack that raced along the curve of the braincase. Molten silver was running in hot droplets down the wire mesh, propelled away from the storm and falling toward Malus, splashing in sizzling droplets against his breastplate.

The highborn dimly sensed the engines of the portal trying to awaken, but something was wrong. They had lain idle too long with no hand to tend them, and now the paths that directed the shade's power were spinning out of control. There was a groaning sound in the air, and Malus saw the irregular arch start to twist and deform like heated wax.

A shudder passed through Malus's soul. The terrible storm was swelling. At first he thought it was because the arch was failing, but then he realised that the raging energies were being pushed aside by the passage of those ageless beings, as sea dragons shoulder aside the freezing waters of the ocean. They were reaching across the storm.

They were reaching for him.

Ehrenlish's cries had reached an agonising crescendo. Bloody froth burst from Malus's throat as the torrent of incantations poured into the air. He could feel the shade's stark terror. It, too, felt the rising of the ageless ones, and in a fleeting moment of clarity Malus caught a glimpse of the fate that awaited Ehrenlish, and even his hardened soul quailed at the thought of it.

The gate wavered in the air and flew apart into molten gobbets of rock that were sucked into the hungry maw of the storm. The great sorcerous engines failed in a clap of thunder and a blaze of terrible light, and a huge, clawed hand coalesced from the energies of the storm itself, closing about the sizzling surface of the skull. The bone turned to dust at the touch of that impossible hand, and the silver wire flared into mist, and the otherworldly storm that had seethed beyond the gate vanished as though it had never been, taking the shade of Ehrenlish with it.

Malus fell to his knees in the place where the Gate of Infinity had once stood. Steam curled from the joints in his armour. It felt like an eternity before he could hear the sound of his own heartbeat again, or put intent into coherent thoughts in his numbed mind.

When he could focus his eyes again, Malus could see a white road of skulls stretching ahead of him to a huge, stone edifice made of enormous slabs of the blackest basalt. It was a square, tiered structure with no windows or carven images that hinted at the glories held within. It was a temple of power, a place built not for venerating the unseen but to serve the ambitions of the worldly. The very sight of it lit the flames of desire in Malus's savage breast.

The highborn rose to his feet, suppressing flashes of pain with a ruthless effort of will. Here was a triumph beyond all imaginings. He could sense it calling out to him. With the power secreted within the temple he would bend the entire world to his will.

Someone was calling his name. Malus turned, trying to focus on the sound.

'My lord! They're coming!'

It was Lhunara. She and the rest of the warband sat astride their cold ones, facing back down the road from whence they'd come. Just at the bend of the road, nearly a hundred yards away, Malus saw the beastman herd had gathered. A tremor went through their massed ranks, and isolated voices howled challenges at the distant riders. Malus guessed the mob had seen the storm come undone, and they were now working up the courage to attack.

The highborn glanced back at the temple. Sure enough, a low wall surrounded the structure, broken by what appeared to be a single gate. Malus raced forward and leapt into Spite's saddle. 'To the temple!' he cried, hauling on the reins. The warband turned as one and raced down the road, and the beastman herd broke into bloodthirsty cries and charged after them.

In moments the cold ones were racing through the plain gate of the temple wall, turning left and right across broad stone tiles worked with runes and carvings of daemonic skulls. 'Bar the gate!' Malus ordered. He checked the height of the walls. There were no parapets, but a druchii standing on a cold one's back could peer over it. 'Lhunara, get the men against the wall! They can fire over it when the herd tries to force the gate.'

Vanhir and Dalvar pushed heavy gates made from basalt slabs into place. Thick iron bars fitted into holes in the bottom of each gate thudded into place into corresponding holes carved into the road. 'This won't hold them forever, not if they bring hammers,' Vanhir told Malus. 'What do we do when they breach the gate?'

Beyond the gateway the road ran straight up to a simple entryway at the side of the great temple. Malus had already slid from the saddle and was walking swiftly towards the shadowy portal.

'Hold them off,' the highborn said simply, and disappeared inside.

MALUS'S FOOTSTEPS ECHOED hollowly down the narrow processional leading into the temple proper. No torches lined the walls, nor ironwork stands holding globes of greenish witchfire – instead the black walls seemed to radiate a kind of power that thinned the darkness somehow, like water added to ink. He could see clearly in any direction, but the weight of abyssal darkness hung about his shoulders all the same.

The silence in the great temple was palpable, like the funereal stillness of a tomb, and yet the highborn could sense a faint tremor of power suffusing the air. It was not so fierce and uncontrolled as the storm that had raged outside; rather, it seemed ruthlessly harnessed and infinitely patient, waiting to be summoned to life.

The processional led to a large, square chamber similarly devoid of ornamentation. Row upon row of humped shapes lined the floor to either side of the aisle, and it took a moment for Malus to realise that they had once been the shapes of servants. In life they had worn metal vestments and mantles of some kind, and those ceremonial clothes still remained, bent in positions of supplication towards the narrow aisle. The highborn wondered what kind of power – or awesome, numbing fear – could drive more than a hundred slaves to bend their heads to the stone floor and remain there, waiting in vain for the return of their terrible overlords, until finally they died there. The same could be said for the two massive suits of armour that still stood to either side of the doorway at the far end of the chamber. Their occupants had long since fallen to dust, but their empty armour still maintained their endless vigil.

Malus passed through the doorway into what appeared to be a large chamber for prayers and sacrifices to the four gods of the north. Great statues stood at four different points within the room, each with its own stained altar. The darkness here was palpable, pressing against him like a hundred clammy hands sticky with blood.

The great statues of the Ruinous Powers glared down at him with implacable hate, demanding his subservience and adoration. Muttering a prayer to the Dark Mother, the highborn crossed the room without sparing the idols more than a passing glance, and stepped through a doorway.

The space beyond was nothing less than cavernous. Heat and the stench of sulphur smote his face and neck. Malus stepped onto a floor of slate tiles that stretched across an open area the size of a small plaza back at the Hag. Ahead, he could see a dim, red glow through the haze of darkness, silhouetting a huge shape that seemed to descend from the vastness of the ceiling above.

Malus walked for nearly fifty yards across the tiles, until he reached the edge of a precipice. The statue of an immense, winged daemon crouched at the very brink, its horned forehead bent to the tiles in a gesture of supplication. Frowning, the highborn stepped around the statue and peered into the abyss beyond. Hundreds of feet below was nothing but fire and seething, molten stone… and a line of flat-topped boulders that seemed to hang in the air above the magma.

The highborn glanced at the large shape hanging above the fiery pit and saw that it, too, was an enormous, rough-hewn pillar of stone, carved with wide stairs that spiralled upwards to the temple's next level. Unfortunately, they were also more than thirty yards away.

Malus stepped back and regarded the statue of the daemon once more. He noticed that its knobby back could also be seen as a set of cunningly carved steps. Carefully, he placed one boot on the top of the daemon's head and took a step up. The stone easily supported his weight.

The highborn climbed the short flight of 'steps' along the daemon's back, until there was nothing but reeking air before him. Peering down, he saw the first of the floating boulders, perfectly in line with the statue's back. A bit ostentatious, Malus thought, staring up at the distant staircase. But effective. The sorcerers were jealous of their power indeed. The question was how to make the boulders rise for him.

Force of will, Malus thought. What is sorcery, after all, but bending the world to one's will? How else did Kul Hadar and Ehrenlish fight one another? How else did I force Ehrenlish to obey my commands?

Malus looked down at the stepping stones. *Rise*, he thought, focusing his will on them. *Rise!*

The stones remained where they were.

Rise, damn you! Malus thought fiercely, adding his rage to the force of his thoughts. *In the name of dead Ehrenlish, obey your new master. Rise!*

Nothing happened.

A growl escaped Malus's lips. He cast about for another name to hurl at the implacable rock. 'In the name... in the name of Tz'arkan, RISE!'

At once, Malus felt the power in the air thrum like a plucked chord. The stepping stones trembled, and then began to rise.

The highborn smiled triumphantly. Tz'arkan, eh? What kind of name is that, I wonder?

The stepping stones rose smoothly and silently through the air, their faceted lower halves glowing from the heat of the magma below. They formed a perfect set of steps that curved upwards and met the stairs high above the blazing pit. Steeling himself, Malus stepped from the daemon's back onto the first stone, and was gratified to discover it was as stable as the very earth.

In minutes the highborn climbed the floating boulders to the staircase. As he stepped from each one, the stone plummeted back to its original position deep in the pit. By the time he reached the curving staircase, Malus felt like a petty god himself. The steps themselves appeared to be carved from alabaster; each riser worked with a cunning relief of dozens of small, naked figures, writhing in torment. Their faces were upturned, pleading for mercy, even as their shoulders and backs supported the weight of each stair. This is a place made for conquerors, Malus thought.

His smug grin faded a third of the way up the stair when he stumbled upon the body. It wore robes of a finer cut and a jewelled mantle that was similar to, but far richer than, those in the entry chamber below, and the hot, dry air had mummified the corpse almost perfectly. Malus was struck by the corpse's gaping mouth, frozen in a rictus of terror. Nor did he miss the curved dagger in the body's right hand, and the long, neat cuts along the withered veins of both forearms.

* * *

THERE WERE BODIES everywhere, perfectly preserved by the heat. All of them had died violent deaths, slain by one another or dead by their own hand.

The second floor of the temple was given over to five large sanctums and the smaller quarters of the attendants who ministered to the needs of Ehrenlish and his cabal. Huge, broad columns of basalt, carved in the likeness of terrible daemons, supported the arched ceiling, and cold braziers made of bronze and dark iron stood at regular intervals along the broad corridors. Inserts of dark sandstone had been fitted among the black granite blocks of the walls. Each panel contained a bas relief of corpse-choked fields or ruined cities burning beneath the twin moons.

The doorway to each sanctum was carved with thick bands of magical runes, though the violence that marred the entire floor had made itself felt against these guardian wards as well. The bands of runes were broken by the blows of hammers and axes, though on two occasions Malus also found the blackened husks of the servants who'd tempted their masters' arcane power. The rooms themselves were torn apart; ancient brown bloodstains marked the thick tapestries lining the walls and lay in pools across the marble floors. All of the rooms were piled with riches – urns full of gold and silver coin sat amid broken bookshelves and piles of ancient books. Malus could only imagine the sorcerous wisdom contained within those pages – what would Nagaira or Urial have given for one hour alone in these rooms? Suits of armour and fine weapons lay scattered along the floor, evidently ignored in the frenzy of slaughter that came upon the sorcerers' servants.

At one point Malus stumbled into a servant's room that had been turned into a slaughterhouse. A large, oaken table had been drawn into the centre of the sparsely furnished room and a wide assortment of cleavers and saws had been laid by its side. A mummified corpse still lay tied to the table, its right leg and arm sawn away. They ran out of food when Ehrenlish and his army failed to return, Malus thought. *Why didn't the stepping stones work for them? Surely they had better knowledge of the workings of this place than I?*

The aura of power was much stronger here. It pulsed along the walls and hummed along his bones. *Perhaps that is what eventually drove them mad*, Malus thought. *Trapped here, slowly starving to death, and that tremor constantly running through one's body. It would be enough to drive me to murder.*

Seeing the sanctums of the lost sorcerers finally brought home the realisation that whatever power the temple contained, it was not meant to travel. This wasn't some magical sword or arcane relic like Ehrenlish's skull. Perhaps a source of power tied to the land, like Hadar's crystals? Clearly the cabal was able to draw upon its strength from a great distance, but if they had living quarters in the temple, it seemed they couldn't be separated from it for very long.

The notion vexed Malus. I'll have to find some way to make it work for me as well, he thought, but couldn't imagine how. I may have to treat with that treacherous goat Hadar after all. Give him access to the temple and the power, and entrust him with its safekeeping. Putting so much trust in the beastman seemed the height of lunacy, but what else could he do?

I'll taste of the power for just a short time, enough to deal with my family and become Vaulkhar, and that will be enough, Malus thought. It was a bitter drink to swallow, but the history of Ehrenlish and his cabal hinted that the power didn't come without cost. Better a brief flirtation and escape rather than the kind of obsession that consumed one from the inside out.

There was a ramp at one end of the level, surrounded by the quarters of the five sorcerers, that led upwards to the third tier of the temple. The ramp itself was carved with skulls and worked with hundreds of runes, and the doors were formed of solid gold. Ten years' worth of raiding wouldn't purchase all that gold, Malus thought with avaricious wonder. I could pull those down, break them up and return to the Hag a wealthy man. But then, if those are merely the doors, what manner of glories lie beyond? The great doors were perfectly balanced, and swung open at the lightest touch.

Beyond lay a large chamber dominated by a tall pair of basalt doors, flanked by huge statues of fearsome, winged daemons. The floor was made of polished basalt slabs, blacker than night, and inlaid with an intricate series of interlocking magical wards, worked in gold, silver and crushed gems. The greatest of the wards was only a third of a much greater circle that evidently ran beneath the far wall and encompassed part of the chamber beyond the basalt doors.

At the foot of the great doors lay a heap of mummified bodies – one with its arm still outstretched against a basalt slab. Long brown streaks of dried blood made four perfect lines that stretched from the door's golden handle to the mummy's ragged fingertips.

The air here trembled with power. It tasted like copper and ash on Malus's tongue. He set ripples of it in motion as he stepped across the threshold, like he was wading out into an ocean of invisible energy. It lapped around him, plucking at his hair and roiling with his breath. The feel of it left him giddy with greed, but a small part of him was also troubled. So much strength here. Why couldn't these wretches bend it to their will?

He crossed the lines of the wards with great care, even though they had been worked in such a fashion that no mere man could harm them. When he stepped across the first of the rune-inlaid barriers he felt a new kind of power settle over him, like an iron fist closing around his chest. It was so potent that for a moment he thought he couldn't breathe – and then he realised that his heart wasn't beating, either.

Once, in his early years of flirtation with Nagaira, she had taken him into her sanctum and showed him some of her oldest magical tomes. One of them was about wards of stasis and binding, the magical arts of trapping spirits and objects in one place and holding them there until the spell expired.

He was standing in such a ward now – in *layers* of them, each one supplying energy to the others in a weave of incredible complexity and strength. Standing within the wards effectively stopped his body from one heartbeat to the next. He could stand here for thousands of years and not die.

With a creak of ancient, leathery skin, one of the mummies turned to stare at Malus with yellowed, rheumy eyes.

The highborn drew his sword, watching in horror as five bodies – not living, but certainly not dead – rose awkwardly to their feet. Two of the figures brandished knives, while the rest reached out to him with gnarled, wrinkled hands. They tried to speak, their desiccated mouths working, but only a thin whistle of air leaked from their ruined lungs. They staggered towards him, their faces contorted with a mixture of anger, fear – and greed.

The first mummy to reach him swung its dagger wildly at the highborn's head – Malus rocked back on his heels, dodging the blow, then leaned back in and slashed at the creature's knife arm. The limb tore away in a puff of dust, but the mummy simply dropped its shoulder and rushed at him, knocking Malus off his feet. His sword hand cracked against the basalt tile and the blade went skittering across the floor.

A rotted hand groped for Malus's throat, and the mummy's face was inches from his own, still uttering its thin, whistling cry. The other creatures were on him moments later, tearing at him with their hands. The highborn caught sight of the second knife-wielding mummy circling around to stab at his unarmoured head.

Paper-dry fingers closed around his neck. The other mummy's knife flashed downwards, and Malus pulled the one-armed mummy into its path. The blade plunged into the back of the one-armed mummy's skull with a sound like a cracking eggshell, showering the highborn with stinking dust and flecks of dry skin. Malus pulled his leg up underneath the one-armed mummy and kicked the withered corpse back over his head, crashing it into its knife-wielding companion. Both were knocked off balance and fell backwards – landing outside the boundaries of the wards. They hit the floor and exploded into dust as the stasis effect of the magical barriers deserted them.

The other mummies recoiled from Malus with wordless cries of despair as they saw the fate of their companions. The highborn rolled to his feet, recovered his sword, and remorselessly attacked the ancient figures. Within moments their limbless torsos were hurled across the barrier and dashed into dust.

What madness is this, Malus thought, wiping the brownish powder from his face. They lingered for centuries, trying to open those doors, and yet when I appeared to try the same, they attacked me. Was it out of greed, or fear? Or both?

Malus stepped towards the doors. He felt the power flow past him like a receding wave, retreating into the chamber beyond. There was a faint click, and the basalt doors swung silently open.

The room beyond looked like nothing so much as a vast treasure chamber. Piles of gold and silver, jewels and ornate relics lay heaped everywhere, surrounding an enormous, faceted crystal set in the centre of the room. Unlike the green crystals that the beastmen held sacred, this stone was lit with a shifting, bluish glow, not unlike the ambience of the northern lights. The aura of power coalesced around the crystal, sending arcs of blue lightning flickering over its surface.

At last.

Malus approached the crystal, eyes gleaming with anticipation. You were so certain I would fail, sister. You had no idea with whom you were dealing!

The highborn laughed, gazing at the fabulous wealth that surrounded him. Gold enough to beggar Hag Graef, he thought. And it is only the beginning. His eyes alighted on a gold ring, set with an oblong ruby almost as long as his finger. The flickering light of the crystal played across its surface, giving it the deep colour of fresh blood. Malus plucked the ring from the pile of treasure, savouring its weight and the rich colour of the gem. A ring of blood befitting a conqueror, he thought. The Dark Mother grant this is only the first of the glories that will be mine!

Malus slid the ring upon his finger. The instant it settled into place the power that surrounded the crystal struck the highborn full in the chest. Fire and ice and black corruption seared along his bones. It was a sensation greater than pain and terror and madness combined.

The power that flooded him was coldly, cruelly aware. It was as merciless as a winter storm, as relentless as an avalanche. The highborn's will wasn't merely broken; it was swept away as though it had never been.

Malus screamed in agony and soul-numbing terror as the terrible power hollowed out his soul in a single, awful instant. He fell to his knees, and only then became aware of the thunderous laughter echoing through his mind.

Darkness threatened to overwhelm him. Then a voice reverberated through his skull, whispering with all the intimacy of a lover.

'It is you who are the fool, Malus Darkblade. For want of a bauble you have become my willing slave.'

Chapter Twenty-One
GRIP OF THE DAEMON

MALUS DOUBLED OVER, smoke rising from his body as he fought against the presence that had forced its way into his body. It wasn't the same as the experience with Ehrenlish – this was many, many times worse. The spirit that possessed him permeated flesh and bone, curling around his heart like a serpent and leaving nothing but emptiness where his soul had once been. He raged against the spirit's icy touch, focusing all his will to force the presence from his body but making no impression whatsoever. Fell laughter echoed through his mind.

'Release me!' Malus groaned.

'Release you? But I've only just acquired you. Do you know how long I've waited for a servant like yourself?'

With a roar the highborn hurled himself at the crystal. He tore his sword from its scabbard and rained blows upon the gleaming surface. Steel and crystal rang like the clashing of bells, but when he staggered back, his strength spent, the faceted surface was unmarked.

'That's a poor way to treat such a fine sword, Malus. If you keep that up you'll ruin the edge.'

'What are you?' Malus cried, frantic with rage.

'I? Compared to you, I am as a god.' A callous chuckle reverberated through the room. 'Your kind, with their rudimentary perceptions, would call me a daemon. You could not pronounce my name if you had a thousand years to make the attempt. For our purposes, you may call me Tz'arkan. That will suffice.'

'A daemon?' Malus staggered at the thought. A daemon? Inside me? No. I will not allow it! The highborn fell to his knees and dragged his dagger from its sheath. He pressed the broken tip to his throat. 'I am a slave to no one, be they daemon or god!'

'If you drive that blade home, mortal, you will not only die a slave, but you will remain my slave for all eternity,' the daemon said, its voice cold and grim.

'You are lying.'

'Strike then, and find out.'

The highborn's mind raged. Do it. He lies. Better to die than to live like this! But doubt nagged at him. What if he is telling the truth? What reason does he have to lie? With a bestial growl Malus let the dagger fall to the floor. 'You said I might remain a slave.'

'That's better,' the daemon said, approval in its stony voice. 'Clever little druchii. Yes, I would make a bargain with you. A trade: your soul for my freedom. Set me free, and I will relinquish my hold on you. What could be more fair than that?'

Malus frowned. 'I am no sorcerer, Tz'arkan. How may I free you?'

'Leave the sorcery to me, little druchii. You know the story of the temple, I presume? Of that worm Ehrenlish and his lickspittle cronies? You must know – it was Ehrenlish's screams I heard when the great storm was dispelled. How I have longed to hear that sound, Malus! I knew that sooner or later that fool's skull would turn up, but the way you used him to open the gate... it was glorious. For that, you have my gratitude.'

'Get on with it, daemon,' the highborn snarled. 'Unlike you, I can die of old age – or boredom.'

'Not within these wards, little druchii – at least, not for a very, very long time. But I digress. Ehrenlish and his cronies – vile, craven little slugs that they were – succeeded, at great cost, in trapping me in this crystal, many thousands of years ago.'

'Trapped you how?'

'How they did it is not important, Malus. It is enough to say that they did. They bound me to this place and made me their slave. I'm certain you can appreciate how horrible that was.'

'All the more reason for you to release me,' Malus snarled.

'Do not make light of my tragic circumstances, little druchii,' the daemon replied coldly. 'The five sorcerers drew upon my vast power to serve their own pitiful schemes. But they trifled with powers far beyond mortal ken, and that proved to be their undoing. One by one they met with terrible fates, until at last that fool Ehrenlish walled himself up inside his own skull and was lost to history for millennia. But the wards those fools laid upon me still remained. I curse their names for all eternity, but I will admit they did their work well when construct-ing this awful prison! As soon as Ehrenlish was gone I began clawing at the walls of my cell. I was able to amuse myself with the acolytes and slaves that the sorcerers left behind, but little else. Slowly, slowly, I was able to extend my reach a little further beyond my prison. Within the last hundred years I was able to extend the limits of my awareness to the walls of the temple itself. But I could go no further. The wards were too potent even for one such as myself.'

'So you admit you have your limits? Some god you are,' Malus sneered.

The daemon ignored him. 'The wards can be unravelled, little druchii. The sorceries involved are beyond the pitiful skills of any mor-tal sorcerer living today, but I know the words and the rituals that must be performed. However, I need a token from each of the five lost sor-cerers – five talismans that can be used to undo the spells they once wrought. Each are potent magical artefacts in their own right: The Octagon of Praan; The Idol of Kolkuth; The Dagger of Torxus; The Warpsword of Khaine; and the Amulet of Vaurog.'

'What do I know of talismans, daemon? I am a warrior and a slaver, not some sorcerer or thin-necked scholar. These men died millennia ago. How am I to find these things, if they even still exist?'

'For your sake, little druchii, you had best pray they may still be found. Already the sands are running from the hourglass. Even as we speak your life is slipping from your grasp.'

Malus straightened. 'What! What are you talking about?'

'I have claimed your soul, Malus. Do you not remember? I hollowed you out like a gourd so I could fit the merest sliver of my essence into your frail little frame. That is how we are able to communicate right now, and how I am able to know your every thought. I am not one to let my servants go about unattended, you see.'

'Yet you are killing me? Is that it?'

'It is more fair to say that you killed yourself the moment you let your greed get the better of you,' the daemon said smugly. 'When I claimed your soul your body began to die. In fact, you would be dead right now if it weren't for my power. But not even I can halt the inevitable. If your soul is not restored within a year, your body will per-ish, and your spirit will be mine forever.'

'A year?' Malus exclaimed. 'I have only a year to find five long-lost relics? You ask the impossible!'

'Perhaps,' the daemon readily agreed. 'But there is no way to know until you try. And if you fail, well, I'm certain there will be others who will seek out the temple, especially now that the Gate of Infinity is no more.'

Malus ground his teeth in frustration. 'I could just stay here,' he said defiantly. 'You said yourself that I could linger here a very, very long time.'

'Oh, clever, clever little druchii,' the daemon said. 'You are right, of course. You could linger here for hundreds and hundreds of years, slowly shrivelling to a withered husk like those wretches you fought beyond my door. By all means, stay then. I will wait for another willing servant. Feel free to amuse yourself with the baubles Ehrenlish and his cronies heaped about me, though I must confess even this much gold loses its lustre after the first century or so.'

'Curse you daemon!' Malus snarled. 'All right. I will find you your trinkets!'

'Excellent! I knew you would come around sooner or later.' The daemon sounded as though he'd just succeeded in teaching a pet a demanding new trick. 'When you have found all the talismans you must return them here before the year is out, and I will take care of the rest.'

'And then you will free me?'

'Not only will I set you free, you have my oath that I will never try to enslave you again. And just to show you that I have your best interests at heart, I will reveal to you that one of the talismans, the Octagon of Praan, is very close by. I can sense it, even in my confined state.'

'Where is this trinket, then?'

'Upon the mountainside,' the daemon replied. 'The beastmen venerate it. At night I can hear their braying chants, calling out to the talisman for protection. Stupid creatures. Ironic that you may have to kill them all to pry their talisman of protection from their grubby little paws.' The daemon sounded inordinately pleased at the prospect.

Slowly and deliberately, Malus picked up his dagger and slid it back into its sheath. The highborn rose to his feet. 'I'll do whatever I must,' he said coldly, his willpower once again reasserting itself. 'In a year's time I'll return here, and we will finish what we've begun.'

'Indeed we will, Malus Darkblade. Indeed we will.'

'Do not call me that!' Malus seethed.

'Why not? Am I mistaken somehow? Darkblades are flawed things, are they not? Step before the crystal, Malus. There is something you must see.'

The highborn frowned in consternation, but after a moment he relented and stepped before the crystal.

'Good. Now look closely.'

The blue glow faded, revealing a crystal facet that gleamed like polished silver. It was like looking into a mirror–

And Malus saw what he had become.

His skin had turned pale as chalk. Distended black veins ran along the back of the hand that bore the ruby ring, disappearing beneath the wrist of his vambrace. They seemed to pulse with a steady flow of corruption. His eyes were orbs of purest jet.

'Gaze upon what you have become – a man with no soul, bound in service to a daemon. And you say you are not a flawed thing, Malus Darkblade?'

The daemon's laughter pealed like thunder as Malus fled from its prison.

MALUS FLED THROUGH the precincts of the temple, slipping in the dust of the dissolved mummies as he plunged down the ramp to the apartments of the doomed sorcerers. The bodies of the acolytes mocked him with their slack jaws and wide, staring eye sockets. They seemed to reach out to him as he passed, offering their knives or their hanging ropes. They offered him the charity of the damned.

His boots rang along the stone. He flew down the spiral staircase, feeling the heat of the magma on his face and fighting the urge to fling himself into the flames. When he came upon the mummified corpse lying on the steps he kicked the body into the lake of fire in his place, envying it its fiery plunge.

The stepping stones were waiting for him when he reached the bottom of the stairs, levitated into position at the will of the daemon upstairs. What a fool he'd been to believe that he had called them from the depths with the strength of his will! He crossed from one stone to the next with as little regard as he would have paid to the stepping stones of a river.

Beyond the plaza and the lake of fire, the statues of the gods seemed to laugh at his anguish, leering at his foolishness in assailing the lair of the daemon. This is what you get for spurning us, the abominable faces seemed to say. You and your Dark Mother. Did she hear your prayer in the stone halls above? Did she grant you victory over your foes?

He threw himself at the statues, howling like a fiend, but he had not the strength to throw those huge edifices down. If anything, the idols only seemed to mock him all the more.

Malus flung himself from the presence of the four gods, staggering through the ranks of the eternal servants. He dashed their obedient bodies into dust, screaming curses at their craven poses.

Distantly he could hear the sound of screams and the ringing clash of steel. Beastmen and druchii alike cried out in rage and pain. Malus drew his sword and ran towards the promise of battle.

Can I ever spill enough blood to drown the memory of my reflection?

Malus stumbled into the cold light of day and beheld the carnage at the temple gate. The beastmen had made a hole with their heavy, two-handed hammers, and dozens of corpses lay in mounds just beyond the breach. Two of the four nauglir lay dead, their bodies pierced and rent by the blows of sword and axe. A third trembled and bled from mortal blows that were slowly stealing away its life. Only Spite survived. Leaner and quicker than his fellows, he nevertheless bore a score of wounds across his armoured hide.

Malus's three retainers stalked amid the battlefield like carrion crows, their black armour splashed and streaked with the blood of their foes. They had cast aside their empty crossbows long ago, and held red, dripping blades in their hands. They worked with the dispassionate skill of butchers, peering among the corpses and dispatching any wounded that they found. There was no telling how many assaults they had already fought off, biding their time between each wave in the same fashion. They were so intent on their business that they didn't notice Malus until he was almost upon them.

It was Lhunara who saw him first. She was covered in gore, her hair matted and her face painted crimson like one of Khaine's murderous brides. There were scores of dents and creases in her armour, and she held a battered sword in each hand. Her expression was a mask of fatigue.

'You've come none too soon, my lord,' she began. 'They've tried to rush us three times now, and only just retreated. Between us and the cold ones we've killed close to eighty of them, but–'

The words died in her throat as Lhunara registered the change in her lord's face. Her eyes met his and they widened in horror. 'My lord, what–'

Malus howled like a wounded beast and buried his sword in Lhunara's skull.

Dalvar and Vanhir saw the blow fall and cried out in horror and dismay. The highborn leapt at them even as Lhunara's body was falling to the ground.

Nagaira's man moved to the left, his hand drawing back and snapping forward in a blur of motion. Without thinking, Malus swept his blade around and knocked the thrown dagger aside. He rushed at the rogue, snapping a blow at his head that Dalvar blocked with the long knife in his left hand. The rogue's right hand drew another long fighting knife and lunged in, stabbing for one of the joints in the highborn's articulated breastplate.

Malus caught Dalvar's wrist in his left hand and punched the retainer across the face with the pommel of his sword. Stunned, Dalvar stabbed for his throat but the thrust went a little wide, scoring a jagged cut along the line of Malus's jaw. The highborn snarled and thrust the point of his sword into the rogue's left armpit, where the armour afforded no protection. The point caught on the joint of the arm. Dalvar stiffened, his face going white with pain, and Malus leaned against the blade, grating against gristle and bone and sinking slowly deeper into the druchii's chest.

Dalvar shrieked and spasmed violently, trying to pull away, but Malus still held his other wrist in a death grip, keeping him in place. The rogue stabbed wildly at him with his dagger, but Malus's outstretched sword arm was in the way; the point of the retainer's dagger gouged him deeply at cheek, temple, ear and throat, but none could dig deep enough to kill. With every blow, every blossom of pain, Malus only pushed harder on his own blade. The point grated free of the joint, pushed past the ribs and sliced through muscle, lung and heart. Dalvar let out a strangled gasp, retched a torrent of blood and fell to the earth.

When Malus spun to face Vanhir, he found the retainer waiting for him several yards away.

'I want to look you in the eye when I kill you,' the knight said, showing his pointed teeth. 'I had much grander plans for your destruction, Darkblade – wondrous creations that would have taken years to end your miserable life. If I am to be denied those glories, I at least want to see the life flee from your pitiful eyes.'

Malus hurled himself at the highborn knight, raining a flurry of blows at his head, shoulders and neck. Vanhir moved like a viper, blocking each blow with the skill of an expert duellist. The dagger in his left hand rapped a staccato drumbeat against Malus's breastplate, vambrace and thigh, probing for weak spots in the armour. When the highborn drew back for another combination of blows, Vanhir's sword flicked out and laid a long cut across Malus's neck, narrowly missing the artery. The highborn was a skilled swordsman, but Vanhir was a master, an artist of the blade.

Now Vanhir pressed his advantage, alternating attacks with sword and dagger. Malus blocked the first sword but took a shallow knife wound through a gap in his right vambrace. He swept aside a lightning thrust – and then he flung himself onto the knight, sinking his white teeth into Vanhir's throat.

Vanhir screamed and writhed, smashing the pommel of his sword into the side of Malus's head, but the highborn would not be shaken off so easily. He bit deep, tasting a rush of coppery blood, then wrenched his head to one side and tore out the side of the knight's throat. Vanhir fell back, clapping his hands to the torrent of blood spilling from his ravaged neck, but it was a futile gesture for a mortal wound. Within moments the life faded from Vanhir's eyes, his gaze freezing in an eternal glare of unremitting hate.

Malus Darkblade threw back his head and howled like a maddened wolf. It was a cry so savage and unhinged that even the herd of battle-hardened beastmen, now advancing slowly down the road for their fourth assault on the gate, paused in fear and wonder at the sound.

The vision of Lhunara's face still hung before his mind's eye, tormenting him. The look of horror on her face when she'd realised his failure had been more than he could bear.

Malus staggered to his feet, wiping Vanhir's blood from his mouth with the back of his black-veined hand.

They had all served him faithfully and well, friend and foe alike, he thought. Better they die than witness his awful shame.

Chapter Twenty-Two
BLOOD ON THE WIND

SPITE GROWLED AT Malus's approach. The cold one's eyes were glazed with pain and its flanks heaved with exertion. The nauglir dimly sensed something amiss with his master, yet could not understand what.

'Easy there, terrible one,' Malus said calmly, watching Spite's eyes carefully. If the pupils widened suddenly and his inner eyelids closed, Malus would be fighting for his life a heartbeat later.

'It's just me, Malus. We've done what we came here to do. There's blood on the wind and it's time to ride.'

For a heart-stopping moment it looked as though Spite had forsaken him. The nauglir growled again and his pupils widened, but then the beastmen advancing on the gate let out a ragged shout, distracting the great beast, and Malus took advantage of the moment to leap into the saddle. Spite grumbled and tossed his head, but Malus dug in his spurs and the cold one leapt forward obediently.

The highborn drove Spite right for the gate, kicking the nauglir into a run just as he reached the hole the beastmen had made. Malus leaned against Spite's neck and he still endured a fearfully close call as the cold one shouldered through the hole and scattered broken bits of stone in a wide swathe before him. Once they were through, Malus straightened in his saddle and spurred his mount into a charge, right into the face of the advancing beastmen.

In other circumstances the sight of a lone rider wouldn't have been enough to sway the mob of warriors. But they had been fighting a vicious, close-quarter battle at the temple gate and had seen three separate assaults hurled back by the crushing jaws and cruel talons of Spite and his kin. The sight of the onrushing nauglir caused them to waver, and the moment's hesitation was enough. Malus and Spite ploughed into them, hurling broken bodies left and right. The highborn slashed at upturned faces and throats, screaming like a banshee, and the beastmen fell back from the frenzied attack.

All but a familiar knot of huge beastman champions hefting large, two-handed weapons. Yaghan and his chosen warriors howled their war-cries and tried to rush at Malus, but the press of the retreating mob held the champions at bay for a few crucial seconds. The highborn hauled on the reins, whipping Spite's tail through the press of beastmen, then spurred the cold one into a run, breaking free of the disordered mob and racing headlong down the road of skulls. It took only moments for Yaghan to rally the beastmen with howled curses and oaths, but by the time the weary mob took up the pursuit, Malus was already around the bend in the road and well out of sight.

The highborn's mind raced, trying to force the horrors of the last hour from his mind in order to formulate a plan. Somhow, he had to sneak back into the beastmen camp and find where the Octagon of Praan was kept. He was sure that the only person who knew for certain where to find the relic was Kul Hadar himself. Slipping into the camp in broad daylight would be next to impossible. He would have to find a place to lie low for the night, and slip into the shaman's tent when the opportunity presented itself.

But first there was the matter of the howling mob on his trail.

Malus looked back over his shoulder. None of the beastmen had reached the bend yet, and there was another turn in the road just ahead. As the nauglir raced around the second turn, Malus hauled back on the reins. 'Stand,' he said, and leapt from the saddle. Then he unclipped Spite's reins and stowed them in his saddlebag. 'Run, Spite,' he said, looking the cold one in the eye. 'Hunt. Wait for my call.'

Nauglir were not bright creatures; some would even go so far as to call them stupid, but with enough patience and repetition, they could be trained to respond to simple commands. Spite knew these orders well; when Malus struck him on the shoulder the cold one trotted off, heading for the trees by the side of the road. He would make his way into the forest, looking for food and likely find a spot to lie down and lick his wounds. If things went well Malus could call for him later that night. If things didn't go well, it was better that Spite was free and able to hunt on his own.

As the cold one loped away, Malus sheathed his sword and dived into the underbrush on the side of the road closest to the herd camp. He stayed low and moved as quickly and stealthily as he could. Sure enough, within moments he heard howls nearby, and then the thunder of more than a hundred bare feet as the beastman mob ran past him along the road of skulls. If he was lucky they would run on for quite some distance before realising they'd lost track of their quarry. By then he hoped to be deep in the middle of the forest.

He was just beginning to congratulate himself on his tactics when he raced around an upthrust spur of rock and ran headlong into a beastman coming the other way.

Druchii and beastman went down in a tangle of limbs. Malus didn't know if the warrior was part of the mob that had been chasing him or not. He tore his dagger from its sheath and buried the blade in the beastman's chest. The warrior let out a bubbling moan and tried to hit the highborn with his club. Malus took the blow on his armoured shoulder and drove the knife again and again into the beastman's chest and neck. Within moments the warrior went limp, but already Malus could hear shouts coming from the direction of the road.

He gathered his feet underneath him and ran, holding his arm up in front of his face to ward off the worst of the brambles. He heard cries and howls behind him, and once again he was amazed at how easily the beastmen could move through the dense undergrowth. Malus ran on for another fifty yards and then slowed almost to a crawl, crouching low and looking for a fallen log or a depression in the ground he could hide in. After a few moments he found a dip in the ground that was partially covered by thick, green ground creepers, and he lay prone beneath them, struggling to control his breathing.

Within minutes there were sounds of pursuit all around him. Beastmen ran past on either side, grunting and growling to one another as they searched the woods for him. Malus lay as motionless as he could, still clutching the bloody dagger to his chest. The sounds of pursuit raced away to the north-west – and then Malus heard another beastman heading his way at a trot, moving directly in line with his hiding place.

There was no point moving. The searcher would either stumble onto him or pass on by. Malus lay on his back and listened.

Closer… closer. The warrior had to have seen the creepers by now – would he turn aside? Closer still. He wasn't turning away. Furred legs thrashed through the thick bed of vines. A hoof sank into the loam a scant two inches from Malus's thigh. In a burst of movement, the highborn sat up, grabbed the beastman by one of his curving horns and pulled him down onto the tip of his knife. The blade pierced the warrior's throat, plunging through and severing his spine. The beastman fell hard on Malus, spasmed once, and died without a sound.

The highborn lay there with the beastman atop him, warm blood flowing over his chest and pooling in the hollow of his throat. As far as Malus could tell, the larger beastman completely covered the parts of him that weren't already hidden by the creepers. Once his breathing settled, Malus rested his head against the cold ground and waited for night to fall. Within moments he was asleep.

MALUS AWOKE WITH a start, his breath misting in the cold night air. The body of the beastman had grown stiff; dried blood crackled faintly as the highborn moved. He slowly, carefully rolled the warrior's body off him and sat up, wincing at the stiffness in his limbs. The highborn looked around at the forest growth and for a moment his exhausted mind did not know where he was or how he'd gotten there. But then the throbbing pain of his wounds penetrated his consciousness, and he felt the sense of emptiness in his chest, and remembered.

He rose wearily to his feet and tried to take his bearings. In the distance he could hear the sounds of the herd and the crackle of bonfires. It sounded like a solemn gathering indeed, Malus thought with a merciless grin. Enjoy the bitter fruits of your victory, Kul Hadar. You should have never tried to match wills with me.

There was no way to tell for certain, but it sounded like at least half the herd's survivors had returned to camp. If Hadar followed the same ritual as Machuk had, he would be by the fire, drinking and eating with the rest of the herd until almost dawn. Malus would have to sneak to the edge of the woods and see if he could spy the imposing form of the shaman among the rest of the beastmen around the bonfires.

Then there remained the challenge of slipping through the camp undetected. Although many of the beastmen would likely be intoxicated in the wee hours of the morning, his silhouette would still give him away as not being a member of the herd. He needed some way to change his appearance.

Malus looked down at the body by his feet. He considered the beastman for a moment, then bent over the body and began skinning it.

HE WORE THE beastman's skin over his armour like a cloak. It hung poorly, but it only had to fool the herd from a distance, and then only for a momentary glimpse. Or so he hoped.

Malus crouched at the edge of the woods, scanning each of the three bonfires as carefully as he could. As far as he could tell, Kul Hadar was nowhere to be seen. Not a part of the herd, are you Hadar? No wonder they eventually ran you off.

The good news was that he counted less than a hundred beastmen in camp. Between those lost to Urial's riders and the terrible battle at the temple gate, the herd had been decimated. Those that he could see around the fire seemed well and truly drunk.

The highborn stepped from the woods and began his ascent to Kul Hadar's large tent. He kept to the shadows, moving no faster than a walk, and tried to put tents and shelters between himself and the bonfires whenever possible. No one challenged him as he moved deeper into camp.

As he approached Kul Hadar's tent, Malus noted that the smaller satellite tents were dark. If those belonged to Yaghan and his champions, it likely meant that they were still out searching for him in the woods. That would make his task much easier.

The highborn circled around to the rear of the great tent and pressed himself against the layered hides. He could smell wood smoke, and faintly heard someone moving quietly inside. Malus pulled out his dagger and, quietly and carefully, cut a slit in the hide long enough for him to be able to pry the leather apart and peer inside.

There was a figure sitting next to an iron brazier in the centre of the tent, facing the central door flap. He heard a faint murmur, like chanting. Kul Hadar was possibly praying to his gods for protection, or deliverance, or to pass the blame for the defilement of the grove onto someone else. Malus grinned fiercely to himself and began to slowly widen the slit, cutting carefully in the direction of the ground. When the slit was large enough for him to slip through, he let the skin of the beastman fall to the ground and crept quietly into the tent.

The interior of the tent was carpeted in thick rugs and hide-covered pillows; either Machuk or Hadar before him had lived like an Autarii Urhan, lounging like country lords on plump pillows. They muffled Malus's movements as he crept closer to the figure chanting by the fire. When the highborn was slightly more than an arm's length away, the sound of chanting suddenly stopped, and the horned figure tensed. Without hesitation, Malus leapt at the beastman, grabbing one horn and placing the dagger to the figure's throat. 'Not a sound, Hadar, or I'll slice you from one horn to the other.'

The cloaked figure let out a bleat of alarm and Malus knew at once that it wasn't Hadar he had caught. Within moments, hanging panels around the perimeter of the tent were pushed aside, revealing connecting entrances with the satellite tents ranged around the central tent. Yaghan and his champions rushed inside, weapons held ready. In their wake stepped Kul Hadar, clutching his staff and baring his fanged smile.

Furious, Malus cut the throat of the beastman he'd caught, stepping back as Hadar's decoy convulsed and bled onto the piled rugs.

The shaman was undeterred. 'When Yaghan and his warriors lost track of you in the forest, he came to me and asked what you might do next.' Hadar's horned head shook from side to side. 'I told him that if you weren't still running, it meant you would be coming back here. Predictable, druchii, predictable. What I do not understand is why?'

Malus grinned wolfishly. 'I'm here to deal with you Hadar,' he said. 'I'm looking for a talisman, something called the Octagon of Praan. I've been told you have it.' The highborn held out his hand. 'Give it to me and I'll share with you everything I've found in the temple.'

The beastman threw back his head and laughed, a coarse, braying sound. 'You amuse me, druchii. Here, I'll make you a counter-offer. Put down that knife and tell me everything you know about the temple, and I promise I won't skin you alive before I sacrifice you in the sacred grove.'

'An interesting offer, Hadar. Let me think about it a moment,' Malus said, and threw his knife at the shaman's head. Hadar knocked it out of the air with his staff, but by that point Malus had drawn his sword and was charging across the tent.

Yaghan roared, and the champions rushed forward. One burly warrior made to grab Malus, and the highborn gave him a backhanded swipe with his blade that severed most of the champion's fingers. As the warrior bellowed in agony, Malus reversed his stroke and ripped open the beastman's throat.

Another of the champions lashed out with a gnarled fist and struck the highborn just below his right temple. Malus's vision went red and spots danced before his eyes. Another set of powerful hands grabbed the highborn's sword arm and pinned it; the gnarled fist lashed out again and Malus received another stunning blow to the head. He felt his left arm being grabbed and pinned back, and then when his vision cleared Yaghan was standing before him, brandishing his enormous battle axe. The champion showed Malus the cruel edge of both axe heads, and with a swift movement he reversed the axe and drove the weapon's butt into Malus's midriff.

There was the sound of crumpled metal and an icy shock convulsed his body. The highborn looked down as Yaghan drew back the butt of his axe and pulled its four-inch-long triangular spike from the hole it had punched in his gut. Dark blood bubbled out of the hole, and then the pain hit, wiping everything else away.

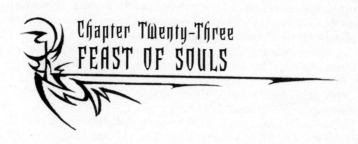

Chapter Twenty-Three
FEAST OF SOULS

THEY TOOK HIS swords and armour away and beat him with their fists until his robes and kheitan were soaked with blood. Blood still seeped from the wound in his gut, and the pain made any movement all but impossible. They lashed him to one of the thick poles in Hadar's tent, and the shaman questioned him at length about what he'd found in the temple.

Malus told him everything. He even overstated the amount of treasure waiting in the room with the terrible crystal. Let the beastmen kill one another trying to get there. If the Dark Mother was kind, Hadar would actually succeed, and Tz'arkan would claim him as he'd claimed Malus. Hadar said he didn't believe a word, and once again threatened to skin the highborn alive. Malus just laughed at him, which under the circumstances was torture in and of itself. Soon he would be in the clutches of a daemon for all eternity, the highborn said. What could Hadar do that would possibly compare to that?

'You do not have to die as yet,' the daemon's voice echoed in his head. 'If you wish it, I can heal your wounds. I can lend you great strength and speed. I can–'

'No,' the highborn muttered.

'No? You're refusing me? You would rather suffer as my slave for all eternity?'

'Shut up,' Malus hissed.

A heavy blow rocked the side of his head. Pain exploded through his midsection, and Malus passed out for several seconds.

When he came to, Hadar was crouching on his knees, looking up at Malus. 'Don't die on me yet, druchii,' the shaman grunted. 'We still have some things to discuss before you go up the slope to atone for your sins in the grove. Now, what does Tz'arkan want with the Octagon of Praan?'

The highborn blinked slowly, trying to focus his thoughts. 'He wants to be free. The Octagon belonged to one of the sorcerers who imprisoned him.'

'All the more reason to keep it from him, then,' Hadar said. 'Praan was the great shaman who founded this herd, many centuries ago. The talisman is one of the herd's most sacred treasures.'

Malus wasn't listening. His head had drooped to his chin, and a thin stream of bloody drool trickled onto the rug. Hadar pushed the highborn's head back and thumbed one eyelid open.

'He's nearly finished,' Hadar told Yaghan. 'Take him to the circle. I must prepare myself for the sacrifice.'

As the champions untied Malus's bonds, Hadar retreated to the far side of the tent, where a copper bowl brimmed with clear water. The shaman began washing the blood from his hands and face, purifying his body for the ceremony to come. 'You know, Malus, for all the carnage you have wrought, I look upon you as a blessing from the gods. Truly I do. You brought the Skull of Ehrenlish, killed Machuk and opened the Gate of Infinity for me. Now you have given me priceless information about the dangers of Tz'arkan and the temple, knowledge I will use to approach the crystal on my own terms and bend the daemon to my will. And finally, thanks to your foolishness, I will cut your throat in the circle of stones, and your blood will purify the grove you so recently defiled.' He turned to face Malus as the champions prepared to carry him from the tent. 'I look forward to eating your heart at the bonfire later tonight, Malus. You have done a great service for me and my herd.'

Hadar's deep laughter accompanied Malus into the darkness.

MALUS LEFT A trail of blood behind him the entire way up the hill. His limbs were growing cold, and his vision came and went. He had never been so close to death before; he could sense it, just at the edge of his being, seeping into his body like a winter chill.

The daemon spoke inside his head every step of the way, offering to heal his wounds. The highborn savoured the subtle edge of desperation mounting in Tz'arkan's voice. The daemon might be telling the truth about his eternal servitude after death, but it was still clear to Malus that Tz'arkan would much rather keep him alive. He also found it interesting that the daemon couldn't heal him without receiving permission. What other limitations did he have? The thought quenched some of the pain he felt. It was good to have even a thin sliver of control over his own fate.

Yaghan and the remaining champions, four in all, carried him effortlessly up the mountain slope. The dark trees rustled hungrily as they passed, no doubt sensing the spilled blood on Malus's body. The standing stones had been shattered by the magical energies unleashed there earlier in the day, but the circle within was clear of debris. Someone, perhaps the surviving priests, had cleared the many bodies away. Many of them were probably being served around the cook fires downslope.

There was a handful of priests still clearing away debris outside the sacred circle. They bowed to the champions as Yaghan barked orders to his warriors. The beastmen stepped reverently into the circle and laid Malus on the stone, then retreated beyond its border. They hadn't bothered to bind him, and why should they? He was unarmed and nearly dead.

At least, for the moment.

Malus carefully opened his eyes. The champions were standing around the outside of the stone circle with their weapons grounded. Yaghan stood off to one side, watching both his warriors and the activities of the priests.

'Tz'arkan,' Malus whispered, the words coming forth in a faint hiss. 'You said you could heal me. Make me stronger and faster.'

'That is so. I can make you stronger and faster for a short time, but there will be a price to pay later. Do you wish it?'

'Yes,' Malus said, and hated himself for it.

Black ice raced through his veins, freezing his blood and causing his wounds to burn. Every muscle clenched at the pain; his shoulders and legs came off the stone slab and hung there for several agonising seconds. Then he collapsed against the stone, half-delirious with the absence of suffering, and when his senses cleared he realised that he was whole again. Whole and powerful.

He didn't want to think how much deeper Tz'arkan had sunk his talons into him after he'd made that request. He would pay whatever price he had to and count the cost later.

Malus slowly turned his head. He spied a large stone outside the circle, less than a foot from where one of the champions stood. As quietly as he could he rolled onto his side and scrambled for it.

It felt as though he was made of fine steel wire, light and strong. He all but flew the intervening feet over to the rock, and plucked it from the ground as though it were a pebble. The champion was just starting to turn, his eyes going wide, when Malus took the rock and crushed the beastman's skull. The champion's eyes bulged and blood flew in a lazy spray as the warrior toppled to the ground. Malus had the champion's great sword in hand and was rushing to the next warrior in line before the first one had hit the ground.

The next champion bleated out a warning and raised his axe as Malus struck, slashing the beastman along the midsection and cutting him in two without breaking stride. The highborn raced through an expanding cloud of blood and viscera and set his sights on the next warrior, who had stepped forward and raised his sword to parry the highborn's attack. Malus slipped effortlessly under the beastman's guard and disembowelled him with a swift slash of his blade, then left the champion clutching at its guts as he sought out the last of Yaghan's warriors.

The remaining champion was running towards him, axe raised high. Out of the corner of his eye, Malus saw Yaghan attempting the same, approaching from the side and a little behind the highborn. Malus focused his attentions on the beastman in front of him – and without warning the steel was gone from his step and the attacking champion seemed to leap directly in his path. The highborn howled inwardly. Cursed daemon and your paltry gifts, he raged.

'You asked for help and I gave it,' the daemon replied coldly. 'Ask, and you may taste of my strength again.'

Acting instinctively Malus ducked left and swept low with the great sword, just as the champion's axe plummeted towards his head. The beastman missed, and Malus's sword sheared off the champion's right leg at the knee. The warrior toppled forward with a scream, and Malus took two steps past and then spun to receive Yaghan's charge.

Yaghan came on like a charging bull, roaring a challenge and holding his axe high. If he hits me solidly, even once, I'm dead, the highborn thought. Without armour, the two-handed axe would split him like kindling.

Malus watched Yaghan approach, waiting until the axe started to fall before dropping the point of his sword and ducking to the left. The axe whistled into the ground less than a finger's width away, and Malus took the opening this presented by raising the point of the blade enough to stab deep into the champion's massive right bicep. The champion howled and swept the axe at Malus with a backhanded stroke that he barely ducked in time.

Before the highborn could fully recover, the powerful champion reversed his stroke and slashed for the highborn's head. Malus ducked lower still and threw himself forward, this time digging the point of the blade through Yaghan's thickly muscled thigh. Flesh and muscle parted easily before the sharp point, tearing a deep trench from front to back along the outside of the champion's upper leg.

The highborn propelled himself past Yaghan as quickly as he could – but not quickly enough. Another lightning fast backhand stroke made a glancing blow on his right shoulder, making a deep, painful cut. Blood poured in a hot stream down his arm and the highborn stumbled. Malus gritted his teeth and spun to face the champion while he tried to plan his next move.

Again, Yaghan dictated the exchange, rushing forward and knocking Malus's sword aside with a powerful blow that nearly wrenched the blade from the highborn's hands. But instead of remaining still, Malus rushed forward as well, so when Yaghan's backhand swing came again, the highborn was inside the weapon's arc and could not hit. Again, Malus threw himself past Yaghan, and again chopped at the champion's thigh in passing. Blood now poured down the beastman's leg.

Yaghan turned about and rushed again almost immediately, but he was slower now, and his swing a tiny bit less powerful. As he charged, Malus spun and suddenly thrust his sword at the beastman's face, causing the champion to check his advance instinctively. As soon as he did, Malus dropped the point of his sword and buried it deep into the champion's wounded thigh.

This time the leg collapsed out from under the beastman. As he fell, Malus raised his blade and rushed in, bringing it down on Yaghan's outflung left arm. The heavy blade chopped nearly through the thick limb, leaving it hanging by a thin strip of muscle.

Yaghan let out a bellow of anguish and fell forwards in a pool of his own blood. Yet despite his terrible wounds, the champion tried to push himself back upright with his one working arm. Malus raised his sword and spared the champion further anguish. The blade sang against flesh and bone and Yaghan's head went bouncing down the steep mountain slope.

A chorus of yells went up from the priests, almost immediately answered from the camp below. Malus thought he could make out Kul Hadar's bellow among the mingled cries. He had little doubt the shaman and the rest of his herd would be storming the grove in moments.

If he were going to claim the Octagon of Praan it would be now or never. Fortunately, Hadar had given him the one clue he needed to uncover its resting place. Where better to keep the most sacred relics of the herd?

Gripping the bloody sword in both hands, Malus ran for the cave at the top of the cleft and the holy sanctum within.

Chapter Twenty-Four
THE DAEMON'S CURSE

THERE WERE TWO priests hiding just beyond the cave mouth; Malus stabbed one through the chest while the other pushed past him and ran braying down the slope. More crystal formations lent a greenish glow to the small, rough-hewn chamber. Scattered around the room were small altars to numerous beast-headed gods – minor deities, perhaps, that the herd worshipped in addition to the terrible Ruinous Powers that ruled the wild north.

In truth, the space wasn't so much a discreet chamber as it was an exceptionally broad bulge in a rough-hewn passage that led deeper into the mountain. Alert for signs of danger, Malus pressed onward.

The passage ran for more than fifty yards in more or less a straight line. The farther Malus went, the more he began to notice old, discarded bones – many cracked for the marrow within – and smell the stench of rotting meat. A guardian, Malus thought sourly. But what sort of guardian, and where is it hiding? More importantly, does it sense my presence?

Just ahead, the highborn could see more greenish light. The passage appeared to end in another small cave, lit this time by a glowing crystal that had been placed in an iron brazier instead of growing straight from the ground. In the pale glow Malus could see a broad shelf of natural stone along the far wall of the chamber. Resting on that shelf and gleaming in the greenish glow sat a large, octagonal medallion made from brass and affixed to a long chain. Runes covered the surface of the medallion, hinting at the power locked within.

'Yes – that's it! The Octagon of Praan! Seize it!' urged the daemon.

But Malus was far more interested in the stench of rotted meat that hung in the air of the small chamber. He crept carefully and quietly to the threshold and slowly surveyed the room. The highborn heard no sounds nor saw any movement.

That's strange, he thought. What is causing the smell? And then he saw the body of the stag heaped in a broken lump on the floor near the Octagon itself. Its back and neck were broken, causing the body to bend in opposite angles from one another. One side of a magnificent rack of antlers had been snapped off, and rested on the floor near the body. Both forelegs had been torn away at some point in the past, and the body rested in a black pool of rotting blood. Malus guessed it had sat in the cave for a week or more. Perhaps a sacrifice, he thought. Though those marrow-bones back there didn't crack themselves.

The highborn surveyed the room again. Nothing moved in the shadows. Maybe there was a guardian previously, and it was killed in one of the battles? The idea seemed plausible, especially since the chamber appeared quite empty. No time to waste, Malus thought decisively. I do know for a fact that Hadar will be here at any moment, and I don't relish being trapped in a dead-end tunnel.

Malus crossed the small cave, reaching for the talisman. When he was halfway across something huge and hairy landed on his back and knocked him flat onto the rocky floor. A knotted club smashed into the middle of his back, knocking the breath out of him. Another blow hit hard against his ribs and sent waves of fiery agony shooting across his chest.

The highborn tried to rise, only to discover that his attacker was sitting on his lower back and pinning him in place to deliver his blows. The club smashed down on his right shoulder next, and the pain of that atop the cut he'd received there, nearly knocked him out.

His attacker was in a perfect place to avoid the blows of the large sword in Malus's hands. Thinking desperately, the highborn reversed his grip on the sword so he held it underhand, and stabbed backwards as hard as he could. The point of the sword bit into flesh and his attacker let loose a savage howl that set his hair on end. It leaped off him, and when it did Malus raced quickly across the floor towards the Octagon. Panting in pain, he turned to face his attacker and his eyes went wide with shock.

If the massive guardian of the Octagon had once been a beastman, there was little resemblance left any more. The creature was massive, with huge, broad shoulders and short, trunk-like legs. The powerfully muscled body was covered in irregular patches of fur, and the stunted, misshapen head looked as though it had been made of wax and left half-formed. One bloodshot eye watched him intently.

Malus noted that the creature wasn't carrying a club. The damage it had done was with fists alone.

The guardian of the Octagon clapped a hand to the deep wound in its side and let out a howl that was part angry and part anguish. Without warning it turned and scrambled up the wall behind it, alighting on a rough ledge of rock that sat above the cave entrance.

For a split second Malus thought that the creature was just going to sit there and lick its wound, but as soon as it reached the ledge it let out a snarl and leapt at him once more.

With his back to the shelf there was no place to run. Had Malus been a beginner in the arts of combat he might have panicked. Instead he set the pommel of his great sword against the rock shelf behind him and pointed it directly at the creature's chest.

The guardian let out a wail and Malus struck the sword at a point just below its ribs. The broad blade drove itself up to the quillons in the creature's chest, spilling blood and bile in a torrent onto Malus in the heartbeat before the monster's bulk slammed against him. He hit the rock shelf hard and gasped at the pain that flared across his back. Then the creature let out a strangled cry and grasped the highborn's head firmly in one enormous hand. The guardian's other hand tightened on Malus's shoulder, and then the monster started to twist.

It was trying to twist his head off.

Malus gritted his teeth and tensed his neck, battering the huge hands with his fists, but it was like the chicken fighting the hands of the farmwife. He grabbed at the hilt of the sword and tried to twist it in the wound – anything to force the creature to release him. But the monster only howled in pain and redoubled its efforts.

Slowly, inexorably, Malus's head turned. When it reached the limit his spine would allow, it started to bend further. Pain shot along his vertebrae, and his vision dissolved into a white haze. The highborn started to shout, a single long, painful note as he felt his bones continue to flex and wondered how close he was to the breaking point.

Suddenly, the pressure eased, dropping off almost to nothing. Slowly – and equally painfully – Malus straightened his head, and the guardian's body slumped to the side. Its melted face was ashen, and huge quantities of its blood lapped against the highborn's boots.

Uncaring, the highborn sat down in the sticky fluid and tried to get his breathing under control. He'd been stabbed, cut and beaten dozens of times, but he'd never had to suffer an attack like that before.

'Get up,' the daemon urged. 'Hurry. Kul Hadar could be here at any moment!'

'Let him come,' Malus snarled. 'He can't twist my head off.'

'No. He puts his faith in axes,' Tz'arkan answered sarcastically. 'Now go.'

Malus climbed painfully to his feet and reached for the Octagon. 'Put it on,' the daemon said.

'Why? What does it do?'

'It absorbs magical energy. Spells directed against you will be consumed by the amulet, no matter how powerful. It is a most useful talisman.'

Suspicion warred with desperation in Malus's mind. What if the daemon were lying? Then again, could he afford not to take advantage of such a valuable talisman? In the end, the looped the chain over his neck with a barely repressed curse. The daemon might not be telling the truth, but neither would he put Malus in a position where he could no longer serve his interests.

With a great deal of effort, Malus recovered his sword and made his way back down the passage. His worst fears of facing Hadar and his mob at the mouth of the shrine turned out to be unfounded. They waited before the ruins of the stone circle, evidently unwilling to defile the sacred cave with further violence.

The highborn noticed with some surprise that Hadar had less than fifty of the herd with him. *Is your support waning, Hadar, or has the herd gotten its fill of bloodshed for the time being?*

The ones that did come, however, were the true believers. When they saw he wore the Octagon, the beastmen let out howls of anger and outrage.

'There are almost fifty of them,' the daemon said. 'You have neither armour nor mount. You will need my help if you are to prevail.'

'No,' Malus said angrily. 'I've bartered enough of my flesh to you today. You'll get no more.'

'You'll die!'

'Perhaps… and perhaps not. Now shut up and observe.'

Malus stepped from the cave. 'It appears I won't be serving your herd quite so well as you imagined, Hadar.'

'Remove the Octagon from your unclean neck at once!' Hadar roared, and the rest of the true believers howled their agreement.

Malus pretended to hold up the medallion between thumb and forefinger and study it intently. 'If this trinket is so sacred, and your faith so strong, why don't we put it to the test?'

For a moment Hadar didn't answer. The rest of the faithful eyed him expectantly, and the shaman knew he'd been trapped. 'What do you have in mind?'

Malus spread his hands. 'What else? I challenge you. If you win, your faith is clearly superior, and the medallion is yours. But if you lose…'

Malus and Hadar locked eyes. Finally, the shaman said. 'It is not worth considering, druchii. I will not lose.'

The druchii grinned. 'Then let us begin.'

'No!' Tz'arkan raged. 'You fool. You set no terms for the challenge!'

'Terms? What terms do I need? While I wear the Octagon, his magic can't affect me, and I fear that stick of his far less than Yaghran's axe. The advantage is mine.' And besides, Malus thought grimly, I want to be certain that, whatever else may happen, Hadar dies by my hand. He owes me a debt of pain.

Malus was already walking down the hill, sword held at the ready. Hadar shrugged out of his robe and hefted his heavy staff. His lips pulled back in a feral smile.

That's odd, the highborn thought to himself. What does he have to smile about?

Then Hadar spoke a string of words and the air seemed to warp around the shaman. His already imposing frame swelled even further, appearing far more powerful than before. Hadar roared like an enraged bear – and then barked out another string of magical words. By the time he'd finished speaking he had crossed the ten or so yards between himself and Malus.

The next thing Malus knew, the shaman's staff smashed against his sword hand and the great sword went spinning off into the grass. Hadar followed up with a backhanded swing that crashed into the highborn's chest and sent him flying in the opposite direction.

He fetched up alarmingly close to the dark trees, his ribs throbbing as though he'd been kicked by a cold one. It took a moment before he could breathe again, and in that time Hadar was standing over him, striking down at his head with his terrible staff. Malus summoned all his strength and leapt away barely in time.

'You lied to me!' Malus raged at the daemon as he ran headlong for his lost sword.

'No, I told you exactly what Hadar's limitations were. His magic can't affect you directly. You were the fool who thought you knew better than I in matters of sorcery.'

Suddenly a shadow fell over Malus, and instinct made him duck his head. Instead of killing him, the staff struck him across his shoulders and flung him face-first to the ground. His entire left arm was numb from the blow, and his right throbbed in agony. Worse, he was now several yards downslope from where his sword lay. Realising the danger in hesitating, Malus scrabbled to his feet and staggered forward, his right hand running through the grass before him as he tried to find something he could use as a weapon.

The faithful laughed to see their foe capering like a fool in the grove he'd defamed. Hadar stalked after him, summoning his power once more. 'You were stupid to challenge me in my place of power,' Hadar said. 'Here I can work my magic with impunity, drawing strength from the land itself. What do you have that can compare?'

'Let me help you,' the daemon whispered. 'I can give you the strength and speed to surprise him. Just say the word.'

'No,' Malus replied.

The staff smashed down on him again, this time striking the high-born in the lower back. Malus cried out in pain and fell face-first. His one good hand fumbled frantically through the grass – and finally closed on something small and hard.

Hadar rose above him, his staff poised to strike. 'I had expected better of the warrior who bested Yaghan,' the shaman said. 'But then, the earth is not your ally, is it?'

Malus rolled onto his back and snapped his right hand forward, fingers pointing up at the bottom of Hadar's jaw. The shaman had just enough time to register the motion before the small, charred boot knife punched through soft flesh and drove upwards into Kul Hadar's brain.

'Perhaps not, beastman,' Malus answered coldly. 'But from time to time she supplies me with what I need.'

The shaman swayed on his feet for the space of several heartbeats, then crashed to the ground.

I thought that knife had landed somewhere over here, the highborn thought as he climbed to his feet. Malus went and reclaimed his sword, ignoring the shocked cries and the horrified looks of the true believers. Then he turned on them, brandishing the point of the sword in their faces.

'Hear me, animals,' Malus growled. 'Your shaman is dead. Your champions are dead. Your relic has been plundered – all by my hand alone. Your herd has been broken – leave now, or try your faith against mine and perish, as Kul Hadar did. Now choose.'

The true believers stared at Malus for several heartbeats, clearly weighing their convictions. One beastman stepped forward, opening his mouth to speak, and Malus stabbed him through the throat. The rest fled, filling the grove with wails of despair.

Malus watched them go. Once they were lost from sight, he let the great sword fall to the ground and walked over to Yaghan's headless body. Bending down, he picked up the champion's fallen axe. Then, studying the black-boled trees carefully, he went to gather some wood for a fire.

THE LOGS BLAZED hotly in the stone circle, the heat reflecting from the slab and keeping the chill of the night at bay. Malus carved off another piece of meat with his boot knife and slipped the morsel into his mouth. It was tough and chewy, but by no means the most stringy meat he'd ever had. A little gamy, but that was all right, too. He sat back on his haunches and watched the northern lights dance overhead.

There had been much shouting and howls of despair in the herd camp throughout the afternoon, but as evening wore on the place fell silent. Malus wandered down from the grove – itself a great deal less demonstrative than before – and found the place deserted. He went through Hadar's tent and found it expertly pillaged. Except for his belongings – they sat in a neat pile on the dirt floor where rugs and pillows had once lain. Malus had armed himself, and, feeling more relaxed at that point, went into the woods to find Spite.

The nauglir now wandered near the bottom of the cleft, helping himself to Hadar's fallen champions. He'd let Spite eat his fill, and then begin the long trek south, back to the Hag. The daemon's words still echoed in his mind: *Already the sands are running from the hourglass. Even as we speak your life is slipping from your grasp.*

He had the Octagon of Praan, but that still left four talismans to go, and he hadn't any idea how to find them. And of the two people he knew who might have the information, one likely wanted him dead and the other had actively tried to kill him by sending him into the Wastes in the first place.

'Your sister sought to teach you a lesson,' Tz'arkan said. 'If she wanted you dead she would have kept you in the city where Urial could get to you.'

Malus bit back a curse. It was going to be a long time before he grew accustomed to the daemon's presence in the back of his mind. 'You may have a point,' the highborn grudgingly agreed. 'She may have expected me to turn back once the going became too dangerous.' He grinned. 'It appears my sister does not know me as well as she thinks.'

Then as he thought about the possibilities, his face grew cold. If that's true, then Nagaira never meant to sacrifice Dalvar and her men at all.

'Perhaps, but that assumption worked out in your favour, putting rest to a potential threat of betrayal. Simply tell her your warband was wiped out on the journey north. It is nothing but the truth.'

Malus nodded, but his expression was troubled. He'd lost a great many valuable resources during the journey. Some, like Lhunara, would be almost impossible to replace.

Yet the expedition hadn't been a total loss. He would return with enough wealth from the daemon's treasure chamber to pay off his debts and begin forming the power base he'd always needed...

'You are very free with my trinkets, Darkblade,' the daemon warned.

'If I'm free with your gold, you'll be free in turn,' Malus replied. 'I can't search for your relics if I wind up on the wrong end of an assassin's blade.'

Tz'arkan fell silent. Malus afforded himself a brief, smug grin. It was true that he'd left the Hag as a highborn and would return as a slave, but between now and then he would find a way to conceal the mark of the daemon's bond. As bad as his situation was, it still lent him advantages that no one else realised he possessed. He planned on making use of those advantages where they would do the most good.

He would overcome this setback. Eventually, he would be free again. He was capable of making sacrifices and suffering lasting torments if they brought him closer to his goals. That was the essence of who the druchii were – taking strength from darkness and making it their own.

The highborn leaned back against the burnt stump of one of the standing stones. He would find a way to rebuild his ties to Urial or Nagaira. The highborn was willing to pay whatever price was required. He was nothing if not a reasonable man.

Malus cut another slice of Kul Hadar's heart and chewed it thoughtfully, contemplating the future.

BLOODSTORM

Chapter One
PRODIGAL

THE NAUGLIR LET out a hiss like hot steel quenched in blood, its muscular legs pumping furiously as the huge reptile scrambled around the narrow turn. Clots of snow and black cinders sprayed from beneath the cold one's claws and Malus Darkblade twisted in the saddle as he fought to keep his seat. Sibilant shouts echoed in the cold air behind Malus, rising over the thunder of hooves. A crossbow bolt buzzed past his ear like an angry hornet. The highborn bared his teeth in a feral grin as he regained his balance and put the spurs to Spite's flanks once more. Just ahead the Spear Road fell away into the dreadful Valley of Shadow and in the distance he could spy the knifelike towers of Hag Graef rising from the clinging tendrils of last night's fog.

Another bolt whipped a hand span from the highborn's face – then a third slammed like a hammer blow between Malus's shoulders. The broad, steel head of the crossbow bolt punched through the thick cloak of crudely stitched beastman hide Malus wore and slapped into the backplate of his armour with a flat *crack*. The silver steel plate and the thick leather kheitan beneath robbed the shot of much of its lethal force, but the bolt's tip tore into his back like a talon of ice. The highborn let out a wordless snarl of pain and bent as low as he could against Spite's heaving back. The gang of brigands galloping in Malus's wake let out a chorus of savage cries as they sensed the chase was nearly at an end.

It had been nearly three months since Malus and his retainers had slipped from Hag Graef and headed north, hunting a source of ancient power hidden in the Chaos Wastes. This was not the triumphant return he'd dreamt of all those months ago.

Countless leagues of snow and blood and starvation had left their mark on rider and mount. The cold one's scaly, armoured hide bore dozens of scars from sword, axe and claw, and Malus's saddle was cinched tightly over sharply etched ribs. The highborn's cloak of coarse, greasy black fur was tattered and rent and the silver steel armour beneath was tarnished and scarred from constant wear. His robes and kheitan were stiff with old sweat, blood and grime and his boots were patched with rags and scraps of deer hide. Malus's dark eyes were sunken and fever-bright, his cruel features paler and even more sharply defined. With hollow cheeks and thin, cracked lips, he seemed more wight than man.

Death had dogged his path from the moment his journey began. Every retainer who'd ridden from the Hag into the tainted north had died there, some by Malus's own hand. Yet he hadn't returned from the Wastes empty-handed: four large saddlebags bounced heavily on Spite's gaunt flanks, bulging with a Drachau's ransom in gold and gems.

Nor had he returned entirely alone.

Spite plunged down the long, steep slope toward the valley floor and for a moment the sounds of pursuit fell away on the far side of the ridge. Malus reached back and drew his crossbow from its saddle hook. His path back to Hag Graef had been fraught with peril: packs of fierce beastmen, twisted, Chaos-tainted monsters and gangs of druchii thieves had all sought to spill his blood, hungry for his flesh or the bags of treasure at his side. The highborn's sword was notched and pitted and his bolts were nearly spent. 'I didn't come all this way to die within sight of home,' Malus swore, calling on every blasphemous god he could name.

'Then kill them,' a cold voice replied, welling up in Malus's chest like blood from an old wound. 'There are but eight of them, little druchii. Let your cold one feast on their sallow flesh.'

Malus snarled, resisting an urge to pound at his breast with a gauntleted hand. 'Bold words from a daemon, who knows nothing of hunger or fatigue.'

'You have your hate, Malus,' the daemon Tz'arkan whispered, the words buzzing in his skull like flies. 'With hate, all things are possible.'

'If that were true I would have been rid of you long ago,' the highborn seethed, working the arming lever on the crossbow and readying it to fire. 'Now shut up and let me concentrate.'

He could feel the daemon's consciousness recede, his bones vibrating with Tz'arkan's mocking laughter. There were times, late in the night, when Malus would awaken and feel the daemon writhing within his chest like a clutch of vipers, slithering and tangling around his beating heart.

Desperation had driven him north, seeking power to use against his enemies. He sought the power to thwart the schemes of his father and his siblings, to bathe in their blood and drink deeply of their pain. And he'd found what he sought in a temple far to the north, standing before a great crystal surrounded by circle after circle of magical wards and the piled riches of a dozen kingdoms. Giddy with power-lust and ravenous greed, Malus had been oblivious to the cunning trap surrounding him. The highborn had plucked a single ring from the treasure heaped in the room – a perfect ruby cabochon, like a shimmering drop of blood – and had slipped it on his finger. And the terrible daemon bound within the crystal had claimed Darkblade's soul in return.

The steel bowstring locked into place and one of Malus's last bolts was levered into the firing channel. Spite had nearly reached the base of the slope as the first of the druchii brigands crested the ridgeline with a lupine howl. Malus twisted in the saddle and fired with an ease born from months of experience. The black-fletched bolt struck the brigand below the ribcage, piercing the rusted mail the druchii wore and tearing upwards through his vitals before lodging in the man's spine. The brigand's howl cut off with a choked cry and he toppled backwards out of the saddle.

Tall stands of darkpine and witchwood rose from the dark soil of the valley floor, their branches heavy with snow. Perpetual twilight reigned beneath the trees; in the narrow confines of the valley the sun's light reached the city and its surroundings for a few short hours each day. The Spear Road wound a sinuous course among the copses of trees, but Malus spurred his mount directly ahead, off the road and into the shadowy wood.

Malus bent low against Spite's neck as the nauglir crashed through low-hanging branches and leapt the rotting boles of fallen trees. Speed was of the essence. The thieves had been as patient as wolves, tracking him for days and gauging his strength. Now they knew he and his mount were almost spent and they knew that the safety of the city walls was less than a mile away. If they didn't pull him down in the next few minutes they would be cheated of their prize.

Sure enough, shouts and muffled hoof beats echoed across the snowy ground behind Malus. The highborn readied his crossbow and twisted at the waist, aiming backwards one-handed at the black shapes darting between the trees. He fired out of instinct and caught one of the brigands' horses in mid-turn – the animal lost its footing with a terrible shriek and crashed to the ground in a spray of dirt and snow, throwing its rider into a stand of fallen timber. Two of the bandits fired their weapons in response and a bolt struck a fan of bright sparks as it glanced from Malus's left pauldron. The blow knocked the highborn forwards – and his crossbow was smashed from his hands by a pine bough.

Pine needles lashed at the side of Malus's face and then suddenly the trees fell away on either side and Spite was lunging through drifts of piled snow. The cold one was losing speed rapidly. Ahead the black ribbon of the Spear Road crossed a narrow, snowy field and less than a quarter of a mile away loomed his home, the great City of Shadow. 'The race is nearly won, beast of the deep earth,' Malus rasped to his mount. 'A few more furlongs and then we will see how brave these dogs are.' As if understanding the highborn's words, Spite put on a final burst of speed, charging across the open ground for the basalt walls of the city ahead.

Malus drew his sword, holding it high in hopes of catching the attention of the men on the ramparts. The thunder of hoof beats brought his head around – the five remaining bandits had emerged from the woods and were lashing at their horses' flanks with whip and spur. Their pale faces stood out sharply against the dark background of the hooded cloaks they wore. Their eyes were intent, teeth bared against the icy wind.

The bandits were gaining ground, but slowly, too slowly. Malus was halfway to the city walls within moments and could spy the tall helmets of the city guard rising above the spiked battlements of the gatehouse. 'Open the gate!' he cried, with all the strength he could muster. If the guardsmen heard, they gave no sign.

Spite leapt onto the roadway, flat feet crunching across the pressed layer of cinders. Malus caught sight of several stubby poles with black fletching jutting at an angle from the frozen ground – the heavy bolts the city guard had fired at him months ago still lay where they had fallen, perhaps left as a warning to future travellers. He was less than a hundred paces from the tall city gates, yet the portal remained shut.

Malus hurled a torrent of curses at the guards on the battlements, hauling back on Spite's reins to stop the beast's headlong rush. The gate wasn't going to open in time – if at all.

The wounded nauglir stumbled to a halt right in front of the tall doors. Malus hauled on the reins and brought the beast sharply around, then lashed out at the dark iron with an armoured boot. 'Open the gates you lowborn worms!' Malus roared.

Then the air around the highborn was filled with the angry buzz of man-made hornets. Three crossbow bolts shattered against the city's iron gates and two more struck Malus in the back. One bolt tore through his heavy cloak and skimmed the druchii's backplate with a harsh, clattering sound, while the second punched through his cloak, his left pauldron and part of the backplate it overlapped. Malus felt a stabbing pain in his shoulder and threw himself instinctively to the ground, taking shelter between Spite's bulk and the gate.

The sound of hooves had stopped. Spite turned his head to face his attackers, managing a weak hiss. Malus chanced a quick look over the nauglir's hindquarters. The bandits had reined in, right in the middle of the road, eyeing the city's gatehouse and debating their chances. The highborn could feel blood staining his robes and seeping down his back. 'Why aren't they opening the damned gate,' he muttered fiercely. 'Why aren't they shooting at these curs?'

'Biding their time, perhaps,' Tz'arkan said, faintly amused. 'The bandits kill you, they kill the bandits and then they have six bodies to loot.'

'I wouldn't sound so smug, daemon,' Darkblade said through gritted teeth. He planted the point of his sword in the ground and groped over his shoulder, trying to pull the crossbow bolts free from his back. 'There are five of them and I'm down to sword and knife. If they put a bolt through my eye, how will you ever escape that cursed temple?'

'Do not fear for me, Darkblade,' the daemon said. 'I have waited thousands of years in my prison and I can wait thousands more if I must. You should worry about the consequences if you fail me and I claim your soul for eternity. But that need not happen. These fools are fodder for your blade, if you allow me to lend you a little strength.'

Malus clenched his fists. The daemon had claimed him in the temple for one reason only – to be free from the prison he'd been bound into millennia ago. Darkblade was his agent in the world of mortals, seeking the keys that would unlock the magical wards trapping Tz'arkan in his crystal cell. And for all that the daemon threatened him with eternal torment, Tz'arkan was quick to lend the highborn a measure of his power when things took a turn for the worse.

There had been several times on the long journey home when Malus had been forced to accept Tz'arkan's gifts: knitting torn flesh and broken bone, staving off fever or frostbite or giving him unearthly speed and strength in battle. Each time, when the tide of unearthly power faded, it felt as though the daemon's taint had spread a little further through his body, strengthening Tz'arkan's hold over him.

And yet, Malus thought, did he dare refuse?

Suddenly the sound of hoof beats thundered through the air and Malus heard Spite utter a warning hiss. 'All right,' the highborn seethed. 'Lend me your strength one last time, daemon.'

'One last time,' the daemon answered mockingly. 'Of course.'

The power hit like a rush of black, icy water, racing through his body in a torrent that made every muscle strain at its fleshy bonds. Malus's head snapped back, his mouth dropping open in a wordless snarl. He could feel the veins on his face and neck writhe like serpents, pulsing with corruption. When his vision cleared, his senses were sharp and the world had slowed to a turgid crawl. The sound of the oncoming horses was like the slow, purposeful beat of a temple drum.

The bandits came forward in a rush, hoping to kill their prey swiftly and escape before the guards on the walls changed their mind. Malus heard two riders split off to the right, towards Spite's head, while the other three circled wide around the cold one's tail. Grinning like a wolf, Malus raced at the trio to his left.

Once again, the highborn was amazed at the way he raced across the ground, his steps so swift and light they didn't seem to actually touch the earth at all. He was on the brigands before they knew it, their attention focused on Spite and his deadly tail. The first horse caught wind of Malus and let out a terrified shriek, its eyes rolling back in its head with fear as it sensed the daemon inside him. It tossed its head and tried to back away, and Malus leapt in and sliced through its reins with a flick of his wrist. The animal reared and the rider lost his seat, tumbling backwards onto the road. Before he could recover, Malus buried his blade in the bandit's neck, spraying a jet of bright crimson across the churned snow.

A crossbow bolt droned lazily past his head. Malus turned in time to see the second bandit hurl the empty crossbow at his face. He batted the weapon aside with his sword and rushed forward, savouring the dawning horror in the bandit's eyes as the brigand tried to draw his sword in time. Malus's sword flashed, severing the bandit's right leg at the knee. Druchii and horse screamed alike and the bandit fell beneath the horse's hooves as the animal bolted, fleeing Malus's daemonic visage.

Malus heard another horse scream then saw the third bandit yank savagely on his reins and kick his lathered mount into a gallop, racing back down the road. The remaining two brigands joined him, frantically lashing at their horses' flanks.

They were about ten yards from the gate when the bolt throwers on top of the walls went into action. The metal strings snapped and sang and bolts three feet long streaked through the clear air piercing man and horse. As the bodies tumbled across the snowy ground Malus fell to his knees, guts heaving as the daemon's power leached from his body. He retched black bile onto the cinder-covered road and heard the sound of chains as the city guard began to winch open the great gates.

A small spark of something akin to panic welled up in Malus's brain. Control, he thought fiercely, trying to overcome his helpless nausea. Push back the daemon. Hide his traces...

There was no sin in Naggaroth save weakness: the Witch King commanded the fealty of conquerors and slave masters – anything less was prey. Malus well knew that if his people discovered Tz'arkan's hold over him they would slaughter him out of hand. It did not matter that the daemon's gifts made him the equal of any ten druchii – the fact that he'd allowed himself to fall into Tz'arkan's trap and become the daemon's slave made him unfit to live.

Over the long months in the wilderness Malus had struggled to master the telltale signs of daemonic influence that warped his thin frame. With an effort of extreme will, he slowed his racing heart, causing the black veins to recede from his neck and face. His skin, a chalky bluish-white, smoothed into a uniform alabaster tone. As the first of the guards charged out onto the road Malus wiped bile from his lips and forced himself to rise without the slightest sign of his exertions.

The armoured guardsmen of the city raced from the gateway, long knives gleaming in their hands. Spite raised his head from the carcass of one of the brigand's horses and roared a warning at the interlopers, his blocky snout smeared with blood and scraps of flesh. The warriors ignored both Malus and his mount, inspecting each of the brigands in turn and slitting their throats with quick, expert knife strokes, then searching the bodies for valuables. The highborn headed back towards Spite, keeping a wary distance until the nauglir had eaten his fill of horseflesh.

'Two dead and the rest put to flight in as much time as it takes to tell of it,' said a voice from the shadows of the city gate. 'A most impressive display, dread lord. Your time in the wilderness has suited you well, if I may be so bold.'

Malus turned at the sound of the voice, his fist clenching around the hilt of his sword. A guard captain stepped into the light, clad in fine armour and wearing a silver-chased sword at his hip. There was a wry look in the captain's dark eyes that Malus didn't care for one bit. There was something familiar about the man.

'Bold words from a craven captain,' Malus hissed, 'who hid behind stone walls while I fought alone. When the Vaulkhar hears of it you and your children's lives will be forfeit.'

Malus expected the man to quail at the words, but instead the captain smiled faintly and his dark eyes shone with cruel mirth. The highborn fought the urge to bury his knife in the man's mocking eyes – remembering who he was talking to. It was the same captain he'd bribed to escape the city months ago. His face had picked up a few new scars in the meantime, but judging by his new armour he'd clearly put Malus's gift to good use.

The captain stepped from beneath the gate arch and approached the highborn. 'You are of course free to make your complaint to your father the Vaulkhar,' he said calmly, 'but I don't think it would be a pleasant reunion, dread lord. In fact, it could be a fatal one.'

Malus studied the captain with narrowed eyes. 'And how would you know such a thing?'

'Because there is a standing order for the city guard – issued by both your father and the Drachau himself – that Malus, son of Lurhan, is to be arrested on sight and delivered to the Vaulkhar's tower.' The captain smiled. 'Does your father always treat his children like criminals, dread lord?'

The captain's audacity was breathtaking – but it was a carefully calculated ploy, Malus saw. The man was nothing if not ambitious.

Malus stepped closer to the captain. 'So you kept the gates closed as a favour to me, then?'

'Of course, dread lord. If I'd sounded the alarm and opened the gates, the commander of the watch would have to be informed and that would have necessitated your arrest.' The captain glanced around at his men. 'At the moment I'm just giving my men a break while I discuss business with a noble acquaintance.'

Malus grinned mirthlessly. 'Indeed?'

The captain nodded. 'Certainly. I know very well what your father and the Drachau are offering for your arrest. I'm curious to know what you'd offer to avoid that unfortunate fate.'

The highborn stared at the captain and began to laugh. It was a harsh, bloodless sound that drained the amusement from the captain's face. 'As I seem to recall I promised you a reward when I returned to Hag Graef,' Malus said. 'Allow me into the city, captain and I shall double it.'

'Is that so?' The captain considered Malus carefully, weighing the risks. Malus could see the avarice in the man's expression. 'I'll take the payment now if it please you, dread lord.'

'Are you certain that's wise, with all these men around? They'll want a cut, too and then where will you be?' The highborn took a step closer and spoke in a conspiratorial whisper. 'Do you know of a flesh house in the Corsairs' Quarter called the House of Brass?'

'I know of it,' the captain said warily.

'Then I have a favour to ask of you. Carry a message to Silar Thornblood – he is one of my sworn men – and tell him to meet me there this evening. You will find him at my tower in the Hag. Accompany him tonight and I will see you amply rewarded for your efforts.'

The captain cocked his head suspiciously. 'My dread lord is a cruel and canny man,' he said. 'So you understand if I have reason to believe this is some sort of deception.'

Malus grinned. It was hard not to admire such brazenness. 'Do I dare deceive you captain? If I do, you report me to my father and I can't have that.'

The captain thought it over for a moment, gauging the odds. 'Very well,' he said evenly. 'I will look forward to our rendezvous, then. What message shall I deliver?'

'Say that his lord is returned from the Wastes,' Malus said. 'That will tell him all he needs to know.'

THE HOUSE OF Brass was a den of pleasures that catered to highborn druchii in a seedier district of the city. Malus knew the proprietor well, having spent entire nights in one of the private suites entertaining disreputable guests and would-be allies. It was one of the first places the Vaulkhar's men would think to look if they knew he'd returned to the city, but he was certain that Mistress Nemeira knew him well enough that she'd never dare betray him. The House of Brass was a maze of chambers and narrow corridors – some hidden behind concealed doors and wall panels – that occupied half a city block at the border between the Corsairs' Quarter and the Slavers' Quarter. There were even secret escape routes from the building that supposedly led outside the city walls; Nemeira charged extra for their use.

Malus took another sip of wine and settled deeper into a mound of thick cushions. The room was decorated in the autarii style, with piles of thick rugs and pillows laid around braziers in a rough cloverleaf pattern around a circular hearth. His grimy, ragged clothes and kheitan had been taken away – to be burned immediately, Nemeira had said sternly – and his ravaged armour had been carried off to be mended by an armourer the proprietor knew well. After a long, scalding bath and vigorous scrubbing by two attendants, he'd changed into robes of rich silk and ordered the best wine the house could provide.

Weariness pulled at him with ever-strengthening fingers. Since the brigands had picked up his trail a few days before there had been precious few opportunities to sleep and no chance to forage for food. Exhaustion threatened to overwhelm him even as his mind roiled with suspicion.

There was a light scratching at the door. Malus set his wine aside, his right hand straying to the sword lying on the rug beside him. 'Enter,' he said.

The door opened silently and a human slave entered, head bowed and eyes downcast. 'Your guests have arrived and await your pleasure, dread lord,' she said softly. 'Will you see them?'

'Bring them in, then fetch wine and food from the kitchen,' Malus answered.

Now we'll have some answers, he thought. And a bit of pleasant diversion afterwards. He'd had hours to contemplate the long list of excruciations he would inflict on that upstart captain. It would be a fine way to celebrate his return to Hag Graef.

In moments the door opened again to admit three druchii. Silar Thornblood entered first, his tall frame slightly stooped due to the chamber's low ceiling. The young druchii wore full armour and his hand rested warily on the hilt of his sword. Behind him slipped a dark shadow wrapped in a heavy, hooded cloak. As the figure stepped into the light of the nearest brazier, Malus caught sight of Arleth Vann's pale, cadaverous face. His eyes glinted golden in the firelight, as cold and merciless as the stare of a hungry wolf. The last to enter was the guard captain, who eyed the room's luxurious furnishings with an equal mixture of suspicion and desire.

Silar caught sight of Malus and his expression changed from one of wariness to genuine surprise. 'When the captain sought me out I was sure this had to be some trick,' the young druchii said.

Malus rose, accepting Silar's formal bow. 'Well met, Silar – and you, Arleth Vann,' the highborn said, nodding his head to the hooded druchii. 'Though I'm curious why both of you elected to come.'

'I had to be certain we weren't followed,' Silar replied, his expression turning grim. 'Obviously you've heard about the warrant for your arrest. The Vaulkhar has his eye on us night and day, hoping we will lead him to you.'

Before Malus could reply, the guard captain took a step forward. 'Forgive me, dread lord, but I have no wish to intrude on you further. If we could conclude our business now, I'll be on my way.'

'Intrusion? There is no intrusion, captain,' Malus said easily. 'You have done me a great favour and you are my guest this evening.' He gestured at the cushions. 'Sit. We have much to discuss and I've been without stimulating company for quite some time.' He fixed the druchii with a hard stare. 'I insist.'

Malus's two retainers turned to regard the captain and the enterprising druchii's face went pale as he realised the snare he'd stepped in. 'I... yes... of course,' he said uneasily.

'Excellent,' the highborn said. 'I regret that I can't share the hospitality of my own apartments, captain, but I expect that my half-brother Urial has taken out his frustrations on them in my absence, eh, Silar?'

Silar turned to Malus, his brow furrowing in concern. 'You mean you haven't heard?'

Malus's good humour faded. 'Heard what?'

Without a word, Silar pointed to the hadrilkar around his neck. It was not the silver steel that Malus was familiar with, but pure silver, worked in the sigil of the Vaulkhar himself.

'Your tower has been confiscated by your father, along with all the property within,' Silar said, his voice grave. 'He has claimed your retainers, your slaves – everything. You've been disowned, cast out of the Vaulkhar's household.'

Chapter Two
THE FORSWORN

'DISOWNED?' MALUS'S MIND reeled at the thought. 'Why would my father do such a thing?'

'It's your own fault,' Silar replied flatly.

The guard captain's eyes went wide at Silar's thoughtless honestly and from his expression it was clear he expected Silar's head to go bouncing across the carpets at any moment. 'I told you that torturing the Naggorite hostage was reckless.'

'Fuerlan?' Malus spat. 'What does that toad have to do with any of this? He laid hands on me – *me* – in the Court of Thorns and dared to presume my acquaintance. I was well within my rights to *kill* him for such an affront.' The highborn folded his arms and glared at Silar. 'His excruciations were complex and intricate. They were a gift. If the fool had any sense of honour he would thank me for what I did.'

'Except that Fuerlan is a hostage. He's the Drachau's property and the Drachau is the one responsible for his punishment.' Silar spread his hands. 'Can you not see the political implications? It is an affront to Naggor at the very least.'

Malus shot Silar a venomous glare. 'So the Drachau reacted poorly to Fuerlan's torture.'

'He ordered your father to kill you with his own hands,' Silar replied. 'I expect it was the best way he could think of to avoid the threat of the

Witch King's wrath. Balneth Bale couldn't very well demand justice if his most bitter foe had already taken steps to deal with the matter.'

Malus considered the problem. 'So when the Vaulkhar couldn't find me in the city, he confiscated my property?'

Silar smiled ruefully. 'Remember the nobles who invested in your slave raid? The ones who lost a sizeable fortune when your stock were slaughtered outside Clar Karond? They all got together and called their debts due a few days after you left. And since you were gone, they were able to petition your father instead. He settled your debt and disowned you by claiming your property to cover his loss. Now do you see what one reckless act has caused?'

'I do, indeed,' Malus answered coldly, his patience at an end. 'And I would do it again under the same circumstances. That's my privilege as a highborn, Silar. Do not forget that.'

Silar bowed his head. 'Of course, dread lord. I only wish to show you the depth of the problem you've returned to.'

The highborn laughed bitterly. 'It is more tangled than you know, Silar Thornblood. At least now I don't have to worry about assassins from the Temple of Khaine since my father has covered my debt.'

'Not so, my lord,' Arleth Vann spoke, the thin whisper rising from the shadows at the far end of the room. The former temple assassin sought out the shadows instinctively, like cleaving to like. 'The debt of blood still stands between you and the Lord of Murder.'

'But that makes no sense!' Malus shouted, his temper rising. 'My former allies have been repaid – why would they continue to keep Khaine's worshippers hounding my trail?'

'When our slave stock was wiped out several months ago, we assumed that your former backers hired the services of the temple to punish you for your failure,' Arleth Vann continued. 'I think perhaps we were too hasty in making that assumption. The nobles you chose to back your slave raid were picked specifically because they had little influence but moderate fortunes and ambition. And you ensured that each of these nobles invested the vast majority of their influence and funds in your enterprise to guarantee their continued support.'

Malus felt the slither of invisible snakes across his heart. 'What a tangled web you've woven, Darkblade,' the daemon chuckled. 'I've never seen a spider ensnare itself so tightly. Perhaps I made a mistake when I chose you as my saviour.'

'If you doubt my abilities then leave me and let the Outer Darkness take you!' Malus hissed – then stiffened, realising he had spoken aloud. Silar bristled, his eyes shining with suppressed anger, while Arleth Vann's face remained a pale, implacable mask. The highborn strode swiftly to where his wine cup sat and took a long swallow.

'So now you believe these nobles didn't approach the temple after all?' Malus said sharply.

'No, my lord,' Arleth Vann replied. 'I made a number of enquiries after you left for the Wastes and it appears that you chose your backers very well indeed – several of them invested more than they could truly afford and were on the verge of ruin when our enterprise failed. Even if they had combined whatever coin they had left, it would not have been enough to secure the temple's assistance. Someone else is responsible for the blood debt – and continues to maintain it even now.'

Malus went to take another drink from his cup and discovered that he'd already drained it dry. With a supreme effort he controlled the urge to hurl the cup across the room. 'So,' he said, setting the cup carefully on the floor, 'after three months travelling to the Chaos Wastes and back, I've returned home to find that I'm an outcast, the city guard has orders to arrest me on sight and the Drachau, my father the Vaulkhar *and* the Temple of Khaine are all actively trying to kill me.'

For a long moment, no one spoke. The guard captain glanced longingly at the door, suddenly very uncomfortable. Silar and Arleth Vann exchanged looks. 'That... would be an accurate assessment,' Silar said hesitantly. 'I trust the expedition to the Wastes went well?'

'DEAD, MY LORD? *All* of them?' Silar regarded Malus with a look of shock and horror combined.

The house servants had come and gone, leaving plates of spiced foods and fresh bottles of wine. Malus was already on his third cup. The warmth of the wine seemed to fill the empty feeling in his chest and still the shifting coils of the daemon within. 'We knew when we set out that the journey was not without risk,' the highborn said grimly, his mind filled with disquieting images of the fight outside the temple.

'What was in the temple, lord?' Arleth Vann inquired. He sat cross-legged to Malus's left, his hands resting easily on his knees. The former acolyte had touched neither food nor wine. 'Did you find the source of power you sought?'

Dimly, Malus could feel Tz'arkan stirring in his breast. The highborn leaned back, bringing the bottle to his lips. 'Another piece of the puzzle,' he replied. 'There was power there, but I haven't the means to unlock it yet. I lack the keys, which brings me back to Hag Graef.'

'The keys are here?' Silar said, frowning.

'It is possible they no longer exist at all,' Malus said darkly. 'But then we thought the same thing about the temple itself. There are four arcane relics I must unearth before I can unlock the power in the temple and I have less than a year to find them.'

'Less than a year?' The guard captain asked, intrigued in spite of himself. He had appropriated a bottle of his own when the servants arrived, but had otherwise laboured to avoid catching anyone's notice.

'Yes,' Malus answered, biting back a surge of irritation. 'If I cannot unlock the wards in the temple within the space of a year, my... claim is forfeit.'

The highborn heard the daemon's voice whisper mockingly, but the sound was too faint to hear over the buzzing in his head. Malus chuckled. 'If this keeps up I may stay drunk for the next nine months!'

Silence fell over the druchii. Malus caught Silar and Arleth Vann's worried glances and realised he'd thought aloud once more. 'Think nothing of my mutterings,' the highborn said with a casual wave of his hand. 'I spent one too many months alone in the Wastes with nothing but my own voice for company.'

Malus took another drink, then straightened and set the bottle carefully on the carpet. 'Time is of the essence. I must gain access to an arcane library and begin searching for references to these relics, which means that I need to contact my sister Nagaira. This also means I will require trusted agents to be my hands and eyes in the Hag and elsewhere in the city.'

Silar nodded, looking at the floor. 'We have not forgotten our oaths to you, my lord,' he answered. 'But we must now answer to the Vaulkhar as well.'

'Not so,' the guard captain said.

Malus raised an eyebrow. 'And how is that?'

The guard captain paused a moment, collecting his thoughts and drawing a little more courage from the bottle clasped in his hands. 'Oaths of fealty are paramount,' he began. 'Not even the Witch King himself can usurp a druchii's oath of service to another. So long as you live and your retainers haven't forsworn their oaths, the Vaulkhar can't claim them as his own. He *can* claim to command them in your absence, since you owe fealty to him as father and Vaulkhar and aren't here to contest ownership.'

'And that isn't likely to change, so long as I want to keep my head attached to my neck,' Malus growled.

'True – but you can designate a representative to act as your executor,' the captain said, offering a faint smile. 'A signed writ presented to the Vaulkhar would free your retainers from his control.'

Malus regarded the man with narrowed eyes. Was there no end to his temerity? 'And who would you suggest assume this role?'

The captain smiled. 'I would consider it an honour to serve, dread lord.'

'Despite the fact that the two most powerful highborn in Hag Graef want me dead and the Temple of Khaine besides? Despite the fact that I've just returned from a journey that cost the lives of each and every one of my retainers?'

'Even so, dread lord. Honestly, it's a much better reward than a bag of gold or a handful of gems. There are far better chances for advancement serving a highborn than commanding a barracks of guardsmen.' The captain winked knowingly. 'I have a feeling there will be plenty more opportunities for coin serving in your household anyway.'

Malus shook his head. He had no reason to trust the conniving druchii whatsoever. But for the moment he could be useful, he thought. 'Your ambition is going to get you killed, captain…?'

'Hauclir,' the druchii answered, bowing his head.

'Hauclir? Like the famous general?'

'The one the Witch King later executed for treason, yes. My father had poor judgement when it came to choosing patrons, it seems.'

'Indeed,' Malus said. 'I'd venture to say you suffer from the same affliction. But nevertheless,' the highborn said wearily, reaching over and drawing his sword, 'I have a need and you will fulfil it.' He rose and Hauclir followed suit.

'The Dark Mother watches and knows what lies in our hearts,' Malus intoned, placing the tip of his blade in the hollow of Hauclir's throat. 'This steel is sworn in her service. Do you swear to pledge your life to mine, to serve as I command and to die at my call?'

'Before the Mother of Night, I swear it,' Hauclir answered. 'Let her steel strike me down if I am false. I shall wear your collar until you release me from it, in death or in reward.'

Malus nodded. 'Very well, then, Hauclir. You are mine now. May you live long enough to regret it.' He tossed the naked blade on the carpet. 'Tomorrow, you and I will create this writ you spoke of. 'For now,' the highborn said, sinking back onto the rugs, 'I intend to drink every last drop of wine in the room and sleep like the dead. Get out.'

The retainers bowed as one and slipped quietly from the room. Malus reached for his bottle and drained it dry, savouring the silence.

A WHISPER OF sound brought Malus out of dreamless slumber. Weeks of travelling alone in the Wastes had honed his senses to a razor's edge and conditioned his reflexes for instant action. At first the highborn held perfectly still, listening intently for the sound to repeat itself. When he heard it again – the faintest brush of a bare foot across the piled rugs – he opened his eyes ever so slightly, focusing on its source.

The braziers had burned low, filling the centre of the room with a faint reddish glow and leaving the walls in impenetrable shadow. Malus lay against a mound of cushions, bare feet pointed at the nearest brazier and empty wine bottles strewn around his legs. Another empty bottle was still clutched in his right hand. After his erstwhile retainers had left, Malus had drunk himself into a stupor. Now, only a few hours later, the highborn was faintly surprised at how little of the alcoholic fog remained.

Across the room a druchii servant cleared upended cups and plates with swift, silent movements. The slave worked his way quickly through the detritus. Within moments he was carefully pulling away the bottles around Malus's knees.

The highborn suppressed a flash of annoyance at his own paranoia, forcing his eyes to shut and trying to sink back into sleep. *It's going to take some effort to start ignoring the servants again,* Malus thought sourly.

He sank back into slumber. Then suddenly he remembered: *Mistress Nemeira didn't keep druchii slaves.*

Malus bolted from the cushions just as the assassin's dagger struck home, its keen blade sliding through the silk robe and sinking into his shoulder instead of opening his throat. It felt like a shard of ice – suddenly the highborn's left hand went numb. The assassin loomed over Malus, his eyes shining like molten brass. *An acolyte of the temple,* Malus thought furiously, fighting a surge of panic.

The assassin jerked his dagger free – Malus felt the hot flow of blood stain the fine robe and plaster it to his chest – and the highborn caught the man's wrist. Malus lashed at the man's head with the wine bottle in his other hand, but the assassin grabbed the highborn's wrist with effortless speed and then they were rolling across the rugs in a flurry of kicks, bites and head-butts.

Teeth sank into Malus's right forearm. He drove his knee into the assassin's groin and bashed his forehead into the man's temple until he felt the killer's jaws loosen. Malus jerked his weapon-arm away, hoping to pull free and land a blow, but the assassin responded by biting at the highborn's throat. Malus twisted, trying to use his weight to turn the assassin's dagger towards its wielder and drive it into the man's chest, but the numbness in his hand was intensifying and he could feel his grip start to weaken.

The acolyte twisted sharply at the waist and they rolled again. Malus's right shoulder struck something hard and unyielding and waves of heat beat at his face and arm. With a cold grin the assassin loomed above him, drawing his knife blade inexorably higher, the light from the brazier painting the acolyte's face with a daemonic leer. The blood on the knife-blade seemed to glow in the sullen light and Malus could feel his grip starting to give way.

Roaring with desperate fury Malus twisted his body with all his strength and threw the acolyte against the iron brazier, knocking it over in a shower of angry sparks. Caught off-balance, the assassin rolled onto the hot coals and Malus let go of his bottle to grab the man's chin and hold his head to the fire. The assassin stiffened and smoke curled around his shoulders. His black hair blazed into bluish flame, but still he struggled to pull his knife-arm free and plunge the blade into Malus's chest. Malus felt his strength fading with every moment, but the assassin's eyes remained fever-bright and focused on his destruction. Then without warning the acolyte let out a tortured scream and dropped his knife, his hands groping for the flames searing his skull.

Malus let go and rolled away, his eyes darting about the room for his sword. The rugs had started to burn and the air was full of acrid smoke. The highborn's left arm hung uselessly at his side. Where did I put that damned blade, he thought furiously, trying to cudgel his wine-fogged memory into focus.

Three sharp, stabbing pains in his right shoulder tore a shout from the highborn's throat. At once, searing pain blossomed at each of the tiny wounds, blazing like a fire wasp's sting. Malus staggered, his right hand groping at his back and pulled three slim, brass needles from his shoulder. He heard the crackle of burnt leather and turned to see the assassin rolling to his feet. The acolyte's hair was gone, his scalp blackened and his face grey with pain, but his pale eyes shone with murderous intent.

Malus leapt for the door, shouldering the thick oak aside with a hiss of pain and raced down the dimly lit corridor. There were no guards or servants about; few guests stayed overnight at the flesh house and the highborn reckoned it was close to dawn. The muscles in his chest spasmed as the needles' venom spread – it was difficult enough to breathe, let alone sound an alarm. Even if he could, he found himself wondering who, if anyone, might respond. Had Nemeira betrayed him after all? Had the acolyte followed Silar and Arleth Vann?

It won't matter if I'm dead in the next few minutes, he thought angrily. Revenge is the luxury of the living.

The highborn couldn't hear the assassin behind him, but Malus knew that didn't mean anything and he wasn't about to waste energy looking over his shoulder. He plunged on down the corridor, fighting for each ragged breath. For a moment he was tempted to call out to Tz'arkan, willing to beggar another piece of himself if the daemon could burn the poison from his body, but for once he found that he couldn't focus on Tz'arkan's presence. Damn that wine, he thought angrily.

Within moments the corridor began to turn to the right and angle slightly upwards. Malus turned the first corner and stumbled over the body of a naked slave. The human's face was turned to the ceiling, staring sightlessly with one blue eye – the other was a red ruin, pierced by the single thrust of a dagger. Malus fell headlong, scraping his forehead on the stone floor, but got his feet back underneath him and lurched on, fearing the bite of that selfsame dagger in his back.

He followed the curve of the corridor until it emptied into the main room of the flesh house, a circular chamber offset with dozens of veiled niches and set with plush divans that surrounded raised daises or delicately-wrought cages. Witchfire globes burned dimly around the perimeter of the empty room, shedding a pale greenish glow. At once, Malus caught sight of two druchii sprawled on the floor, both wearing the dark leather kheitans of Nemeira's guards. Both lay on their stomachs and judging by the huge pools of blood their throats had been expertly slit.

The highborn saw the curved swords at their hips and for a moment was tempted to grab one, but he knew that in his present state he couldn't possibly survive another fight with the acolyte. At the far end of the chamber the house's double doors stood open to the night air and the caustic yellow nightfog spilled across the threshold, filling the house's vestibule.

Gritting his teeth, Malus charged for the doorway. The fog would burn in his open wounds, but the assassin would be hard-pressed to find him in Hag Graef's twisting, shadowy streets.

Just as Malus crossed the threshold something buzzed past his ear and two more of the acolyte's brass needles struck the wooden doorjamb to his right. The highborn risked a quick look over his shoulder and saw the burned man at the far end of the room, leaning against the wall for support. Without hesitation he charged out into the fog-shrouded street, trying to remember if there was a connecting lane or alley mouth on the opposite side.

He reached the opposite side of the street and immediately saw the shadow of an alley mouth just a few yards away. Without skipping a beat Malus angled from the opening – and failed to notice the robed shapes rising from the shadows of a nearby shop front until it was too late.

There was a hissing sound in the air and a fine net of steel wire wrapped around Malus's torso. Fine hooks sank into his skin, binding the net to his body and then the acolyte jerked back on the thin chain attached to the net and pulled Malus off his feet. He roared in pain as he hit the slick cobblestones, the hooks sinking deeper into his flesh. The highborn tried to roll to his feet, but the acolyte pulled him onto his back with a flick of the wrist.

The second robed acolyte rushed forward, grabbing Malus's ankles and pressing them to the cobbles with all his weight. The druchii looked surprisingly young – little more than a child really – evidently an initiate accompanying the assassin and providing assistance where required. They had him trussed like a blood moon sacrifice and Malus watched helplessly as the burned acolyte staggered from the fog, his dagger held high.

There was a sharp *pop pop pop* as three crossbow bolts punched through the brittle leather kheitan the assassin wore and dug deep into his vitals. The killer looked down uncomprehendingly at the black fletching sprouting from his chest and then toppled onto his side.

Cloaked shapes rushed out of the fog like nighthawks, glittering steel clenched in their hands. The acolyte at Malus's feet started to rise, his hand going for his dagger, but a curved sword sliced into his neck and the boy's severed head bounced into the highborn's lap. The shapes rushed past and then Malus heard a brief struggle behind him. Steel clashed on steel and for a moment the chain attached to the net pulled painfully tight. Then came the sound of a keen edge biting into flesh and the tether went slack.

Malus couldn't move. He wasn't sure if it was the tension of the net, or the fact that his muscles were frozen by the assassin's poison. The highborn fought for every searing breath, his eyes searching the fog for signs of his rescuers. Then the cloaked figures returned, their silver nightmasks gleaming beneath the shadows of their black hoods.

'The Dark Mother smiles upon us tonight, brothers,' one of the figures said, his deep voice rumbling from behind the mask of a leering daemon's face. 'A moment later and our lord would have been very wroth indeed. Instead the temple has flushed our prey for us and wrapped him in silver for the Vaulkhar's pleasure.' The daemon's face lowered until it was inches from Malus's own. He could see the druchii's black eyes behind the silver eye sockets and hear the man's breath whistling through the slits carved between the daemon's fangs. Then darkness crowded at the edges of his vision, rising like a black tide and Malus knew nothing more.

Chapter Three
DREAMS OF BLOOD AND MADNESS

I T SEEMED AS though he fought on a raging sea of blood, beneath a sky that writhed and thundered and rained bone and ash.

He stumbled and lurched across the twisted landscape and a horde of angry ghosts clawed and gibbered at him every step of the way.

They reached for him with their misshapen hands and howled in tongues of fire, their eyes nothing but orbs of nacreous light. A withered elven sorceress leapt upon his back, sinking her cracked nails into his chest and tearing at the side of his face with her jagged teeth. A hulking, slithering creature formed of naked, roiling muscle undulated across the ground and lashed him with saw-edged tendrils of ropy flesh. A pack of hounds circled him hungrily, their gaping mandibles dripping green threads of venom.

He roared his fury at the storm and lashed at the ghosts with his blade, but their bodies parted like jelly beneath each stroke and flowed back together again.

THE MAELSTROM DISSOLVED in a blaze of pale light. Dark clouds coalesced out of the haze, taking the shape of faces. A woman bent over him, propping one eyelid open.

'His wounds are mending, dread lord.' The woman's lips were moving, but her voice didn't quite match their movements.

A man regarded him from an impossible distance, his face cruel and cold. 'More hushalta then,' the man said, harshly. 'I tire of waiting.'

Cold fingers pried open his lips and a thick fluid tasting of burnt copper poured down his throat. He choked, his body spasming, but strong hands pinned him in place.

The light dimmed, the faces receding into a reddening mist. Red faded to black and a familiar voice spoke in the darkness.

'You fool,' Tz'arkan said.

HE LAY UPON a bed of writhing bodies. Pale hands bore him up, caressing his body, clutching him in their hungry embrace. Lips pressed against his skin, tasting him, worshipping him. The air hung heavy and still, fragrant with incense and trembling with the moans and sighs of a hundred rapturous voices.

Faces rose around him, haunting sirens with hungry looks in their depthless eyes. They reached for him, running their hands across his bare chest, each delicate fingertip leaving a trail of heat across his flesh.

One siren climbed languidly onto him, her dark hair seeming to float around her fine-boned face. She stretched across him like a cat, long fingers reaching for his face. Her red lips twisted in a sensual smile as she laid her long nails against his cheeks and sank them deep into his skin.

Blood ran cold and thin down the sides of his face. She dug deeper, taking handfuls of flesh and pulling downwards, like skinning the hide from a hare. Flesh, muscle and tendons pulled away in a glistening mat, exposing his neck and the upper part of his chest.

He writhed in the grip of the sirens, but they held him fast. Now they tore at him as well, pulling away hunks of bloody skin. He felt the flesh of his entire left arm slough away like a soggy sleeve and when he wrenched it away he saw that the limb beneath was corded with muscle and wrapped in a pebbly, greenish-black hide. Then the pebbles ruptured into hundreds of tiny mouths, lapping at the streaks of blood running from wrist to elbow–

SOMETHING WAS DRAGGING at his feet. Malus opened gummy eyes and saw his toes scuffing along smooth flooring stones. Two druchii held him by his arms, dragging him easily along a passage lit by witchlights.

It was a struggle to raise his head and take in his surroundings. His mouth felt like dried leather. Hushalta, he remembered. They had been feeding him hushalta for days. His skin felt taut and slightly feverish, but whole. It's a wonder my mind is still intact, he thought dimly.

'That remains to be seen,' a faint voice echoed in his head.

Cool wind played across his face, stirring his lank hair. Chains clinked softly; pure crystal tones that made his blood run cold. Then the strong hands holding his arms released him and Malus fell to his knees on the slate tiles of a large, circular chamber. Globes of witch-light gleamed from ornately worked iron sconces around the perimeter of the room, illuminating bas-reliefs worked into the stone walls depicting a series of famous massacres from the long wars against the elves of Ulthuan. A mass of chains tipped with cruel hooks depended from the high ceiling in the centre of the chamber. The metal links clinked softly together in the cool air.

He could feel the eyes of others upon him. The highborn drew a shuddering breath and straightened, meeting the reptilian stares of the druchii who awaited him.

Lurhan Fellblade, Vaulkhar of Hag Graef, stood bare-chested before his son, his powerfully muscled upper body marked with dozens of scars from his service to the Witch King. His black hair was pulled back from his face, accentuating his fierce eyes and prominent, aquiline nose. The warlord's sheer presence filled the chamber, eclipsing every other person in the room.

Two broken men stood in Lurhan's shadow, their eyes gleaming with hate. One was tall, nearly as imposing as the Vaulkhar himself, though the druchii's right arm was hidden beneath layers of black robes. Urial had the same sharp, angry features as his father, but his face was gaunt and his pale skin had an unhealthy, bluish cast. His thick hair had been almost completely white since returning from his years in the Temple of Khaine and his eyes were the colour of molten brass.

The second druchii was bent and trembling, his sunken eyes like dark pits in a bloodless face lined with a network of fine scars. A thin, black beard shadowed his narrow chin and his hair was shaved but for a long corsair's topknot. The wretch wore a provincial-looking kheitan of red leather worked with the sigil of a mountain peak. Silver rings glittered from the scarred ruin of his ears. Fuerlan, hostage to the court of the Drachau, glared at Malus with a look of fear and rage combined.

Behind Lurhan and his companions a trio of druchii slaves worked with a cluster of silver chains that hung from the centre of the room's ceiling. Large, sharp hooks were attached to the chains at different heights. Small tables stood nearby, holding arrangements of gleaming tools laid out on silk cloths.

The two retainers backed away from Malus, retreating to the shadows by the doorway. The highborn returned his gaze to Lurhan and made an ostentatious bow. 'Well met, father and Vaulkhar,' Malus rasped. 'It's an honour to be invited into your tower at long last. Though considering your choice of company, perhaps it's not the privilege I thought it to be.'

Lurhan let out an angry hiss. 'Insolent churl! Do not presume to speak to me as an equal. You have been a stain upon the honour of this house from the moment of your birth! Would that I could have given you to the cauldron when you were but a babe.' Beside the Vaulkhar, Urial stiffened slightly, but his cold expression betrayed nothing of his thoughts. Unlike Malus, he had been thrown into the Lord of Murder's cauldron, his malformed body offered as a sacrifice – and emerged unscathed as one of Khaine's chosen.

'Speak to you as an *equal*, dread Lurhan? I think it is you who are presuming here,' Malus said slowly, trying to keep his speech from slurring. The sound of his words reverberated through him as though he was speaking underwater – doubtless a lingering effect of the restorative drugs. 'We could never be equals. I could never even rise to the level of the rest of your misbegotten brood. *You* saw to that. You gave me just barely enough support to survive, just enough to fulfil your obligations to my mother and then left me to wither.'

'You are not here to speak, you misbegotten bastard, but to suffer,' the Vaulkhar said. 'It was not enough for you to indebt yourself to a handful of petty nobles – a debt that I was forced to pay when you could not – no, you also stained the honour of the Drachau himself by laying hands on his hostage and jeopardising the truce with Naggor.'

'A truce to a feud *you* started,' Malus shot back. 'The Witch King himself ordered you to raid Naggor and take Eldire from her brother, but it was you who claimed conqueror's privilege and brought her back to the Hag instead of sending her to Naggarond.' Malus staggered back upright, fixing his father with a glare of pure hatred. 'Has she served you well, father? Has she shown you the future and steered you down the path of glory? Or did you find, too late, that she shares only what she chooses and then only when it suits her arcane schemes? But are you bold enough to cross her even now, with the Drachau ordering my death?' He grinned wolfishly. 'Do you dare tempt her wrath by killing me?'

Lurhan gestured and the druchii slaves approached, their robes whispering around their bare feet. 'I will not kill you,' the Vaulkhar said. 'I will *hurt* you. You will suffer agonies for days on end, until you beg me for release. Yet I will do everything in my power to help you cling to life, each and every day. I will salve your exposed nerves and lave your raw flesh and turn a deaf ear to your pleas for mercy. If you die it will be because *you* wish it. You can chew off your own tongue and choke on your blood, or simply will your heart to stop beating – I have seen it happen to far stronger druchii than yourself. No, I will not kill you. That is your own choice to make.' He studied his son critically as the slaves dragged Malus to his feet. 'No druchii has ever survived my attentions for more than five days. I think you will be dead within three and Eldire will have no one to blame but her own weak-willed son.'

The slaves dragged the highborn towards the waiting chains. Malus glared over his shoulder at the Vaulkhar. 'I have never failed to disappoint you, father,' he snarled. 'Mark my words, I will do so again and you will live to regret it.'

Lurhan chuckled cruelly and went to inspect his instruments. The highborn tried to struggle, but his limbs were leaden and useless.

Bestir yourself, daemon, Malus thought fiercely. I need no persuading now. Lend me your power!

The daemon uncoiled itself in the highborn's breast. 'Very well, you shall have it,' the daemon answered. 'When the time is right.'

Malus was forced once more to his knees. Hands pulled the tattered robe from his back. One of the slaves studied the chains thoughtfully and reached for a gleaming hook, oblivious to the highborn's cry of rage.

THERE WAS NO end to the pain.

Malus hung from the silver chains, twisting slowly in an agonising breeze. Even when the Vaulkhar put down his spattered tools, the air alone was enough to torture his exposed nerves and muscle.

He felt shrivelled and hard, like petrified wood. His wounds no longer bled. For a while he was able to measure time by the steady drip of blood upon the tile, but now there was no procession of minutes and hours. There were only periods of agony that gave way to irregular stretches of unrelieved suffering. As he hung from the chains and waited for the Vaulkhar's return, he could feel his life slipping away, receding like a tide. Yet every time his spirit ebbed, something dark and vital flowed into the space it left behind and lent him a small measure of strength. Sometimes the daemon whispered to him in a language whose words Malus could not understand, yet etched themselves deeply into his bones.

Each time Lurhan was done with him the Vaulkhar's slaves would carefully tend his ravaged body with sophisticated salves and potions. A foul mixture of wine and hushalta was poured past his torn lips using a thin metal tube. It was not enough to allow him to sleep, but it did cause him to dream.

THE TILES BENEATH him groaned.

He looked down, feeling the hooks pull painfully at the muscles of his shoulders. The slate was buckling, becoming concave; there was another long moan, then with a sharp crack the tile shattered, falling in upon itself. Below was absolute darkness, like the heart of the Dark Mother herself.

Such darkness, he thought. Such power. Take me from this place and loose me like a thunderbolt upon those I despise.

Something moved within the blackness. It seemed to shift and settle, though he could not say how he knew this; he simply felt the movement, as though the ancient blackness pressed against his ruined skin.

An armoured gauntlet rose from the darkness, its steel fingertips shaped into curved claws. The long fingers, almost delicate in their craftsmanship, unfolded with slow, malevolent grace.

The hand closed on his right foot and pulled.

He screamed in agony as the hooks in his back, arms and legs all pulled cruelly taut. Pierced muscles pulled away from his bones until the tendons creaked.

A second hand rose from the blackness and seized his other foot. Then, hand over hand, they began to climb upwards.

He felt his muscles began to tear. His skin trembled in waves of bright, burning pain. His throat seized, but the screams continued to come, making ragged, gasping noises each time the hands moved a little higher.

A helmeted head emerged from the blackness: peaked and plumed in the manner of a druchii knight, faceless and menacing. Little by little the armoured figure rose from the darkness, tearing him into pieces with each slow, methodical movement.

One hand rose high enough to close around his throat. His body seemed to sag against the hooks as his bones hung free from its fleshy sheath. The thin screams were stifled by the steel fingers gripping his neck.

The helmet rose until the black eye sockets were level with his own. He could feel the knight's breath: it was cold and rank, like the air from a tomb.

Its free hand reached up and pulled the helmet off. A multitude of thin, black braids fell loose from the helm; spiders and centipedes scuttled among clots of loam crusted into the hair. The knight's skin was grey and shrunken with rot, the muscles long since turned to foul-smelling ichor. A single, deep gash ran from the top of the knight's head to just above the left brow and the eye beneath was a swollen, black orb, the pupil gleaming with grave mould.

Lhunara's blackened lips pulled back in a gruesome smile, revealing jagged yellow teeth.

THERE WAS NO sensation of regaining consciousness; no fumbling, dawning awareness as the drugs failed to overcome his pain. One moment there was darkness and fever-dreams and the next moment his eyes were open and she was standing before him.

She was a statuesque figure in black, robed in the severe habit of the convent. Her alabaster face, stern and composed, seemed to float like an apparition in the darkness of the chamber. Long, black hair was drawn back in a single, heavy braid wrapped with silver wire, and a silver circlet wrought with tiny, arcane runes adorned her forehead. Her slim hands held a chain of gold, shaped from large, flat links set with precious stones. Unknowable power stirred in the depths of her violet eyes. She was utterly perfect, an image of the Dark Mother herself made flesh and he desired her with every fibre of his being.

Malus was certain she was another apparition, until the woman glided soundlessly forward and slipped the heavy chain around his neck. The instant the cold metal touched his skin a jolt passed through him from head to toe. In its wake his terrible pain faded and the last vestiges of the drugs vanished like morning mist. He was clear-headed and alert and suddenly he realised who it was standing before him.

'Mother?' Malus said wearily.

Eldire's penetrating gaze surveyed the ruin of her son's naked body. 'Lurhan has outdone himself,' she said coldly. 'I doubt even the Drachau himself could have done better. This will be something to remember, years from now. You will wear these scars with pride.'

Malus attempted a weak smile that was little more than parchment lips pulling away from a yellowed skull. 'Will I be some wight, boasting of my scars in the barrow-field? I will stay here until I die, Mother. Lurhan made this clear.'

'He said no such thing, child. He said he would make you suffer until you were willing to kill yourself. A craven distinction, but it is the only stratagem the great warlord has at his disposal.' She laid a hand on his cheek, brushing away layers of dried blood. 'Yet you have lingered well beyond his expectations.'

Malus did not question how Eldire knew what had been said between him and his father. Druchii witches were kept mewed up in convents in each of the great cities, forbidden to walk among the citizens by decree of the Witch King – yet the strongest among them had their ways of reaching beyond the convent walls.

'How long?'

'Today is the fifth day,' Eldire said. 'Your father is furious. The Drachau has commanded him to kill you, but if he does he will face a reckoning with me. This was the best way he could attempt to appease both of us and now the gambit looks likely to fail.'

Malus took a deep breath and tried to focus his thoughts. 'I was right. Whatever agreement you forged with Lurhan included producing a child. If he kills me, then he loses your gifts.'

Eldire seized his chin with surprisingly strong fingers. 'Do not pry into affairs that are none of your concern, child,' the witch said sternly. 'It is enough for you to know that every day past today it will become increasingly obvious that Lurhan is intent on torturing you unto death. Then the Vaulkhar will have to decide whose displeasure he fears more. So you must endure a bit longer.' She leaned close, peering deeply into her son's eyes. 'You are stronger than even I expected, child.'

'Hate is a cure for all things, mother. You taught me that–'

'That is not what I mean,' she said sharply. 'Your body is stronger than I expected it to be after so much punishment. Something has changed about you... something that was not there when you went into the Wastes.'

Without warning, Malus felt a fist clench around his heart. The coils of the daemon tightened – or were they shrinking, fearful of attracting Eldire's notice?

'I–it was a difficult journey,' Malus gasped. 'I was forced to return to the Hag alone and the Wastes consume the weak-willed.' He managed a defiant grin. 'I suffered much worse than this for weeks at a time.'

Eldire frowned. 'And was your journey successful? Did you find what you sought?'

Malus stiffened. 'Yes... and no. I found power there, but not the sort that would serve one such as me.'

'Nonsense,' Eldire snapped. 'Are there swords you cannot wield, because they were not made for your hand? Are there towers you cannot shelter in, because they were not made with you in mind? Power is shaped by the wielder. It is made to serve, in the way a slave is bent to the master's will.'

Malus started to formulate an answer when a thought suddenly occurred to him. Now it was his turn to regard Eldire suspiciously. 'How did you know of my trip north? Who told you?'

The witch laughed mirthlessly. 'Am I not a seer, child? Do I not ride the winds of time and space?'

'Of course,' Malus agreed. 'But you haven't taken such interest in my doings before.'

'That is not true,' Eldire said, stepping close. 'You are mine, child. Born of my flesh and blood. My eyes are upon you always.' She reached up to stroke his matted hair. 'I know your ambitions, your secret hatreds and desires. And if you love me, I will give them all to you, in time. Do you love me, child?'

Malus stared deep into her violet eyes. 'As much as I have ever loved anyone, mother.'

The witch smiled and kissed him gently on the lips. 'Then you will survive, you will grow powerful and in time you will conquer, my beloved child. Do not forget.'

With that she drew away. Malus felt the chain lifted from his neck. He opened his mouth to reply, but the ocean of pain that the chain had held at bay fell upon him with crushing force. He was borne under and knew nothing more.

AFTER THAT THERE were no dreams.

They stopped giving him hushalta and only the barest taste of watered wine. He lost consciousness many times, but whenever he opened his eyes again Lurhan was there, his fine knives working at Malus's ravaged body.

'Why won't you *die*?' The Vaulkhar said it again and again. 'What is it that keeps you in this ruined husk? You're weak. I know it. Why won't you stop this?'

It took ages to remember how to speak. Drawing in a tendril of breath was a heroic effort.

'S... sss... spite,' he finally gasped, with a faint rattle of laughter.

As time passed, Lurhan's work became frenzied and crude. He turned to larger knives and cut deeper and deeper.

And yet the highborn lingered.

Malus could feel the black stain of the daemon's taint stretching throughout his body, like the roots of some enormous tree. Huge tap-roots and tiny, hair-like capillaries, reaching from his tortured brain to the tips of his toes. If he concentrated his attention he thought he could still perceive the difference between the two – the demarcation where he ended and Tz'arkan began – at least, for now.

He felt himself jerk against the chains. There was a pressure on his neck. He dimly realised Lurhan had grabbed him, but he couldn't feel anything clearly any more. Something bright flashed before his eyes. Another knife, he supposed. A large one.

'It's over, Malus,' Lurhan hissed. 'It must end now. It *must*! Beg me to end your life. I will make it quick and your agonies will end. It is no dishonour. No one will fault you.'

Again, Malus fought to draw breath. 'Do... one thing... for me...'

'Yes?' Lurhan leaned close, almost pressing his ear to his son's rav-aged lips.

'Tell me... what... day... it is.'

Lurhan let out a savage cry of anger. The knife felt blessedly cool, like a soothing piece of ice, as it slid between his ribs. The slaves cried out in alarm, calling to the Vaulkhar, but Malus paid them no mind. It felt as though his consciousness was seeping away, draining like wine from a pierced skin. The coldness spread through his chest, taking away the pain and he surrendered gladly to it.

THERE WAS CLOTH against his face, light and cool. His arms were folded tightly against his chest and his legs were bound together. With effort, Malus opened his eyes and saw only a thin layer of fabric resting against his eyelids. There was a smell of unguents and spices in the air.

Am I in my barrow-shroud, he thought?

'But for me, it would have been,' a voice said in his mind. Malus paid it no heed.

'Much of his skin and the flesh beneath is gone, or carved into ruin,' a diffident voice said. 'My master preserved most of his face and his eyes. A great many of his nerves were separated and splayed as well. Truly, I have never seen a more extensive series of excruciations. How he survived for seven days is truly a mystery to us and his injuries are far beyond our power to heal.'

A shadow moved between Malus and the dim light. Delicate fingertips, light as wasp's wings, brushed across his face. Swift, precise movements peeled back the cloth covering his eyes. For a moment, even the witchlights were dazzling.

'I can help him,' a voice spoke from the brilliance. As Malus's eyes adjusted, he saw a blurry shape looming over him. Cool fingertips brushed his cheek and the figure leaned closer.

'There are powers beyond bandages and unguents that will make him whole again,' Nagaira said, her lips twisting into a smile. 'His mother has commanded the Vaulkhar to deliver him to me and I will show her that her faith in my power is not misplaced. It is the least I can do to have my beloved brother in my arms once more.'

Chapter Four
MASKS OF FLESH

VOICES CIRCLED MALUS for days; they chanted and whispered in words that sent shivers through the air around him. Blurred figures swayed and gestured before his shrouded eyes. Sometimes in the dead of night shapes swooped before his vision, chittering sounds that were almost recognisable and leaving his skin tingling painfully in their wake.

Attendants with soft, perfumed hands waited on him, peeling back the shroud one thin layer at a time. He emerged from his agony like a dragon from its egg, his shell wearing away inexorably as flesh and muscles knit and strength flowed back into his frame.

As time passed and he could perceive more and more of the world through his thinning shroud, he began to take in greater detail of the acolytes who performed the healing rituals over him. Though he could not grasp the arcane tongue they spoke, their voices became distinct and familiar. All highborn druchii, both women *and* men, always chanting in groups of six. Nagaira led them in every ritual, her voice commanding and the others answering in a discordant chorus. Each time the rites were performed, Malus felt Tz'arkan respond, slithering against his ribs and whispering in blasphemous pleasure.

There was a pattern to the rites that Malus eventually discerned – once at the hour before sunrise and once again at the hour before sunset, and two short rites at the rising and setting of the moon. By this he reckoned that he had been a guest of his sister for at least five days. The fact that she hadn't slipped a knife into his eye or turned his skull into a drinking cup vexed the highborn to no end.

It had been Nagaira who had tricked him into undertaking the deadly journey into the Wastes – embarking on an elaborate plot to pit him against his brother Urial over a trivial slight. Because he had left her without warning the previous summer in an audacious plan to further his fortunes with an impromptu slave raid, she had decided to retaliate. She had spurned the advances of her younger brother Urial and blamed it squarely on devotion to him. The result had been a cunning ambush just outside Clar Karond that had cost him all of the slaves he'd so painstakingly harvested over the summer and put him at knife points with his cabal of investors. With his enemies smelling blood and circling nearer and assassins from the Temple of Khaine sworn to kill him, it had been all too easy to seduce him with a story of a hidden temple and ancient power lost in the Wastes.

Nearly two score druchii – several of them Nagaira's own retainers – and more than ten times that number of slaves had perished over an imagined slight. Malus's relationship with his half-sister had never been more than a series of brief, often violent affairs, so he was hard-pressed to understand why she'd been so affronted. Not that a highborn ever needed a compelling reason to engage in a petty game of revenge. Druchii women were widely considered the deadlier of the sexes when it came to drawn-out contests of spite. With fewer options to exercise their lust for violence they had plenty of time to contemplate elaborate, bloody-minded intrigues.

On the sixth day the routine changed. He was awakened by the chanted cries of the morning ritual and again by the evening rite. By this time only a single, thin sheet of fabric wrapped his body, the material stiff with layers of dried body fluids and healing unguents. His eyes reacted well to the shifting glow of the witchlights and Malus could easily discern the figures that surrounded the bier upon which he lay. The acolytes all wore layered robes of ebon wool that were dense with painted symbols in a sharp, spiky script. Their heads were covered in voluminous hoods that sheltered their faces in concealing darkness. The highborn had no doubt it was more than mere affectation; any one of them caught practising sorcery by one of the Witch King's agents forfeited not just their rank and properties, but their very souls as well.

When the time came for the rite at moonrise, Malus watched five acolytes enter the room and surround his bier in a carefully proscribed circle. The highborn felt the daemon stir expectantly as the acolytes raised their arms and began to chant. It was an invocation of some kind; Malus had heard the general form many times now. The chant lasted for some time, much longer than Malus had been expecting. Then, at its zenith, another figure stepped into view.

It was an elven slave, clad only in a thin cotton shift. Her golden hair had been carefully cleaned and pulled back to reveal a graceful, swan-like neck. A circlet of steel gleamed dully from her brow and her perfect face was rapt with a kind of horrified ecstasy. Behind the slave came Nagaira, pacing silently in heavy robes and a breastplate of cured human hide set with precious stones. The sapphires caught the light and described a spiral pattern that plucked at Malus's eyes. Unlike her acolytes, Nagaira's face was uncovered, her eyes bright and her head held high.

The chanting of the acolytes altered, becoming a slow susurration of breath, like the flow of the sea or the hissing of blood through artery and vein. Moving as if in a trance, the elven slave mounted the bier and slowly, lightly climbed onto him. She weighed little more than a willow wand, and the stiff sheets crackled faintly like brittle ice as she straddled his body. Malus's eyes narrowed appraisingly – and then the slave raised a curved, sickle-like blade in her hand. Her eyes bulged with horror as she watched her own hand move slowly and deliberately, drawing the razor-sharp inner edge of the blade across her throat.

Fat drops of hot blood spattered against the sheet like drops of rain, spreading like constellations before the highborn's eyes. Slowly, then gathering speed, the crimson rain fell, soaking the fabric and plastering it like a caul against his skin. The sodden material shrank against the skin of his face, pulling taut over his mouth and nose. His nostrils filled with the bitter tang of blood and he began to struggle, forcing his arms to move and pull at the clinging material. For a heartbeat it resisted and then the shroud parted like rotten cheesecloth, pulling from his naked body with a wet ripping sound. There was a final, gurgling whisper and the slave pitched off the bier, her blade ringing against the stone tiles. With a groan of pain Malus pushed himself upright, his bare face and chest streaked with fresh gore.

'Rise, dreadful wyrm,' Nagaira said, her eyes glinting lasciviously. As one, the acolytes fell to their knees, shouting in their arcane tongue. 'Stretch your wings and slake your thirst with the blood of the innocent.'

The highborn found himself in a small, hexagonally shaped room. Witchlight glowed from hemispherical lamps set in a cluster directly overhead and the black marble walls of the chamber were carved with hundreds of arcane runes and dusted with ground silver so that they glowed a pale green. The floor surrounding the bier was likewise carved in an intricate pattern of lines and circles, their glittering lines obscured by spreading pools of blood. Malus wiped the elf's vital fluids from his face with the back of his hand. 'If there was magic in your sacrifice, sweet sister, I regret that it failed to touch me.'

The druchii witch laughed. 'Her death had nothing to do with the rite. That was completed at nightfall. But it's been almost a fortnight fretting over your torn little husk and I needed to spill some blood.' She leaned forward and touched a pale finger to a crimson drop on the bier, then placed it against her tongue. 'She was a maiden you know. A princess, supposedly, from Tor Yvresse. You have no idea how much she cost.'

Tz'arkan slithered beneath his ribs. 'Such a fine one, she is! If only she had come north instead of you, little Darkblade. What a savoury prize she would have been.'

Malus paid the daemon little heed. 'A fortnight? I reckoned I'd been here only six days.'

Nagaira shook her head. 'You lingered at the edge of death for many days, sweet brother. I confess there were moments when I wasn't sure that even my skill could bring you back. But that is past now.'

She stepped around the bier, a wolfish smile playing across her face. Nagaira was the shortest of Lurhan's six children, rising little higher than the level of Malus's eyes. Her figure was softer and curvier than the rest of the Vaulkhar's lean brood, but her face was every bit that of her fearsome father, with a sharp nose and a black stare that could cut like a knife when she wished. She stepped up to Malus and took the remnants of the bloodstained shroud in her small, strong hands. The cloth parted easily and she tossed it casually aside. 'I took great pains to restore your vitality, brother,' she said. 'I'm eager to see the results of my handiwork.' The witch stood on her tiptoes and kissed him lightly on the lips. 'Cold as ever,' she said with a grin. 'And tasting of the battlefield.'

Nagaira snapped her fingers and a slave materialised from the shadows near one of the chamber walls. The human carried a gleaming goblet with both hands and offered the brimming vessel to Malus. The goblet had a thick stem of wrought silver, shaped in the manner of a curling nauglir's tail. The skull that held the dark wine had been recently boiled and still carried its sheen of fine oil. The top of the head had been sawn cleanly away, leaving a smooth, rounded lip to drink from – clearly a work of superior craftsmanship. 'What's this?' Malus asked.

'A gift from me to welcome you home. You drink from the skull of a temple acolyte who sought to kill you while you convalesced here. Such a fool he was, to think that stealth and silvered steel would be enough to prevail in *my* house.'

'Pray he did not have companions like the pack that brought me down in the Slavers' Quarter. If word of your sorcery gets back to the temple you will have the wrath of the Witch King to contend with.'

Nagaira shrugged. 'If he did not come alone, his companions remained beyond the wards of my tower. Had they trespassed, I or my companions,' she indicated the robed figures, 'would have known of it.'

Malus drank deeply of the wine. It was thick and sweet, fit for a merchant's table. The highborn grimaced. Nagaira had many terrible powers at her command, but she still had horrible taste in wine. 'You appear to have gone to great expense on my behalf,' he said at length. 'Such generosity is surprising – considering how you sent me and six of your own men to die in the far north.'

Nagaira's smile turned cold and an appraising look came into her eyes. 'Leave us,' she said in a tone of icy authority. The acolytes rose to their feet and glided soundlessly from the room, followed by the slave.

'So you have acolytes now, sister?' Malus said with a raised eyebrow. 'When did you abandon the pretence of scholarship and consider yourself a witch in deed and name? Father has turned a blind eye to your studies for too long and it's made you reckless.'

'Those fawning students are from some of the most powerful houses in Hag Graef,' she said simply. 'Do not concern yourself about Lurhan, or even the Drachau – my influence runs deeper in this city than you realise. There are many more than those five, sweet brother, all pursuing their devotions in secret. In fact, summoning them here to assist in these rites is a greater honour than you know.'

The highborn growled deep in his throat. 'An honour that no doubt comes with a steep price.'

Tz'arkan chuckled, an oily resonance in his chest. 'You are learning, Malus. That's good.'

'I think of it as an investment, brother. You and I have unfinished business.'

'Oh? What business would that be?'

Nagaira laughed, though the sound held little mirth. 'Don't be stupid. We agreed to share in whatever you brought with you out of the Wastes. Now you've returned and I know you didn't come back empty-handed, my agents have found your cold one being tended to in the nauglir den beneath the House of Brass. The great beast is standing watch over a fortune in coin and gems, but I care little for those. What else did you find in the hidden temple?'

Malus met her eyes and sought to plumb their depths. Was she serious? Had there been more to her scheme than simple revenge? If so, then she put me on the trail of the temple because she already had an inkling of what was there, Malus thought. But how much did she know and how much did she merely suspect? But there were no secrets waiting to be read in the witch's black eyes – he could sooner sound the deeps of the Outer Darkness itself.

'I found a daemon,' he said simply.

Nagaira's eyes widened. '*Tz'arkan*,' she breathed.

Malus felt the daemon surge inside him, pressing against the inside of his chest at the sound of its name. The highborn's fingers curled into claws. It had become difficult to breathe. 'So… you knew… all along,' he said haltingly. He wondered if his sister understood how close she was to dying just then.

'I… suspected,' she replied, wetting her lips. Suddenly her self-assurance was gone. 'After I had a close look at the skull inside Urial's tower, I was able to focus my research while you were away. There are numerous references to the daemon in my library, but I hardly dared hope that we had discovered his very prison!' Suddenly she grew still and studied his face with care. 'Did you look upon the great prince? Did he speak to you?'

Malus hesitated. Within, the daemon had fallen still. 'I saw the prison where he resides. It is a great crystal, larger than two men and wider than the bole of an elder oak. My sword made no mark on it, no matter how hard I struck it.'

'No, of course not,' Nagaira replied, a distant look coming over her face. Suddenly she was the arcane scholar once more. 'The Tome of Al'khasur says that the great prince was bound in a raw, black diamond birthed in the raw energies of Chaos itself. There are sorcerers who would spill the blood of entire nations just to possess a *fragment* of that stone, much less the great power trapped within. Nothing less could contain the Drinker of Worlds.'

Tz'arkan swelled and Malus suddenly felt his heart begin to labour fitfully. He leaned against the bier for support, gritting his teeth. 'Clever, clever druchii. I have not heard that name in a very long time. Oh, she is fine! How I would love to possess her.'

'Be… my… guest,' Malus gasped.

Nagaira misunderstood his meaning. 'The stone is priceless, true enough, but nothing compared to the power harnessed within. Did the great prince bless you with his favour? What did he say?'

'He wishes to be free,' Malus answered. 'What else?'

The witch leaned close. 'Did he say how?'

Suddenly the daemon receded, shrinking inside the highborn's chest to wrap tightly around his heart. 'Answer with care, Malus,' the daemon warned. 'Answer very carefully indeed.'

'There are a number of items the daemon wants me to find,' he said carefully. 'Together, they will unlock his prison and return him to the sea of souls.'

Nagaira snorted. 'Return? Set him loose across the face of Creation is more like,' she said. 'The Drinker of Worlds would love nothing better. Tell me: what are these items?'

The highborn smiled. 'Tut, tut, sweet sister. Haven't I given you enough already?'

'I brought you back from death's clutches, brother,' Nagaira warned. 'The way I see it, the balance of the debt is still yours to bear.'

Malus raised his hands. 'Truce, then. I will give you the name of one of the relics. Do you know of an object called the Idol of Kolkuth?'

Nagaira frowned, her dark brows furrowing with thought. 'I have seen that name... somewhere...'

'No games, sister,' Malus hissed.

'Have you any idea how many books I have in my sanctum?' Nagaira shot back. 'How many scrolls and carvings? I read the name *somewhere*, but I can't place it just yet.' She grinned. 'Give me time, though. I'll find it.'

'Time is not something I have in ample supply,' the highborn said. 'The daemon warned me that I had a single year to retrieve all the items, or else the effort would fail.'

The witch cocked her head quizzically. 'Why would he say that? What does a year have to do with anything?'

'Am I a sorcerer, sister? How should I know? The daemon said I had a year, no more. And I have already spent the better part of three months just getting back to Hag Graef. So you can see that time is of the essence.'

Nagaira sighed. 'Well, if time is so short it would make much more sense to research all of the items at once.'

'Am I mistaken, or do you not wish to share in this power? If I can't gain it neither will you and you only get the name of one relic at a time. Don't try to barter with me like some fishwife.'

The witch's voice went cold. 'I could simply wring it out of you like a blood-soaked rag.'

The highborn smiled. 'After all the work you just went through to restore me, sweet sister? What a waste.'

She glowered at him a moment – then threw back her head and laughed. 'Oh, how I've missed you, dear brother,' she said. 'No one else vexes me as sweetly as you. In fact, you will be pleased to know that I have prepared a great celebration in your honour.'

'A celebration?' Malus said, as though unfamiliar with the word.

'Oh, yes! A grand feast of wine and flesh, of powders and spices and sweet blood. You will get to see just how deep my connections run – many of my allies are eager to meet you and there is much you could reap from such acquaintances. I daresay you would taste a bit of the power I know you've coveted your entire life.'

'And how many of the temple's devoted will find their way into the celebration and try to plunge their knives in my throat?'

'Let them come,' the witch smirked, tapping the edge of Malus's goblet with a long fingernail. 'I could use a few more goblets for my guests.' Her eyes widened. 'And speaking of the fete, I have another gift for you.'

She reached into the sleeve of her robe and produced a carefully wrapped bundle a bit larger than her hand.

'I should be scandalised at the way I lavish you with costly things,' she said, setting the parcel on the bier and carefully unwrapping it. 'All of the guests at the fete must wear one of these,' she said, holding the object up to the witchlight. 'I think this one will suit you well.'

Malus reached out and took the object from her hand. A skilled craftsman had used very keen knives to remove the top part of a druchii's face, peeling away the flesh down to the muscle. The hide had then been mounted on a mould and carefully cured back into its former shape, then painted with what appeared to be intricate tattoos. It was an exquisite mask, the tattoos forming the image of a dragon's eyes and snout.

'Masks on top of masks,' the highborn said, pressing the cured skin to his face. It fitted perfectly.

Chapter Five
RAIMENT OF BLOOD

I T WAS ANOTHER two nights before the grand revel began. At Nagaira's command, Malus was installed in one of the tower's apartments and afforded every luxury. A steady procession of slaves presented themselves before him, bearing new clothes, weapons and armour. There were black robes of watered silk to caress his skin and fine outer robes of indigo-dyed wool and a kheitan of the toughest, most supple dwarf hide he had ever seen. An armourer from the Princes' Quarter delivered a hauberk of fine mail and a fearsome harness of articulated plate that fitted over it. A weapon smith from the famous Sa'hreich forges appeared with an exquisite set of vraith and a human slave to test them upon. The sleek blades were forged with runes that kept the edges razor-keen and able to turn aside all but the most terrible sorcerous weapons without harm. Gifts fit for a prince and accompanied by every form of luxury he could imagine, from wine to flesh to exotic spices and vapours.

Yet for all that, Malus understood that he was a captive.

His every request to return to his own tower was met with a cunning denial. Nagaira claimed that he wasn't yet fully recovered from the healing rites and needed to regain his strength. Then it was because his tower had lain unused for more than two months and needed to be prepared for his arrival. Then it was because the grand revel was imminent and the slaves couldn't be spared to move his possessions until

313

afterwards. Several times he lost patience with Nagaira's calm protests, but each time he found himself quickly drained by any heated exchange of words. After a while he began to hope that it was because he was still recovering – the thought that she might have somehow magically rendered him unable to resist her suggestions was too awful a fate to contemplate.

He had at least been permitted to meet with his retainers the day after the completion of the rites. From Silar he learned that they had been returned to Malus's service the day that he had been given into Nagaira's keeping and they had tried to take charge of him immediately thereafter. Nagaira had refused every attempt and there had in fact been points where Silar had considered bloodshed in order to rescue his lord. It was only after the failed assassination attempt in the witch's tower that the retainer grudgingly admitted that he was better protected under Nagaira's care than he would be in his own tower and further plans to retrieve him were abandoned.

Unfortunately, their presence was intermittent at best. There was a palpable tension between Malus's men and Nagaira's; evidently word had spread about the deaths of Nagaira's retainers in the north and somehow that translated into antagonism towards his own. Malus had too few retainers to countenance a violent rivalry between the two camps, so he was ultimately forced to dismiss Silar and the rest to his tower. Had Nagaira wished him ill she'd had plenty of opportunity to harm him already, though it was clear that she had embarked on a comprehensive campaign to keep him isolated from the outside world. For the moment, he was willing to bide his time and wait to see what her next move would be.

'AND WHAT AM I to wear to this... revel?' Malus frowned at Nagaira from a high-backed chair near one of the tower windows, sipping wine from his attempted killer's skull. He looked out over the sharp spires of the city, wreathed in sickly nightfog. It struck him as odd that he felt his confinement more keenly in Nagaira's possession than he ever did hanging from chains in the Vaulkhar's tower.

'Do as you will,' Nagaira answered with a fleeting smile. She stood before a tall mirror, attended by a pair of druchii slaves. Her hair was pulled back in a thick braid and bound in wire; tiny barbed blades glittered evilly from the rope of black hair. The witch's naked body was covered in a spiralling tattoo she'd taken all day to paint; it reminded him of the marks she'd laid on her body before the raid on Urial's tower, twisting and pulling at his eyes. This time, however, it seemed to shroud her in a dark allure and his blood raced with each passing glance. 'Just leave that cold armour here – I think you'll find it inconvenient before too long.' As the spoke the slaves slipped a silken robe over their mistress, binding it loosely with a belt formed of silver skulls.

Grunting, Malus rose from the chair and pulled his kheitan from a dressing-chest. He could countenance leaving the plate and mail behind, but he wanted some measure of protection, even at a revel in his honour. By the time he was done buckling the light armour around his chest, Nagaira was regarding him from behind her own mask. It looked to be druchii hide like Malus's, pale and fine, with long strips of flayed skin around the temples that hung down past the witch's shoulders. More tattoos traced arcane patterns across the mask's cheeks, but these were more for ornamentation, Malus sensed, than any sorcerous purpose. 'Ready?' she asked, her voice breathy behind her mask.

'I've *been* ready, woman,' the highborn growled. 'Didn't this revel start an hour ago?'

Nagaira laughed. 'Of course. But you must be the last to arrive. Did your mother teach you nothing of society as a child?'

'My mother was locked in the convent almost from the moment she arrived in Hag Graef. She had little time for revels.'

His half-sister gave him a languid smile. 'Then this will be an education for you,' she said, beckoning to Malus. 'Come.'

She led the way from her apartments, down the long, curving stair from her quarters near the top of her tower. The two highborn passed numerous armed retainers on the stairs, accoutred in full armour and holding naked steel in their gauntleted hands. For all her pride in her magic, Malus noted that Nagaira was leaving nothing to chance. If the temple sent their acolytes into the tower tonight they would pay a very heavy price.

Other than the guards, the halls and stairways were deserted. Before, they had buzzed with activity as Nagaira prepared for the revel – the highborn hadn't realised how many slaves his half-sister had owned until she'd set them scurrying to work like a swarm of ants. Now the silence and stillness of the tower was unsettling by comparison.

The descent lasted several minutes, ending at last on the tower's ground floor. The large, circular room was empty, save for a handful of guards standing watch over the spire's ground floor entrance. The tall, double doors were the way in which most of the tower's visitors came and went – everyone from slaves to traders and guests from the city. Now the doors were securely barred with lengths of cold iron set securely into heavy brackets on either side of the doorframe. The centre of the chamber was dominated by a tall, imposing statue of a druchii maiden and a crouching manticore, worked in imposing black marble. The expression on the maiden's face seemed both inviting and menacing all at the same time – not that there were any guests to admire it.

Dan Abnett & Mike Lee

Malus cast a sidelong glance at Nagaira. 'A fair turnout. I can't say I was expecting any differently for a revel held in *my* honour.'

Nagaira grinned, her eyes glinting with mischief. 'Stupid boy. When will you learn that nothing in my demesne is what it appears to be?'

With that she stepped forward swiftly, marching up to the towering statue – and disappearing inside it.

Tz'arkan stirred. 'A passable illusion,' the daemon observed. 'It would appear that your sweet sister has a great many talents – sorcerously and otherwise. I wonder where she learned them all?'

'Perhaps she has a daemon of her own to torment her,' Malus growled under his breath, then steeled himself to follow.

There was nothing more than a slight tingle as he passed through the illusory image – he had to close his eyes at the last moment because he couldn't quite convince himself that he wasn't about to walk face-first into a massive piece of carved marble.

A small hand on his chest brought him up short. When he opened his eyes he found that he was standing next to Nagaira at the top of a narrow, curving stair that disappeared below the floor. A circle of magical symbols enclosed the stairway landing and the air had a dusky shimmer to it. From the corner of his eye Malus could almost make out the lines of the statue, seen from the inside out, but the illusion vanished the instant he tried to view it directly.

'Well,' the highborn responded. 'What else haven't you been telling me, dear sister?'

'Come and find out,' she said, taking his arm.

They descended into darkness, Malus's booted feet echoing soft in the confined space. A faint smell rose up the stairwell, tickling his nose with its spicy odour. Just as he was about to ask where the stairs were leading, he turned another tight corner and found himself looking out over a large, subterranean chamber suffused with pale green witchlight.

Figures awaited them, all concealed behind masks of flesh. These druchii stood in concentric rings surrounding the spiral stairs – six in the first ring, twelve in the next, eighteen in the one beyond that – all facing him and all raising their arms in a gesture of supplication as he appeared. They cried out as he approached, filling the chamber with an exultant chant in a language he could not comprehend.

Beyond the masked circles lay a sea of writhing flesh.

Scores and scores of slaves filled the rest of the chamber, sprawled on the stone in a drugged delirium or climbing over one another in the throes of desire. Braziers situated around the room filled the air with incense and mind-altering herbs. Malus's heart quickened to see such a tempting feast laid before him. His skin tingled with each breath and for once even the daemon seemed to echo his kindled desire.

The chants of the supplicants washed over him and trembled in his bones. It was like nothing he had ever felt before and it left him intoxicated. Is this what it is like to be worshipped, Malus thought?

It was something he could grow to like.

Nagaira continued down the stairs, drawing Malus along with her. At the bottom another figure waited – a druchii in robes of newly-skinned human hide, still glistening with blood. The surface of the robe was tattooed with intricate runes and spiral patterns and a censer steaming with a pungent kind of musk hung on a golden chain from the figure's neck. Instead of a mask, the figure wore the skull of a great mountain ram, its bony snout hanging well below shoulder height and its long, curved horns gleaming like polished teak in the artificial light. The skull was painted with symbols and the figure's tattooed hands held a goblet brimming with thick, red fluid that steamed in the air.

The figure radiated a palpable aura of power and authority, one to which even Nagaira seemed to defer. Malus eyed the figure warily. This is no mere wine-soaked orgy, he thought. What have you drawn me into now, sister?

As they approached, the figure raised the goblet, offering it to Malus. Nagaira led him to the cup and spoke, her voice pitched to carry across the cavern. 'The Prince of the Revel is come! The cup is placed before him!' She turned to Malus, her voice still clear and carrying, but her words were focused directly to him. 'Anoint yourself with the nectar of desire and inflame the hunger of your heart. Drink deep!'

'*Drink deep!*' The masked figures intoned, their voices trembling with anticipation.

'Yes. Drink.' Tz'arkan whispered. Did the daemon's voice tremble as well?

Moving slowly, as if in a dream, Malus reached out and took the goblet from the figure's hands. It was heavier than he imagined and he raised it carefully; for some reason he feared to spill the thick, sloshing liquid. He raised the cup to his lips and drank.

Hot blood filled his mouth, bitter and salty. It slid like oil over his tongue and down his throat and it filled him with *hunger*. Not just his desires, but the appetites of each and every supplicant who had poured some of his or her blood into the cup. If he closed his eyes he could almost see them in his mind, tasting their pleasure as they slaked their terrible hunger.

Flesh. Food. Wine. Murder. Every appetite, every scintillating taste, reverberated through him in waves of heat and cold. His body shook and the supplicants roared.

'*Slaanesh! He is come! The Prince of Pleasure is come!*'

His consciousness tumbled like a leaf in the maelstrom of desire. Slaanesh! Malus's mind reeled. Nagaira, you foolish girl, what have you done?

Nagaira reached up and pried the cup from his grasp. He was surprised to discover that once he'd begun drinking, he hadn't paused until the cup was dry. Streamers of anointed blood ran down his chin and stained the front of his kheitan. She raised it high and the exultation of the supplicants fell silent.

'The Prince of the Revel has drunk deep and accepted the blessing of Slaanesh! Offer yourselves to him! Drink deeply of your desires and praise the Prince of Pleasure! Worship before the throne of flesh!'

The supplicants roared with a single voice. '*Slaanesh!*' The name of the Ruinous God reverberated through the cavern until the air itself seemed to curdle with an unholy presence.

Within Malus, the daemon seemed to swell until it filled him from head to toe, wearing him like an ill-fitting skin. It drew strength from the supplicants' ecstatic cries, as though it claimed some of the worshippers' devotion for itself.

In that moment, Malus Darkblade felt like a god.

Nagaira pressed against him, the heat of her nearly naked body radiating through Malus's silken robes. She pointed to the glistening bodies beyond the circle of supplicants. 'There lies your feast,' she whispered huskily. 'All of it has been prepared in your honour, you who have stood before the Drinker of Worlds. And that is but a foretaste of the gifts that await you.'

She reached out and propelled him forward. The ram-headed figure stepped aside and the rings of supplicants parted before him. He walked alone and as he passed each ring of worshippers he felt their hands caress him, strike him, claw at him with desire. Malus walked among them as a king, a god and he could feel their devotion to him surrounding him like a silken cloak.

All his life he had known nothing but hate and it had sustained him like bitter wine. Now he tasted absolute power and he knew that he would do *anything* to keep it.

It would not be enough to see his siblings destroyed and his father broken beneath his hand. It would not be enough to wear the armour of the Vaulkhar and go to war in the Witch King's name. No amount of gold or slaves, no lofty title or terrible authority would ever be enough for him. The entire world might not be enough to slake the hunger that now seethed inside him.

But he would feast upon it nonetheless.

Thunderous laughter filled his ears – drunken, lustful and triumphant. He could not be sure if it was his or the daemon's, but it mattered not one whit as Malus revelled in the delicacies that the Prince of Pleasure laid before him.

MALUS LAY UPON a bed of moaning bodies, his naked skin hot and streaked with sweat and blood. His dark hair was matted with wine and other fluids and his nerves sang with the effects of the drugged smoke and whetted desires. The air shuddered with release: whispers, moans, screams and cruel laughter, all mingled in a storm of sybaritic devotion. Every breath filled his lungs with a thick musk of drugs, blood, sex and wine. It was the taste of ecstasy and the highborn was surprised to find that it sharpened his mind like nothing ever had before.

He understood, among other things, why the Witch King had outlawed the Cult of Slaanesh among the druchii. The cold doctrine of Khaine was one thing – hate shaped the soul and sharpened it like a sword and like a sword it could be wielded against the enemies of the state. But desire was something else altogether. It had no limits, nor could it be shaped to suit the whims of a king. Hunger had no respect for states or boundaries – it existed to consume all in its path. Such hunger, when directed at the king on his throne, was a dangerous thing indeed.

Though legends claimed that the Prince of Pleasure was once the centre of worship for the peoples of lost Nagarythe, when the druchii made their way to Naggaroth the Witch King murdered the priests and priestesses of Slaanesh and elevated the Lord of Murder instead. Though cults of Slaanesh were said to linger amid the great cities of the Land of Chill, the Witch King's agents ruthlessly persecuted them, executing any worshipper they could find and enslaving their families as well. The thought that such a cancer lay unseen in the Vaulkhar's household brought a cruel smile to Malus's lips.

Of course, Nagaira had only trusted him with this knowledge because now he was tainted as well. Malekith would make no distinction between family members if the cult was uncovered, from Lurhan the Vaulkhar on down. The question was *why*. Clearly his half-sister had been part of the cult for some time; indeed she appeared to enjoy considerable rank among its members. Yet she had been utterly circumspect prior to this. If she'd wanted to initiate him into the cult it would have been easy to do so – he was brutally honest with himself and recognised that the taste of desire he'd felt tonight would mark him forever. In fact, if it weren't for the daemon's damned hold on him he had little doubt that he would have joined the cult gladly and then worked to manipulate it to his ends.

Ironically, he was certain that Tz'arkan was the reason that the cult wanted him in the first place.

Dimly Malus sensed the presence of other druchii surrounding him. He stirred slightly, glancing about with half-lidded eyes. Half a dozen supplicants approached him with a mixture of deference and fear. Malus remembered little of the last few hours – it had been a tempest of gluttony, rapine and slaughter. As prodigious as his own magically fuelled appetites had turned out to be, he had also been aware that the daemon had driven him to even deeper depths of depravity. The supplicants behaved as though he were Slaanesh incarnate and he allowed that he had probably come as close to the Prince of Pleasure as any of the cultists had witnessed before.

One of the supplicants bowed low before him. She was entirely naked save for her mask, her pale skin dappled with patches of dried blood and vomit. Like Malus, her black hair was matted with the fruits of her excess. 'Is the wine sweet, my prince? Is the flesh tender and delectable? Are the screams melodious? Are your desires sated by this grand feast?'

He looked at her and smiled. Part of him wanted to reach for her, but his body refused to move. 'No,' he said at last. 'I still hunger.'

A ripple of reverent approval ran through the supplicants. Another of the masked druchii, male by the sound of his voice, said 'Truly you are blessed above all others, great prince. All have marvelled at your hunger, the sublime rapaciousness of your fleshly desires. Truly you are marked by the Drinker of Worlds and we are blessed by your presence.'

A third supplicant, a man covered in scores of bleeding cuts, opened his crimson-stained hands in a gesture of deprecation. 'We regret that our offering is so meagre, great prince,' he said. 'There are even fewer initiates in the city than elsewhere in the land. Well, enough to say that there are few of us here, but those of us who do honour the ancient beliefs are powerful indeed.'

Malus considered the man thoughtfully. They all spoke with high-born accents and though the masks muffled their voices somewhat, he fancied that some of their voices were familiar to him. He had no doubt that many of the supplicants were scions of the highest-ranking households in the city. Nagaira received a generous allowance from Lurhan, himself the second most powerful man in Hag Graef, but not even she could have afforded the enormous expense this revel would have demanded. 'Only the most ancient and proudest households in the city would dare uphold the ways of lost Nagarythe,' he said carefully. 'It is an honour to have been a guest among such exalted company.'

The bleeding druchii bowed his head politely. 'You must not think of yourself as a guest, great prince. Your journey north has transformed you. We have all seen with our own eyes how you have been marked by the Drinker of Worlds. Indeed, you would hold a place of great prominence among us – if you were to assume a role in our meagre cult.'

'It is no small thing to set oneself against the laws of the Witch King,' Malus replied. To the highborn's surprise, the man nodded readily.

'The power of Malekith is great and terrible,' the supplicant agreed. 'And his will is the law of our land. But we serve a power far greater, do we not? Does Malekith not defer to the priests of the Temple of Khaine?'

Yes, Malus thought, but they serve his interests. This cult is a threat. 'Of course you are correct,' he answered smoothly. 'But that does not lessen the risk.'

The female druchii knelt at his feet. 'We have worshipped the Prince of Pleasure in secret for centuries,' she said proudly. 'While we are few in number, we protect our own.'

'Indeed,' the male supplicant agreed. 'And we take care of our fellow believers. All are one in the crucible of desire. It would be a great sin if we were to let a true believer's appetites go unfulfilled.'

The implication in the highborn's words stirred the ambition in Malus's heart. 'Be careful, brother,' he said companionably. 'You've seen for yourself that my appetites are considerable indeed.'

That drew a respectful chuckle from the supplicants. 'True enough, but we also expect that you could give us much in return.'

Ah, but what is it you want from me, Malus thought? What is Tz'arkan to you and how do you know about him? More to the point, what else do you know about the daemon that I don't?

For the first time it occurred to him that perhaps Nagaira's efforts were infinitely more cunning than he'd given her credit for. What were the odds that the hidden temple in the north just happened to hold a daemon held in high regard by her cult? Was it possible that everything that had happened to him since returning from his slave raid had been an elaborate plot to make contact with a patron of the cult?

Ah, sister, I continue to underestimate you, he thought. You are *far* more dangerous than I realised.

Yes, it did indeed make sense. The question was, how could he turn it to his advantage?

Chapter Six
LEGENDS AND LIES

MALUS CONSIDERED THE suppliants thoughtfully. 'How may a humble son of the Vaulkhar serve the Prince of Pleasure?'

The bloody druchii held out one crimson-stained hand. 'That is not for me to say, great prince. Such matters are for you and the Hierophant to discuss – and he awaits the pleasure of your company.'

Reluctantly, Malus took the man's hand and allowed himself to be pulled to his feet. His limbs trembled from the exertions of the night until he stilled them with an effort of will and then gestured for the suppliants to precede him with a wave of his hand.

They crossed back through a ruin of spent bodies – some living, others dead. Scores of slaves littered the cavern floor in twisted heaps, as gruesome as any battlefield Malus had ever seen. His bare feet padded through cooling puddles of congealing blood and sticky wine. The revel had run its course and now Nagaira's household slaves worked their way through the detritus left behind, inspecting the bodies and dispatching those who physically survived but whose spirit had been shattered by the rapacious suppliants. As Malus watched, one slave rolled a catatonic victim onto his back and began strangling him with a silken cord. The slave made no attempt to resist.

Once past the towering spiral staircase the group crossed to the opposite end of the chamber and passed through an oval archway into an adjoining space. The walls were raw stone and rough-hewn, more like a cave than a finished room and Malus suddenly realised that they were most likely in a sealed-off part of the Burrows, the twisting maze of tunnels and caverns hollowed out of the rock beneath Hag Graef. He wondered idly if Nagaira's slaves would bother hauling the bodies up to the surface, or simply open a concealed passage that connected the chamber with the rest of the tunnels and let the wild predators that roamed there come and eat their fill.

The space was small in comparison to the revel chamber, perhaps fifteen paces across at its widest point. The bodies of a dozen slaves hung from chains around the perimeter of the chamber, their vital fluids mingling on the rough stone floor. In the centre of the space sat the druchii wearing the ram's skull who had anointed him at the base of the curving stair. The Hierophant reclined on a throne formed of living bodies – naked slaves were contorted and clasped together to form the seat, sides and backrest to support the reclining druchii. The slaves had been paralysed with some kind of poison to lock their limbs together and a palpable sense of agony hung over the Hierophant's throne. Acrid, pale green smoke rose to the low ceiling from two small braziers set to either side of the living chair, sending a burning tingle through Malus's nostrils.

The Hierophant's sharp, lacquered nails sliced thin tracks along the pale skin of his armrests. His eyes were bright and hard within the dark oculars of the ram's skull, glaring a challenge at Malus as he approached. Nagaira stood to one side of the throne, her expression inscrutable.

'Your appetites are prodigious, great prince,' grated the voice within the skull. The bone made strange echoes, distorting the Hierophant's words. Still, Malus fought to keep his expression neutral. He knew that voice from somewhere…

'When a man is given food, he eats.' Malus bowed deeply before the leader of the cult. 'With such a great and wondrous feast set before me, how could I not revel in it?'

The supplicants looked to one another and nodded in approval, but the Hierophant seemed unmoved. He leaned forward in his seat, his long fingers twining restlessly together. 'It is said you are but recently returned from the north.'

'Indeed, Hierophant.'

'I have also been told that you discovered something there of great interest to us. Is that so?'

Of interest to whom, Malus wondered, and why? He could think of several reasons why a Slaanesh cult would take interest in a bound daemon – favours and patronage alone would lend them great power – but the highborn sensed that there was more at work here. The Hierophant is cautious, distrustful, Malus reasoned. But if Nagaira had

steered him into the Wastes for the express purpose of finding
Tz'arkan, did that mean she had acted without the Hierophant's
knowledge? Was she making a play for power within the cult?

Malus kept his expression carefully neutral. 'I found a great temple
in the Wastes, hidden in a valley at the foot of a cleft mountain.'

'We know of this place,' the Hierophant said curtly. 'The Tome of
Ak'zhaal speaks of it and the sacred power bound within. But the temple is warded by the most powerful of barriers, by the very warp itself–'

'It was,' Malus answered.

The supplicants bent their heads and murmured excitedly to one
another. The Hierophant silenced them with an upraised finger. 'What
of the priests within?'

'Long dead, Hierophant.'

'And you took the boat across the poison sea to reach the daemon's
sanctum?'

'No, I climbed a stair of floating rocks over a sea of fire,' Malus said,
allowing his irritation to show. 'Surely your tome speaks of this as well.'

The Hierophant leaned back, tapping a bloodstained nail against the
bony ram's snout. 'Indeed. So you stood before the great crystal and
beheld the power within?'

Malus nodded. 'In time, yes,' he answered slowly.

'And the Drinker of Worlds spared you. Why?'

The highborn smiled. 'You will have to go ask him yourself. I could
draw you a map if you like.'

Malus sensed the supplicants stiffen in shock. For a moment, the
Hierophant was utterly still – even his taloned hands were frozen in
mid-gesture, a flourish of blood-stained points. A brief smile played
across Nagaira's lips.

Is this what you were hoping for, Malus thought? Did you draw me
into this web merely to cross swords with this high priest?

'It had been reported to me that you required our help, great prince,'
the Hierophant replied acidly. 'You are seeking certain relics on the
daemon's behalf, arcane objects lost to the mists of time. A great
scholar with access to an exceptional library might be able to locate
references to these lost artefacts, given time. You do not strike me as
much of a page-turner, however.'

Malus glanced sidelong at Nagaira. 'Forgive me, Hierophant. You are
better informed than I realised. I wasn't aware that you were offering
me your help. What I heard moments ago sounded more like an inter-
rogation than a meeting of allies.'

The highborn could hear the cold smile in the Hierophant's voice.
'That is because we are not allies, great prince. At least, not yet. The
anointed of Slaanesh are all one and we act to protect one another
against the persecutions of the unbelievers. But you surely understand

the precariousness of our situation. We can only extend our aid to those who are truly worthy.'

'I have been touched by the Drinker of Worlds. Is that not enough?'

'No. We only have your word that such a thing occurred. Your knowledge of the temple is correct in every particular, but you could have read the Tome as easily as myself – or had the facts related to you by... a third party.'

Malus noticed Nagaira stiffen slightly at the thinly-veiled implication.

'On the other hand, we cannot dismiss an opportunity to spread the glory of the Prince of Pleasure, no matter how... unlikely... such an opportunity appears. So I shall offer you a proposition.'

'Tell me.'

'I will place all the power of our cult at your disposal – our riches, our influence, even our strength of arms if we must – but only on the condition that you consign your soul in service to Slaanesh with a holy initiation. As I said, we take care of our own. Join us and all that we have will be yours as well.'

Malus considered the Hierophant's words, his mind working furiously. 'I will think on it,' he said.

The Hierophant visibly recoiled, his nails sinking deep into the armrests. Runnels of blood streaked the pale flesh and pattered on the floor. 'What? What is there to consider? You have *no* chance of completing your quest without our help.'

'I serve at the whim of the Drinker of Worlds, great Hierophant,' Malus said coldly. 'And while you are especially well-informed as to my intentions, there is still much you do not know. I must now decide whether it is in the interests of my daemonic patron–' Malus couldn't bring himself to say *master* – 'to enmesh myself in the petty agendas of your cult and place myself under your authority, or to continue my quest alone.'

Now the Hierophant glared angrily, first at Nagaira and then at Malus. 'Such insolence! Have we not lavished you with gifts of flesh and wine? Have we not honoured you with a grand revel the likes of which Hag Graef has never before seen?'

'Indeed, indeed, Hierophant – and I thank you for your lavish entertainments. But the great daemons do not want gifts. They want only to be *obeyed*. Think on that, if you still crave the Drinker of Worlds as your patron. Meanwhile, I shall consider your proposition with great care.'

The Hierophant rose abruptly from the chair, his hands bright with fresh blood. 'Consider it well, great prince, but keep this in mind as well. The night of the new moon approaches, when the Prince of Pleasure accepts initiates into his service. You have until then to decide.'

And then what, Malus thought? Will you kill me to keep your secret cult safe? One look in the Hierophant's eyes stifled his sarcastic reply, however.

Ah. I see. That's *exactly* what you mean.

Malus bowed once more. 'Then may the Prince of Pleasure speed my thoughts, Hierophant, and I hope you will excuse me so that I may rest and begin my deliberations.'

The Hierophant made no reply, but it was clear the interview was over. Nagaira bowed deeply and led Malus from the room.

Nagaira took Malus by the arm as they crossed the carnage of the revelry floor, pointedly oblivious to the tension hardening every muscle of the highborn's body. 'What a wonderful night,' she whispered, stealing a glance back the way they'd come. 'I knew you'd find a way to liven up the festivities.'

HOURS LATER, THE highborn lay awake in his bedchamber, listening carefully as the bustling of the servants gradually dwindled away. Moving slowly and carefully, the highborn eased from his bed. From the darkness beyond the narrow windows, Malus estimated it was only a few hours before dawn. He slipped on his silk robes and belted a dagger around his waist, then crept from his apartment into the corridor beyond.

The halls were as silent as a tomb. Days of frenzied preparations, followed by the monumental task of cleaning up the remains of the great revel had taxed the capacity of Nagaira's household to the utmost. Malus expected that nearly all of the house servants were occupied with tasks or taking what opportunity they had to rest before their mistress summoned them again. He was certain that the same could be said for the guards – after days at a heightened state of readiness it was only natural that they would relax as soon as the revel was concluded.

It was perhaps the only opportunity he would get to work his way out of the snare his sister had laid for him.

The meeting with the Hierophant had not only confirmed his fears about Nagaira but expanded their dimensions in troubling ways. Not only did she know much more about Tz'arkan and the nature of his imprisonment, she had shared the knowledge of his predicament with the members of the cult. The witch was using him to usurp the role of the Hierophant and using the power of the cult to gain greater influence over him. No matter which way he turned, she was always one step ahead of him, drawing him deeper into her web.

His only alternative was to take matters into his own hands and quickly, before she left him with no room to manoeuvre.

Malus reached the tower's main stair and turned right, heading down. The next landing ended in a door; he pushed it open quickly and quietly, paying no heed to the guard standing watch on the other side. The guards were well used to his presence and he had the run of the tower except for Nagaira's topmost sanctum. Malus continued down the stairs without a backward glance and the guard made no attempt to challenge him before he disappeared around the curve of the staircase.

The next landing ended in yet another door, which Malus opened much more slowly and carefully. Beyond was a small room, lined with racks of long spears and heavy crossbows. A circular table occupied the centre of the guardroom and two of Nagaira's men were slumped in their seats, snoring softly. The highborn shut the door behind him as carefully as possible, then crept the rest of the way down the staircase past the room. To Malus's left a short corridor led to a heavy, iron-banded door. A single globe of witchlight cast long shadows from its sconce at the midpoint of the hall. Malus plucked the globe from its iron holder and moved quietly to a thin arrow-slit just to the right of the door.

Malus could see another black, needle-like tower rising against the night sky – *his* tower, one of several granted by the Drachau for Lurhan and his family. A narrow bridge connected Nagaira's tower with his own; it was a treacherous walk in high winds, but had Malus wished he could have been within the relative safety of his own quarters in moments.

To do so however would have also meant braving the intricate band of runes surrounding the tall, arched bridge door. Malus had no idea how Nagaira's sorcerous defences worked, but he reckoned that at the very least she would be instantly alerted if he tried to cross one of the tower's warded thresholds.

The highborn raised the witchlight globe to eye level, counted three heartbeats and then lowered it once more. After three more heartbeats he repeated the process and then paused, his eyes straining to pierce the predawn darkness.

One moment stretched into the next, until Malus felt his patience starting to fray. Then his eyes caught sight of faint movement on the narrow span. A swift shape was flowing like dark water across the bridge, keeping low so as to avoid silhouetting itself against the faint starlight.

Malus watched as the figure reached the near end of the bridge and straightened its hooded head to peer at the arrow-slit. He did not need to see the druchii's face to know it was Arleth Vann. The assassin's whisper carried easily despite the wind keening across the bridge. 'I have the parcel, my lord. All is in readiness.'

Once it had become clear that Malus was to remain in Nagaira's tower without the support of his retainers, he had gone to some pains during one of their infrequent meetings to establish a contingency plan in the event he needed to escape. 'Give it here,' he whispered to Arleth Vann, readying his hands.

The assassin's arm emerged from his cloak, holding a narrow, square bundle shaped like a book. With a sharp flick of his wrist, the retainer sent the package across the intervening space and through the arrow-slit like a hurled dagger. Even prepared, the speed of the throw took Malus by surprise, the package striking him sharply in the chest. He fumbled with the parcel for a heartbeat and then clasped his hands around it. It was dark cloth bound with cord and he cut the bindings free with his blade and then turned his attention back to Arleth Vann.

'I'm not coming out yet,' he whispered. 'But soon. How goes the restoration?'

'It goes well,' the retainer replied. 'Silar has everything well in hand. He and Dolthaic have hired mercenaries to defend the tower until you can choose new retainers. Your mount has been brought back to the stables and is almost completely mended.'

Malus nodded. 'Well done. Now go back across and get some sleep. Keep to the same vigil, though – when I come out, it will likely be within the next couple of days, at right around this time.'

The hooded head bobbed. 'Yes, my lord,' he whispered and then was gone, like a shadow passing over the moon.

Malus returned the witchlight to its sconce and tucked the parcel within the folds of his robe. The men in the guardroom snored on as he climbed back up the staircase and slipped through the door. At the next landing the guard there watched him calmly and admitted him into his mistress's apartments with a deferential nod of his head.

Once past the guard, Malus drew out the bundle and unwrapped it. A layer of black cloth enclosed a box made of thin wood. Inside was a small, disassembled hand crossbow with five poisoned bolts, a set of lockpicks that he barely knew how to use – and most importantly of all, a smaller wrapped bundle the size of his palm. He plucked the cloth bundle from the box and slipped the rest back into his robe, then unwrapped the one key he truly needed to escape Nagaira's grasp.

The cloth contained a heavy, octagonal brass amulet fitted to a long chain. The amulet's surface was covered with intricate runes that Malus would have been hard pressed to describe, much less understand. What he did know was that the Octagon of Praan was a potent magical relic, capable of absorbing any magic directed at the caster, no matter its power. Since he'd fled the camp of Kul Hadar's beastman herd the octagon had rested at the bottom of a saddlebag hung from Spite's saddle and so it had gone undetected by ally and rival alike until Malus had directed Arleth Vann to make it ready for his use.

Malus slipped the amulet's chain over his head, letting the cold weight of the octagon rest against his chest. He was certain that it would defeat any magical defence in the tower that was aimed at him – but what about simple alarms triggered by his mere presence? He had no answer for that and the notion set his teeth on edge.

Only one way to know for certain, he thought grimly and started up the stairs.

There had been guards outside the entrance to Nagaira's sanctum the last time he'd visited. He hoped that with the mistress in bed the guards would be elsewhere. Malus rounded the corner of the spiral stairs, ready with a half-hearted excuse in case he was challenged – and found the small landing deserted. A pair of tall double doors stood closed, their surface gleaming with patterns of glowing green runes. Further runes etched the arched doorframe, rising to a stylised etching of a manticore leering down from the keystone of the doorway.

Malus swallowed nervously, pleased that there was no one about to witness his apprehension. After the sights he'd seen while raiding his half-brother Urial's tower – himself a sorcerer of sorts – he had some small idea of the kind of power those protective runes held. Yet they can't touch me, he told himself. The medallion will protect me. It *will* protect me.

He laid a hand on the door's latch. The metal felt cold and there was a strange ripple that disturbed the surface of the gleaming runes – as though he'd dipped his hand in a reflecting pool.

Steeling himself, Malus tripped the latch and pulled the door open, then stepped swiftly inside. There was a faint, oily sensation as he crossed the threshold, but nothing more. Breathing a quick sigh of relief, the highborn eased the door shut.

The sanctum was dimly lit by banked witchlights, plunging much of the room into deep shadow. The sanctum occupied the highest rooms in Nagaira's tower, making them consequently the smallest. A circular stone hearth – now cold – occupied the centre of the chamber, surrounded by two plush divans and a number of low tables. The tables, as well as every other bench, shelf, niche and pedestal, were covered with stacks of scrolls, books and other paraphernalia. Tall bookshelves lined every wall, groaning with the weight of grimoires and dusty tomes. At the far end of the room Malus saw a short ladder rising up to the floor above. He'd never gone up there, but now that he thought about it, he remembered that Nagaira had mentioned once that there was nothing up there but more stacks of books and scrolls.

For the first time Malus surveyed the room and took in the sheer vastness of the knowledge contained therein. Hundreds, perhaps *thousands* of works and not one of them kept in anything like a logical order.

He'd had it all wrong. Getting past the deadly wards wasn't the hardest part of his plan. Finding the one book he needed in this scrivener's maze was. And he had only a few hours before dawn, when the household slaves would start roaming the halls again.

The Hierophant had let slip the name of a book: the Tome of Ak'zhaal. If the high priest hadn't merely been making empty boasts, the tome contained details about Tz'arkan. Somewhere within its pages might also lie the resting place of the Idol of Kolkuth. And outside of the city convent, he could think of no better library.

'But where does the Tome of Ak'zhaal lie?' Malus muttered to himself. 'Blessed Mother, what if it isn't even written in druchast at all?' The highborn bared his teeth at the thought that the knowledge he sought could be under his very nose, concealed behind the illegible scrawls of some demented mage.

The daemon stirred, its chuckle rumbling through Malus's skull. Tz'arkan had lain quiescent since the mad feasting of the revel and the sudden voice caused the highborn to jump. 'Impetuous druchii! Only now do you think of these things? Did you imagine the sorcerers of old would write their secrets in your childlike alphabet?'

'How should I know? One set of scratchings are as good as another, are they not?'

'No. They are not.'

'You sound like you know many languages, daemon.'

'Of course. I know every spoken and written tongue this pitiful world has produced. In fact, I had a hand in creating–'

'Excellent. Then you can translate these writings for me, can't you?'

For a moment, the daemon made no response. 'Yes. I suppose,' it said peevishly.

'Good,' Malus said, eyeing the nearest bookshelf. 'Because we have precious little time to do our reading.'

Chapter Seven
THE ALTAR OF THE LOST

IT HAD TAKEN nearly two hours to cover a third of the books contained within the main room, to say nothing of the stacks of volumes kept in the room above. He had fought to keep his frustration in check – if he and Tz'arkan were truly integral to Nagaira's schemes then the books she had been consulting would be close by, not gathering dust in some far corner of her sanctum. Dawn was close at hand when Malus almost literally stumbled over the Tome of Ak'zhaal. As he had rushed to the next bookshelf in line he spied a large leather-bound book on the floor near one of the divans, hidden underneath a platter littered with bits of old cheese and breadcrumbs. The runes on the book's spine meant nothing to him – and yet when he looked at them it felt like a film of oil slid over his eyes and he instinctively knew what the ancient writing meant.

Even then, much of the text was indecipherable to him. Parts of it were history, parts of it references to sorcerous arts that completely escaped him. Malus scanned page after page, hungry for references to Tz'arkan and coming up wanting again and again. His attention wandered, after another half an hour he found himself listening for the sound of a hand on the door-latch and wondering what he would say to the slave – or worse, his sister – when he was discovered.

Then, two-thirds of the way into the book the references began. Initially, the comments were things he already knew: Tz'arkan was a mighty daemon that had once walked the earth during the First War, many thousands of years ago, but he had been tricked and bound into the service of five powerful Chaos sorcerers. With the daemon's power and knowledge at their disposal the sorcerers became fearsome conquerors, driving their foes before them. In the end, however, the daemon's diabolical gifts proved to be the sorcerers' undoing – one by one they were torn apart by rivals, driven mad by greed and bloodlust or consumed in sorcerous conflagrations too powerful for them to contain.

According to the book, the sorcerer Eradorius was the master of the enigmatic Idol of Kolkuth, a relic of a lost age even in those ancient times. Eradorius was the first to realise the peril of the daemon's gifts – and as a result he was the first of the five sorcerers to die. Beset by treacherous lieutenants who hungered for his power and fearful that his fellow sorcerers were scheming to assassinate him, Eradorius fled his enormous palace and his legion of retainers and sought refuge on a tiny island in the storm-wracked northern seas. There, he hoped to cheat the daemon's revenge by fleeing to a sanctuary that no enemy – mortal or daemon – could breach.

The highborn took a deep breath and returned his attention to the great book lying open on the low table by the divan. He carefully turned the page with the tips of two fingers, noting with alarm how the aged vellum crackled beneath his touch.

In the Time of Ash and Crimson the sorcerer Eradorius, known to the sons of Aenarion as one of the terrible Lords of the Black Stone, did leave the fastness of his citadel at Harash-Karn and rode the ash-laden winds like a great wyrm. Darkness and terror followed in his wake and the lesser minions of the Ruinous Powers quailed and cursed at his passing.

The sorcerer rode the heavens for seven days and nights, until the slate-coloured seas of the north stretched below him as far as his eyes could see. He soared above those cold and hungry waters until at last he spied a gnarled finger of stone rising from the icy mists – the isle called Morhaut, which in the tongue of the First Men means the altar of the lost.

Upon this haunted stone the dread mage alighted and stretched forth his claw-like hand to bend the cursed isle to his will. He used the secrets the Cursed One had given him and tunnelled deep into rock and air and the passage of years. A tower was built by Eradorius, raised with power and madness, reaching to the sky and sinking into worlds beyond, to a place without walls or passageways or doors. He dug into the bedrock of the world, seeking the empty place beyond, where the earthbound daemon could not find him. And there he passed from the ken of his fellows and from the talons of the Cursed One and was lost for all time.

'Morhaut,' Malus growled, his face grim. 'Of course. I should have known.'

The highborn felt the daemon stir within his breast. 'Oh? Why is that?'

Malus fought the urge to throw the old book across the room. 'Because it's little more than a legend and every druchii who's gone searching for it has never been seen again.'

He leapt to his feet and went to a large map that hung in a wooden frame against one of the sanctum's walls. 'I heard several versions of the story on the slaving cruise last summer,' he said, his eyes roving over the huge expanse of yellowed parchment. 'It's an isle of lost ships going back to the First War, surrounded by deadly reefs and impenetrable mists.'

The highborn traced a finger along Naggaroth's rough eastern coast, then north-east from the straits near Karond Kar. North and east, over a wide swath of hungry grey sea. 'Mother of Night,' he cursed softly. 'I'll need a whole *fleet*. Raiding ships and fighting men and damnable sorcery as well.'

'How grandiose,' the daemon sneered. 'You let that little taste of adoration go to your head, or you're simply looking for a reason to squander more of my treasure.'

'Would that were the truth,' Malus snarled. 'I'd throw every bit of your gold to the slaves in the Market Quarter if it meant an easy path to your damnable relics. No, the waters in the north are teeming with marauders. A single ship wouldn't last a week on those seas.'

'Marauders?'

Malus nodded. 'Norscan raiders claim the north seas as their own and there are marauder strongholds on nearly every island. They come south in the summer and make coastal raids against Ulthuan and the human lands, much as we do. Some of the more foolhardy bands even raid Naggaroth from time to time, or harry our raiding ships as they return home laden with plunder.'

'Indeed? I can see why you care little for them. They sound much like druchii.'

'They are *nothing* like us,' Malus snapped. 'We raid other lands for the gold and flesh to sustain our kingdom. The weak suffer so the strong may survive – that is the way of the world and we are its finest predators. These marauders exist only to destroy. They burn and slaughter without reason, without purpose. They are wasteful and ignorant, like animals.' The highborn's scowl deepened. 'Worst among them are the Skinriders.'

'You seem quite the expert on these marauding humans,' the daemon sneered. 'For a scholar, you have strange interests.'

'The Skinriders have been a thorn in Naggaroth's side for years, preying on our raiders as they return home loaded with flesh for our markets,' Malus replied acidly. 'They take the skin of others to cover their own raw, suppurating bodies. They worship a daemon god of pestilence and are rewarded with terrible strength and vitality. But the skin sloughs from their diseased bodies like putrid wax and they suffer constant agony unless they can clothe their raw flesh with untainted hide. Such are the rewards for placing faith in the words of daemons.'

'You insult me, little Darkblade. I am among the most honourable of beings. I have obeyed your every request to the letter, have I not? Do not blame me for your own lack of imagination or wit. Are not these Skinriders mighty warriors, blessed by their patron?'

'They are. In fact, they infest the northern sea like a plague – even the other raiders pay them tribute in fresh skins and sacrificial victims. In fact, legend has it their strength is so great and their sorcery so potent that they have claimed the most dangerous island in the region as their stronghold.'

'The Isle of Morhaut.'

'Now you begin to see the scope of the challenge set before me,' Malus answered grimly. 'Thus: a fleet, soldiers and a sorcerer. And soon. Damnably soon. The spring thaws begin in little more than a week and the corsairs at Clar Karond will be putting to sea as soon as they are able.'

'Ah, yes. The sands are trickling from the hourglass. You must find another way, Malus. There is no time for such elaborate schemes.'

Remembering where he was, Malus glanced at the nearest window and saw that the sky had nearly paled to the grey gloom of morning. The slaves were doubtless already stirring in the lower levels of the tower, preparing for the day. 'I have little choice, daemon,' Malus growled, dashing back to the divan and returning the tome to its place on the floor. 'If I can't raise such a force on my own I'll have to convince someone else to give me one.'

'The revels have left you unhinged, little druchii. Who would give you such power? The Drachau? The Witch King himself?' Tz'arkan laughed mockingly.

'I'd have better luck with my own father,' Malus said bitterly. Suddenly he straightened, his dark brows furrowing. 'On the other hand…'

The daemon squirmed beneath his ribs. 'Yes?'

Malus grinned like a wolf. 'I'm a fool. All the pieces are right in front of me. I just need to begin pulling some strings. It's *perfect*.'

The highborn could feel the weight of the daemon's attention settle on him like a mantle of ice. 'What lunacy are you contemplating now? Tell me!'

Malus raced for the door, his mind hard at work as the pieces of his plan came together. Tired as he was, there would be no sleep for him today. 'First things first,' he said, as much to the daemon as to himself. 'If I don't get back to my bed before the tower slaves awaken things could become awkward indeed.'

DOWN ON THE arena floor a slave screamed in terror, kicking up a spray of red-stained sand as he threw himself to one side before the cold one's charge. The young human almost made it, but he timed his leap a fraction of a second too late and the nauglir's jaws closed on the man's scabby legs. Razor-sharp fangs as long as knives snipped off both limbs just below the knee, sending the human tumbling in a bright fountain of blood. The cold one's black-armoured rider hauled at the reins, trying to check his mount's headlong rush and circle back to the slave while the highborn in the stands hissed in derision or shouted words of support.

The small arena shook beneath the combined weight of a dozen cold ones as the swirling game of shakhtila neared its end. Of the three score slaves who began the game less than a third still survived and they were scattered all over the playing field. Most of the survivors still clutched their flimsy spears or hefted short blades, their faces pale and heads turning wildly as they tried to keep all of the cold ones in sight. As Malus watched, the legless slave tried to drag himself by his hands across the arena floor, but two red-armoured riders from the opposing team caught sight of the man and spurred their mounts towards him. The druchii in the lead brandished a bloody sabre, while his team-mate hefted a long, slim spear. The riders expertly controlled the speed of their beasts, racing in a line as straight as an arrow right at the hapless man. Before the slave could register his peril the sabre flashed down, severing the man's head and the spearman following close behind caught it on the sleek steel point while the grisly trophy was still spinning in the air. The black rider howled in impotent fury as the red spearman raised his trophy to the small audience watching from above.

The arena was one of the most luxurious in the city, catering solely to the wealthiest households in Hag Graef. The lavishly-appointed viewing boxes surrounding the arena could normally hold little more than two hundred druchii and their retinues, but today the riders performed for fewer than two dozen nobles, all dressed in gleaming armour and chains of silver and gold. Many of them raised jewelled goblets in salute to the red team's point, while others picked at delicacies proffered on silver trays or argued with one another over the merits of the different riders. They were all young, rich men who wore their two swords with ostentatious pride and carried themselves with the reckless assurance of the all-powerful. Yet the highborn could not help but notice that each and every man, regardless of what they were doing, had positioned themselves so that they could watch every move by the statuesque woman who reclined in their midst.

Malus stood at the top of a marble stairway leading down to the viewing boxes from the lesser galleries above. With a start of surprise he caught himself checking the state of his own attire, adjusting the position of the enamelled plate armour and the arrangement of the paired swords given to him by his sister. With the octagon in his possession it had been a relatively simple matter to bypass Nagaira's wards and escape without raising an alarm. Silar and his men had been surprised at his sudden arrival in his refurbished tower, but a few sharp commands had set them scurrying to enquire about the location of the person he wished to meet.

Silar and Arleth Vann had tried to insist on sending him with a proper retinue, but once again, Malus was forced to order them to remain behind. His instincts told him that their presence would have only complicated things further; the last thing he needed was for an overheated noble to misconstrue a word or gesture that would lead to bloodshed. He had enough feuds to contend with as it was.

Malus took a deep breath, collecting his wits and started down the stairs. No less than three of the nobles leapt to bar his entrance to the viewing box, their hands straying to the hilts of their swords. So many young fools with so much to prove, he thought, careful to keep his disdain from showing on his face.

For a fleeting instant Malus wasn't sure how to address the men. It was a complicated tangle of etiquette: on the one hand each one of them clearly outranked him in terms of personal wealth and prestige, on the other hand they were also retainers and he had a blood-tie to the woman they served. There was also the fact that he'd likely killed more men in battle than all of the retainers combined and he wasn't in a mood to kowtow to anyone. 'Stand aside, hounds,' he said with an easy smile and a glitter of menace in his eyes. 'I'm here to speak to my sister.'

The leader of the trio, a sharp-featured man with finely-pointed teeth and a row of gold rings glinting in each ear, leaned forward and made to draw one of his elaborately ornamented swords. 'This is a private party, Darkblade. If you want the pleasure of my lady's company go make an appointment with her chamberlain, otherwise we'll chuck you into the arena for the nauglir to chew on.'

Malus met the highborn's stare. 'You're too close,' he said calmly.

'Am I?' The noble leaned in slightly closer, almost nose-to-nose with Malus. 'Do I make you uncomfortable?'

Malus grabbed the elbow of the noble's sword arm with his left hand and punched the druchii in the throat with his right. The retainer's eyes bulged and he doubled over, gagging and gasping for breath. With a shove Malus sent the man crashing into one of his fellows, sending both sprawling in a heap.

The third retainer's eyes went wide. Before he could more than half-draw his own blade Malus darted in until they stood almost nose-to-nose. The noble back-pedalled, trying to get enough room to finish drawing his sword and Malus helped him along with a hard shove in the middle of his chest. The retainer let out a yelp and tumbled backwards, falling over a pair of seated retainers and losing his grip on his blade.

Angry shouts filled the spectators' box and a dozen blades rasped from their scabbards, but over the din of the rising scuffle and the thunder of the combat below a woman's smooth voice cut through the tumult and stopped every man in his tracks.

'Enough. *Enough!* If my brother wishes to speak to me so badly he'd risk his own precious skin then I'll hear what he has to say.'

The retainers stopped cold. Even the man Malus had struck in the throat somehow stifled his hacking gasps for air. Her presence filled the spectators' box like a burst of cold winter sunlight and the nobles instantly subsided. They returned to what they'd been doing before the sudden interruption, making a path for Malus to approach the reclining form of his sister Yasmir.

She was watching him with an expression of mild curiosity and in spite of himself Malus felt as though he were being drawn into her large, violet eyes. He realised at that moment that the magical allure Nagaira used on him at the revel had been nothing more than a feeble imitation of Yasmir's personal glamour. She was every inch the ideal of druchii beauty: lithe and sensual, with perfect alabaster skin and a fine-boned face that seemed to glow against a backdrop of lustrous black hair. Not even Eldire's fearsome presence could compare; she had built a persona based on magic, vast influence and guile. With Yasmir, her glamour was effortless, like sunlight gleaming on the surface of a glacier. There was great danger there, of that he was certain, but he was nevertheless blind to it.

'Well met, sister,' he managed, struggling to regain his poise. It occurred to him that this was the first time in his life he had actually spoken to Yasmir; as the third oldest of Lurhan's six children, she had been nearing adulthood by the time Malus was born. Aside from mandatory observances like the annual Hanil Khar, they never saw one another. 'I... I had no idea you had an interest in sports.'

Yasmir smiled, the expression disturbingly unaffected and genuine. 'I would say it depends on the nature of the game,' she replied. Her voice was melodious and soft as sable fur. There was not a single rough edge to it and it made Malus wonder if she had ever had to raise her voice for anything in her entire life. 'Vaklyr and Lord Kurgal seek to prove whose fighting skills are superior, so they and their retainers are vying for heads in the arena. Lord Kurgal's red team appears to have the lead and Vaklyr's men are losing more than just the game.' There was an eerie gleam of mirth in her eyes. 'What do you think of their riding ability, Malus? Rumour has it you're quite the expert on cold ones.'

Malus shrugged. 'Lord Kurgal has served our father for many years as Master of Cavalry. He and his men are the true experts. I merely dabble in breeding nauglir when it amuses me.' He attempted to cover his unease by studying the movements of the riders in the arena. 'Vaklyr is too eager. Too aggressive. He's clearly trying to win more here than just a game.'

It was obvious that he'd walked in on the latest spat between Yasmir's ardent rivals. They were constantly vying with one another for her attentions and his sister always managed to give them just enough reason to hope to keep them coming back again and again. It was said that Yasmir had slain more of Hag Graef's knights than any enemy army. He had never really stopped to think how much craft such manipulations required, but now he was being shown a taste of it. *Lurhan should order you to choose a husband,* Malus thought, *or pack you off to the temple where you can do no more harm.*

Yasmir laughed, a clear, pure sound that sent shivers along Malus's skin. 'Vaklyr is an ardent one,' she agreed. 'So passionate and unbridled. I fear he won't ever amount to much, despite his family's connections, but right now his artless desire is entertaining.' She regarded Malus almost languidly. 'What is it that you desire, brother? I must say, this visit comes as a great surprise.'

Again, Malus was taken aback by the sheer frankness of her question. *Does she know nothing of guile,* the highborn thought? And then it struck him: of course she did. She simply didn't feel the need for it. Yasmir was relaxed, open and genuine as a show of *strength*. Adored as she was by many of the most powerful nobles in Hag Graef, she had little reason to fear anyone, save perhaps the Drachau himself.

'I have come to enlist your aid, sister,' Malus said, summoning up a smile of his own. 'There is a matter I wish to propose to our elder brother once he returns to Clar Karond with his ships.'

To his surprise – and annoyance – Yasmir laughed again. 'Seeking another backer for a slave raid, Malus? I don't think you could win the support of a tavern full of drunken sailors, much less a corsair lord like my beloved brother.' At the mention of Bruglir, Lurhan's eldest son, a real look of hunger came over Yasmir's features. They saw one another for only a month or two at a time, just long enough to refit the raiding ships in Bruglir's fleet before he set out to hunt the seas once more. When he was at Hag Graef the two were inseparable. It was the one deterrent that had served to keep the nobles at the Hag from pressing a case for Yasmir's marriage. No one wished to cross the man who would be the next Vaulkhar – a man who was also reputed to be one of the finest swordsmen in Naggaroth and one of the most powerful corsairs in memory.

Malus felt his smile falter a bit and felt a flash of annoyance. Once again, he fought to regain his balance. 'Were I acting by myself, you would undoubtedly be correct, sister,' he said. 'But that's why I wish to enlist your help. Everyone knows that you alone have Bruglir's utter confidence. If you were to speak on my behalf, even the great corsair lord would have to listen.'

'Perhaps,' Yasmir said languidly. 'You're a bit better at flattery than I imagined, Malus. Have you been practising with Nagaira? You're quite the couple these days.'

'I… no,' he caught himself stammering. Once again, the irritation flared. He could hear the retainers chuckling quietly to themselves. 'I didn't think to win you over with mere flattery,' the highborn said. 'I plan to pay well for your aid, dear sister.'

For a moment, Yasmir was silent. Malus sensed a wave of tension ripple through the nobles. 'And what, pray tell, can you offer me that these worthies cannot?'

Malus turned back to Yasmir with a wolfish smile. 'Our brother Urial's head, of course.'

Yasmir sat bolt upright, her careless demeanour wiped away. Now her eyes were brilliant and intense. 'That's a fearful offer to make, brother.'

'I can think of no finer gift for you, dear sister,' Malus answered. He knew that was the one thing that she wanted nearly as much as Bruglir himself. Urial had made no secret of his infatuation for Yasmir, even though his twisted body and mind repulsed her. Yet he continued to pursue her affections and such were his ties to the temple and to the Drachau himself that no man dared raise a hand against him. 'As well-informed as you are, you are clearly aware of the… difficulties between Urial and myself. We are already at swords' points over other matters – I can either negotiate with him or end his threat to me in a more permanent fashion.'

'If you kill Urial, it will cost you. The temple will neither forgive nor forget.'

Malus shrugged. 'I am already at war with them, sister. So far I find it most agreeable. Regardless, that would not be your concern, would it? Urial would haunt you no more and I would face the consequences in your stead.'

Yasmir regarded him at length, her expression intent. 'Before you left for the north I would have thought you incapable of such daring,' she said. 'But now? I confess, it is a very tempting offer.' She leaned back against the divan and stretched out her hand. Instantly a young lord leapt to her side with a goblet of wine. Yasmir gave the man a brief, luminous smile and then turned her attention back to Malus. 'What do you wish of me?'

'Merely your support. I intend to speak to Bruglir in Clar Karond as soon as his fleet puts in. If you lend your aid and persuade him to join the expedition, then I will take care of Urial in turn.'

Yasmir smiled enticingly. 'Suppose I ask for payment in advance? A show of good faith?'

Now it was Malus's turn to laugh. 'You are wondrously beguiling sister, but please.'

'I was merely thinking of you, dear brother. Why, you could likely see to the problem right now. If you hurry, I expect you could catch him before he reaches the stables. I don't expect he can walk very fast with that twisted leg of his.'

Malus's smile faltered and no amount of willpower could bring it back. 'I beg your pardon, sister?'

Yasmir regarded him with a look of innocent surprise, though the look in her eyes belied the gesture. 'Why, he was just here, brother, pressing his nauseating case for my affections. When one of my men reported that you'd entered the arena he became very agitated and took his leave.'

'Did he? How interesting,' Malus replied. 'Perhaps he and I will have a conversation about you after all. Something to encourage him to seek his entertainment elsewhere.' The highborn's mind raced. How many retainers had Urial brought with him? How many more could he call on at short notice? *I have to get out of here.*

'Would you? That would please me very much,' Yasmir said.

Malus bowed deeply. 'Then may I count on your support with Bruglir?'

'For your efforts with Urial? Of course.'

'Excellent,' Malus answered. 'Then I will take my leave. I expect Urial and I will have much to discuss in the near future.' *Just not right here and now,* Malus hoped. He cursed himself for leaving his men at the tower.

He gave no time to Yasmir to respond. The nobles glared hatefully at him as he passed, but he gave the hounds little heed.

A roar went up from the arena floor as another man bled for Yasmir's pleasure. Malus had the feeling that he wouldn't be the last.

Chapter Eight
THE BLESSING OF STEEL

MALUS TOOK THE steps to the upper gallery two at a time, fighting the urge to draw his sword as he approached the dark portal leading to the spectator ramps beyond. Bad enough for Yasmir and her aides to see him run – he wasn't about to start jabbing his blades into every deep shadow he passed.

All was not entirely lost. He had no mount in the arena stables, having walked the short distance from the fortress. That worked to his advantage somewhat, it was likely that Urial would set up his ambush there. If he moved swiftly he could take a somewhat circuitous route down to the ground level, out through one of the arena's many open gates and onto the crowded city streets. It was late in the afternoon, when much of the city's business was conducted, so one more highborn walking the streets wouldn't attract too much attention.

His skin felt cold beneath the weight of his armour, black ice moved sluggishly through his veins. Malus thought about turning to Tz'arkan for aid. The daemon was strangely quiet, like a cat studying an unsuspecting mouse and the silence made the highborn uneasy. How deeply had Tz'arkan sunk his roots while Malus hung in the Vaulkhar's tower? How close was he to surrendering himself entirely to the daemon? Malus could no longer say for certain. And death brought no salvation either; if he died Tz'arkan would claim his soul 'til the end of time.

So I'd best survive then, Malus thought grimly, with nothing but my swords and my blessed hate. Just like old times.

The highborn plunged through the dark archway, his eyes momentarily blinded as he adjusted to the lack of light and that was the moment Urial's men made their move.

A sword struck his left pauldron, glancing off the curved metal and cutting a small notch in the highborn's ear. Another blade whispered through the air from his right, but Malus ducked instinctively and the keen edge missed his skull by less than a finger length. The highborn hurled himself forward with a shouted oath, crashing into yet another swordsman, whose blade clanged ineffectually from Malus's breastplate. The retainer, caught by surprise, tried to back-pedal out of the way, but Malus continued his rush, pushing the warrior off his feet.

Malus's sword flashed from its oiled scabbard as he fetched up against the far wall. His eyes were adjusting, the pain in his cut ear making his blood sing and lending a cold, clear focus to his surroundings. There were five men on the shadowy spectators' ramp, all of them in black robes and kheitans. They wore close-fitting hoods and silver caedlin, even in the light of day; the delicate masks were worked in the shape of skulls, their dark oculars devoid of interest or pity. They all held large, curved swords, wielding the great blades two-handed and moved with the speed and grace of skilled swordsmen. Fortunately for Malus, none of the retainers wore heavy armour – only hauberks of black mail that covered their torso and part of their upper arms. It lent him a distinct advantage, Malus thought, but how much? Urial, the highborn noted, was nowhere to be seen and he wasn't sure if that was a good sign or a bad one.

The man Malus had knocked down was already back on his feet and the five men rushed silently at him, instinctively forming a semicircle that sought to pin his back to the arena's outside wall. But Malus wasn't about to give them the advantage; with a snarl he rushed at the nearest man, swinging viciously. The retainer's blade was a blur of motion, flashing in the half-light. He blocked Malus's stroke easily and turned the move into a cut aimed for the highborn's skull, only realising too late that Malus's stroke was only a well-timed feint that reversed itself and swept low, slicing through the retainer's right leg. The sword had been forged by a master and its fearsome edge parted robes, skin and muscle with equal ease. Blood flowed in a torrent, splashing on the stone floor and the retainer collapsed with the faintest of groans. Malus had already leapt past the grievously wounded man and charged down the spectators' ramp, heading for the street.

Footsteps whispered along the stone in Malus's wake. Something hard rapped against his back, but the strong steel turned aside the hurled dagger and sent it ringing along the floor. The ramp curved and Malus raced around the corner, momentarily out of the line of fire.

The ramp switched back upon itself and now he was just one level above the street. Here the outer wall of the arena was pierced by tall windows that let in shafts of pale daylight to relieve the gloom. On impulse Malus leapt for the nearest window, turning as he jumped and tried to force his way through the tight space. He crashed through the thin glass, cold air rushing against his face as he plummeted to the street below.

Malus rolled slightly in mid air, taking the fall on his armoured back. The impact jarred him to the core and knocked the wind from his lungs, but the instant his vision cleared he was rolling on the paving stones, trying to regain his feet. There were shouts of surprise and muffled curses from passing druchii nearby, but Malus paid no heed, gasping for breath and groping about for his sword. Even now he could imagine Urial's retainers racing down the ramp to ground level, swords ready at their sides.

When the highborn staggered to his feet, however, it wasn't a skull-faced retainer standing in the arena's open gate, but Urial the Forsaken himself, his eyes burning like molten brass.

Like Malus, Urial wore full armour for his visit to Yasmir. Two short, slender swords were buckled to his waist, looking more like an adolescent's practice blades than true weapons of war. Sheathed in steel, his deformities were almost invisible unless one knew where to look. There was no one in between them; for a fleeting instant Malus was tempted to rush at his malformed half-brother and fulfil Yasmir's wish then and there. But then Urial raised his good arm and pointed at Malus and his thin lips moved in silent incantation.

The highborn turned, his mind driving him to panicked flight even though Malus knew that it was too little, too late. Pain flared along his body in a wave. Malus staggered, his mouth opening in a silent scream. Every nerve, every fibre hissed like red-hot iron.

Dimly he sensed a presence rushing at him. Finding his voice, he uttered a bestial snarl and lashed out with his blade. The retainer was caught by surprise, hurled backward with his throat gaping wide. The highborn turned and forced his limbs to work, stumbling, then lurching, then shambling down the paved street as fast as he could.

The streets of the Highborn Quarter teemed with groups of servants going about the business of their masters, their arms laden with parcels bought from the craftsmen's shops that filled the area. There were few highborn about; this late in the day many of the city's nobles had already retired to their towers, preparing themselves for whatever diversions the night promised. Small groups of druchii retainers and lesser nobles strolled along the narrow streets, busy on errands or scheming quietly to themselves.

The searing pain was fading. Malus gasped for air with lungs that seemed full of jagged glass. Druchii stepped from his path, many placing hands to sword hilts or spitting curses as he passed. Keep going, he thought. Keep going. Find a large retinue and mingle with them, turn a corner, find an alley. *Keep moving.*

Malus looked about wildly, trying to find his bearings. By sheer good fortune he'd gone the right way outside the arena; the Hag's towers loomed above him less than a quarter-mile distant. He continued to run, shoving through huddled clusters of slaves, weaving around groups of low-born druchii and looking for another group of highborn he could lose himself amongst. Just ahead was a corner and a large number of armoured druchii. He was almost upon them when they stepped left and right, clearing a path before him – and the knot of armed temple acolytes running towards him from farther up the street.

'Mother of Night,' Malus gasped, his eyes widening. He fumbled his second sword from its scabbard as well. It looked like close to a dozen holy warriors, wearing dark red robes and silver breastplates. Each one held a gleaming draich in their hands – the two-handed executioner's sword favoured by the warriors of Khaine and wielded with terrible skill. Their expressions were fierce in the fading light and Malus knew that his running was at an end.

'Damn you all!' Malus roared back, raising his blades defiantly. 'Come ahead then and pour out your blood upon my steel!'

The highborn readied his weapons as the acolytes came on and the highborn saw death glinting in their brass-coloured eyes. Then a sharp blow struck him at the base of his skull and the world dissolved in a flare of white light.

THE AIR SHOOK with the howls of the damned.

Once more he ran across a heaving plain of blood-red earth, while the sky churned and vomited ash and bone dust from its depths. Multitudes of ghosts surrounded him, reaching for him with gnarled hands and clashing jaws. Already his fine armour was rent and pierced in dozens of places, though no blood flowed from the cold wounds beneath.

His sword passed effortlessly through them. Gelid, pulpy bodies and misshapen skulls all turned to sickly vapour as his blade bisected them, only to coalesce once more in the wake of the blade's passing. At best, he could only clear a path before him with each stroke as he ran, pushing ahead towards a goal he only dimly understood.

The horizon before him was a flat, featureless line as dark as old brick, standing out sharply against the swirling grey sky. A single tower stood there, square and black, silhouetted against both earth and sky alike. It seemed impossibly far away and yet it radiated a solidity that the rest of the alien landscape did not. It was a source of sanity in a vast plain of madness and he fought his way toward it with the manic intensity of a drowning man. Yet no matter how hard he struggled or how many steps he took, the tower grew no closer.

'Awaken, Darkblade! The sons of murder approach and the time of your death is at hand!'

Malus opened his eyes, yet for long moments he could not tell if he was indeed awake. There was a red haze to the air, a kind of indistinct shimmer that blurred the geometry of walls, doorways and ceilings. Even the solidity of objects seemed inconstant; one moment the dark stone surrounding him was dense and oppressive, then it became pale and translucent, lit from behind by an angry red light. There was a buzzing in the air, harsh and somehow metallic. If he focused on it he could make out the sound of voices: bloodthirsty, exultant, agonised.

There was pain. It came and went with the shifting solidity of his surroundings. Strangely, the less distinct things were, the sharper his pain became. He lay against a rack of brass needles of varying lengths, holding him nearly upright in the centre of a small, octagonal room. Each beat of his heart trembled through the scores of thin needles and reverberated back along his bones. When the walls faded to smoke, the agony was indescribable, leaving him gasping for breath when tangible reality wavered back into place. He could not move an inch; the needles were artfully placed to paralyse his muscles, pinning him like a living specimen in a display of grotesqueries.

He faced a set of double doors with iron hinges and brass facings. At the archway above the door were set a pair of faces worked in gleaming silver. The faces were exultant and bestial, their eyeholes were black voids; empty and yet somehow aware. He looked into those depthless pits and knew at once where he was.

'May the Outer Darkness take you, daemon!' Malus said, his words coming out in a hoarse whisper. 'You sat silent while Urial's men surrounded me!'

'This half-brother of yours is not like your zealous but self-absorbed sister,' Tz'arkan replied acidly. 'His sight is sharper than most. Had he sensed my presence he would have spared nothing to destroy you then and there and no aid I could have given you would have made any difference.'

'So you deliver me into his hands instead? You allow him and his damned temple lackeys to drag me to his tower? We stand at the gateway to the realm of murder! What would you have me do now?'

'I would have you save yourself, fool!' The daemon's voice was more agitated than Malus had ever heard it. Was there fear in the daemon's voice? 'Urial and his priests draw near, Malus. If they take you through the doorway standing before you, that will be the end. You will not emerge from the red place they will take you.'

Malus gritted his teeth and forced himself to move, pouring every ounce of his black will into drawing his right arm free from its bed of needles. Veins bulged from his temples and neck and his entire frame quivered with the strain, but his limbs would not budge. When the next wave of torment washed over him the sensation was so intense Malus was certain his heart would burst. The fact that it didn't was likely another testament to Urial's infernal skills.

'Spare me your insults and help me, cursed spirit! Lend me the strength to overcome these blasted needles, if nothing else! I can't get away if I can't move!'

'I cannot, Darkblade. Not here. It is too dangerous.'

Malus managed a bitter laugh. 'Too dangerous? For whom?'

But Tz'arkan did not reply. The doors swung open, the iron hinges groaning in torment. A group of blood-soaked druchii waited at the threshold, their hands bearing bowls and brass knives. Slowly and silently they filed into the room, half turning left, half turning right. As they surrounded him the room grew less and less distinct and a tide of irresistible pain swelled where each brass needle pierced his skin.

Urial was the last to enter the crowded room. Like the priests, he wore thin robes of white, soaked with blotches of fresh blood that somehow steamed in the thick air. Without the concealment of armour or heavy clothes there was no disguising Urial's gaunt physique. Muscles like thin steel cords stood out sharply across his narrow, bony chest and angular shoulders, lending his face an even more cadaverous cast than normal. His ruined sword arm was clutched tightly to his side. Even more shrunken than the rest of his body, Urial's right hand was twisted into a gnarled, paralysed claw, the palm turned upwards and the fingers curled inward as though shrivelled by an open flame.

The former acolyte of Khaine walked with a pronounced limp, dragging a crippled left foot, but his eyes were bright and he held himself proudly, like a king rather than a cursed cripple. Strange runes had been incised into the skin of his chest and arms. His white hair had been bound in a thick braid that lay over his right shoulder, hanging down almost as far as his waist. A third of its length was red with blood. In his left hand Urial held a long, broad-bladed dagger, its blade worked with fearsome sigils. There was a red haze around the weapon, as though blood coalesced from the very air around its sanctified edge. Heavy crimson drops fell from the blade's wicked point, spattering heavily on the stone tile below.

The tide of pain rose with every step Urial took. Once more focusing every iota of his will, Malus made his head bow in greeting. 'Well met, brother,' he wheezed through clenched teeth. 'It's... an honour to be invited into your sanctum, but you needn't put on such... a show for my sake.'

No emotion showed on Urial's face. His eyes regarded Malus with the same kind of dispassion as a priest inspecting a sacrificial slave. When he spoke his voice was resonant and harsh, like the penetrating note of a cymbal or bell. 'The honour is mine,' Urial said, without the slightest trace of modesty or compassion. 'There is no greater offering to the Lord of the Blade than to sacrifice one's own kin. I have been patient and dutiful in your pursuit and now Khaine has provided by placing you in my hands.'

'Blessed be the Murderer,' the priests intoned.

'I... I have wronged you, brother,' Malus said, his mind working furiously for a way to distract Urial from his deadly purpose. 'And the blood of your possessions lies on my hands. I wish to make amends.'

Urial paused, his brow furrowing ever so slightly. 'You will,' he replied, sounding faintly bemused. 'Your severed head will rest on a great pyramid of skulls, where you will gaze adoringly upon the glory of Khaine. I will see to it.'

'Blessed is he who slays in Khaine's name,' the priests intoned.

'But... is it not said that all warriors look upon the face of Khaine in the fullness of time?' Again, Urial paused. 'Yes. That is so.'

'Then what need is there to hurry things along?'

'You broke into my tower. You stole my possessions, killed my slaves and defiled my sanctum with your unclean presence,' Urial answered harshly. 'And there is the matter of the blood debt to the temple. An oath sworn before the Lord of Murder cannot be denied.'

'The call of blood is answered in sundered flesh,' said the priests.

'But it was a debt that you invoked against me,' Malus countered. 'And thus you could absolve it if you desired. I was deceived... '

Now Urial's expression became one of complete puzzlement. 'I did not invoke the blood debt,' Urial said. 'Nagaira did.'

For a moment, Malus couldn't speak. He struggled to accept what Urial had said and realised the full scope of the deception that had been built around him. 'Blessed Mother,' he said to himself, 'she played me at every turn. Everything she said was a lie.'

Urial nodded gravely. 'Such is the way of all flesh – a path of weakness and deception redeemed in the blood of the slain.' He stepped forward, raising the dagger. 'Soon you will know the truth, brother. The blessing of steel wipes all deception away.'

But Malus was no longer listening, caught up in a wave of cold, clear fury that washed his pain and fear away. 'Take this blessing from me and save it for one more deserving. It was Nagaira who made me her cat's paw, who told me of the skull in your keeping and who provided the means to violate your sanctum. She is the one who deserves your attention. I was merely the sword in her hand.' As he spoke, a plan took shape in his mind. 'I wish to atone for my crimes, brother. I wish to cleanse my soul with the blood of the unbeliever. If you will stay your hand, I will reward you and the temple with a rich gift of slaughter that will grant you the favour of Khaine.'

A stir went through the assembled priests, but Urial's expression was stern. 'You beg for *mercy* from a servant of Khaine?'

'No! I ask for the chance to serve his cause and provide a greater sacrifice in his name.' He looked his brother in the eye. 'What if I were to tell you that the Cult of Slaanesh is thriving within the very walls of the Hag itself?'

Urial's eyes narrowed suspiciously. 'The temple has long suspected this. Our agents search for signs of the apostates in the Hag and elsewhere.'

'The stain runs deeper than you know, brother. It reaches into the most powerful houses in the city,' Malus replied. 'Stay your hand and I can deliver them to you – our sister Nagaira stands high in their esteem. Think on that. Imagine the sacrifice *she* would make.' After a moment, he added, 'and there is more.'

Whispers filled the air as the priests reacted to the news. Urial silenced them with a look. 'More? What more can you offer?'

'Yasmir.'

Urial stiffened. He rushed at Malus, surprisingly swift for the deformities that warped his body. 'Do not dare impugn her honour, Darkblade! She who is pure and beloved before the god!'

'No! I did not mean that, brother – stay your hand!' Malus lowered his voice so only Urial could hear. 'I mean to say that I can bring her to you.'

Urial stared at Malus, his eyes wide and uncomprehending. 'Her thoughts are for Bruglir alone,' he said woodenly. 'And she refuses to give him up.'

'Of course,' Malus agreed. 'Of course. You know that as well as I. But all warriors see the face of Khaine in time, do they not?'

Urial stared hard into Malus's eyes, his expression unreadable. 'They do. They do indeed,' he whispered.

'This can be arranged, brother. I can see to it. But I would need your help. My plan requires a sorcerer of great skill.' He attempted a shrug but forgot the paralysing effect of the needles. 'I confess that I had planned to use Nagaira in my schemes, but this is so much more fitting. One might even see the hand of Khaine at work in this.'

After a long moment, Urial lowered his blade. Something glittered in his eyes, but whether it was desire or madness, Malus couldn't say. Perhaps there was little difference between the two.

'Perhaps,' Urial said at last. 'I cannot deny that your offer would make a glorious gift to Khaine. I also cannot deny that you have more twists in you than a viper. This could all be a lie.'

Once again, Malus bowed his head respectfully. 'That is so and I cannot convince you otherwise. So you must ask yourself: what have you to lose if I'm lying and what do you stand to gain if I'm telling you the truth?'

Urial's expression changed. It was not a smile, but rather a slight softening of his severe features. 'Well said, brother,' he replied, gesturing to the priests. 'I have little to lose by sparing you a little while longer. But tell me, how will you deliver the apostates into our hands?'

The priests of Khaine surrounded Malus, gripping him with their bloodstained hands and lifting him from his bed of pain. His cry of pain transmuted itself into a harsh laugh of triumph.

'Did I not mention it before, brother? I am to be initiated into their cult tomorrow.'

Chapter Nine
THE WITCH'S GIFT

MALUS WAITED IN shadow, preparing for the battle to come. Nagaira had been furious upon learning of his escape. It was well past nightfall by the time he had completed his plans with Urial and left his half-brother's tower. After that there had been nothing for it but to cross the grounds of the fortress and enter his own tower to inform his men of the part they would play in his upcoming initiation. The Octagon of Praan was left behind, locked in an ironwood chest within his own quarters, leaving the highborn to cross the narrow, windy bridge connecting his spire with his sister's. The guards were not surprised to hear his knock. They had been given orders to keep a watch for him the moment Nagaira realised he had gone.

Malus leaned back in his chair, his face twisting in a smile at the thought of his sister's wrath. He had never seen her so angry before – she hurled questions at him like thunderbolts, demanding he account for every step he'd taken upon leaving her tower. He'd mollified her somewhat when he told her that he was ready to undertake the initiation. For a moment she'd been pleased – and then her interest had become sharper than a razor as the witch demanded to know how he'd made his way from her demesne without her being any wiser. That had led to a string of threats and curses, both real and implied, that had lasted much of the night, until finally she summoned her retainers and banished him to his chambers, there to await his time before the anointed of Slaanesh.

The following evening a procession of servants swept through the room, bearing clothes, food and libations to prepare him for the ceremony. The slaves stripped away his armour, kheitan and robes, clothing him in a robe of expensive white Tilean linen and a belt of pebbled hide unlike anything he'd seen before. A circlet set with six precious stones was placed on his brow and braziers were lit in his room to fill the air with pungent incense. Then he was left to wait in silence, breathing the spiced air and feeling his skin tingle as the herbs did their work on body and mind.

Hours passed while Malus listened to the steady commotion of servants and guards outside as Nagaira made her preparations for the ritual. Then, as the hour drew close to midnight and the coals in the braziers had burned low, the door to the chamber swung wide and Nagaira swept in like a cold wind. Unlike the seductress of the previous revel she now carried herself as a priestess, clad in white robes and a breastplate of hammered gold worked with sorcerous runes. She wore another mask this time, a horned skull smaller but no less fearsome than the Hierophant's and like him she bore a brimming goblet in her hands.

'The hour is nigh, supplicant,' Nagaira said gravely. 'Drink with me as we await the Prince's pleasure.'

Malus considered his options carefully. The wine was likely drugged, but he could think of no plausible way to refuse. He took the goblet from her carefully and drank without a word. The wine was thick and sweet, with a resinous aftertaste. More traders' wine, he thought, suppressing a grimace. The highborn passed the wine back to the witch and was surprised to see her drink as well.

'We are all one in the crucible of desire,' she said, reading the expression on his face. 'After tonight we will be bound together more tightly than family, more intimate than lovers. As you dedicate yourself to the Prince, he shall dedicate himself to you and your devotion will be rewarded six-fold. Glory awaits, brother. Your every desire will be fulfilled.'

'I pray so, sister,' he said with a wolfish smile. 'With all my heart.'

A robed supplicant entered amongst whispers and bowed to Nagaira. Malus was startled to see that the druchii wore no mask and recognised the man as one of the Drachau's personal retainers. 'The Prince awaits,' he said, favouring Malus with a conspiratorial smile.

Nagaira stretched forth her hand. 'Come, brother. It is time to join the revel.'

Malus took her hand. As she turned to lead him from the room a quick pass of his free hand reassured him that the dagger within his robes was still securely in place.

They descended once more to the base of the tower, walking in silence and passing through shadow. The witchlights had all been dimmed and after a time Malus felt as though he were being drawn along through a sea of darkness, pulled by a hand of gleaming alabaster. The wine, he thought, trying to focus. The more he concentrated the more his focus broke into fragments, as though he were grasping at quicksilver. Not even his anger could avail him, it glowed like a dead coal, sullen and without heat.

Before he knew it they had reached the bottom of the long, curving stairs. The tall statue shed its own cold light in the darkened room, lit from within by its own sorcery. Its light shone dimly on helmets and breastplates, spear points and pauldrons. Rank after rank of Nagaira's warriors bore witness to their descent, their pale faces limned with pellucid fire.

They stepped slowly down the narrow, hidden stair. They sank downwards into air that was humid and sweet with the taste of incense and oiled flesh. A strange, piping music rose from the darkness. It was eerie and discordant, a song wrought for inhuman ears that set his teeth on edge and yet filled his heart with a terrible longing that was as alien as it was irresistible.

As they turned the final corner it seemed as though they looked down on starlight. Hands held aloft tiny globes of witchlight, throwing strange shadows and shifting currents of light across the assembled supplicants. None wore masks save the terrible Hierophant, who stood at the far end of the chamber across a sea of slowly undulating bodies. Naked, writhing slaves covered the stone floor of the room, lulled by the incense and stoked by the strange refrain of the unearthly flutes.

The moment the supplicants saw him they began to chant, filling the air with a husky litany in maddening counterpoint to the pipes. Malus felt the hairs on the back of his neck stand straight as a strange kind of tension crackled through the air of the chamber. There was a kind of pressure he could feel on his neck and shoulders, as though the blasphemous song had summoned the attention of a being that moved in a realm beyond mortal comprehension. A feeling of dread began to steal into Malus's heart. It swept away the lingering effects of the drugged wine, but left in its place an atavistic fear that threatened to rob his limbs of their strength.

The supplicants parted to let him and Nagaira pass. She drew him onward, towards the waiting Hierophant, who stood in the company of two attendants. One attendant bore a scourge of leather whose tails were studded with silver barbs; the other held a golden basin and a curved dagger made of bone. The Hierophant stood with his hands clasped before him. His long pale fingers waved languidly, like the legs of a hunting spider. Malus felt a sudden shock of recognition. Could it be?

Nagaira bowed before the Hierophant. 'I come bearing gifts for the Prince Who Waits,' she intoned. 'Will he come forth?'

The chanting and the piping flute stopped. Silence descended, heavy and oppressive. Malus felt the awful presence in the chamber increase. His sight seemed to waver at the edges as *something* pressed against the fabric of reality and the highborn felt his heart grow cold.

'The Prince will come forth!' intoned the Hierophant, raising his hands to the ceiling. The supplicants cried out in joy and terror combined and an awful groaning filled the darkness of the chamber. Then there came a tremendous crash of mortar and stone and the air shivered with rapturous war cries.

'The call of blood is answered in sundered flesh!'

The draichnyr na Khaine took the chamber by storm, pouring from breaches in the chamber walls with their curved draichs held high. The warriors were clad in heavy coats of mail reinforced with brass pauldrons, breastplate and helm. Their great swords flickered like willow wands, harvesting a bloody path through the scores of panicked slaves around the perimeter of the room.

Malus snatched his hand from Nagaira's and swung his fist at the side of her skull mask. The movement felt leaden and clumsy and the blow only glanced the goat skull's bony snout, knocking it askew. Cursed drugs, Malus thought. Nagaira recoiled from the blow, cursing herself and temporarily blinded by the skewed mask. As her hands clawed at the goat skull Malus tore the dagger free from his robes.

There was a great shout that ripped through the pandemonium, searing the air with is power. Malus turned to see the Hierophant brandishing a bottle of heavy, dark glass above his head. The highborn could feel the hatred from the high priest like a red-hot spear point pressed against his flesh. 'Mother of Night, what's he doing?'

'Sating his lust for vengeance,' Tz'arkan replied coldly. 'Did you expect the anointed of Slaanesh to be helpless?'

Before Malus could answer the Hierophant shrieked an invocation that smote his ears like a thunderclap, then saw the high priest dash the bottle against the stone floor. A roiling, purplish fog boiled up from the broken glass, expanding and gathering strength as it grew.

There were faces in the smoke – leering, obscene faces that made mockery of mortal senses. Malus snarled a bitter curse. The bottle had been a magic vessel containing the bound spirits of a horde of fearsome daemons.

The cloud of chittering, shrieking spirits enveloped the room, howling through the air like a chorus of the damned. More arcane commands reverberated through the chamber and the daemons descended on the panicked slaves. Malus saw one nearby human fall to the ground, choking and writhing as one of the spirits forced its way into the slave's nostrils and mouth. In moments the human began to change colour, the skin stretching as the muscles beneath swelled. Grasping hands twisted and deformed, the flesh splitting and falling away to reveal blood-streaked pincers formed of melted bone. With a shout, Malus leapt upon the possessed slave, plunging his dagger again and again into the creature's eyes and throat. One huge pincer smashed at the side of his head, sending him sprawling.

Malus rolled onto his back, blinking stars from his eyes as the possessed slave reared to its feet. Purple ichor poured from its ruined eyes and a terrible wound in its neck, but the daemon guided the slave's body unerringly as it advanced on the fallen highborn. The creature loomed over him, pincers snapping, then Malus caught a flash of brass above his head as an executioner swept past, swinging his bloody draich. The great sword sheared through the slave's bulbous torso, snapping ribs like dry twigs and lodging deep in the creature's spine. The possessed slave toppled, lashing out as it fell and catching the executioner's helmeted head in one over-sized pincer. The creature's dying spasms ripped the executioner's head from his shoulders in a fountain of gore and both bodies fell onto the stunned highborn.

This is *not* going according to plan, Malus thought savagely, kicking himself free from the corpses. His robes were wet with gore and he'd lost track of his dagger. He kicked the body of the dead slave over onto its side and wrapped his hands around the hilt of the draich. With a curse and a heave the corpse's spine parted and the long blade pulled free.

The chamber echoed with the sounds of battle. Chaos reigned in the darkness as the executioners and possessed intermingled in a swirling, confused melee. Sorcerous bolts lashed at warriors and possessed slaves alike as the supplicants loosed their spells indiscriminately into the mass. There was no way to tell who had the upper hand, but Malus was certain that sheer numbers lay on the cultists' side.

A bolt of purple fire roared close by and in the flare of light Malus caught sight of the Hierophant, his hands working in a complicated series of gestures. The highborn couldn't guess at what the high priest was doing, but he knew that he didn't care to see its results.

Time to see who is really under that skull, Malus thought with a savage grin, and charged at the Hierophant over the heaped bodies of the dead.

The highborn stayed low, his great sword down and to one side to attract as little attention as possible. He expected one of the possessed slaves to leap upon his back at any moment, but their attention appeared entirely occupied by the remaining executioners. A fatal mistake, Malus thought, closing in for the kill.

He approached the Hierophant from his right side, his hands tensing on the hilt of the draich. Two steps short of striking range a blur of motion from Malus's left was all the warning he had as the Hierophant's dagger-wielding attendant leapt for his throat.

Instincts honed on a dozen battlefields caused Malus to plant his left foot and pivot, swinging his right leg around and reversing the stroke of his sword in a cut aimed for the attendant's midsection. The cultist's dagger flashed downwards, scoring a line across Malus's forehead as the draich opened the supplicant's belly. The attendant doubled up around the blade as he fell, nearly dragging Malus from his feet. The highborn planted a foot on the man's shoulder and hauled at the blade – and cords of raw fire raked across the side of his face as the second attendant lashed at him with his scourge.

Pain bloomed in Malus's right eye and he fell to his knees with a savage curse. The scourge fell again, the silver barbs shredding his right sleeve and biting deep into his shoulder. Another blow to the side of his head knocked the highborn to the ground, the hilt of the draich twisting from his grasp. Malus fell onto the disembowelled supplicant, smelling the stink of blood and spilt entrails as the man shuddered in the throes of death.

His left eye caught a gleam of metal on the floor and Malus threw himself upon it as the scourge clawed across his back. The highborn's hand closed on the hilt of the supplicant's sacrificial dagger and he rolled onto his back in time for the scourge-wielding cultist to aim another blow at his head.

Malus threw up his left hand and caught a handful of the scourge tails against his palm. Roaring with pain he grabbed hold of the leather thongs and pulled, dragging the supplicant off his feet and onto the highborn's up-thrust dagger. The curved blade punched through the man's breastbone and lodged against his spine, slicing his heart in two. Malus watched the hate fade from the druchii's dark eyes and threw the corpse to one side.

Not six feet away the Hierophant still performed his enigmatic ritual – too caught up in the intricacies of his spell to notice the life-and-death battle going on around him. Malus rubbed his right eye against the sleeve of his robe and was relieved to discover that he could still see through a thick film of blood. He grabbed the pommel of the draich and pulled the weapon free, then without a moment's hesitation he swung the gore-stained sword at the Hierophant's head.

At the last moment Malus realised his error. Without thinking he'd aimed the blow for the front of the Hierophant's neck instead of its unprotected rear. As it was, the blade bit into the ram's skull mask the high priest wore, shattering it and turning the blade slightly on impact. Rather than a decapitating blow, the sword tore a long, ragged gash across the Hierophant's throat and across his right shoulder, spinning him around in a spray of bright blood and fragments of yellowed bone.

The Hierophant fell to one knee, blood spilling from the shattered snout of his mask. Malus stepped in, bringing his sword back for a second stroke, when the high priest flung out a scarred hand and shrieked a bubbling curse. Heat and thunder enveloped Malus and he felt himself thrown through the air. The impact knocked him senseless, sending the draich spinning from his hands.

It felt like an eternity before Malus's vision cleared. Much of his ceremonial robe had been burned away and the skin of his chest, arms and face stung from minor burns. Either he'd been hit with only a glancing blow or the high priest had failed to cast the spell properly. Malus sat up with a groan and saw the Hierophant staggering into the small chamber that had housed his throne of flesh not two nights past. Malus reclaimed his sword and lurched after the high priest, determined to finish what he'd begun.

When the highborn reached the entrance of the room he was prepared for another sorcerous barrage, but instead he discovered the Hierophant stepping through a narrow archway on the opposite side of the room – an escape route formerly concealed by some kind of embedded spell. Runes glistened along the doorway as the high priest stepped through. At once, the runes flared painfully bright and Malus sensed the danger burning within. He turned and flung himself back into the main chamber as the doorway erupted in a flare of purple fire, collapsing the small room in a shower of rock and earth.

A pall of dust and a thunderous concussion swept through the chamber, staggering the survivors still fighting around the curving stair. Malus regained his feet and saw that the cavern was lit again by young temple initiates bearing witchlight globes on slender poles. The slaves were collapsing, caught by the blades of the executioners or literally falling apart as the daemons possessing them lost strength and returned to their own blasted domain.

The supplicants were dead or dying, their bodies steaming from acids that burned from the depths of their ghastly wounds. Pale, blood-spattered sylphs glided among the cultists, fresh gore steaming upon their envenomed blades. Their long hair was unbound and flowed around their naked bodies like a mane. Malus felt his breath catch in his throat at the sight of the beautiful, unearthly women stalking silently among the carrion. The anwyr na Khaine were a rare sight outside the temple, called forth only in times of war or great need. Their poisoned blades and savage skill had clearly turned the tide and now they searched among the dead for more blood to shed in the name of the Lord of Murder.

Malus caught sight of Urial, attended by a bodyguard of executioners as he surveyed the bodies of the supplicants from a respectful distance. When the witch elves walked among the slain it was never wise to come between them and their prey. The highborn hastened to his side, slipping and sliding among the ruin of hacked and torn flesh littering the chamber floor.

'Where is Nagaira?' Malus called to him.

Urial shook his head, hefting a bloody axe with his one good hand. 'Our sister is not among the slain.'

Malus spat a savage curse. 'She must have slipped up the stairs during the battle! Hurry!'

The highborn raced for the stairs, darting among the witch elves and feeling the hairs on the back of his neck prickle as their attention turned his way. Carefully averting his eyes he leapt up the steps two and three at a time, wondering how much of a lead Nagaira had on him and whether her guards were still waiting on the floor above.

It was bad enough that the Hierophant had escaped, he thought. Now that she'd seen the depth of his treachery he didn't dare let Nagaira slip through his clutches as well.

He emerged from the illusory statue into the midst of a raging battle. Urial's plan of attack had been savage and thorough: even as he and the executioners struck the initiation chamber via the twisting passageways of the Burrows, his own personal retainers had hacked their way through the ground floor entrance and attacked the guards stationed there. As close as the battle had been down below, the fight at the base of the tower still hung in the balance, with Nagaira's rogues on their home ground and enjoying greater numbers than the invading druchii. The witch's retainers had rallied and had pushed Urial's men back towards the broken doorway, leaving a narrow path behind the defender's ranks that led to the main staircase. Without hesitation Malus ran for the stairs. The climb seemed to last forever. Distantly he thought he heard the rumble of thunder, but he knew that a storm this time of year was impossible. A few moments later he passed a burning slave running the opposite way, his agonised screams echoing up and down the stairway long after he'd disappeared from sight.

He reached the guardroom just below the sanctum without realising it at first, stumbling into a smoky chamber that reeked with the smell of burnt hair and charred flesh. Half a dozen bodies lay on the stone floor, tossed about like straw dolls by a sudden, violent explosion.

Armoured figures suddenly rushed at him through the smoke, bloodstained swords held ready. At the last moment the lead warrior checked his rush and raised his hand to the rest. 'Stop!' Arleth Vann ordered to his men. 'My lord! We nearly took you for one of the cultists.'

Malus paused, gasping for breath in the foetid air. 'Nagaira? Where is she?'

Arleth Vann nodded towards the ceiling. 'She tore through here like a storm, just as we were finishing off the last of the bridge guards,' he said. 'Killed two of ours and four of hers with some kind of thunderbolt and kept on going.'

'How long ago?'

The retainer shrugged. 'A few minutes, no more. Silar took the rest of the men after her.'

Malus nodded. He'd hoped his men would have been able to storm across the bridge and seize the sanctum during the chaos of the attack, but battle had a way of unravelling even the simplest of plans. 'Well done. Now take your men back across the bridge. Urial and his acolytes will be here any moment.'

Another thunderclap shook the air above the tower, this time sending drifts of dust raining from the ceiling. Fighting a strong sense of foreboding, Malus charged up the stairs.

The antechamber to the sanctum was full of smoke and swirling lights. The double doors leading to Nagaira's study were gone, leaving nothing but a jagged hole in the crumbling wall. Silar and his men lay on the floor, their armour smoking. Several were contorted in agony or lying motionless amid piles of jagged rubble.

A howling wind roared through the room, whistling through the ragged hole leading from the sanctum itself. A raging storm of multicoloured light blazed within.

'You are too late!' Tz'arkan cried. 'Leave this place before the spell she's cast consumes you!'

Yet Malus couldn't bring himself to give up, not within sight of his quarry. Seeing the power at work in the room beyond, he was certain that he didn't dare let his sister get away.

The highborn paused long enough to pull Silar upright and order the men out of the room, then he hurled himself through the jagged opening.

Within the confines of the sanctum the storm threatened to take his breath away. The light was blinding, a shifting pattern of sights and strange sounds that grew in strength with each passing moment.

The ceiling of the room was already gone, consumed by the ravening energies unleashed by the witch's spell. Her robed form hung in midair, surrounded by the vortex, her skin glowing with unearthly patterns of light. Nagaira saw Malus and her face lit with a triumphant smile. At that moment he knew that for once the daemon had spoken wisely. He'd made a terrible mistake.

'There you are, little brother,' Nagaira said, her voice one with the howling storm. 'I've been waiting for you. I have a gift to repay you for your treachery.'

The air curdled around the witch – and began to bleed. A nimbus of Chaotic energy took shape around her, split with jagged arcs of purple lightning.

Tz'arkan writhed inside Malus. 'Get out of here, you fool! She's calling down the storm of Chaos itself!'

Malus snarled, furious at the thought of retreat. As he turned to go, he caught sight of a leather-bound tome at the foot of a shattered divan. On impulse he leapt for it, just as a bolt of purple energy tore through the space where he'd stood. The arc of power played along the far wall, carving a path through the stone and leaving a wild pattern of flesh, scales and viscera etched in its wake.

The highborn's hands closed around the Tome of Ak'zhaal as another burst of lightning turned the remains of the divan into a puddle of stinking slime. The vortex surrounding Nagaira was swelling, increasing in velocity. Malus rose to his knees and flung the draich at her one-handed. It shattered into droplets of boiling steel before he'd reached his feet and started for the antechamber.

More lightning reached for him as he ran and the witch's voice rose in a shriek of thwarted anger. The air crackled and moaned around him. He felt his hair writhe and melt into the dried gore on his skin.

He did not stop upon reaching the antechamber; if anything, he spurred himself to greater speed, racing for the stairs. Nagaira's shriek rose to an unearthly wail – and then went silent.

The explosion that followed turned the world inside out.

A wave of energy washed over him as he tumbled down the stairs and he felt the fabric of the world come undone. For a single, endless heartbeat he hung from a precipice of sorts, dangling at the edge of infinity. Entire universes stretched before him, each one greater and less sane than the one before.

Worse still he glimpsed the impossible beings that crouched in the emptiness between the universes – and for a moment, *they* glimpsed *him*.

Malus screamed in pure, mindless terror – then the wave collapsed back in on itself and the entire top of Nagaira's tower exploded in a ball of unnatural light.

His head struck the edge of a stone step with a blinding flash of blessed pain, snapping his awareness back to the physical world. Malus rebounded off walls and staircases until he spilled out into the wrecked guard room below.

The pain was intense and sweet. It reminded him of his place in the world. For a long while, all he could do was clutch the great tome in his arms and laugh like a madman, grateful to be blinded once again to the awful expanse beyond the world of flesh.

Malus had no idea how much time had passed before he realised he wasn't alone. When the laughter finally died and he focused his eyes on the smoky room around him, he saw Urial looming over him. There was a strange look in his brass-coloured eyes.

'She is gone,' was all Malus could say.

Urial nodded. 'It is perhaps for the best. The question is: will she return?'

The thought chilled Malus to the bone. 'Mother of Night, I pray not.'

Once more, Urial stared intently at Malus, then surprised the high-born by bending over him and extending his good hand. His grip was surprisingly strong and he pulled Malus effortlessly to his feet. 'Best to save your prayers for later,' he said, his expression inscrutable. 'The Vaulkhar's troops have entered the tower to restore order and they have been commanded to escort us to the Drachau's tower. It would appear that we have some explaining to do.'

Chapter Ten
WRIT OF IRON

Nagaira's tower continued to burn, its upper storeys wreathed in seething white flame that rose for more than a hundred feet into the night sky. The eerie glow of the burning tower shone like a white borealis through the crystal skylight set in the arched ceiling of the Drachau's inner court. It threw elaborate patterns of light and shadow across the tiled floor, writhing knots of white light and inky shadow that drew Malus's attention away from the undisputed lord of Hag Graef. Every time he bent himself to the task of focusing on the man presiding from the dais in the centre of the great chamber the shadows would twist and writhe at the edges of his vision. He caught the hint of patterns there, of meaning where none ought to be.

Malus and Urial had been brought into the Drachau's presence, only to be made to wait while he received reports from his lieutenants and the arrival of the Vaulkhar. It was all Malus could do to remain on his feet, his body was battered and torn and the cut across his scalp had bled so much he was dizzy and weak. But the Drachau offered him no comforts, nor would it have ever occurred to him to ask for any. Weakness was not tolerated in the presence of the Drachau, only the strong were fit to stand in his shadow and await his pleasure.

The highborn could not say how long he stood in silence, fighting a desperate battle to remain upright and conscious. At some point he heard the great double doors swing wide and the warlord of Hag Graef swept in like a storm, clad in his red-enamelled armour and wearing the ancient blade Render at his side. It was a testament to the majesty of the great court that Lurhan's fierce presence did not fill it like a turbulent sea. As it was, Malus could feel an electric tension in the air as his father approached and knew that the infamous Vaulkhar seethed.

Uthlan Tyr, the Drachau of Hag Graef, also wore a suit of fine plate armour – not the great relic armour worn at ceremonies like the Hanil Khar or on the field of war, but a mundane harness that was suitable for everyday use and worth a highborn's ransom. While the Vaulkhar carried his helmet tucked under one arm the Drachau disdained the great dragon helm of his station, his long, black hair pulled back from his face with a fine gold circlet and spilling down over his shoulders. He had a thin, almost boyish face despite being nearly eight hundred years of age and his small eyes glittered like chips of onyx beneath an imposing brow. He and Lurhan were distant cousins and both shared the sharp patrician nose of their ancestors and a defiant set to their pointed chins. Unlike the Vaulkhar, Tyr's hand rested on the pommel of a naked blade, its chisel point grounded on the wooden floor of the dais. It was a draich, similar to the weapon Malus had used at the tower, but the slender, curving sword had the hallmarks of a master craftsman and its blade was etched with runes of power that parted steel as easily as skin. It was said among the highborn houses of Hag Graef that Lurhan had fought in more battles than he had hairs on his head, but Uthlan Tyr had killed far more men than he. For the Drachau, spilling blood was as natural – and necessary – as breathing. Malus had little doubt that his life – and possibly even that of Urial as well – was balanced precariously on the keen edge of that blade.

The Vaulkhar climbed the steps of the dais and knelt before his lord. 'My men have secured the tower,' Lurhan said, his voice hoarse from shouting commands over the din of battle. 'Nagaira's retainers fought to the death rather than surrender. There were only a handful of slaves left alive in the tower and they have been taken by my men for questioning. The… chamber… beneath the tower is a charnel pit. It would appear that no less than two hundred slave stock were butchered there, many of them clearly twisted by the effects of powerful sorcery. Worse yet, there were three score highborn found below, slain by poisoned blades or the draichs of the temple executioners.' Lurhan turned to regard Urial coldly. 'When we arrived the bodies were being mutilated by a band of temple brides.'

Urial met his father's eyes with his own impassive stare. After a moment, the Vaulkhar glanced back to his lord.

'These were no mere highborn, dread one. They were the sons and daughters of some of your most powerful allies. When news reaches their kin the gutters will run with blood, mark my words.'

The Drachau's eyes swept contemptuously over Malus and settled on Urial. 'Explain yourself,' he commanded.

A lesser noble would have quailed beneath Tyr's murderous glare, but Urial was undaunted. 'I stand before you not as your vassal but as an agent of the Temple of Khaine,' he answered. 'This is a temple matter: you trifle with it at your peril.'

Lurhan's face went white with rage, but Malus was shocked to see the Vaulkhar hold his fury in check. The only sign of tension in the Drachau himself was a slight tightening of his hand on the pommel of his sword. His tone remained even as he said, 'Go on.'

'The Temple of Khaine has excised a canker growing in the very heart of this city. The Cult of Slaanesh had spread its rot through the highest orders of Hag Graef's nobility — including the Vaulkhar's daughter, Nagaira.'

'Have a care, Urial! Now it is you who dance the razor's edge,' Lurhan said, his voice full of quiet menace.

Does he fear that he will be implicated as well, Malus thought? Or does he know that the taint of the cult runs even deeper in his house and fears what the Drachau will say? He had been so focused on his own schemes that he'd failed to appreciate how politically damaging the events of the evening could be. A few carefully chosen words from Urial and the Vaulkhar could find himself kneeling before an executioner in the temple courtyard. The Drachau would have no choice but to order Lurhan's death, if for no other reason than to avoid the same fate should word reach the Witch King.

The notion restored a bit of the fire in Malus's veins. Lurhan and the Drachau had reason to be afraid and that gave Malus a small amount of power over them.

'These are grave accusations,' Tyr said carefully. 'Where is your proof?'

Urial scowled at the Drachau? 'Proof? We are the anointed of Khaine. We need provide no proof.' The former acolyte raised his hand to forestall the Drachau's angry protest. 'That said, I realise that these events have placed you in a precarious position, so I will provide you with some amount of detail.'

He indicated Malus with a nod of his head. 'This all began with your order to torture my brother to death for his recent indiscretions. After the Vaulkhar had tormented Malus beyond the endurance of the strongest druchii it was determined that he had fulfilled your wishes to the best of his ability and Malus was released into the care of his sister.'

The Drachau shot the warlord a stern glance, then returned his attention to Urial. 'This much I know,' Tyr said darkly.

Urial nodded absently, his expression vague as he focused on the chain of events laid out in his mind. 'While Malus was being treated by

Nagaira – treated with both drugs and outlawed sorcery, I might add – she took advantage of his weakened state in an attempt to seduce him into her debased cult.' Urial's expression cleared and he eyed Malus coldly. 'Malus and Nagaira have been companions – some would say *more* than companions – for some time. She has used her forbidden knowledge to support him on more than one occasion. I believe she has been intent upon subverting him for some time now.' Tyr gave a snort of disgust. 'This libertine? What would be the point? He has nothing to offer!'

'So it would appear,' Urial said, his voice neutral. 'And yet it is a fact that the cult held a revel in his honour shortly after his recovery and that he was brought before their Hierophant and invited to join their ranks.'

Urial turned towards Malus, his pronounced limp the only outward sign of the exhaustion the crippled druchii felt. 'As soon as he was able, Malus came to me with this information, as was proper. He put forth a plan to use his proposed initiation as a trap to eliminate the heart of the cult here in the city.'

'By rights he should have come to me, first!' Lurhan growled. 'The honour of our house–'

'The honour of your house or any other comes second to the affairs of the temple,' Urial said flatly. 'It is our duty to keep the souls of the druchii pure, free from the weakness of our traitorous kin in Ulthuan. This is not merely the commandment of Khaine, but the wish of Malekith himself. Do you care to dispute this?'

'You have made your point, Urial,' the Drachau interjected. 'Continue.'

'Malus gave us the location of the initiation chamber, suggesting it was part of the tunnels burrowed beneath the city. I despatched scouts into the Burrows and located passages that had been walled off to isolate the chamber from the rest of the network.' Urial shrugged. 'After that it was a matter of alerting the temple and rousing its holy warriors to do Khaine's sacred work. We burst through the walls just before the culmination of the ceremony and attempted to capture the apostates.' The former acolyte gave a wintry smile. 'Fortunately, they chose to resist.'

Suddenly the white glow in the night sky flickered and went out. The Drachau glanced at the skylight above with evident relief, then returned his attention to Malus. 'What of this Hierophant Urial spoke of?'

'I fought the Hierophant in the initiation chamber,' Malus said hoarsely. 'Though I gravely wounded the high priest, he managed to escape. I believe that he would be easy to locate, however. Like his supplicants, he must be a high-ranking noble – someone close to the most powerful leaders in the city.'

Malus looked squarely at his father. 'I would suggest a search of all the spires in the Hag, my lords. Find the noble with the ruined throat and you will have your chief apostate. I expect you will not have to look very far.'

'What are you implying, you misbegotten churl?' Lurhan took a step towards Malus, his hand going to the long hilt of bone rising above his left hip. 'Bad enough that first you and then your sister defile our honour – now you try to heap more disgrace upon us?'

'I imply nothing,' Malus shot back. 'If you are so covetous of your house's honour then send your troops to my brother Isilvar's tower. Drag him here from his dens of flesh and ask him what he knows of this damnable cult. I warn you, though – he might not be fit to say much.'

'Be silent!' Lurhan roared, descending the steps like a thunderbolt as his hand tightened on the hilt of his blade.

'*No further!*' The Drachau leapt to his feet, pointing at Lurhan with the point of his own blade. 'Restrain yourself, Vaulkhar. Methinks your children are right: you place the honour of your house above the security of the state and that is a grave mistake. This high priest must be rooted out and the sooner the better. We will search the Hag, as Malus has suggested, because it serves our interests. Now,' he commanded, 'tell me of Nagaira.'

Malus made as if to reply, but Urial answered first. 'She is no more,' he said.

The Drachau nodded. 'And the fire?'

'Born of a Chaos storm, dread lord. Nagaira unleashed a powerful spell in an attempt to escape and to destroy evidence that might have led us to her patron.'

'Patron?' The Drachau frowned. 'You mean the Hierophant?'

'Not at all, dread lord. I mean the person responsible for teaching her the forbidden arts of sorcery and supplying her with the extensive library that filled the upper portion of her tower. It has long been an open secret that she flouted the Witch King's laws,' Urial glared accusingly at Lurhan, 'but no one chose to act upon it. Possibly because no one realised she'd become much more than a mere scholar of the arcane… or possibly because of the identity of the patron involved.'

'And tell me Urial, who would that patron be?'

Heads turned at the sound of the cold, powerful voice. Eldire seemed to coalesce from the shadows themselves, gliding soundlessly across the tiled floor towards the dais. No one had heard the tall doors part to admit her. Malus frankly wasn't certain that they had. The Vaulkhar's fierce expression disappeared, his previous fury suddenly forgotten. The Drachau eyed Eldire warily but held his tongue in the face of the seer's unexpected arrival.

Urial faced the sorceress, his face hard and expressionless. 'I... have my theories, but no evidence as yet. Still, there cannot be but a handful of people in the city who could possess such knowledge... and the majority of those reside in the witch's convent.'

'I imagine so,' Eldire replied coolly. 'The rest would be criminals against the state, after all, teaching the arcane arts to those with no right to possess it. Men like yourself, for example.'

Malus bit his tongue, careful to keep his face neutral as the air grew thick with tension. Urial stiffened, his expression growing strained, but he made no reply.

'You come into my court unannounced, Yrila,' the Drachau hissed.

'I am here to report that the city's coven has extinguished the fire at the tower,' Eldire said dryly. 'I had thought you would be pleased to hear it. Shall I tell my sisters to re-ignite the blaze and wait until you are ready to summon us?'

'You are too impertinent by half, Eldire,' the Drachau said querulously. 'Tell me of the damage.'

'The energies released by the spell consumed almost half of the tower – had it gone unchecked it would have continued to burn so long as there was stone to feed it. The entire city could have been lost.' Eldire glared at Urial. 'If Nagaira did indeed have a patron then he greatly underestimated her power. The spell she unleashed was beyond the power of a single sorcerer to control. As it is, the rest of the tower will have to be demolished, as the taint of the Chaos magic has seeped through it to the very foundation. Left unchecked that taint will spread throughout the entire city.'

He, Malus wondered, or *she*? The highborn eyed his mother with newfound respect... and uncertainty. Were you mentoring Nagaira? If so, why – and what do I have to do with it?

Tyr considered the news and nodded gravely. 'Then you have done your duty well, Yrila. Now, what of the bodies of the highborn in the initiation chamber?'

Eldire smiled. 'The bodies of the cultists were given to the fire, my lord. It seemed like the appropriate thing to do.'

'You *burned* them? All of them?' The Drachau was incredulous. 'It's monstrous! Their kin will be up in arms when they hear of this!'

'As of this moment these cultists are *missing*, not dead.' Eldire said sharply. 'The Chaos magic consumed them entirely – what little was left was not even recognisable as druchii, much less who they really were. Tomorrow the story will spread through the Hag that Nagaira and her household were consumed in a sorcerous conflagration, one that no doubt my husband and the Temple alike – ' Eldire glared forcefully at both Lurhan and Urial in turn – 'will decry as the just fate of all those who would dabble in the forbidden arts. An investigation will be promised and punishments threatened for any other unlawful sorcerers found in the city. If your allies wish to come forward at that point and publicly proclaim that their sons or daughters were present in the witch's tower when it burned then I should be greatly surprised.'

The Drachau sat back upon his throne, rubbing his chin thoughtfully. 'What of the presence of the executioners, to say nothing of the Brides of Khaine that were there?'

Urial shrugged. 'They entered by way of the Burrows and left in the same manner. Only my retainers and the Vaulkhar's troops were seen entering the tower and it can be truthfully said that they were there to put an end to Nagaira's sorcery.'

Tyr nodded, a sly smile spreading across his narrow face. 'Then that is the story we shall tell,' he declared. 'Doubtless there will be private complaints, but that can be mended with time and favours. That only leaves one last matter.'

'What is that, dread lord?' Malus asked. He had his own matters to discuss, if the opportunity presented itself.

The Drachau's expression turned cold. 'Whether to kill you now or execute you publicly as a cultist of Slaanesh.'

'*Execute* me? This cult was uprooted thanks to me—' Malus looked to Urial for support. The former acolyte said nothing, eyeing the Drachau warily.

Uthlan Tyr smiled cruelly. 'You know the law, Malus. Any druchii that tastes of the forbidden fruit of Slaanesh must die. By your own admission you have done so, have you not?'

'But you cannot execute me without admitting that the cult was here, hiding under your very nose,' Malus shot back. 'And then your allies will call for your hide, dread lord.'

Tyr rose from his chair. 'Then we shall slay you now, far from prying eyes.' The Drachau ignored Eldire's murderous look, turning instead to Lurhan and Urial. 'Have you any objection to this?'

Lurhan looked to Eldire, then to his lord. 'It is my duty to serve,' he said, a little nervously. 'Do as you will, dread lord.'

The Drachau acknowledged his warlord with a nod. 'Urial?'

Urial stared hard at Malus. Anger, desire and frustration alike warred behind his eyes. Finally he turned to the Drachau and shook his head. 'No. For now he is an agent of the temple and beyond your grasp, Uthlan Tyr.'

Tyr recoiled, his eyes widening in surprise. 'Are you mad? Have you not been baying for his blood all winter?' The Drachau held out his sword to Urial. 'Here. Strike off his head yourself. Bathe in his tainted blood! Is that not what you want?'

Urial's jaw clenched. A bitter smile twisted his lips. 'What I do, I do for the good of the temple,' he said. 'There is a task he must do for me. Until then, no man shall threaten him while I live.'

The Drachau shook his head. 'You are a fool, Urial!' He lowered his sword. 'I am no oracle, but I warrant you'll never have another chance like this again.' Tyr glared at Malus. 'This is twice now you've escaped death at my hands, Darkblade. Your luck cannot last forever.'

Malus smiled, sensing an opportunity. 'Doubtless you are correct, dread lord. Thus, I must press my advantage while I'm able. I demand you present me with a writ of iron.'

Uthlan Tyr laughed. 'Shall I give you my concubines and my tower as well?'

'No, that won't be necessary,' Malus answered, his tone calm and even. 'The writ alone will suffice.'

'Enough with your impertinence,' Lurhan growled, raising his fist. 'The Drachau must heed the wishes of the temple, but not I!'

'No, you have other oaths to consider,' Eldire said. 'And the consequences of breaking them would be far more terrible.'

Lurhan stopped in his tracks, his face turning pale. Tyr's alarm grew as he watched the exchange. He turned to Malus, all trace of humour gone. 'What makes you think I would give a man such as you so much power?'

'For all the proper reasons: I seek to serve the state in a great endeavour and to bring honour and glory to you and the city,' Malus replied. 'And to ensure my silence over what really happened within the tower, of course.'

'Just what endeavour do you speak of? Do you plan to drink the city dry, or exhaust all the flesh houses in the Corsairs' Quarter?'

Malus surprised Tyr with a hearty laugh. 'Will you give a writ for such a thing? If so I would be glad to have it. No, I need your authority to form an expedition. I will need ships, sailors and skilled raiders and time is short.'

'For what purpose?'

The highborn considered his response carefully. 'I have recently discovered the lost Isle of Morhaut,' he said. 'And I intend to drive the Skinriders from the northern sea.'

Uthlan Tyr shook his head, his expression incredulous. 'That's impossible. Where did you learn such a thing?'

'How I did so is unimportant,' Malus said. 'Consider what I am offering instead. The Skinriders have harassed our raiding ships and competed with us for plunder. If I am successful we will double our harvest for years to come. Not to mention the fact that the island is legendary for the ships and treasures lost on its shores. As author of the writ you would not only share in the glory, but the plunder as well. The fortunes of our city have suffered greatly in the long feud with Naggor – that can change in the space of just a few months. All I need is the writ.'

The Drachau started to protest, but Malus could see a spark of interest in the ruler's eyes. 'You wouldn't stand a chance. The Skinriders would kill you before you got within a mile of the island.'

'For a man who was about to have me executed, your sudden concern for my welfare comes as a bit of a surprise.'

The Drachau looked to Urial. 'What does the Temple say about this fool's errand? Did you not just say you have a task for him to perform?'

Urial sighed. 'Issue the writ, Uthlan Tyr. I like it no better than you, but in this he also serves the temple's interests.'

The Drachau's hand tightened on his sword. 'I am beset from all sides then,' he said in quiet exasperation. 'Very well Malus, you will have your writ of iron,' Tyr said. 'May it bring you a bounty of blood and fire.'

'Of that I have little doubt, dread lord,' Malus replied, a steely look of triumph on his face. 'And I swear you will share the fruits of it in the fullness of time.'

Chapter Eleven
DOORWAYS OF THE DEAD

HE WAS LOST.

There was a door in front of him, black wood with a silver knob worked in the shape of a leering daemon's face. He pushed it open and saw a hexagonal room beyond. Four staircases rose from the centre of the room, climbing into thin air in four different directions.

The same it's all the same it's all the same… his voice echoed in his head. He pulled the door shut.

A roar echoed behind him. Closer now than it had been before.

Before? When?

The roar echoed again, much closer now. He yanked the door open and found a staircase descending into darkness.

Now he could hear footsteps. Heavy, ponderous footfalls drumming like the beating of a bestial heart. Thud-*thud*, thud-*thud*, thud-*thud*–

He ran down the stairs, fleeing the sound of the footsteps.

The staircase curved abruptly, straightened, then curved back the other way. He raced through an arch – and found himself descending a staircase surrounded by open air, leading to a hexagonal room. Three more staircases rose up from the room, heading in three different directions.

There was a door of black wood set into one of the walls. As he reached the bottom of the stairs it shook on its hinges beneath a powerful blow. A roar thundered on the other side of the splintering wood.

* * *

MALUS AWOKE WITH a shout, sitting bolt upright amid a tangle of bed sheets and groping in the darkness for a weapon. By the time his hand closed on the hilt of the sword leaning beside his bed he realised that he had been dreaming and fell back against the mattress with a shuddering sigh. The cut on his forehead throbbed in time with his racing heart and the ragged scabs on the right side of his face stung as his cheek stretched into a weary grimace.

Pale moonlight slanted silver-blue through the windowpanes of his sleeping chamber. The night sky was unnaturally clear, with not a shred of cloud in the sky. Malus couldn't recall the last time he'd seen such a thing – clouds always hung heavy over the Land of Chill, especially during the late winter months. He wondered if it had anything to do with the fire the previous night, or the sorceries used to extinguish it. Everything felt strange, somehow unsettled.

With a groan Malus pushed himself back upright and rose shakily from the bed. He moved haltingly, the muscles in his back, shoulders and hips singing painfully with each shuffling step. In truth, he felt better than he'd been when he first stumbled back to his tower after the meeting with the Drachau. Delirious with fatigue and loss of blood he'd wandered the fortress for more than an hour before finally fetching up against the black oak doors at the base of his spire. Thinking back now, he couldn't remember how he'd got inside – an image stuck in his mind of falling inwards as one of the doors was pulled open and hearing Silar's surprised shout, but little else.

Malus staggered to the large, circular table that dominated a corner of the sleeping chamber. Among the piles of clutter was a tray with a wine bottle and a goblet. Next to the tray sat the Tome of Ak'zhaal. The highborn snatched up the bottle and pulled the cork with his teeth, spitting it into the nearest corner. He took a deep drink, barely tasting the vintage and opened the book at a random page.

…Stone he built upon stone, raised with sorcery and madness, as Eradorius built a tower beyond the reach of years…

A soft knock sounded at the door. Malus frowned, thinking again of the sword beside the bed. He reminded himself that with Nagaira gone, the blood debt to the temple had lapsed and forced himself to relax. 'Enter,' he said.

The door creaked open – few highborn cared for oiled hinges in places where they slept – and one of his retainers stepped into the room. It took a moment before Malus recognised Hauclir's scarred face. The former guard captain was sporting a few new cuts on his face from the recent battle, including a dramatic wound that ran at an angle from his forehead, across his nose and down to his chin.

'Do you typically block your opponent's blade with your face, Hauclir?' Malus said by way of greeting.

'If the tactic's good enough for my lord and master it's good enough for me,' Hauclir deadpanned. 'Forgive the interruption, my lord, but your brother Urial is here. He insisted on speaking to you at once, despite the unholy hour.'

'What time is it?'

'The hour of the wolf, my lord.'

'Mother of Night,' Malus cursed, taking another drink to fortify himself. 'The man is indeed a monster. Bring me a robe, then send him in.'

Hauclir scanned the room quickly, went and snatched up a discarded sleeping robe from the end of the bed and tossed it to Malus. The highborn let the bunched-up cloth bounce off his chest and hit the floor. He stared pointedly at the garment and then looked archly at his new retainer.

'I've already worn that.'

'Excellent,' the former captain answered. 'Then we're sure it fits.'

'I see,' Malus answered. 'Any other night I'd have your backside hung from a meat hook, but I'm too tired to bother just now. Go and get my brother and bring him here.'

Hauclir bowed. 'At once, my lord,' he replied and slipped quietly from the room.

Malus shrugged the silk robe over his shoulders, careful of the cuts and gouges across his upper back and right arm. No sooner had he cinched up his belt than the bedroom door groaned wide and Urial walked slowly into the room with Hauclir in his wake. The retainer made a clumsy attempt at presenting Urial after the fact, then sketched an awkward bow and retreated from sight.

'You keep the hours of a bat, dear brother,' Malus said around a swig of wine. He offered the bottle to Urial, who eyed it with disdain.

'Sleep is for the weak, brother,' Urial replied. 'The state never rests, nor does its true servants.'

'I was saying something very similar just a moment ago,' the highborn said, setting the bottle carefully on its tray. 'Why are you here?'

Urial scowled at his brother, drawing an object from his belt. It was a plaque of dark metal set in a frame of yellowed bone, about a foot long and four inches wide.

For all his fatigue and his numerous minor hurts, Malus's heart skipped a beat upon seeing the Drachau's writ. 'What are you doing with that?'

'By law and custom the Drachau presents his writ to the temple, who then delivers it to his chosen agent. We do this to bear witness that the delegation of power falls into the proper hands and to act as a guarantor of its temporary nature.' Urial held the plaque before him, his expression strained. He took a deep breath and spoke the necessary words:

'Malus, son of Lurhan, the Drachau Uthlan Tyr of Hag Graef desires you to perform an extraordinary endeavour in the service of the state and invests in you all the similar authority and power of his station, that you may accomplish the task set before you with honour and dispatch. He binds you with this writ of iron. Bear it before you and no druchii in the land will bar your way.'

All of a sudden Malus was glad for the wine warming his insides and steadying his nerves. Without preamble he reached out and plucked the writ from Urial's stiff fingers. The iron plates were thin and surprisingly light; they opened on tiny, oiled hinges to reveal the lettered parchment and elaborate seals protected in the shallow space within. 'It's smaller than I imagined. Is it true that if you fail they melt down the iron plates and pour them down your throat?'

'I certainly hope so,' Urial muttered. 'If my researches are correct you are only the eighth highborn in the history of the city to receive one.' He shook his head incredulously. 'And got it by blackmailing the Drachau, no less. The very idea is appalling.'

'Did your researches mention how the other seven acquired theirs? I expect it was exactly the same way,' Malus said absently, inspecting the parchment with a growing sense of wonder. Within the scope of the writ he effectively had the power of the Drachau himself.

'Be that as it may, this authority does not extend to the temple or its agents,' Urial said archly. 'Let us be clear on this from the start. Now perhaps you will explain to me how this will deliver Yasmir from her wanton existence and into the sacred bounds of the temple?'

Malus closed the covers of the writ and suppressed a frown. He'd hoped to put this conversation off for a while longer. 'Very well,' he said with a sigh. 'For years our sister has lived like a princess of lost Nagarythe, using her beauty and her wiles to drink the lifeblood of every enterprising nobleman in the upper reaches of the city's court. They surround her with riches and influence out of proportion to her station, each one hoping to convince her to ask for their hand in marriage. Not one of them has the courage to ask her themselves. And why is that?'

'Because she is the focus of our elder brother's affections,' Urial growled, his good hand clenching into a fist.

'Indeed and Bruglir is a very powerful, very jealous and extraordinarily murderous man,' Malus said. 'He fights duels just to test the sharpness of his swords. Any man who presses his case for Yasmir's hand must answer to Bruglir and so far our father has shown no interest in restraining him.' He gave Urial a curious look. 'I've always wondered why he never raised a hand to you. It's not as though you made any secret of your desire for her.'

Urial's expression hardened. 'Isn't it obvious? Because he knows without doubt that I'm no threat to him.' The former acolyte abruptly turned and plucked the bottle from the tray. No emotion showed on his face as he carefully filled the goblet, but the bitterness in his voice was evident. 'Yasmir told me once that she complained to him about me and he laughed at her. It was the first and only time he'd ever done such a thing, or so she claimed. It made her very angry for a time.'

'The point, however, is that the cornerstone of Yasmir's existence is Bruglir. Without him she becomes… vulnerable.'

Urial nodded thoughtfully, taking a cautious sip of the wine. 'So you plan to kill him.'

'Better to say that I intend to put him into a position that is very likely to end his life,' Malus said carefully. 'I don't dare try to kill him myself. In the first place I don't want to risk Yasmir's wrath if I'm caught and in the second place I'm not sure I'd succeed if I tried.' Malus smiled. 'No, he will meet a glorious death driving the Skinriders from the north seas and then Yasmir will have to decide where her best interests lie.'

'An intriguing plan,' Urial said, swirling the wine in his cup. 'But where do I fit into this? You mentioned that you needed a sorcerer.'

Malus nodded. 'Yes, indeed.' He pointed to the Tome of Ak'zhaal. 'If my researches are correct, the Isle of Morhaut is protected by powerful sorceries. I will need a magic-wielder of great skill to penetrate them so we can reach the island.'

Urial eyed the book quizzically, as though noticing it for the first time. 'Never in my life would I have imagined such a thing.'

'What? That I need your help?'

'No, that you can actually read.' Urial stepped forward, setting the goblet down and turning the pages of the tome gingerly with his gloved hand. 'So you actually intend to fight the Skinriders?'

Malus shrugged. 'Only so far as I must. What I'm really after lies within a tower on the island – a sanctuary built by a sorcerer named Eradorius during the First War.'

'The First War? That was thousands of years ago! What makes you think such a place still exists?'

The highborn didn't answer for a moment. 'Call it intuition,' he said. 'I saw things in the Wastes that were even older than Eradorius's legendary tower, so I know that it's at least possible.'

Urial looked up from the book, his brass-coloured eyes boring into Malus's own. 'Does this have anything to do with the skull you took from my tower?'

Malus met Urial's stare unflinchingly. 'It was Nagaira who suggested robbing you of that skull. I suspect it had something to do with her plans for the cult.'

'That doesn't answer my question.'

'It's as much of an answer as you're going to get,' Malus said flatly. 'Does it matter, so long as Yasmir is yours in the end?'

Urial glanced one last time at the yellowed pages of the tome, then slowly and deliberately closed the cover. 'No. I suppose not.'

Inwardly the highborn breathed a sigh of relief. 'Excellent. Now the three of us need only prepare for a trip to Clar Karond in the coming weeks. I want to be there the moment Bruglir and his fleet puts in for supplies. With luck I can use the writ to hurry the process along and we can be on our way north within a month.'

'The three of us?' Urial inquired.

'We need Yasmir to accompany us on the voyage,' Malus said. 'While I may have a writ from the Drachau, neither you nor I are well-loved by our brother and we will be hundreds of leagues from civilisation and surrounded by his army of cut-throats. I intend to use Yasmir to keep Bruglir under control.'

'Ah, I see. And who will control Yasmir?'

The highborn chuckled. 'I will, of course.' And you will be the rod I will hold over her, Malus thought.

Urial nodded thoughtfully, his finger tracing the runes inscribed in the cover of the tome. 'An interesting plan, brother. But I am concerned about the lengthy delay. Many things can go awry in a month's time. The Drachau could even grow impatient and rescind the writ if he wished.'

Malus spread his hands. 'I can't make the winds blow any faster brother. I expect Bruglir hasn't even begun the voyage home yet. The straits around Karond Kar will be frozen for another couple of weeks at least.'

Urial gave Malus a wintry smile. 'Forgive my ignorance. Unlike the rest of you I was never allowed a hakseer-cruise of my own. Father wouldn't risk the embarrassment of being unable to hire a crew to go to sea under the command of a cripple. Still,' he added, his smile turning conspiratorial, 'what if I said that it was possible to go to Bruglir now? To meet him while his ships are still at sea and begin your expedition immediately?'

Malus's eyes narrowed. 'So magic is only heretical when it's being performed by someone outside the temple?'

'Do not seek to confuse the debased rituals of a cultist with the blessings of the Lord of Murder,' Urial growled.

Malus's first instinct was to dismiss the offer. He didn't care for the notion of being dropped into the middle of Bruglir's fleet with no warning or preparation, no time to sound out members of his brother's crew and perhaps test their loyalties with a little gold coin. On the other hand, time was the one commodity he needed most but had the least to spare. *I need every day I can get,* he thought ruefully. Then a sudden realisation made his heart skip a beat. *Does he know? He had the skull of Ehrenlish in his possession for many months – does he know about Tz'arkan and the five relics? Does he suspect what I'm after?*

'Does it matter?' Tz'arkan said. 'Does it change the fact that you must reach the island and recover the idol and that you need his sorceries to succeed?'

'No,' Malus muttered, half to himself. 'No, of course not.'

Urial nodded brusquely. 'Then deliver the news to Yasmir and prepare for the journey. You and she may bring one member of your retinue each if you wish – more than that would be too dangerous to risk.'

'What?' Malus stirred from his internal reverie with a start. 'I mean – yes, of course. When will you be ready?'

'We can depart this evening,' Urial replied, almost enthusiastic at the prospect. 'The moon and tides will be propitious. Come to my tower at nightfall, just before the rising of the fog and we will be on our way.'

Before Malus could think of a response, Urial turned on his heel and limped from the room, leaving the highborn to wonder just what he'd got himself into.

He held up the writ and considered its iron cover, shaking his head ruefully. *Absolute power indeed,* he thought.

THE FIGURINE WAS little more than one foot tall; formed from a single piece of obsidian, it depicted a priestess of the temple drinking the brains from the skull of a defeated foe. It was more than a hundred years old, carved by the infamous artist Luclayr before his spectacular suicide. Easily worth more than a highborn's ransom, the figurine made a sharp whirring sound as it spun through the air and exploded into razor-edged shards inches from Malus's head. The highborn ducked instinctively, grimacing at the shower of razor-sharp splinters.

'A sea voyage? With *him*?' Yasmir's violet eyes glowed with hatred. She stalked through the shadows at the far end of her sleeping chamber, her half-open silk robe trailing in her wake like the shroud of a wight. Her skin was luminous where the weak daylight touched it – she was the classic druchii beauty, at her most alluring when moved to anger. Even Malus had to admit that she was breathtaking, but as he plucked splinters of black glass from his cheek he also mused that the lovelier she became, the more attention he had to devote to staying alive.

'This was not our bargain,' Yasmir hissed. Another object – a wine goblet – struck the wall near the highborn with a hollow clang. 'You asked for my help convincing Bruglir to back your expedition. *Nothing* more. In return you promised to kill Urial, not put us at the mercy of his blood magic!'

'Plans change, dear sister,' Malus said, readying himself to dodge another missile. 'The Drachau took a keen interest in my plan and gave me his unstinting support, as you have seen,' he pointed to the writ, lying open on a small table near the centre of the room. 'With the writ in hand I was able to command Urial to transport us directly to Bruglir's ship rather than wait so many weeks for his fleet to make port. Time is of the essence, Yasmir and so I must regretfully insist that you accompany me.'

'Insist!' The word came out in a hissing screech. A barrage of shoes flew across the room, then another small piece of statuary moving too fast to identify before it shattered against Malus's breastplate. The rest of her furious reply tapered off into a wordless screech of frustration; she had read the writ with exacting care and knew that she had no real power to resist his summons.

Malus watched Yasmir's fit with considerable interest, wondering when the last time was that she'd been dictated to about anything. He'd first called upon her early in the day, only to be told by her slaves that she was indisposed. Hours passed, morning to noon and then well into the afternoon and after being rebuffed for a third time Malus had produced the writ and shoved the frightened slaves out of the way. Her retainers had rushed at him like angry cadaver bees, but for once their highborn upbringing proved useful, as one glimpse of the iron plaque had been enough to stop them in their tracks. And so he'd barged into her bedroom just behind a cloud of stammering slaves and sent Yasmir's rich and powerful bed partners scrambling for their robes.

At first she'd reacted to his intrusion with the same languid calm she'd displayed at the arena – until she saw the writ. Then her composure gave way to anger. She's grown too accustomed to being in a position of control, he thought. Take that away and she becomes fearful. And dangerous, he reminded himself.

'Our bargain still stands, dear sister. It is merely the circumstances that have changed,' he said, trying to sound conciliatory. 'I still need your help to encourage Bruglir's co-operation and I need Urial's magic to penetrate the sorcerous defences surrounding the island. Once that's done we can dispatch him at our leisure. In the meantime, you will be able to enjoy the company of your beloved Bruglir for weeks more than you normally would. Haven't you always wished to sail with him on his long sea raids, taking part in the bloody battles and choosing the choicest baubles from the treasure trove as befits a corsair queen?'

Yasmir paused. 'There is something in what you say, I suppose. It's not as though I wouldn't have Bruglir and his crew to keep that vile temple-worm away from me.' Malus heard her take a deep breath and then she stepped back into the light, drawing her robe securely about her graceful body. 'Very well,' she said, attempting a small measure of her former composure. 'Just one companion, you said? And we are to leave in...?'

Malus considered the light outside. 'In just a few hours, sister: just before the fog rises. I tried to tell you earlier, but–'

'Yes, yes, I know.' She drew herself up to her full, regal height. 'I shall be ready at the appointed time. Let it not be said that I do not honour my bargains to the letter, Malus. See to it that you do the same.' Yasmir scooped the iron plaque from the table and held it out to Malus. 'This writ won't count for much a thousand leagues from the Hag. On the seas the only law will be our dear brother the sea captain.' Her full lips quirked in a cruel smile. 'Disappoint me and it might be your head rolling along the deck beside Urial's.'

Malus took the plaque from her hand. 'I expect nothing less,' he said.

'WHY ME? WHY not Silar Thornblood, or Arleth Vann?' Hauclir looked up at the ominous bulk of Urial's spire from the barren courtyard outside its iron-banded doors. The former guard captain's face was faintly green in the early evening light; like almost everyone else in Hag Graef, he'd heard legends about the dread tower of the Forsaken One. Malus eyed him with some amusement and wondered what the man would think if he told him that all of the stories were true.

'Because Silar runs my household and is still in the process of rebuilding it. And Arleth Vann doesn't mix well with members of the temple,' the highborn said. 'You, on the other hand–'

'I'm expendable,' Hauclir answered, his face grim. The retainer wore full armour over his kheitan and robes and carried a single sword at his hip. A large pack hung from one shoulder, carrying clothes and supplies for both him and his lord.

Malus clapped Hauclir on the back. 'Come now, Hauclir, it's not like that. *All* of my retainers are expendable. You're just more expendable than the others at the moment.'

'And to think, I *asked* for this,' Hauclir grumbled, shifting the pack on his shoulder.

'Indeed you did,' Malus nodded. 'Delightful, is it not?'

Just then Malus caught sight of a group of druchii entering the courtyard from the opposite side. Yasmir walked amid a group of mournful retainers, several holding witchlight globes aloft on long poles to light their path. A slave walked several paces behind the party, almost doubled over with a huge pack on her shoulders.

Malus bowed as she approached. 'Well met, sister. Are you looking forward to being reunited with our noble brother?' The highborn savoured the stricken looks on Yasmir's entourage as she nodded.

'Indeed I am. It's the one part of this cursed voyage that I expect to enjoy at all.'

Yasmir was dressed all in black, with fine woollen robes and a long shirt of fine black mail that covered her arms and hung to just above her knees. A wide belt of nauglir hide circled her narrow waist and she wore two long daggers, one at each hip. Though the fog hadn't yet risen she wore her silver caedlin. Unlike many highborn who wore nightmasks worked in the shape of monsters or daemons, Yasmir's mask eerily mirrored her own features, almost like a death mask. Malus imagined the shock strangers must have upon seeing that ethereal mask – and then have it pulled away to reveal the startling reality beneath.

'Then send your hounds away, dear Yasmir. The moons have risen and Urial awaits.'

To her credit, Yasmir offered no melodramatic farewells – she simply beckoned to her slave and walked away from the noblemen without a single word. Malus felt the heat of their stares on his neck as he led Yasmir to the tower's tall doorway. As he raised his fist to strike the aged wood, the portal swung soundlessly open, spilling a wash of crimson light onto the cobblestones outside.

One of Urial's skull-faced retainers silently beckoned the highborn and their retainers to come inside. Malus found himself entering the tower with some trepidation. He could not help but feel a chill upon seeing the ranks of silver masks lining the walls of the circular room, all too aware of the malevolent beings that watched from behind the masks' sightless eyes.

Urial waited in the centre of the room, standing before a large brass cauldron brimming with blood. Beyond the cauldron rose what appeared to be a very tall mirror-frame of etched brass. The glass within the frame was missing and Malus saw that a small set of steps had been set before the empty brass oval. Half a dozen of Urial's retainers stood at a discrete distance from their master, along with a handful of robed acolytes, their heads bowed in concentration. Malus could hear them chanting in a language that set his hair on end.

'Your timing is good,' Urial said. 'The moon is in the proper alignment. Once the doorway is open you will have to move quickly, however – we will have little time.' With that, he turned to the cauldron and spread his arms wide.

A sonorous chant rose from Urial's lips, echoed by the acolytes nearby. Yasmir looked to Malus; the highborn shrugged and walked towards the cauldron.

Within the brass vessel the blood was beginning to stir, as though churned from within by invisible hands. Steam rose from its surface, forming a reddish haze before the mirror frame. The chanting increased in volume and Malus saw a thick tendril of steam begin to twist like the funnel of a whirlpool, extending inexorably towards the empty brass frame.

The churning mist reached for the space within the wire oval and flattened as though it touched an invisible plane suspended within the wire. Blood radiated across this plane in concentric ripples, shimmering with unnatural power, until they reached the wire rim and rebounded back towards the centre. Malus could now hear a faint howling sound coming from the crimson mirror – was it the souls of the damned? No, he realised. It was the wind off the sea, cold and unbound.

Suddenly the funnel dissipated. The cauldron was empty and a sheen of bright blood, like a bubble formed in a pool of gore, glistened and trembled within the wire. 'Quickly now,' Urial said, his voice strained. 'Step through! It will not last more than a few moments.'

Once again, Yasmir looked to Malus – she had plucked her mask away and he could see the fear deep in her eyes. He gave her a mocking smile and stepped lightly up to the wire, gritting his teeth against his own palpable unease. This close to the portal Malus could hear other sounds above the wind: the creaking of wood and rope and the groan of a ship's hull as it surged through the waves. He hesitated only a moment, then with a deep breath he stepped into the swirling pattern of blood.

Chapter Twelve
THE SEA RAVENS

For the space of a single heartbeat it felt as though Malus hung above an impossibly vast space, filled with howling wind and the rushing presence of a multitude of angry ghosts. Then an icy shock washed over him, like a torrent of freezing water and he fell.

He felt no rush of air against his body, only the un-moored feeling in his guts as he plummeted through darkness. The further he fell the faster he went, until it seemed as though he were coming apart from within, unravelling like a tumbling skein of muscle, flesh and veins. Malus focussed his terrible will to hold the screams at bay. Then without warning his foot struck solid wood and a harsh slap of cold sea air struck his face as he staggered across the heeling deck of a druchii ship under weigh.

Unearthly darkness still clung to Malus's eyes as he lurched drunkenly across the deck. He blinked furiously, trying to see past the viscous blackness. Sights swam in and out of his vision, curious double-images that showed two or even three different versions of the scene around him. Malus saw the dark, polished deck of the ship gleaming in the early moonlight, then the image blurred and he saw the main mast cracked through and the debris of battle littering the blood-stained planks in the full light of day. He blinked and shook his head fiercely and when he opened his eyes again there were black-robed shapes rushing across the deck with naked steel in their hands. The shapes blurred, becoming bloody and torn, then resolved themselves once more.

The highborn clenched his jaw against a stream of curses and closed his eyes, focusing on steadying his feet against the rolling of the ship. *What sorcery is this,* he thought? *Did the hushalta forever twist my body and mind, or is this something else entirely?*

'Whatever it is,' he whispered to himself. 'It stops, here and now.'

The words stirred the daemon, provoking it to slow laughter. 'Here and now? There is no such thing, little druchii. If you cannot understand this then you are truly lost.'

Before Malus could reply, however, the thudding of boots across the wooden deck reminded him of more immediate concerns. The highborn opened his eyes and saw a score of druchii corsairs, armed with swords, bill-hooks and axes rushing towards him. Their faces were covered in heavy scarves rimed with frost, but there was no mistaking the anger and alarm in their dark eyes. The highborn raised his hands, showing open palms, only realising then as they continued to rush towards him that the crew had no interest in talking to him whatsoever.

The highborn's first instinct was to reach for his swords, but he knew that if he did it would only confirm the crew's worst suspicions. His disoriented mind raced furiously, trying to think of a proper response, but before he could speak the air crackled with electricity and a body thumped onto the deck behind Malus. The sailors recoiled and the highborn turned to see Hauclir on one knee before an oval-shaped crimson haze that waxed and waned in density just a foot above the deck. The retainer stared wildly about at his surroundings, his face a mask of pure terror.

'What manner of madness is this?' said one of the sailors, his eyes darting warily from Malus to Hauclir and back again. The air crackled with invisible lightning once more and the corsairs shrank back a step. The sailor glared sharply at the men to either side of him. 'Stand fast, you black birds!' he commanded in a leathery voice and the corsairs regained a measure of resolve.

Yasmir and her slave stepped through next. The highborn staggered slightly under the burden of Urial's spell, but with a blistering curse she banished the strange effects and straightened imperiously before the gawking sailors. Her slave, a pale human woman with bright red hair and vivid blue eyes, took one step and collapsed to the deck, convulsing uncontrollably.

'I am Yasmir, daughter of Lurhan the Vaulkhar of Hag Graef,' the druchii woman declared angrily, as though the band of armed corsairs facing her were more of an insult than a deadly threat. 'And I wish to see my brother at once.'

The leader of the corsairs stepped forward, riding the heaving deck with the ease of a veteran sailor. 'The captain has no interest in seeing you,' the man said with a harsh laugh. 'I've the watch while he is below so you'll be speaking to me, sea-witch, or I'll have the lads see you off with kisses of steel.'

Yasmir drew back, her face luminous with rage as she reached for the long knives at her belt. Malus stepped forward, drawing the plaque from his belt. 'I am Malus, son of Lurhan the Vaulkhar and I bear a writ of iron compelling your service in the name of the Drachau of Hag Graef! Put away your blades, or your lives are forfeit!'

The gruff-voiced sailor rounded on Malus. 'You're eight weeks' sail from the harbour of Clar Karond and the only law on this deck is the captain's.' Despite his bluster, the sailor's eyes were growing wider by the moment as he struggled to understand what was happening. Malus knew that the man could just as easily give in to his growing unease and order his men to attack if something didn't happen to change his mind.

That was when the air trembled with a hideous ripping sound, like a giant being torn in two, followed by a sharp thunderclap that sent nearly everyone on deck reeling. There was a bright flash of red light in the place where the shimmering crimson fog had hung, leaving Urial and six of his retainers standing in a tight circle on the pitching deck. If the former acolyte and his skull-faced men felt any distress at the effects of the spell, they gave no outward sign.

Several of the sailors fell to their knees, stunned by the blast of noise. Malus struggled to keep his expression neutral, even as his mind raged. *Six* men and every one a deadly warrior. Urial had lied to him!

Yet this was not the time for recriminations. Malus mastered his anger and moved quickly, taking advantage of the sailors' stunned reactions. He rushed to the side of the corsair officer, speaking in low, insistent tones. 'We've come a long way in an unpleasantly short amount of time on an important mission of state,' he said. 'If you deny the power of the writ in favour of the captain's law, then it is for the captain to decide what to do with us, not you.' Malus gestured sharply at the reeling corsairs. 'Send these sea ravens back to their roosts and call out your captain. Believe me when I say he'll speak with us once he realises who has come aboard.'

For a moment, no one spoke as the sailors picked themselves up off the deck and their officer struggled with the decisions laid before him. The only sounds were the cold wind whistling through the rigging and the groan of the masts under minimal sail in the face of the rough weather. The two moons broached like whales through the silver clouds scudding overhead, painting the ship in silver light.

The corsair shook himself out of his dreadful reverie and waved back his men with a curt gesture. He turned to Malus. 'The captain is not to be disturbed,' he said, a little shakily. 'He is below with his sea mistress.'

Yasmir's slave let out a strangled cry, then went silent. Malus turned to see his half-sister standing over the human, her boot across the slave's throat. The slave pawed weakly at her mistress's leg, her body writhing as she struggled for air. Yasmir's expression was beautiful and terrible to behold. '*What* did you say, seabird?' Her voice was cold as steel.

The officer's eyes widened further and his shoulders hunched, as though realising for the first time who it was he was addressing. 'Dragons Below take me,' he cursed softly to himself – or given whom he faced, perhaps it was a prayer. 'I… I meant to say he is below with the first officer, dread lady,' he said to Yasmir. 'Deep in their plans, belike, charting our course for the coming week.'

'Where?' Yasmir demanded. Small white fists pounded desperately at her lower leg. The slave's face was bright purple, her eyes bulging in their sockets.

'In… in the captain's cabin, dread lady,' the officer replied dully. 'But when he's in his cabin the crew is not to disturb him–'

'Except for his first mate, evidently,' Yasmir said venomously. 'Fortunately, we aren't part of Bruglir's crew, but his *beloved kin*.' Abruptly she took her foot from her slave's throat. The human rolled onto her side retching and gasping for air. Swift as an adder, Yasmir drew one of her long blades from its scabbard and took the slave by her hair. With a single, smooth stroke and the sound of a razor parting flesh the slave's forehead thumped back to the deck. Blood poured from the human's slashed throat in a swiftly spreading pool.

Yasmir straightened, bloody knife scattering red droplets across the lower half of her robes. 'Take me to my darling brother,' she said with a terrifying smile. 'Whatever the captain's plans, I assure you they are about to change.'

As the procession filed swiftly through the shadowy central passageway of Bruglir's ship, Malus had a moment to reflect that this made the second time in less than a day that he had barged into the bedchamber of a powerful and murderous druchii noble. It seemed an odd way to conduct affairs of state, but he had to admit it opened up interesting possibilities for the future.

While women marched to war alongside men they were expected to put down their weapons in time of peace and pursue other interests appropriate to their gender, like managing households or finding ways to murder their husband's enemies. Notable exceptions to this rule were the priestesses of the temple and sailors on the black-hulled druchii corsairs. The call of the sea was a sacred thing to most druchii. They regarded the black waters with equal measures of reverence and fear, for it was the raging ocean that drowned their ancestral home of Nagarythe, ages ago and thus it was the only link they had to the glories of their past. As the ocean claimed their birthright, the druchii claimed the ocean itself in return, riding its waves to gather the plunder and the glory that kept their people alive. Though the druchii called upon their women to give up their swords in times of hateful peace, they would never ask them to give up the sea.

It had never occurred to Malus that Bruglir would keep a sea mistress. Many captains did, Malus knew, but he'd always assumed that Bruglir was as devoted to Yasmir as she was to him. All at once his tangled web of deception took on a wholly different dimension and his mind raced as he considered the many possibilities.

The pirate officer led the way, moving with the reluctant step of a condemned man with Yasmir looming over him like a thundercloud. Malus followed close behind, with Urial bringing up the rear. He hadn't stopped staring at Yasmir since she'd taken her knife to her maddened slave and the expression on Urial's face was one of almost rapturous desire. The sight was both pathetic and deeply disturbing all at the same time.

There was no guard at the captain's door – for a man like Bruglir, it was a show of his own prowess that he needed no protection from daggers in the night. Eyeing the bloody knife still gripped in Yasmir's hand, Malus wondered if that policy might be changing in the very near future.

The druchii officer stopped at the door, bracing himself and preparing to knock, but Yasmir put a hand to the side of the sailor's head and pushed him aside with a startling show of strength. For a moment Malus thought she was going to put a boot to the thin panel door, but she turned the doorknob with fluid speed and stood in the doorway like one of Khaine's ecstatic brides, arms spread and bloody knife held high.

'Hello, beloved brother,' Yasmir said in a cool and sultry voice. 'Have you missed me?'

The captain's quarters lay in darkness, illuminated by squares of moonlight that waxed and waned with the whim of the clouds. Two figures clutched one another on the broad bed, their naked skin limned with lambent silver. At the sound of Yasmir's voice they leapt apart, one with a startled curse and the other with a yowl like a scalded Lustrian tiger. There was a rasp of steel and a woman stepped into the moonlight, naked as the blade in her hand. She was lean and hard as whipcord, her pale skin a dusky white from endless days at sea. Her body was made of hard muscle and scar tissue, a grizzled veteran's share of desperate battles and bloodletting. Bruglir's first mate had a striking, if severe face, marred by a long scar that ran from above her left temple down to her upper lip. The sword stroke had blinded her left eye and pulled her lip upwards in a permanent snarl. Her one good eye was black as jet and bright with fury.

'Begone, jhindara!' The corsair commanded, brandishing her sword. It was a short, heavy blade, broad and single-edged like a cleaver and nicked from hard use. 'Try to take him and I'll leave you squirming in your own guts!'

Yasmir's laugh was easy and light. 'Who is the witch and who the saviour, you scarred little churl?' She drew her second knife and seemed to float towards the corsair, her expression soulless and intent as a hunting hawk. 'Dance with me and we will see who the Lord of Murder favours more!'

'Stand fast!' roared a commanding voice that brought both women up short. A tall, powerfully-built figure leapt between the two. Bruglir had his father's height, standing half a head taller than Yasmir and had an unusually broad-shouldered frame that added to his imposing stature. The corsair lord very much resembled the Vaulkhar in his youth, with a chiselled brow and a hawk-like nose that lent him a ferocious presence even in repose. A long, black moustache hung down to his pointed chin, adding to his already fierce demeanour. 'She is mine, Yasmir, part of my crew by oath and by blood and you cannot have her.'

Yasmir regarded her beloved with dreadful intensity. 'She is yours, but are you not *mine*, beloved brother? Was that not the promise you made to me, the oath you renew again and again each time you return to the Hag?' Her voice rose in pitch and intensity, like a raging wind. 'And if this... this deformed wretch is yours, then by rights she is mine as well, to do with as I please. Is she not?' She leaned close to Bruglir, her lips nearly brushing his, her knives quivering in her hands. 'Answer me,' she whispered. '*Answer me.*'

The room was about to erupt into bloodshed. It was a particular kind of tension that Malus could almost taste, like the charged air that heralded a sudden storm. Thinking quickly, the highborn stepped into the room, brandishing the plaque. 'Actually, as of now all of you belong to *me*,' he loudly declared. 'And until I no longer have need of you, you will stay your hand or answer to the Drachau *and* our father upon our return to the Hag.'

Bruglir turned at the sound of Malus's voice, his natural scowl deepening as he saw first Malus, then his brother Urial. 'What's this? The Darkblade and the temple worm both fouling the deck of my ship? He glared at Yasmir. 'You brought them here?'

'No, brother,' Malus answered. 'More the other way around. I'd thought you would be pleased to see your beloved sister, but it appears

I stand corrected.' He eyed Yasmir carefully. 'A druchii woman may take as many lovers as she pleases, but when a druchii man commits himself, he is expected to remain faithful as a measure of his strength. Honestly, brother, I expected better of you.'

Bruglir's expression turned incredulous, then pale with anger. 'I don't know how you managed this, Darkblade, but–'

Malus stepped forward and held the plaque under Bruglir's nose. 'You haven't been paying attention, brother. Listen carefully. I bear a writ of iron from the Drachau of Hag Graef, placing you and your fleet under my command for a campaign against the Skinriders. I act with the Drachau's will in this and any man who bars my path will answer for it with his life.'

'The only law at sea is the captain's law,' the first officer spat, her eyes still boring into Yasmir's.

'But if the captain ever wishes to set foot in his home again – and still claim the mighty fortune he's amassed there over the years – he'll see the wisdom in making his law *my* law as well.'

Bruglir snatched the plaque from Malus's hand, flipping open the cover as though he expected to find nothing there. His brow furrowed as he read the writing on the parchment inside and examined the seals thereon.

'There are ten of us, all told,' Malus continued. 'I'll require a cabin for myself and I assume Urial will require one as well. Sister?'

Yasmir still glared murderously at the first mate. She bit out her reply as though snipping veins between her teeth. 'I'll take her cabin,' she said. 'It's clear that she isn't using it.'

'Do you take us for fools?' the first officer snapped. 'You didn't come by boat, but by sorcery. So there's no one back home to know what actually happened to you. We can toss your innards to the sea dragons and sail for home–'

'Tani, *enough*,' Bruglir ordered wearily. The first officer glared hotly at her captain, but fell silent. 'Get dressed and go topside.'

Tani nodded curtly. 'Your will, sir.' She snatched a salt-stained sea robe from the deck by the bed and shrugged into it, never taking her eye off Yasmir and switching her heavy cleaver from hand to hand as she dressed. For a moment it seemed as though another confrontation loomed as Yasmir blocked the first officer's path to the door, but at the last moment the knife-wielding druchii stepped aside.

Bruglir followed her to the door, then closed it in Urial's face. He turned to Yasmir, holding up the plaque. 'Is this some kind of forgery?'

Radiant and hateful, Yasmir shook her head.

'Then it appears my worst nightmare has come true,' the captain said sourly, throwing the plaque onto the disordered bed. He turned to Malus. 'For the moment, you have me,' he said, his voice devoid of any emotion, though his eyes were pools of malevolence. 'But this remit has its limits. Sooner or later, the Drachau will rescind it and then I will destroy you.'

Malus managed a smile. 'I might have feared you more had we not also met your sea mistress,' he replied. 'If I were you, I'd be more worried about your own odds of survival once the writ runs its course.'

Bruglir looked to Yasmir and found himself staring into eyes as flat and cold as the blades in her hands. 'Damn you, Darkblade,' he hissed. 'If I do nothing else, I swear before the Dragons Below that I will ruin you. But until then,' he snarled, 'I and my fleet are at your command.'

THE WRIT OF iron evidently carried little weight with Urial's skull-faced retainers; they formed a wall of flesh and steel between Malus and their lord as he approached Urial by the port rail. His head hung low and he managed another aching dry heave as his stomach continued to rebel against the motion of ship and sea.

Malus threw back his head and laughed, savouring his half-brother's suffering. 'Now this is rich irony,' he said aloud. 'A gift from the Dark Mother herself.'

Urial turned until his back was to the rail. Dried vomit dotted his cheeks and chin and a thin stream of bile hung from his slack lips and twisted stubbornly in the cold wind. 'Hateful thing,' he grunted, sliding to the deck. 'I've slain men for less.'

Malus grinned cruelly. 'Would you care to see my hot blood roll across this pitching deck?'

'By the Bloody-Handed God, *shut up*!' Urial groaned, his eyes rolling in their sockets like a pair of thrown dice. The highborn pushed past the retainers and leaned against the rail, drinking deep of the salt air. It surprised him how much he'd missed the sea once he'd returned to the Hag. 'You know, in the old times, a druchii who couldn't get his sea legs was believed to be bad luck and thrown overboard to the Dragons Below.'

'If the sea is steady down in the depths, then throw me in,' Urial moaned. 'They can have me and may they choke on my bones.'

Malus looked out into the darkness. Before his recent slaving cruise he would have been utterly blind, staring out into the inky night, but his experienced eye could discern subtle shades among the blackness, revealing a long coastline of craggy cliffs less than ten miles off the beam. The wind was blowing westerly off the port bow as Bruglir's flagship tacked northward, her sleek hull slicing through the sullen waves.

'You lied to me,' the highborn said, his voice level.

'I did not.'

'You said more than one retainer each would be too risky.'

Urial nodded. 'Indeed – because I planned on bringing six men of my own. You didn't expect me to trust your word that Bruglir and Yasmir would honour the writ, did you?'

Malus shrugged, concealing his anger. 'No, I suppose not.'

'What did our illustrious brother have to say?'

'His fleet is scattered along the coast, looking for the last pickings before heading home,' the highborn said. 'We'll be turning soon, riding south before the wind as he seeks them out. He thinks it will be three or four days before he's got them all together and we can make our way north.'

With a heartfelt groan Urial gripped the rail with his good hand and pulled himself upright. 'What coast is that, yonder?'

Malus gave Urial a sidelong look. 'That's Bretonnia. We're close to Lyonnesse, I think.'

'Ah,' Urial nodded, sounding relieved. 'That's good.'

'Why?'

'Because I feared it might be Ulthuan, in which case I would be greatly disappointed,' Urial answered. 'I hope to see the home of our kin some day. I expect it's grand and mountainous, rising from the sea like a crown.' He grinned in the darkness. 'I dream of going there and watching those white cities burn.' Suddenly he turned to Malus. 'There's something I've been meaning to ask you.'

'You may ask,' Malus said, his voice promising nothing.

'Back at the Hag, you told the Drachau you'd found the Isle of Morhaut,' Urial said. 'How? The location's been lost for at least two hundred years. Even the temple's vast library holds no mention of it.'

'Oh. That.' Malus looked at Urial and grinned. 'That was all a lie. I haven't the slightest idea where the forsaken island is.'

Chapter Thirteen
PROMISES OF DEATH

'YOU LIED TO the Drachau,' Yasmir said, her voice chillingly pleasant. 'By all rights, that writ of iron you hold isn't worth the metal holding it together.'

Malus folded his arms and frowned at his half sister, trying to adjust his back into a more comfortable position without giving her the impression he was squirming. With Yasmir in the first officer's cabin there were precious few berthing spaces left for the unexpected arrivals short of sleeping with the regular crew. Urial was one deck below with the ship's chirurgeon, consigned to share a dank, lightless cell packed with jars of unguents, salves and animal parts. After some negotiation, Malus had managed to secure the ship's chart room for himself; it was a musty alcove that smelled of rot and old paper, crammed with boxes of rolled-up maps and one long chart table that ran the length of the outside bulkhead. The table was currently acting as his bed, supporting a thin bedroll of straw ticking and a pillow made from a spare cloak. Malus attempted to recline on his makeshift divan, back propped against his poor excuse for a pillow and craning his head a little awkwardly due to the curvature of the bulkhead behind him.

'I was right there when you stood in Bruglir's cabin and told him that our first task was to uncover the location of the lost island,' Yasmir continued. Only her pointed chin and her sensual smile could be seen beneath a black half-veil of Tilean lace that concealed the rest of her features. Malus couldn't imagine what had possessed her to bring such a thing on the voyage, but now she wore it whenever she left her cabin. It was the sort of thing a wife wore while keeping a death vigil over her husband – yet no matter what she was doing, Yasmir's lips were always smiling, as though she were tickled by some secret amusement. It had only been a day since their arrival on Bruglir's ship, but Malus was starting to wonder if perhaps the recent upheavals she'd suffered had pushed his radiant, pampered sister close to the edge of madness.

'You led the Drachau to believe you already knew where the Isle of Morhaut was – if Bruglir had spent more time reading what the writ actually said rather than checking its authenticity, he would have found you out and you would be hanging by your neck from the mast right now.'

'Fortunately he was somewhat distracted,' Malus answered calmly, his expression implacable. 'I hadn't realised you were so punctilious on matters of legality, dear sister.'

'Only where my freedom is concerned. You used that writ to try and make a slave of me! You have no idea how abhorrent such a thing feels!'

'Indeed, sister. You're quite right. I never stopped to imagine what it might be like,' Malus replied coldly. He spread his hands. 'Very well. You're free. What will you do now? Spread the news to your beloved?'

Yasmir laughed, a bubbling sound of artless joy that set Malus's teeth on edge. 'By the Mother, of course not! Let him toil in chains for as long as you'll have him.' She bent over him, her face inches from his. Malus could smell her sweetened breath and almost feel the silken brush of her lips and it disturbed him how much his body seemed drawn to hers, like iron to a lodestone. She whispered, 'There is a price for my silence, Malus. Will you pay it?'

'You know I will,' he said, squirming against the bulkhead now for entirely different reasons. Damned confined spaces! He should have guessed she'd been up to something when she'd barged into the chart-room unannounced. Now she was using every method at her disposal to keep him off-balance and he couldn't do a single thing about it.

'I want that scarred sea whore dead,' she said, the words spilling like pure venom from her smiling lips. 'I don't care how, but she must die and the sooner the better.' Malus attempted a laugh. 'I've already promised you Urial's head, sister! Is there no end to your greed?' But the false mirth died beneath Yasmir's implacable will.

'It is the price of your continued survival, brother,' Yasmir whispered. 'For now, you and I are partners, because I have an interest in seeing Bruglir suffer. He must atone for what he has done to me and the humiliation he endures from serving you is sweet. So I have no problem letting this campaign of yours continue. I'll even support it so long

as it suits my needs. But the woman must die. Only then can I make
Bruglir devote himself entirely to me. Do you understand?'

'If you want her dead why not kill her yourself?'

For just a moment Yasmir's zealous smile faltered. 'Don't be a fool,
Malus,' she hissed. '*Of course* I can kill her, but that would gain me
nothing. If she dies by my hand then Bruglir becomes my enemy and
makes my plan that much harder.'

'So you would rather I make an enemy of him instead?'

'Of course, if that's what it takes,' Yasmir replied. 'But you are the
leader of this expedition. I'm certain you can find some crafty means
of sending the vile woman to her death that still keeps your own hands
clean. Think on it, brother. Think carefully. The sooner the better, or I
may lose my patience and tell Bruglir the truth.' Her dazzling smile
glowed beneath the blackness of the veil. 'It's possible that he might be
so grateful at escaping the writ that he'd kill the whore just to please
me, but I don't want to take that chance unless I feel I must.' With that
she turned on her heel and opened the door into the shadowy passageway, slipping gracefully from sight.

Before Malus could slide his feet off the table Hauclir ducked into
the cramped room, gnawing on a chunk of bread and holding a
wooden platter of cheese, sausage and apple slices in his hand. He held
the food out to Malus. 'It appears our timing was good; they raided a
human village not two days ago and were able to refill their stores.
Before that they were down to eating rats while dodging Bretonnian
coastal patrols. Your brother is a madman for staying out as long as he
does.' The guardsman pointed at the cheese, a small half-round the size
of his palm. 'I think that's from a goat. You should try it.'

Malus took the proffered plate with a glare for his retainer. He
pressed his fingertips to the platter and studied the number of cheese
crumbs they picked up. 'Hauclir,' he said sourly, 'while it is your duty
to test my food for poison, you don't have to eat half the cheese to do
it.'

Hauclir paused in mid-chew. 'Test for poison, my lord?'

BRUGLIR'S FLAGSHIP WAS a long, ebon sea-blade named *Harrier*, built by
the shipwrights in Clar Karond and wrought with the best craft and
sorcery that the captain's ample fortune could buy. With three stepped
masts and a long, narrow hull she could fly along the water with all her
sails set and her crew knew the dance of wind and wave as well as they
knew the lands of their birth. For some, the sea was the only homeland
they'd ever known and all that they ever longed for when tied up in
port.

But the qualities that made *Harrier* sleek and swift also made her difficult to handle in heavy weather; her tall masts and narrow beam

made her prone to rolling dangerously in rough seas, which was what the nimble corsair faced now. Winter still stubbornly refused to yield to spring along the Bretonnian coast and a sharp wind still blew westerly from the open sea before a wall of heavy grey clouds. The ocean was the colour of unpolished steel, surging and crashing against the hull of the raider as she worked her way southwards into the areas where the remaining ships of the fleet were hunting for prey. For the last three days Bruglir had collected his scattered ships, using prearranged rendezvous points and surreptitious signals made in the dead of night. Eight other raiders now trailed along in the *Harrier's* wake, their captains growing more nervous by the hour as a fleet of black ships was bound to attract the attention of watchers along the coast.

Muffled shouts and pounding feet had brought Malus topside with Hauclir in tow. There was a subtle change in the atmosphere, an undercurrent of tension that he recognised from his raiding cruise the previous year and had learned to pay attention to. Something was happening and the crew was on edge.

A cold, salty wind slapped at the highborn's face as he emerged on deck, prompting him to reach back for the woollen hood hanging at his shoulders. He'd changed into his armour and wore a cloak of raw wool to keep the water from the expensive steel. The *Harrier* rolled drunkenly as it staggered against another hissing wave and the sailors up in the rigging relayed instructions to one another from the woman standing at the ship's wheel below. Malus caught sight of Tanithra, the first officer, casting a weather eye on the storm front standing out to the west as she led the ship a merry dance along the sullen sea. Off to port, between *Harrier* and the coast, Malus saw two new corsairs, their raked prows pointing north as they tacked against the wind.

Hauclir staggered as the ship reeled in the opposite direction as the wave surged past. The former captain had yet to find his sea legs, though his stomach had apparently adjusted easily enough. 'Looks like two of our scattered sea birds came and found us for a change,' he shouted over the waves and the rushing wind.

'So it would appear,' Malus answered, scanning the deck. Other than the day watch, the rest of the crew were below, knowing that they would have to suffer their turn in the freezing wind and spray soon enough. 'The question is why.'

The highborn turned and headed aft, towards the citadel. From the citadel the captain would command the ship in battle, able to look down on the main deck and across to the raised deck of the redoubt at the bow of the ship. The ship's wheel stood upon the citadel, just forward of a pair of powerful bolt throwers that could fire massive steel-headed bolts at enemy ships approaching the *Harrier* from the aft quarter or stern. Two short stairways led up from the main deck, one to port and one to starboard. On impulse, Malus crossed to the starboard stair. As he did, another wave surged against the hull and the corsair heeled over like a bottle bobbing in the surf. Hauclir staggered with a sharp curse, inadvertently bumping into Malus and sending him reeling towards the side of the staircase.

The highborn flung out a hand to steady himself and suddenly a powerful wave of vertigo seized him. His vision swam and a cacophony of sound waxed and waned in his ears – discordant, clashing noises and cries of anger and pain. Wetness, warm and thick, soaked across his palm. Malus reeled, holding up his hand to see a stain of deep red in his wavering sight. *Here is where I died*, a thought echoed crazily in his mind.

Then strong hands seized him by the shoulders and held him fast. Malus shook his head fiercely and the world seemed to snap back onto its moorings once more. He looked over his shoulder to see Hauclir bracing him with both hands.

'My apologies, my lord,' Hauclir said, somewhat sheepishly. 'How does anyone get used to this incessant tumbling?'

Malus shook himself free of Hauclir's grip. 'Perhaps I should have you walk the deck all night tonight until you learn.'

'Will that be before or after you've ripped out my fingernails and gouged out my eyes with a fish bone?'

'Eh?'

'So far you've promised to rip out my nails for being late with breakfast and then said you'd gouge out my eyes for airing out your good cloak and getting it soaked with salt water.'

Malus frowned. 'All that since we came aboard?'

'All that since this morning. Yesterday, you said–'

'Never mind,' the highborn muttered, grinding his teeth. 'When we get back home I'll have you fed to the cold ones and we'll leave it at that.'

Hauclir nodded, his face impassive. 'Very well, my lord. I'll make a note of it.'

'Are you *mocking* me now, you impertinent wretch?'

'Just trying to help you keep track of things, my lord. I'm here to be of service.'

'Indeed? Feel free to begin at any time.'

Malus worked his way around to the bottom of the staircase and made for the citadel deck, his retainer trailing obediently in his wake. 'Your pardon, my lord,' he said stiffly. 'I know I'm no good with clothes and meals and such. Perhaps if you gave me some task that suited my skills?'

'Extortion, you mean? I can manage that myself,' Malus growled. 'Though I confess you show a particular kind of artistry in that sort of thing.'

'Ambition is a virtue, my lord,' Hauclir said archly. 'As to my professional skills, I'm swift with a knife or a cudgel, I know how to deal with inconvenient bodies and I've got a good sense of what's going on behind a person's eyes, if you take my meaning.'

'Were you a guard in the Drachau's service, or a thug?' Malus asked, climbing the stair.

'Is there a difference, my lord?'

'No, I suppose not. All right, then. What do you make of our current situation?'

'Thrown to the cold ones my lord, with a steak round our necks.'

The image brought a sharp bark of laughter from the highborn. 'That good, eh?'

Hauclir shrugged. 'The crew is wagering which of your siblings will slip you the knife first. Every one of them – even that flat-eyed cripple Urial – all study you like a strange kind of insect. Right now they're more interested in what you are and what you're about, but sooner or later you can see in their eyes that they're going to crush you and move on.'

'None of this comes as much of a surprise,' Malus said. 'So you're well acquainted with the crew now, are you?'

Hauclir shrugged. 'They're a clannish lot, like most sea ravens, but they gamble and drink and complain like guardsmen, so I've had a chance to chew the fat with a few of them.'

Malus paused at the top of the stairs, tapping his chin thoughtfully. 'All right then, here's a task for you. I want you to find out how the loyalties of these sea birds lie. How well-loved are Bruglir and his first officer? If the illustrious captain were to die, who would they follow?'

The retainer considered the command, then nodded. 'Easy enough to do, my lord.' He eyed his master and chuckled. 'You've promised each one of your siblings the other's head, it appears. Have you decided which one you're going to kill?'

Malus looked back at Hauclir, his smile cold and his black eyes glittering. 'I'm going to see them all dead or broken in the end, Hauclir. Who lives or dies by the end of this cruise depends on who remains useful to me for the future. Including you.'

Hauclir straightened, his eyes widening at the highborn's menacing tone, then collected himself. 'As you command, my lord,' he said stiffly, then turned and headed below.

The citadel deck was more than sixty paces long and twenty in width and with only the day watch topside it was sparsely manned. Four lookouts, two to a side, stood at the ship's rails, scanning the grey horizon and the rocky cliffs of Bretonnia with long spyglasses. A tall sailor with a heavy boarding pike stood guard at the head of each of the stair rails and the first officer performed a solitary dance with rudder and

sail, her fingers light on the polished teak wheel. A junior officer paced
the perimeter of the entire deck, keeping an eye on every member of
the crew and seeing that each one kept to his task with eagle eyes. The
guard at the top of the starboard rail, a scarred veteran of many cruises,
eyed Malus with the wary belligerence of an old watchdog but stepped
aside to let the highborn pass.

Malus paced slowly across the deck, sidling close to the first officer.
The corsair's scarred face was intent, her good eye distant as she gauged
forces described by the trembling of the hull and the warp of the sails
overhead. Yet he could sense that she was also aware of him, keeping
close track of his movements with the same intensity as she measured
wind, tide and the positions of the ships around the *Harrier*.

The highborn walked to within an arm's length of the wheel and
stood to one side of the first officer, staying upwind so his words would
carry easily to her. 'What news? I didn't think we were due to meet any
more of our companions until well after dark.'

'There's a Bretonnian coastal squadron hunting south of us,' the first
officer rasped, her rough voice carrying easily over the wind and waves.
'Drove *Bloodied Knife* and *Sea Witch* off their patrol and pushed them
towards us. Their captains came aboard a short while ago and are talking in Bruglir's cabin.'

Malus frowned, looking out at the churning, slate-coloured waves.
They came across in this? 'Is there a problem?'

She shrugged. 'It could be part of a snare, working with another
squadron further north to drive us together and bottle us up against
the coast.' The first officer spared a moment's vigilance to throw Malus
a vicious glare. 'I don't doubt every coast watcher from Lyonesse to
Broadhead is calling for the coastal guard, watching us lumber along
together like this. Probably think we're an invasion fleet.'

'Can the Bretonnians catch us?'

Again, the corsair shrugged, scrutinising the storm front bulking
along the western horizon. 'The Bretonnians can read the weather as
well as we,' she said, 'and their fat old scows can handle these seas a little better than we can. It's possible, if their captains are hungry enough
and bold enough.'

'They can't be bolder than Bruglir and his captains,' Malus said confidently. He eyed the first officer appraisingly. 'Tanithra Bael,' he said
slowly, using the officer's full name. 'You're an officer of no small
repute yourself. I heard your name spoken more than once when I was
rounding up my own crew at Clar Karond last year. Yet you're serving
as second to Bruglir. I would have thought you'd be captaining your
own ship.'

Bael's expression didn't change, but Malus saw her spine stiffen
slightly. 'All things in their time,' she growled. 'Women can sail with the

corsairs, but female captains are still rare. If I struck out on my own I'd have a hard time raising a crew, even with my reputation. Bruglir has promised me the next ship that comes available and we'll handpick the crew from all over the fleet.' She smiled then, imagining a vessel that sailed every night in her deepest dreams. 'Then the great captain and I will turn the seas red!'

The highborn nodded thoughtfully. 'But you've been serving as his lieutenant for more than seven years. That's a long time to wait for a ship, isn't it?'

Tanithra's smile faded. 'Fine ships take time to build,' she replied. '*Harrier* here sat in her cradle for almost ten years while the shipwrights laid on their sorceries. My time will come.'

'Of course, of course,' Malus agreed. 'But now there is the matter of his sister–'

'What of her?' Tanithra said hotly, this time turning to face him with both hands still clutching the wheel. 'He dallies with her a few weeks each year while I stay with the ship for her fitting-out. It makes no difference to me what he does on dry land. At sea, he's mine. If Yasmir had tried to drive me from his bed instead of taking my quarters, you would have seen then where Bruglir's real affections lie.'

Malus nodded. In truth, he'd been a little surprised that Yasmir hadn't tried to press that very point. Perhaps she'd sensed the truth as well and refused to acknowledge it? Something to consider, he thought. 'Still,' he continued, 'now *she* knows of *you*. You can't expect a proud and pampered highborn like her to let such an insult go unanswered. And she has the ear of many powerful nobles back at the Hag. She could make Bruglir's ambitions to succeed his father very difficult indeed.'

Tanithra glanced at him warily, her expression troubled. 'Perhaps,' she said, then gave a shrug. 'But that's years in the future. By then I'll have my ship and the rest will see to itself.'

The highborn nodded, though inwardly he smiled cunningly. 'I'm certain you're right,' he said. 'So long as Yasmir does nothing to poison Bruglir's mind against you, or find a way to murder you, or affect changes at home that force her beloved to give up the sea between now and then your position is perfectly safe.'

The first officer nodded, then Malus watched her expression darken as the full weight of his words made themselves felt. She turned back to the wheel, her face intent. Malus allowed himself a brief, outward smile, watching his seed take root.

Just then came a faint cry from the bow, the words tattered by the rushing wind. Tanithra became alert at once, her worries forgotten. After a moment a sailor at mid-deck repeated the cry, relaying the message to the stern.

Malus leaned forward, trying to catch the words. 'What's he talking about?'

'Maiden's favours,' Tanithra snapped, muttering a sharp curse. 'Square sheets – Bretonnian sails sighted ahead.' She sought out the junior officer of the deck and called out to him in a clear, piercing voice. 'Sound the call to battle! Topmen aloft and stand ready to unfurl sail!'

The junior officer stopped in mid-stride at the sound of Tanithra's voice and without hesitation put a silver horn to his lips and winded a skirling, moaning note that shivered along Malus's bones. Almost immediately the deck beneath his feet shivered as the crew of the corsair leapt to action, bounding for their positions on or below deck. Within moments Malus heard eerie echoes of the horn's cry riding the wind – the other ships of the fleet had heard the *Harrier's* war-horn or had seen the danger for themselves and were readying themselves for action.

Dark-robed figures boiled from the hatches like angry birds, some heading aloft on frost-rimed rigging while others stood ready with spear and shield or pulled oilskin covers off the menacing bolt throwers fore and aft. Tanithra glanced over at Malus, her one eye cold and hard like a stormcrow's.

'Here's where we see what those Bretonnians are made of,' she said, showing a wolf's hungry smile.

Chapter Fourteen
KNIVES IN THE DARK

'HERE COMES ANOTHER one!' one of the druchii lookouts yelled, pointing aft at one of the Bretonnian ships. Few of the veteran sailors on the citadel deck even turned their heads, but Malus couldn't help but watch in horrified fascination as a black dot arced skyward from the bow of the lead human ship and seemed to climb lazily into the air.

The dot was a sphere of polished granite, lobbed from a siege cata-pult mounted in the Bretonnian warship's bow – they were so large that only one could fit per ship, or so the corsairs claimed and domi-nated the bows of the broad-bellied coastal ships. They were a recent innovation of the coastal guard and if the corsairs had little regard for the Bretonnians' seamanship, they had a grudging respect for their marksmanship. The aft lookouts marked the flight of the stone with dreadful intent and as Malus watched, the dot seemed to freeze its motion for a single heartbeat, then swell with terrifying speed. It seemed to be aimed right for him, a ball of stone the size of his chest and heavy as three men and Malus found his mouth go dry. Then at the last moment he saw that the shot would fall short and the stone whizzed into the ship's wake less than ten paces from the hull, striking the water with a sharp *slap* and a high, narrow plume of white.

'That's the closest one yet,' Hauclir said, standing just behind Malus's left shoulder. He'd raced topside with the sound of the horn, fully

armoured in the space of five minutes and ready to fight. The guard at
the top of the citadel stair had tried to block the former captain's way,
but Hauclir had frozen the man in his place with an officer's baleful
stare and joined his lord for the long sea chase that had transpired over
the course of the afternoon.

Bruglir had reached the citadel within minutes of hearing the horn,
dismissing his visiting captains to their ships and sizing up the lookout's
reports. As soon as the captains had pulled away in their long boats he'd
ordered flags set to turn the fleet northward, away from the approaching
human squadron. The Bretonnians looked to number no more than five
ships – twin-masted vessels with square sails of sapphire or crimson,
arrayed in an echelon trailing off to port – but it appeared Bruglir had
no intention of offering battle and risking damage to his fleet, not with
the closest friendly port hundreds of leagues west and no chance of
heading there any time soon. The corsair captain hoped to stay ahead of
the Bretonnians until nightfall, when the black ships could easily shake
their pursuers in the darkness. Unfortunately, tacking against a strong
wind and fighting a heavy sea, the druchii ships could make little headway. The waves slapped at the flat of the blade-like corsair hulls and
slowed their advance, while the broad-bellied coastal guard ships wad-
dled like fat old ducks over the swells and pressed doggedly ahead,
closing the distance slowly but steadily. Malus looked to the cloudy sky.
It was little more than two hours until nightfall. With their course
reversed, *Harrier* and her sister ships *Sea Witch* and *Bloodied Knife* were
strung out at the rear of the corsair fleet, closest to the approaching Bretonnian ships. The highborn tried to gauge the rate of the human ships'
advance against the passage of hours and found he couldn't be certain
who was going to win the race.

'They are hoping to hit one of our masts or our rudder,' Bruglir said,
glancing back to eye the Bretonnian ships' progress. The captain stood
close by the wheel while a junior officer tended the helm. Tanithra had
gone forward to the fortress deck, her appointed station during battle.
'The Bretonnians have the range – now it's just a matter of gaining a
few more yards and letting fate take its course.'

Malus frowned. 'And if they don't hit us in our vitals – can we keep
our distance until nightfall?'

The captain frowned, his long moustache nearly touching his enamelled breastplate. 'No. Not likely.' With a pained look Bruglir turned to
Urial, who stood close by his men, axe in hand. 'Have you some sorcery that could lend us speed?'

Urial regarded the captain inscrutably. 'No,' he said. 'The ways of the
Lord of Murder do not lend themselves to flight.'

'Of course not,' Bruglir said with a derisive snort. 'Dark Mother forbid the temple contribute anything but mayhem,' he grumbled.

Not even Malus could keep a look of surprise from his face at the naked scorn in Bruglir's voice. *I fear your years at sea may have kept you out of the petty feuds at home, but it's poorly prepared you for political realities at the Hag, Malus thought. You'll be a short-lived Vaulkhar indeed if you alienate the Temple of Khaine.* 'Why don't we shoot back?' he said, pointing to the bolt throwers standing ready at the stern.

Bruglir shook his head. 'The winds are too high and a bolt wouldn't do much to slow those big sea-cows anyway,' he said.

'Have you no dragon's fire aboard?'

The captain scowled at him. 'We've a few, yes, but I'll not fire them off unless I must. Each shot is like firing a bag of gold into the sea and I have a feeling we'll need them much more where we're going,' he said darkly. 'No, there's another option open to us.' He pointed to the storm front to the west, now much closer as the fleet had been tacking slowly but steadily away from the coast. 'We head into the squall line and lose them in the storm.'

'Won't that be dangerous?'

Bruglir shrugged. 'Some. As dangerous to them as to us, certainly and they won't be able to see more than a dozen yards in any direction. The fleet will be scattered, but that's not much of a concern. So long as we don't bump into someone in the storm, we should escape with no trouble.'

Malus didn't want to think about the consequences of a collision in the middle of a raging winter storm. 'When will you decide to head into the storm?'

One of the lookouts cried out, then a flat, droning sound filled the air a split-second before a dark stone struck the *Harrier's* stern. Sailors dived for cover as the round stone shattered a section of the stern rail just to the left of the portside bolt thrower and ploughed through one of its crew. The hapless sailor literally flew apart in a welter of blood and viscera and the stone rebounded from the deck's teak planking, racing in a black streak across the citadel and striking the sentry at the top of the starboard stair. Malus watched as the stone shattered the man's steel armour and flung his dead body into the air, carrying him over the side and into the embrace of the sea.

Malus straightened, only then realising he'd crouched to the deck instinctively from the first impact. 'Clear the deck!' Bruglir roared, even as unhurt sailors leapt to drag their wounded fellows below decks to the chirurgeon and the bolt thrower's crew tossed the pieces of their mate into the sea with a hurried prayer to the Dragons Below. The captain turned to his signal man. 'Flags aloft,' he ordered. 'Signal the fleet to turn three points west by north. If scattered, rendezvous at the Pearl Sack.' The officer repeated the message and headed to the rail, readying his flags of red and black.

'Come about three points to port,' Bruglir ordered, his voice carrying easily to mid-deck and the topmen aloft in the shrouds. 'Loose the top-gallants and the stays! We'll see how stiff their spines are with ice rattling along their decks!'

Malus watched as the corsairs put on more sail and the ship responded, surging like a game horse into the heaving waves. Ahead, the other ships of the fleet were beginning their own course changes. A motion out of the corner of his eye caught his attention – Urial was beckoning to him with a nod of his head.

'Stay here,' Malus told Hauclir, then crossed the tilting deck as the corsair came about. Urial, he noticed, appeared to have finally found his sea legs, leaning unconsciously with the change in attitude of the wooden deck.

'What's happening?' Urial asked as Malus drew near. There was a subtle tension in the former acolyte's pale face. Was he anticipating battle, Malus thought, or something else?

'We're turning into that storm yonder,' Malus said. 'Bruglir hopes to evade the Bretonnians in the squall.'

Urial frowned. 'The famous sea captain won't offer battle?'

'He's taking the long view,' the highborn replied. 'There will be major battles aplenty where we're headed and he must conserve his force. I would do the same in his position.'

'But if the Bretonnians find us in the storm?'

'Then it will be a fight indeed,' Malus said. 'Close and brutal. Men are apt to die.'

Urial's eyes shone at the prospect. 'Indeed,' he said eagerly. 'Even a great sea captain could find a knife in his side from an unknown quarter, if an attacker were bold enough.'

Malus's eyes widened. He leaned close, his voice dropping to a harsh whisper. 'I haven't forgotten my promise, brother,' he said. 'But now is no time for assassins' knives. We need Bruglir to command his fleet. If he dies, the captains will look to their own, either fighting to control the fleet or turning for home. I can't have that. Not yet.'

Urial's face twisted into a grimace. 'So long as you remember your vow, Malus,' he hissed, 'you have my support. But my patience has its limits.'

'Of course, brother,' Malus said tightly, trying to conceal his irritation. 'Tell me, have you seen our sister since the horn was sounded?'

'No. She remains below, I think,' Urial said. 'I'm a trifle disappointed. I'd hoped that the prospect of battle would draw her from her cabin.'

Or she could be down on the mid-deck, stalking among the crew and waiting for a chance to get close to Tanithra, Malus thought. He wasn't sure how Bruglir would react if his first officer wound up dead with a knife in her back. Would he retaliate against Yasmir? There was no way to tell. For a moment Malus contemplated sending Hauclir forward to keep an eye on Tanithra, but he dismissed the notion almost as quickly. What could the retainer do? Come between the first officer and a murderous highborn lady? What would that achieve besides his death?

The wind picked up across the deck, buffeting Malus's hood and blowing a spray of fine ice crystals into his face. The sky was darkening as the *Harrier* crossed the squall line, plunging into the winter storm. Soon it would be hard to see more than a few feet in any direction and danger could fall upon them with little warning, striking from almost any quarter.

Even within, Malus thought, his eyes scanning the crew. An old proverb came to mind as the storm swept over them.

When darkness falls, the knives come out.

THE STORM LASHED at them like a tremendous serpent, battering hull, mast and sail with invisible coils of blustering, icy wind and hissing across the deck and rigging in a spray of ice and freezing rain. The teak planks and thick, hempen ropes were coated with a thin film of ice in moments, making every step treacherous and potentially fatal as the *Harrier* pitched and rolled in the fury of the storm.

It had been nearly an hour and a half since the ships disappeared into the grey haze. The deck crew crowded along the railings, peering into the formless gloom in search of dark shapes that could prove to be another ship. There were no friendly vessels in a storm like this; a collision with another corsair would be just as deadly as one with a Bretonnian and equally sudden.

Malus shivered beneath the heavy weight of his cloak. Despite layers of protection the icy wind found its way to his bare skin, soaking him to the bone in moments. Ice rimed the edge of his hood and crackled across his shoulders. He stood clutching the starboard rail not far from Urial, peering into the haze like everyone else. The highborn could tell the difference between sea and sky only in subtle gradations of grey. Everyone was tense, many fingering the hilts of their swords and dreading the sight of a dark shape looming from the haze in front of them.

Gritting his teeth, Malus turned away from the grey murk and cast his eyes over the crew instead. Bruglir still stood by the helm, ramrod straight in the face of the wind. White ice crusted the front of his cloak and the toes of his boots, but for all that he seemed unfazed by the howling fury of the wind. The helmsman beside him clutched the wheel in a death grip, trying to emulate the example of the captain. Urial stood with his retainers just a few feet further down the starboard rail, partially shielded from the icy wind by the tall robed figures of his warriors.

Hauclir stood at Malus's shoulder as ever, one hand steadying himself on the rail. The former guardsman had his hood back and stared bare-headed and slit-eyed into the storm. Malus leaned towards him. 'Do you want to lose your nose and ears to frostbite, you fool?'

The retainer shook his head. 'I've had frostbite more times than I can count, my lord. A bit of my mother's blackroot poultice and the skin's as good as new. No, I can't stand not being able to see all the way around me in a situation like this.' He hunched his shoulders. 'The hair on my neck is standing straight up, like there's someone out there pointing a crossbow at me. How long are we going to stay in this?'

Malus shrugged. 'Until the captain is satisfied we've slipped past the enemy. It will be dark soon, so I expect he'll try to head out to calmer waters then.' Though I have no idea how he'll manage it, the highborn thought. 'We're through the worst of it,' he continued, trying to reassure himself more than Hauclir. 'Every moment likely carries us further away from the Bretonnians–'

Just then a splintering crash echoed distantly over the howling wind to starboard, turning into a long, grinding crunch of breaking wood. 'A collision!' one of the sailors shouted, pointing uselessly off into the haze. 'Something's hit the *Bloodied Knife*!'

'Or two fat Bretonnian scows kissed hulls in the mist,' another sailor offered weakly.

'Silence on the rail!' Bruglir hissed like a rasping blade. The men fell silent. Malus looked back at his older brother – and saw the great, dark shape coalescing out of the murk on the opposite side of the ship, bearing down like a thunderbolt on the unsuspecting corsair.

Every man on the port rail seemed to cry out at once and Bruglir leapt into action without thought. 'Hard to starboard!' he roared at the helmsman, adding his own hands to the wheel and spinning it for all it was worth. The ship began to heel over, but slowly, too slowly. Malus watched men flock from the port rail like a flight of black birds startled from a bough. 'Hang on!' he bellowed, reaching for the rail and then the *Harrier* bucked like a bitten mare as the Bretonnian ship crashed alongside.

Wood splintered and snapped in a long, rending groan as the two ships met and the deck of the *Harrier* pitched further and further towards the heaving sea as the heavier human ship pushed her over. Black-clad sailors clung desperately to the icy rigging as the spars of the ship's three masts sank closer and closer towards the hungry sea. Malus held to the starboard rail with both hands, feeling his guts shrivel as it seemed as though the ship would be borne over and capsized. Then at the last moment the *Harrier* hit the bottom of a wave trough and started up the next and the hull heeled back to port, biting back at the flank of the human ship.

Bruglir's last-minute course change had saved them. Rather than be struck nearly amidships by the Bretonnian's prow the corsair had shied away and been scraped along her entire length instead. Yet now the two ships were stuck fast, their spars tangled together in one another's rigging and Malus watched as the human crew recovered quickly from the impact and flung boarding lines across the rail of the druchii ship. Already the Bretonnians were rushing forward, axes and billhooks in their hands as they prepared to come to grips with their prey.

'Sa'an'ishar!' Bruglir roared into the howling wind, brandishing his sword in the air. 'All hands repel boarders!'

The Bretonnian ship was broader in the beam but lower to the water and so the corsair's citadel deck rose above the enemy's main deck. Sailors scrambled back to the port rail, hacking at boarding lines with short-hafted axes, but on the main deck below a wave of boarders surged over the rail and came to grips with the stunned druchii sailors. In the rigging above, topmen cut at the enemy's rigging and traded crossbow bolts with Bretonnians fighting to keep the two ships bound together.

Malus drew his sword, trying to work some feeling back into numbed fingers as he gripped the leather-wrapped hilt. He turned to Urial and the sailors standing around him. 'Down to the main deck! Keep the humans from the citadel stairs and drive them back to their own ship!'

Urial understood at once what Malus was saying. He raised his rune-inscribed axe high, its razor edges crackling with a nimbus of crimson energy. 'Blood and glory!' he cried and threw back his head to howl up at the storm. A jolt like lightning surged through the gathered corsairs, galvanising them to action. They took up Urial's cry and raced for the stairs, weapons held high. Malus pushed his way through the press, knowing that every moment that passed meant a dozen more boarders climbing aboard the embattled *Harrier*.

The surge of men for the stairs created a bottleneck at the top of the stairway. Malus beat at the backs of the men with the flat of his blade, but they could move no further or faster. Snarling, he pushed his way to the railing that looked out over the main deck and saw that the humans had driven a broad wedge of men onto the corsair, almost completely isolating the fortress deck and the citadel from one another. There were enemy boarders fighting at the base of both citadel stairways, keeping reinforcements from reaching the embattled pockets of corsairs surrounded on the deck below.

Hauclir pulled up short, peering over Malus's shoulder. 'They've almost got us,' he said. 'What now?'

'Follow me!' Malus cried. He leapt onto the rail and hurled himself at the men below, screaming like a raksha.

The humans barely had time to look up before Malus crashed onto
them, bearing down three men with his own armoured body and splitting the skull of a fourth with a downward sweep of his blade. They fell
to the deck in a welter of shouted curses and a tangle of thrashing
limbs. A man's face bellowed at him and Malus ground the pommel of
his sword in the human's eye. A hand tried to reach around and grab
his throat. A blade clattered off his right pauldron and someone kicked
at his hip. The highborn thrashed like a landed fish, slashing wildly in
an attempt to clear a space where he could stand. Then came another
pounding impact as Hauclir landed almost on top of him, laying
about with his own sword and a three-foot cudgel in his left hand.
Men cried out and scattered from the highborn as his retainer killed or
maimed every man he could reach, his face as calm as a butcher's as he
went about his work. The highborn rolled clear, pulling his feet up
beneath him and surging to his feet close by the staircase.

The din was incredible. Scores of humans and druchii shrieked their
war cries and hammered at one another with furious abandon, the
clamour blotting out even the howling wind and ringing in Malus's
ears. His feet slipped and skidded in a slush of blood and ice as the
enemy boarders recovered from his reckless attack and surged towards
him, hacking with short, heavy cutlasses or trying to get a billhook
around one of his legs. A gap-toothed human lunged at him with his
cutlass and overextended, burying the point in the wood of the staircase. Malus opened his throat with a swipe of his blade and shoved the
man backwards with the heel of his boot. Another boarder grabbed at
his ankle and tried to pull him from his feet; Hauclir, to his left, spun
on one heel and struck the man's hand from his wrist with a powerful
stroke of his sword.

Crossbow bolts snapped through the air from all sides, fired from
men in the shrouds or from the decks of both ships. A human in front
of Malus coughed up a gout of dark blood and pitched over, a black
druchii bolt jutting from his back. A boarder lunged for Hauclir, striking the retainer a glancing blow across his temple with a cutlass; Malus
buried the point of his sword in the man's armpit, sliding past muscle
and joint into the vital organs beyond.

The press of bodies was lessening. Malus found he had more room to
swing before him and to his right more corsairs were forcing their way
down the staircase and joining the battle. Then he saw a knot of black-
cloaked figures surge from the base of the stair, their great draichs whirling
in crimson arcs as Urial's men tore into the enemy. A great cry of despair
went up among the human attackers and Malus responded with a bloodcurdling cry of his own as he surged forward, sword ready.

Suddenly Malus's vision blurred and his stomach heaved as a wave
of vertigo crashed over him. The roar of battle echoed and re-echoed

crazily in his ears, as if he were hearing not one but multiple versions of the same tumultuous din. The men before him doubled, trebled and quadrupled in his eyes. It was the same feeling he'd experienced earlier in the day, in the very same place by the starboard staircase.

All at once a premonition of doom swept over him. Without thinking, Malus dropped to one knee, bracing himself on the slick deck with an outflung hand. The highborn closed his eyes and shook his head savagely, the hairs on the back of his neck standing on end as he expected one of the boarders to try and take advantage of his confusion. But no blow fell and after a moment the world seemed to settle back onto its moorings. Malus surged to his feet and saw the boarders in headlong retreat, falling back to the portside rail as the two ships began to pull apart. As they did, they parted like water around a luminous figure in their midst, her naked body clothed in a raiment of steaming blood and Malus realised at once what had happened.

Yasmir had emerged onto the deck in the midst of the enemy, her twin knives in hand and heedless of her own life had danced among them like a temple priestess, taking a life with each sinuous stroke of her arm. Awed and terrified by the beautiful, deadly figure, they fell away from her on every side and that allowed more sailors to join the fight by rushing down the portside citadel stairway. These men had started hacking at the boarding lines connecting the two ships. Within moments the *Harrier* had been cut free and the boarders, who moments before had thought themselves on the verge of triumph, now found themselves facing the dire fate of being trapped aboard a druchii raider. Already men were clambering onto the port rail and hurling themselves through the opening gap between the two ships, preferring to risk death in the deadly waters below than to be captured by the vengeful crew of the druchii ship. Yasmir stood amid heaps of the enemy dead, bathed in gore and laughing with sheer, mad joy at the slaughter she'd wrought. The attackers had laid not a single mark upon her.

Malus took a few more steps towards the routed enemy and stopped, suddenly weary. He lowered his bloody sword and gasped for breath in the freezing air, watching the Bretonnian ship heeling away to port. Someone on the citadel deck had trained the portside bolt thrower on the ship and had shot away her wheel, leaving the vessel at the mercy of the storm. A terrible wail went up from the survivors as the broad-beamed ship rolled helplessly in the waves and was swallowed by the swirling haze.

The highborn surveyed the scene upon the main deck. Bodies lay everywhere, steaming in the cold. Druchii sailors moved among them, dispatching the enemy wounded and throwing the bodies overboard. The corsairs moved hesitantly, almost reverentially, as they pulled at the corpses surrounding Yasmir. She watched them with something like a murderer's serenity as they worked. Urial and his men approached her and fell to their knees. The former acolyte's face was a mask of holy ecstasy.

Malus turned away in disgust. His left hand felt like ice. The high-born looked down at his blood-soaked palm and a shiver went through him. I've seen this before, he thought, feeling the cold hand of dread settle over him.

Like a man in a dream he walked back to the starboard stairway. Just short of the staircase he stumbled over the body of one of the enemy dead, catching himself with his left hand as he fell against the stair.

Next to his hand a black crossbow bolt jutted from the wood. It was at chest height, right where he'd been standing just minutes ago.

Here is where I died, he thought. Or would have died, but for the premonition I received. How was this possible?

The laughter of the daemon was his only answer.

Chapter Fifteen
THE BLACK SAIL

I T WAS ONLY an hour past dawn when the lashing storm lost its
strength and the clouds gave way to early spring sunshine. They
found themselves well out to sea, with no trace of land in sight,
bearing north by north-west on a general course towards Ulthuan.
Dark sails of human hide caught the freshening wind and soon the
Harrier was flying across the waves like a bird on the wing.

Bruglir took the ship north and east, following the northern raiding
route around the eastern coast of the elven homeland. They reached
Ulthuan within several weeks, passing it late in the night; Urial stood
a watch of his own then, peering into the darkness like a wolf, lost in
private thoughts of fire and ruin.

Yasmir had retreated to her cabin once more after the last of the boarders had been slain. One moment she'd stood on the mid-deck among the
piles of the dead, then the next she was gone. Her quarters were just down
the passageway from the chart room where Malus tried to sleep; from time
to time, always late at night, he heard faint whispers coming from that
direction. Once, he'd risen from his makeshift bed and crept to the door.
Peering into the dimly lit passage, he saw Urial kneeling outside her door,
head bent as if in prayer and chanting softly under his breath, as though
he knelt before a shrine to the Bloody-Handed God.

Amid the blood and mayhem of the confused battle in the storm it
was a wonder that neither Tanithra nor Urial had been murdered, to

say nothing of Bruglir himself. Of all the highborn on the ship, the only person to narrowly escape assassination that night had been himself.

And why not? They had little reason to fear him outside of the writ. Bruglir and Tanithra had a fleet of ships and men to avenge them. Yasmir had her suitors. Urial had the temple. He had nothing. The thought was enough to keep him in his own cabin after nightfall, drinking bottles of wine that Hauclir had pilfered from the galley.

He'd suffered no more dreams or waking visions since the battle in the storm. Malus suspected that the copious amount of wine he drank had something to do with it. It certainly seemed to keep the daemon quiescent, which made the effort worthwhile all by itself.

A week after breaking out of the Bretonnians' trap the *Harrier* reached the Pearl Sack, a secret meeting point among the tiny atolls where lost Nagarythe once lay. By the time Bruglir's ship arrived, the rest of the fleet lay waiting at anchor in the sheltered cove, riding indigo waters that threw back pearlescent reflections when the pale sun hung high overhead.

There were two ships missing. The *Bloodied Knife* was presumed lost, having collided with a Bretonnian ship in the storm. Another, the *Dragon's Claw*, had simply disappeared. She'd last been seen sailing with much of her sails set; possibly she'd been lost, or perhaps so damaged that she'd been forced to abandon the cruise and limp back to Clar Karond. The fleet waited three days in the hidden cove, lookouts scanning the seas for telltale signs of approaching ships, but finally Bruglir declared he could wait no more and ordered his remaining ships under weigh. The sooner they dealt with the Skinriders the sooner they could set course for home.

'The problem,' Bruglir said, scowling at the chart spread on the table before him, 'is that the Skinrider ships don't carry maps.'

Sunlight slanted through the open windows in the captain's cabin, carrying with it the rushing sound of the *Harrier's* wake and the salty smell of the sea. They were four days north by north-west from Ulthuan, almost parallel with the straits leading to Karond Kar, some three hundred leagues due west. They were at the fringes of the wild northern sea; from this point forward, each day would carry them further into the realm of the Skinriders.

The chart spread across the pitted surface of the captain's table was the best reference any druchii sailor had of the seas north-east of Naggaroth and to Malus's eyes it said precious little of value. Lines depicting ocean currents made serpent trails across the open sea, weaving in and out among long chains of tiny islands without description or name. Coastal areas of the great continents were marked with the names of the twisted Chaos tribes that claimed them: Aghalls, Graelings, Vargs and others. The cartographer had drawn tiny depictions of tentacled things pulling ships apart or dragging them below the waves.

The highborn sat in a chair opposite the captain, drinking watered wine from a pewter cup. Since leaving Ulthuan most everything in the galley had begun to be rationed, as no one knew for certain how long the voyage would be. It was a prudent move, Malus knew, but terrible for the crew's morale. It certainly wasn't doing *his* mood any good.

'Come now, brother. I'm no sea bird like yourself, but even I know that's impossible,' he replied sourly. 'How do they navigate?'

Bruglir shrugged. 'They have small hideouts on many of the islands in the area,' he said, indicating the spray of tiny dots on the page with a sweep of his hand. 'I think they keep their charts locked away there. When their captains make port they study what they need to reach their next stop and press on. That's the only possible explanation I can think of.' The captain's moustaches twitched in an expression of distaste. 'The Skinriders are hideous, loathsome creatures, but they are clever in their own way.'

'What about torture?'

'How?' Bruglir snorted in disgust. 'Their skin turns to mush and slides from their bones. Their flesh seethes with pestilence and their veins are filled with corruption. Open them up with your knives and all you get are diseases raging like a fire through your crew.'

Malus scowled into the depths of his cup. 'Then we'll have to raid one of their hideouts.'

Bruglir nodded. 'My thoughts exactly. But such a thing is easier said than done.' He leaned back in his high-backed chair and folded his arms. 'You aren't the first highborn to try and exterminate these vermin. I even attempted it myself several years ago. No one has succeeded, for two reasons. Firstly, the whole area is like a hornet's nest – every little bolt-hole on these islands is within a day's sail of another, so word of an attack spreads very quickly. Each hideout keeps at least one vessel crewed and ready to sail at a moment's notice. At the first sign of trouble it will flee and spread the alarm and within two days the seas around the island will be full of Skinrider ships seeking vengeance. Secondly – and most importantly – there is the problem of plague. Their ships are bad enough, but their hideouts are cesspits, seething with every imaginable sickness. Bring a single scrap of parchment back aboard your ship and your crew would be decimated within days.'

'I spoke to Urial before leaving the Hag and he says he has a means of combatting the Skinriders' pestilence,' Malus said. 'Can you guarantee that you can keep any Skinrider ships from escaping during the raid?'

Bruglir pursed his lips thoughtfully. 'I have enough ships to cordon off a small island,' he said, 'and the Skinriders are indifferent sailors at best. Nothing is certain, but I believe our chances are good.'

'Very well,' Malus nodded, not entirely happy with the answer. 'Have you an island in mind?'

A scarred finger tapped a speck of ink on the chart. 'This one,' Bruglir said. 'The Skinriders may have a name for it, but it's just a knob of rock jutting from the sea, perhaps three miles across. They've kept a small way station there for years because it lies so close to our northern raiding route. We'll have to approach the island carefully – there will be scouts and regular patrols in the area, so I plan on separating the fleet into three small squadrons and disperse us on different courses. *Harrier*, *Sea Dragon* and *Black Razor* are the fastest, so we'll travel together. We can be there in two days' time.'

'And you're certain that there will be charts there?'

'Am I a Skinrider? Of course I'm not certain,' Bruglir growled. 'But it's the best place I can think of to look.'

'Then that will have to do,' Malus said, rising to his feet. He finished the wine and set the cup on the table. 'I'll inform Urial to begin his preparations.' Halfway to the cabin door the highborn paused, then looked back at the captain. 'You also might want to give your crossbowmen some time to practise, as well. The man you ordered to murder me during the boarding action was a terrible shot.'

Bruglir's eyes widened slightly. 'Did someone try to murder you, brother? I had no idea. Perhaps it was Tanithra – she's talked of nothing but slitting your throat since you brought our dear sister on board.'

Malus smiled. 'That's an idle threat, brother. Your first officer may not like me, but she gains nothing from my death. She's more likely to try her hand at Yasmir than to attempt to kill me. You, on the other hand, have much to gain by my death, not least of which is freedom from the power of the writ.' The highborn chuckled. 'And as for Tanithra, I'd be more concerned for my own health were I you. She has to know that Yasmir is going to force the issue between the three of you sooner or later and she has a great deal riding on the choice you must make. Choose wisely. I daresay your life depends on it.'

Without waiting for a reply, Malus turned on his heel and left the cabin, his boots thudding softly on the creaking deck. Hauclir, who had been leaning against a bulkhead outside the cabin, rose from his reverie and trailed along in his master's wake.

'Did you tell him about the crossbow bolt?' Hauclir asked.

'Yes,' Malus said over his shoulder, making no effort to conceal his annoyance.

'What did he say?'

'He denied it, just as I expected he would. But it let me plant the seed I needed to about Tanithra. What have you learned from the crew?'

'Some interesting things, as a matter of fact,' Hauclir said, checking the passageway fore and aft for potential eavesdroppers. 'If you'd asked these birds three weeks ago whom they'd follow in place of Bruglir, they'd have said Tanithra, hands down.'

Malus paused. 'And now?'

'Now they don't much care for her feud with Yasmir. Seems these sea ravens have got it into their heads she's some kind of saint, what with her beauty and her strange airs and the way she cut through those Bretonnians back during the storm. Have you seen the door to her cabin lately? Sailors have taken to carving little prayers into the wood, asking for her protection on the voyage. '

'Indeed? That *is* interesting news.' Malus tapped his chin with a long forefinger. 'It appears she's enamoured more than just my brothers. And they don't care much for Tanithra's ire?'

'No, my lord. They think she's putting them all at risk by plotting against Yasmir.'

The highborn considered this and smiled. 'Excellent. Feed the fire, Hauclir. Spread the rumour that Urial fears if Yasmir were to be murdered that Khaine himself will take vengeance upon the crew.'

Hauclir eyed Malus warily. 'So you've settled on how you'll play your hand?'

'Nearly so,' the highborn responded. 'But don't worry, Hauclir,' he said, turning and clapping his retainer on the shoulder. 'You're still in the running. I may kill you yet before this whole thing is done.'

TWO MOONS SPREAD a blanket of silver across the restless sea. He breathed and the air stank of corruption, a foetid reek that sank into his lungs like a thick mist and festered there. His skin felt loose and greasy, sliding over flesh and bone.

In the distance he saw a tall mast and a black, triangular sail, rising like a dreadful banner on the horizon.

The air rippled like water, turning grey and cold and he couldn't breathe. There were bony hands wrapped around his throat, bending him backwards beneath the surface of a pool of slimy water. He thrashed and kicked, snarling and spitting filthy liquid from his mouth. He pushed back with all his strength, forcing himself upwards – and found himself face to face with a horrific creature, its rotten form swathed in drapes of pus-stained skin that hung from its frame like a poorly-stitched robe. He could feel the pulpy flesh of the creature's fingers weep rotten blood as they tightened around his throat. Its eyes were little more than grey-green orbs of mould, burning with hate from the depths of a faceless hood made of rotting human skin. He opened his mouth to speak, but his throat filled with the stink of rotting corpses, choking off his words in a surge of bitter bile.

Another sickened creature joined the first, grabbing him by the shoulders and forcing him back down towards the water. They were going to drown him in the bilges of the ship! More hands grabbed at his arm, waist and leg, lifting him off the ground. His head dipped back into the filthy, cold water. He writhed in their stinking grip, but they held him fast...

MALUS FELL FROM the chart table with a strangled cry, tangled in sweat-stained bed sheets. He hit the deck with a painful thud, rapping his elbow hard against the polished wood. But the bright flare of pain did little to dispel the waves of vertigo or the blurring vision that left him dizzy and confused.

'Damn this!' Malus rolled onto his back, screwing his eyes shut and gritting his teeth at the waves of dislocation that rippled through him. 'Bestir yourself, daemon! Help me!'

Tz'arkan slithered against his ribs. 'But Malus, I've already done all I can. You must find your own way out of this labyrinth.' The daemon chuckled cruelly to itself, as though amused by some private joke.

The highborn snarled, beating the back of his head against the deck until the pain forced the dizziness from his mind. After a moment he opened his eyes, teeth bared at the ache in his skull. It was late and the twin moons hung low in the sky, sending a shaft of silver-blue light slanting through the small porthole above his makeshift bed.

He studied the pale light and a powerful feeling of dread came over him. Malus levered himself to his feet, pulled on boots and sword-belt and headed topside.

The night was cool and windy and the deck of the ship was silent save for the rumble of sails and the creak of the hull as the *Harrier* sped north. Off to starboard Malus saw the rakish silhouette of one of the corsair's sister ships, her sleek bow slicing effortlessly through the steel-grey waters. The highborn stood at the rail for several long moments, his eyes straining to pierce the darkness along the horizon. Finally he gave up and made his way forward to the fortress deck.

The upper deck at the bow was twice the length of the citadel, mounting four bolt throwers instead of two and coiled boarding ropes with hooks stowed by the rail. Ruuvalk, the ship's second mate, stood nearby, smoking from a long-stemmed pipe and idly supervising the bow lookouts. The sailor gave Malus a suspicious stare. 'Come to stand the wolves' watch with us?'

'There's a ship out there,' Malus said. 'A tall mast with a triangular black sail.'

Ruuvalk stiffened, his expression suddenly alert. 'Where?'

'I… I don't know.' The highborn looked about, now cudgelling his brain to remember the image of the ship in his dream. He compared the image in his mind with the one before him, looking off the starboard bow. 'There,' he said, pointing. 'Somewhere out there.'

The lookouts on the starboard side turned in that direction, unable to resist the highborn's commanding tone. Ruuvalk stared at Malus, slowly shaking his head. 'Pardon, dread lord,' the corsair said carefully, 'but are you drunk?'

'Sail ho!' One of the lookouts flung out a hand, pointing to the north-east. 'Four points off the bow.'

Ruuvalk's eyes went wide. With a parting glance at Malus, he rushed to the rail, forcing himself in between the lookouts. 'Damn me, a black triangle,' he muttered, staring into the darkness. 'A Skinrider scout, I warrant. Have they seen us?'

'Most like,' the lookout said grimly. 'She's come about sharply. Looks like she's getting ready to make a run for it.'

'Damn! I thought we'd get closer than this before the alarm went out,' Ruuvalk muttered. 'We've got calm seas and a good wind, though. Those plague dogs haven't got away yet.' He leaned back from the rail and looked to the stern. 'Black sail off the starboard bow,' Ruuvalk bellowed to the junior officer of the deck. 'Sound the call to battle! Lay on full sail and come three points to starboard.'

As the first wailing notes of the war-horn echoed through the night air Ruuvalk turned back to Malus. 'If we hadn't known where to look, we'd have never seen her. She could have turned tail and slipped over the horizon with no one the wiser. How did you know she was out there?'

Malus met the sailor's stare, considering any number of possible answers. Finally he shrugged and settled on the truth.

'I saw it in a dream.'

THE SKINRIDERS' SHIP was once a Lustrian vagabond, or so the druchii sailors called her – low to the water and broad at the stern, long and twin-masted, but with sharp-edged triangular sails instead of a Bretonnian's squares. She was nimble enough, like a dancer in the face of the druchii corsairs, but she couldn't cut through the waves like the black hulls of her pursuers and little by little the druchii ships closed the distance, stalking the vagabond like a trio of hungry wolves.

Hauclir grunted softly as he tightened the last set of the buckles on Malus's armour. The highborn rotated his arms slowly, testing the way the harness fit, then nodded curtly to his retainer and returned to the group of druchii watching the pursuit from the bow. Bruglir and Tanithra stood side-by-side at the rail, occasionally sharing observations in low, professional tones a short distance from the starboard lookouts. The starboard bolt throwers had been uncovered and made ready, the crews idling near their mounts. As Malus walked to the rail his progress was momentarily checked by a trio of grunting sailors carrying an open-topped barrel full of water. Three long bolts jutted from the barrel, their steel heads wrapped in cotton and submerged in the dirty water. The sailors inched along the deck, mindful of the explosive dragon's breath bolts they carried. Even with the steel heads and their glass bulbs cushioned in layers of cotton batting, a greenish glow from the sorcerous compound turned the sloshing water bright emerald.

One of the lookouts suddenly pointed. 'Arrows!' he cried. Black-shafted arrows made a momentary flurry of splashes in the water between the two ships. After two and a half hours of pursuit, the corsairs were only just now coming into firing range. The moons had set and the pale glow of false dawn was lightening the sky to the east.

'How much longer?' Malus asked, leaning against the rail to the captain's right.

Bruglir turned away from Tanithra and eyed him with evident distaste, as though he'd barged his way into a private function. 'A few minutes more. We'll start by trying to cut their rigging and spill their sails, then pull alongside and set them afire.'

Malus grunted. 'I'm surprised they're not coming about and trying to put up a fight.'

The captain shrugged. 'Spreading the alarm is more important. Every minute they remain under weigh is another minute that might bring them closer to another Skinrider ship. If they can spread the word, they've won. Nothing else matters to them.' Bruglir turned to the bolt thrower crews. 'Try a ranging shot. Let's see how close we are.'

Malus watched absently as the crews ratcheted back the heavy steel cables and loaded standard bolts onto the long tracks. The Skinriders fired another volley of arrows, again falling short of the druchii ship. The bolt throwers banged on their mounts; two seconds later one of the six-foot bolts buried itself in the planks of the vagabond's stern with a splintering crash.

Bruglir nodded approvingly. 'Switch to mast cutters,' he ordered.

Suddenly, Malus stiffened. 'Alarm…' he muttered. Then the highborn turned and beckoned to Hauclir. 'Go and get Urial and bring him here.'

As the bolt thrower crews reloaded, Malus tapped Bruglir on the arm. 'We must capture the Skinriders' ship,' he said to his half-brother.

Bruglir looked at Malus as though he were mad. 'That leaky old scow? If you're hungry for prize money there's little to be had in that worm-ridden old hull.'

'Prize money be damned,' Malus hissed. 'That scout is our way into the Skinriders' hideout. We can sail in close and make our way into their camp without raising any alarms!'

The captain shook his head. 'That vessel is a plague den–'

'Their hideout will be even worse. You said so yourself. Better to see if Urial can combat their pestilence here than once we're ashore, don't you think? Send me over with a boarding party and cast off. If we can't protect ourselves from the sickness onboard, you've only lost a few dozen crew.' And the man holding a writ over your head, he thought, but didn't say so aloud.

Perhaps Bruglir read the unspoken thought in Malus's eyes, because his expression became pensive. 'Who will command the prize?'

Tanithra surprised them both. 'I'll do it. Let me pick my boarding party and we'll sail her right into the pirates' cove,' she said. The first officer glanced at her captain, then turned her gaze back to the vagabond with a frown. 'Probably the closest I'll get to a real command.'

If Bruglir caught the bitterness in Tanithra's voice, he gave no sign. 'Very well,' he said brusquely. 'Round up your men, Tani. I'll need to pass signals to *Black Razor* and *Sea Dragon*.' The captain headed aft to the citadel, where the signalman and his lanterns waited. Tanithra followed close behind, calling out the names of men who would seize the Skinrider ship.

The men at the bolt throwers finished winding their weapons and now the loaders were fitting special bolts into the firing tracks. Instead of a pointed steel head, these had large, crescent shapes like sickle blades. They were capable of inflicting horrific damage to a ship's crew, but their primary function was to sever rigging and split sails. At close range the curved blades could split masts like saplings. The bolt throwers banged and the mast cutters arced across the water. One landed somewhere on the deck and the other clipped the rearmost mast, scattering a fan of splinters from the blow and spinning away in a glinting pinwheel to crash into the water on the other side.

'You called for me?'

Malus turned to Urial. 'Back at the Hag you said you could counter the pestilence of the Skinriders. Well, your powers are about to be put to the test.' He nodded at the enemy ship. 'We're going over there in just a few minutes. Can you be ready by then?'

Urial nodded. 'I must pray. Summon me when it is time,' he said, limping away.

Malus turned his attention back to the developing battle, just in time to catch sight of another flight of arrows arcing from the stern of the enemy ship. This time the raiders were in range and black arrows drummed against deck and hull. A sailor staggered backward with a vicious curse, clawing at the shaft jutting from his shoulder.

They were close enough now that Malus could see the archers standing by the stern rail; broad, misshapen men wreathed in dirty grey vapours, fitting arrows to dark recurve bows made of sinew and horn. They looked like the hideous creatures of his dream, their bodies covered with ragged surcoats of crudely stitched hide that covered their arms, chest and much of their heads. His nostrils wrinkled as he caught a faint stench trailing from the fleeing scout; it was the sickly sweet smell of rotting meat, like a battlefield under a hot summer sun.

The bolt throwers fired again. Splinters flew from the scout's port quarter, then sprung rigging and shroud lines leapt into the air as the mast cutter slashed through the lower half of the aft sail. As Malus watched, the second bolt skimmed right over the stern rail and tore through the archers. Two men caught squarely by the curved blade simply exploded in a rain of green and yellow bile. What horrified Malus even more was another man who was struck a glancing blow that tore through his chest like a sword stroke. Thick fluid burst from the man's body in a putrid spray of bilious green. He staggered back a step – then bent to retrieve his dropped arrow as though nothing had happened. Malus felt his mouth go dry.

With half her sails gone, the scout lost speed quickly. 'Bolt throwers! Make ready to fire grappling lines,' Tanithra ordered as she strode purposefully across the fortress deck. Men streamed up the stairs in her wake, some carrying crossbows while others hefted spears, swords and shields. The shield men pushed their way up to the rail, while the crossbowmen crouched and began to load their weapons. An eager kind of tension began to spread among the men as the druchii looked forward to the prospect of battle.

More Skinriders took up position at the stern and began firing arrows as quickly as they could ready their bows. The druchii boarders crouched behind their shields as the arrows struck home. Minutes passed and the *Harrier* swept down on the vagabond like a hunting hawk. 'Get Urial,' Malus ordered Hauclir. 'It's nearly time.'

Tanithra crouched close by Malus's side. She wore a hauberk of light mail over a jerkin made of cork – steel armour was useful in a fight but a death sentence if one went over the side – and carried her cleaver-like sword unsheathed at her side. 'Will your bloody handed sister not be joining us?' she asked darkly.

Malus shrugged. 'She's not mine to command, Tanithra. Khaine alone knows her mind these days.'

A stir went among the crowded boarders. Malus looked over and saw Urial working his way through the group, touching each man on the head and muttering a short phrase as he went. Each man he touched shook himself like a dog, then watched the crippled man limp away with a look of mingled fear and awe.

Tanithra raised a little to peer over the shield wall. 'Bolt throwers ready! Take aim! Fire!' Both weapons fired as one, the heavy boarding ropes uncoiling with a frenetic hiss. Malus straightened as well. He could see the Skinriders clustering along the port side of the ship, brandishing rusty swords and axes and taunting the druchii in a harsh, croaking tongue. The grappling lines sped in a flat line for the hull of the enemy ship, the barbed heads biting deeply into the planks of the ship's port quarter.

The first officer turned to the boarders. 'Belay and haul!' Tanithra ordered. The men raced to a pair of great wooden windlasses set just aft of the bolt throwers and began to wind them as fast as they could. Within moments the boarding ropes grew taut and the two ships began to draw relentlessly together. On cue, the crossbowmen pushed their way to the rail, sniping at Skinriders who tried to dislodge the ropes or cut them with their blades.

Malus felt fingertips brush his forehead and a voice mutter words that crackled in the early morning air. At once a wave of heat washed through him; for a brief moment the cold touch of the daemon faded and he felt vibrant and powerful. I'm *invincible*, his body seemed to say, but then the cold tendrils of Tz'arkan coiled once more around Malus's heart and the fire Urial had kindled dwindled to a sullen coal.

'He cannot have you!' Tz'arkan said with surprising intensity. Whether the daemon meant Urial or perhaps Khaine himself, Malus wasn't certain.

A sickening miasma settled over the fortress deck, as though the ship were downwind of a charnel house. The smell of rotten blood, festering skin and spilled entrails made a stench that Malus could almost physically see. There was a discordant buzzing in the air. At first the highborn thought it was the sound of distant voices, but then he realised it came from swarms of huge black flies, hanging over the refuse that choked the deck of the Skinrider vessel.

At this range the exchange of missiles was fierce. One druchii swordsman fell limply to the deck with an arrow buried in his eye. Another let out a yell and staggered backwards, staring in shock and surprise at an arrow that had penetrated his shield and the arm beneath. Crossbow bolts were raining down on the enemy crew as well, striking bodies with a glutinous *slap!* that sparked gobbling cries of rage and pain. The image of the Skinrider shrugging off the blow of the mast cutter hung in his mind. What had he got himself into this time? Malus turned to Tanithra. 'If we kill their captain will they surrender?'

The druchii threw back her head and laughed. 'Skinriders don't surrender,' she said. 'The fight is over when the last of them is dead. And don't forget to make sure you've killed your man – crush his skull or sever his head. With these things, nothing else is certain.'

Just then the two ships met with a bone-jarring thud. Malus pitched forward, propping himself up with an outflung hand, but Tanithra leapt nimbly to her feet. 'Away boarders!' she cried and with a thunderous chorus of war screams the corsairs leapt to obey.

Chapter Sixteen
THE RAIDING PARTY

THE CROSSBOWMEN AT the rail let fly a ragged volley of bolts and then dropped to their knees. Tanithra and the first wave of boarders vaulted the rail and dropped onto the Skinrider ship, their weapons glinting in the weak morning light. Almost immediately the sounds of battle rose from the deck of the enemy ship. Malus surged forward with the second wave, checked his grip on his sword and leapt nimbly to the rail.

A desperate battle was raging less than twelve feet below. The volley of crossbow bolts had killed or wounded a handful of the Skinriders, but the rest had held their ground by the rail, awaiting the druchii onslaught with inhuman determination. Tanithra and her corsairs had literally fallen on them from above, slashing and stabbing, but the Skinriders had not retreated an inch. Tanithra fought against two of the corrupted raiders, warding off their blows with savage parries of her heavy sword as they pushed her step by step back towards the rail.

Roaring out a warcry of his own, Malus vaulted the rail and dropped onto the Skinrider ship, aiming to land beside one of the raiders hammering at Tanithra. As he fell, however, another Skinrider rushed at the female druchii, reaching for one of her legs with a short-hafted bill hook and stepped directly into Malus's path. The highborn's feet struck the Skinrider on his hooded head and both he and Malus collapsed to the noisome deck in a clatter of weapons and armoured limbs.

The deck planks stank of rot, covered in puddles of brown and yellow fluids and mounds of decaying refuse. Malus's furious snarl caught in his throat as he choked on the miasma rising from the corrupted ship. He slipped and slid in the greasy fluids, trying to get his feet as the Skinrider he'd landed on pulled a corroded dagger from his belt and leapt at him with a gurgling cry.

Malus checked the Skinrider's rush with a raised boot, planting his heel in the raider's shoulder. The Skinrider's knife jabbed against Malus's breastplate; the tip of the blade snapped, but the raider only stabbed all the harder, searching for a vulnerable point to sink the weapon into the highborn's chest.

Malus slid backwards along the slippery deck, unable to find purchase until his head and shoulders fetched up against the ship's port rail. The Skinrider loomed over him, dagger raised, but the highborn moved with the speed of a striking snake. He made a backhand slash with his sword, striking the raider at the base of his jaw and shearing through his skull from right to left. The Skinrider's head burst like an over-ripe melon, pouring out a stinking mush of rotting blood, brains and squirming maggots. Cursing viciously, Malus got his boot planted on the raider's chest and kicked the corpse away.

Roaring and spitting, Malus leapt to his feet, sparing a glance at Tanithra, who was still locked in combat with two raiders less than five feet away. Both of her foes were intent on battering through her defences and so Malus caught them unawares as he darted towards the nearest one and sliced the raider's head from his misshapen shoulders.

Tanithra despatched her opponent and added her own sword to the battle going on to her right. More boarders were coming across as the initial counterassault faltered and the druchii were widening their hold on the stern of the enemy ship. Malus looked aft and saw the ship's wheel, guarded by the ship's captain and a pair of Skinriders with spears. The highborn drew his second sword with his left hand and circled to starboard, hoping to catch the raiders unawares. He stepped around the raised coaming of the aft hold – a large square hatch fifteen feet across and a third again in length – and as he rounded the hatch's starboard quarter he ran headlong into a crouching group of Skinriders coming the opposite way.

There was but a moment to react and Malus threw himself at the enemy with a snarl of rage. The first raider tried to rise, bringing up a battered buckler to shield his head, but the highborn knocked it aside with his left-hand sword and beheaded the man with a sweeping stroke from his right. Malus kicked the raider's body backwards onto the next man in line and surged forwards, both blades singing through the air in a deadly, interlocking pattern.

The raiders fell back, more and more of them forced to their feet and exposed to the fire of the crossbowmen nearby. Bolts buzzed angrily through the air, tearing through bloated muscle and sacks of rotting viscera. A Skinrider suddenly leapt at Malus, stabbing for his belly with a broad-bladed spear. The highborn pivoted on the ball of his right foot and let the spear point slide past, then slashed open the raider's throat. The Skinrider staggered and Malus gave him a backhanded stroke that completed the job and sent the raider's head bouncing wetly across the deck. The highborn threw back his head and shouted in exultation, lost in the joy of the slaughter.

A Skinrider roared in response and charged at him, empty hands reaching for his throat. Acting instinctively, Malus levelled his sword and ran the man through, the steel blade sliding cleanly between the raider's ribs and bursting from the man's back. Too late, Malus realised that his blade was now trapped – and the Skinrider was still coming, his swollen lips twisted in a grimace of rage.

Another raider dashed around the first and came at Malus from the side, throwing himself on the highborn's sword arm. Malus barely had time to cry out before the Skinrider he'd impaled crashed against him, spattering the highborn with stinking fluids from the gaping wound in his chest. Malus staggered against the blow – then his boot stepped in something slick and went out from under him and he fell backwards, crashing against the aft hatch cover. The rotting wood gave way and the highborn and his foes were falling through cold, foetid darkness.

Malus felt a spine-jarring crash as they landed in the bottom of the aft hold below. Something like old bone crunched beneath his shoulders and the weight on his left arm fell away with a grunt, but then there was another grinding, splintering crunch of rotten wood and he was falling again, this time landing in a pool of reeking fluid that closed greasily over his head.

The bilges! They'd landed among the bones of the decrepit scout, thrashing about in the polluted water standing in the bottom of the hull. The image from Malus's dream returned with sickening force, just as the raider he'd stabbed tightened his rotting hands around the highborn's throat and forced him deeper into the filthy water.

Malus thrashed and heaved, trying to gain some kind of leverage, but his right arm was trapped underneath the weight of his attacker. His left hand was empty – at some point on the way down his off-hand sword had been torn from his grasp – and he beat uselessly at the rotting hood. Flailing desperately, the highborn grabbed hold of the hood, groping with his fingers for an eye socket. He found one and sank his thumb into it, feeling cold, thick liquid run down his wrist. The Skinrider thrashed and Malus pushed against him, managing to pull his head out of the foul water. He gasped for breath, gagging at the

vile taste in his mouth and blinking furiously at the oily water stinging
his eyes. All he could see was a ragged hole far above him and a patch
of grey light – everything else was dark in the cavernous space below
the hold. The raider was weakening. Malus remembered the dagger at
his belt and fumbled for it – just as the Skinrider he'd shaken off in the
hold above dropped down through the hole and threw himself against
Malus's shoulders.

The highborn drew in a mouthful of air as his head was once more
pushed beneath the water. It felt as though a wall had fallen on him –
no matter how hard he fought against the weight of the two men he
couldn't budge them an inch. There was a roaring in his ears and the
skin on his cheeks began to tingle. He tried to speak, to call for the daemon's power, but his mouth filled with reeking water. Precious air
burst from his throat in a cloud of bubbles. His chest began to ache
and the need to breathe was like a fist twisting in his lungs.

Suddenly there was another heavy impact, strong enough to drive
the back of Malus's head against the curved ribs of the ship – and then
the weight on his chest was gone. The highborn flailed weakly, no
longer certain if his hands were out of the water or not until a strong
grip seized him and pulled him from the bilge.

'You shouldn't go running off on your own like that, my lord,' Hauclir said casually. 'It's hard enough work guarding your back without
having to chase after you all the time.'

Malus managed to roll onto his knees in the stinking water, coughing and spitting as he tried to shake the oily liquid from his hair and
ears. 'The damned Skinriders took me on a tour of their ship and I
wasn't in a position to argue,' he gasped. 'How go things topside?'

'The last I saw, Tanithra had killed the Skinrider captain and was
sending men forward to finish off the last of the crew,' the retainer said.

'And she's welcome to them,' the highborn said, rolling over the body of
the raider that had trapped his blade and grabbing the long hilt with both
hands. The sword came free with a sucking sound. 'Mother of Night, these
Skinriders *stink*,' he said, feeling his gorge rise. 'Let's find the stairs and get
back on deck and pray there's a stiff wind blowing.'

By the time Malus and his man had reached the open air the battle was
finished. Tanithra's men had forced the surviving crewman into a tight
knot at the far end of the bow and then methodically slaughtered them
with crossbows and blades. The bodies were stripped of their hide surcoats and thrown over the side and the dead corsairs were wrapped in
their cloaks and taken aboard the *Harrier* after one last benediction
from Urial.

The next few hours were spent taking on supplies and tools from the
Harrier to repair the damaged mast. The boarders bent to the task with

a will, splicing severed ropes and hauling a spare hide sail from one of the holds below. By midmorning the vagabond's damage was repaired and the ship was ready to get under weigh.

'If the wind remains favourable you should reach the hideout by midnight,' Bruglir said, shouting at Malus and Tanithra from the fortress deck of the *Harrier*. 'We'll be just over the horizon to the south-west, waiting for your return. Remember to keep a sailing watch ready so that you can leave as soon as you've secured the charts.'

The highborn nodded. 'How many raiders are there likely to be on the island?' Malus asked, shading his eyes with his hand as he looked up at the captain.

Bruglir shrugged. 'There is no way to know. Maybe a couple of ships, plus a small garrison. Their numbers change with the season and the whims of the raiders. With luck, you'll have little problem slipping into the camp.'

'Just be where you say you'll be after midnight. I've no doubt the Skinriders will chase us to the Outer Darkness and back once they realise what we've taken.'

'Cast off!' Bruglir ordered his men. 'We'll be waiting, Malus,' he said, then raised his arm to Tanithra in salute. 'Good hunting, captain! Take good care of your new ship!'

The crew on the fortress deck laughed as the *Harrier* pulled apart from the rotting vagabond. Tanithra returned the salute, but only Malus could see the corsair's teeth clench at the hoots of derision thrown her way. 'I'm sure he's speaking in jest,' the highborn said.

Tanithra didn't reply, staring darkly at Bruglir's dwindling form. Inwardly, Malus smiled in satisfaction. Things were coming together nicely.

THEY'D OPENED EVERY hatch cover to let in the sea breeze, but it still did nothing to lessen the stench. Malus leaned against the bulkhead, staring up at the square of night sky overhead and listening to the hiss of the sea against the ship's hull. Things could be much worse, he reminded himself. The handful of sailors on deck had been forced to put on the hide surcoats they'd stripped from the bodies of the dead crew.

Two score druchii corsairs sat in the reeking hold, cleaning their weapons or gambling with one another in tense, whispered voices. They kept a respectful distance from Malus and Urial, giving up the aft part of the hold to the highborn. Hauclir rested his head against the bulkhead to Malus's right, snoring softly and rocking in time to the swaying of the ship. As tired as he was, Malus couldn't bring himself to sleep. The stench was terrible, but more than that he feared what terrible visions waited for him in his dreams.

Malus sought out his half-brother, who sat on the deck just a few feet away with his bad leg stretched out before him. 'I've a question for you, brother,' he said.

Those cold eyes turned his way, fixing him with an owl-like stare. 'You may ask,' Urial said, promising nothing.

The highborn grinned mirthlessly, hearing his words thrown back at him. 'How is it that seers can peer into the future?'

Urial blinked. 'Because there is no such thing.'

'None of your sorcerer's riddles, brother,' Malus growled. 'I'm tired and I smell like a midden heap and I'm in no mood for games.'

'Then listen and learn,' Urial said, leaning towards him. 'Imagine that you are standing in the middle of a river.'

Malus grunted. 'That's easy enough. I've been dreaming about a bath for hours now.'

'In the middle of a river, all you are aware of is the water rushing past your waist. Your only point of reference is the spot on the riverbed where you are standing. All else is in motion, changing from moment to moment before your very eyes. That is how most mortals perceive the flow of time.'

Malus considered this, frowning in thought. 'All right.'

'Now imagine stepping out of the river and standing on the bank. Your perspective has changed. You can look back at the river and see its course in both directions. If you want, you can catch a glimpse of a floating piece of wood and trace its course along the moving stream. You can see where it came from and where it will go, because you can see the totality of its course. That is how seers perceive the future – by altering their perspective and taking in the totality of existence.'

Malus thought about what the acolyte had said, formulating his response. 'Is… is it possible for someone who isn't a seer to alter their perspective in this way?'

For a long time Urial was silent. 'It is possible,' he said at last. 'If a man were to step outside the realm of the physical world he could look back at the river of life and view its course. Or he might receive visions if he were being possessed by a potent enough spirit.' The acolyte studied him intently. 'Why do you ask?'

Before Malus could reply, a hooded figure peered over the lip of the hatch, barely discernible in the abyssal darkness. 'We're sailing into the cove,' he whispered. 'Landing party topside.'

Glad for the interruption, Malus nudged Hauclir with his boot. The retainer was awake in an instant and rising silently to his feet. Malus, Hauclir and four corsairs, all hand-picked for their ability to move and kill silently, gathered together near the topside ladder.

Urial rose as well and limped forward. 'You are all still protected by the aegis of the Bloody-Handed God,' he said in a low voice. 'But the power of the enemy will be much stronger within the camp. Touch nothing save what you must, or even my power may not be enough to protect you.'

'Next thing you'll say is that we can't kill anyone,' Hauclir said sourly.

Urial smiled coldly. 'Have no fear on that score. Spill blood in Khaine's name and his blessing will remain strong.'

'Then let's go do our holy duty,' Malus growled, nodding for the men to follow him as he started up the ladder.

The sea breeze was cool and brisk as Malus made his way onto the deck, but he had barely a moment to savour it. Tanithra was waiting for him at the top of the ladder, draped in one of the raiders' stinking hides. The lower part of her face was all the highborn could see from beneath the surcoat's crude hood, but he sensed that she was worried. 'We have a problem,' she hissed and pointed over his shoulder.

Malus turned. The island cove spread before him, the waters glittering in the pale moonlight. Six Skinrider ships lay in the anchorage, every one a seagoing raider twice the size of the little vagabond. It was almost midnight, yet Malus could see crewmen swarming over the big ships, clearly readying them for sea. Longboats scurried to and fro between the squadron and the shore, carrying supplies to the waiting ships. The highborn bit back a curse. 'Someone's planning a major raid,' he growled.

'And I'll wager this old boat was out scouting for them,' Tanithra said. 'We don't have much time before whoever's in charge realises we're not supposed to be here and sends someone to ask a lot of awkward questions.'

'Then we're going to have to hurry,' Malus said, forestalling the question he read in the corsair's eyes. 'I didn't come this far to leave empty-handed. Be ready to sail the instant we return.'

Malus scanned the rocky shoreline until he found the point where the Skinriders were loading the grounded longboats with supplies. From there, he gazed deeper inland, following the antlike procession of labourers until he spied a squat tower, almost invisible against the background of dark fir trees about half a mile from the shore. He pointed to the tower. 'That's where the charts will be kept,' he told the assembled druchii. 'We'll have to move overland – the shore is too exposed.'

Malus dashed silently to the starboard rail, where a group of sailors had lowered the ship's longboat into the placid waters of the cove. Without a backward glance Malus threw his leg over the rail and clambered down a rope ladder into the boat. He was no sooner settled in the bow when Hauclir landed in the boat behind him, holding a loaded crossbow. The retainer passed the weapon to Malus and settled down beside him. The remaining members of the landing party took their positions swiftly and silently. At a nod from Malus the portside oarsman pushed them away from the hull of the vagabond with his oar and within moments they were rowing towards the shoreline, their course largely concealed by the bulk of their anchored ship.

The trip to shore seemed to last forever. Malus listened to the faint sounds of the Skinriders at work on the distant ships, expecting to hear a thin cry of alarm at any moment. His attention was so fixed on the sounds carrying in the night air that the sudden grounding of the boat in the shallows took the highborn by surprise. Two sailors leapt from the boat, landing in the water with scarcely a splash as they stabilised the boat for the others to disembark. Malus stepped over the gunwale and stalked quietly into the shadows as the corsairs dragged the heavy boat onto the shore.

There was little light beneath the trees, but compared to the tangled woods of the far north the forest on the island was almost free of undergrowth. The landing party moved silently beneath the tall trees, drawn by the sounds of the loading crews. Malus was surprised to find no sentries or patrols keeping guard over the wooded approach – likely every man that could be spared had been dragooned into readying the ships for sea.

The Skinrider camp was actually a small fort, with a wooden tower three storeys high rising amid a cluster of wooden buildings surrounded by a wooden stockade. The corsairs crouched at the edge of the forest and watched a steady stream of men pushing wheelbarrows past the stockade's open gates. Tall torches had been driven into the ground at regular intervals along the route, providing ample light for the labourers – and the guards standing watch at the entrance.

Malus felt Hauclir crouch silently down beside him. 'All this hustle and bustle will serve us well,' the retainer said. 'The inside of that compound is likely to be busier than a beehive – one more group of labourers isn't likely to attract any unwanted attention. And the guards will all be focusing their efforts on the traffic moving through the gate.' He indicated the tower with a jerk of his head. 'Let's have a look on the back side of the stockade and see if it can be scaled.'

The corsairs rose silently and slipped like shadows beneath the towering fir trees, circling around the camp's perimeter until they stood by the wall directly opposite the gate. There they sank onto their bellies and crawled through the sparse scrub and fern until they had a clear view of the stockade and the square tower beyond. After several long minutes of study, Malus and Hauclir exchanged looks. There were no sentries to be seen. The appalling lack of defences made Malus's hair stand on end. There was something here that he wasn't seeing, but he couldn't imagine what it was and there was no time to waste puzzling it out. Finally he shrugged and waved two of the corsairs forward.

The men rose from cover and raced across the cleared area leading up to the wall. They disappeared in the shadow of the wall, then Malus heard a low whistle. The scouts had determined that the wall was scalable. The highborn rose to a crouch and the rest of the raiding party followed.

The logs were made from the local fir trees, broad and sturdy and pegged together by thick iron nails. White mould grew in the chinking between the logs and swarms of insects crawled along the wood's countless fissures. The highborn made a conscious effort to ignore the squirming carpet of life covering the palisade and focused on the faces of the scouts. 'Wall's not too high,' one of the men said. 'We can boost a man up and go over in relays.'

Malus nodded. 'All right. Hauclir, you first.'

Hauclir gave his lord an impertinent stare. 'I live to serve,' he whispered and put his boot into one of the scouts' interlaced hands. With a faint grunt the scout propelled Hauclir upwards and the retainer immediately found good handholds on the wall. He wedged his armoured form between the pointed ends of two of the logs and then bent down, reaching for the next man. Moments later a second man straddled the top of the wall and both men together began pulling the rest of the raiding party up and over as fast as they could grab them.

Malus was last to go. The two druchii took his hands and pulled him up to the top of the wall as though he were a straw doll. Without pausing he swung his legs over the palisade and dropped to the other side, drawing his crossbow as he landed. From his vantage point Malus could see that the square tower was built at the far end of a long feasting hall, similar to ones the autarii or even the barbarian norsemen liked to build. There were lights burning beyond narrow arrow slits set into the walls of the great hall and sickly-sweet smoke rose from the hall's two chimneys. Nearer to the wall were two square wooden buildings, their windows dark and shuttered. The raiding party was taking cover in the shadow of these buildings and Malus raced to join them. Within moments Hauclir and the remaining corsair were off the wall and ducking behind the building opposite the one where Malus crouched.

They watched and listened for several minutes. There was no sign of activity around the corsairs. Malus waited as long as he dared, then rounded the corner of the small building and led the raiding party to the tower.

The closer they came to the tower, the more Malus felt a kind of tension in the air, like the sky just before a summer storm. Sorcery, he thought bitterly. He was getting all too familiar with the sensation.

Up close to the tower, it looked as though there were plenty of footholds for a skilled climber. The walls were made of the same fir logs as the palisade, though some kind of glistening membrane had been stretched across their surface. Malus reached out a hand and touched it and it parted like rotting parchment, releasing a horrid stench like a ruptured bowel. Squirming insects poured from the hole and raced along the ground. Beneath the membrane the wall appeared chinked with some kind of moist red clay.

Malus eyed the tower with a grimace. 'No wonder they don't rely on guards,' he hissed. 'Who in their right mind would want to seize such a place?' He looked up, gauging the length of the climb. Finally he sighed and reached for a handhold, splitting the membrane further and filling the air with more noxious gas.

The corsairs, accustomed to scrambling up wet rigging day and night, scaled the tower with ease. Malus and Hauclir quickly fell behind, taking the climb one hand and foothold at a time. There was a narrow window frame inset at each storey and the raiders took special care to pass them with wide margins.

Malus and Hauclir were almost at the second storey when suddenly a silhouette leaned out of the open frame and looked left and right along the wall. The highborn froze, pressing himself against the insect-infested wood and praying to the Dark Mother that the diseased creature didn't think to look directly below him. The crossbow, still cocked and loaded, was slung on his back, for all intents and purposes a thousand miles away.

The highborn watched the hooded form of the pirate scan the walls of the tower one last time and then pause in thought. Was he trying to explain away the strange sounds he'd heard? After a moment the figure receded – then abruptly leaned back out and looked down. Malus found himself staring into a pair of sickly grey eyes only five feet from his own.

There was a rustle of fine metal, like the unravelling of a necklace, then Malus sensed Hauclir make a sudden, sweeping move off to his right. A fine length of chain lashed like a whip through the air and wrapped tightly around the Skinrider's throat. The hooded man barely had a moment to gasp for air before the retainer hauled backwards and pulled the man from the window. The body hurtled silently past them and hit the ground with a wet *smack*!

Malus glanced at Hauclir and gave him a nod of approval and the two resumed their climb. Minutes later they joined the rest of the raiding party.

The top of the tower was crenellated and afforded a commanding view of the entire camp. The four corsairs lay on their bellies in the middle of the floor, keeping out of sight. Malus crawled over to them. One of the druchii pointed towards one of the floor's corners. The highborn spied a trapdoor there, inset with a dark iron ring.

As Hauclir settled down beside the corsairs and gasped for breath, Malus crawled to the far side of the tower and rose up enough to peer over the battlements at the activity below. There was a large open field just past the main gate of the camp and it was packed with crates and barrels, many protected from the elements by large hide tarps. The torchlight field was swarming with Skinriders – possibly the entire camp and a sizeable portion of the crews of the anchored ships.

Movement near the gate caught Malus's attention. A Skinrider had run up empty-handed to the gate and was speaking excitedly to the sentries. After a moment the most senior of the guards appeared to reach a decision and pointed to the tower. Without hesitation the man ran on. Clearly he had news for someone.

Malus turned to his men. 'It looks like someone in the cove has noticed the ship,' he said in a low voice. 'We've run out of time.'

Chapter Seventeen
THE EMERALD FIRE

MALUS EDGED BACKWARDS from the battlements, his mind racing. Had the ships in the cove already attacked the vagabond and killed Tanithra and the rest of the crew, or were they asking for permission to challenge the new arrival? Worse still, what if some sharp-eyed lookout had spotted the longboat?

On the other hand, it could have nothing to do with us whatsoever, Malus the highborn thought angrily. There was no way to be certain, but it seemed wise to expect the worst.

He crawled to the trapdoor inset at the north-east corner of the floor, motioning for Hauclir and another druchii with a crossbow to join him. Malus pointed to Hauclir and then at the iron ring, then rose into a crouch, aiming his crossbow at the doorway. The second druchii mirrored his movements on the opposite side of the door.

The retainer took up the ring with both hands, took a deep breath and swung it open slowly and carefully. Reddish torchlight rose from the doorway and transformed the three druchii into hellish figures doused in crimson and orange. The stench of rot and rendered fat rose in a smoky cloud from the spaces below.

Below, Malus saw the top of a curving flight of stairs and a broad landing lit by torches fitted into sconces along the walls. Much of the landing lay in shadow, but he could clearly see a wooden door almost directly below. Malus passed the crossbow to Hauclir without a word and reached for the ladder waiting below the open door.

Descending into the tower was like sinking into a steam bath. The air was rank and humid and seemed to tremble with a life of its own. It pressed against Malus's exposed skin like oil, sliding greasily into every crevice and hollow and his flesh tingled sharply at the touch. He edged stealthily towards the door and drew one of his swords. There was an indistinct rumble of noise rising up the stairwell from the floors below – Malus imagined the long hall filled with Skinriders preparing for their voyage. By now they would be looking curiously at the messenger darting through their midst.

The highborn eyed the progress at the ladder – Hauclir was the last man to descend, already half way to the floor with the rest of the corsairs spread out around the stairs and looking to him for orders. Malus told two men with crossbows to cover the stairway and motioned the rest to accompany him. Then he turned and laid a hand on the door's iron ring. Moving cautiously, Malus eased the door open and peered through a narrow gap into the room beyond. The chamber was dimly lit; light from two banked braziers cast a faint glow across what looked to be a table of some kind. A figure struggled weakly on the platform, apparently bound there by rope. The stink of spilled blood hung heavy in the room, along with the familiar odour of decay.

Malus swung the door wide and rushed into the room, sword ready and peering into the dimly lit corners for waiting foes. But for the wretch twitching on the table in the centre of the room, there was no one there. The highborn looked about for a moment with a mixture of relief and consternation.

The room was like a rustic shrine to the Bloody-Handed God. The wooden table in the centre of the room was worn and stained with layer upon layer of dried gore and the wooden floor was tacky with pools of old blood. The shuddering figure bound spread-eagled to the tabletop was naked and had been – rather crudely, Malus noted in passing – skinned from the waist up. Maggots, flies and red wasps crawled over the glistening flesh. Yellowed teeth shone from the tortured gums and exposed musculature of the jaw; the mouth worked, but nothing more than a tortured whisper rose from the man's ravaged throat.

Hide curtains had been stretched across alcoves lining three of the room's walls. In the midst of the wall opposite the door stood a life-size statue of what appeared to be a broad-shouldered Skinrider, his hood decorated with a pair of massive, downward-curving horns and his right hand extended towards the skinning table as if demanding the portion of flesh that was due him. The Skinriders had laid voluminous hide robes on the armature of the statue, lending the figure a disturbing degree of life. The folds of the robe shifted slightly in the draft created by the open door.

Hauclir stood in the doorway, studying the room with a grimace of distaste. 'What is this place?'

Malus shrugged. There was an undercurrent of tension in the air, ebbing and flowing like the slow beat of an unseen heart. More sorcery, he suspected. 'Some kind of shrine, perhaps,' he said, pointing at the statue with his sword. 'Whatever it is, it's important to the Skinriders. Search the alcoves.'

The corsairs went to work with their knives, slashing open the curtains and examining the items stacked behind them. There were dusty tomes and scrolls, jewelled skulls and gilded weapons, jars of arcane liquids and sealed boxes inscribed with curious runes and bound with silver wire.

'Looks like a treasure room,' Hauclir said, eyeing a matched pair of bejewelled swords with an avaricious grin.

'Remember what Urial said,' Malus warned. 'Touch only what you must, unless you want to end up watching your skin melt from your body.' The highborn studied the stacks of plunder carefully. 'Unusual treasures,' he muttered. 'Not a sack of coin among them, which means that the bulk of their treasure is stored somewhere else. So they're keeping only their most valuable items here.' He frowned, poking at one of the books with the point of his blade. 'If that's so, then the charts must be up here as well.'

His gaze ran along the alcoves, peering into their shadowy depths. There was something about the room that wasn't quite right, but he couldn't place what. He turned in a complete circle, studying the walls, until finally returning to the horned statue looming over the corsairs across the room. The robes shifted silently and then Malus realised what was missing.

'There was a window on this level,' he said as he stepped up to the statue. The highborn reached out with his sword and pushed the hanging robes aside. Behind the hanging cloth wasn't the body of a statue, but a narrow wooden door.

Grinning like a wolf, Malus grasped the door's iron ring and pushed. The door swung open, revealing a second room lit only by a narrow band of pale moonlight from the window opposite. From where he stood, Malus could see wooden bins filled with tall rolls of parchment and his heart quickened. Then, from the deep shadows in one of the room's far corners, he heard the faint rustle of chains.

'A torch,' Malus said, holding out his hand. 'Quickly!'

Hauclir was by his side in moments, having taken a torch from one of the sconces by the stairwell. Malus tore the robes from the wall, stirring up a cloud of iridescent flies as the stained cloth tumbled to the floor. Holding the torch high, he edged slowly inside.

The room was indeed a repository for the camp's sea charts, the bins arranged around a wooden table similar to the layout aboard the *Harrier*. There was a sharp rattle of chains as the torchlight spilled into the room; Malus oriented on the sound and walked forward, sword held ready.

Ruddy light pushed back the shadows, finally reaching the corner and revealing a huddled, emaciated figure shackled at wrists and ankles, its naked body covered in grime and weeping sores. The human raised thin arms as if to shield itself from the bright light, then suddenly it froze. Above the hissing of the torch, Malus heard furtive sniffing.

The human stiffened. His face, shadowed by a fall of greasy, black hair, turned towards the highborn. Malus saw that the slave's eyes had been put out, leaving raw, burnt holes where hot metal had cauterised the wounds. The human sniffed the air like a hunting hound and began to tremble. His toothless mouth gaped as the wretched creature pointed a crooked finger at Malus and unleashed a horrific, paralysing shriek.

It was no mere noise that erupted from the human's throat, but a sorcerous force that cut through the druchii like a freezing wind. The scream froze the corsairs in their tracks, their hands pressed to their ears in shock and pain. And the sound went on and on, long past the point when a mortal's lungs would have failed.

Teeth bared, Malus roared back at the slave, feeling the paralysis waver in against the heat of his rage and he ran across the room, his sword held high. The curved blade flashed downwards and sent the creature's head bouncing across the floor.

The sudden silence was deafening. Malus staggered, trying to clear his head, but the rising thunder of scores of feet pounding up the tower stairs quickly focused his thoughts. He rounded on his men. 'Take those braziers in the skinning room and anything else that will burn and empty them onto the stairs – throw the torches, the robes, everything! With luck this tower will burn like a candle wick.'

Hauclir leapt into action, snapping orders at the men with the forceful tone of a proven officer and the corsairs leapt to obey. Satisfied his orders were being carried out, Malus turned back to the wooden bins and pulled out the largest and thickest charts he could find, binding them in sheaves with twine he pulled from his belt. The sheaves then went out the narrow window as quickly as he could throw them.

There were screams from the stairwell behind him and the thump of crossbow strings. The braziers were tipped over with a loud crash and then a general commotion ensued, punctuated by the clash of steel. Malus grabbed the wrist of the slave and dragged the body into the centre of the room until the chain pulled taut. About eight feet each, he calculated and began hacking off hands and feet. Once the chains were free, he pulled at the iron staples holding the chains to the walls, but no amount of tugging would tear them free. He turned back to the doorway. 'Bring me an axe!'

One of the corsairs dashed into the room, bleeding from a cut to his forehead. 'The stairs are burning, lord,' he gasped. 'But the Skinriders keep charging through the flames. I don't know how long we can hold them.'

The highborn pointed at the wall. 'Get three of those chains loose – only three – and we won't have to hold them long at all.'

'Your will, my lord,' the druchii said and bent to the task. A few sharp strokes later and he was holding three chains in his free hand. Malus took them and rushed to the doorway. 'Fall back into the skinning room!' he called to the men defending the stairwell. 'And bar the door!'

As the corsairs retreated from the burning landing, Malus went to work on the chains. He threaded one chain through the closed mana-cle of the second, drawing them together until the two manacles met. Then he picked up one of the U-shaped staples from the floor and threaded it first through the closed manacle of the chain still stapled to the wall and then through the last link of one of the freed chains. Malus held out his hand for the axe and used its hammer-shaped back to beat the soft iron staple shut. With one quick check of his handi-work he tossed the now-elongated chain out the window. 'It won't reach all the way to the ground,' he said, passing back the axe, 'but it will be close enough. Now go!'

The corsair nodded and went out of the window without a word. Malus leaned out and watched the man scramble down the length of the chain and nimbly drop the last few feet onto the ground. Satisfied, he ran back into the skinning room. The corsairs had dragged the heavy skinning table and its tethered victim across the room and braced it against the door and now they watched the smoking portal with mounting dread.

'Everyone out of the window,' Malus ordered. 'Once you're on the ground grab as many charts as you can and then run for the wall!'

The corsairs leapt to obey. Hauclir retreated to stand by the high-born's side. 'Something's going on,' he said, eyeing the door warily. 'The shouting's stopped, but I think I can hear chanting over the sound of the fire.'

Tz'arkan stirred. 'I smell sorcery,' the daemon whispered. 'Potent sor-cery. You've made someone very angry, Darkblade.'

'Out of the window,' Malus snarled. 'Hurry!'

'You first, my lord,' Hauclir insisted and then the door across the room exploded in a ball of greenish flame.

Shards of burning wood buzzed lethally across the room, trailing streamers of fire. The heavy skinning table flew over Malus and Hauclir and shattered against the head and shoulders of the horned Skinrider, showering both druchii with debris. There was a figure in the doorway, limned by firelight; Malus caught a passing glance of a naked, skinless form, the thick layers of muscle across his chest incised with complex magical runes and eyes that were globes of seething green fire. Everything else was a blur as he turned and ran for the open window as fast as his feet could carry him.

Malus leapt upon the chart table and snagged the chain with his free hand. There was the sound of steel striking flesh behind him, followed by a torrent of words that hissed venomously in the air. There was a flash of greenish light and a powerful blast smote Malus in the chest, hurling him through the window. He fell for almost twelve feet before his body slammed back against the wall of the tower, partially slowing his descent. Still half-blind with pain, he managed to get his legs around the chain and control the speed of his plunge the rest of the way down. When his feet hit the ground it surprised him so much his knees went out from under him and he collapsed on his side. Hauclir hit the ground beside him a heartbeat later, his robes smouldering and much of his short hair burned away.

Hands pulled at him, trying to draw him to his feet. Malus staggered upright, looking up at the tower. Green light seethed from the narrow window and the square tower top was haloed in angry flames. Malus glanced at his retainer. 'What did you *do*?'

The retainer rose shakily to his feet. 'I threw my knife at him. I didn't think he would be in much shape to cast his spells with a blade sticking out of his chest.' He ran a hand across his scalp, his palm coming away black with charred hair. 'Apparently that was a mistake.'

'Or perhaps it's the reason we're still alive.' The highborn said. 'Let's not push our luck any further. Grab some charts and let's get out of here.'

Despite his orders, none of the corsairs had fled for the wall. Any other time the gesture of loyalty would have pleased him, but now he jostled and shoved at the men to get them moving. Hauclir may have wounded the sorcerer, but Malus knew from experience how difficult such men were to kill.

He was just a few paces short of the wall when the wooden palisade was lit by a flare of greenish light. Energy sizzled through the air and Malus looked back to see a jagged bolt of emerald lightning arc from the top of the tower and play along the ground in the wake of the fleeing corsairs. Malus could see the dark form of the sorcerer silhouetted in the window frame. 'Hurry!' he cried to the laden druchii.

The first man reached him and leapt into Malus's waiting hands. The highborn caught the foot and propelled it upwards, hurling the corsair skyward. The man nimbly caught the top of the wall and swung one leg over, reaching down for the next man in line. Malus sent him upwards as well and the second corsair settled into place and reached down to help the others across.

Another arc of lightning crackled through the air, burning a jagged line across the ground and licking up the side of one of the camp's out-buildings. The log structure didn't explode so much as disintegrate, rotted into a steaming mush by the sorcerous bolt. Howls and angry cries echoed from the far side of the hall. Malus helped the third and fourth men up and over the palisade. Only Hauclir was left and this time he made no attempt to bring up the rear, his face sickly with fear as he put his foot in Malus's hands and leapt for the top of the wall.

A crowd of running Skinriders turned the corner of the outbuilding closest to the hall just as the sorcerer let loose another bolt. This time the lightning clipped the corner of a nearby building and then boiled across the ground to within a yard of where Malus stood. Shouting a startled curse, he leapt for the outstretched hands of the men on the wall. They grabbed him on the first attempt and all but hurled him over the row of sharpened logs.

Malus staggered as he hit the ground, turning back to yell for the men on the palisade when there was another flash of green light. The corsairs straddling the wall were blotted out in a blaze of emerald fire and the men below were caught in a shower of steaming flesh and bone. The highborn stumbled and fell backwards, staggered by the horrific effects of the blast. Not only the two druchii, but a sizeable portion of the wall they sat upon was simply gone. Through the wisps of steam rising from the ravaged logs, Malus saw a figure wreathed in green fire step lightly from the top of the tower and descend on a seething pillar of emerald light.

'Blessed Mother of Night,' Malus breathed, his eyes wide. He scrambled to his feet, turning to his stunned, gore-slicked men. 'Fly, you sea birds, fly!' he said, breaking into a run.

By the time the palisade dissolved under the sorcerer's magical bolts the druchii were gone, running for their lives through the shadowy depths of the forest.

Chapter Eighteen
THE DRAGON'S KISS

IT WAS AS if Malus was back in the Chaos Wastes again, hunted through the forests like an animal. The dark woods echoed with howls and cries of fury as the Skinriders poured from the camp into the shadows beneath the trees. To the highborn it sounded as though the raiders were fanning out in a wide circle, which told him that they were poor trackers to begin with and unsure of the direction he and his men had fled in. The surviving members of the landing party raced along in a ragged line behind Malus, leaving little trace of their passing. Every yard of distance they gained from the Skinrider camp made their trail that much harder to find.

Malus paused to gain his bearings. Off to the right he thought he could see the waters of the cove through the gaps between the trees. He reckoned that their longboat was two and a half miles from the camp and they'd covered half that distance so far. The cries of the raiders were fainter now, but he knew from experience that sounds could be deceiving inside a thick wood. Hauclir and the surviving corsairs caught up to the highborn, their faces taut with fear. Malus jerked his head in the direction of the trail and ran on.

There was a loud shout in the distance, followed by a chorus of baying voices.

Several minutes later Malus veered off the path and headed towards the shore. There were no landmarks to point out his location but the terrain and the amount of time they'd been travelling felt right to him. He plunged from the trees onto the rocky shoreline and was relieved to see the longboat just a dozen yards away.

There were shouts from further up the shoreline. Malus turned to see a knot of Skinriders brandishing torches and charging across the rocks. 'Hurry!' he called to his men.

The corsairs were already at the longboat, pushing it into the cold water. Hauclir waited nearby, a crossbow in his hands. Malus raced like a madman over the treacherous shale. 'Get in the boat, damn you!' he roared.

Hauclir waited until the highborn ran past, firing a parting shot down the shoreline before wading out into the surf and clambering aboard the boat. The corsairs were already at the oars and as Malus grabbed his retainer by the collar and pulled him aboard they dipped the oak paddles into the water and accelerated into the bay. The Skinriders pulled up at the edge of the water, shouting and cursing. Arrows buzzed through the air and made thin splashes in the sea. One struck the hull of the longboat with a sharp *thunk*!, making Malus duck. The remaining arrows fell short as the longboat pulled steadily out of range. The highborn watched the crowd fire a few more arrows, then after a moment they turned and began lumbering down the shoreline towards the camp's landing area.

The sky above the camp roiled with black smoke and rising clouds of bright cinders. It appeared that the Skinriders were having little luck extinguishing the burning tower. A large mob had gathered at the landing and longboats were rowing furiously between the shore and the six raiders at anchor in the bay. Malus looked back over his shoulder at the vagabond, growing closer with every broad sweep of the oars. He saw pale-faced figures racing along the decks; Tanithra and the rest of the corsairs had cast off any pretence of deception and were readying the ship to sail as quickly as they could.

Minutes later the longboat pulled up alongside the reeking hull of the captured scout. Malus and Hauclir scrambled up the rope ladder onto the ship, clutching crumpled sheaves of stolen charts under their arms.

Tanithra was waiting for them on the main deck, her expression tense. 'So much for guile and secrecy,' she said.

'Sorcery makes a mockery of us all,' Malus growled. 'Where is my esteemed half-brother?'

'He went below as soon as the thunder started onshore.'

Malus grunted. 'Let's hope he's preparing a surprise for their sorcerer. How soon can we make sail?'

'We're taking in the anchor now.' She nodded at the crumpled charts. 'Did you find what you were after?'

'I have no idea,' Malus said with a shrug. 'The Skinriders weren't being very obliging.' He handed his load of charts over to Hauclir and went to the rail, looking out at the Skinrider ships. 'What do you think they're going to do?'

'Normally, I'd say they would scatter, spreading the alarm to the rest of the nearby hideouts. But if they know you've run off with their sea charts, I'd expect they'd chase us all the way to Clar Karond to get them back.' She pointed at the frantic efforts of the Skinrider longboats. 'The good news is that a lot of their crews were ashore and their ships aren't ready to sail. The captains over there will have a hard time sorting themselves out.'

At that moment the crowd on the shore scattered like rats as a figure wreathed in green fire moved in their midst. When the sorcerer reached the water's edge he raised his hand and rose on a crackling pillar of emerald lightning. Higher and higher the sorcerer rose, like a fiery arrow shot into the air over the bay, then he plunged slowly and steadily down onto the deck of one of the nearer enemy ships. Skinriders scrambled across the deck, backlit by the angry glow of the sorcerer's presence.

'I think the captains are going to be encouraged to hurry,' Malus said, his voice tinged with dread. 'Let's get out of here.'

DAWN FOUND THE vagabond well south of the Skinriders' island, racing along the waves with the wind strong and bearing on her starboard quarter. Tanithra had put on all the sail the little ship had and with her hands on the wheel the scout was as nimble as a race horse, plunging headlong for the horizon with a pack of sea wolves loping in her wake.

Two hours after leaving the bay the lookouts spotted the sails of the lead Skinrider pursuers. A mix of Tilean and Bretonnian ships, they were twin-masted like the vagabond, but could hang a greater weight of sail and thus gain more power from the steady wind. Druchii ships like the *Harrier* could have sailed effortlessly away from the broad-beamed raiders, but Tanithra and Malus could only look on with mounting unease as their pursuers slowly and steadily closed the gap between them.

As the sun was rising Urial came on deck, joining Malus and Hauclir at the stern, his expression troubled. The former acolyte carried his rune-inscribed axe, clutching it more like a talisman than a weapon of war. 'No sign of Bruglir yet?'

Malus shook his head. 'It shouldn't be long now, or so Tanithra says. An hour perhaps, or less.'

'We may not have even that much time,' Urial replied, glancing back at the Skinrider ships. 'I can feel the sorcerer on board the lead ship. He is summoning terrible power to unleash against us.'

'Isn't there something you can do to make us go any faster?' Malus said, a trace of exasperation slipping into his voice.

'My skills lie in different disciplines than wind and waves,' Urial said. 'I believe I can counter much of the Skinriders' spells, but I will be sorely tested in the process.'

Malus shook his head. 'The Skinriders won't need spells to finish us. Those big ships mount catapults, just like Bretonnian coastal ships. They can smash us to kindling or turn us into a flaming wreck and there's little we can do about it.'

'Then we'd best pray that Bruglir is where he said he would be.'

Before Malus could respond a lookout cried, 'They're shooting!'

A rough-hewn rock arced high into the air from the bow of the lead Skinrider vessel, speeding towards the vagabond. Malus watched its trajectory, feeling his throat go dry. The small boulder fell well short of the fleeing ship, striking the water with a tremendous splash.

'A ranging shot,' Malus said, his expression grim. 'We're still out of reach, but not for too much longer. If you've power of your own to summon, I suggest you get started now.'

The highborn left Urial at the stern and joined Tanithra at the wheel. Her one good eye flickered from sail to horizon to the nearby sea and back again as she constantly made small adjustments to the wheel. The expression on her face was strained, but Malus thought he saw a faint smile on her lips as she led the sea chase.

'I don't suppose we can go any faster?' Malus asked.

Tanithra gestured at the nearest mast. 'Why don't you climb up there and blow into the sail? Put that hot air to some good use.'

Malus grinned. He was growing to like the rough-edged corsair.

A cry echoed from the forward mast. 'Sails on the horizon!'

Malus bent, trying to see beneath the low booms of the sails and past the bow at the distant sky. He couldn't see a thing, but Tanithra let out a shout and pointed just slightly to starboard. 'There! Two points to starboard! But I only count three ships. Where are the other six?'

'Who knows?' Malus replied. 'Four against six is much better odds than we had a moment ago!'

Tanithra altered course to intercept the oncoming druchii ships, just as the Skinriders tried another shot. The boulder spun through the air and ploughed into the water close enough to douse the stern with spray. 'More like three against six,' Tanithra said angrily. 'There's nothing we can do against those ships.'

Malus managed a gallows laugh. 'Well, we're doing a pretty good job of drawing their fire.'

Two more boulders plunged into the sea around the vagabond, one ahead and the other behind the little ship. The Skinriders were redoubling their efforts to cripple or sink the fleeing ship. One of the corsairs at the stern shouted, pointing aft. Malus turned and saw a greenish-black nimbus surrounding the lead raider, the air curdling like a bruise as the enemy sorcerer mustered his strength.

The druchii ships had seen the vagabond and her pursuers and two of the ships turned to starboard, angling to intercept the captured scout while the third held its course and continued north. If the vagabond held its course it would pass between the druchii ships and lead the Skinriders into a crossfire. Malus watched the sleek corsairs slicing through the grey water like sharks, moving swiftly even with the wind on their bow. Looking aft, Malus saw the Skinrider formation spread out to meet the new threat. Two ships angled to the south-east and one ship angled to the south-west, heading right for the druchii ships. That left three raiders bearing down on the vagabond.

Malus saw a speck of green fire appear at the bow of the closest enemy ship. The sorcerer had revealed himself at last. Urial straightened, spotting the enemy sorcerer as well and raising the axe as if to ward off a blow.

A stone flew from the bow of the lead Skinrider ship. Malus watched its trajectory and saw that this time their luck had run out. 'Take cover!' he yelled to the men at the stern. The corsairs scattered left and right as the boulder struck the aft rail in an explosion of long, needle-like splinters. The rock crashed along the deck like the hammer blows of a god, making the ship buck and quiver with each blow. It missed the wheel by less than a yard, struck the aft mast a glancing blow and plunged through a hatch cover.

Tanithra spun the wheel hard to port. 'Lyrvan!' she called to one of the corsairs nearby. 'Get below and see if that rock went through the hull! If we're holed below the waterline we're finished!'

Wounded men writhed on the deck, clutching at splinters jutting from arms, legs and torsos. One corsair kicked in his death throes, his lifeblood spreading in a vast pool from the jagged piece of wood jutting from his throat. There was a dark blur as another boulder whipped through the air over Malus's head and punched a hole in the aft sail before plunging into the sea on the other side of the ship. The Skinriders were mediocre sailors, but their aim was another matter entirely. The three Skinrider ships pursuing them hadn't altered course at all and looked as though they would cut across the vagabond's stern, heading south as the scout moved to the south-west. For the moment they were closing the range rapidly. The highborn gritted his teeth in frustration, wishing for a way to pay the enemy back, blow for blow.

Then came an angry sizzling sound that cut through the air from farther south. Malus looked back in time to see a tongue of green flame streak through the sky and plunge onto the deck of one of the pursuing ships. The sphere of dragon's fire fixed to the bolt shattered and spread a sheet of all-consuming magical fire across the bow of the raider. Hooded figures fled from the hungry flames, many of them blazing like torches. The druchii cheered and Malus joined in.

With surprising agility, the other two pursuers came about, pointing their bows directly at the vagabond and trying to pull away from the corsairs further south. Malus saw the sorcerer clearly now and watched the blazing figure raise his hands into the air. The highborn felt his heart grow cold and cried out a warning just as the sorcerer unleashed a jagged arc of lightning. The green bolt seemed to reach directly for Malus – then diffused with a sharp thunderclap against a hemisphere of reddish light just a few feet from the ship's stern.

The air hissed and crackled to Malus's right. He turned and saw Urial staring defiantly at the enemy sorcerer, his axe held high. The runes inscribed in the weapon's twin blades glowed a fiery red and the air around them shimmered with heat. For a fleeting moment the highborn felt a surge of relief – then a stone from the second raider passed overhead and struck the aft mast with a splintering crash. Iron fittings flew across the deck and ropes parted with a sharp snapping sound as the mast toppled sternwards like a felled tree. Tanithra was forced to dive across the deck as the mast crashed against the wheel. The vagabond began to heel over into a port turn, heading back towards her pursuers.

Malus raced across the pitching deck, knowing even as he did so that his efforts were in vain. The wheel was buried beneath hundreds of pounds of oaken mast and tangled in a web of frayed rigging. He looked back over his shoulder and saw the bow of the Skinrider ship pointed at them like an axe blade and drawing closer with every passing second. There was no way they were going to avoid a collision.

'Ready boarding ropes!' Malus roared. 'Brace for impact!'

The Skinrider ship struck the vagabond amidships with a thunderous boom of broken timbers, stopping the smaller craft dead in the water. Malus was hurled from his feet as the deck canted sharply to starboard, throwing him against the fallen mast. For a moment it looked as though the vagabond wouldn't recover from the blow, but then she swung heavily back upright, grating against the prow of the enemy raider. The two ships were locked together and Malus saw that for the moment there was as much shock and confusion on the enemy ship as there was on his own. The enemy sorcerer was nowhere to be seen.

Men shouted in fear and rage and the highborn struggled free of the entangling ropes, drawing his sword and raising it into the air. 'At them, sea birds!' he cried. 'Away boarders!'

The corsairs responded with a savage yell, eager to repay the Skinriders for the punishment they'd endured. Boarding ropes were cast onto the raider and the druchii clambered aboard, striking savagely at the stunned raiders. Hauclir and Urial joined Malus by the wheel. Urial moved with a surprising degree of strength and agility and his eyes were fever-bright. The axe still glowed brightly in his hand. Malus eyed him appraisingly. 'Do you think you can make it onto the enemy ship?'

'It's either that or swim!' Tanithra interjected angrily, coming around the end of the fallen mast with her sword in hand. 'Between that first stone and the collision, this old tub has sprung her seams. She's sinking fast!'

There was a blaze of greenish light on the enemy ship and men shrieked in terror and pain. 'Hauclir, get below and grab the charts!' Malus commanded. 'Tanithra, take command of the boarders. Urial and I are going to kill that sorcerer!'

Malus ran to the port side of the sinking ship with Urial close on his heels. He leapt onto the splintered rail, grabbed a quivering boarding rope and nimbly scaled his way up onto the deck of the enemy raider.

The highborn landed amid a scene of carnage. Dead raiders lay everywhere, spilling corrupted blood and vile fluids onto the deck. Arrows and stones buzzed through the air, fired by Skinriders high in the ship's twin masts. Another flare of emerald caught Malus's eye and he saw the enemy sorcerer at the waist of the ship with his back to the main mast. Crossbow bolts and broken, rusting weapons protruded from his chest and in his rage he lashed out at every man within his reach, be they friend or foe. A bolt of jagged lightning played across a knot of Skinriders and corsairs locked in fierce melee, reducing all of them to blackened bones and stinking mush.

Urial pushed in front of Malus. 'Stay behind me,' he said, his mouth twisted into a fierce grin. He made for the sorcerer at a steady, deliberate pace, holding his axe at the ready with his one good hand. Malus drew his knife with his left hand and followed warily behind him.

The press of battle around the mast all but vanished as the combatants fled in every direction to escape the sorcerer's fury. Malus watched the Skinrider straighten painfully, his eyes and open mouth blazing with green fire as he spoke words of power and surrounded himself with a nimbus of energy. The weapons piercing his body disintegrated, decaying in an instant.

Two fleeing Skinriders stumbled across Urial's path. The axe flashed in a crimson arc and the two raiders fell to the deck, their bodies ruptured and steaming. The fiery light surrounding the axe seemed to glow slightly brighter as Urial spoke in a thunderous voice.

'Servant of Corruption! Slave to the Lord of Decay! The cleansing fire of the Bloody-Handed God is upon you! Redeem yourself upon the razor edge of his mercy or I will cast your soul into the Outer Darkness for all time!'

Druchii and Skinrider alike reeled from the unearthly power seething through Urial's voice. Even Malus, who had walked at the edges of the Realm of Murder and peered across the Abyss into undreamt-of worlds, heard the voice of Khaine resounding from his mouth and was amazed.

The sorcerer reeled back as though struck, his shoulders striking the main mast hard enough to send cracks shooting along its length – then he rebounded, opening his mouth wide and vomiting a torrent of black bile at the axe-wielding druchii.

The virulent gout of acidic slime washed over Urial's wards and burst into crimson flames, spattering the deck with burning globules that ate through the oak planking in an instant. Malus crouched low, bent slightly forward as though advancing against a storm wind and let the blazing mess fly over him. They advanced steadily upon the sorcerer and the axe in Urial's hand was glowing now like a desert sun.

Words of power burst from the sorcerer's drooling lips and every surviving Skinrider within thirty paces groaned in pain and terror. Arcs of greenish fire played across their bloated bodies and they staggered awkwardly, as though no longer in full control of their limbs. Then a single, despairing wail rose from a dozen cankered throats and the raiders hurled themselves at Urial.

The devoted servant of Khaine met their frenzied charge with a joyous laugh and the slaughter began in earnest. The Skinriders struck a ward made of enchanted, razor-edged steel; the axe whirled in a hungry blur, hurling the raiders back with shorn limbs and shattered torsos, their blood burning in an offering to the Lord of Murder. But such was the mindless fury of the raiders' charge that Urial's advance faltered. Swords clashed against his armour and gangrenous hands groped for his throat for fleeting moments, each blow slowing the druchii a bit more, until he was nearly at a standstill. The sorcerer gave Urial a mocking, fiery smile and then spread his hands, rising slowly on a crackling pillar of emerald lightning.

'Oh, no you don't,' Malus said coldly, stepping around from behind Urial and hurling his knife.

The keen blade flew straight and true for the sorcerer's heart. The Skinrider's blazing eyes widened and at the last moment he brought up his hand and took the silver steel dagger through his palm. The sorcerer snarled in pain and uttered a virulent curse as he clenched his fist and dissolved the knife in a rain of glittering rust. It was only a moment's distraction, but it caused the sorcerer's ascent to falter and in that instant of hesitation Malus hurled himself at the servant of decay.

He crashed into the sorcerer's chest, surprised to find rock-hard muscle instead of the bloated, bulbous flesh of the other raiders the highborn had fought. Malus rolled onto the sorcerer and raised his blade, but the Skinrider seized him by the throat and caught his sword wrist in an iron grip. And then he began to draw Malus downward, towards his blazing eyes and fiery lips.

Tz'arkan writhed and hammered beneath Malus's ribs and the highborn looked into the twin orbs of the sorcerer's eyes and saw the face of another daemon staring back at him.

Malus felt Urial's blessing begin to sputter, like a candle that had reached the end of its wick. The pure fire scouring his skin began to wane, leaving an unhealthy fever in its wake. Black smoke rose from the possessed sorcerer's hungry mouth and Malus could feel vermin writhing within it as the vapours slid down his throat. He could feel the corruption blooming in his lungs and taking root in his guts. Thick trails of pus leaked from his eyes, oozing down his cheeks.

The sorcerer drew Malus downwards until their faces were inches apart. The highborn could feel the presence of the pestilential spirit roiling within the Skinrider. The possessed man chuckled, his true voice bubbling up from corrupted lungs. 'Look into the face of a daemon and despair,' the sorcerer said.

Malus met the sorcerer's eyes and gave a cold laugh of his own. 'As you wish,' he said. 'Show him your face, o Drinker of Worlds.'

Black ice surged through his veins, freezing the pestilence in his flesh and swelling his limbs with inhuman power. The highborn's eyes were swallowed in utter blackness, the endless cold of eternal night. His fingernails stretched into talons and his teeth sharpened into terrible fangs. The sorcerer stiffened. The daemon inside him quailed before Tz'arkan's fury and the Skinrider screamed in terror.

Malus plunged his left hand into the sorcerer's belly, his razor-edged talons tearing out the man's guts. 'Slither, slither little worm,' Malus said in a voice not his own. 'Flee down your burrows of tumour and rot, but you'll not escape me.'

His sword tumbled to the deck. The sorcerer writhed and shrieked, begging for mercy and the highborn tore the man apart. He emptied the man's chest, split his ribs and reached up his throat and into the man's skull, until at last he pulled free a long, black worm that twisted madly in his dripping hands. Malus crushed it in his fist, sensing Tz'arkan's ecstasy as the lesser daemon was hurled screaming back into the nether realms.

It was long moments before Malus realised the daemon's presence had subsided. He was sitting on the deck and a roaring noise echoed in his ears. Tendrils of frozen mist rose from his gore-splashed armour. There was little left of the sorcerer that was still recognisable.

After a moment, the roaring resolved itself as the sounds of battle and Malus remembered where he was. A thrill of terror ran down his spine as he grasped the implications of what he'd done. He looked about wildly, expecting to find Urial standing above him, his fiery axe poised to strike.

Instead he had given in to his own unearthly master, transported by the ecstasy of battle. He'd slain every Skinrider the sorcerer had thrown at him and grown drunk on bloodshed, charging further aft where the fight for the ship still raged. He'd fallen upon the ship's defenders like a thunderbolt and the corsairs, recognising the touch of the divine, had taken heart and redoubled their efforts as well. There had been no one to witness Malus's transformation save the dead and for the moment he was alone among them.

The highborn rose to his feet, feeling weary to his bones. All around the ship, the sea was red with fire. Off to starboard, the last of the three ships that had chased after the vagabond now drifted with the wind, its deck a raging inferno. A trio of black ships slipped past the blazing hulk, gliding effortlessly south before turning back upwind. Farther off to starboard the *Harrier* cruised north, battered but unbowed. The raider that had turned her way at the start of the battle was now a blazing pyre sinking below the waves.

Off to port the battle had not gone so well. The *Black Razor* drifted in a burning embrace with a Skinrider ship – one vessel had boarded the other and in the furious battle that followed both ships had caught fire and no one had been able to extinguish the flames. The Sea *Dragon* was sinking slowly, the waves lapping over her rails as the sea poured through the jagged holes punched through her hull. But her killer had little time to savour her victory. The last Skinrider ship was now well to the south, trailing burning rigging and a broken mast and dogged by three more druchii corsairs that harried her like wolves.

Bruglir had never been outnumbered, Malus realised. He'd divided his force into three squadrons and sent two of them off to east and west, just over the horizon. When the battle had begun he'd signalled them and they'd swept down on the Skinriders' flanks, closing on them like a set of jaws.

The sounds of battle at the stern suddenly subsided. Malus turned and saw the Skinrider captain drop his sword and fall to his knees before Tanithra – evidently the blazing visage of Urial and his axe had been enough to force an uncharacteristic surrender. Tanithra let out a shout of joy and struck the man's head from his shoulders and the crew let out a long cry of victory.

The cries of celebration were so loud that Malus almost didn't hear the thin wail coming from the bow. The highborn frowned. That sounds strangely familiar, he thought. Then he remembered: Hauclir!

Malus rushed to the bow. The vagabond was gone, swallowed by the hungry waves. The highborn peered over the side and saw the retainer hanging from a boarding rope, clutching bundles of soggy charts. Malus let out a startled shout and hauled on the rope for all he was worth, wishing he still had a little of the daemon's strength left in him.

Long minutes later Hauclir rolled over the rail. Water ran from his pale face and hair and poured in a flood from beneath the weight of his heavy armour. He still held the charts in a death grip and the look he gave Malus was both insubordinate and horrified at the same time.

'The Dark Mother forbid,' Hauclir said shakily, 'but if we're ever on another sinking ship and something's been left below, you can damned well go get it yourself, my lord!'

Chapter Nineteen
ISLAND OF THE LOST

'THERE IT IS,' Bruglir declared, tapping a point on the yellowed parchment map with one gauntleted hand. 'That's the Isle of Morhaut.'

Malus folded his arms beneath the heavy cloak he wore, fighting against another bout of shivering. The icy touch of the daemon had yet to lapse, even though the battle on the Skinrider ship was more than four hours past. It was close to midday and the heaving northern sea gleamed like polished steel beneath diffuse, pale sunlight. The druchii corsairs were going about barefoot and shirtless, basking like lizards beneath the welcome heat, but Malus still felt frozen to the core. He'd told Tanithra and the rest that he'd been soaked fishing Hauclir from the water and the winter cloak had merited only passing interest from Bruglir and Urial. The highborn leaned over the captain's table, squinting at the mosaic of finely-scrawled lines and bizarre notations on the Skinriders' map. He'd seen sorcerer's tomes that were clearer and simpler to decipher. 'How can you be so certain? Everything is in some kind of pidgin language.'

'Actually it's Norse,' Bruglir answered, 'Look here.' His finger retreated from the tiny mark representing the island and pointed to eight larger islands scattered across the approaches to the northern sea. 'Three of these islands are well-known as being major Skinrider camps and we can assume that the other five are significant outposts as well. You'll notice that all of them have clearly defined courses laid out that connect them to one another.' His fingers traced the long, curving lines that ran from one rocky outline to the next, each one annotated in strange runic script. 'Now, what else do these islands all have in common?'

Malus studied the map. When Bruglir pointed it out, the answer leapt from the jumble of lines and runes. 'They all have a course plotted to a centrally-located island that's smaller than all the rest.'

The captain nodded. 'Exactly. This central island is their headquarters. Nothing else makes sense.' He reached over and leafed through a sheaf of druchii charts piled on a nearby desktop, finally settling on one and laying it out. The thin vellum rested on the Skinrider chart and showed the markings beneath, creating a composite picture of the same area. 'See how the island doesn't even appear on our charts?' Bruglir smiled cruelly. 'This is the secret they fought so hard to try and protect. Now we know where their heart lies – and we can tear it out and hold it up to their disbelieving faces!'

Malus gritted his teeth against another wave of trembling and surveyed the other druchii sharing the cabin. Tanithra nodded to herself as she studied the map, her expression thoughtful. Urial the Forsaken stood rigidly erect, his eyes bright and fierce. Clearly the ecstasy of battle still sang in his veins and the look he gave his older brother nearly amounted to an outright challenge. The highborn wondered if Urial had ever fought in a true battle before today. Clearly the taste was to his liking. Malus considered the changes that had come over Yasmir since their arrival on the *Harrier* and wondered what this would mean for his plans. Very soon now he was going to have to act and he couldn't afford to have Urial or anyone else doing something unpredictable.

The battle with the Skinriders had gone on for another hour after Tanithra and her men had captured the raider. Three of the enemy ships were totally destroyed, their hulls savaged by the sorcerous fire of the dragon flame bolts. Of the three remaining, two were stripped of everything useful and then set adrift with blazing pitch scattered across their decks, as there wasn't enough spare crew to man them. The *Bloodied Knife* was given to the flames as well – her captain and nearly all of the crew were dead and her rigging all but completely destroyed during the fight. The majority of the crew of the Sea *Dragon* had been lost as well, freezing to death in the cold waters before another ship could arrive to rescue them. That just left the ship Tanithra had taken – and clearly expected to keep, judging by her pointed requests to Bruglir for more crewmen and supplies.

Once the battle had concluded the *Harrier* had pulled alongside the captured raider. Malus and Urial had gone aboard with the charts and the highborn had sent Hauclir to dry himself out and learn what had transpired in their absence. Now the remainder of the fleet was tacking northward, working slowly but surely towards the Island of Morhaut.

'All right,' Malus said. 'It appears that everyone agrees with your conclusions, captain. What next?'

Bruglir shrugged. 'Providing we encounter no other Skinriders on the way we'll reach the island within the week,' he said. 'After that, it's up to Urial to get us past the island's defences – if he's capable.'

Urial stiffened further, a flush rising on his pale cheeks. 'Oh, I'm capable of many things, brother,' he said with surprising venom. 'You're going to learn that very soon indeed.'

Malus cleared his throat in the sudden silence. 'What do you know of the island's defences, Urial?'

For a moment Urial and Bruglir continued to lock eyes over the spread charts. Finally Urial turned away. 'There are few concrete details, unfortunately,' he said to Malus. 'The libraries at Hag Graef contain few references to the island at all, but I was able to unearth some information about Eradorius, the sorcerer who resided there and supposedly created the defences thousands of years ago.' Urial's brass-coloured eyes shone like heated coins. 'It appears that Eradorius was a servant of Chaos during the years of the First War – a conqueror and a master of arcane lore who was a terrible foe of Aenarion and his twisted kin, until he fled from his castle of iron and bone and took refuge on a distant island in the northern sea.'

Malus felt his mouth go dry. 'Fled, you say?'

'So it would appear. Most likely his lieutenants turned on him, coveting his wealth and power,' Urial replied. 'Whatever it was that Eradorius feared, he devoted all his remaining power to try and escape it. According to legend he laid many sorcerous wards around the Isle of Morhaut, meant to destroy anyone foolish enough to approach it.'

Tanithra frowned. 'Wards?' she said with a grimace, as though disliking the taste of the word. 'Like what? Storms of blood and flocks of daemons?'

Urial chuckled. 'No. Such defences require great power to maintain and wouldn't have survived without regular infusions of power. No, these wards were more subtle, twisting an intruder's perceptions so that they more than likely wouldn't even notice the island at all.'

'And if they did?'

'Then they would become forever lost.'

Tanithra shook her head. 'I don't understand.'

The former acolyte spread his hands. 'That was all the legends said. I will know more once I've had a chance to study the wards first-hand.'

'We will use the captured raider,' Bruglir said. 'Once Urial has found his way through the defences we'll take the rest of the fleet in.'

'So does that mean I'll get the crewmen I need?' Tanithra asked.

Bruglir took a deep breath and straightened to his full height, his head brushing the beams overhead. 'After the last battle the fleet has few sailors to spare,' he said carefully. 'I don't want to leave our ships undermanned with another major battle looming.'

'You're leaving one dangerously undermanned right now,' Tanithra shot back.

'I have no intention of taking the raider into battle,' Bruglir replied. 'Once we've found the way past the island's wards and have a sense of what lies beyond, we'll scuttle the ship. It has no value to me as a prize.'

Tanithra's jaw dropped. Her dark eye flashed with anger. 'You're talking about *my ship*, captain. I won her with blood and steel and no one decides to scuttle her but me.'

'You had a ship, Tani and you lost her in the battle,' Bruglir answered coldly. 'And every captain on every ship in this fleet serves at my pleasure. I'll need you back here on the *Harrier* when the battle begins in earnest.'

Malus gauged the reactions of the two corsairs carefully. He cleared his throat. 'Brother, you are being unfair to your first officer. She handled the vagabond with great skill and she led her crew to victory over an enemy more than twice her size. Even I know that the law of the sea dictates her claim to the prize.' He paused for effect. 'If this is about Yasmir–'

'This is about my command of this fleet,' Bruglir snapped. 'Something that your precious writ has no influence on whatsoever. This meeting is concluded,' Bruglir said coldly, then bent to the charts before him. 'We will reach the Isle of Morhaut in six days. Now get out.'

Malus turned on his heel, concealing a fleeting look of amusement. He reached for the cabin door but Tanithra swept past like a fast-moving thunderhead, all but shouldering him aside as she stomped down the passageway. Hauclir, waiting just beyond the door, barely leapt out of her path in time.

Urial followed close on Malus's heels, pulling the door closed behind him. 'Is this your plan?' he asked the highborn in a harsh whisper. 'Provoke Tanithra to murder?'

Malus cast a glare at Urial over his shoulder. 'I'm sure I don't know what you're talking about, brother,' he hissed. 'After all, this is a ship under weigh and even *discussing* what you're talking about is grounds for public vivisection.'

But the former acolyte was unfazed by the thinly veiled warning. He stepped close to Malus, his voice dropping into a lower but no less intense register. 'She won't kill him,' Urial whispered. 'The other captains would tear her apart in an instant. I had expected you to take more of a direct hand in this.'

Malus turned until the two were practically nose to nose. 'Why, so the captains can tear me apart instead?' The highborn looked Urial up and down. 'You have grown a bit overbold since we took that raider, brother. If you're so keen for Bruglir's blood, why not challenge him yourself?' He nodded at the cabin door. 'You looked as though you were working up to it back there. What's preventing you?'

Urial stepped back, a snarl twisting his features, but if he'd intended an intemperate reply he appeared to master himself at the last moment and his face settled into a stolid mask. 'I merely wish to remind you of your obligation,' he said. 'I might decide to call your debt due before we reach the Isle.'

'Don't be stupid, brother,' Malus hissed. 'Like it or not, we will need Bruglir to defeat the Skinriders. You've suffered his existence your whole life; can you not wait a few days more?'

'My patience is limitless,' Urial said flatly. 'My trust, however, is not. Think on that, Malus,' he said, pushing past the highborn and continuing down the passageway.

The highborn watched his brother turn a corner and disappear from sight, shaking his head in disgust. 'And to think I feared them once upon a time,' he muttered. 'Such artless fools!'

Hauclir shrugged. 'On the other hand, even the wiliest rat dies if you stamp on him hard enough.'

'Are you calling me a rat?'

'Not at all sir,' the former guard captain deadpanned. 'Just saying there's a lot of big boots stamping around on this ship, that's all.'

'Have a care one doesn't land on your head.'

'It occupies much of my waking moments, my lord.'

The highborn failed to smother a sigh of exasperation. 'Tell me you've spent the remainder of your precious time serving my interests.'

'It wounds me to hear you say such a thing my lord,' Hauclir replied archly. 'Of course I have.'

'Then what transpired while we were away from the ship?'

The retainer fell in alongside Malus as they headed for the chart room. 'Yasmir never left her quarters, though there are rumours that she has collected the crew's offerings into a sort of shrine in her cabin. Urial's men watched her quarters day and night.'

Malus nodded. 'So that's why he left them behind. Interesting. What were their orders?'

Hauclir snorted. 'Who knows? Perhaps they were watching to see if she'd show herself. They didn't try to enter her room, nor did they interfere with the crew's offerings.' Hauclir glanced about, his voice dropping into a near-inaudible whisper. 'They also did nothing when Bruglir visited her in the dead of night.'

The highborn smiled. 'So the great captain is being cautious. And how did the visit go?'

The retainer shrugged. 'There weren't any loud shouts and Bruglir left with the same number of limbs he arrived with. Make of that what you will.'

'How do you know of this?

'One of the hands caught sight of the captain leaving Yasmir's quarters shortly after midnight. Everyone down in the ship's mess is talking about it.'

Malus nodded thoughtfully. 'Then I believe an agreement has been reached. That's excellent news.'

Hauclir's brow furrowed in consternation. 'It is?'

'Oh, yes. That fits my plan perfectly.' They had reached the highborn's cramped quarters. Malus pushed the door open and paused in the doorway. 'Now all we must do is reach the island and penetrate its wards and everything will be in place.'

'I see, my lord,' though from the expression on Hauclir's face it was clear that he did not. 'What shall I do in the meantime?'

'Take a bath. You smell like dead fish,' Malus answered, closing the door in the retainer's face.

THE WIND WAS brisk off the port bow, whistling through the rigging and slowing the captured raider to a near crawl as she approached the spot where the Isle of Morhaut was believed to be. Malus stood close by the ship's wheel, dividing his attention between scanning the northern horizon and watching Urial's preparations just a few feet away.

Urial knelt close to the deck, a brass bowl in one hand and a rune-carved brush in the other. The wind blew thin streamers of congealing blood from the surface of the bowl, painting livid streaks in his hair, but Urial paid it no mind, absorbed in the task at hand. He had painted a small circle on the planks with his brush and now turned slowly in place, decorating the inner arc of the figure with complicated sigils. Tanithra stood at the wheel, her expression savage and brooding.

She had returned to the captured ship immediately after the conversation with Bruglir, now almost six days past and the great captain had not summoned her back since. In that time Hauclir reported that Bruglir had visited his sister twice more, both times in the dead of night. Once, there were sounds of what might have been a struggle, but what actually happened in the cabin was anyone's guess. Malus believed that Bruglir was trying to make amends, having offered to kill Tanithra at the earliest available moment in order to redeem himself. Urial haunted her quarters like a wraith, watching the comings and goings of Bruglir with something akin to righteous indignation but taking no action of his own. At this point Malus felt that the only reason Urial hadn't sent his men to murder Bruglir in his sleep was that he needed to pin the captain's death on Malus in order to gain Yasmir's affection. The highborn wondered how much longer Urial's patience would hold out.

Malus had busied himself in the intervening days by drinking up every bit of liquor to be had on Bruglir's ship. Despite Hauclir's protestations each and every night that he'd scrounged up the very last of the ship's spirits, somehow Malus's combination of wit and malicious threats brought the retainer to his door the following evening with a new bottle in hand. As much as the highborn hated to admit it, he was beginning to find the former guard captain indispensable.

He needed to drink to keep the dreadful chill of the daemon's influence at bay. Though not as strong as it had been in the wake of the sea battle a week ago, it was still painfully evident, enough for Malus to fear that he'd finally crossed some threshold into the daemon's clutches that there would be no coming back from. That thought was bad enough to keep him awake at night; worse still was the fact that he was having more and more strange dreams, each one more intense and terrifying than the one before.

There was no rhyme or reason to them, as though they were images painted on a hundred different cards and then tossed to the wind, fluttering and falling in chaotic patterns that hinted at meaning but ultimately revealed nothing.

Corridors and stairways, he thought. Doors opening onto the same rooms, over and over again. It was as though it was the same scene replaying itself endlessly in his mind. The only difference was the footfalls. Each night they seemed to get a little closer. Huge, thundering footfalls, like the tread of a giant. And he knew, with the omniscience of the dreamer, that when those footfalls finally reached him, he was going to die. It was only a matter of time.

'What if they are not dreams,' Tz'arkan said. 'What if you see the future, like drowning in the bilges on the pirate ship?'

'That cannot be,' he hissed. 'These sights are pure madness. Nothing in this world can be so twisted and malign.'

'Even so, little druchii. Even so.'

'Be silent! Do you hear me? Be silent!'

Malus felt eyes watching him. He looked up and saw Tanithra studying him warily.

The daemon chuckled. 'She thinks you mad, Darkblade.'

'And why not?' Malus muttered. 'She's probably right.'

His work complete, Urial set the brush aside and straightened, holding the bowl with both hands. 'Furl all the sail you can and still make headway,' he told Tanithra. 'Once we begin threading the maze we will need to move slowly and deliberately.'

'With this wind off the bow we'll have to struggle to make headway at all,' she said, never taking her eyes from the horizon.

But Urial shook his head. 'If my theories are correct, it won't be the wind propelling us inside the maze.'

At that, Tanithra turned, but if she was expecting a more detailed explanation, she was to be disappointed. Urial had already bowed his head over the bowl and was muttering a long, breathless chant. Once again, Malus looked to the north, but the horizon seemed like an empty plain of featureless slate. He looked back astern and in the far distance he could still spy the black sails of Bruglir's fleet. The corsairs would stand well out to sea while the captured ship attempted to penetrate the island's wards.

The chanting was growing louder. Or rather, it was making its presence felt more intensely – he couldn't hear an increase in volume, but the air was trembling with each syllable. He could feel each ripple against his skin, like tiny wavelets stirred by an invisible hand. They washed over him and radiated away from the ship in ever-widening circles, reaching to the horizon.

Something was happening ahead of them, perhaps a mile off the bow. There was a mist gathering in the air, slowly spreading to the east and west like an unfolding screen.

Urial straightened, raising the bowl to the sky as if making an offering to the divine. His head tilted back and he poured the bowl of blood onto his upturned face. Crimson soaked into his white hair and pooled in his open eyes and mouth. The blood steamed as though freshly spilled, rising in curling tendrils from his eye sockets. When he looked down and smiled, his eyes were orbs of purest red, shining with power.

'I can sense it out there,' he said, his voice sounding clear but somehow diminished, as though he spoke from a great distance. 'It is like an unravelling of the world. Tanithra, do exactly as I say, without the slightest hesitation and all will be well. Now, take in your sails. We will be at the threshold in just a few moments.'

'All hands! Furl sail!' Tanithra cried at the men in the rigging. 'Smartly now, sea birds, if you value your lives!'

The mist was thickening, filling the sky ahead of them. It had no discernible shape – just a vast, shifting mass of curdled air, blown by a wind not of this earth. The last sails were brought in and Malus could feel the ship slowing in the water as she came up against the windborne waves. She rose on the white-capped swell and then as she nosed over the crest Malus could feel the ship gather speed, as though she were a wagon at the top of a high hill. He felt his guts come unmoored as the ship plummeted down, down and down, falling forever and then the mist closed over them, blotting out the sun.

'Three points to starboard!' Urial cried. 'Steady! Steady! Now two points to port! Quickly now!'

Malus could see nothing. The air shrieked and whistled, but he felt no wind against his face. The ship twisted and yawned, first one way and then another, as though she were caught upon four different seas at once.

To the highborn's horror, the world began to waver about the edges, as though he stood upon the verge of another waking vision. He fought against it with all the rage that was left to him and prayed to the Dark Mother that it would be enough.

Someone screamed. Urial continued to shout course changes to Tanithra. Malus looked over and saw the hard-bitten corsair bent almost double, her one eye tightly shut even though they were wrapped in shadow. Yet her hands still plied the wheel, driving the ship through its countless gyrations as it fought a storm unlike any other.

Suddenly, the wind dropped to a muted growl and Malus heard the pure tone of a ship's bell echoing out of the mist. Through the swirling mists to port the highborn thought he saw the rough outline of a railing, then a ship's deck strewn with debris and stricken with age. Boards were warped and covered with mould and fittings were pitted with rust and grime. And yet Malus saw scrawny shapes scrambling along the deck, clad only in tattered rags and sniffing the air like animals. One turned towards the highborn and he saw the figure point and throw back his head to let loose a long, plaintive wail bereft of sanity or hope. Before he could see more the raider abruptly turned to starboard and the ragged figure was swallowed by the mist.

He could hear more cries now, coming from lookouts at the bow and high up in the masts – he shivered at the thought of men high above the deck, surrounded on all sides by the unearthly smoke.

'Ten points to port!' Urial said, his voice sounding even fainter than before. Something made Malus look in that direction – a premonition perhaps, or the unseen manipulations of another waking vision – and abruptly saw a wide-beamed shadow looming from the mist, heading directly at them! If they didn't turn the ship would strike them on the beam and break them in half.

'Hard to starboard!' Malus cried. 'Put her hard over or we're lost!'

'NO!' Urial roared. 'Steady as you go.'

The ship loomed before Malus, pointed at them like a dagger aimed for his heart. 'Brace for impact!' he cried, flinging up his hands in a vain attempt to ward off the blow he knew to be coming.

And yet, nothing happened.

Malus lowered his arms and his mouth gaped in horror. The ship was passing *through* them, like an apparition, yet it looked as solid as the one he was standing on.

Then Malus realised that he recognised the grim figures watching him as the ship passed by.

It was *their* ship.

Malus saw a pale, grim-faced Hauclir watching him stonily from the apparition's bow. Other crewmen became apparent, each one grim as death as the ships passed one another. He saw Tanithra, still bent before the wheel and blind to the madness surrounding her. When he saw the gaunt, pale-faced apparition at Tanithra's side, Malus started as though stung.

Is that what others see when they look at me, he thought? He watched the ghostly version of himself recede into the distance until the ship was once more swallowed by the mist. Then the deck he was on plummeted once more before coming to a bone-jarring halt. The highborn staggered, his heart in his throat at the fear that he would be thrown about like a cask of ale and tossed overboard into the ghostly storm. And then he realised that the moaning was gone and the mist receding like early morning fog.

They were sailing across dark water beneath a dark sky and before them an island reared up from the water like the ruins of a drowned kingdom. The isle's steep cliffs were piled with the broken debris of hundreds of years of lost ships. Directly ahead of the raider lay a sheltered cove with long stone sea walls like two curving arms, their surfaces studded with twin towers that jutted into the sky like broken teeth. The shoreline of the cove was piled with the jumbled detritus of countless shipwrecks and upon the dark and refuse-strewn waters rode almost a dozen ships at anchor – Skinrider ships, some larger and far more powerful than the captured vessel the druchii had arrived in. High on the cliffs overlooking the cove rose a ruined citadel, crumbled and broken by the weight of centuries and the ceaseless gnawing of the sea wind. Pale fires burned in the citadel's windows and the arrow slits of the malevolent towers on the sea walls. Everywhere lay the crushing pall of enormous age, as though this were a place the rest of the world had forgotten long, long ago.

They had reached the Isle of Morhaut.

Chapter Twenty
THE COIN OF THE REALM

THE RAIDER DRIFTED from the bank of mist, riding uneasily on choppy grey waves. A breath of wind, reeking of rotting bone and wet mould, brushed Malus's face and pulled at the furled sails high above.

No one spoke. Even the sound of the water slapping at the hull was muted somehow – it was as though everything lay buried beneath an invisible mantle of incalculable age. Finally, it was Malus who broke the silence. 'We should lower some sail and learn what we can before returning to the fleet.'

Tanithra didn't seem to hear him at first. She turned to look at him, moving as though in a dream. 'Why is the sky dark? The sun was shining when we went into the fog.'

'It's this place,' Urial said. 'It… is elsewhere. A place that is no place, teased from the fabric of physicality like a thread pulled from a tapestry.'

The corsair shook her head savagely. 'Stop it! You're making no sense!'

Malus managed a quiet, bitter laugh. 'Such are the ways of sorcery, Tanithra. I like it no better than you. Focus instead on what you *do* understand. Like those towers yonder,' he pointed to the citadels rising from the sea walls, 'and the ships in the cove. What are we facing here?'

Tanithra gave him an uncertain look, but turned her attention to the island just a few miles away. 'We'll have to get closer,' she said after a moment. 'At least with all this darkness we should be able to make a fairly close run in towards the cove and then head back into the mist without raising any alarms.' She snapped out a series of orders to the men in the rigging. Moments later the mainsails were unfurled and the raider gathered headway, running before a mild wind that now blew from the south – if such a direction had any meaning in a place like this.

Malus turned to Urial. 'Can you sense any other wards between us and the island?'

Urial shook his head. His eyes still glistened red. 'No. But... it is difficult to be certain. The very air here seethes with power. A skilled sorcerer can conceal much beneath such a shroud.'

The highborn sighed. 'I shouldn't have asked.'

The former acolyte shrugged. 'For what it is worth, the sorcerer we fought on this very ship wasn't particularly skilled – merely a receptacle of a great deal of power. I don't think the Skinriders are any better sorcerers than they are sailors.' He turned about, taking in the dark vista around him. 'They are merely skulking in the ruins of a much greater power.'

'Eradorius, you mean.'

Urial nodded. 'He was one of the mightiest sorcerers in the time of Aenarion.' He paused as his eyes fell upon the ruined tower. 'I wonder what he was fleeing from?'

'That was millennia ago. Does it matter?'

Malus's half-brother fixed him with a bloody stare. 'Time is a river, Malus, remember that.'

'You highborn and your riddle games,' Tanithra growled, shaking her head. 'If I were you, I'd be more concerned about the twelve ships anchored in the cove.' She surveyed the distant hulls with an experienced eye. 'The smallest of them is as big as *Harrier*. Big Tilean and Empire warships, not the clapped-out scows we've been facing. I'd wager these are the Skinrider chieftain's prize ships, the fist he uses to keep his men – and the other North Sea raiders – in line.'

Malus frowned. 'Can we outrun them?'

Tanithra nodded. 'Oh, yes. We can sail circles around them, even in this awkward beast.' She patted the wheel almost affectionately. 'But we can't outfight them on the open sea.'

The highborn considered this and shrugged. 'Then we catch them at anchor and burn them. A swift raid into the anchorage with Bruglir's ships and a dozen dragon fire bolts and the Skinriders are broken.'

Tanithra chuckled coldly. 'A flawless strategy, Admiral – but they've anticipated this.' She pointed towards the towers rising from the sea walls. 'If you look closely you can see that those citadels have stone throwers situated to fire on the approaches to the anchorage, all the way up to the gap between the sea walls themselves. That's plunging fire, lobbing stones in an easy arc right down onto a ship's deck. A skilled crew could hole a ship in minutes and we know that the bastards are good shots, if nothing else.'

Malus shook his head in consternation. 'Then we put on all the sail we have and give them as little opportunity to fire at us as possible. We can be in and out of their reach again in minutes. You said yourself that stone throwers only cover up to the entrance of the cove.'

The corsair grinned mirthlessly. 'That's right. Now why do you suppose they would do that?'

The highborn considered the sea wall for a moment, trying to put himself in the minds of the raiders tasked with defending the cove. 'Because... they don't *need* to fire past that point.'

Her grin widened. 'Just so.' She pointed to the tower on the left. 'Look closely near the base of the tower.'

Malus did, but it was Urial who spotted it first. 'There's a chain leading from the tower into the water behind the sea wall.'

'That's right. A harbour chain, stretching across the mouth of the cove from one tower to another. If a ship hits that she'll be stopped dead in the water, helpless in the shadow of those two towers while the crew tries to turn her around and escape.' She looked back towards the stern. 'And with the wind coming up from the south, a ship would actually be *pushed* against the chain, making their job that much harder.' Tanithra nodded sagely. 'It's a tactic the Bretonnians perfected after they got tired of us raiding their seaports and the Skinriders have put it to good use here.'

'All right. How do we drop the chain?' Malus asked.

Tanithra shook her head. 'I expect the tower guards only allow in ships that they recognise. We can't break the chain from out here. We'd have to get into one of the citadels and lower it from there.'

Malus studied the towers at length, tapping meditatively at his chin. Plans swirled in his head as he considered the problem. He began to discern a way to thread them all together and a slow smile spread across his face as the pieces fell into place. 'Then that's exactly what we'll do,' he said. 'Turn us around. I think we've seen enough.'

Urial studied Malus warily. 'You have a plan, then?'

'Dear brother, I *always* have a plan.'

BRUGLIR FOLDED HIS arms and leaned back in his chair. 'That's the stupidest plan I've ever heard.'

Malus was unfazed. 'We don't have to fool them, brother. Just *tempt* them and even then only for a short time.'

The captain frowned. 'But Karond Kar?'

'Our ships fight the Skinriders every summer as they return to Naggaroth. They wait for us to head back with full holds and then try to steal our plunder. And what do they take? Gold? Gems? No. They take the slaves and as many of the crew as they can. Now think of Karond Kar and how many slaves pass through there every month. Thousands, all shackled and ready to transport.' Malus took a sip of wine from one of the captain's cups. 'The challenge will be in convincing them we aren't trying to attack them long enough for them to listen to our ruse.'

Bruglir's fierce glower swept over Malus, Urial and Tanithra in turn, as though he believed he was being made the victim of some kind of elaborate joke. 'So while we're talking to their leader, a landing party slips off the ship, somehow enters one of the sea wall towers and lowers the chain just in time for our fleet to attack the anchored ships.'

The captain thought it over once again and once again shook his head. 'A great deal can go wrong.'

'There is a certain element of risk in every daring plan,' Malus replied. 'Don't worry about what might go wrong – we'll be working to ensure that doesn't happen. Consider instead what will occur if things go *right*. The Skinriders will be broken, their treasure houses will be ours and you will return to Hag Graef as a hero. A *very wealthy* hero, I might add. You could buy a ship for each and every man in the fleet – every woman, too, for that matter,' he added, nodding towards Tanithra.

The druchii captain continued to brood, tapping at the table with a gloved finger. Finally he sighed. 'How would we co-ordinate our actions? The fleet will have to come in effectively blind.'

Malus looked to Tanithra. They had discussed this at length on the way back to the rendezvous. 'After we pass through the mist, the fleet waits two hours before starting its own passage. We will have men waiting in one of the towers by that point, ready to drop the chain.'

Bruglir thought it over. 'And if the Skinrider chieftain doesn't believe your story?'

The highborn shrugged. 'It doesn't matter, ultimately. By that point the fleet would be on the way and our men in place in the tower. Those of us brought before the chieftain will just have to put up a stiff fight and try to hold out until help arrives.'

'Your chances would be almost non-existent.'

Malus nodded. 'It's a risk I am willing to take.'

Bruglir rose to his feet, hands clasped behind his back. 'And it's a risk you've no compunction demanding of the rest of us, too.' He spread his hands. 'It ultimately doesn't matter what I think. Your writ trumps my authority in this case.' He sighed. 'Very well, Malus. We'll follow the plan. But the Dragons take you if it fails.'

Suddenly Tanithra shot to her feet. 'There's one more thing,' she said. 'If I lead the ship into the harbour and bring down that chain, I'll have something in return,' she said, the words coming out in a rush. 'I'll have command of the captured ship. I'll have bought it with blood twice over by that point. And I'll not ask for any extra hands. I'll sail her back to Clar Karond and hire my own sailors–'

Bruglir cut her off with a sweep of his hand. 'You won't be leading the raider in, Tani. You'll lead the landing party, but I'll have overall command.'

'*You?*' Tanithra exclaimed.

'Of course,' the captain snapped. 'The survival of the entire fleet will depend on the outcome of this raid. Did you think for a moment I wouldn't take a personal hand in its execution? You'll have the task of dropping the chain while Malus and I distract the pirate chieftain.'

Tanithra's face went pale. When she spoke, her voice trembled. 'You… you promised me a command. Years ago, during your hakseer-cruise. And I've served you faithfully. I let you dally onshore with that sister of yours and never said a thing–'

'The business of the highborn isn't of any concern to you,' Bruglir said coldly. 'And don't presume to remind me of my obligations. You'll get your command. Perhaps once we put in at Clar Karond. You heard Malus. There will be gold aplenty then.'

Tanithra started to reply, her eye glittering with rage, but abruptly she reined herself in. She took a deep breath and stilled her trembling hands. 'Yes, captain. Of course. A little longer then.' The corsair stood straight, her head high. 'Will that be all?'

Bruglir studied her for a moment, a flicker of concern in his eyes. 'Yes. I believe so. We will make preparations tonight, then I'll transfer to the raider at dawn and we will set the plan in motion.'

Malus rose to his feet. 'Of course, brother. Until then.'

They filed from the captain's cabin. Tanithra brought up the rear, walking slowly and carefully, as though she'd lost her sea legs since entering the room. Outside the cabin Urial turned and gave Malus a meaningful glance: the endgame approaches, his brass-coloured eyes said. Your move.

The highborn merely nodded and Urial walked away.

Hauclir straightened from his now-habitual spot against the bulk-head, his expression curious. Malus shook his head fractionally then walked away without a word, vanishing around a nearby corner. That left just Malus and Tanithra. When Malus turned to look at her, he was secretly delighted to see the stricken expression on her face.

'Are you about to return to the raider?' Malus asked, feigning casual interest.

Tanithra frowned, looking at Malus as though he'd suddenly grown out of the deck. Her expression hardened. 'What else? I have no intention of staying here.'

Malus smiled. 'Then I'll go over with you – if you'll allow me to get some things from my cabin first?'

A look of weary disgust played across her scarred features, but Tanithra managed a shrug. 'As you wish,' she said, motioning him to lead on.

Malus made his way down the cramped corridors to the chart room, offering no other comment until he'd pushed open the door and stepped inside. He reached deep inside a chart bin and held up the last bottle of rum. The highborn drew out the cork with his teeth and offered the bottle to Tanithra, who stood out in the corridor with her arms folded tightly against her chest. 'It would appear that Bruglir has decided to redeem himself in his sister's eyes,' he said quietly.

Tanithra shot Malus an angry glare, but after a moment she stepped inside and took the proffered bottle. 'He wouldn't have had to make the choice in the first place had you not brought her aboard. She'd *never* set foot on the *Harrier* before this.'

'How was I to know? It's not as though Bruglir spoke of you at the Hag. Believe me, had I known about you and my brother I would have left Yasmir at home.' He watched the corsair take a long pull of the fiery liquid and reached for the bottle himself. 'Of course, this also provides you with a unique opportunity.'

Tanithra snorted in disgust. 'Opportunity?'

'Oh, yes,' Malus assured her, taking a drink of his own. 'You now have a chance to split them apart for good.'

'I could split her easily enough on the edge of my sword, but that will just poison Bruglir against me,' she said bitterly.

'Then have Bruglir do the poisoning instead of you.'

Tanithra frowned. 'I'm not in the mood for more of your riddles, highborn.'

Malus passed back the bottle. 'Let me explain. What if we were to make Yasmir think that Bruglir was going to betray her?'

The corsair's eyebrow rose. 'We?'

Malus paused. 'Of course. I don't have any interest in seeing the two of them together any more than you do. So why not work together? Consider this,' he said, forestalling her reply. 'What if Yasmir was to believe that Bruglir was going to sacrifice her to the Skinriders?'

Tanithra paused, the bottle halfway to her lips. 'Why in the Dark Mother's name would she think such a thing?'

'Because we are going to seize her in the dead of night, smuggle her onto the raider and make her think it was Bruglir's idea,' he replied.

'We'll let her overhear that Bruglir plans to give her to the Skinriders in order to buy his way into their confidence.'

'What then?'

Malus shrugged. 'You'll be remaining behind with the landing party while the rest of us go and speak to the pirate chieftain. Turn her over to the pirates if you want. Once the attack begins, they'll throw her in a cell and she'll be rescued later, but by then the seeds of hatred will be sown in her heart.'

'She'll try to kill him.'

The highborn nodded. 'And Bruglir will be forced to slay her with his own hand. A rather neat conclusion and a fitting way to punish him for his fecklessness.'

Tanithra said nothing, her expression thoughtful. She took another drink from the bottle. 'Do you really think we could do such a thing?'

'Of course.' Malus stepped around her and closed the cabin door. 'Return to the raider. I'll stay behind and have my man keep watch on her cabin. Bruglir will likely visit her tonight, so return to the *Harrier* with a handful of trusted men just past the hour of the wolf. Once Bruglir's gone back to his quarters we'll make our move.'

Tanithra regarded him in silence. 'You know, I never spent much time in the Six Cities. I was born on a ship off the coast of Lustria and I can count on one hand the number of times I've spent more than a week ashore. My father was once a captain himself. He told me that betrayal is the coin of the realm in Naggaroth. Until just now I never knew what he was trying to tell me.'

She passed the bottle back to Malus. 'Tell me more.'

THE SHIP ROCKED gently in calm seas, silent at last after many hours of frenzied preparation. Malus reclined on his makeshift bed, the Tome of Ak'zhaal open in his lap. The hour of the wolf was close at hand; from where he sat he could glance through the tiny porthole and track the progress of the twin moons through the night sky. He was far too tense to sleep and thanked the Dark Mother for it.

Malus turned a page of the book with a gloved fingertip. He waited in black robes and an unadorned kheitan that belonged to Hauclir, as well as a shirt of fine mail of the type favoured by the corsairs aboard ship. A glass of watered wine rested on a sheaf of maps on a nearby shelf.

On a whim he'd taken the book from his bag as a way to pass the time. He turned the pages, puzzling over the strange diagrams and sketches, but after a few hours he found that he could understand the spidery script. He wondered if that was a reflection on how deep the daemon's taint ran in him, but feared to speculate further.

His finger traced the drawing of a square stone, its surface inscribed with a complicated sigil. The words beneath it were foreign to him, yet they gave up their secrets as his eyes passed over them.

Stone upon stone Eradorius built his tower, but its foundations he laid on darkness eternal, where there are no paths and no sun to mark the seasons. And there he laid passageways where there were none before, each to his own desire and not bound by the ways of the living world. The crooked passage he made straight and the straight he bent back upon itself so that no man knew the way into his sanctum save he.

Yet still Eradorius was afraid, knowing the fate that waited for him. So he made a guardian to watch over the twisting ways and commanded that it let no man pass into his sanctum, but that it should feast upon them and grow in strength. This it did, growing in strength and bestial cunning and its tread was like thunder in the twisting ways and its breath was like the desert wind.

Malus stopped. His heart went cold. 'Mother of Night,' he said softly. 'I haven't been dreaming at all.'

'Clever, clever little druchii,' the daemon purred. 'You aren't such a fool after all. That's reassuring.'

'Why didn't you tell me?' Malus cried. 'What profit did you gain by tormenting me?'

Tz'arkan laughed, a sound like rattling bones. 'That question answers itself, little druchii! Your fear is sweet. Your madness more so.'

'But how can this be? I saw corridors turn back upon themselves! Crossed the threshold from one room and entered it again on the other side! It's not possible!'

The daemon's laugh pealed inside his head. 'Foolish little ape! The answers are right in front of you, yet you refuse to see them! You refuse to *believe* in them, because you cannot see past the tree you shelter in. How pitiful you are, Darkblade. What am I to do with you?'

Malus fought with all his will to keep from hurling the ancient book across the small cabin. 'You may begin,' he said through clenched teeth, 'by giving me some answers!'

'Ask the questions,' Tz'arkan said with a sneer. 'I will answer them.'

'Did Eradorius come here to escape the fate of the other four sorcerers?'

'He did.'

'How?'

'By going where I could not.'

'But where?' Malus glowered at the tome. 'Wait – you were bound inside the crystal. You were trapped here, in the physical world.'

The daemon said nothing.

'Eradorius fled beyond the physical world to escape you, didn't he?'

'Yes.'

'But how?'

'I cannot explain it to you,' the daemon said. 'Your pitiful brain could not comprehend it. Suffice it to say that he used potent sorcery and leave it at that.'

Malus paused. 'Yet he also created this impossible labyrinth to protect him. He still needed to protect himself from intruders, so his tower must still somehow touch upon this world, correct?'

'Indeed,' Tz'arkan said. 'Physical form cannot exist in the realms of ether, little druchii. It must be… anchored, if you will, in order to retain its form. So the tower's foundations still touch upon the physical realm.'

'The tower still exists, then?'

'I do not know for certain,' the daemon replied. 'It has been many thousands of years. If the anchor was destroyed the tower and everything inside it would be lost within the ether.'

'Don't you know?'

'Did I not mention that he fled *where I cannot go?*' the daemon replied archly.

Malus set the tome aside and swung his legs over the edge of the table. 'You're still not telling me everything you know.'

The highborn could feel the daemon's wicked smile. 'Of course not. You haven't asked the right questions yet.'

'What do you want from me?' Malus cried angrily. 'You lure me into your damnable trap and set my feet on this impossible quest and then you keep me ignorant of the challenges before me! What do you hope to achieve? Is it not enough that you've taken my soul? Must you have my sanity as well?' He grabbed the glass of wine and hurled it against the wall. 'Answer me! ANSWER ME!'

Silence fell, broken only by the lapping of waves against the hull. It took several moments before Malus realised he wasn't alone.

He turned to find Hauclir standing in the doorway, his expression impassive. Malus fought down a surge of panic. He searched the retainer's eyes for signs of suspicion, but could find none. 'Yes?' he said at length.

'It's time, my lord,' Hauclir said, his expression inscrutable.

Malus straightened, running a hand through his dark hair. 'Very well,' he said, pulling up a voluminous hood that swallowed his face in shadow. 'Let us begin.'

Chapter Twenty-One
THE HOUR OF THE WOLF

'CORRECT ME IF I'm wrong, my lord,' Hauclir grumbled as they made their way down the dark, narrow passageways of the *Harrier*, 'but I fail to see how this plan of yours will accomplish anything except getting the two of us killed.'

'Your boundless faith in my skills never ceases to amaze me,' Malus replied. With the hood concealing his face, he was a black-robed apparition, a patch of night gliding among lesser shadows. 'I should think it obvious; by the end of the day I intend to see Bruglir and his sea mistress dead and myself in command of the corsair fleet.'

'And you plan to accomplish this by kidnapping your sister?'

A faint chuckle escaped the darkness within the hood. 'It will be the spark to the tinder that's built up between her, Bruglir and Tanithra. Consider how... changed Yasmir has become since she discovered Bruglir's betrayal. Now imagine how she will react when she thinks he's betrayed her again – and worse, intends to give her as a gift to the Skinrider chieftain.'

'Except for the fact that she'll be trussed up like a festival pig and thrown in the bottom of our cargo hold by the time she realises any of this.'

Malus nodded. 'That's where you come in.'

'Ah, yes. I should have guessed.'

'When Bruglir and I go to speak to the Skinrider chieftain you will remain behind, ostensibly to join the landing party that will lower the chain. Before that happens, I want you to go below and free Yasmir. Tell her that Urial learned of her capture and you and I have been trying to find her ever since.'

Hauclir nodded, his expression thoughtful. 'She'll try to kill Tanithra. You know that.'

'I'm counting on it. She was always known as being skilled with those knives of hers, but after seeing the carnage she wrought when we were boarded weeks ago, there's something almost supernatural in her ability to kill.' The highborn paused, considering his words carefully. 'For the first time I'm starting to wonder if perhaps Urial's obsession with her is motivated more than by simple lust. She might actually possess the touch of the divine.'

'So that's why you decided to side with her?'

'I'm siding with her because Bruglir must die. Otherwise he'll certainly kill me as soon as we've beaten the Skinriders. And if he dies, Tanithra must die as well, because I can't afford anyone else vying with me for control of the fleet.'

'And Urial?'

'For the moment we still need one another.' Malus said. 'I need him to get inside Eradorius's tower and he will need me to intercede with Yasmir on his behalf.'

The former guard captain considered the scheme for several moments in silence. 'So instead of merely kidnapping the lover of the Vaulkhar's heir, you're actually setting a plan in motion that's guaranteed to unleash a storm of bloodshed on your own allies just hours before a major battle?'

'That's a rather superficial way of looking at it, but essentially correct.'

Hauclir sighed. 'Well, I suppose it could be worse. Though at the moment that's only a theory, mind.'

'Enough moaning,' Malus said. 'What of Urial? Are you certain he's stopped watching Yasmir?'

'He hasn't even visited her cabin door since his return and his retainers haven't been seen either. I expect he's been busy drafting the charts that will direct the rest of the fleet through that damnable mist.'

'And you gave him my message?'

'I told him just as you said: the time for paying debts is almost at hand. He gave me a nod and disappeared inside his cabin. That's the last I've seen of him.'

'Very well. Maybe that will be enough to keep him out of our way for the next few hours. After that he can do as he pleases.'

Before Hauclir could respond the two druchii turned the corner of an adjoining passage and came upon half a dozen corsairs waiting impatiently just a few feet from Yasmir's cabin. Like Malus, most of the corsairs were clothed in black and concealed their features with hoods or leather masks. Only Tanithra kept her face uncovered and her expression was nothing short of joyfully murderous. Two of the corsairs carried a rolled-up sheet of sail hide between them, while the rest held black-coloured coshes in their hands.

'You took your time getting here,' Tanithra hissed. 'I've got men topside loading supplies onto the longboat, but we've only got a few minutes before they're done.'

'Calm down,' Malus said smoothly. 'Yasmir is likely asleep by now. We'll knock her out, roll her up and be gone before anyone knows what's going on.' He nudged Hauclir, who nodded sheepishly and pulled a black sailor's scarf over his face. 'Do your men know the plan?'

'Aye.'

Malus nodded. 'Good. And remember: no one speaks until we're aboard the raider and *no one* mentions any names save Bruglir's in her presence.' He turned to the corsairs. 'Let's go.'

Without waiting for a response, Malus slipped quietly down the passage until he reached Yasmir's cabin door. The thin wood was literally covered with votive runes and the names of sailors asking for Khaine's blessing. Here and there the tracks of the carved symbols were coated with dried blood. Malus ran his fingertips over the symbols. A feeling of intense apprehension suddenly gripped his heart, but with an effort he pushed it aside.

He held out his hand. Hauclir laid the handle of the cosh against his palm. The highborn took a last moment to make sure the corsairs were in place. 'Remember,' he said in a barely audible whisper. 'Move fast. Don't give her any chance to react.'

Heads nodded. Malus took a deep breath, pushed the door open and rushed soundlessly into the dimly lit cabin beyond.

The air inside was hot and stuffy. The deck planks were tacky with splashes and loops of spilled blood, sticking noisily to the soles of his boots. Across the cabin six candles had burned low, spilling long trails of wax over the lip of a narrow shelf and extending gleaming pillars all the way to the deck.

The cabin's single narrow bunk was empty, its blankets neatly arranged. Yasmir knelt in the centre of the room, her black hair unbound and spilling like a mantle across her naked shoulders. Her skin glowed in the soft candlelight, showing the gleaming red trails of the intricate patterns of cuts on her arms, legs and shoulders. Her back was to the corsairs as they swept into the room, but Malus took one look at Yasmir and knew that things had already gone terribly wrong.

He was halfway across the room when she rose to her feet, turning with an almost languid grace at his approach. Her face was beatific, unmarred by the razor edges that had decorated much of her naked body; her violet eyes were half-lidded and serene, as though she moved in a dream. It was the serenity of the executioner, the elegance of death incarnate.

Long, narrow-bladed knives made silver arcs in her seemingly delicate hands as she rushed towards Malus and instincts born of bloody-handed experience told him that if he let her reach him he was dead. She smiled, spreading her arms like a lover as she came to him and Malus threw himself to the deck rather than fall into that deadly embrace.

Malus rolled across the blood-spattered planks. He piled into a table and chair, knocking empty bottles of wine and a tray of breadcrumbs onto his head. Then came the sound of razor-edged steel slicing leather and skin and Malus heard a bubbling gasp where he'd stood only moments before.

Two bodies hit the deck with a single, muffled thud. Malus had ducked out of Yasmir's deadly rush and the two corsairs behind him had borne the brunt of her charge instead. Her knives had struck like adders, killing the men as they gaped at the unearthly vision before them.

Yasmir passed between the dead men as they fell and the corsairs beyond scattered like sheep before the wolf. One man who didn't move quite fast enough died with a knife through his temple and then there was no one between Yasmir and Tanithra. The female corsair snarled a wordless challenge and drew her heavy sword from its sheath. Malus scrambled to his feet, knowing that he would never reach the two women in time. For all her skill, Tanithra would be dead in moments and Malus was going to need an entirely new plan.

Suddenly there was the dry rustle of metal links and Yasmir fell forward. Hauclir pulled for all he was worth, dragging Yasmir backward by the chain he'd looped around her ankle.

Tanithra lunged for Yasmir and Malus leapt as well, determined to reach her first. His half-sister rolled onto her back as he loomed over her and her hands blurred in the air. Malus gritted his teeth and lashed out with the cosh, striking Yasmir squarely in the forehead. The back of her skull struck the deck with a sharp *thump* and she went limp. The highborn toppled to the deck beside her and Tanithra came up short, checking her sword stroke at the last moment.

Hauclir was beside Malus at once, standing between his lord and the female corsair. One of Yasmir's daggers jutted from the retainer's shoulder. 'Are you all right?' he whispered in a strained voice.

The highborn nodded, rolling onto his back. He gritted his teeth and reached down to his right thigh, his hand closing on the knife hilt and drawing the weapon from his leg. A hot rush of blood poured over his thigh, soaking into the woollen robes.

The retainer knelt, ignoring the blade in his own arm and probed Malus's leg through the hole in his breeches. 'Missed the artery by less than a finger's width,' he said grimly, then reached up and pulled Yasmir's other blade free. 'Let's hope she isn't the sort to poison her knives. I hear that's fashionable among the ladies this season.'

Malus ignored him, gritting his teeth against the swelling tide of pain as he glared up at Tanithra. 'I suppose you were planning to knock her out with the flat of your blade?'

'Of course not,' Tanithra spat. 'If she'd taken another step I'd have hacked her open like a sausage. You saw what she did to my men.'

'Then it's good for us that my man got to her first,' the highborn replied. Biting back a groan he pushed himself to his feet. 'Get her wrapped up. Now.'

'What about my men?' Tanithra exclaimed, pointing to the bodies in the middle of the room.

'Keep your damned voice down!' Malus hissed. 'Leave them. No one will come calling on Yasmir until the battle's done and by then it won't matter if they're found. Now get her tied up before she regains consciousness and we have to do this all over again!'

Tanithra snapped her fingers and the surviving corsairs leapt into action, binding Yasmir's hands and feet and gagging her with a strip of hide before rolling her up in the sail. With a grunt the two men levered the wrapped hide onto their shoulders and the female corsair ducked her head through the open door to make certain the coast was clear. Satisfied, she gestured to the men, who rushed from the cabin and down the passage.

Malus limped after Tanithra, wincing with every step. It surprised him how tempted he was to call upon the daemon to heal him, even in front of witnesses, but he steadfastly resisted the urge. 'Get back to the raider,' he told her, 'and see to it she suffers no accidents along the way. Remember, Bruglir must be made to kill her, or else you gain nothing by her death.'

Tanithra regarded him with an implacable stare. Saying nothing, she pushed past the wounded highborn and trailed after her men.

Once she was out of earshot, Malus turned to Hauclir. 'Do you have Yasmir's knives?'

The retainer nodded, pointing to where the hilts of the two weapons protruded from his belt. Hauclir's eyes never left Tanithra as she receded down the passageway. 'That one's not to be trusted, my lord,' he said, his voice tight with pain. 'She's too unpredictable.'

Malus shook his head. 'The die is already cast, Hauclir. She won't kill Yasmir now that I've reminded her of the consequences and she has no one else to turn to. We hold the upper hand.'

'For now, my lord,' Hauclir said darkly. 'For now.'

* * *

MALUS WALKED SLOWLY onto the deck of the captured raider, trying to conceal his limp as he climbed the narrow stairway. With great reluctance he'd allowed Hauclir to give him a small draught of hushalta and the stab wound ached fiercely as the drug did its work. The narcotic effects of the drink had kept him below as Bruglir and Urial had come aboard and the raider made its way once again through the mists surrounding the island. Already the sands were flowing through the glass; in less than two hours the rest of the fleet would follow Urial's charts and the attack would begin.

The highborn stepped onto the main deck under a dark sky, with the narrow towers guarding the island's sea wall looming ominously above the captured ship. They were less than half a mile from the opening to the cove and closing fast under a full spread of sail. Already Urial was moving among the crew, touching each man and imparting the blessing of Khaine to ward them from the corrupting touch of the Skinriders. Bruglir stood at the bow, studying the cove with a sharp eye. The highborn turned and caught sight of Tanithra at the helm, her expression grim. Hauclir was nowhere to be seen. Malus imagined that he was already below, waiting in the shadows near the cargo hold where Yasmir lay.

Malus worked his way forward, moving slowly and deliberately to the bow. He'd removed the light mail and now wore his customary full armour and the twin swords Nagaira had given him. Bruglir, by comparison, wore battered but functional plate armour and a single sword that had been well-cared for and obviously saw regular use. The highborn was irritated to see that his half-brother managed to arm himself like a knight of simple means and yet appear regal and heroic at the same time. Malus stood at the bow rail and squinted into the gloom. 'Any sign they've lowered the chain yet?'

'Not yet,' Bruglir answered. 'They'll likely wait until the last moment.' He pointed to the towers on the sea wall. 'Probably wondering what we're doing here and trying to find someone who recognises the ship.'

It hadn't occurred to Malus that the men standing watch at the tower might not be familiar with the captured raider and bar its entry on general principles. The thought was both absurd and terrifying all at the same time. 'You don't suppose they can tell we aren't Skinriders?'

Bruglir chuckled. 'Not unless they've stuck hawk's eyes in their skulls. They'll know us by the cut of our sails and the shape of our hull and that's all.' He nodded to the big ships anchored in the cove. 'Things will get interesting when we have to run *that* gauntlet, however.'

They were almost at the entrance to the cove. Malus eyed the tower to port. From this distance he could see how roughly it was made. Parts of the circular wall and the facings of the tower had fallen away and the top of the citadel was ragged and uneven. The firing positions near the top of the tower looked well-made, though and were perfectly sited to fire on ships approaching the cove. He couldn't see the squat stone-throwers or their piles of carefully hoarded stones, but he knew they were there. The windows of the citadel gleamed with pale light.

'There!' Bruglir pointed into the darkness ahead. Malus followed the gesture but all he saw were turgid waves and more shadow. 'Someone must have recognised us. They're lowering the chain.'

The captured ship sailed past the towers into the cove. Now that they were on the other side of the sea wall, Malus spied the huge links of the sea chain running from the portside tower, the greased links still playing out into the water as the barrier was lowered into the depths. Again, he was struck by the nature of the tower's construction. He supposed that the Skinriders had found their way to the island, saw the sea walls were undefended and did what they could to rectify the problem. It was crude but effective work, the highborn had to admit, but where did they get the materials?

Muted orders from the helm set the riggers to work overhead. Sails were brought in, slowing the ship. Bruglir placed a boot on the rail and leaned forward, resting his arms on his bent knee as he studied the distant coast. 'Those big ships draw too much water to move close to shore, but we should be able to tie up somewhere if we can find a pier.'

They were already coming up on the nearest Skinrider ships – two large Empire warships with old, wide mouthed brass culverins gaping like dragon's jaws both fore and aft. Malus wondered if the Skinriders still had powder for those huge cannon and if they could still fire without bursting apart. If they could the damage they would wreak would be appalling.

Hooded figures moved on the warship's main deck, shambling to the rail and looking down on the smaller raider as it sailed by. The druchii made no effort to conceal themselves and Malus fancied that he heard shouts of consternation on the deck of the towering warship as it receded into the distance.

The Skinrider armada was scattered across the breadth of the cove, maintaining enough distance from one another to allow them to get under weigh without risking a collision. Tanithra guided the ship past the two older Empire vessels and wove a seemingly meandering course past a Bretonnian guardship and two Tilean arrow-ships, their decks bristling with serried ranks of crude bolt throwers. Bruglir caught sight of a stone pier at the far end of the cove and barked orders to Tanithra. The clear, carrying orders, spoken in druhir, brought a chorus of startled shouts from the Skinrider ships nearby. Within moments a Norse horn winded an eerie, skirling note from the closest vessel, a sound soon taken up by every other ship in the cove, like the baying of a pack of wolves.

Shouts and gibbered cries echoed across the cove as the Skinrider crews boiled like ants from below decks and rushed to get a look at the interloper sailing past. Many carried lanterns gleaming with pale light and in their sickly glow Malus saw that these raiders were not merely skinless, but also hideously bloated and gangrenous, their bodies twisted by the corrupting power of the vile god they worshipped. Clouds of insects raged in the air above their putrefying bodies, stirred to frenetic activity by the Skinriders' distress. Officers – or what Malus presumed to be officers – bawled commands at the pestilent crew, ordering them back to work. Long-limbed, swollen figures climbed the rigging of the ships like gangly spiders, scrabbling for the stays binding up the tattered sails.

'Are they going to weigh anchor?' Malus mused aloud.

Bruglir shook his head. 'Unlikely. I expect they just want to be prepared in case they're called into action.'

'So they'll respond all the more quickly when your ships arrive,' the highborn said grimly and was surprised when Bruglir laughed.

'Believe me, once that chain falls it will be like wolves among the sheep. We could tell them right now that the fleet was coming and it wouldn't make any difference. In two hours this cove will be burning from end to end and we'll be hauling gold by the ton from their treasure houses.' The captain's dark eyes glittered with avarice and Malus smiled.

The captured raider came about slowly, aiming for the pier. It was made of cut stone, far better built than the ramshackle towers of the Skinriders and Malus wondered who might have made it. How many people had claimed this island in the thousands of years since Eradorius landed here? For the first time he felt a real tremor of doubt. What if the tower was no more and the idol long since taken by some enterprising sailor?

His dreadful reverie was broken by a roar that reverberated from the shoreline. A mob of Skinriders had rushed to the edge of the long pier, brandishing corroded weapons and thundering a challenge at the approaching corsairs. Lanterns bobbed on long poles above the mob, throwing their diseased faces into flickering relief.

Bruglir glanced at Malus and grinned. 'They've given us a welcome fit for a king,' he said dryly. 'I wonder if there will be slave girls and carafes of wine?'

Malus and the corsairs nearby laughed and everyone took heart from the sepulchral sound. Before, Bruglir seemed diffident about the plan, but now that the enemy was before him he had come alive, fearless in the face of peril and his men responded in kind. It was a revelation that filled Malus with surprise and bitter envy.

The raider pulled up alongside the pier. Bruglir turned to the men on deck. 'Cast away lines and make fast!' he ordered and the men leapt to obey. Heavy ropes went over the port side and men followed with nimble assurance, heedless of the raging mob howling at them only a few yards away. The captain smiled, pleased with his men's courage. 'Ready the gangplank!' he cried.

There was a groan of coiled ropes and the deck beneath Malus shifted as the big ship slowed against the pier. Almost immediately the raider's gangplank came down with a rattle and bang and Bruglir was on the move, forcing Malus to grit his teeth and lumber along painfully in his wake. Urial administered the last of his benedictions, hefted his axe and moved to join them, his masked retainers taking formation around him like a murder of brooding crows. Three heavily armed corsairs already waited at the gangplank, ready to provide escort for their captain.

'Tani, you have the ship,' Bruglir called. 'You know what you must do.'

Tanithra said nothing, watching the captain depart with a resentful scowl. Farewell, Tanithra, Malus thought. The Dark Mother grant we never meet again.

The highborn made his way carefully down the bouncing gangplank. Bruglir and his men were already halfway down the pier, forcing Malus to hobble along quickly to try and catch up.

Malus noted similar movement at the far end of the pier. Someone with rank had evidently asserted their control over the mob, because the shouts had fallen silent and the crowd was making way for a tall figure flanked by a handful of guards. As the figure approached the druchii on the pier, Bruglir started forward as well, intending to meet the Skinrider halfway. As soon as they were within shouting distance, Bruglir spoke something in a harsh, guttural language and Malus was surprised when the Skinrider answered in accented druhir.

'Don't humiliate yourself trying to speak our tongue,' the Skinrider said, his voice a harsh, bubbling rasp. The raider was clothed in thick hide that reminded Malus of a cold one's scales, crudely stitched together around his broad-shouldered, muscular form. Over the hide the Skinrider wore a Norscan's heavy chain hauberk that hung to his knees and his skinless hands gripped the haft of a huge, double-bitted axe. A black woollen mantle with a voluminous hood covered the raider's head, concealing most of it in shadow. When the Skinrider spoke, Malus could see gleaming muscles moving the raider's jaw and torn lips pulling back from pointed teeth. 'I can understand your pathetic mewlings well enough.'

Bruglir glared haughtily at the man. 'Do you speak for your chieftain, Skinrider? Because I did not sail for thousands of leagues to be met at the shore by a pack of his lapdogs.'

The Skinrider's jaw shifted in what Malus took for a smile. 'It is well that my men cannot understand your pulings. They would tear you to pieces for saying such things.'

'Then explain it to them, skinless one, or spare me your empty threats. I've come with a rich offer for your master.'

'Tell me what it is and I will decide if it is worth my master's attention.'

'Dogs have no place in their master's business,' Bruglir sneered. 'Take me to him and you will have served your purpose.'

'You think me a fool to allow you into my lord's presence? A pack of filthy, treacherous dark elves not worthy to lick the excretions from my master's feet?'

Bruglir laughed in the man's face. 'Does your great chieftain fear a dozen druchii that much?' The captain took a step forward. 'Are all the legends about the infamous Skinriders mere bedtime tales, meant to frighten soft human children?'

The Skinrider roared in anger, meaning to raise his heavy axe, but Bruglir fixed him in place with a single look. 'Raise a hand against me, you slug and it will be the last mistake you ever make,' the captain said.

A tense silence stretched between the two men. Finally the Skinrider lowered his axe. 'Follow me,' he growled.

The Skinrider turned, bellowing a command in Norse to the men at the end of the pier. Bruglir followed with a disdainful scowl, but to Malus there was no mistaking the cold glitter of triumph in his eyes.

Savour it while you can, the highborn thought. He followed along like a ghost in his brother's wake, smiling secretly to himself as he watched his scheme unfold.

You play your part well, brother, thought Malus as they began the long climb to the citadel on the cliff. But you forget that I am its author and this is a tale writ in blood.

Chapter Twenty-Two
DARKNESS FALLS

THE CITADEL WAS built upon the bones of the dead.

From the pier at the base of the cliff the Skinriders led the druchii through an empty village of stone houses, their walls covered in moss and their roofs rotted to dust many centuries past. They had the appearance of a cairn-yard, the stone outlines arrayed like barrows in orderly rows and left for the ravages of time. As they walked through the narrow lanes between the buildings Malus noticed how still and silent the air was; not a breath of wind or wild sound disturbed the funereal silence. Open doorways and empty windows seemed to tug at them as they passed by, tempting them with ancient mysteries hidden in their abyssal shadows. The highborn thought he could feel unseen stares scrutinising him from those ruined buildings – the flat, implacable gaze of restless ghosts, waiting in the darkness for the fleeting warmth of a mortal too curious for his own good.

Past the haunted village was a broad, slightly sloping field that had been cleared of trees at some time in the distant past – Malus could see dozens of mounds of very old tree stumps rising from the grass and low shrubs. A path worked its way across the field and forked on the other side. The left-hand path began to climb the cliff face in a long series of switchbacks that rose to the citadel, while the right hand path led to the wooden gates of a log stockade built against the base of the cliff itself. Vines climbed the logs of the palisade and green moss grew from the chinks between them. The narrow firing slits in the two corner towers and the windows of the stockade house that rose from behind the wall were black and empty as those in the village, but here the blackness exuded malignant, debased hatred. Even the Skinriders gave the abandoned structure a wide berth and Malus once more wondered how many other seafarers had come to the island over the millennia, seeking fortune or safe haven but finding only madness and ruin instead.

It was a long and arduous climb up the cliff face. The paths were steep and narrow and the Skinriders set a relentless pace. About midway up the cliff they began to encounter gaping holes high in the cliff walls, often in groups of two or three set side by side and exuding thick streams of smoke or mist that reeked of decay. Once or twice he heard a high-pitched rumble, like the hiss of a hot spring reverberating through the stone.

After a time the highborn tried to distract himself by looking out over the cove and the surrounding shore. He saw more abandoned buildings, broken monuments and even the rotted hulls of ships, all piled on top of one another over the progression of years. The twin towers of the sea wall stood in stark relief against a wall of mist that rose into the dark sky in every direction. The highborn tried to work out how long it had been since they'd passed through that barrier themselves. Had it been an hour? An hour and a half? How close were the ships of the fleet and was the landing party in position to lower the chain? There was no way to tell, he finally admitted to himself. Time was slippery on this side of the mist. It wasn't long before he caught himself stealing glances out to sea, dreading the sight of tall masts and black sails that meant the fleet had somehow arrived early and was headed for disaster.

They had reached the top of the cliffs before Malus realised it. The path turned sharply and entered an arched alcove that ended in a crumbling, stone stairway. He could feel the weight of the citadel looming over them, a pile of old stone built by skinless, diseased hands and mortared with blood and bone.

The stink of rotting blood was thick in the air. Up close, Malus could see the crumbling, rust-coloured cement clinging to smooth, glassy bricks that could have been ten thousand years old. He ran his fingers over the surface of one brick and felt a tingle of power sink through his fingertips. Something nagged at the back of his mind; a sense of familiarity that he couldn't quite place. Before he could consider it further the stairway made a turn to the left and Malus rose into a realm of utter madness.

The stairway emerged into the base of the citadel – or so Malus suspected, since he could see no walls from where he stood. The air was thick and humid, suffused with a greenish glow that shone through narrow, stitched curtains of skin that hung from somewhere high above. Streaks of blood and bile ran across the surface of the glistening hides, the pulsing flow drawing Malus's attention. After a moment he squeezed his stinging eyes shut and turned away, unable to shake the sense that there were *patterns* in the flow of sickly fluid, promising knowledge and power if he would open his eyes to them.

Clouds of blue and black flies hung like smoke in the air, filling the space with a keening buzz that played counterpoint to a chorus of ragged screams that echoed from somewhere high above. Drops of blood spattered down from the heights, falling upon the druchii's head and shoulders in a warm, bitter rain.

The curtains of skin made close spaces and narrow lanes in the interior of the citadel; Malus wondered if the whole structure was in fact an empty shell, partitioned by tapestries of torture and disease. The flaps of skin swayed in a faint breeze, seeming to reach for the druchii as they followed the Skinriders through the stinking labyrinth.

He turned to Urial, who was marching stolidly along behind Malus with his axe held across his chest like a sceptre. 'Have you any idea how long it's been since we entered the mists?' Malus whispered.

Urial shook his head. 'I can't say for certain, but it feels as though our time is nearly up.'

Malus nodded, his head turning this way and that as he attempted to keep his bearings in the confusing maze of rotting skin. 'I feel the same way.' He shot the former acolyte a pointed look. 'We may have to find our own way out when things become heated.'

Urial shrugged. 'If we are in an audience with their chieftain when our friends arrive we might be able to turn the situation to our favour,' he whispered, 'but if we've been here as long as it seems then there should already be alarms sounding from one of the sea wall towers. We've heard nothing yet and that worries me.'

The highborn felt a chill run down his spine – the faintest, teasing caress of Fate. 'Tanithra is a seasoned raider,' he replied quickly. 'There's no telling how many times she's stolen upon a watchtower in the dead of night and cut the throats of the men inside.'

'Perhaps you are right,' Urial said, but his expression was grim. 'We will know soon enough.'

It seemed as though they walked for a long while down the green, fleshy corridors, turning this way and that without apparent rhyme or reason. The drippings from the ceiling stained their shoulders and the sleeves of their robes. One of Bruglir's retainers stumbled and doubled over, retching violently. The rest of the procession filed on by, saying nothing. As bad as it was, Malus expected it was going to get much worse.

At length the procession came to a halt, bunching up in a group at the top of another curving stairway. This one led down, following the rough-hewn wall of a circular shaft that sank down into the cliff. A pillar of mist like the ones in the cliff wall outside rose from the depths, filling the inside of the tower with the festering stink of corruption. As Malus sidled through the crowd to stand beside Bruglir he heard a clattering sound echo from overhead. Pieces of glossy black brick flashed in the green light as they tumbled into the pit, bouncing from one wall to the next.

The huge armoured Norscan stood to one side, his axe propped on one mailed shoulder. The raider's skinless chin and white teeth gleamed eerily in the light as he spoke. 'Our lord waits below,' he said, pointing with a clawed finger. He made a rasping sound that might have been a chuckle. 'Present your gifts to him, druchii and he will make a place of honour for you at his side.'

A twinge of uneasiness passed through Malus, but before he could consider the situation more carefully Bruglir shot the Norscan a defiant look and started downwards, moving quickly and purposefully along the dripping stairs. Without hesitation Malus followed in his wake, casting a quick glance over his shoulder to check the progress of the rest of the party. Bruglir's retainers were the next to move, casting angry glares at the highborn for inadvertently shaming them. Urial came next, his shoulder pressed to the rough wall as he negotiated the steps with his twisted leg. His eyes were fixed on the mist and the depths below, as though trying to discern what lay at their source.

Just beyond Urial, Malus saw a Skinrider slide between the fleshy curtains and bow his head before the Norscan. The Skinrider's shoulders were heaving and he spoke to the tall warrior in quick gasps. The highborn felt his heart skip a beat as the Norscan stiffened and shot Malus an accusing look. That's it then, Malus thought. He's learned about the attack on the tower. But just as Malus went for his sword the Norscan pushed the messenger aside and rushed off the way he'd come, leaving the Skinrider loping along in the big warrior's wake.

Now what was all that about, Malus thought? Perhaps the raiders had learned something was amiss at one of the towers, but weren't certain exactly what. The Norscan suspects, though, the highborn thought. Urial caught his eye with an arched eyebrow and Malus shrugged in reply, then turned and went down the stairs.

Bricks continued to fall in a steady trickle from the top of the crumbling tower, sometimes striking the rock wall close enough to shower the druchii with dust as the projectiles hurtled past. The further they descended the thicker the air seemed to become, until Malus fancied that the tendrils of mist had taken on a life of their own. They swirled about his head and plucked coyly at his lashes with sticky, ghostly fingers, pulled at his lips and reached down his throat. He could feel Tz'arkan stir angrily in his breast, like a bear cornered in its den. Every time the mist seemed to thicken in his lungs, he could feel the daemon swell, scattering the fog and pushing it from Malus's body.

The descent seemed to last an eternity. After a time the air quivered with a stentorian hissing, like a dragon's hot breath issuing from below. Malus was reminded of the hot geysers that blasted skyward on the Plain of Dragons in Naggaroth, but as they descended still further he could hear an undertone to the loud exhalation of steam. There was a curious, piping note that rose and fell in pitch, almost too faint to hear beneath the sharp blast of trapped air. The sound seemed to come from dozens of sources at once, rising and falling in perfect unison. Despite the close atmosphere the tremulous wail chilled him to the bone.

As they descended further the mist thickened, surrounding them and making their footing difficult. Malus stumbled ahead, barely able to see where to put one foot ahead of the other and trying to focus on the hazy outlines of Bruglir's shoulders and head. The highborn took another step – and came up short, realising that their descent had ended at last. He walked forward hesitantly, enveloped by stinking clouds of pestilence, until Bruglir's tall form resolved itself out of the haze. The captain had his hand on the hilt of his sword, peering warily into the mists around him. He caught sight of Malus and for a moment he actually seemed relieved. The hissing sound – and the chorus of cries that rose beneath it – resounded thunderously from the rock walls around them.

Then, without warning the mist billowed – and then abruptly receded, retreating like an ebb tide towards an irregular circle of grey light that grew in brightness and definition as the fog thinned. After a moment Malus realised that the circle was one of the rough openings that decorated the side of the cliff. A stiff wind had blown up, racing across the cliff face and drawing the steam away for the moment.

Any sense of relief the highborn might have felt vanished in a single instant as he saw what the mists were concealing. Beside Malus, Bruglir recoiled with a startled curse.

They stood in a natural hollow within the cliff, with a rough but relatively level floor that stretched almost eighty paces across. In the centre of the chamber lay a circular pit approximately fifteen paces at its widest point. Steam rose in gusts from a thick, heaving surface of red and yellow. Arms, legs and hairless heads rolled and bobbed in the horrific stew; lifeless fingers seemed to wave as the hands rose and fell with the escape of trapped gases. The gangrenous air over the mass seethed with flies, their buzzing rasp lost in the reverberating voice of the pit.

With growing revulsion Malus's shocked mind took in every detail of the pit's hideous contents and a small part of him realised that it was a stew of melting bodies, tossed in by the hundreds and left to ferment in the steam. The whole surface heaved with an eruption of stinking gas and as the highborn watched, the heads riding the surface of the mass rolled back on melting necks and *moaned*. Their voices were the source of that terrible symphony of pain that rose with the steam and the highborn was stunned in awe and horror at the sight.

'Mother of Night and the Dragons of the Deep Sea,' Bruglir whispered. 'What monsters are these?'

'Supplicants of the Ruinous Powers,' Malus said gravely. 'Worshippers of the god of pestilence and decay. You knew this from the beginning, Bruglir. You said it yourself.'

'Yes, but…' the captain's voice trailed away as he tried to grapple with the enormity of the scene before him. 'I never imagined…'

The surface of the pit heaved again, but this time it wasn't the roiling pressure of steam behind the motion; the fleshy skin of the human stew stretched like a caul as a powerful figure rose from the depths before the stunned druchii. Malus watched the clinging mass of skin and jellied bone drape like a cloak around a broad-shouldered, muscular figure. Yellow-green folds of soft skin stretched from the tips of huge, downward-sweeping horns and then parted, tearing a hole that settled around the top of the creature's head like one of the Skinriders' crude hoods. Two green points of light burned where the beast's eyes should be and the flesh of the hood ran down its dark cheeks in a mockery of tears.

The Skinrider chieftain raised his powerful arms, draped in sleeves of skin and bone and turned his blazing eyes upon the druchii. Malus met that baleful stare and understood that the creature before him might have been a man long ago, but now a fell daemon possessed the body standing before him. Tz'arkan noticed as well and this time Malus sensed the daemon recoil warily in the face of this new threat.

'Come forward.' The daemon's voice was like the death-rattle of a god, a sound like pooled blood and pus bubbling from a diseased wound. Malus's guts shrivelled at the sound and he heard Bruglir groan in dismay as the captain took a lurching step forward and then another. Malus felt the pull as well, though it seemed distant and dreadful rather than an iron fist that defied resistance. He could hear the rest of the party take halting steps toward the daemon and the highborn joined in rather than reveal his advantage to the chieftain.

'Ah,' the daemon sighed, 'the flesh of Naggaroth. The sweet blood of the lost elves. Bones like fine, cool ice. You are welcome here. I will savour you in my embrace and you will entertain me with song.'

The daemon spread his powerful arms in welcome. Malus saw the molten heads in the chieftain's raiment shudder, the mouths working in a chorus of madness and horror. Milky eyes rolled in their sockets, focusing on the druchii lumbering helplessly to their doom.

'You will not defile the chosen sons of Khaine!'

The words cut through the air like the shriek of a red-hot iron against skin. Urial the Forsaken limped fearlessly towards the daemon, his axe held high. His pale cheeks were deeply slashed and his own blood burned like a fiery brand from the razor edges of the arcane weapon. Urial's voice thundered in the cavernous space. 'The chosen of Khaine are not for you or your master to touch! They are marked for fields of gore, not the stinking pit of human mud!'

Bubbling laughter echoed from the towering figure. 'And what will you do, poor cripple, if I choose to take them anyway? Will the Bloody-Handed God make his presence known through a flawed vessel such as yours?'

Urial met the daemon's blazing eyes and smiled. 'My body is weak, yes, but my faith is like shining gold. Go ahead, daemon. Tempt the wrath of the Lord of Murder and feel the full measure of his terrible vengeance.'

The chieftain started to reach for Urial with one taloned hand – and then hesitated. The former acolyte faced him with the fiery zeal of the true believer and in that moment Malus saw the faintest tinge of doubt creep into the daemon's eyes. 'Very well,' the chieftain said at length and the highborn felt the being's terrible presence lift from him like a collar of iron. 'Say what you have come to say and I will decide if it is worth your lives.'

Bruglir took a silent breath, composing himself and then took a measured step forward. There was no mistaking the terror in his eyes, but the captain's voice was steady and sure. 'I and my men wish to join your ranks, terrible one. We wish to become Skinriders ourselves.'

Another croaking chuckle. 'Indeed? You chosen sons of Khaine would abandon your god and your precious white skin and serve me like dogs? Why?'

Malus swallowed. Think quickly brother, he prayed. He couldn't say a word to prod Bruglir, or else the daemon would know he was being fed a lie.

To Malus's great relief, the captain barely skipped a beat. 'Why, revenge, of course,' he said. 'My father is dead and my brother Isilvar has betrayed me. He has taken my home and slaughtered or enslaved every member of my household. I am an exile, hunted by the best assassins my brother can buy. Where else can I find sanctuary? Where else can I ally myself with a force powerful enough to make my brother – and all Hag Graef – pay for the way they betrayed me?'

The daemon studied Bruglir in silence, folding his clawed hands over one another like a fearsome mantis. 'Tell me. What form would this vengeance take?'

'With your leave, I would command a raiding fleet that would sack the slave tower of Karond Kar, then cross the inner seas and strike Hag Graef itself. There are hidden tunnels that lead into the city – we could strike swiftly, in the dead of night and put half the city to the torch before anyone realised their peril! Think of it – we could return with holds full of every kind of flesh to fill your great cauldron and entertain you for *years*. We would return with enough wealth to make you the undisputed lord of the northern seas for a very long time to come.'

The daemon leaned towards Bruglir. 'And what do you stand to gain from all this?'

Bruglir shrugged. 'The best is reserved for me, of course. I see my enemies broken and driven before me. I burn everything they hold dear and paint them with the ashes. I hear their cries of anguish as I feed them into your stew pot one by one. And I get to continue terrorising them for decades, taking what I will and destroying that which does not please me. What man could wish for more?'

'Indeed.' There was a wet, slithering sound as the chieftain rubbed his greasy hands together. 'And how will you lead my fleet down the deadly straits and assault the tower of Karond Kar?'

To Malus's surprise, Bruglir rose to his full height and drew a deep breath, evidently ready to launch into a long-winded plan that the captain must have been rehearsing for several days. He'd planned for everything, Malus saw with a touch of admiration. I'd thought to kill you last of all, the highborn thought ruefully. Now, you may have to be the first, brother. My congratulations.

Just as the captain began to speak however there was a commotion on the stairs. Malus turned to see the Norscan warrior advancing across the chamber at the head of a large band of Skinriders wielding swords and spears.

The alarm has sounded at last, Malus thought, reaching slowly for his sword.

'What is the meaning of this?' said the daemon, anger bubbling in his voice.

'A runner has arrived bearing news,' the Norscan said.

'And it is worthy enough to trouble me?'

'It is,' said a voice from within the mass of Skinriders. 'There is a druchii fleet approaching, aiming to catch your ships at anchor and burn them, then sack your tower and stake you out to die in the sun.'

A shock ran through Malus's body. Bruglir and Urial turned at the sound of the voice, their eyes widening in recognition.

'What of the great chain protecting the cove?'

'They meant for it to fall,' said the voice. The raiders parted as the speaker worked her way towards Malus and the rest. 'While you wasted your time talking to these liars, a landing party was to slip into one of the sea wall towers and lower the barrier.

'I should know,' Tanithra said with a cold smile. 'It was a task they entrusted to me.'

Chapter Twenty-Three
BLOODSTORM

TANITHRA STEPPED FROM the crowd of Skinriders, one hand resting on the hilt of her sword and the other dragging a naked figure by her long, raven-black hair. Yasmir was still gagged, bound at the wrists and hobbled by ropes around her ankles. Her lithe body was scraped and bruised from head to toe, but her violet eyes blazed fever-bright, tinged with fury – and a kind of fearlessness – that made Malus wonder how much of her sanity still remained. The female corsair was flanked by almost a dozen members of the captured ship's crew, their faces and arms stained with spatters of blood. Hauclir, Malus noted, was nowhere to be seen. Had he escaped the bloody mutiny or died with the rest of the crew?

'The Dragons Below take you, damned mutineers!' Bruglir took a step towards Tanithra, his sword glittering in his hand. The big Norscan and six Skinriders moved to meet the captain, ringing him in a half-circle just beyond sword reach. Malus turned slowly in place, sizing up the situation as the rest of the Skinriders fanned out around the rest of the druchii with swords and axes held ready. He bit back a curse, thinking furiously. The sea chain was still in place and time was rapidly running out.

Bruglir barely took notice of the huge Norscan and the Skinriders. His face was an alabaster mask of rage. 'I gave you a place on my ships and a life on the red tides! And this is how you repay your oaths to me?'

'You speak to *me* of betrayals?' Tanithra shrieked, her face contorting into a mask of near-bestial hate. 'I kept my oaths to you for *years*, commanding the crew of the *Harrier* better than any of your other captains. I tolerated your dalliances with this pampered witch–' she hauled Yasmir nearly upright with a savage jerk of her hair, 'and I waited for you to make me a captain, as was my right. That ship down at the pier was mine by right of blood, but you took it from me. You convinced me then and there that you weren't going to keep your oaths to me, o great and mighty captain. So it is *you* who are forsworn, not I.' She looked to the daemon towering from the charnel pit and nodded in salute. 'So I will seek a ship of my own with another great leader and buy it with your blood.'

Bruglir snarled like a wounded wolf and took another step towards his sea mistress, his sword trembling in his hand. The Skinriders growled in response and Bruglir's retainers took their place beside their captain with naked steel in their hands.

Malus hissed in frustration, casting about for some way to salvage the situation before everything spun out of control. He looked to Urial, but he had forgotten everyone else save for the pale figure in Tanithra's grip. Urial clutched his axe, his face stricken with fear and rage. His six retainers held their greatswords in their hands, waiting on their master's command. One wrong move, one hasty word and a storm of bloodshed would erupt. The highborn turned to the Skinrider chieftain. 'She lies, great one,' Malus said hastily. 'We've long suspected she might be an agent for the Witch King and now she reveals herself in an attempt to protect Naggaroth from your fleet.'

Tanithra threw back her head and laughed with bitter fury. 'You are slick as an eel, Malus Darkblade!' she cried. 'You've poured your poison in our ears all along, twisting our minds with your lies! But I was not the fool you took me to be.' Once more she tightened her fist in Yasmir's hair and gave her a rough shake. 'Did you really think I wouldn't see through your scheme to kidnap this wretch from her cabin? You thought to provoke Bruglir to kill Yasmir *and* me while you lurked like a rat in the shadows!'

Malus felt the hairs on the back of his neck prickle as both Bruglir and Urial rounded on him. 'Viper!' Bruglir hissed. 'Would that you'd died in that winter squall. You've brought me nothing but ruin since you stepped aboard my ship!' He levelled his blade at Malus's throat. 'The Darkness take your damned writ! After I've killed every last one of these mutineers I'll hold your beating heart in my hands!'

'*Silence!*' the chieftain thundered and Malus once again felt the daemon's will settle on him like a heavy cloak. Bruglir groaned, swaying on his feet and his sword fell slowly to his side.

Slowly, ponderously, the chieftain stepped from the pit, his raiment of soft, living skin trailing behind him like a noble's gown. He towered head and shoulders above every other person in the room, even the huge, axe-wielding Norscan. 'I see the truth of things now,' the daemon said. He pointed to Tanithra with a taloned finger. 'And I accept your service. Already you have served me well, druchii and soon you will enjoy the blessings of the Great Father. Name your reward.'

Tanithra smiled in triumph. 'There are seven ships and more than three hundred souls sailing into your clutches, great chieftain. Leave me just one of those ships – just one – and I will be content.'

The daemon hissed in pleasure. 'And you will accept the benedictions of the Great Father Nurgle?'

'Oh, yes,' the corsair said. 'Melt this scarred hide from my body, great chieftain.' She pulled Yasmir to her feet, glaring into the highborn's violet eyes. 'I'll wear this one's perfumed skin instead.'

'No!' Bruglir cried, his eyes wide with desperation. 'Spare *me*, great chieftain! Slay the rest – take all the ships and the men. I ask nothing from you and I can still deliver Naggaroth into your hands!' With an effort he turned his head to indicate Yasmir. 'She will be a sweet sacrifice indeed, great chieftain! A highborn woman, worshipped like a saint by my crew! Take her into your embrace!'

The daemon moved in a blur, lashing out at the druchii captain with a backhanded blow that flayed the skin from the right side of his face. Bruglir fell with a shriek of terror and pain and his retainers cried out in frustration and despair.

'Fear not, druchii. You will indeed deliver Naggaroth to me. You will sing to me its secrets as you melt within my grasp.' The daemon stepped past the stricken captain, its eyes focused on Yasmir. 'But you are right. I can smell the musk of divinity rising from her tender skin. I will save her for last and let you watch as she submits to my will.'

It was all spinning out of control. Malus watched Bruglir roll to his feet, skin hanging in wet, grey strips from his cheek and the bone beneath already rotting from the daemon's touch. His retainers struggled to draw their blades, their faces contorted with hatred even as the Skinriders standing nearby moved to strike them down. The highborn started to speak, thinking to seduce the great chieftain with promises of hidden treasure in the tower of Eradorius. But his voice was lost in beneath a wild roar as Urial the Forsaken hurled himself at the Skinrider chieftain and the killing storm broke in all its fury.

Urial slashed one-handed at the chieftain, but the axe blade had tasted little in the way of blood or magic so the attack was awkward and weak. The chieftain recoiled from the gleaming blade nonetheless and the Skinriders responded with shouts of rage. They rushed at Urial in a shambling tide, only to be met by the whirling draichs of his silver-masked retainers. The daemon hissed and spat words of fell power, causing Urial's axe to blaze like a brand and Malus felt the chieftain's oppressive will vanish in the battle.

Malus drew his sword with an ululating war scream and spun on his heel, slashing at the pair of Skinriders who were charging at his back. He caught the first man across the eyes, dropping him to his knees and knocked aside the downward-sweeping blade of the second raider. Knocked off-balance, the man stumbled forward and Malus's back-handed return stroke sent the Skinrider's bulbous head bouncing across the cavern floor. The highborn stepped past the toppling, head-less body and thrust his sword through the blinded raider's throat. The keen edge parted the spine and burst through the back of the man's neck, pushing him over backwards.

As Malus put his boot on the raider's chest and made ready to tear his trapped blade free a powerful sense of vertigo washed over him. His knees trembled and the walls seemed to blur. He heard footsteps behind him and the sound of steel slicing flesh and watched the ghostly image of his own head tumbling through the air.

Without hesitation the highborn ducked – and the world snapped back into focus as Bruglir's sword hissed through the air where his neck had been a heartbeat before.

Malus aimed a savage cut at the captain's knees, but Bruglir deftly parried the stroke and responded with a lightning-fast cut at the high-born's head. Malus blocked the stroke, just barely and threw himself into a powerful thrust at Bruglir's eyes. The captain batted the sword aside but gave ground, allowing Malus to rise to his feet and press his attack, aiming a vicious series of cuts at Bruglir's head and neck.

The captain's face was a creeping horror; as Malus fought he could see black rot blooming across the muscle and bone of Bruglir's flayed cheek. Already the captain's right eye was turning milky-white and the veins of his neck blackening with corruption. He responded with a feint to Bruglir's throat and a sudden chopping stroke at the captain's right knee, but the bent joint brought the blow up short and a sudden stab of pain from his wounded leg caused him to stumble. The blow glanced from Bruglir's armour and Malus was left unbalanced and off-guard, his neck exposed to the captain's sword. A chill raced down his spine as Malus waited for the blow to fall, but a thunderous clash of steel caused the highborn to look up just as the Norscan's heavy axe crashed into the back of the druchii captain's shoulder. The blow spun Bruglir half around, tearing through the straps of his left pauldron and causing the armour plate to flap loose like a broken hinge.

Bruglir roared in pain – a cry tinged with madness and fear and aimed a backhanded stroke for the Norscan's neck. The warrior caught the blade on the haft of his axe and pressed downwards, forcing the blade to the floor. His left hand shot out and closed around Bruglir's throat, the muscles on the back of his skinless hand standing out like steel cords as he squeezed the life from the wounded captain. One of Bruglir's retainers leapt at the Skinrider, stabbing into his shirt of heavy mail, but the huge warrior slashed upwards with his axe and smashed the blade into the retainer's face. Blood and bone splattered in all directions and the druchii fell with a strangled cry.

Malus lunged forward with a shout, swinging his sword in a short arc that severed the Norscan's hand at the wrist. Dark blood sprayed over Bruglir and Malus both and the Skinrider reeled backwards with an anguished roar. The Norscan swung his axe one-handed at Malus, forcing him to dodge backwards, then the highborn twisted to parry a thrust from Bruglir that narrowly missed his throat. Malus stabbed once again at Bruglir's ruined face and was surprised when the point scored muscle and bone just beneath the captain's milky eye. The captain screamed in shock and pain and fell back and the highborn slashed wildly at the Norscan, raking his blade across the warrior's mail shirt.

Despite his terrible injuries, Bruglir's ferocity and skill were barely diminished. He pivoted slightly until he could see Malus with his left eye and aimed a series of punishing blows at the highborn, battering aside his guard and making a ragged cut across Malus's neck. Before Malus could respond the Norscan lunged at him from the right with an overhead blow that the highborn barely knocked aside.

Thinking quickly, Malus feinted with a thrust to the Norscan's eyes, then lunged between the two attackers and towards Bruglir, aiming a blow at the captain's left side. Bruglir pivoted to keep his good eye on Malus, his breath coming now in wheezing gasps – and the Norscan's axe blow, aimed at Malus, struck the captain in the back of the head instead. Bruglir stiffened, his head haloed for a single moment in a corona of bright red, then collapsed to the ground.

The Skinrider cursed, trying to pull the axe free one-handed and Malus turned and swung his sword down in a single motion, cutting off the warrior's axe arm at the elbow. The Norscan roared in fear and pain – until the highborn's next stroke split his skull from crown to chin. Malus pulled the pus-streaked sword free as the body crashed to the ground and swayed on unsteady feet, trying to look in every direction at once. Only a dozen feet away Bruglir's last retainer fought a desperate battle against two Skinriders; a rusty spear jutted from the man's shoulder and his left arm dripped long streamers of blood, but he fought the pair of raiders with berserk ferocity.

Urial and the daemon still fought, the former acolyte's axe leaving trails of molten light in its wake as it slashed at the chieftain. For all Urial's fury, however, the daemon's speed was fearsome – though its robe of flesh was tattered and rent, the deadly axe had yet to bite into the chieftain's rotting body. Urial's retainers had leapt into battle with the Skinriders and reaped a terrible harvest of ruptured bodies and severed heads. Now they fought a two-way battle between the surviving raiders and Tanithra and her mutineers. Two of the silver-masked warriors were already dead, pierced and hacked into torn mounds of flesh.

As Malus watched, Tanithra traded blows with one of Urial's retainers, her heavy sword almost a match for the fearsome draich the retainer wielded. The warrior stepped forward, bringing his blade down in a diagonal slash that meant to split the corsair in two. At the last moment however, she ducked and leapt inside the blow, letting it pass harmlessly to her right, then brought her sword up in a disembowelling cut. The retainer collapsed, clutching vainly at his spilled guts and Tanithra charged headlong at Urial, leaving Yasmir bound like a sacrificial goat on the cavern floor.

Malus bared his teeth in a predatory snarl and swung wide of the daemon and Urial, circling around to where Yasmir lay. He watched Tanithra descend on Urial like a hawk, but before the highborn could shout a warning Urial seemed to sense the corsair's presence and he turned with surprising speed, knocking her blade aside but then finding himself forced back on the defensive as Tanithra pressed her advantage, hammering at him with a non-stop rain of punishing blows. One of the silver-masked retainers abandoned the melee and ran to his master's aid – only to be seized by the possessed chieftain. The daemon's hand closed about the retainer's sword wrist and Malus watched with horror as the limb melted like a candle held to the flame.

The highborn fell to his knees beside Yasmir, gently rolling his half-sister onto her side. 'I'm going to set you free, sister,' he hissed into her ear as he worked at the knot securing her gag. In a moment the greasy rag was pulled free and Malus drew his knife, turning to the ropes binding her ankles. He could feel her eyes upon him, though she said not a word. There was a serene, passionless cast to her face amid the chaos and slaughter that Malus found both seductive and deeply disturbing. 'Tanithra's lies have doomed us all,' he continued, sawing carefully at the ropes. 'Bruglir is dead at the enemy's hands and the daemon rages unchecked.'

There was another terrible, bubbling shriek. Malus stole a frantic look over his shoulder and saw another of Urial's retainers dissolving in the daemon's hands. A draich protruded from the chieftain's skull; the daemon reached up with one hand and crumbled it in a rain of blood-red rust. Then Malus locked eyes with the chieftain and the daemon snarled a challenge, tossing the melted warrior aside and striding purposefully towards him.

Malus sliced through the ropes around Yasmir's ankles. He reached for her wrists. 'Sister, we're going to have to run,' he began and then a shadow fell over him.

He looked up. A Skinrider loomed over him, a bloody axe dangling in one gloved hand. The highborn's eyes went wide and he tensed himself to leap – until the raider dropped the axe and reached for the drooping hood. With one hand he pulled the slimy surcoat free and Malus stared in shock at the stained face of Hauclir.

The retainer hefted a stitched leather bag, like a wineskin, its rough seams dripping water. 'You're going to want to duck, my lord,' Hauclir said and flung the bag at the daemon.

Malus looked back at the chieftain. The daemon saw the ungainly projectile lobbed at him and caught it deftly with one hand. Smiling, the creature closed its fist, crushing the bag in a spray of water – and smashing the globe containing the dragon's fire hidden within.

In the blink of an eye the daemon was engulfed in a cloud of ravenous green fire. The sorcerous compound seethed across the chieftain's body, eating through muscle and bone as though they were old parchment. The daemon whirled, shrieking and beating at the hungry flames, but the dragon's fire was not to be denied. The surviving Skinriders fell back, crying in dismay as the possessed man let out a long, tormented scream and ran, leaving pools of burning fat in its wake as it hurled itself through the hole in the cavern wall and out into the open air three hundred feet above the cove.

'Blessed Mother of Night,' Malus rasped, unable to tear his eyes from the burning puddles of human tallow stretching across the cavern floor. 'You stole a globe of *dragon's fire?*'

Hauclir grunted, wiping vile fluids from his face with the back of his hand as he drew one of Yasmir's needle-like daggers from his belt and began sawing at her bindings. 'You had me stealing from Bruglir's brandy cabinet. Taking a globe of dragon's fire was much less dangerous by comparison.' He shrugged. 'I thought it might come in handy somewhere down the road.'

Malus shook his head ruefully and turned to reply as the last of Yasmir's bindings fell away. He caught a glimpse of violet eyes and luminous skin as she moved with the soulless grace of a hunting cat, rising like smoke between the two men and plucking her knives from Hauclir as though he were a child. The highborn looked up at Yasmir with a mix of wonder and fear, black daggers glinting balefully in the green light. Her face was serene, her mind lost in dreams of slaughter as she faced Tanithra's smoking form.

The druchii corsair stood less than ten feet away, smoke rising from deep wounds burnt by drops of dragon's fire flung from the chieftain's writhing body. She swayed on her feet, the last foe still standing in the bloodstained chamber and her sword was pointed unerringly at Yasmir's throat. Urial lay nearby, knocked senseless by a glancing blow to the head. He'd been less than a heartbeat from death when Yasmir had risen, drawing Tanithra's undivided attention.

'Ah, how I've longed for this,' Tanithra hissed through scorched lips. She managed a halting, hateful smile. 'Bruglir escaped me, but we'll dance, you and I and I'll make you pay.'

Yasmir said not a word. She opened her arms like a lover and rushed at the battered corsair, her black hair flowing behind her like a cloak of raven's feathers. Tanithra made as if to shout, raising her sword, but Yasmir flowed effortlessly past her guard and wrapped her naked arms around her foe. Tanithra stiffened, drawing a single breath, her eyes going wide as she looked into depthless violet pools and felt twin daggers slide beneath the base of her skull and into her brain.

Malus watched his sister stare into the corsair's dying eyes, watching the light fade from them and feeling Tanithra's death tremors on her naked skin. At last, the corsair's body went limp and Yasmir stepped away, letting the corpse crumple to the ground. Then she turned her gaze upon Malus.

For the space of a single heartbeat they stared into one another's eyes. Slowly and deliberately, Malus set his sword upon the floor and then bowed deeply, until his forehead touched the rough stone.

When he rose from his bow she was gone.

It was several moments before Malus realised the melee was over. Bodies and pieces of bodies were scattered everywhere. One of Urial's surviving retainers was checking out each one and killing wounded Skinriders with a stroke of his sword. The other silver-masked warrior was helping Urial to his feet; his face was smeared with blood and his armour was pierced in a few places. Bruglir's man knelt by the body of his captain, his eyes hollow with shock.

Malus turned to Hauclir. 'Where... where did she go?'

The retainer pointed upwards. 'She went upstairs like a puff of smoke. Hunting for more raiders to kill, I reckon. Those eyes of hers were hungry.'

Urial groaned as he was pulled upright. 'You looked into those eyes,' he said, staring at Malus. 'What did you see?'

The highborn started to speak, then thought better of it. Finally, he just shrugged. 'Plains of brass and rivers of blood,' he said. 'I saw death. No more, no less.'

Hauclir raised his hand. 'Wait. What's that sound?'

Malus looked to his retainer and strained to hear what Hauclir was talking about. After a moment he heard it, too; a chorus of piping wails, riding the winds above the sheltered cove.

'Horns,' he said. 'Our fleet's arrived and they're sailing to their deaths.'

Chapter Twenty-Four
ACROSS THE RIVER OF TIME

BLACK SAILS STOOD out in sharp contrast to the misty horizon, rising like upswept raven's wings from the surface of the grey sea as the druchii fleet bore down on the Skinrider ships nestled in the small cove. Malus and Hauclir stood at the lip of the ragged opening in the cliff side and watched the frenetic movements on the decks of the anchored ships as the raiders prepared for action. The huge, broad-bellied ships were not meant for cut-and-thrust duels close to shore; for all their seagoing power and greater numbers they were almost helpless in their present position, sheep before a sleek pack of wolves. Except, that is, for the sea chain.

Malus ground a fist against the rock wall. 'Surely they can see that the damned chain is still up!'

The retainer nodded grimly. 'Most likely they do and are expecting us to drop it at the last minute, the better to surprise the raiders.'

But it was the druchii who were heading for a brutal surprise. With the wind at their backs they would be forced against the heavy iron chain and pinned there while the stone throwers in the sea wall citadels would smash them to bits.

Careful not to put any weight on his aching leg, Malus leaned out from the cliff opening. Hundreds of feet below, he could see the abandoned village near the shore, now seething with bands of Skinriders who had answered the call of the horns. The highborn studied the rock walls to either side and tested the strength of the wind. Far below, in the open field between the village and the abandoned stockade, he saw a smouldering shape still licked with the occasional tongue of emerald flame.

'No climbing down this,' he snarled. And even if we could, the chain towers are at least two or three miles away. We'd never reach them in time.'

'Pity we can't ride on green lighting like the Skinriders can,' Hauclir said ruefully. He peered down at the smoking remains of the chieftain. 'Not that it seemed to work so well for him, mind.'

Malus stiffened. 'Not lightning perhaps, but...' He turned to Urial. 'We need to get to the tower across the cove. What about that spell you used to get us to the *Harrier*?'

Urial leaned wearily on his axe. The blood and magic it had drank was all but gone now, leaving the wounded druchii pale and exhausted. He shook his head. 'What I did was build a bridge,' he said, his voice little more than a whisper. 'I need a resonance with the destination. Last time I used Yasmir's connection to Bruglir to bridge the distance...'

'You need a resonance? A connection?' Malus limped quickly across the chamber and scooped a small object from the floor. He held it up, revealing a broken chunk of glossy brick. 'All of these towers are made from the same scavenged brick. Would that be enough?'

Urial closed his eyes, concentrating on the problem. 'Perhaps,' he said at length. 'Yes, it's possible. But I would also need a frame – an enclosed circle that we could step through.'

Malus frowned, his gaze sweeping the room. Finally he pointed to the opening in the cliffside. 'Use that. And do it quickly – time is running out.'

Urial studied the irregular opening, his expression uncertain. 'The geometries are poor,' he said. 'I cannot guarantee the spell will work. If it fails, you will step through and plummet to your death.'

'The alternative is to be marooned here!' Malus snapped. 'The Skinriders will sink or capture every ship in the fleet – worse, they will kill every druchii the sharks don't get to first. We have no other choice.'

Faced with the alternatives, Urial nodded quickly and snapped orders to his surviving men, then limped to the opening. The retainers rooted through the bodies until they found the severed head of the Norscan warrior and brought it to their lord. Urial took the grisly trophy, inspected it like a servant buying a melon at market, then used his axe to split the skull in half and tossed the lower section aside. Then he passed the axe reverently to one of the retainers and went to work, dipping his fingers in the Norscan's brain pan and daubing crimson sigils around the rim of the opening. When he was done, he held out his hand for the piece of brick; Malus handed it over and surveyed his meagre force. Urial's two surviving men were unhurt and despite having to conceal himself in the stinking surcoat of a Skinrider, Hauclir seemed none the worse for wear. Bruglir's surviving retainer had spent several long minutes whispering over the body of his fallen captain before rising silently and taking his place with the rest of the party.

Six men to storm a citadel, he thought. It would have to be enough, somehow.

Bruglir held the segment of the Norscan's skull in both hands and began to chant. At first, nothing happened. Then a single, trembling tendril of steam rose from the brain pan, flowing towards the opening as though drawn by the wind. The tendril waxed and waned in strength, spreading blood and brains across the pane of sorcery until a thin red sheen gleamed across the rough opening.

Malus frowned. Something didn't look quite right. For one thing, he could still clearly see the grey sky beyond the faint membrane.

'Quickly now!' Urial hissed, his voice tight with strain. 'I cannot hold this for long!'

The highborn felt a touch of dread. It was one thing to speak boldly of a blind leap to death or glory and another thing entirely to come upon that last, momentous step. Then another thought struck him. What if the spell was only an illusion? What if Urial saw this as an opportunity to eliminate him? 'Are you certain the bridge is established?' Malus said.

'Of course I'm not sure!' Urial shot back. 'Hurry!'

No time for doubt, Malus thought, drawing his bloody sword. If the spell doesn't work we're likely dead anyway.

Taking a deep breath, the highborn ran forward, gritting his teeth against the pain in his leg and leapt through the opening.

HE STUMBLED ACROSS a heaving plain of blood, under a raging crimson sky. Howls of the damned filled his ears. Malus looked over his shoulder and saw a black tower rising in the distance just before a wave of searing cold washed over him…

Malus fell, rolling across a rough stone floor littered with refuse. Hoarse shouts echoed around him, sounding surprised and angry.

The highborn rolled onto his back. He lay on the floor of a circular room, its stone walls slick with slimy moss. A crumbling stone stairway rose along the outside of one of the walls, rising to a partially-collapsed ground floor and an open doorway that led somewhere outside. Just a few feet away he could see a faint crimson oval shining in the dimness, wavering and insubstantial. The spell had worked.

Then Malus heard shouts and heavy footfalls and remembered that he wasn't alone.

He rolled quickly to his feet, sword in hand and realised with a start that the Dark Mother had blessed his audacious plan – he stood only a few feet from an enormous capstan, not unlike the ones used to haul in ships' anchors except that it was far larger. Massive links of rusted chain were wound around the huge wooden drum. Urial's spell had taken him directly to the sea chain.

The rest of the chamber was heaped with bits of broken wood and piles of rubble from the collapsed floor above. When Malus had arrived there were Skinriders loading rubble into a large basket suspended from a rope and pulley system running through the gaping hole above – more ammunition for the stone throwers at the top of the tower, the highborn surmised. Now the raiders had recovered from the shock of his sudden arrival and rushed at him with everything from swords to chunks of broken brick.

There was an electrical crackle and the thud of a body behind Malus and the charging Skinriders pulled up short at the sudden flare of magic. The highborn took advantage of their hesitation and charged at them. His blade flashed, slicing though the skull of one raider and he stepped over the corpse's body and swung at the next man in a single, fluid motion. The Skinrider blocked the cut and fell back with a startled shout, piling into the men behind him. Malus pressed his advantage, hammering at the raider's guard until he was able to draw the man off-balance and bury his sword in the Skinrider's neck. The keen edge split the man's spine and left his head hanging by little more than a strip of flesh and diseased muscle.

Dismayed by the ferocity of the highborn's attack, the surviving Skinriders broke and ran for the stairs, shouting an alarm to other men somewhere above. Malus chased them all the way to the base of the stair, then turned at the sound of a sharp thunderclap to find Urial and the three surviving retainers staggering over to the capstan. 'Look for a lever to release the chain!' Malus cried.

'No need,' Urial said wearily, pushing the retainers aside. He raised his axe over his head and spoke a word of power, then brought the blade down on the taut chain. Iron links parted like soft cheese and the unwound links disappeared through the feed chute in the wall with a thunderous rattle, followed by a churning splash in the sea outside.

Ears ringing, the druchii looked at one another, unsure what to do next. Hauclir blinked like an owl. 'Well,' he said. 'That was easy.'

No sooner had he spoken then the entire tower shook beneath a tremendous blow. A section of wall just above ground level blew apart, showering the druchii below with jagged stones and enveloping them in a pall of gritty dust.

Malus whirled, coughing in the dust cloud and heard something large slither wetly through the opening. Peering into the haze, the highborn caught a glimpse of two pinpoints of greenish light rushing at him and leapt to one side barely in time as a seething mass of shifting flesh landed in the spot where he'd stood.

The daemon was a pulpy mass of melted bodies, welded together by magic and supernatural will. Arms and legs protruded haphazardly from the pulsating mass; some hands still clutched corroded weapons while others grasped spasmodically at the air. Distorted faces gaped and moaned across the yellow-brown mass. As the highborn watched in horror the shape contracted, producing a head on top of a thick neck of maggot-ridden flesh that rose above the amorphous body and vomited a stream of brown bile at Urial and his men. Urial brought up his axe in an instinctive move and the arcane weapon blazed with light, deflecting the spray away from its wielder. Urial's two men were not as fortunate as their master, however. They howled in agony as the acid splashed across them, melting armour, cloth and flesh with horrifying ease.

Without thinking, Malus threw himself at the daemon, slicing a deep cut into the fleshy mass that oozed steaming bile but otherwise seemed to have little effect. The long-necked head, still dripping bile from its malleable jaws, snapped around and regarded him with blazing eyes. The creature's body bulged and long tentacles studded with jagged bits of teeth burst from the mass, wrapping around Malus's waist and throat.

There was a wild scream of fury from the other side of the daemon and Bruglir's man clambered *onto* the creature, running up onto the monster's side and swinging his blade at the towering neck. The thick cord of foul muscle parted in a fountain of acidic bile and the head bounced wetly across the floor. At that, the creature's entire body seemed to recoil, hurling the frenzied retainer into the air, then it gave a huge spasm and lunged at the airborne druchii with a giant maw like a frog snapping at a fly. It swallowed the man whole and Malus grimaced at the sizzling sound as the monster's stomach juices dissolved the man in seconds.

The highborn slashed his sword through the tentacles around his throat, the blade slicing through them like they were pliable vines. The ropy tendrils around his wrist constricted, drawing him closer to the monster. Malus saw the skin near the tendrils bulge and a new head began to emerge from the depths of the creature, green eyes burning with hate.

Gangrenous skin stretched like a caul as the head pushed free of the daemonic mass. Its mouth opened – and uttered an agonised scream as Urial buried his enchanted blade in the monster's body.

Sensing his opportunity, Malus reached forward and grabbed the taut tendrils pulling at his waist and used them to haul himself even closer to the daemon, thrusting forward with his sword at the same time. He stabbed the creature right between his fiery green eyes and a jolt like lightning shot up his sword arm, throwing him back onto his back. There was a hideous crackling sound, like popping grease and the daemon's fleshy body lost its stability, melting into a spreading pool of bile and rotting flesh. Staring at the ceiling, the highborn saw a pall of greasy yellow mist rise from the body – and fly like a tattered wraith through the gaping hole in the wall above.

Moments later a pair of strong hands grabbed Malus by the arms and pulled him upright. Hauclir was breathing heavily, covered in brick dust and bleeding from a cut on his forehead. The highborn jerked loose of his retainer's grip. 'Your timing could have been better,' he snapped. 'That thing nearly turned me into paste!'

'An unforgivable breach of duty, my lord,' Hauclir muttered darkly. 'Part of the wall fell on me and I selfishly tried to free myself instead of immediately seeing to your safety.'

'Just help me up.'

Grunting painfully, Hauclir managed to drag Malus upright. Urial was already staggering up the splintered stairway, the ichor of the daemon still smoking from the edges of his axe. The highborn pushed away from his retainer's steadying hands and started after his half-brother.

'What was that image that flew up from the daemon's body?' Malus asked as he clambered up the stairs.

'Something that ought not to be,' Urial answered, his voice troubled. He reached the open doorway and looked out over the cove. Malus reached him a moment later and took in the scene unfolding before him.

The sea chain had fallen and the druchii wolves were in among the herd. Six nimble corsairs – a seventh was sinking at the mouth of the cove, holed through by stones from the towers – slipped past the huge Skinrider ships, loosing their heavy bolts at point-blank range into the hulls of the enemy ships. The heavy steel heads punched fist-sized holes at the waterline of the raiders, opening their lower decks to the sea. The Skinriders responded with showers of arrows and bolts of their own, but their heavy war engines could not be brought to bear on the corsairs at such close quarters. Already two of the enemy ships were sitting low in the water as their holds slowly flooded. Bodies and debris already littered the surface of the cove and here and there Malus saw churning splashes in the water as the sharks began to feed.

'The butcher's bill will be steep, but we've a good chance of winning,' Malus said grimly. 'The confines of the cove favour us and Bruglir's corsairs know their work well.'

'No,' Urial said bleakly. 'We are doomed. Each and every one of us.'

The fatigue and fear in Urial's voice brought Malus's head around. He pointed a bloodstained finger at the outskirts of the abandoned village on the far side of the cove.

Malus squinted, trying to make out details of what was happening at the shore. At first he could make nothing out beyond a huge crowd of Skinriders – and then he realised that none of them were moving. They were frozen in place, as though held in the grip of an unseen fist.

Then he saw a flash of greenish fire among the raiders and realised what was happening. 'The daemon,' he said. 'It's using the Skinriders to make another body.'

Urial nodded, his expression dark. 'It shouldn't be possible. The spirit should have been hurled back into the Outer Darkness when its first vessel was destroyed. But something is allowing it to remain here, rebuilding its strength and striking at us again.'

'There are just the three of us left and my power is nearly exhausted. It will keep coming until we are dead and then it will slaughter everyone in the fleet. They'll be helpless to stop it.'

'It's the island,' Malus realised. 'The tower of Eradorius–'

The words died in Malus's throat. Now he remembered why the bricks in the citadel – and here, in the sea wall tower – looked so familiar to him. Moving as if in a dream, he knelt, groping among the broken bricks lying on the floor. He found one that was mostly intact and turned it over in his hands until he found the symbol carved in its surface.

Urial watched the highborn with a bemused frown. 'What are you talking about?'

Malus traced the incised symbol with his thumb, feeling a fist of ice settle in his gut. 'You recall I told you that I sought the Isle of Morhaut to find an item hidden in a tower there. The tower was built by a sorcerer named Eradorius.' He held up the brick. 'And the Skinriders tore it down to build their damned citadels.' With a sudden burst of rage he hurled the stone across the chamber. 'Who knows? It might have been nothing more than ruins for hundreds of years before the raiders even arrived. We'll never know now.' Or what happened to the cursed idol, the highborn thought. For the first time since Tz'arkan stole his black soul Malus felt utterly lost.

'What does that have to do with the daemon?'

'The tower was built to escape *another* daemon. Eradorius used his sorcery to create a sanctum that was outside time and space. He created a place that was a realm unto itself, separate from all the others.' He pointed outside. 'That daemon hasn't been hurled back into the Outer Darkness because its pull cannot reach him here. No doubt that's why it picked this island in the first place.'

Urial looked at Malus as though he were mad. 'But you just said the tower was destroyed long ago.'

'The tower stood *outside time*! It was set apart...' the highborn's voice trailed off as his eyes widened in realisation. 'Outside time. Of course. It's on the shore of the river!'

Hauclir clambered up beside Malus and peered carefully into his eyes. 'I think you need to sit down, my lord,' he said warily. 'You may have taken a hard knock to your head.'

Malus pushed the retainer away. 'The tower was placed in a realm beyond the reach of time and space. It still exists in a sense – and the idol is still there.' He reached for Urial. 'When we crossed from the chieftain's citadel to here, you saw the red plain? The tower on the horizon?'

'You think that was the tower you speak of?'

'Yes!' He paced up and down, one finger tapping meditatively at his chin. 'It was all there, right in front of me all along! Why didn't I realise it before?' He turned back to Urial. 'You have to use your sorcery to send me there. Now.'

'But... but the resonance...'

Malus gestured at the scattered bricks. 'We have all the resonance we need!'

Urial shook his head. 'You don't understand. The... place you're speaking of is not of this world. It sits on a nether plane, if you will, rather than sitting at the other end.' He paused, his face suddenly weary. 'I can open a door and send you through, but it will have to be held open on this side for you to return through. And I don't know how long I can hold such a portal open. If it fails, you will be trapped there for all time.'

'And how is that any worse than being eaten alive by that vile thing?' Malus pointed to the distant village, where the daemon was still consuming the Skinriders. 'Open the gate! I'll take my chances on the other side. If I'm successful, the power binding the daemon here will fail and it will be drawn back into the Outer Darkness. It's our only chance!'

Urial seemed about to argue further, but one brief look at the chaos on the far shore convinced him. 'Very well,' he said hollowly and headed back down the stairs in search of blood.

'You mentioned an idol, my lord,' Hauclir said quietly. 'How will we know how to find it?'

'We? No, Hauclir. You're staying behind.'

The retainer squared his shoulders. 'Now see here, my lord–'

Malus cut him off with a curt wave of his hand. 'Be still and listen. You must stay behind to watch over Urial,' he said quietly. 'If he means some secret treachery I'll be helpless to stop him, so you must be the knife at his back. There's also the Skinriders.' He pointed to the upper floors of the tower. 'They may think us dead after the daemon's attack, but then again they may not. If they come down here you'll have to hold them off long enough for me to return.'

The retainer clearly didn't like what he was hearing, but there was little he could do about it. 'Very well, my lord,' he growled. 'And what if you don't return?'

'If it were me, I'd take my chances with the sharks.'

'You think I can swim to one of our ships?'

'No. I think you should jump in the water and hope the sharks get you before the daemon does.'

THERE WAS NO shock of icy cold or sense of dislocation. Malus stepped through the portal and it was as though he walked in the land of his nightmares.

The ground heaved beneath his feet and the sky churned overhead. The wind cried and moaned in his ears but he could not feel it against his skin. He looked back over his shoulder and saw the oval of pearlescent light floating in the air. Some kind of iridescent mist curled from its edges and somehow the highborn could sense how fragile it was, like a bubble that could burst at any moment. He could just make out the figures of Urial and Hauclir standing before the doorway; Malus raised his sword in salute and then turned his eyes to the dark horizon where the tower stood.

It was tall and square, its glossy black surface gleaming under the directionless light that permeated the nether realm. The tower seemed far more solid that the Chaotic landscape around it, like an island rising from an angry sea. From where Malus stood it seemed leagues distant. He took a deep breath and began to run.

The terrain flashed by beneath his feet. His weariness was gone and the pain in his wounded leg had vanished. Then he realised with a start that Tz'arkan was no longer curled like a viper in his chest. The thought almost caused him to stumble. Was it possible, he thought? Could I have found a realm where he truly cannot reach, as Eradorius believed?

Laughter echoed like thunder through Malus's body, loud enough to send a tremor through his bones. 'Foolish little druchii,' the daemon said. 'Look at your hands.'

Malus stopped. With a growing sense of dread he held up his hand and saw the dark grey skin and pulsing black veins writhing like worms at his wrist. His nails, not quite talons, were black and sharp.

The strength he felt was Tz'arkan's. The daemon hadn't disappeared – only spread through every part of his body, rushing through him like blood.

'You see,' the daemon said. 'Here I am suspended between your pitiful world and the storms of Chaos that empower me.' Tz'arkan's awareness rumbled through him. 'I could never have reached this place from my prison – you were *my* bridge, in a sense.' The daemon chuckled. 'Yes. This place pleases me. I could remain here for a very long time.'

Malus fought to suppress a surge of terror. 'And trade one prison for another? Let's just get the damned idol and be done with it.'

'Why, Malus, if I didn't know any better I would think you were tiring of my company.'

The highborn ran on.

THE GHOSTS OF his dreams awaited him in the shadow of the tower.

They clawed their way free of the clotted, bloody earth, reaching for him with clawed, bony hands, flailing tentacles or barbed hooks. Some were human, some elven; many were twisted monstrosities from some sorcerer's nightmare. They crawled, leapt, flapped and slithered towards him as he ran across the plain.

A skeletal human with white parchment skin and a mane of snow-white hair reached for his throat; Malus swung his sword through the wraith's head and the figure wavered like smoke. An undulating mass of blue-veined flesh slithered across the ground and wrapped a thorny tentacle around his leg; the needle-like spikes pierced layers of leather and flesh with ease, leaving his flesh icy and numb. He snarled and slashed downwards and the blade passed harmlessly through the creature.

'What are these creatures, daemon?' he said.

'They are the lost,' Tz'arkan replied. 'Beings who found themselves thrown upon the shores of the island. When they died, their ghosts remained. Now they hunger for your life force, Darkblade. They haven't had such a sweet morsel in a very long time.'

The skeleton's hands closed around his throat. Malus aimed a cut at its head – only to have a withered elven prince grab his sword arm and trap it against its armoured body. Something locked its jaws on his leg, biting through armour and robes. The cold was seeping inexorably through his body now, sapping his strength. He could hear his heartbeat hammering in his chest. 'What can I do to stop them?' he cried as he struggled in their grasp.

'Why Malus, my beloved son,' the daemon whispered. 'You have but to ask for my help.'

The ghosts pulled him off his feet. He fell beneath a sea of grasping hands and snapping jaws. A creature like an octopus slithered onto his chest and wrapped its tentacles around his face. Its jade-green eyes glittered with malevolent intelligence.

'Help me, damn you!' Malus cried. Tentacles pushed past his lips and crawled over his tongue. 'Help me!'

'And so I shall.'

A new wave of cold roared through him – not the icy touch of the ghosts but a flood of black ice that surged from his chest and spread through the rest of his body. Dark steam rose from his pale skin and frost crept along the length of his blade. The ghosts recoiled – all save the octopus-creature, which could not unwind itself swiftly enough. Its skin blackened and its eyes turned pale blue and it let out a whistling shriek before Malus struck it with his hand and shattered it into pieces.

The white-haired skeleton recoiled from him, arms raised as if to shield itself from harm. Malus leapt to his feet with a roar and slashed his blade through the ghost's chest. The body blackened in an instant and shattered as it hit the ground. The highborn caught the elven prince in full flight; he laughed like a madman and slashed the prince across the back of his neck.

Everywhere the ghosts were in retreat, receding from him like ripples in a pond. He slew a one-eyed bear, stabbing deep into the creature's flank and then ran down two human sailors who cried for mercy with faint, piteous voices as his sword severed their heads.

Just beyond the sailors ran a druchii corsair. Drunk with slaughter, Malus leapt after him, smoking sword held high. The corsair looked over his shoulder at his pursuer, his dark eyes wide with terror. Malus recognised the scarred form at once, but the withered face was a cruel mockery of Tanithra's fierce visage.

The sight brought Malus up short, reminding him of the reason he'd come to this cursed place. He watched her stumble across the broken land for a moment more, then shook his head and resumed his journey to the tower, more determined to reach the idol than ever.

Chapter Twenty-Five
THE TOWER OF ERADORIUS

THERE WERE NO high walls or imposing gates guarding the Tower of Eradorius; the single dark portal at the base of the featureless structure beckoned almost welcomingly to Malus. Only the invisible currents of power coursing across his skin belied the illusion of safety. The closer the highborn came to the tower the more he felt the warping presence of the power contained therein.

'Tread carefully, Malus,' Tz'arkan warned. This close to the tower the daemon's presence seemed to pulse within him, waxing and waning to the beat of Malus's heart. 'The most difficult task is yet to come.'

The highborn frowned. 'The Tome of Ak'zhaal says that Eradorius is dead.'

'Perhaps, but his labyrinth still remains,' the daemon said. 'Eradorius built a maze so subtle that he himself was trapped within it. Think on that and be wary, Darkblade.'

'Spare me your feeble attempts at wisdom,' Malus sneered, crossing the last few yards between him and the tower and stepping through the open doorway. 'A maze is naught but an exercise of the mind. Eradorius was mad. But I…' He fell silent, feeling a pall of dread settle over him.

'Yes, Malus?'

'Nothing,' the highborn snapped. 'I grow weary of your taunts, daemon. Let's see what secrets this labyrinth holds.'

Past the doorway lay a short corridor that led to a space Malus first took to be an open-air gallery of some kind. Diffuse green light permeated the interior of the tower, seeming to come from every direction at once. Sword ready, the highborn stepped into the chamber.

The room's ceiling was lost in a luminous emerald haze. The highborn saw three doors of dark wood, one to the left, one to the right and one directly ahead of him. Door rings of polished silver gleamed in the light. Malus regarded each one in turn. As he did, he could not shake the sensation he was being watched, but he could not pinpoint its source.

'The doors are identical,' he said at last. 'No markings, no tell-tale footprints in the dust. Nothing to show the proper path.'

'All paths lead to the centre of the labyrinth,' the daemon whispered. 'As you said, it isn't a test of the feet, but of the mind. Are you certain you are ready to follow it to its conclusion? This maze is *aware*, Darkblade. It studies you even as you study it. And it will destroy you if you let it.'

The highborn laughed coldly. 'If I *let* it? What sort of devious trap is that?'

'Why, the very worst kind,' the daemon said, but Malus was no longer listening. Acting on impulse, he crossed the room in three quick strides and pulled open the door opposite the one he came in.

Beyond was nothing but utter blackness, an emptiness so deep it pulled at him, drawing him into its all-encompassing embrace. Malus felt a cold wind on his face and he plummeted into blackness.

A soft weight pressed against his side. Arms enclosed his chest, rising and falling with the rhythm of his breath. Malus started, sitting bolt upright amid a tangle of silken sheets.

The air was cool and fragrant with incense. The bed was low and broad, built for a druchii's tastes and surrounded by layers of drapes to trap body heat. Through the sheer drapes Malus could see an arch of pale light opposite the foot of the bed. All else was plunged into shadow; the woman by his side moaned softly in her sleep and rolled languidly onto her back. The faint light limned a bare shoulder and part of one alabaster cheek. Her lips were strikingly red, as though painted with fresh blood.

Malus reeled from the sight, stumbling awkwardly from the bed and landing naked on the dark slate floor. The icy shock of the cold tiles brought everything into sharp focus: he was in a richly-appointed bedroom somewhere in Naggaroth. How else to explain the furnishings, or the grey slate tiles, or the peculiar quality of the light streaming in through the drapes across the room?

The highborn's eye caught a hint of movement in one of the chamber's shadowy corners. He looked about hurriedly for a weapon and saw his swords draped across an expensive divan near the bed. The sword rasped icily from its scabbard as he launched himself across the room towards the source of the movement. For a fleeting instant he thought he saw the shape of a hooded figure, little more than a deeper shadow among the dark folds of the hanging drapes, but when he reached the corner there was no one there. Malus probed the heavy drapes with the point of his blade, but no one lurked within their depths.

Malus turned back to the bed dominating the large room, unable to shake a strange feeling of foreboding. Without thinking, he crossed to a nearby table and plucked a goblet of wine from a silver tray. He'd set the wine there just before bed; he could remember it clearly, as though he'd done it only moments before, but the very act of touching it felt wrong somehow.

'Come back to bed, you scoundrel,' the woman said, her voice sending a shiver down his spine. 'I'm cold.'

He could think of nothing he wanted more than to return to her side and breathe the scent of her creamy skin – but even that held an undercurrent of foreboding that he couldn't explain. 'I... I thought I saw something.'

To his surprise, she laughed at the thought. 'Are you jumping at shadows? Here in the Vaulkhar's tower? Even the Drachau is not so well protected as you now.'

Malus froze, the goblet half-raised to his lips. 'What did you say?'

He heard her turn onto her side, silk rippling across her bare skin. 'Not even the Drachau is as well protected as you are. Surely you realise this? No one else would dare move against you now. Isn't that what you've been working towards all these years?'

Malus carefully set the goblet on the tray, fearful that it would drop from his nerveless fingers. Moving as though in a dream, he walked to the window opposite the bed and pulled the heavy drapes aside.

Watery grey light flooded into the room. Beyond the narrow window Malus saw the blade-like central spire of the Drachau's citadel. It loomed only a few storeys taller than the tower the highborn watched from – a cluster of smaller spires rose in a black thicket below, comprising the towers of the Vaulkhar's household.

He stood in Lurhan's tower, not his own. Was this the Vaulkhar's very bedchamber? His heart went cold. This was wrong. Terribly, lethally wrong. 'I shouldn't be here,' Malus said to the woman on the bed.

The light from the open window shone against the hanging curtains surrounding the bed, rendering them opaque. He heard her body whispering against the sheets and imagined her sitting up, wrapping one arm around her knees. 'You didn't complain last night,' she said with a breathy chuckle. 'What difference does one day make? Tonight the Drachau will put the hadrilkar around your throat and then this will all be yours in truth.'

She moved again and this time Malus saw the silhouette of her body take shape as she crawled closer to the sheer curtains. 'I doubt anyone will gainsay your taking ownership of Lurhan's possessions a day early,' she said. The curtains parted and he saw her, outlined in pale sunlight. She reached for him with a slim hand.

Malus felt his mouth go dry. Terror and longing seized him with equal strength. Desire raced along his nerves like fire. 'My brothers will kill me for this,' was all he could manage to say.

Her violent eyes regarded him quizzically. 'Your brothers? They wouldn't dare,' she said with a laugh. 'You were the one Lurhan chose above all the rest.' She smiled, her red lips pouting wryly. 'And to the victor go the spoils.'

Malus's hands ached. He looked over to see his fist clutching the thick drapes in a white-knuckled grip. Terror washed through him in waves, even as a part of him reacted to her words with insatiable lust. He took a step, then another and then he was running across the room, reaching for the gleaming silver ring set into the dark-panelled door to the left of the bed. She called after him as he pulled the door wide, sending a spear of longing through him as he plunged into the darkness on the other side.

He smelled blood and the stink of ruptured bodies.

The chamber was close and hot with the presence of so many bodies, living and unliving. Sorcerous fire boiled from the broken vessel of a witchlight high on one wall of the hexagonal room. Broken by a flung missile in the furious battle, the wild flames set monstrous shadows capering across the smooth walls.

Uthlan Tyr lay on his back, his sightless eyes staring towards the ceiling as the last of his life blood pumped from the terrible wound in his chest. His sword dangled from one half-open hand. Malus looked down on the Drachau and felt a hot rush of triumph mingled with fear. The Drachau's servants and retainers lay scattered about the room; Malus's retainers had taken them entirely by surprise, hacking them apart in an explosion of carefully planned violence. Tyr and his men never stood a chance.

There was a sound permeating the thick walls of the chamber – it was the muffled voices of a thousand noble throats, rising and falling like the surf. In the centre of the room stood a suit of elaborate plate armour on a stand of blooded oak. Silar Thornblood and Arleth Vann waited by the harness, their faces splashed with gore and their eyes alight with the heady rush of battle.

Malus wore simple robes and an unadorned kheitan. There was no hadrilkar around his neck, nor was there the familiar weight of a pair of swords at his hip. Greenish light played on the razor-edge of the blade in the Drachau's stiffening hand. Without thinking he reached for it, but a voice cut through the thick air, bringing him up short.

'Do not touch the Drachau's sword,' the voice said. It was deep and even, surprisingly calm in a room that reeked of the battlefield. 'Take nothing from him nor let his blood stain your clothes, or the ancient armour will consume you.'

Malus turned at the voice. A hooded figure stood by his side, his form concealed beneath heavy black robes. An aura of icy power radiated from the man, taking the highborn aback. He began to ask the man who he was, but an all-too-familiar sense of foreboding made him pause. The figure turned to regard him, the cold voice washing over him from the blackness beneath the hood. 'Your triumph is not yet complete, Vaulkhar. The highborn of Hag Graef await. Don the armour and accept their fealty and then no one will be able to challenge your rule.'

The highborn turned back to the ornate harness. On a nearby stand rested the great enchanted draich that the Drachau carried during the ritual of the Hanil Khar. All at once he knew where he was – how many times had he dreamt of this very moment? How often had he languished in his tower and planned how he would seize the city for himself in the fullness of time?

Fear gripped him. He looked back at the hooded figure. 'Am I dreaming?'

'Ask the Drachau if this is a dream,' the figure replied. 'No doubt he wishes it were so.' The figure stepped closer. 'This is real. You have made it so, Malus. Do you doubt yourself now, on the verge of your greatest triumph?'

The highborn took a deep breath, trying to master the doubts that threatened to overwhelm him. What had the hooded man said that had frightened him so? Something about time?

He knew what awaited him. Once he donned the armour the highborn of the city would bow before him as their Drachau and offer their yearly fealty to him, thinking he was Uthlan Tyr. Once the oaths were sworn, they would belong to him and his usurpation would be complete. With dreamlike languor he stepped to the arming stand and let his retainers begin fitting the harness to his body. Each piece that locked into place sent a thrill of power tingling along his skin.

Malus longed to surrender himself to the feeling of that power, but part of his mind shrank from it. He tried to focus on what was wrong, but realisation eluded him, slipping like quicksilver through his grasp. As they fitted the ornate breastplate into place he turned and looked back at the way he'd come.

Just as he did so Malus caught sight of another hooded figure – this one wearing robes and an indigo-dyed kheitan – who stepped back into the darkness beyond the doorway. A frisson of pure terror struck him like a knife. 'There!' he said, pointing at the archway 'A man skulking at the threshold!'

Arleth Vann rushed silently to the doorway, knives glinting in his hands. He peered into the darkness. 'There's no one there, my lord,' he said, shaking his head.

'There was a man, damn you! I saw him with my own eyes!' Malus's hand clenched into a fist. 'He saw... he saw everything!' He *knows*, Malus thought fearfully. He knows I'm not who they think I am. The realisation made his blood run cold. 'We have to stop him.'

As he spoke he felt Silar slide the vambraces onto his arms and lock them in place. Then came the helm, settling like a crown of ice onto his brow. The hooded figure stepped forward, holding up a curved piece of silver steel. 'Put on the mask,' the figure said. 'Wear it and no one will know.'

Malus felt the mask lock into position over his face. His breath rumbled through the mask's vents and steam rose before his eyes. Heat suffused his limbs and the air around him took on a crimson sheen. Once again, he felt a surge of power so sweet his body ached in response, but at the same time he felt cruelly exposed.

The hooded figure turned, gesturing towards a narrow staircase that curved along the wall and rose into darkness. Malus moved to the steps, dimly aware of his retainers bowing their heads in supplication as he passed. High above waited the dais and the great throne where he would preside over the unknowing throng and accept their devotion. Unbidden, his feet began to climb the steps. The muted roar of the assembled throng called to him, promising him power and glory – everything he had craved for so long.

So long, he thought. So much time.

Malus stopped. 'Time,' he said to himself. He looked back at the hooded figure on the steps behind him. 'This is an illusion.'

'Time is an illusion, Malus,' the hooded figure replied. 'You have crossed the river and stand upon its shore, remember?'

The highborn shook his head, forcing himself to remember through sheer effort of will. 'This isn't real. This isn't really happening. I'm lost in the labyrinth.'

'You are wrong,' the hooded one said. 'This is entirely real. You made this happen, Malus. Is this not what you always wanted, deep in the darkest places of your heart?'

The highborn staggered, falling back against the hard-edged steps. 'Yes,' he said, the word rumbling from the mask. 'Is this my future?' he whispered. 'Does this glory await me in years to come?'

For a moment the figure regarded him in silence. 'All this and more.' The figure pointed past Malus, to an opening at the top of the stairs. Blackness lay beyond. 'Go forth and claim your destiny,' he said.

The roar of the throng washed over him, tugging at his soul. Malus let himself be pulled along, climbing the stairs into the darkness.

THE HEAVY FLAPS of the tent fell away from his armoured form and Malus stepped into the cool, salt air. Rising before him were the tall cliffs of Ulthuan and a forest of spikes rose from the sloping ground in between. More than five thousand elven warriors writhed on those gore-stained spikes, singing a chorus of agony to the fire-tinged sky. The sight staggered him; it was breathtaking in its glory. For a moment he was overwhelmed at the vista of torment spread before him, but then, bit by bit, he became aware of the great pavilion, bordered by tall banner-poles bearing the colours of the Six Cities and the armoured champions standing guard around the tent. He looked down and saw that he wore the rune-carved armour of the Drachau and a shock passed through him.

This was his army. Naggaroth had marched to war and as tradition demanded, the Drachau of Hag Graef marched at its head. This terrible victory belonged to *him*.

Malus strode from the tent, his stride clumsy on the fine, white sand. As far as he could see along the curving shore there stretched the largest druchii army he had ever seen. Thousands upon thousands of warriors, all busy at their tasks preparing for the next battle ahead – every one serving at his whim. 'Blessed Mother,' he breathed. 'Let this all be true.'

'It is,' a familiar voice said behind him.

Malus turned. The hooded figure stood some distance away. 'Why do you show me these things?' the highborn asked.

'I? No. This is your doing. These are the truths the labyrinth has revealed to you.'

The highborn took a step forward. 'So you admit it! I *am* still in the tower and this is all illusion.'

'You are in the tower of Eradorius *and* you are on the shore of Ulthuan,' a hint of impatience in its icy voice. 'Time and space have no power over you. You see what your mind wishes you to see. No more. No less.'

'And what are you? Are you the guardian of this place?'

The figure made no reply.

Malus sneered at the figure's silence. 'Is this how you guard the tower's secrets? By plying me with sweet visions of future success?'

'Success?' the figure echoed. 'Do you imagine your tale ends in triumph, Malus Darkblade?'

Malus's sneer faded. Cold fear gnawed at his guts. 'What do you mean?'

Before the figure could reply the flaps of the pavilion tent parted again and Malus saw a knot of armoured men issue forth, their

expressions grim. He saw Silar and Dolthaic among them, their faces
bearing the scars of war, but recognised no one else. They approached
him swiftly, their eyes darting this way and that. They have the look of
conspirators, he thought, one hand edging towards the knife hilt at his
belt. Yet what would it gain them to conspire against me?

Then he realised. When the armies of Naggor marched, they did not
do so alone.

Silar was the first to reach him. When the retainer spoke, his voice
was strained. 'You cannot put off the Witch King's summons forever,'
Silar hissed. 'You must act, now, or all is lost!'

'Act?' Malus frowned. 'What would you have me do, Silar?'

Before Silar could reply, Dolthaic stepped between them. 'Do nothing rash, my lord!' he said. 'You have given Malekith a great victory
today! He can't suspect you!'

The highborn's mind whirled as he tried to grasp the events unfolding before him. Suspect him? Did Malekith have cause to suspect
anything? Yet even as he asked the question, the answer rose unbidden.

Of course he does.

Silar pushed Dolthaic aside. 'What does it matter if he suspects or
not? After what you have done today the entire camp is offering sacrifices to your name! Malekith won't countenance a threat to his rule,
real or imagined. When you go to his tent, you must be prepared to
strike! Now, while the army is behind you! Think of what you might
achieve!'

A riot of emotions raged in Malus's breast. 'Shut up,' he said. 'Both
of you just *shut up* and let me think.'

His mind reeled. It's an illusion, he thought. It doesn't matter, he
tried to tell himself.

But what if it wasn't?

He tore his eyes away from the pleading looks of his men, his gaze
wandering across the crowd of armoured retainers – and just as he did
he caught sight of the hooded man slipping away from the rear of the
group and stealing silently across the sands.

'A spy,' he said, his eyes widening with shock. He pointed at the man.
'Stop him!'

Silar and Dolthaic turned, following the panicked gesture. Dolthaic
looked back at Malus, his brow furrowing with concern. 'What spy?
There's no one there.'

'Are you mad? He's right there!' Malus raged, but the men were blind
to the retreating figure. Some kind of foul sorcery, Malus thought. He's
watched me from the beginning. He knows my secrets and he's going
to betray everything to the Witch King!

The shock of his fear hit him like a physical blow and he realised at
that moment how terrified he was of having the glories he'd seen taken

from him. And then he thought he finally understood the peril of the sorcerer's labyrinth. The guardian had made his deepest desires come true – and it was going to use them to destroy him.

Malus shoved his way through the press of men, drawing the knife from his belt. He stumbled through the ankle-deep sand, eyes fixed on the back of the hooded man as he disappeared around the side of the pavilion. The highborn bent every iota of his will into forcing his legs to work, gaining speed to keep the guardian from reaching Malekith's tent.

The highborn rounded the corner of the pavilion and caught sight of the hooded man again, now just a few yards away. He moved calmly and quietly, unaware of Malus bearing down upon him like a hunting hawk. The highborn's face twisted into a vicious snarl. The fear he felt – and the ferocity it lent him – was almost exhilarating in its intensity. You're not going to expose me, he thought furiously. You're not going to show me for what I really am!

He leapt upon the figure, knocking him down. The man barely struggled, apparently stunned by the impact. Malus rolled him over, pressing his knife to the man's throat.

'You think me a coward?' Malus drove the knife downward, feeling the hooded man's throat begin to part beneath the blade. 'You think me weak, a flawed thing like the rest of my family? How strong are you, then, with my knife digging into your neck?' He laughed wildly at the thought. His face was inches from the darkness within the hood. The man lay still, offering no resistance. 'Just as I thought. It is *you* who are the weakling! *You* are the coward, skulking and scheming in the shadow of your betters! Let us see your face, guardian! Show me your real guise, or must I drag your guts across the sand in order to compel you?'

The hooded man did not move. Anger flared fever-bright in Malus's breast. 'Do you hear me, weakling? Show yourself. *Show yourself!*'

He ground the knife deeper into the man's throat. The very air seemed to shimmer around the form, rippling like a disturbed pool.

The knife in his hand wavered, swimming in and out of focus. One moment it was pressed to the hooded man, the next it seemed to be aimed at his own neck, as though he were standing before a mirror. He roared in anger, pressing the knife deeper – and felt the point an inch deep in his own neck. Warm blood ran down his throat, soaking into the robe beneath his kheitan.

Malus's vision swam. A wave of disorientation swept over him, then suddenly he was kneeling in the square chamber within the tower of Eradorius, surrounded by three doors panelled in dark wood.

He was a heartbeat away from driving his own knife into his throat.

The highborn fell backwards, drawing the knife point from his neck. Pain bloomed beneath his chin and the sensation was almost exhilarating. 'An illusion…' he panted, 'all… an illusion.'

A shadow fell over him. Malus looked up and saw a hooded figure standing over him, his face lost in shadow. His breath felt like a cold wind against Malus's cheek.

'Who is the coward now, Malus Darkblade?' the figure said. 'Who skulks and schemes in the shadows of his betters?'

For a moment, Malus was startled into speechlessness by the figure. A lesser man might have broken beneath the shock of the revelation he'd been given, but the highborn was sustained by the fire of the hatred still burning in his heart.

'Do you think to break me with but a glance in the mirror?' Malus rose slowly to his feet. 'Did you think I would die from the shock of my own ugliness? If so, you are wrong. I am not broken. I am not defeated. My hate is strong and while I hate, I live.'

Malus rushed at the hooded figure, grabbing a handful of his robe with one hand. 'You've held a mirror up to my face – now let's have a look at yours, Eradorius!'

The highborn tore away the robe with a convulsive wrench of his hand, revealing a black-skinned figure whose muscular form swelled before him until it towered over him like a giant. A lantern-jawed face leered down at Malus, smiling a lunatic grin full of pointed fangs. Green eyes glowed eerily from the almost-human face and a long dragon's tongue licked from fleshless lips.

'Clever, clever little druchii,' Tz'arkan said. 'But yet so very wrong.'

Malus recoiled in shock – and the daemon struck like a viper, his mouth growing impossibly wide as it closed around the highborn's head and shoulders and swallowed him whole.

HE LAY IN blackness, coiled around a daemon's heart.

The darkness around him was empty, like the blackness between the stars. Malus had never known such cold could exist – it sank into his body and sucked the life from it, spilling his living essence into the blackness like a wound carved into his very soul. The cold spread like death itself – no, not death, because to Malus death was a force unto itself, like a storm or a raging fire. This was *nothingness*, utter and absolute and it filled him with fear.

There was heat in the heart of the daemon – heat nurtured from the lifeblood of worlds. Malus pressed himself against that horrid, unnatural organ, forcing his cold skin into the slime and feeling the souls squirming within. Hundreds of souls, *thousands* of them, all frozen in a single moment of pure, soul-shattering terror. He felt each and every one, like a shard of razor-edged glass and he crushed them against his flesh, savouring their brief warmth. He howled in agony and ecstasy, propelled by the mingled passions of entire civilisations as the Drinker of Worlds consumed them. For one titanic heartbeat Malus was pierced by the collective madness of an entire people – then they were gone.

Then came another beat of the daemon's heart and *another* multitude of souls shrieked in transcendent agony. Malus howled in absolute horror even as he forced these needles of crystalline passion deeper into his soul.

Tz'arkan had possessed him – now *he* was inside the daemon, feeling what it felt as it looked out upon the raging storms of purest Chaos. He saw with the daemon's eyes as universes span through the ether, each one trembling with the dew of countless souls. He could feel each soul on each world in each universe, taste a lifetime's passions in the space of a single breath.

Tz'arkan moved among worlds unnumbered and Malus realised how insignificant he was before such power. When the daemon spoke, all of Creation trembled.

'See the power of my will, mortal, and despair. Give yourself unto me, and all this will be yours in return.'

Malus felt himself fraying beneath the sheer pressure of Tz'arkan's awareness. He was dying. He could feel it. And with that realisation all his fear simply fell away.

Go on, he thought. Destroy me.

The storm of Chaos raged around him. Nothingness ate at his soul. Yet he did not die.

Destroy me, Malus raged! I'm nothing but a speck to you – wipe me away!

He hung suspended over the maelstrom of Creation… but still he did not die.

Is this some kind of trick, Malus thought? And then, he realised: of course it was. It was just another turn in the labyrinth, another gambit to break his spirit.

All of it was in his mind. He knew this. And if it was in his mind, Malus thought, it was subject to his will.

You had your chance, Eradorius, he seethed, summoning his hate. Now you'll dance to my tune.

Malus bent his will to the raging storm around him. Show me your secrets, sorcerer! Open your mind to *me*!

The highborn's will blazed like a new-born star in the firmament of madness and Creation collapsed like a bursting bubble. Malus fell into darkness, but his descent was marked by laughter, wild and triumphant.

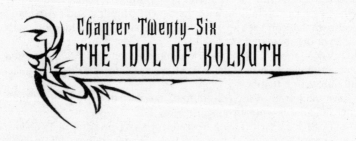

Chapter Twenty-Six
THE IDOL OF KOLKUTH

THERE WAS NO ceiling. He was standing in the centre of the square tower, surrounded by staircases reaching up to galleries that rose as far as his eyes could see. It was a vertical labyrinth that twisted and turned back upon itself and stretched upwards seemingly without end. The tower had looked simple and straightforward on the outside, but the reality was anything but, shaped by the insane sorceries of Eradorius and the Idol of Kolkuth.

The maze of the mad sorcerer was revealed at last, stripped of its illusions but no less daunting for all that.

Gritting his teeth, Malus chose a staircase at random and started upwards. It was a narrow, twisting stair, without rails or supporting walls to anchor it, but the stone was steady beneath his feet nonetheless. It carried him up to the second gallery, then turned right, leading into a small room. From there, four more staircases climbed upwards towards the top of the tower.

Stay consistent, he told himself. These things have a pattern to them. Make the same choice every time so you don't lose your place.

He went to the very same position that the first staircase occupied in the room below and started upwards. The stairway climbed up into the diffuse green light – and ended at a wall. There was a moment of vertigo – Malus's head swam and his feet seemed drawn to the wall as if by gravity. He took another step – and walked out onto the wall. Malus blinked, unable to orient himself for a moment.

The light was streaming down on him from above. He looked up to see the galleries of the tower stretching endlessly overhead.

He was back in the room where he had begun.

'Blessed Mother of Darkness,' Malus cursed. 'This is madness.'

'You have never spoken more truly in your life,' Tz'arkan replied. If the daemon had any awareness of the visions Malus saw within the labyrinth, it gave no sign. 'The labyrinth is a reflection of Eradorius's own tortured mind. You will wind up like one of those twisted ghosts on the plain before you come to fully understand the maze and its maddened paths.'

'I don't want to understand the damned place,' Malus seethed. 'I just want to reach the idol.' He tried to think of the resources he had at hand. 'We need some means of laying a trail.' Yet he had no chalk or string to hand. Malus bared his teeth. 'Is there something you could do to mark our path, daemon?' he asked reluctantly.

'Nothing could be simpler,' Tz'arkan said and pain bloomed from the back of Malus's right hand.

The highborn cried out, raising his sword arm – and saw the black veins on the back of his hand bulge and writhe like river eels. The skin of his hand distended as one of the veins took on a life of its own, extending itself as a pulsing tendril and burying itself in a crack between two paving stones. The line grew taut, but Malus guessed there was more length to be played out, as though his veins were just one long skein of twine he could unravel as he walked. He could feel the entire length of the living cord, like an extension of his own skin. It was the most revolting, unsettling sensation he had ever felt in his life.

'I bet you never thought you had such depths to draw upon,' the daemon chuckled. 'We can unravel you for miles before you spill your organs on the floor.'

Cursing quietly to himself, Malus picked the left-most stair and started upwards once more.

He could not tell if he had been climbing for hours or days.

Malus had made quite a few wrong turns at first, ending up in places he'd been before and using the cord to retrace his steps. Over time he'd grown sensitive to the feeling in the vein stretching out behind him and was able to sense when he began to turn back towards it. So long as he kept it playing out behind him, he knew he was making progress and so he slowly but steadily climbed higher up the tower. Already, the floor of the tower was many hundreds of feet below. He was making progress, of that he was certain.

Unfortunately, he was equally certain something was stalking him in the sorcerer's great maze.

He'd begun to hear distant sounds – thumps and scrapes, like something heavy lurching across the stone floor. Once or twice when his path took him near the centre of the tower he would peer down at the galleries below and would catch a glimpse of shadowy movement. Was it one of the ghosts from the plain, or did the tower have its own guardian to keep interlopers away from its innermost secrets?

Whatever it was, Malus had few options. He wasn't about to retrace his steps and try to confront it – that could well be what the creature wanted in the first place. No, he decided, if it wanted to stop him then sooner or later it would have to confront him and when it did he would deal with it.

It wasn't long after making the decision that he began to hear the sound of deep grunts and long, snuffling breaths, as though some huge beast was sniffing the air for his scent and loping along his trail. The sound came from every direction it seemed – above, behind, left and right, as though the creature were circling him in the twisted maze. Fighting a growing sense of uneasiness, Malus pressed on. *The closer it gets, the closer I must be to my goal,* he thought.

Then, without warning, he came upon a door. It was a simple wooden affair, but it was the first one he'd seen since entering the tower. Malus laid a hand on the iron ring and pulled it open – and heard an enraged bellow echo from somewhere behind him. *Now we're making progress,* the highborn thought.

Beyond the door was a room with another set of stairs – the sight looked disturbingly familiar. Thinking quickly, he picked one staircase and started upwards. It led to another door and room virtually identical to the one he'd just left.

In the room just behind him, something huge smashed against the door with a thunderous crash and Malus remembered the dreams he'd had of this very moment. Without knowing why, he began to run. As if hearing his hurried footsteps, the guardian of the labyrinth bellowed in his wake and the door behind him banged against its frame as the creature burst through.

Malus ran on, focusing on the tendril playing out from his hand and using it to steer his course ever higher. Thunder followed after him as he ran, the beast smashing aside each door he left behind. Whatever it was sounded enormous and powerful and filled with mounting rage. He'd have tried to taunt it if he'd had any breath to spare.

Suddenly the highborn swept through another identical square room and up a flight of stairs – and found himself once more at the rail of a gallery overlooking the tower's centre. He was so high now that the floor was invisible in the greenish light. The highborn was further surprised to see that only one staircase lay available to him and it led up. Sensing he was near the end of the cursed maze, he sped on, only absently realising that the sounds of pursuit had stopped.

The staircase climbed without support into the open air above the gallery, winding around and around as it led upwards to a central point. It ended in a landing and a pair of rune-inscribed doors.

At last, Malus thought. Grinning triumphantly, he grabbed one of the iron rings and pulled the door open – and a huge creature leapt through the doorway with a thunderous roar, brandishing an enormous axe!

It was the guardian of the maze, Malus realised, hurling himself backwards barely in time to avoid a deadly sweep of the monster's blade.

The creature was huge, towering head and shoulders over Malus. Its powerfully-muscled body looked brutish and human, but its skin gleamed like brass and its head was that of an enraged bull. The creature swung its axe in broad, powerful strokes, but compared to the druchii it was clumsy and slow. Malus let out a savage cry and lunged beneath the monster's guard, swinging at its muscled belly. Just at the apex of his swing, however, his hand was pulled up short – the cord leading from his hand was binding him. The blade struck the monster but the blow was weak and the keen edge glanced harmlessly from the guardian's side. It advanced on him, swinging its axe at the highborn's neck and Malus was forced to retreat.

'What are you doing?' Tz'arkan raged. 'Kill it!'

Malus planted his feet and darted forward like a viper, lashing out at the monster's knee. This time there was enough slack in the cord that the blow struck with full force – and rebounded with a harsh clang. 'My blade can't penetrate its hide!' Malus cried in horror. 'It's as though it were solid brass! Can't you do something?'

'It's all I can do to keep the cord from breaking!' the daemon answered. '*You* think of something!'

The axe sliced at him in a short, backhanded blow and Malus saw it coming a fraction of a second too late. It struck a glancing blow across his breastplate, but the impact threw him off his feet. For a sickening instant he plummeted through the air, catching himself at the edge of one of the stairs at the last moment. His feet dangled over the tower's central chasm and Malus let go of his sword and fought for purchase on the smooth stones with his hands.

A shadow loomed over him. The guardian stepped ponderously towards him, his huge feet picking their way through loops of Malus's living cord. The highborn snarled fiercely, winding a length of the cord in his hand.

'I've seen how well you fight, beast,' he said, watching the creature's movements carefully. 'Let's see how well you keep your feet!'

Just as the guardian reached him it stepped through a loop of living cord. Malus hauled back on the black line with all his might, pulling it taut just as the monster moved forward. The huge creature stumbled, arms flailing for balance and then with a despairing bellow it pitched over and plummeted over Malus's head and into the central chasm. The highborn let go of the cord and listened as the monster's bellow receded into the distance. By the time Malus had climbed back onto the stair and rolled, panting, onto his back, it struck bottom with a sound like the tolling of an enormous bell.

Beyond the double doors at the top of the stairs was a small, octagonal room. Inside lay a complicated set of sigils inscribed into the floor, surrounding a stone pedestal. At the feet of the pedestal lay a skeleton, contorted in a pose of agonising death. Upon the pedestal stood an idol worked from brass, barely a foot in height.

The Idol of Kolkuth. Malus saw it and expected to feel triumph, but instead felt only a sort of weary disgust.

'All this blood and intrigue for a piece of brass scrap?' he said.

'Can mere brass twist time and space to its master's whim?' Tz'arkan replied. 'Take it, Malus. The second relic is within your grasp.'

Powerful energies throbbed in the air of the small chamber. Malus studied the skeleton warily. 'Is that Eradorius?'

'Indeed,' the daemon said with some amusement. 'So much effort to build a tower where he thought I could not find him. The madman built a maze beyond the ken of mortal men and placed an implacable guardian to keep it safe – but in his paranoid zeal he gave the guardian too much power and it not only kept others out, but trapped Eradorius within. Wondrous irony, is it not?'

Malus stepped forward, the toes of his boots brushing the outer edge of the sigil – and a powerful wave of disorientation flooded through him. It was as though he was a piece of wood tossed on a stormy sea – and yet at the same time everything felt familiar, as though he'd been here many times before.

Time and space, twisted within the arcane loops of the sigil, the highborn realised. Malus took another step towards the idol and his mind filled with visions.

He hung from hooks in the Vaulkhar's tower, delirious with agony.

He stood on the deck of a heaving ship in the middle of a fight, ducking at the last minute to avoid a crossbow bolt fired from a would-be assassin.

He stood in the middle of a swirling melee and narrowly avoided a decapitating stroke from Bruglir's sword.

All points led to this moment. Malus took another step and the visions continued, stretching past him into the future.

He raised his arms in triumph over a swathe of blood-stained sand, holding a druchii's severed head in his hands.

He saw Yasmir striding towards him across a bridge made of skulls, naked and luminous, her daggers glinting in her hands.

He saw a tower backlit against a seething crimson sky, besieged by an army that blackened the snowy earth and cried out for his blood.

Malus staggered, stumbling forward and the visions came more quickly.

He saw himself upon a throne of red oak with a Vaulkhar's torc around his throat.

He saw himself at the head of a vast army of druchii, charging up a road towards a waiting elven army with the high cliffs of Ulthuan towering above him.

He stood in the great tower of Naggaroth, looking out over a landscape full of darkness and storms.

The highborn's questing hand closed on something cold and hard. He plucked the idol from its resting place and there was a flash of blinding white light.

MALUS STAGGERED FROM Urial's portal into the midst of a raging storm. Wind and rain lashed at the citadel, howling through the hole battered by the Skinrider daemon. The cold rain felt like a blessing from the Dark Mother as the highborn fell to his knees. Steam curled from the seams in his armour and he gasped greedily at the damp air.

Urial staggered, his strength all but spent, reaching out to prop himself against a nearby wall with a trembling hand. Hauclir stood at the foot of the tower stair, surrounded by the bodies of half-a-dozen Skinriders. Blood and bile pooled at the retainer's feet, thinned by the driving rain.

Hauclir rushed to Malus's side. 'Are you well, my lord?'

Malus nodded. 'Well enough for now,' he said. 'How long have I been gone?'

'Only a few minutes,' Hauclir said, shouting over the wind. 'One minute things were the way you left them and then all of a sudden we heard this terrible cry and the wind blew up.'

'It was the daemon,' Urial said wearily. 'The magic surrounding the island has failed and the spirit was drawn back into the Outer Darkness.'

'What about the storm?' Malus asked.

'The world is reclaiming the island,' Urial answered. 'It is a storm of time breaking over the isle and everything upon it.' As he said this there was a series of sharp noises and a huge spiderweb of cracks radiated through the bricks that comprised the nearby wall. 'We'd best be getting out of here!'

The druchii staggered into the wind and spray. Outside was a scene of terrible devastation. The Skinrider fleet was burning or in the throes of deadly boarding actions with the survivors of the druchii fleet. Of Bruglir's seven vessels, only three survived and of those two looked too damaged to return to sea. There were loud reports echoing from the cove as the sorcery that held the Skinrider ships together began to fail, causing rotting seams to burst apart and masts to break from their mountings. On the shore a pall of smoke rose from the abandoned village as building after building collapsed under the avalanche of years.

There was a terrible groan from high overhead. As one, the highborn scrambled down the slope of the sea wall and found an overhang to duck under just as the citadel behind them collapsed. Ancient bricks exploded into powder as they struck the sea wall. A stone thrower weighing as much as a dozen men arced overhead and landed in the cove with a tremendous splash. Across the water there was another grinding roar as the chieftain's tower collapsed as well, spilling its contents down the face of the cliff.

As the last of the bricks broke apart or splashed into the waters of the cove the wind and rain abated, dwindling almost to nothing. Out in the cove the Skinrider ships were settling into the water as their holds flooded. Shattered hulls blazed across the length of the harbour, sending plumes of smoke high into the sky. Distantly, Malus heard the war screams of the druchii corsairs as they recovered from the shock of the storm and hurled themselves upon their demoralised opponents. The battle was over; now the slaughter and celebration would begin.

WHEN THE WIND shifted in the right way Malus could hear the screams of the dying Skinriders.

They'd taken a few hundred prisoners in the wake of the battle and the survivors of Bruglir's shattered fleet had sated their lusts for pain upon their enemies' already tortured bodies. Despite the popular wisdom that the raiders were beyond suffering, the druchii found ways to make the Skinriders suffer for what they'd done.

The cavern beneath the ruined citadel still stank with the miasma of decay, but Malus barely noticed. He moved across the cavern floor, picking his way carefully among the twisted bodies. Every now and then he could faintly hear the cries of other druchii sailors as the corsairs searched for their living saint. Urial remained convinced that Yasmir had survived the battle and would be found unharmed. The crew certainly believed him and that was all that mattered. When the corsairs weren't looking for Yasmir they were breaking open the treasure vaults deeper beneath the citadel and hauling chests of gold out into the light of day. Hauclir had taken charge of the recovery efforts, which were proceeding apace.

Malus knelt beside the body of a druchii in corsair's armour. The corpse was stiff, but the body had yet to putrefy in the cool air. He rolled the dead figure on its back, frowning when he discovered that it wasn't the one he sought. The highborn sat on his haunches, surveying the carnage. His eyes lit on another figure, this one closer to the sacrificial crater. Nodding to himself, Malus made his way to the body.

It had been three days since the battle in the cove. Since he'd emerged from the portal Malus's sleep had been free of portents. Now it was his waking thoughts that filled him with unease.

He reached the corpse and knew at once that he'd found who he sought. With a grunt of effort Malus rolled the body onto its back and considered it thoughtfully. After a moment he drew a thin-bladed knife from his belt and bent over the ravaged face. The razor-edged blade sank effortlessly into the loose skin. The highborn smiled faintly as he worked, making cuts with long, smooth strokes.

There would be a reckoning when he returned to Hag Graef, Malus knew. Lurhan would be furious when he learned of the death of his firstborn son. Bruglir had been the Vaulkhar's chosen successor, his pride and joy, but he was also a pragmatic man. Another son would have to step forward and take Bruglir's place.

The highborn set the knife by his side and lifted his prize away with gentle fingers. In a few months he would return to the Hag as a conquering hero and both the Drachau and his father would have to treat him as such. From there, the possibilities were limitless.

Malus raised Bruglir's face to the light and carefully laid it over his own. 'Masks on top of masks…' he smirked. It suited him well.

REAPER OF SOULS

Chapter One
SHIP OF THE DAMNED

THE WHISPERING DRAGGED Malus Darkblade back from merciful oblivion. With a snarl he opened sleep-gummed eyes and fumbled in the darkness for the bottle by his side, already wincing in anticipation of the taste of sour wine. Then he realised with a jolt that the low, urgent voice wasn't muttering in his head, but somewhere in the room nearby.

Malus bolted upright from the tangled sheets, sending a clatter of empty bottles rolling from the ruined bed onto the wooden floor. His mind reeled, and for a few sickening moments the motion swirled in counterpoint to the pitch and roll of the ship around him. The hairs on the back of his neck prickled at the hint of danger, even as he clenched his teeth and tried not to be violently ill. Malus blinked in the blackness of the captain's cabin, an involuntary groan escaping his lips.

The voice whispered again, this time a little louder and more intelligible. 'Forgive me for waking you, my lord–'

Malus squinted in the direction of the voice. The silhouette of a man stood at the foot of the broken bed, limned by the faint glow of a witchlight lantern burning in the passageway beyond the open cabin door. The highborn glared coldly at the apparition, trying to focus his wine-addled thoughts. 'Gods Below, Hauclir,' he grated. 'If I could kill you with just my eyes you'd be a steaming puddle on the deck. Do you have any idea what time it is?'

'Just a bit past midnight my lord,' the retainer said. 'That's why I'm here. It's happened again.'

The words brought the highborn up short, a vicious curse dying on his thin lips. He bent his head and drew a single, hissing breath, summoning the cold clarity of his rage. When he lurched from the bed his brain still felt swollen and his mouth tasted like a midden heap, but his thoughts were cold and clear.

Wreckage littered the captain's cabin of the corsair ship *Harrier*. Resources were scarce. After the battle she'd fought at the Isle of Morhaut almost a month ago, there were always more pressing repairs to be made as the wounded vessel limped home. Squares of triple-layered canvas were nailed over broken window frames on the stern and port side of the cabin. Cabin doors scavenged from other parts of the ship were nailed over holes in the port bulkhead and the ceiling where catapult stones had punched through the ship's ensorcelled oak. One stone had crossed the cabin and smashed the frame of the polished thornwood bed before coming to rest in the pile of horsehair mattresses; the other was still buried halfway in the deck between the bed and the room's large map table. Smashed sea trunks, piles of clothes, bits of armour and discarded weapons were piled among chunks of jagged wood and broken crockery. Still wearing a fine coat of blackened mail over his dark leather kheitan and robes, Malus paused only long enough to pull on his boots, then, with practiced familiarity, he wove among the piles of debris and grabbed his heavy cloak and sword belt from the charred map table.

'Let's go,' he said as he swept past his retainer and into the passageway beyond.

A long, deep-throated groan echoed along the cramped corridor as the *Harrier* sank into the trough between two waves. Malus adjusted his footing to the sloping deck without breaking stride and shrugged into his woollen sea cloak. In the back of his wine-fogged mind he began counting the seconds as the ship reached the bottom of her descent. *Harrier* was wallowing in the heavy seas, not riding along the surface of the waves as she should. The highborn counted to five before he felt the hull tremble as the ship nosed into the oncoming wave and then slowly began to rise again.

Malus wondered how much water had just washed along the upper deck and poured into her holds, adding to the weight of the gold and silver loaded there. Too much weight and the ship could spring her seams, drawing yet more water into the ship, until the moment finally came when *Harrier* would sink to the bottom of a trough and keep on going, straight into the jaws of the Dragons Below.

The plunder had been a necessary evil, Malus thought ruefully as he buckled on his swords. He'd led nine ships and more than a thousand men deep into the North Sea, to find and destroy the lair of a band of Chaos-tainted pirates called the Skinriders. The confrontation with the Skinrider chieftain's personal war fleet at the island's anchorage had been a brutal, close-quarters battle between the nimble druchii corsairs and the Skinriders' larger, heavier warships. In the end, only *Harrier* and less than a hundred sailors from among the nine ships had survived. Had Malus tried to deny the druchii the spoils of their victory he had no doubt they would have killed him on the spot.

As it was, he was captain only by default. *Harrier's* true master and her first mate were both dead and he commanded by virtue of his highborn rank and the writ of authority he carried from the Drachau of Hag Graef. Malus reached the ladder at the end of the passageway and steeled himself for the climb to the upper deck. Like the mounting pressure in the ship's holds below, he wondered how much longer his authority would hold.

The ship's ladder climbed through the corsair's citadel, the aft section of decks that contained the quarters for the ship's officers, the chart room and the work space for the ship's chirurgeon. Malus rose as far as the main deck and turned down a cramped, dimly-lit passageway that ended at a sturdy oak door. Two corsairs stood to one side of the door in the fitful glow of a failing witchlamp, their weather cloaks dripping a steady stream of saltwater onto the deck. The druchii sailors straightened perfunctorily as Malus approached, but their eyes were downcast and their expressions sullen. The highborn brushed by them without a glance – he assumed they were part of the watch and as such they had no business being away from their posts. If he acknowledged their presence it meant he had to deal with the infraction and at the moment he wasn't certain how such a confrontation would play out. The realisation galled him to the core, but his rage was muted beneath the weight of gallons of bad wine. At the moment, Malus wasn't certain if that was a good or a bad thing, but it was definitely a *necessary* thing, so long as the balance of power on the ship remained precarious.

Malus pushed the door open and got a sharp spray of cold water against his face and neck that cut through the buzzing in his head like a flensing-knife. A gust of damp wind threatened to pull the heavy door from his hand.

Bracing himself and clutching his cloak tightly about him with one white hand, the highborn stepped carefully out into the night. A sharp wind was blowing from the north, making the *Harrier's* sails rattle and bang, keening like a tormented spirit among the frayed rigging above. The chill air buffeted the highborn from above and behind and the deck beneath him heaved as the ship was pummelled by the cold, slate-grey waves. Weak globes of witchlight cast eerie pools of greenish light along the main deck, but beyond the ship's smashed and splintered rails there was nothing but darkness and the crashing of the sea. It was a mild summer night, as far as the North Sea went.

The highborn paused, finding his feet and Hauclir brushed past him, heading for the main mast. The former guard captain wore dark robes and an indigo-stained kheitan of human hide under a shirt of fine, blackened mail. He wore no heavy cloak to ward off the wind and spray – after years standing watch on the battlements of Hag Graef he was hardened to far worse weather than this. Like the sailors, his skin was a dusky shade of pale, owing to a lifetime spent in the harsh elements, but the scars criss-crossing his hands and face were a testament to battles of a different sort.

The retainer was stocky for a druchii, with powerfully muscled arms and legs. He wore a short, businesslike sword and a heavy, knobbed cudgel at his belt. He was a far cry from the avaricious, dandified officer Malus had first encountered at Hag Graef's Spear Gate more than five months before, choosing simple utility and efficiency over jewelled weapons and fine robes. His long black hair was bound back into a thick braid tucked into the back of his kheitan and his angular cheeks were fringed with a rakish black beard he'd grown since the battle at the lost isle.

Despite an utter lack of respect for Malus's rank and an insolent streak that was almost suicidal in its frankness, Hauclir had proved himself a surprisingly capable and loyal retainer since entering the highborn's service. It was a difficult dance, acting as insubordinate as possible while remaining just indispensable enough not to be slain out of hand and Malus had to admire the man's dedication and craft.

Hauclir led Malus to the mainmast, altering his course at the last minute to swing wide of a portion of the deck near the mast's iron fitting. Malus's boot came down in a puddle of sticky gore.

'Mind your step, my lord,' Hauclir muttered just a moment too late, then pointed halfway up the length of the mast. 'Look there.'

The shape was a darker shadow against the *Harrier's* black sail; Malus thought he could just hear the creaking of a rope as the body twisted in the shifting wind. As he looked up he felt warm, heavy drops spatter against his face, smelling of hot copper. Though he couldn't see any details, he knew well enough what hung there – a naked man, his belly opened and his guts pulled out and his eyes no more than red, weeping hollows emptied by crude, clawing hands. Malus growled deep in his throat. The haze of bad wine was starting to thin and a painful buzzing was beginning in the back of his head. 'How many does this make?' he asked coldly.

Hauclir folded his arms, his bearded face twisting in a grimace. 'Eight, my lord.'

Malus craned his head, picking out the other shapes hanging like grisly trophies from the spars of the battered ship. The first killing had occurred the night after the *Harrier* had left the lost isle and began her torturous journey home. At the time, neither Malus nor Hauclir had known what to make of it. Was it the settling of some old score, or an obscure offering to the Dragons Below for a safe return home? The highborn had only been on two cruises in his entire life: his traditional hakseer-cruise upon reaching manhood and a single slaving cruise to the Old World many years later. He was a novice in the ways of the sea and Hauclir had never set foot on a ship before the expedition against the Skinriders. Bruglir, Malus's illustrious brother, had commanded *Harrier*, but he and his first mate had died in the battle and the crew regarded Malus as an interloper at best. The highborn was reluctant to begin scourging the handful of survivors for information. So he had refrained, willing to ignore the murder as an isolated event and focus on making port in Naggaroth. At first it had seemed like the proper course of action. Then, three days later, another body appeared.

Hauclir studied the bodies and theorised that it had to do with the treasure lying in the corsair's hold. Every sailor aboard could claim a drachau's ransom in gold as their share of the loot, but greed was a fever that only grew when fed and sailors were wont to gamble as a way of passing time. The former guardsman concluded that the dead men were hapless souls caught cheating at dice or hassariya and were strung up in a form of sailors' justice to warn off other gamblers.

Malus mustered the crew the next morning and ordered a stop to the killings, then Hauclir and a cadre of sailors gathered the crew's swords and locked them away in the ship's armoury. The crew turned sullen at the order, but they obeyed, and after some consideration Malus declined to press things further by ordering the bodies be cut down. Hundreds of leagues from Hag Graef he knew perfectly well that he had only as much authority as sailing tradition and the crew's morale lent him.

It was only after the fifth killing that Hauclir noticed a worrying trend – there were only a handful of sailors on board whose loyalty Malus could count on and one by one they were being gutted and left to hang.

Enquiries were made. Sailors were flogged. The morale of the crew worsened, but no one knew who was behind the killings or even why they were committed. Malus ordered the bodies to be cut down, but at the end of the day they still hung from the ship's spars. Given the choice of pressing the issue and perhaps sparking a confrontation, Malus had gritted his teeth and let the matter slide, unwilling to risk eroding his authority further. He decided on ordering Hauclir and his chosen men to lay in wait for the killers, hoping to catch them in the act and then publicly torture those responsible in the most brutal way he could imagine.

Three more men had died since. Malus rubbed his forehead, trying to clear his thoughts and banish his growing headache. 'How did this happen?' he asked, his voice leaden with menace.

Hauclir started to respond, then caught himself. After a moment he shook his head. 'I don't know,' he said grimly, showing fashionably filed teeth. 'I was watching from the citadel deck. I had men in the masts above and men at the bow. Duras was walking the deck every fifteen minutes, but just after the change of the watch, there it was.'

'It would have taken two men at least,' Malus growled, his fists clenching. 'The body is gutted like a pig for the feast, yet there is no trail of blood?'

The former guard captain shrugged. 'It could have been wrapped in a spare piece of sailcloth and already tied at the wrists. All they would have to do is throw the line over the mast spar and haul away.' Hauclir cast his eyes about in the cavern-like gloom, his expression tight with anger and frustration. 'The deed could have been done in less time than it takes to tell of it and it's as dark as a witch's heart out here. I could have had a man standing at the foot of the mast and still not have caught anyone.'

Malus could feel the rage simmering in his chest as the effects of the wine began to recede. 'Enough of this,' he hissed. 'My patience is at an end. Pick ten men at random and start skinning them. I want names.'

'We can't do that,' Hauclir said.

The highborn turned and struck the retainer across the face with the back of his hand. The flat *crack* was lost on the wind in an instant, but Hauclir rocked back on his heels, blood spurting from a split lip.

'I am the captain of this ship,' Malus snapped, 'and no one sheds the blood of this crew save me, by law and by custom. I should have started flaying men alive as soon as this began.'

'We couldn't have done so then and we dare not try it now,' Hauclir said levelly, wiping away a stream of dark blood with the back of his hand. His eyes were bright with pain, but his expression was cold and disciplined. 'By the time we'd filled out our crew with survivors from the rest of the fleet there was perhaps one man in ten whose loyalty we could count on. Now there are two. Believe me, my lord, I've faced more than one mutinous barracks in my time and I know for a fact that once you've shown your hand, only one of two things can happen – the men either back down and accept your authority without question, or they turn on you like a pack of starving nauglir. If you press the issue I don't think there is much doubt which way they'll go.'

'And you think it better I appear weak and let these killings go unchecked?'

Hauclir took a deep breath. 'I think we avoid starting a fight that we can't win, my lord.' He jerked his head in the direction of the ship's wheel. 'Old Lachlyr says we're no more than twenty leagues from the north coast of Naggaroth – how he knows is a mystery to me, but these sea birds have their own instincts about such things. He says we'll sight land by dawn tomorrow and from there it's another day or two down the Slavers' Straits and into the Sea of Chill. We could make port at Karond Kar in three days, pay off the crew and be rid of them. There won't be another killing before then, so you can avoid a confrontation altogether and keep our skins intact.'

'Unless these men are being killed because there's a mutiny afoot and the killers are eliminating the loyal crew members before making their move?' Malus considered the dangling corpse thoughtfully. 'They could be hanging the victims as a warning to others so as to keep them in line. Sighting land tomorrow might be the signal to make their move and seize the ship and the entirety of the gold for themselves.'

The retainer shook his head. 'No, I've already thought of that. Why wait? If enough of the crew were willing to kill us and claim all the gold they could have done it any time they liked. Why go to all the trouble to hunt out the loyal ones? These aren't subtle men, my lord. If anything, they've turned more feral since we left that damned island.'

Malus muttered a dark curse, but had to admit that Hauclir was right. At first the crew's spirits were high in the wake of the battle and the looting that had followed, but once they'd returned to the open sea the mood of the sailors had become increasingly tense. First it had been just the original men of the *Harrier*, but it had gradually spread to the other survivors as well, like a strange fever. Pain sharpened in time with his thoughts and the buzzing in his head was growing louder. The highborn gritted his teeth. 'There's some purpose to these killings, Hauclir. If it's not mutiny, then what is it? It's too regular to be anything but a plan…' The highborn's voice trailed off as his eyes narrowed in realisation.

The pause brought Hauclir's head around. 'My lord?'

'The killings,' Malus said. 'How do you know one won't happen before we reach Karond Kar?'

Hauclir frowned. 'Well, each man was killed about four days apart, just at…' The retainer's eyes widened. 'Just at the change of the moons.'

Malus nodded, his expression turning murderous. 'Exactly. This isn't mutiny, Hauclir. This is *sorcery*.' The highborn turned on his heel, striding quickly back the way he'd come.

It took several moments for the full weight of Malus's words to sink in. Hauclir's eyes widened and he hurried after the highborn. 'But what does it mean, my lord? Where are you going?'

'To the source,' Malus said angrily. 'My dear brother has some explaining to do.'

THE OAK DOOR had become a grisly shrine.

At first it had been merely carvings – sailors incised their names into the door or the frame, hoping for a blessing, or inscribed small prayers for the death of their foes. Some of the prayers had been embellished over time as the carvers returned and sought to rededicate themselves to their god. Flowing lines of druchast, elegantly carved by calloused hands, were surrounded by vivid depictions of battle scenes comprised of scores upon scores of artful lines cut into the wood. Even Malus was impressed at the artistry and skill of the devoted sailors who had spent hours working their prayers into the steel-hard surface of the door.

Later, however, the offerings became less artful and more direct. Names were painted in blood, or sometimes the aspirant merely pressed a bloody palm print to the door's wooden surface. Then someone took a carpenter's nail and put up a severed hand taken from a Skinrider. Severed ears became popular, as well as scalps.

From there it was only a matter of time before the devout began piling severed heads at the foot of Yasmir's door.

The stench was profound. Malus had not been in this part of the ship since the *Harrier* had left the Isle of Morhaut and the gory spectacle had been gruesome even then. The highborn counted two score Skinrider heads before giving up in disgust. The pain in his head was much sharper now, beating against the back of his eyes like a drum and an invisible charge seemed to play over the surface of his skin, setting his hair on end. He suddenly found himself craving the taste of that damned sour wine.

Malus paused at the blood-soaked door. As near as he could tell it hadn't been opened in some time, possibly not at all since they'd left the island. During the few sober moments he'd had over the last few weeks it had seemed like a blessing not to have Urial haunting the main deck like some misshapen crow. Now he wasn't so sure.

Urial had been in that room with his half-sister for weeks. Malus had no love whatsoever for Yasmir, but the realisation unsettled him nonetheless.

I must still be drunk, the highborn thought sourly, rubbing a hand across his face. Yasmir was beautiful beyond words and as cunning as an adder. Back at Hag Graef she had held the young nobles of the court in the palms of her hands and made them bleed for her sport. Yet it was her love for her brother Bruglir that made her useful to Malus. He needed Bruglir's fleet in order to reach the island and deal with the Skinriders and with Yasmir's backing he could ensure Bruglir's cooperation. Urial, on the other hand, was a bitter and twisted man who had just as much reason to hate his own family as Malus did. Having been given to the Temple of Khaine as a sacrifice, the deformed infant had survived immersion in the sacrificial cauldron – a sign of the god's favour. He'd become a servant of the temple and had learned many arcane arts and for this reason Malus had need of him as well. So Malus had woven a web of promises and lies that had bound his siblings to him. Or so he'd imagined.

With Urial's influence as a servant of the temple Malus was able to persuade the Drachau of Hag Graef to issue a Writ of Iron, giving him the power to commandeer Bruglir's fleet and seek the lost island. Yasmir's influence was the real iron behind the writ, however; a force that Bruglir could not oppose. Urial, in turn, loved Yasmir and Malus promised that by the end of the campaign Bruglir would no longer stand in Urial's way.

In the end they were all betrayed to one degree or another.

Bruglir was killed in battle with the Skinrider chieftain, but not before being betrayed by his sea mistress Tanithra. Yasmir was betrayed by Bruglir's faithlessness and her hatred for him awakened a part of her that had lain dormant during her sheltered years at the Hag. Her desire for slaughter had transformed her into a living manifestation of death – in Urial's words, a saint of the Bloody-Handed God. Even Malus was forced to admit that her ability to kill with her long knives was supernatural in its terrible grace and skill. The crew saw her fight during a desperate boarding action in the teeth of a late winter gale and afterwards her quarters became a shrine to the Lord of Murder.

Malus raised his hand to the bloodstained door. There was sorcery at work within; he was starting to be able to sense it, like a stench burning at the back of his throat. The buzzing in his head began to take the shape of words, but he focused on the door and its bloody inscriptions instead.

He paused, his hand inches from the dark wood. The skin prickled as it came into contact with currents of unseen power. After a moment, he withdrew his hand. Why knock, he thought? With all that power at his command, Urial no doubt already knows I'm here.

Malus Darkblade raised his boot and kicked the door open in a shower of splinters and twisted metal.

Chapter Two
THE BRIDE OF RUIN

ICKING OPEN THE cabin door was like piercing the side of a furnace. Fierce, rippling waves of heat and a blaze of crimson light flooded into the dimly-lit passageway. A sense of dislocation washed over Malus. He raised his hand without thinking, as if to ward off some unseen blow and the buzzing in his head fell silent. A familiar sensation, like a coil of serpents writhing beneath his ribs, constricted tightly around his heart.

Beyond the doorway the air throbbed with otherworldly power. Complex runes and intricate sigils had been carved deeply into the floors, walls and ceiling and fresh blood poured into the channels to tie the mystical geometries together. When the cabin had been Yasmir's quarters she had rarely left it during the voyage. At the far end of the room she'd raised a shrine of sorts, comprised of the crew's first, crude offerings and meditated at its feet for hours on end. That crude construction was gone now; in its place was Yasmir herself. She sat in a kind of trance in the centre of the room, her body effortlessly poised and her face bearing the serene, merciless countenance of a queen.

Malus stared in shock, heedless of Urial's naked, prostrate form stretched at the feet of his regal sister. Yasmir wore a circlet of gleaming brass upon her brow and from her shoulders hung a mantle of bright red and shining black that pulsed with life in time with her beating heart. She wore a cloak of glistening organs, woven together with threads of dark veins and cable-like arteries. Fresh blood shone in the light like enamel upon her breast and a single drop glimmered like a ruby on one perfect cheek.

The highborn looked upon his half-sister and in that moment he glimpsed her as Urial did: transcendent, sublime, a goddess clad in a raiment of slaughter and for the space of a single heartbeat he worshipped her. Words of devotion came unbidden into his mind. I will bow to you on a carpet of bones, he thought, his heart aching. I will bathe you in the blood of nations and fill the air with the music of murdered innocents. I will beat out a dirge upon the surface of the world and bear you beyond, to stars unnumbered.

Cold, cruel laughter, ancient as the bones of the earth, washed away the worshipful litany in his mind. A voice spoke, reverberating hollowly in his chest.

'Look upon her and dismay, little druchii,' Tz'arkan said, his voice sinking like a razor into Malus's brain. 'She is your handiwork – a goddess of blood given form. But you cannot be hers. You belong to *me*.'

Malus tore his eyes from Yasmir's face, feeling bile rise in his throat. Mother of Night, how he needed a drink! 'I belong to no one, daemon,' he whispered through clenched teeth. 'Least of all to you.'

Would that it were true, Malus thought bitterly. His hands clenched into fists and he felt the ruby ring upon his finger. He bore it like a shackle, no more able to remove it than he could pull off his own hand. Malus had worn it for almost five months, ever since he'd found it in a temple deep in the Chaos Wastes. He'd gone there in search of wealth and power, but too late he'd realised that he had fallen into a trap.

The temple was also a prison for the great daemon Tz'arkan, bound there aeons before by a cabal of Chaos sorcerers and in a single rash act Malus had inadvertently become Tz'arkan's pawn. Every waking moment since then had been devoted to escaping the daemon's clutches, for in a year's time Tz'arkan would claim his soul for all eternity unless he found five relics of power that would free the daemon from his crystal prison. Two were now in his possession: the Octagon of Praan, stolen from the clutches of a clan of beastmen in the north and the Idol of Kolkuth, lifted from its resting place in the Tower of Eradorius on the lost Isle of Morhaut.

Confronting the Skinriders who'd claimed the island as their lair had been nothing more than a ruse to gather the ships and men needed to reach the island and find the tower. The price in men and ships was nothing to the highborn, he'd grind entire continents to dust if that was what it took to win back his soul from the daemon – if any part of it still remained, that is.

The daemon hissed in amusement, slithering around the highborn's labouring heart. Tz'arkan's mocking presence was always in the back of his mind, tempting him with powers far beyond mortal ken, but each time the cold, icy force of the daemon's gifts flowed through his bones it left a stain inside him, corrupting him from within. Wine was the only refuge he'd found from Tz'arkan's influence, but it was a fleeting, wretched kind of peace. There were times, late at night, when he wondered if he drank to escape the daemon's taunting whispers, or to protect himself from the temptation of drawing on still more of Tz'arkan's power.

Just now, however, the thought of tearing his half brother into tiny pieces was very tempting indeed.

'Hello, dear brother,' Malus said, his voice cold with anger. 'You've been quite the recluse these last few weeks. Had I known you were down here knitting a robe from my sailors' guts I would have paid a visit much sooner.'

Urial made no reply. Slowly, purposefully, he climbed to his feet, rising carefully on his one good leg. The former acolyte's naked form was slender, almost boyish. He was lean to the point of emaciation, muscles like steel cord standing out starkly beneath skin so pale as to be nearly translucent. Malus was surprised to see that nearly every inch of Urial's body, from neck to toes, was incised with hundreds of arcane runes. His thick, white hair fell unbound to his waist and when he turned to face Malus his eyes shone in the reddish light like molten coins of brass. Malus's eyes were drawn to Urial's withered right arm and his twisted, foreshortened left leg and he fought a surge of revulsion. His disgust must have shown on his face, because Urial squared his shoulders and drew himself straighter, as though daring his half-brother to point out his weakness. There was a gleam in Urial's eyes that Malus had seen before, on the deck of the *Harrier* during that battle in the winter gale when Yasmir had shown her terrible zeal for killing. He was transported in a kind of terrible ecstasy.

The look of joy on his face unsettled Malus more than anything else.

'Greetings, Malus,' Urial said in his sepulchral voice. 'I had wondered when you would come. A few moments more and you would have been too late.'

Malus's eyes narrowed warily. 'What in the Dark Mother's name are you talking about?'

'Do not blaspheme,' Urial said and this time there was the sound of steel in his voice. 'Not here. This is a holy place, sanctified by the Lord of Murder.'

'This is my ship, brother,' Malus said, taking a pointed step across the threshold into the cabin. 'And my men you have slain.'

Urial smiled. 'Your men? I think not. If anyone on this ship can lay claim to being a mutineer, it is you. You murdered their rightful captain.'

'Bruglir died at the hand of a Skinrider,' Malus snapped. 'You were there. You saw it just as well as I.'

The malformed druchii's smile widened further. 'Ah, but he was trying to kill *you*, as I recall. It was simply his ill luck that he got in the way of that monster's axe.' Urial turned and limped to the cabin's single cot, ostentatiously turning his back on his sibling. Black robes and kheitan were laid out on the horsehair mattress. 'You manipulated him for your own ends, just as you manipulated me.' He began to dress himself, casting a protective glance over his shoulder at Yasmir. 'I might have tried to kill you myself, but I had other priorities. The point is, you are the usurper here, not I. In fact, if anyone can now claim to possess the crew's unswerving loyalty, it is Yasmir. I don't see the men leaving blood offerings at *your* door.'

For a moment, Malus was taken aback. This was a side to Urial he hadn't seen before. What had happened to the dour priest whose iron faith had prevailed against the Skinriders' daemon hosts?

Tz'arkan stirred. 'Beware, Malus. There are dangers here you do not comprehend.'

The highborn shook his head as if to clear the voice from his mind. 'Why did you kill those men?' he asked, focusing once more on Urial.

'Kill them? No. You misunderstand,' Urial replied, shaking his head. 'They were willing sacrifices, brother. They died for the glory of the living saint, to herald her arrival with offerings of slaughter as she steps through the Vermilion Gate.'

'Stop speaking in riddles!' Malus snarled. 'What are you babbling about?'

Urial drew his belt tight, then slipped his kheitan over his shoulders. He turned back to Malus, tightening the kheitan's side lacings and smiling his secret smile. 'There is too much to tell,' he said. 'And you are unworthy. But I will say this: in my own way I manipulated you as well.'

Malus paused. He didn't like where this conversation was leading. 'Manipulated, how?'

Urial finished his lacings and adjusted the fit of the leather, then turned and carefully picked up a dark object from the bed. He cradled it in the crook of his crippled arm and Malus saw that it was an ancient, yellowed skull, bound in brass wire. The white-haired druchii caressed the relic gently with a single fingertip, composing his thoughts. Finally he said, 'Did you ever think it strange that I was born this way?'

Malus frowned. 'No. Some children are malformed. It is the way of things.'

'The way of things? Look at her.' Urial gestured at Yasmir. 'She is perfect – the blood of Nagarythe queens courses through her veins.

Consider illustrious, betrayed Bruglir, a hero among men. They shared the same mother, the same father as myself.' His expression darkened. 'My mother was pregnant with me when Lurhan returned from the black ark with that witch Eldire, your mother.'

'You think *she* twisted your limbs in the womb?'

'Of course,' Urial said. 'She intended to kill my mother and take her place. She used metal salts from the forges and had them slipped into her food. Nothing else explains the wasting sickness that took hold of my mother and slowly sapped her strength for two long months. When she finally died, Lurhan had her servants cut me from her belly in the hope I would survive.' The pale-haired druchii's smile turned bitter. 'According to the servants he took one look at me and said I was the cause of his wife's terrible death. I was given to the temple straight away. I believe Lurhan would have thrown me into the cauldron himself if he could.'

'And not even Khaine would have you,' Malus snorted in disgust. He was growing tired of Urial's smug manner.

To his surprise, Urial laughed. 'You are a fool, Malus Darkblade. Do you think Khaine cares whose skulls adorn his throne? No! There are never enough offerings to sate his hunger. He only spares those who are meant for a greater destiny.'

Malus stared incredulously at Urial. 'You?'

'There have been other men spared by the cauldron, but none as crippled as I. The priestesses at Hag Graef took that as a great omen and sent me to the elders at Har Ganeth, City of Executioners. It was there, years later, that I learned of the prophecy.'

Something stirred within Malus. A vague feeling of unease crept over him. 'Prophecy?'

Urial took the skull in his good hand and looked deep into its shadowed eye sockets. 'It is old, very old. Perhaps one of the first testaments given by the Lord of Murder to his believers, back in the dawning days of the world.'

'And what does this prophecy speak of?'

'It speaks of a man born to the house of chains, touched by the gods and forsaken by men.' Urial stared intently at the skull, as though daring it to contradict him. 'His mother will be taken from him and his father will cast him out, yet by his hate he will prosper.' The former acolyte lowered the skull and turned his gaze upon Yasmir, his expression changing to one of pure desire. 'And his sister shall take up the blades of the Bloody-Handed God and be blessed with his countenance and wisdom. She will be the Anwyr na Eruen and the Lord of Murder shall give her to him as his wife, as a sign that his destiny is at hand.'

Malus frowned at the archaic title. 'The Bride of Ruin?'

Urial nodded. 'Even so.' He took a halting step towards her, a look of rapture on his face. 'When I completed my training at the temple, the elders returned me to Lurhan's household to await the coming of my bride. When I first saw Yasmir at the Court of Thorns I knew she was the one. The years passed and still she remained unmarried, despite the attentions of the finest druchii princes in the city. When she took Bruglir as her lover I was angry at first, but now I see that it was all part of Khaine's great plan. Without Bruglir's betrayal she never would have learned of her true self.' He turned to Malus. 'And without you his treachery never would have come to light. You have served the Lord of Murder well, Malus and I'll see to it that you are rewarded for everything you've done.'

The highborn found himself shaking his head. Suddenly it was hard to breathe. Could what Urial was saying be true?

'More true than you know,' Tz'arkan said with a gruesome chuckle. 'What are men, after all, but the playthings of the gods?'

Malus glanced at Yasmir, his breath catching in his throat. 'And what destiny does your precious Lord of Murder intend for the two of you? Will you bring an end to the world?'

The white-haired druchii merely smiled. 'Nothing so petty,' he said with a smile. He held up the yellowed skull. 'This is one of the most ancient relics of the temple, brother. By rights your life is forfeit just for looking upon it. It is older than even lost Nagarythe and our lore proclaims it to be the skull of Aurun Var, the first of our kind to swear himself to the Lord of Murder. It was he who first heard the prophecy from the lips of Khaine himself and the legend says his shade will speak to the chosen one and set him on the path to his destiny when the time is right.'

Malus eyed his brother warily. A mirthless smile spread across his angular face. 'But the skull hasn't spoken to you yet, has it?'

For a fleeting moment, Urial's self-assurance faltered. 'The prophecy is clear. The skull will speak when the time is right and not before.'

The highborn nodded. 'Yes. Of course. But in the meantime, you still need my help.'

'You've done all that the Lord of Murder requires of you, Malus Darkblade. We need no more from the likes of you.'

Malus bared his teeth at the old insult. 'Do you think Lurhan will simply let you shut his daughter up in one of your temples? He's the most powerful warlord in Naggaroth, brother. You'll need my influence to help convince him that she will be better off among the priestesses.' He spread his hands in conciliation. 'I only ask a small favour in return.'

'And what would that be?'

Malus walked close to Urial. 'I wish to make use of your arcane knowledge, brother,' he said quietly. 'I'm searching for a number of artefacts – ancient relics that have been lost for hundreds of years. One of them is a magical weapon called the Dagger of Torxus.' The highborn shrugged. 'The reasons for my search are unimportant, but–'

'You seek to release the daemon Tz'arkan from his prison,' Urial said coldly.

Malus staggered back as though struck. His mind reeled. 'What are you talking about?'

'Do you take me for a fool, brother?' Urial sneered. 'I guessed at your plan before we ever left Naggaroth. I suspected it when you broke into my tower with that witch Nagaira and stole the Skull of Ehrenlish. She sent you to the north in search of his prison, didn't she?' He snorted in disgust. 'When you told me that she was a priestess in the Cult of Slaanesh I knew I was right. You went to the island to claim the Idol of Kolkuth and now you're after the Dagger of Torxus. What else remains? The Octagon of Praan? The Amulet of Vaurog?' Contempt flashed in his brass-coloured eyes. 'I came with you this far for Yasmir's sake. You'll get no more help from me.'

'But Lurhan–'

'Lurhan wanted you dead before we left Naggaroth,' Urial snapped impatiently. 'Were it not for the Writ of Iron you extorted from the drachau he would have found a way to kill you sooner or later. How do you think he will react when he learns you caused the death of his beloved son and heir?' He shook his head. 'No, Malus. You're finished. You have no value to me.'

'I see,' Malus said. Then with two swift strides he crossed the space between them and snatched the skull from Urial's hand.

The pale-haired druchii's eyes went wide with shock and rage. Malus started to speak – but his body jerked with a galvanic shock as sorcerous power split the air in the room with an angry snarl and a voice smote him like a fist.

GO YE TO THE HOUSES OF THE DEAD, O WANDERER, AND SPILL THE BLOOD OF THE FATHER OF CHAINS.

Malus and Urial alike staggered at the force of the words. The air stank of burnt copper as tendrils of smoke rose from the blood laid in the sigils around the cabin. The highborn looked this way and that, seeking the source of the terrible voice.

THE DAGGER LIES BENEATH THE HORNED MOON. YOUR PATH WAITS IN THE DARKNESS OF THE GRAVE.

It was Yasmir. Her raiment of living organs had fallen away as she stood, revealing her naked, luminous form. Streaks of bright blood gleamed against her neck, shoulders and breasts. Her mouth was wide, her full lips trembling and her eyes were discs of burning brass.

The voice faded as swiftly as it arrived, receding in a thunderous silence. Malus staggered, struggling to comprehend what had just happened.

He met Yasmir's eyes and saw in them nothing but death. Her knives glimmered in her hands.

'Blasphemer!' Urial screamed, his voice twisted with anguish. The white-haired druchii lurched forward, snatching the skull away from Malus. 'Daemon's pawn!' He raised the relic over his head and arcs of crimson fire raced along its surface. 'Mine is the birthright! Mine will be the sword and mine will be the Bride of Ruin! The prophecy will be fulfilled!'

Malus stumbled backwards, away from Urial and Yasmir. She watched him with the soulless gaze of a predator and he had no illusions about what would happen if she reached for him with her slender blades.

Words of power crackled from Urial's lips. An invisible hand grabbed Malus and flung him through the air. He flew through the narrow doorway, striking his shoulder painfully against the frame and crashed into the far wall of the passageway beyond.

When he regained his senses a moment later, all Malus could see beyond the doorframe was a maelstrom of reddish light. A hot wind blew from the doorway like the breath of a dragon, carrying the faint cry of Urial the Forsaken.

'Let the Vermilion Gate swing wide! Rise up, O devoted of Khaine and wash the path of the Ruinous Bride with the blood of sacrifice!'

A groan reverberated through the deck beneath Malus, as though the hull of the wounded ship was bending under an impossible weight. Then he heard the faint sound of screams and the clash of steel from the main deck just above. Cursing bitterly, the highborn rose to his feet and ran to the sounds of battle.

URIAL'S WORDS CAME back to Malus as he burst onto the main deck, sword in hand: *I had wondered when you would come. A few moments more and you would have been too late.*

A pitched battle raged across the deck, the struggling silhouettes thrown into momentary relief as they were forced into the gleam of the witchlights. Daggers shone in the greenish light as the men of the night watch struggled hand-to-hand with shrivelled forms that once were fellow shipmates.

The hanged men had returned to life.

Malus watched a sailor grapple with a grey-skinned monstrosity, driving a dagger again and again into the creature's chest. The monster seized the man's shoulder and held him in a vice-like grip, oblivious to the sailor's blows and closed a hand over the man's face. Slowly, inexorably, the fiend bent the sailor's head back until the druchii's screams were silenced with a splintering crack of bone. The mummified sailor dropped the corpse to the deck and staggered towards the citadel, where two guardsmen stood with spears ready to defend the ship's helm.

'Mother of Night,' Malus cursed, gauging the course of the battle. The men on watch were on the verge of being overwhelmed and the rest of the crew was below deck, unaware of the danger. They were all to be sacrificed at Yasmir's feet.

The highborn looked around at the struggling forms, unable to tell one man from another in the blackness. The crew was at a severe disadvantage, armed only with their knives instead of the curved swords they normally carried at their sides. 'Hauclir!' Malus cried, as he moved to intercept the walking corpse approaching the citadel stairs.

'Here, my lord!' came a cry from the darkness, somewhere near the main mast.

'Get below and rouse the rest of the crew, then unlock the armoury! Quickly!'

The retainer shouted a reply, but Malus paid it no mind, focusing on the shambling figure ahead. The corpse was still heading for the stairs, reaching for the rails with torn, shrivelled hands. Maggots writhed in the dead man's empty eye sockets and tendrils of wrinkled entrails hung from the gaping cavity in his ripped belly. Malus leapt at the monstrosity with a war scream and aimed a powerful blow at the corpse's neck. Flesh parted beneath the sword's master-worked edge – then the blade struck the creature's spine and rebounded with a *clang* that sent a spike of pain racing up Malus's arm. The creature's head turned and seemed to notice him for the first time. The flayed man brushed the sword from his neck just like he would a fly, then grabbed for the highborn with surprising speed.

Malus dodged away from the reaching hand and slashed at it with his blade. Once again, the edge clove through the rancid flesh with ease, only to glance away from the bone with a harsh, metallic sound. The sword deflected from the creature's wrist, carving a length of leathery meat from the corpse's forearm and the highborn caught a bright gleam the colour of burnished copper. The sorcery that animated the flayed men had turned their bones to solid brass.

Once again, the corpse reacted with surprising speed, grabbing the highborn's blade in an iron grip. Razor-edged steel grated against metal bones as the monster dragged the sword out of the way and seized Malus by the throat.

Malus let out a choked cry, drawing in a single gulp of air before the fingers closed like a vice. He writhed in the monster's grip, pulling vainly at the sword trapped in the creature's hand, but the hand around his throat continued to tighten.

T'zarkan stirred, uncoiling slowly in Malus's chest. 'You are out-matched, Darkblade,' the daemon hissed spitefully. 'Urial spent an entire month creating his executioners, but you were too stupid, too deep in your cups to see the peril until it was too late.'

The highborn's mouth worked, but no sound escaped past the corpse's crushing grip. A roaring began in his ears and darkness crept like a rising tide at the edge of his sight.

T'zarkan's voice hissed like an adder in Malus's ear. 'Shall I make you regret your foolishness, little druchii?' Shall I let this puppet of meat and brass crush the life from you? Or shall I lend you my strength?' The daemon's chuckle seeped into his brain like poison. 'What shall I do? Tell me, Darkblade. Tell me what to do.'

Malus grabbed the monster's forearm with his free hand and braced his feet against the corpse's hips, pushing for all he was worth. He could feel his limbs weakening and blackness threatened to over-whelm him. Terror, pure and absolute, coursed like lightning down his spine.

Suddenly, the creature staggered backwards. Malus lost his footing on the corpse's abdomen and slumped to the deck and without warn-ing the monster staggered backwards yet again. The highborn fought to regain his feet and as he did so he noticed the shaft of polished black oak jutting from the creature's right collarbone. The guard at the top of the citadel stair had driven his spear into the corpse's shoulder and lodged it against unyielding bone. Now the corsair threw his weight against the spear shaft, threatening to topple the clumsy monster to the deck. Seeing this, Malus threw his weight against the creature as well and that was enough to overbalance it. The mummified body fell back-wards, landing heavily against the deck and for the briefest instant the vice-grip slipped.

Malus drew in a thin wisp of air, his eyes blazing with hate and rasped: 'Lend me your strength, daemon. Now!'

Tz'arkan's power suffused Malus like a torrent of foul, icy water. His body went taut; black veins bulged along his neck and hands and crept like strangling vines up the left side of his face. His eyes became pools of deepest night and icy mist curled from his lips. The very air seemed to curdle around him, tainted by the daemon's touch. As the power coursed through his limbs he could feel it eating away at his insides, like water carving a path through the soft rock of a mountain. One day it would be his demise, but for now it felt *glorious*.

Malus's free hand tightened on the monster's wrist. Dead flesh pulped and putrid fluids trickled between his fingers. Brass wrist bones creaked, bent, then shattered. The highborn staggered backwards, pulling the limp, severed hand from his swollen throat. He dragged the blade from the corpse's grip, sending five brass-cored fingers rolling on the deck. Still the monster tried to rise, mouth gaping hungrily. Malus lashed out with his blade and sheared through the corpse's neck bones with one fell stroke. The body collapsed, lifeless, as the head bounced across the deck. It fetched up by the port rail, the jaws still working relentlessly. The highborn reached it in two swift strides and kicked it into the heaving sea.

THE BATTLE WAS over within a few minutes once Hauclir and fifty sailors roared onto the main deck and overwhelmed the flayed men. By then more than a third of the crew was dead.

Malus stood in the middle of his half-sister's empty cabin. Visions swam before his eyes. One moment he saw the cabin as it was, with scorch marks on the walls and congealing blood dripping from the sigils carved into the ceiling. The next moment the walls blurred and he saw a cavern lit with ruddy light. A throng of figures in black robes and skull-faced porcelain masks bowed in obeisance beneath the outstretched arms of an alabaster-skinned goddess. She and Urial stood with their backs to a free-standing arch worked from reddish stone; he stood beneath the arch itself, feeling as though he watched the scene from the other side of an invisible door.

'You cannot hide from me, brother,' Malus hissed. 'Wherever you run to, I will find you. I swear it.'

'Did you say something, my lord?' Hauclir asked wearily from his place at the doorway.

The vision faded. Malus shook his head, exhausted. The daemon's gifts were potent, but in their wake he felt utterly spent. 'Just making a promise to myself,' he replied.

Hauclir studied his master's face for a moment, long enough to make Malus uncomfortable. For all of the retainer's rough spots and foibles, he could also be disconcertingly perceptive when he wished. But the former guard captain merely said, 'Where do you think they went?'

'I do not know and for the moment I do not care,' he replied. Malus looked around the cabin, trying to remember the words Yasmir – or the voice speaking through Yasmir – had said. Had it been the skull, telling him where he must go? Was such a thing possible?

The dagger lies beneath the horned moon. Your path lies within the darkness of the grave.

'The helmsman says we'll be at the mouth of the Slavers' Straits in a few hours,' the retainer continued. 'He wants to know where we'll make port.'

Malus glanced back to the centre of the room, where he'd seen the ghostly image of his brother. Urial had escaped with his would-be bride, but when he'd looked back at Malus, the highborn had seen something new in the man's brass-coloured eyes.

Fear.

'Set course for Karond Kar,' Malus ordered, nodding thoughtfully to himself. 'I must pay a visit to the houses of the dead.'

Chapter Three
THE TOWER OF SLAVES

THE HARRIER RODE easily in the choppy waters of the Sea of Chill, her black hull gliding through the pewter-coloured waves with something approaching her former grace. Sunlight glinted fiercely on the grey sea, etching the whitecaps with a silver sheen that was painful to look at after the weeks of darkness and gloom to the north. The Slavers' Straits were hours behind them and nearly all of the ship's crew was on deck, making repairs and speaking to one another in low, sibilant voices.

The men up in the rigging were singing some ancient sailing saga dating back to lost Nagarythe. Their husky voices shifted with the wind, like a chorus of mournful ghosts. The battered corsair was working her way along the sea's ragged northern coast, passing tall chalk cliffs and forested inlets five miles to starboard. From time to time the dark shape of a wyvern would straighten languidly from the top of a high cliff and spread broad, leathery wings before launching into the cold, clear air. They circled high over the water, their keen eyes hunting for sea pike to sate their voracious appetites.

Karond Kar was a sharp-edged splinter of dark grey stone, nearly invisible against the overcast sky, still some leagues north and west on their present heading. Barely a third of its impressive height was visible above a rocky spur of coastline, but like all druchii citadels it carried an air of menace and authority even at so great a distance.

Malus stood at the ship's bow as the crew went about their business, his gaze dark and brooding as he studied the distant tower and wondered how much of what Urial had said was true. He wasn't the sort to put stock in prophecies and the machinations of fate; few druchii did, because it implied a degree of helplessness that was anathema to them. Slavery was a sign of weakness, even on a cosmic scale. The fact that the Temple of Khaine nurtured such notions, even in secret, was disturbing enough. Worse still was the idea that he was somehow tied up in it.

One thing he knew for certain was that his expedition into the Chaos Wastes had not been the bold, unexpected plan he'd thought it to be. Facing debtors and a possible blood feud after a disastrous slave raid the previous summer, he'd been manipulated by his sister Nagaira into thinking that there was a source of great power hidden in the north that was his for the taking. That power had turned out to be the daemon, Tz'arkan and later he had discovered that she, along with his brother Isilvar, belonged to the outlawed Cult of Slaanesh, which worshipped Tz'arkan as one of Slaanesh's great princes. They had sought to use his ties to the daemon for their own purposes, but he'd turned the tables on them in the end, betraying them to Urial and the warriors of the temple.

Nagaira had been a sorceress of considerable power and she had manipulated him because of his ignorance in the arcane arts. Her illegal pursuits were an open secret in the Hag and a matter of some speculation. No one knew how she could have learned so much so quickly outside Naggaroth's witch convents. Malus had no proof, but more and more he believed that his mother Eldire had been Nagaira's secret patron.

Urial claimed Eldire was also the cause of his deformity. Was she orchestrating everything to suit some hidden agenda of her own, or was she also an unwitting pawn of this so-called prophecy? The implications sent a chill down his spine.

'How far back does it all go?' Malus asked himself. 'And where will it lead?'

'Into darkness,' Tz'arkan whispered. 'The darkness waits, Malus. Never forget.'

Before Malus could say more he heard the sound of footsteps. The highborn turned as Hauclir approached, fixing the retainer with a forbidding glare.

'What *now*, Hauclir?' Malus snapped.

The retainer stopped at sword's length and paused, considering his words. 'We're approaching Karond Kar, my lord,' he said.

'Yes, Hauclir, I can see that,' the highborn growled.

Hauclir grimaced, shifting uncomfortably on his heels. 'Once we make port it won't be long before Hag Graef's agents learn that Bruglir is dead and his fleet destroyed. Word will get back to your father soon after, I suspect.'

Malus shrugged. 'It is a possibility.'

The retainer frowned, unhappy with the answer. 'Will we be staying at Karond Kar, then? You said something last night about visiting the houses of the dead.'

'What of it?'

The retainer's jaw clenched, uncertain of how to proceed.

'Spit it out, damn you!' Malus snarled.

'The highborn of old went to the houses of the dead to seek the blessings of the Old Kings before they marched to war,' Hauclir replied, the words coming out in a rush. 'Is that your plan? War with your father?'

For a moment all Malus could do was stare incredulously at his retainer's troubled face. 'There. You have it,' he said. 'I'm going to pit my fearsome army of one against the household of the most powerful warlord in Naggaroth. Have you gone mad?'

Hauclir bristled at Malus's tone. 'Since entering your service I've seen you infiltrate a Slaaneshi cult, blackmail the Drachau of Hag Graef into granting you a Writ of Iron and commandeer a druchii fleet to confront the largest band of pirates in the North Sea. At this point *nothing* you do can surprise me any more.' The retainer folded his arms and returned Malus's glare. 'Why the houses of the dead, then? Do you intend to hide in the barrow city until your father forgets about you?'

The highborn's fists clenched. 'Mind your impertinent tongue, lest I pull it out,' Malus warned. 'It happens that there is something in the barrow city that I need and I aim to get it.'

Hauclir's eyes went wide. 'So you aim to *rob* the tombs of the Old Kings?'

'I won't know until I get there,' Malus replied. 'How is it you know so much about the dead city?'

The retainer was momentarily thrown off guard by the change in topic. 'I... read a bit when I was young,' he said.

'Indeed?' Malus arched an eyebrow thoughtfully. 'Did your readings ever mention a place with a horned moon on it?'

'A horned moon? I don't know...' The retainer's voice trailed off as he considered the question. He cocked his head quizzically at Malus. 'If I recall correctly, one of the princes of Nagarythe wore a silver crescent moon as his house sigil.' The retainer's face brightened. 'Eleuril the Damned! That was his name.'

'The damned?' Malus sighed. 'Why doesn't that surprise me?'

'He was a kinslayer, if I remember rightly. Murdered his father, his wife and his wife's father.'

'And?'

'And he was found out.'

'Ah.'

'The story claims he was strangled in his bed by the ghost of his vengeful wife.' Hauclir shrugged. 'Of course, that's just legend. His wife's family probably had him assassinated. Makes for a good story though. If I remember correctly–'

Malus cut him off with a wave of his hand. 'A dreadful story, I'm certain. Does it mention a dagger, by any chance?'

'As I was about to say, my lord,' Hauclir said peremptorily, 'Eleuril was a worshipper of Khaine and if I remember rightly he was one of the first princes to convert here in Naggaroth. This was back in the earliest days, when Malekith first outlawed male sorcerers and Eleuril was something of a warlock hunter. He took this dagger from a Slaaneshi sorcerer named… well, never mind his name. I can't recall. At any rate, he intended to use the dagger to murder his kin and blame it on Slaaneshi cultists.' He shrugged. 'Who knows? Maybe the dagger was cursed.'

'It certainly seems that way to me,' Malus said darkly.

Hauclir's eyes narrowed suspiciously. 'You're after the dagger, aren't you?'

'What would I want with such a thing?'

'What would you want with that little statue you've got locked up in your cabin, or that strange amulet you were fretting over back at the Hag?' The retainer's tone was mild, but his dark eyes were suddenly intent. 'It seems to me you're going to a great deal of effort to collect a number of arcane objects.'

Malus took a step towards Hauclir, his hand drifting to the hilt of his sword. 'Your keen eye and your suspicious mind serve you well, Hauclir – so long as they aren't directed towards *me*,' he said quietly. 'Remember your oath and serve.'

Hauclir stiffened. 'Of course, my lord,' he said stonily. 'What are your wishes once we make port?'

Malus looked back towards the distant tower. 'That will depend upon our reception,' he replied calmly. 'If we are allowed to drop anchor in the harbour, you will remain aboard and keep watch over the treasure while I make some enquiries.' The highborn folded his arms tightly against his chest. 'If something goes amiss, however, you are to gather my possessions from the captain's cabin and meet me at a flesh house in the Traders' Quarter called the Mere-Witch.'

'Is there reason to believe something may… go amiss, as you say?'

The highborn shrugged. 'It's possible I may have offended certain persons of rank the last time I passed this way.'

Silence fell. Hauclir waited, expecting Malus to elaborate, but the highborn offered nothing more. 'Very well, my lord,' the retainer said at last, then turned on his heel and walked away.

Tz'arkan chuckled hollowly in Malus's head. 'You keep secrets like a daemon,' he said admiringly. 'Is there no one you trust?'

The highborn's lips curled in disgust. 'At the moment I don't even trust myself.'

THE BREAKWATER AT Karond Kar was almost three miles long, built up from stone quarried from the forbidding mountains surrounding the Tower of Slaves. The lords of the tower paid enormous sums to a party of sculptors to work the stone at the base of the breakwater into the shapes of slaves, their taut, agonised bodies appearing to rise from the icy waves to support the stone blocks that held the Sea of Chill at bay. For hundreds of years the breakwater had been known as Nheira Vor – the Great Lament. When druchii corsairs arrived at the tower with their holds full of slaves, the cargo would see the lifelike statues and raise a terrible wail, believing that to be their fate. The lords of the tower never tired of the jest.

Karond Kar was the furthest, bleakest and richest of all the six cities in Naggaroth, enjoying enormous wealth as the clearing house for all the slaves taken by druchii raiders across the known world. It was the perfect localation to serve as neutral ground in buying and selling the land's most precious resource – the tower was too distant and too difficult for an army to besiege overland and possessed a powerful fleet of its own to repel assaults from the sea. The six lords of the tower were old and powerful druchii nominated by the Witch King from each of the great cities and thus enjoyed equal influence in the councils of the tower's drachau. Factors from the most powerful households across Naggaroth maintained permanent residences in the trading town at the foot of the tower and during the summer the population would treble as lesser traders would make the two-week journey by sea to buy stock for the coming year.

This early in the raiding season the tower's anchorage was nearly empty. Nearly every druchii raider wintered at the city of Clar Karond and would have only just departed on their cruises a few weeks before. The eastern side of the anchorage was dark with the hulls of the tower's defending fleet – long, sleek-hulled ships that bore a close kinship with the battered *Harrier*. Malus watched from the citadel deck as one of the tower's ships weighed anchor and put on sail. The deck of the ship was teeming with warriors, the northern sunlight glinting on their sharp-flanged armour and the tips of their spears.

Hauclir leaned against one of the ship's aft-mounted bolt throwers, arms folded, eyeing the approaching warship apprehensively. 'Is this normal?'

Malus nodded. 'They'll want to inspect the cargo for disease, look for any choice prospects they can tell their patrons about, shake us down for a bribe or two, that sort of thing.' He cast a sidelong glance at the retainer. 'Everything you used to do at Hag Graef, only on the water.'

The former guard captain nodded appreciatively. 'Shall I break out some coin from the hold?'

To Hauclir's surprise, Malus shook his head. 'Remember those trophies we stowed in the aft hold? Get some men and bring them topside once the inspectors come aboard.'

Hauclir grimaced, but nodded his head. 'As you wish, my lord.' He stepped to the rail overlooking the main deck, barked a set of orders in a parade-ground voice, then headed below.

The warship was upon them in minutes, cutting across their bow and then turning to pass them to starboard. The warriors and officers crowding the ship's rail eyed Malus and the *Harrier* intently, taking in the ship's damage and the state of her crew. At one point the highborn caught the eye of a tall, richly appointed officer standing by the wheel of the passing ship. The highborn bowed his head in greeting but got only a haughty glare in reply.

After completing her close inspection the tower warship cut across the *Harrier's* wake and slid up along the port side. A broad-chested druchii sailor cupped his hands around his mouth and bellowed, 'Strike your sails and drop anchor in the name of the tower lords and prepare to be boarded!' The tone in the man's voice left little doubt as to what would happen if *Harrier's* crew failed to comply.

'Strike sail!' Malus ordered, loud enough to be heard on both vessels. The weary crew leapt into action and within minutes the ship's ragged sheets were furled. By the time the stern anchor was splashing into the bay the tower warship had lowered a long boat full of troops and was rowing across the waves between the two ships.

Malus drew a deep breath. For a moment he wondered if perhaps he should have ordered Hauclir to prepare a bribe, but pushed the thought aside. 'Lower lines and prepare to receive inspection party,' he ordered, then headed to the main deck to await the inspector's arrival.

The long boat was alongside in a few short minutes and no sooner had her hull bumped against the side of the *Harrier* than the rope ladders went taut and armoured men came scrambling over the port rail. The warriors formed a grim-faced cordon around the rail, naked blades in hand. Unlike most corsairs, the tower men wore full plate harness over their kheitans and mail, offering far greater protection so long as the wearer didn't fall overboard. Malus noted the armour was of high quality, enamelled in sea green and worked with the insignia of a dragon twined about a narrow tower – the sigil of the Drachau of Karond Kar himself.

Ten armed men were crowded together on the main deck, weapons facing outwards, before the inspector himself appeared at the rail.

Malus was surprised to see it was the captain himself. The officer wore a heavy cloak of wyvern hide, fixed to his armour by gold brooches in the shape of sea dragons. His sea-green armour was worked with an ostentatious display of scrollwork and gems glittered from the pommels of the man's twin swords. He looked very young to be a ship's captain, with a face unmarked by the scars of battle. It meant he was well-connected, Malus reasoned.

The druchii officer alighted on the deck of the *Harrier* and took in the condition of the main deck in a single, scowling glance. The captain was tall and whipcord-thin, with gaunt features and a sharply pointed nose. His eyes glittered like chips of obsidian as he fretted with his armoured gauntlets and fixed Malus with a disapproving stare. 'Where is your captain? I am Syrclar, son of Nerein the Cruel, Drachau of Karond Kar.' He looked Malus up and down, his lip curling in disdain. 'I am not in the habit of speaking with the rank and file.'

At that moment Malus would have liked nothing better than to pitch the man into the sea, but instead he managed a cold smile. 'I have the honour of commanding this ship, Lord Syrclar,' he said with a slight bow.

A look of consternation crossed Syrclar's face. 'But this is the *Harrier*. I would know her anywhere.'

'Indeed so, lord.'

'Then where is Bruglir, son of Lurhan the vaulkhar? This is his ship.'

Malus's smile broadened. 'Ah, now I understand your confusion, lord. Bruglir died in battle, on a campaign against the Skinriders to the north.'

Just then, the doors to the citadel opened and Hauclir appeared at the head of a handful of sailors, dragging several bundles wrapped in stained sailcloth. Malus waved Hauclir over. 'You will be pleased to hear, Lord Syrclar, that our campaign was successful.'

Before the young druchii could reply, Hauclir dumped his bundle at the druchii's feet. It fell open, revealing a pile of severed heads, their putrid flesh black with crusted blood and stinking of corruption. Syrclar's guards recoiled at the stench, many uttering curses or prayers to the Dragons Below.

Malus bent down and considered the heads like a servant shopping for melons in the market. He grabbed one of the larger ones and tossed it to the young captain. 'Here, Lord Syrclar, with my compliments. Hang it from a pike in the Slavers' Quarter as a sign that the Skinriders will trouble us no more.'

'Dragons Below!' Syrclar screamed as the grisly trophy smacked wetly against his breastplate, leaving a brownish stain on the green enamel. The head hit the deck and bounced among the guards' feet, sending them scrambling in every direction. The *Harrier's* crew on deck watched the men scramble and hissed in derisive laughter.

Syrclar grew pale with fury, rubbing frantically at the fluids staining his armour. 'Are you mad, bringing these poxed things aboard?'

'We've trophies enough below decks to decorate the walls of every city in Naggaroth,' Malus said proudly. 'We thought it was only fitting, as a symbol of Bruglir's great victory.'

'They're thick with disease, you fool!' Syrclar screamed. 'Every one of you could be tainted.'

Malus glanced around at his men, knowing they were well aware that Urial had cleansed the bodies of any taint before they had been brought aboard. He turned back to Syrclar with a well-rehearsed look of innocent credulity. 'But none of us have come down sick,' he said emphatically. 'Well, not except for Irhan and Ryvar.' The highborn glanced meaningfully at Hauclir.

The retainer took up the thread without missing a beat. 'But we locked Ryvar up in the after hold just as soon as his skin started falling off,' he deadpanned.

Syrclar's eyes went wide with horror. 'And Irhan?' he asked.

'Well, we couldn't rightly lock him away, dread lord. He was the cook.'

The young druchii pressed a trembling hand to the surface of his breastplate. 'Back to the ship!' he commanded his men. 'Quickly!' As they began to retreat back over the ship's rail, Syrclar pointed imperiously at Malus. 'Make anchor here, out in the bay! Do not attempt to dock at the harbour or we'll use dragon's breath and burn you to the waterline.'

'But we have need of food and supplies,' Malus said, sounding aggrieved. 'These men need shore leave–'

'Your men need a priest,' Syrclar said, his voice tight with rage. 'If they have any sense of decency they'll pray for the Dragons to curse you and your house until the end of time.' About a quarter of the inspection party had already disappeared over the rail and the young captain had one leg over the side himself. He paused and shot Malus a furious glare. 'What is your name? My father the drachau will hear of this.'

The highborn suppressed a frown of dismay. The ruse had nearly worked to perfection, he thought, sighing inwardly. 'Malus, son of Lurhan the Vaulkhar of Hag Graef,' he said gravely.

Syrclar paused. 'You're Malus? The one they call Darkblade?'

'I am,' the highborn replied, making no effort to conceal his annoyance.

The young officer studied Malus for a moment, indecision warring with fear. Finally, he swung his leg back over the rail and gestured at his remaining men. 'Seize him,' Syrclar commanded.

Hauclir stepped in front of Malus, his face grave and his hands reaching for his weapons. Malus stopped him with a hand on his shoulder. 'Remember my orders,' he said quietly, then pushed his retainer aside. 'Seize me?' Malus said to the young officer. 'On what grounds?'

'Were you not master of the corsair *Shadowblade* last summer?'

The highborn drew a deep breath. 'I was,' he said.

'And did you not return to Naggaroth five months ago with a cargo of flesh?'

'Yes,' Malus admitted.

'But you did not stop here, as the law of the land requires. The lords of the tower receive a tithe of all slave cargoes brought into Naggaroth, whether they are sold here or not.'

'I am well aware of the law,' Malus said tersely. 'I simply chose to ignore it.'

Syrclar gave the highborn a wolfish smile. 'Then you were doubly foolish to return here, tainted or no,' he said. 'The lords of the tower have long memories and do not forget those who slight them.' He nodded to his men. Two warriors gritted their teeth and took Malus by the arms, while a third stripped the highborn of his weapons.

'By the law of the tower, you will be held captive in the dungeons of Karond Kar until such time as your kin pay the tithe you withheld from us,' Syrclar said with a self-satisfied grin. 'I have no doubt your father the vaulkhar will waste no time paying your ransom, so you shouldn't have to spend more than a month in chains.'

THE HORSES STAMPED and snorted on the cobblestones of the quay, disturbing the gulls that perched with their meals on the rows of statues lining the waterfront. They croaked disdainfully from the helms and armoured shoulders of stone corsairs, or hopped upon the backs of carved slaves bent beneath the weight of granite chains. Syrclar and his men paid the birds no mind, waiting impatiently on their mounts while two sailors lifted Malus into his saddle. When he was seated, one of the sailors bound his hands to a ring on the saddle's cantle with several loops of tarred line and a tight square knot. The second sailor passed the reins to one of Syrclar's men, who nodded to his lord. The young lord raised his hand. 'Sa'an'ishar!' he cried. 'Form up and move out!' A few minutes later the procession began making its way along the waterfront, headed for the Dolorous Road.

Malus felt the daemon stir as his horse jerked into motion near the end of the line. 'It appears once again that you've managed to outsmart yourself,' Tz'arkan sneered. 'Did you honestly think that little fool wouldn't ask your name?'

'It was a calculated risk,' the highborn muttered under his breath. 'And it nearly worked.'

'Nearly worked,' the daemon repeated mockingly. 'Which is to say that it failed.'

'Not entirely. The ship at least is isolated. The crew won't be able to make off with the gold. And I made it ashore, which is one step closer to my goal.'

'So you mean to say that this was part of your plan?'

Malus gritted his teeth. 'Not entirely,' he admitted.

The procession reached the end of the eastern waterfront and turned right into a broad avenue leading inland towards the tower. This was the beginning of the Dolorous Road, the path all slaves took as they were herded to market and the path they all followed back to the ships that would take them to their masters across Naggaroth. It was mid-afternoon and the avenue was largely deserted. Small groups of tradesmen wearing heavy cloaks and riding wagons laden with tools made their way to and from the docks, giving the mounted troop of warriors a wide berth as they passed. A troop of guardsmen marched past, spears at their shoulders. Their officer bowed his head in salute to Syrclar and eyed Malus suspiciously as they marched towards the waterfront.

The avenue continued for almost a hundred yards, fronted on both sides by tall, narrow shops that offered everything from barrels to biscuits; most were doing fitful business with so few ships in harbour. Labourers stood around outside with nothing to do, playing at dice or finger bones or smoking pipes and speaking in low tones.

Malus studied the shops intently, trying to match them to a mental image many years old. He hadn't been to Karond Kar since his hakseer-cruise and much of the time he'd been ashore he'd been rather drunk. He tried to remember where the Mere-Witch lay among the twisting streets and alleys off the Slavers' Quarter and for the first time realised that it might not still exist after so much time.

At the end of the row of shops the avenue emptied out into an enormous square, subdivided by rows of empty pens and raised platforms. This was the first and largest of the slave squares, where cargoes were brought and assessed for their value. Slaves suitable for crafts and hard labour were then taken to a smaller auction square to the west, while those fit for household duty or entertainment were sent to the square to the east. The procession continued across the silent and echoing space, heading further north into a narrower road that lay deep in shadow thanks to the tall houses that bordered it. A glimmer of memory tugged at Malus's mind. Yes, he thought, this was familiar.

The road wasn't perfectly straight; druchii cities were generally labyrinths, meant to confound and kill intruders. The horses walked on into the gloom beneath the tall houses, overlooked by balconies and murder-holes every step of the way. Servants and messengers went about their business amid the residences of the city's merchants and factors, ducking into doorways or down alleys to allow the horsemen to pass.

Malus passed a tall house on the right, its iron-studded door decorated with an ornate stone dragon at its arch. The looming head of the dragon reached so far into the narrow lane that several of the mounted warriors had to duck their heads beneath it as they passed. More memories surfaced: the dragon! I remember cracking my head on that cursed thing, the highborn thought. There will be a branch off the main road just up ahead. That's where it will have to happen.

The highborn's gloved hands tightened on the saddle's raised cantle. He glanced over his shoulder. There were four men bringing up the rear, two with crossbows cradled in their laps. They would be the real threat.

Malus straightened in the saddle, trying to see the side road. The warrior ahead of him looked back at the highborn with a warning scowl, tightening his grip on the reins of Malus's horse.

'Bestir yourself, daemon,' Malus whispered. 'I have need of your power.'

Tz'arkan rasped against Malus's ribs. 'Of course,' the daemon said, unctuously. 'I am always here for you, Malus. You don't know how pleased I am to see that you have come to depend upon me in times of need.'

'Shut. Up.' Malus grated, galled to the core that the daemon was right. How had he reached the point where the daemon's power was just another weapon in his arsenal?

The side road was upon him before Malus realised it – a claustrophobic alley that shot off to the left at an angle to the main road. The highborn clenched his fists. 'Now!' he said.

Black ice thundered through his veins. Malus felt his eyes burn and his muscles writhe like snakes beneath his skin. Wisps of steam leaked past clenched teeth as the highborn bent low in the saddle and hung on for dear life as his horse sensed the change come over him and went mad with terror.

Chapter Four
THE HOUSE OF FLESH

MALUS'S HORSE REARED with a shriek, tossing its head and pawing at the air. The warrior leading the mount was pulled from his saddle and dragged across the cobblestones, trapped by the reins wrapped in his hand. The the air rang with equine screams as the other horses in the procession caught the highborn's scent and panicked.

Sharp curses and shouted commands echoed off the close-set walls as the druchii warriors tried to regain control of their mounts. Malus fought to keep his seat, his head bent close to the rearing horse's neck as it turned and bucked in place. Gritting his teeth, he strained against the tarred cords binding his wrists. Red pain lanced up his arms as the ropes creaked, but refused to give.

A crossbow bolt buzzed past the highborn's spinning head, close enough for him to feel the wind of its passing. Malus caught a glimpse of one of the warriors at the rear of the column, his pale face twisted with rage as he hauled at his horse's reins and tried to fire his crossbow one-handed. Malus watched helplessly as the warrior's finger tightened on the trigger and his guts clenched as the weapon fired with a barely audible *thump*. At the same instant, the crossbowman's horse shied to the right, throwing the man's aim off. The bolt went past Malus's head in a dark blur, followed by the distinctive *crack* of an iron head striking steel plate. A man screamed and the smell of blood filled the cramped space.

Malus closed his eyes and bent his will against the ropes cutting into his skin. The raw pain of his wrists only fuelled his anger further; the greater the pain the more he strained against the bonds. Hot blood flowed down the cold skin of his arms – then there was an intense flash of pain and a sharp pop that was more felt than heard and the rope fell away from his bloodied hands.

The highborn grabbed frantically for the reins as the warriors around him shouted in alarm. A hand closed on his ankle – Malus looked down into the screaming face of the druchii warrior who'd been leading his horse mere moments before. The man still had Malus's reins in a white-knuckled grip and now tried to pull the highborn from his saddle. Malus pulled his boot free and brought it down on the warrior's upturned face. Bones broke and blood sprayed against the horse's shins and the man fell back onto the cobbles. Yanking the reins free from the senseless druchii, Malus hauled his horse's head around, aiming for the side road. 'Run, you cursed nag!' he roared, putting his heels to the horse's flanks. The animal bolted forward with a terrified shriek, sending house servants and traders scrambling into sheltered doorways and alleys as it raced down a lane barely wide enough to allow it passage.

Angry curses and fearful shouts echoed in Malus's wake – at one point a flung earthenware bowl shattered against the wall next to his head – but the highborn only spurred his mount faster, knowing that pursuit was only seconds behind him. He cudgelled his brain for memories as doorways and balconies blurred past to left and right. There was a turnoff… to the north, he thought, but how far? A servant carrying a basket of goods from the market ducked across the horse's path, shouting obscenities as he dashed for the safety of a recessed doorway.

Snarling wolfishly the highborn smashed his mount's shoulder into the fleeing figure, hurling the man against a stone wall and sending a shower of fruit and meat into the air. Malus looked back to see the servant's broken form rebound from the wall and collapse in the middle of the lane. Already the door to the house was open and two servants were dashing out to see to the man, which clogged the path even further.

Malus nearly missed the mouth of the street to the right – he hauled back on the reins at the last moment and sparks flew from the horse's iron shoes as it skidded across the cobblestones. The animal screamed and bucked, trying to throw him from the saddle, but thanks to the daemon's strength he clung to its back like a leech. A loud commotion back the way he'd come told Malus that his pursuers were almost on him. He eyed the northern street frantically, searching for familiar details, but found none. Cursing to himself, he spurred his mount up the road just as a druchii warrior with a spear galloped into view back the way Malus had come.

The warrior threw his weapon with an angry shout and Malus threw out his hand, hoping to snatch it from the air. The spear point glanced along the back of Malus's shoulder blades, popping mail rings and twisting him slightly in the saddle. His hand tried to close on the spear haft but the weapon bounced from his palm and struck the far wall, falling out of reach as the horse shot northwards up the road. The warrior drew a curved sword and gave chase, howling like a vengeful wraith. More riders thundered into the lane in the man's wake, taking up the chase as well.

A crossbow bolt ricocheted off the wall to Malus's right and shattered against the stone overhang of a narrow doorway, showering him with shards of stone. This road was a bit wider than the one before, able to permit two horses to travel abreast. There were more druchii on foot, stepping in and out of the shops lining the street. Many were household servants, evidenced by the torcs gleaming at their throats, while others were highborn, tradesmen or off-duty soldiers. The servants scattered at the sound of galloping hooves, while the soldiers eyed Malus with wary curiosity and fingered the hilts of their swords.

'Out of the way, damn your eyes!' Malus shouted at the people in his path, wishing to the Dark Mother that he had a blade in his hand to add weight to the command. Up ahead, one soldier evidently took exception to Malus's tone and drew his sword. The highborn's mouth went dry. He aimed the charging horse directly at the man, but the warrior stood his ground. At the last second Malus swerved left and the soldier swung his blade in a blurring arc. The blade parted the horse's right rein and struck a glancing blow against the highborn's side. Mail rings popped with a dry crackle, but the armour and the thick leather kheitan beneath absorbed the hit. Malus cursed viciously at the man as he sped past and got an obscene gesture in return.

'What I wouldn't give for a sword,' Malus muttered angrily as he grabbed a handful of the horse's mane with his right hand and scanned the shop fronts along the road. He remembered a line of taverns leading up to the Mere-Witch, but all he saw were bakers and fishmongers. His guts churned at the thought that he'd taken a wrong turn.

'Would you like a sword? Nothing could be easier,' Tz'arkan said, its voice cool and slick with malice.

Yes! He thought at once, but the word caught in his throat when he remembered how the daemon had provided him with a way to navigate the labyrinth back at the Isle of Morhaut. 'But I don't need a spur of sharpened bone growing out of my wrist,' he snapped.

'It doesn't have to grow out of your *wrist*–'

'Leave the weapons to me, daemon,' Malus snarled, leading the horse around a sharp turn – and heading straight for a gang of labourers standing around a heap of fallen masonry.

Malus jerked back on the reins with a startled shout, but the horse was moving too fast to stop. Human and dwarf slaves scattered left and right, shouting in alarm and whips cracked as the druchii overseers tried to keep their chattels in line. One slave didn't move quickly enough and was trampled beneath the horse's hooves, his wild screams cut short as an iron shoe split his skull like a melon.

The mound of bricks spilled across a third of the street – part of a house's facade that had fallen away in an avalanche of stone. With no other options available, Malus bent low in the saddle and put his heels to the horse's flanks, driving it up the loose pile of bricks. The horse gamely leapt for the top of the mound, bloodstained hooves scrabbling for purchase. Near the top, the horse started to falter – then a whip struck Malus's left arm with a sharp *crack*. The highborn roared in pain, but the sound startled the horse enough that it redoubled its efforts, lunging for the top of the mound and plunging over the summit.

Unfortunately for Malus, his pursuers had been familiar with the construction. When they came around the bend they angled for the far end of the mound and as the highborn's horse hurtled down the opposite side of the pile he saw two riders already slightly ahead of him and angling in from the left. One was the swordsman he'd seen before; the other carried a spear in an overhand grip, ready to throw or stab. Of the two, the swordsman was the better rider, leading his mount around panicked slaves and small piles of rock and pulling alongside Malus just as the highborn's horse leapt the last few feet off the brick mound.

Malus threw himself to the right as a backhanded cut tore at his mail shirt just below his shoulder blade. Cursing fiercely, he spurred the lathered horse to greater speed, but the swordsman kept pace, leaning forward in his stirrups and slashing downwards with his sword. The blade struck Malus a hard blow on the left shoulder, just behind the collarbone and a hot spike of pain lanced down his back as the edge bit through the mail and kheitan beneath. The highborn felt his left arm go numb at the blow – and at just that moment his horse screamed in pain and slewed to the left, into the swordsman's path.

The two horses crashed together in a chorus of anguished cries and fierce oaths from their riders. The druchii swordsman's horse struck Malus's mount chest to shoulder and for a sickening instant the highborn feared that his horse would be knocked onto its side. As it was, the two horses grappled with one another, rearing and snapping with broad, square teeth. Malus fought to keep his seat, even as the tower swordsman made a clumsy downward swing at his skull.

Hard-won instincts warned Malus at nearly the last moment. He jerked his head to the side and the blow fell once again on his already-injured shoulder. Fiery pain ignited from the base of his neck to the rounded part of his arm. In desperation he let go of the reins with his left hand and grabbed for the man's blade. By sheer luck his hand closed on the back of the single-edged sword – he felt the edge of the blade against his finger-tips as he grabbed hold of the sword and pulled it towards him. Potent with battle-lust and the daemon's terrible gifts, he all but yanked the surprised warrior from his saddle; the man was drawn far forward, his wrist well within Malus's reach. The highborn let go of the sword, lunging for the man's wrist in an attempt to twist the blade from his hand, but just then Malus's horse bit the other mount on the neck. The swordsman's horse shied back with a cry, toppling the man from his saddle even as Malus's horse gathered itself and leapt forward, fleeing the fight. Malus made a vain grab for the sword as it fell beyond his grasp and was left fighting to stay in the saddle as his horse galloped headlong up the lane and around another sharp turn.

Malus could tell at once that something was wrong with the horse's gait – looking back over his shoulder he saw a black-shafted spear buried deep in the animal's rump. Terror was all that was keeping the animal moving forward, but the highborn knew that it wouldn't last much longer. Still worse, he saw that the buildings had changed from shops to residences, many of which were shuttered or in advanced stages of disrepair. He was definitely on the wrong street. Surprisingly, the highborn heard the sounds of galloping hooves taper off just behind him. He couldn't imagine why, but he wasn't going to question his good fortune. His horse was already slowing as they reached another sharp bend in the road. With luck, he thought, he could find an alley up ahead and continue on foot.

He rounded the corner – and saw at once why his pursuers had reined in. The road ran on for another twenty yards and ended in a cul-de-sac overlooked by half a dozen iron-work balconies. They had him cornered.

Malus pulled awkwardly at the single rein, forcing the half-dead horse to come to a stumbling halt. The highborn looked desperately about for a way out of the trap. He could hear his pursuers, hissing orders to one another as they walked their mounts to the corner. They would be on him in moments.

The highborn heard a door open overhead. He looked up to see two highborn children rush out onto the balcony and peer down at him, chattering excitedly. Malus bared his teeth, wishing he had them in arm's reach.

A thought struck him. He turned the horse in place, studying the overhanging ironworks. Looks risky, he thought, but no more so than a blade in the guts.

Malus urged the staggering horse near one of the stone walls and let it come to a shuddering stop. The first of the riders came around the corner, his spear at the ready. The highborn grabbed the saddle's cantle and drew up his right leg. Placing the foot carefully he stood on the animal's back.

The daemon chuckled as Malus spread his arms for balance. 'You look like one of those ugly seagulls,' Tz'arkan said. 'Is this some strange form of surrender, or do you intend to fly over your captors?'

'Something like that,' Malus said with a mirthless grin. Just as the lead spearman readied his weapon to throw the highborn took a deep breath, bent slightly at the knees – and jumped.

Without the daemon's foul strength surging through his limbs he wouldn't have had a chance. As it was, his fingertips just reached the iron rails of the balcony some ten feet overhead. He grabbed at the rusty metal like a drowning man, his fingers tightening painfully around the hard-edged rails. With an explosive grunt of effort he pulled himself upwards. Below, the spearman let out an amazed cry; a moment later his spear clattered off the stone wall to Malus's right.

Malus pulled himself upright and peered over the rail – only to duck back again as a crossbow bolt rang off the ironwork. Angry shouts echoed up from the cul-de-sac. Malus grinned. Unless Syrclar had a daemon-possessed retainer they were going to be hard-pressed to catch him.

Of course, he still had more climbing to do.

The highborn eyed his next destination – another balcony, eight feet up and ten feet away on the adjoining building. Before the crossbow-man could reload, he pulled himself onto the rail, took a deep breath and leapt into space with a wild shout. He reached his target easily, grabbing the rail with both hands and vaulting over the side. Immediately he looked to the balcony at the next house. Ten feet away and ten feet higher than where he crouched, the two druchii children watched with wide, fearful eyes. He gave them a hungry smile and they fled inside, screaming in terror.

This time Syrclar's men were ready. He leapt into a storm of crossbow bolts and flung spears, the projectiles buzzing around him like a swarm of flesh wasps. Malus made the leap easily. In fact, part of him thrilled at the rush of wind against his face and the effortless way his body carried him from one balcony to the next. His shoulder stung fiercely where the sword had cut through his armour, but that, too, only made Malus feel more alive. Laughing to himself, he pulled himself up to the edge of the rail – and came face-to-face with an axe-wielding retainer who had rushed to the children's aid.

Once again, it was raw instinct that saved Malus. He threw himself backwards as the axe whistled through the air, missing his throat by less than an inch. His fingers slipped as he hit the limit of his reach and for a moment he hung motionless, thirty feet above Syrclar and his men. At the same instant the retainer took another swing with his axe and Malus grabbed for it with both hands. Seizing the haft, he pulled himself forward for all he was worth, pulling the retainer off-balance and sending him hurtling out into space even as the highborn slammed against the balcony rail. The retainer fell and Malus tried his best for one heroic lunge at the man's axe, but through either ill luck or druchii spite, the man carried his axe with him as he fell to the cobblestones below.

'Damnation!' Malus cursed, staring helplessly at the lost weapon. Within the house he could hear the children screaming and an even greater commotion coming his way, so he wasted no time. Still standing on the outside of the balcony he turned to face the next balcony and leapt the fifteen feet between them. Another crossbow bolt buzzed past, but now there were shouts of wonder and dismay from below, as the men feared that their quarry would escape. Malus paused for long enough to give the men a mocking salute, then leapt from the balcony to the edge of the building's roof. The slate shingles were slick and the roof steeply pitched, but the highborn wasted no time circling its perimeter until he faced the building to the west. It was a long leap – close to twenty feet, across a narrow road – but he hesitated barely a moment. Malus closed his eyes and flung himself into space with a howl like a maddened wolf.

'Sweet, is it not?' Tz'arkan whispered in his mind. 'And this is but a trifle compared to the gifts I offer. And yet you turn your face from me, hiding in fogs of cheap wine. Do you see now how foolish you have been?'

Malus opened his eyes to see the tiles of the oncoming building rushing at his face. He landed hard, sending broken tiles slithering off the edge of the roof, then circled the perimeter of the roof, looking further west. There was another rooftop directly adjacent to this one, then another lane that appeared to open into a small square. That looks familiar, he realised with a grin.

'I am my own master, daemon,' he said, a little breathlessly. 'Not you, not my father – not the Witch King himself – may command me. What I do, I do for myself. *You* are the foolish one.'

'Indeed? And what would happen if you were to try leaping to the next building, only to find that I'd withdrawn my generous gifts?'

'Then I'd fall.'

'And?'

'And I'd have to think of something very quickly before I hit the ground.'

'Stupid druchii,' the daemon spat. 'You think you have an answer for everything. You weren't so clever when you stepped into my chamber and slid that ring on your finger. You fell for that one rightly enough.'

'I fell for it, true,' Malus said, leaping into space. 'But I haven't hit the ground yet, have I?'

The highborn was touching down on the adjoining roof before he realised the daemon had gone silent. Malus took that to be a good sign.

Crossing to the opposite side of the building, Malus looked down on a street lined with taverns and teeming with soldiers, sailors and labourers. He looked further north and there, across the square, he saw the grey sign of the Mere-Witch. Malus smiled and gauged the distance to the next roof: another fifteen feet more or less. He gathered his legs beneath him, took a deep breath and leapt.

No sooner had his feet left the edge of the roof than Malus realised the daemon's strength had faded.

He flew for six feet and began to fall like an arrow arcing in flight. Ten feet, twenty feet – he could hear the noise of the crowd below growing louder. At twenty-five feet he hit the wall of the building he'd leapt for, striking hard enough to knock the air from his lungs. He tumbled, striking the edge of a metal balcony, then fell another five feet before crashing into an overhanging sign. Wood cracked, hinges splintered. Malus and the wooden sign fell the last ten feet to land in a tangled pile on the cobblestones.

Figures crowded around the edges of his vision – pale faces, looking down in horror, shock or disgust. Malus felt a set of tentative fingers pluck at the money belt at his waist. With a snarl he slapped the hand away and rolled painfully to his knees.

There was a rumbling in his ears. Malus shook his head, trying to clear it. The sound continued. Then he felt the vibrations in the palms of his hands and realised what was causing it. Hoof beats.

Malus lurched unsteadily to his feet. He should have guessed that the horsemen would simply try to parallel his movements on the ground. It took a moment to tell his left from his right, but once he did he set off for the flesh house at a run.

He was halfway there when he heard shouts behind him. Something clattered on the cobblestones – a thrown spear? Malus didn't stop to find out. Druchii scattered out of his way as he staggered to the double doors of the flesh house and pushed his way inside.

Smells of incense and narcotic vapours tingled in his nostrils as Malus stumbled into the heat and shadows beyond the doorway. Servants stepped hesitantly forward, uncertain what to make of a bloodied highborn in battered corsair's armour reeling drunkenly in the entry hall. An armed retainer stepped forward, one hand outstretched. 'Your weapons, sir,' he said.

Malus laughed, showing his empty hands and pushed past the bemused guard. His body moved purely on instinct, acting on drunken memories of years past. The highborn went left, locating the descending stairway almost at once and rushing downwards into scented darkness.

The stairway swept downwards in a broad, lazy spiral, leading past doorways strung with curtains of soft seal hide. Faint sounds issued from within those chambers: laughter, impassioned murmurs or gasps of pain. Music hung in the heavy air, drifting languidly from some hidden room. Malus continued on, picking up his pace when he began to hear urgent cries echoing from above.

His descent came to an end in a circular room lit with glowing braziers. There were eight doors around the perimeter of the chamber, each one leading to a sumptuous suite reserved for the wealthy or the noble-born; servants came and went through the doors, bearing trays of refreshments. Fantastic beasts loomed over each portal: dragons, manticores, chimeras and the like. One doorway was framed by a pair of crouching nauglir. With a hungry smile Malus crossed the room and pushed the door wide.

Beyond lay an octagonal room lit by the banked coals of half a dozen braziers. Carpets and cushions covered the stone floor, surrounding platters heaped with breads, cheeses and fruit. Flagons of wine glittered in the ruddy light and smoke hung thick and blue in the air. Half a dozen figures in hooded autarii cloaks lounged on the cushions, amusing themselves with a like number of human and elf slaves.

Angry shouts echoed from the stairway. Malus staggered across the room, lurching across the soft and treacherous carpets. Slaves scattered as he made his way towards a platter of roast meat near the centre of the room. His eyes were on the long, broad-bladed knife gleaming beside a long fork at the edge of the platter.

Syrclar and six of his men burst into the room on Malus's heels, their faces flushed and swords held at the ready. The highborn swept past the platter, his hand closing on a curved wooden grip and turned to face his pursuers.

Malus showed his teeth to the men of the tower and raised the long, twin-tined meat fork he'd grabbed by mistake. Slaves scattered to the far corners of the room. The autarii were motionless, watching the scene from the depths of their hoods.

'I suppose you'd like to discuss terms of surrender,' the highborn said.

Syrclar smiled. 'Cut off his hands and pluck out his tongue,' he told his men. 'We'll let his father ransom them back in a jar.'

Malus fell back as the six warriors made their way carefully across the room. He retreated until his back touched the far wall and then waited, meat fork held ready. The warriors spread into a rough semicircle, wary of his strange abilities but confident in their greater numbers.

They were halfway across the room when the autarii sprang into action. Without a word passing between them they drew long knives from their voluminous sleeves and leapt at the tower men. Caught by surprise, the warriors were tackled and pulled to the floor. Knife blades flashed, cutting hamstrings, wrists and throats. Blood soaked the rugs in moments as the warriors thrashed, kicking over plates and flagons in the throes of death.

Syrclar recoiled in horror at the slaughter unfolding before him. The young highborn's sword wavered, then fell to the floor. He turned to run, but Malus crossed the room in three swift strides, running over the bodies of the dying men and grabbing a handful of the lord's long, black hair.

The twin tines of the fork plunged deep into the side of Syrclar's throat. The highborn went rigid, coughing a spray of bright arterial blood. Malus let him go, turning and picking up Syrclar's fallen sword as the young lord fell to his knees.

Malus studied the blade and nodded approvingly. 'Better late than never,' he said with a sigh, then turned and struck Syrclar's head from his shoulders. The headless body remained upright for a few moments, then toppled onto its side, still spurting blood.

The highborn admired his handiwork for a moment, then turned to the hooded figures. 'Would it be too much to ask for a cup of wine?' he asked.

Chapter Five
WILES AND STRATAGEMS

'AH, THERE HE IS,' Malus said as Hauclir was escorted into the rug-lined chamber beneath the flesh house. 'I'd begun to think you'd come to some mischief.' The highborn plucked a fat Tilean grape from a tray next to his cushion and waved his retainer to take a seat. 'Have some wine and some food. Pay no mind to all the bodies.'

Hauclir carefully lowered one of Bruglir's old sea chests and set it gently on the floor, his gaze passing from one bloody corpse to the next. Syrclar's guardsmen still lay where they had fallen, contorted in poses of violent death. The retainer nodded his head at the corpse Malus was using as a footrest. 'I take it that would be part of the young Lord Syrclar?'

'The very same,' he said, turning to spit a seed at Syrclar's severed head. 'He proved a capable hunter, but in the end the prey he cornered proved a bit too much for him.'

Quiet chuckles rose from the men surrounding Malus. With the arrival of their lord they had cast aside their autarii cloaks, revealing black-enamelled armour and silver steel torcs worked with the sigil of a nauglir – Malus's personal insignia. They sipped wine from gold cups and toyed with the young slaves crouching at their sides, eyeing Hau-clir with the predatory welcome of a pack of wolves.

The highborn indicated his retainers with a languid sweep of his hand. 'You know some of these old dogs – Silar Thornblood, my seneschal, Dolthaic the Ruthless and Arleth Vann. The others entered my service while we were at sea – all I can say for them is that they're handy with a knife, which counts for much in my estimation.'

Hauclir nodded absently, taking everything in. The retainer set to watch for him brushed past the former guard captain, returning to his own place amid the rugs and cushions. 'What's all this about, my lord?' he asked, slipping a large and heavy pack from his shoulder and setting it beside the chest.

The highborn shrugged, plucking another grape from the bunch in his left hand. A bottle of wine and a brimming cup sat on a low table to his right. Silar had poured it for him hours ago and he'd yet to touch it. 'Planning ahead,' he explained, popping another grape into his mouth. 'I knew before I left Hag Graef that if I wanted to return home alive my illustrious older brother would have to meet an untimely end. So I made arrangements to meet Silar here instead of going straight home to give my father the happy news.' He favoured his men with a feigned scowl. 'They've been here spending my coin and living like conquerors for the last month or so.'

Wolfish grins and muted laughter spread across the room. Dolthaic the Ruthless, a young druchii with sharp, angular features and a long horsetail of hair pulled into a corsair's topknot raised his goblet in salute. 'If this is how you go about killing your kin,' he said with a sepulchral laugh, 'then I say thank the Dark Mother you have such a large family!'

The other retainers joined in the laughter, some raising their goblets in turn, until a strong voice cut through the merriment like a knife. 'Drink and act like fools while you can,' Silar Thornblood declared. 'Nothing will be the same after this. It's war or exile now that Malus has killed Lurhan's favoured son.'

Malus turned slightly in his seat to face his chief lieutenant. Silar was a young warrior, tall and handsome, his face miraculously unscarred by war. He was a dour, impertinent man at the best of times, but he was loyal and honest and above all, utterly lacking in ambition or guile. On his own he wouldn't have lasted a month in druchii society, but Malus provided him with an honourable position in an influential household, largely shielded from the ruthlessness of day-to-day life. He sat at Malus's right hand, staring gloomily into the depths of his wine cup. The highborn frowned and spat a seed at the man.

'Is it any wonder I left you back at the Hag, Silar?' Malus growled good-naturedly. 'What talk is this of war? Bruglir died in battle, not at the end of my sword.'

Hauclir let out a snort. Malus fixed the man with a merciless glare and the retainer lowered his eyes.

'He died in a battle *you* forced on him,' Silar said forcefully. 'Bruglir was already a hero ten times over, enough so that even the drachau envied him. All Lurhan will care about is that you took his eldest son and heir into the North Sea and got him killed, along with most of his fleet.' Silar shook his head, staring into his cup as though it were full of poison. 'Your father tried to kill you once already and if rumour at the Hag is to be believed, you shamed him in front of the drachau when you forced Uthlan Tyr to give you a Writ of Iron. What do you think he will do when he hears this latest news?' The young retainer took a breath and tossed back a large swallow of wine.

The mood in the room turned sombre. Even Dolthaic's avaricious grin faded before Silar's harsh estimation. Malus frowned in aggravation. 'Speaking of vile rumours, what other news do you have from the Hag?'

Silar shrugged. 'The Witch King declared the campaign season a week earlier than expected, owing to the mild winter. The truce between Hag Graef and the Black Ark of Naggor still holds, miraculously enough. The drachau even went so far as to release his hostage Fuerlan and return him to the ark.' Silar took another sip of wine, judiciously avoiding the incident Malus had caused when he'd tortured Fuerlan nearly to death over a matter of etiquette several months before. 'With no major feuds to settle, the highborn of the city who haven't taken to sea are all out in the countryside looking for something to test their swords on.'

'There was talk before we left that your father was gathering his own men for an expedition to the north,' Dolthaic interjected. 'Probably heading up to one of the northern watchtowers to hunt dragons or some such.'

'Indeed?' Malus said with a raised eyebrow. 'That could be fortuitous. But what of my brother Isilvar? Lurhan vowed to search the city for the Slaaneshi cultists who were meeting in Nagaira's tower. Was Isilvar exposed as their hierophant?'

'No,' Silar said gravely. 'Lurhan made a show of searching all the towers in the drachau's citadel, but Isilvar's servants swore that he'd left the city days before. Of course, no one knew where he had gone and your father seemed content to leave things at that.'

'And the drachau?'

'Lurhan presented the drachau with almost a dozen cultists, dragged by their hair from their residences across the city. Some few of them were high-ranking nobles – all of them, coincidentally enough, well-known enemies of the drachau himself. Uthlan Tyr had them impaled on the walls of the Hag and considered the matter settled.'

'The short-sighted idiot,' Malus hissed. 'So Isilvar escaped the drachau's wrath. Clearly he has more influence with Lurhan than I suspected – or perhaps the vaulkhar fears that if Isilvar is implicated it will taint Bruglir's reputation.' The highborn paused, tapping his lip contemplatively with a round, purple grape. 'It might be interesting to see how things change once news of Bruglir's death becomes well-known. Regardless, Isilvar remains a threat to be eliminated.'

'You sound as though you intend to ride straight back to Hag Graef and preside from your tower as though nothing were amiss!' Silar declared incredulously.

'Why, Silar, that's precisely what I intend to do.'

'Then you're a fool! You'll be placing your head in the nauglir's mouth,' Silar exclaimed, lurching unsteadily to his feet. Wine sloshed from his half-empty cup, adding to the stains on the piled rugs. 'And ours as well, for what that's worth. So far you've been very good at staying one step ahead of the consequences your rash actions have created, but this…' Silar's voice faltered as his sense of propriety warred with pent-up frustrations 'This is something you won't be able to talk your way out of. Can't you see that?'

No one moved. Dolthaic turned away from Silar, busying himself with refilling his own goblet. The newer retainers looked from Silar to Malus with equal measures of surprise and anticipation, expecting at any moment to see the seneschal die. But Malus simply stared at his lieutenant in silence for several long moments, his expression betraying nothing of his thoughts.

'Silar, you have served me loyally and well for many years,' he said at last. Without thinking, he picked up the goblet from the table next to him and idly inspected its contents. 'I think you must be very, very drunk to have spoken so carelessly, because normally you would never dare talk out of your place. So I will refrain from ordering these men to skin you alive and feed your private parts to their nauglir, as it would be well within my rights to do.' The highborn met Silar's eyes. 'You are here to serve. Never, *ever* forget that.'

The retainer's fist closed around the neck of his goblet. The muscles in his jaw bunched as he fought back yet more rash words. Finally, he took a deep breath and tossed the goblet aside. 'Of course, my lord,' he said fatalistically. 'Forgive my impertinence. It won't happen again.'

Malus smiled thinly. 'I'm certain of it. But,' he continued, raising a finger for emphasis, 'your concerns are well-taken, if unfounded, so let me explain to you the way of things.' He sat up from his cushions and paused, realising he'd brought the goblet to his lips. The smell of the dry, dark wine rose from the cup and filled his nostrils and he thought of the daemon's warning. After a moment's consideration, he pretended to take a sip, then pointedly set the goblet aside.

'Let us consider the situation as it stands,' Malus told his men. 'For Silar's sake, we shall not mince words – my father the vaulkhar hates me bitterly and would like nothing better than to see me dead. Until recently, he has been prevented from this because of… certain arrangements he made with my mother Eldire.'

'What arrangements?' Hauclir asked, apparently oblivious to the sheer impertinence of such a question.

'I don't know for certain,' Malus replied. As far as it went, this was true – he had suspicions that Eldire lent her sorcerous powers to Lurhan in return for being given a child, but had no proof that this was the case. 'With Bruglir dead, however, Silar feels that Lurhan will accuse me of the murder of his heir and will have ample justification to seek revenge. He would in fact be *compelled* to act, or risk being seen as weak. So you see, my lieutenant spoke with some degree of good sense.'

Hauclir nodded thoughtfully, folding his arms and leaning back against the sea chest. The other retainers looked to one another with expressions of concern – all except Silar, who began to pace about the perimeter of the room.

'This would indeed be a dire event – if it happens.' Malus leaned back again, settling into the cushions. 'I am not at all convinced that it will. We must remember, that whatever else, Lurhan the vaulkhar is a proud and ambitious man who needs an heir to cement his legacy as the warlord of Hag Graef. That man was Bruglir, but now he's gone. Who remains? Isilvar has lived like a rat in the shadow of his older brother all his life and is currently in hiding because of his ties to a forbidden cult. Urial has close ties to the temple and to the drachau himself, but that can't change the fact that he's a cripple and none of the other houses would accept his authority.'

'The vaulkhar could still find a successor through marriage,' Silar pointed out. He'd clearly spent a great deal of time considering the situation while the retainers waited in Karond Kar.

'He might have previously, but Nagaira was consumed by the Chaos storm she unleashed in her tower and Yasmir…' Malus paused, trying to think of a way to explain what his sister had become, 'well, she's gone. Urial took her away and I don't expect Lurhan will be seeing her any time soon.' The highborn's gaze sought out Arleth Vann, who crouched apart from the others in a corner of the room where he could watch both the door and everyone in the room. Unlike the others, his pale face remained shadowed within the hood of his cloak and he showed no interest in food, wine or slaves. Malus suddenly wondered what the former temple assassin might know of the prophecy Urial spoke of, or where the Vermilion Gate led. Later, he thought. He and I will have a long talk after we've returned to the Hag.

'So you think your father will be forced to call a truce with you because you're the only hope he's got for an heir?' Hauclir asked.

Malus smiled. 'Precisely. So you see, recent events have actually placed me in a rather advantageous position when looked at in the proper way.' He shifted his seat to face Silar as he crossed behind Malus. 'Believe me, Silar, I have no intention to seek exile, much less make war with my father. You know me better than anyone. What do I covet more than anything in the world?'

Silar glanced at Malus. 'To be Vaulkhar of Hag Graef.'

'Just so,' Malus said, a fierce gleam burning in his eye. 'And from there it is just a small step to the drachau's throne. That moment is coming, Silar. I've clawed my way towards it slowly but surely for many years. What we face now isn't calamity, but opportunity, if we have but the will to seize it.' He looked about at the assembled retainers and grinned. 'I've already made you rich men. Soon I will make you *powerful* men as well. Are you with me?'

'I'm with you!' Dolthaic cried, raising his goblet in salute. 'To the Outer Darkness and beyond!'

Malus turned to Hauclir. 'And you?'

The retainer shrugged. 'It's a pointless question. I've given my oath, so of course I'm with you,' he said, then grinned. 'Of course I'll be happy to shower myself with wealth and power if you order me to.'

The other men laughed, raising their goblets. '*Malus!*' They cried and Malus laughed with them. Only Silar watched in silence, his expression sombre.

'What is your plan, my lord?' Silar asked gravely.

The highborn considered the question for a moment. 'Did you bring everything I asked?'

Silar nodded. 'The nauglir are stabled at the city barracks and Spite has your possessions loaded on his back.

'Excellent,' Malus replied. He'd learned during his numerous encounters with brigands on the trek back from the Chaos Wastes that the best way to protect property was to lash it to a hungry nauglir's back. 'Then eat and drink while you can, men, because we'll all have to be gone from Karond Kar by morning. There are things to be done before Lurhan returns to the Hag. Besides,' he said, looking at the body beneath his feet, 'sooner or later someone is going to miss my footstool here and start asking around.'

Malus climbed to his feet and approached Hauclir and the sea chest. His swords, taken from Lord Syrclar's horse, lay nearby, propped against the wall. 'Hauclir, you will lead the rest of the men back to the *Harrier* tonight, where you will oversee the payment of the remaining crew. The rest of the treasure will then be taken off the ship and carried back overland to Hag Graef. You and Dolthaic will remain aboard and sail the *Harrier* to Clar Karond. I'll give you a letter to authorise repairs from the shipwrights. With the men paid and the rest of the gold removed, the crew will likely set a speed record reaching the City of Ships and getting some shore leave.'

'Very well, my lord,' Hauclir said reluctantly.

'Who will act as ship's captain?' Dolthaic asked.

Malus grinned. 'You can have that honour. I don't think Hauclir would want the job if you put a knife to his throat.' He waved Hauclir away from the chest and opened it, then began pulling out pieces of his plate armour. Without thinking, Hauclir began unlacing the battered mail shirt covering the highborn's torso.

'Silar, you and the rest of the men will carry the gold back to the Hag and await my return,' he continued. 'Before you depart tomorrow, however, I will need you to locate and hire a guide to lead me to the houses of the dead.'

'The houses of the dead?' Silar asked with a frown. 'But why?'

Malus affected a shrug, feeling Hauclir's stare on the back of his neck. 'It's the campaigning season, as you said. If Lurhan is to see me as a suitable heir I will have to start building a reputation as something other than a libertine, don't you think?'

'But why go alone? Any guides we find here are likely to be cutthroats and thieves.'

'All the more reason not to tempt them with a fortune in loot, don't you agree?' Malus pulled off the heavy shirt and began buckling on his armour plates. For the first time he realised how good it felt to be back on dry land, dealing with familiar problems like treachery and intrigue.

'Besides,' he said, grinning at Silar over his shoulder. 'If you can find a single druchii in this goddess-forsaken city more ruthless and bloody-minded than me I shall be very surprised indeed.'

HATHAN VOR HAD a face that looked as though it had been held against a grindstone.

'Just here, dread lord, just here,' Vor said, glancing back at Malus through the driving rain. Like the rest of his 'brothers', the guide disdained the use of a cloak or hood and his black hair hung in dripping, ropy strands to either side of his ravaged face.

There wasn't an inch of flesh, from narrow forehead to pointed chin, that wasn't worn down by layer upon layer of crisscrossing scar tissue. Vor's ears and nose were little more than ragged lumps, as though they'd once been gnawed at by rats. His eyebrows were gone and scars at the corners of his large eyes lent them a perpetual squint. The man's cheeks were lined with rows of scars that seemed to penetrate all the way to the bone; they glistened with tiny streams of water in the weak afternoon light. A particularly long and ragged scar pulled the left corner of his mouth up in a perpetual sneer, revealing a row of brown, pointed teeth. It was a hard face to look at, even for Malus; as bad as the Skinriders had been, they wore skins that covered their diseased flesh like a hood. Vor's face was that of a fellow druchii and it was alive. That somehow disturbed Malus more than an entire band of skinned, Chaos-tainted pirates.

The other guides, Vor's supposed brothers, weren't much better. Every one of them had the scarred face of a petty criminals. In Karond Kar, druchii whose crimes and social status were too minor to warrant the efforts of a proper torturer were simply given a scar on their face to mark them as troublemakers. By Malus's estimation, Vor must have been stealing bread or cheating at finger bones – and getting caught at it – every day for the last ten years.

Malus leaned back in his saddle and tried to stretch the kinks from his back. His soaked woollen cloak felt heavier than the plate armour he wore beneath. Rain flowed in sheets down Spite's muscular neck and shoulders, adding a strange lustre to the cold one's dark green scales. As Malus watched, the cold one raised its blunt, toothy snout to the sky and blew a thin plume of steam from its nostrils. Born and bred in dark, damp caverns deep beneath the earth, cold ones thrived in wet environments. At just that moment, Malus envied the nauglir so much it hurt.

They had been travelling the Slavers' Road from Karond Kar for almost two full weeks and Malus could not remember a point during that time when it hadn't been raining. He had learned to eat, sleep and ride while soaking wet. There wasn't a stitch of clothing in his possession that was dry. The bedrolls were soaked, as was most of the food. After the fifth straight day of rain Malus realised that he hadn't got so wet in more than a month at sea on the *Harrier*. He spent the rest of the time afterwards looking for an opportunity to murder someone.

The Slavers' Road ran along the winding coastline of two contiguous seas. Starting at Karond Kar it worked its way south and west along first the Sea of Chill, then the Sea of Malice, before finally coming to an end at the gates of Naggorond, the Witch King's fortress. The journey took many weeks by foot, with dark forests and tall, grey mountains to the west and the broad, slate expanse of the sea to the east. There were no inns or taverns along the route, only despatch-forts that kept food and fresh horses ready to relay urgent messages from Karond Kar to Naggorond and back. They slept in small caves or forest clearings just off the road and ate cold, wet food without dry wood for a fire. Malus, who had not so long ago been tortured without respite for more than a week, considered the trek from the slave tower to have been the most miserable time of his life.

Vor pointed proudly at the veritable wall of dense trees and foliage that stood less than a yard from the road. Viewed through the grey haze of the driving rain the forest looked like a solid mass. 'What am I supposed to see?' Malus snapped. If the man tries to say something clever, like seeing the trees for the forest, I'll kill him where he stands, the highborn thought.

'We leave the road here,' the guide said over the drumming rain. 'Up into the mountains to find the houses of the dead.'

Malus eyed the treeline warily. 'I had been led to believe there would be a road.'

'A road, yes. Stones of black basalt and statues of fierce ladies with sharp teeth,' Vor said, nodding emphatically. 'The barrow road, it is called. But that is another two leagues south and it is forbidden to travel on it. There is a hunter's path here that will take us where we need to go.'

'Forbidden?' Malus frowned within his drooping hood. 'By whom?'

'The autarii, of course,' Vor said, as though explaining something to a small child. 'They guard the city from intruders.'

'What?' Malus asked. No one had told him this! 'Why would they care about the graves of the Old Kings?'

Vor merely shrugged. 'Who knows? They are shades, not normal men. Let's go,' he said, motioning to his men. 'You will feel the rain less under the trees.'

Malus paused as Vor and his seven men trudged up the slight incline and moved one by one into the dense undergrowth. A feeling of dread settled like an icy mantle upon his shoulders.

'That man hopes to cut your throat,' the daemon whispered.

'Of course he does,' Malus said with a shrug. 'Who in Naggaroth doesn't?'

'Surely you do not believe his story of forbidden roads. Look at the scars on his face. He has been an outlaw for many years. No doubt he has murdered a hundred credulous highborn such as yourself.'

'You have a strange sense of humour, daemon,' Malus said sourly. 'Those scars are the marks of an amateur. He's an outlaw all right, but a very bad one. I have no fear of him.' He reluctantly prodded Spite towards the forest, alert to the sudden tension in the reptile's shoulders and back. The highborn could feel it, too, as they passed beneath the dripping boughs.

They were being watched.

Chapter Six
BLOOD AND SALT

THEY WERE AMONG the ruins before Malus realised it. One moment he was walking beside Spite, pushing warily through thick, dripping undergrowth and the next he was pulling up short before a small line of dark grey foundation stones that rose to just above his knees. Ahead the ever-present trees receded to form a clearing of sorts, bound by a square outline of ragged grey walls, the edges of their bricks rounded by great age.

Mossy turf filled the space within the walls, descending steeply to a relatively flat floor some ten feet down – Malus reasoned that the building must have had a lower level at some point that was slowly being reclaimed by the earth. The area within the ruined walls was quite large. From his vantage point Malus could see a large fire pit in the centre of the space, surrounded by a collection of lean-tos made from sturdy logs and roofed with more turf. There was even a spot in one corner that had once been set aside as a small enclosure for horses, complete with a crude fence and a rope gate. Hathan Vor and his men moved into the area with the ease of long familiarity, spreading out to inspect the lean-tos and clear damp leaves from the fire pit.

Malus laid his hand against Spite's shoulder, feeling the tension in the cold one's thick muscles. The sensation of being watched had only grown more intense as the group travelled deeper into the forest, but try as he might the highborn saw or heard no sign of who – or what – was following them. He could tell that Vor and his men sensed it as well, but they seemed to accept it as no more of an inconvenience than the constant patter of the summer rain.

It had to be the autarii, Malus reasoned. Vor said they guarded the houses of the dead and he knew firsthand that they could move like ghosts in their native woods. For the first time he was grateful for the rain, since it gave him good reason to keep his drooping hood pulled over his head. There was one autarii clan in particular that he didn't care to cross paths with again. Of course, the Urhan of the clan had died because of his own traitorous nature, but Malus doubted that the rest of the clan would see it that way. Several times over the course of the day he'd tried to gauge how far away the clan's territories were. A hundred leagues? More? Less? Only the autarii themselves knew for certain. All Malus could do was hope for the best.

The highborn took Spite's reins and led the nauglir down the steep, mossy slope into the ruined enclosure. Spite moved forward with a low grunt, the cold one's broad, clawed feet moving easily over the slick ground. The nauglir's belly scales rasped over the weathered edge of the foundation bricks and Malus was surprised to see the ancient stone bear up under the nauglir's one-ton weight.

The warbeast was slightly sluggish, still slowly digesting the steady diet of horseflesh that Silar had fed it during the long stay at Karond Kar. Nauglir were fierce and powerful mounts, ideal for warfare and the hunt, but their volatile natures made them unpredictable and even dangerous riding mounts unless they were kept well-fed. Malus had learned that lesson well during the trip to the Wastes and back and didn't care to repeat it. If Spite got testy and started eating the guides it would make for an awkward situation indeed.

Malus led Spite to a lean-to on the opposite side of the fire pit from the ones that the guides had claimed. 'Stand,' he commanded his mount and the nauglir settled obediently onto its haunches. The cold one raised its blocky snout and growled, causing Malus to look over his shoulder. Vor was approaching with exaggerated care, watching the cold one intently.

'Don't stare into a cold one's eyes, Vor,' Malus said, turning to face the man. 'They're pack creatures and take it as a challenge for dominance.'

Vor quickly shifted his attention to Malus. 'We'll be making camp here and press on tomorrow.'

Malus frowned, trying to ascertain how much light they had left in the day. 'Surely we have another hour or two before dark,' he said, peering up at the rainy mist hazing the air between the trees.

Vor shrugged. 'This is the way it's done, dread lord,' he said. 'Tonight we pay our respects to the shades, then we can continue on unhindered.'

The highborn's frown deepened. 'Pay respects?' He wasn't certain he liked the sound of that.

'Tonight the shades will take a seat at our fire and share our meat and salt and we will tell them we're grateful to be allowed to visit the graves of our ancestors,' Vor said. 'They'll leave us alone after that.'

'That's all?' Malus asked dubiously.

The scarred druchii smiled. 'Respect counts for much with the autarii, dread lord. Besides, the houses of the dead belong to all the druchii – we have as much right to walk among the towers as they do.'

'Then why do they claim to stand watch over them?'

Vor shook his head. 'I've asked them, but they will not speak of it. Perhaps even they don't remember any more.'

The highborn gestured at the ruined walls. 'Have we reached the outskirts of the necropolis?'

To Malus's surprise, Vor chuckled. 'Oh, no, dread lord. The valley of the Old Kings is still a day's travel away.' He studied the grey bricks with an enigmatic smile. 'The necropolis was built thousands of years ago, not long after our people first came here. These ruins are far, far older. Here, let me show you something.' Vor made a wide circuit around the resting nauglir and made his way to the corner of the structure. Curious, Malus followed.

Vor stood at the base of the wall and touched the bare stone with his fingertips. 'Touch it. It's stone, but it feels like polished steel,' he said. 'Smooth and cold, almost like glass. A few summers ago we found enough loose bricks to line the fire pit yonder. They won't glow or crack no matter how hot the flame gets.'

'Sorcery,' Malus said, his lips twisting in distaste.

'Oh, certainly,' Vor agreed, 'but look there.'

He pointed to a band of discolouration running along the wall some twelve feet up. Malus squinted at the varicoloured patch and realised after a moment that he was looking at a mosaic. As the highborn stared, a pattern emerged. 'It looks like a seascape of some kind.'

Vor nodded. 'An ocean shore, with pale sand and strange fish,' he said. 'If you get close enough, you can make out flowers and tall trees and bright sunlight. Here, on the side of a mountain in a land of grey skies and ice.'

Malus nodded thoughtfully. The sight took him back to a strange city even farther north than where they were now, with canals and a beached ship hundreds of leagues from any sea. The memory sent a strange chill down his spine. 'Who built this?' he said, mostly to himself.

Vor shrugged once more. 'No one knows,' he said, his voice faint with wonder. 'These are old mountains, worn down with age and there are deep hollows no druchii has ever seen, much less explored.' His ruined face twisted in a lopsided grin. 'One day I hope to stumble upon an ancient treasure trove hidden in a cave and then I'll go back to Karond Kar and live like a tower lord!'

'Beware what you wish for, Hathan Vor,' Malus said, surprising even himself at the sincerity in his voice. 'Some treasures become lost for a reason.'

Vor eyed the highborn. 'You sound like you speak from experience. Is it treasure you're hunting in the houses of the dead, or do you intend to leave something valuable behind?'

The sheer artlessness of the question made Malus laugh. 'What druchii travels up into these goddess-forsaken mountains to leave his treasure in some ancient crypt?'

'You would be surprised, dread lord,' Vor answered sombrely. 'There are druchii from ancient lineages – some still powerful, others only a shadow of their former glory – who send their sons each year, bearing gifts for their ancestors. The tradition goes all the way back to lost Nagarythe and some families still keep to the ancient ways.'

The highborn eyed Vor warily. 'And I suppose they provide a lucrative sideline to enterprising bandits who know the way to the crypts,' he said.

Vor laughed. 'No doubt,' he replied, though there was a glint in his eyes that belied his easy tone. 'You haven't mentioned which crypt you are seeking, dread lord.'

'Does it matter?'

'Oh, yes,' Vor said. 'The valley is a long one, twisting through the mountains for almost a dozen leagues. The most powerful houses have their towers at the far end of the valley, so it's a matter of how many more days we must climb.'

Malus considered the question for a moment, then shrugged. He'd have to tell the man sooner or later. 'I seek the tomb of Eleuril. His sigil–'

'The sign of the horned moon,' Vor said, nodding. 'Yes, I know of it. Another two days' travel, then, high up into the valley.' His expression darkened.

'What do you know of this crypt?' Malus asked.

Vor started to speak, then thought better of it. He gave another shrug. 'It is haunted,' he said simply, 'but that is your business, not mine.' The scarred druchii nodded brusquely to Malus. 'I must see to the fire and the evening meal, dread lord. The shades will come at midnight, so rest now if you must. You will need to be present when they arrive.'

The guide turned and walked away without another word. Malus watched him go, wondering if he'd given too away too much. Suddenly the unseen presence of the autarii seemed the least of his concerns.

* * *

DINNER WAS A stew of beans and salt beef boiled over the fire, washed down with water. There was a skin of decent wine in Malus's pack, but he had no desire to taste it. He wanted all his wits about him when the autarii appeared that night.

The food was bland, but the fire was welcome. The guides had the foresight to keep a pile of wood sheltered beneath one of the lean-tos and within an hour of making camp there was a roaring fire casting strange shadows on the ruined walls. There was a circle of old logs surrounding the fire pit and Malus had staked out a spot before everyone else. Now, hours later, he was feeling dry and warm and fighting sleep as Vor and the rest of his band smoked clay pipes and murmured to themselves in low tones. An iron kettle still bubbled next to the fire and two clean bowls waited nearby, set aside for the expected visitors.

Vor crouched next to the kettle, stirring it slowly with a wooden spoon. His scraggly hair was pulled back from his face and bound with a leather cord – if anything, it lent him an even more fearsome appearance in the shifting light.

Malus folded his arms and stared up at the mist and smoke roiling above the leaping flames. 'Tell me of the houses of the dead,' he said, trying to stay alert. 'Is it truly a city of stone crypts?'

Hathan Vor smiled faintly. 'It is a city of fragments,' he said quietly. 'Each crypt is surrounded by buildings and stone gardens – one even has a kind of small market square. But none of them go together, if you take my meaning. It's as if each family created its crypt in the fashion of the tower they'd left behind in Nagarythe, including as much of the surrounding city as they could afford.'

Malus tried to picture it in his head. It was a strange enough notion to imagine interring the dead at all – druchii had been cremated for generations, according to the dictates of the Temple of Khaine. Worship that was forbidden in those days, Malus reminded himself. 'I can understand the towers, I suppose,' he said, 'but why the rest?'

The scarred druchii shrugged. 'No one alive remembers – except Morathi herself, I suppose. Although there are legends, of course.' His smile widened. 'My favourite one claims that the houses of the dead were part of an elaborate spell to raise Nagarythe by the power of necromancy. With each soul interred, the spell would grow stronger, until finally the drowned land would rise from the sea.' Vor chuckled to himself. 'Another legend simply says that the old families hoped to recapture a semblance in death of what they lost in life. I suspect there's some truth to that.'

'Is that why you think the crypt of Eleuril is haunted?' Malus asked.

Vor did not reply. For a moment, Malus thought he'd somehow offended the man, but then he realised that the other guides had fallen silent as well. He straightened, scanning the faces of the men around him – and realised that they were no longer alone.

Two autarii stood at the edge of the firelight – they were so slender, dark and still that for a moment Malus took them to be a trick of the light. Then Vor cleared his throat and said, 'I see you there, children of the hills. It is a dark night. Come and share our fire.' The words had a rote quality to them, almost like a ritual chant, but Malus also noted an undercurrent of apprehension. Something wasn't quite right.

Without a word the two figures glided silently up to the fire pit. They wore long, mottled cloaks of grey, green and black wool, glistening with diamond-bright drops of rain. As one, the shades reached up with slim, pale hands and pulled back their voluminous hoods. Firelight played on angular, fine-boned features and glittered in large, unexpectedly violet eyes. The two shades appeared to be brother and sister; more than that, they could have been twins. Their aristocratic faces were tattooed with identical designs of a coiling dragon, worked in ghostly blue ink. They were strikingly handsome, neither too feminine or masculine and the stillness of their near-identical faces made them both irresistible and disturbingly unreal. Their hair, black and gleaming, was pulled back into a number of tightly-woven braids. Malus noticed that the girl wore hollowed finger bones in her hair. Probably the bones of highborn druchii, he thought apprehensively, remembering that the flesh of druchii nobles was a delicacy to the hill clans.

The two shades took their place by the fire but remained standing, surveying each of the seated druchii in turn. When their gaze settled on Malus, they stopped. The weight of their stares set the highborn's teeth on edge. Vor glanced warily at him.

With a deep breath, Malus reached up and drew back his hood.

The autarii continued to stare at Malus. Vor picked up a bowl. 'Forgive me for not having meat and salt ready for you,' he said hastily. 'You are here early tonight. May we share our food with you and pay our respects?'

The boy turned to face Vor, moving with sombre grace. When he spoke, his voice was clear and pure as a bell. 'We know you well, Hathan Vor,' he said, 'just as we know the rest of your kin. But what of this man?' Violet eyes regarded Malus again. 'Do you know his name?'

'He... he is Malus, son of Lurhan the Vaulkhar of Hag Graef,' Vor said, eyeing Malus nervously. 'He is a highborn, from an ancient lineage and comes to honour his ancestors in the houses of the dead.'

Beneath his cloak, Malus's hand inched slowly towards his sword hilt. He didn't like the way this was going.

The boy shook his head, but it was the girl who replied. 'That is one of his names,' she said, her voice dark and husky as smoke. 'But we know another. In the hills he is known as *An Raksha.*'

Malus swallowed a curse. Briefly he contemplated the odds of killing both shades where they stood. There's probably a dozen more watching from the shadows, he thought sourly. I'd likely not get two paces before a crossbow bolt found my throat. With effort, he forced himself to smile. 'I got that name in recognition of a favour I did for Urhan Beg,' he said conversationally. 'Oddly, I don't recall seeing either of you in his clan hall.'

'All the hill clans know you killed the Urhan and his son,' the boy said coldly. 'Show us your hands.'

The highborn hesitated. Vor stared angrily at Malus. 'Do it!' he hissed.

Slowly, Malus pushed aside his cloak and raised his hands, palms outward. The two shades studied them intently, as though searching for some hidden mark visible only to them.

After a moment, the boy frowned. 'His hands are not stained with the blood of the Urhan,' he said to his sister.

'That does not make him innocent, merely clever,' she said. 'He must still answer to the Urhan's kin.' She turned to Vor. 'You have taken this man's gold.' It was more a statement than a question.

Vor looked from her to Malus and back again. 'I… yes,' he stammered. 'But only that. I do not wear his collar, nor have I sworn any oaths to him.'

The scarred druchii's voice was faintly pleading, but the autarii were unmoved. 'Goodbye, Hathan Vor,' the girl said gravely, then the two shades turned and strode silently into the night.

For a moment no one moved. Hathan Vor didn't even seem to breathe for several long moments. 'They didn't touch meat or salt,' he finally said, his voice hollow with fear. 'We're trespassers now.' Vor looked to his kin. 'Blessed Mother of Night, what are we going to do?'

Malus rose to his feet and slowly drew his sword. He held it out, letting the firelight play on its honed edge and glared out into the darkness. 'If I were you, I'd post sentries and keep the fire going,' he growled. 'It's going to be a long night.'

SPITE'S WARNING HISS was like the rumbling of a boiling steam kettle, bringing Malus out of a dreamless slumber. He blinked in the weak light of false dawn, his hand tightening around the naked blade resting in his lap.

A dark figure stood several feet away, shoulders hunched against the falling rain. It took Malus a moment to recognise the druchii's scarred face. Hadn't he just closed his eyes a moment ago? No, he realised. It had still been dark when he'd finally decided that the shades weren't going to try to overrun the camp.

'What is it?' he grumbled.

'Selavhir is gone,' Vor said gravely.

'Gone,' Malus echoed. 'You mean dead?'

'I mean gone. He's disappeared.'

Malus sat upright, rubbing a damp hand over his face. 'Was he one of the sentries?'

'He had the early watch, then traded with Hethal at the hour of the wolf. I watched him head back to his bedroll.' Vor looked fearfully at one of the lean-tos on the opposite side of the smouldering fire pit. 'But he's not there now.'

Malus stared dumbly up at the mist roiling overhead, trying to cudgel his mind into alertness. 'So he went back to his bedroll, gathered his things and slipped off when you weren't looking.'

Vorn gave a bitter laugh. 'Not even I would be foolish enough to try and walk these woods at night – especially not when they're crawling with angry shades,' he snapped. 'You didn't tell me the autarii had a feud with you.'

'You didn't tell me we'd be sitting down to a meal with a pair of shades back when I hired you at Karond Kar,' Malus shot back.

Vor bared his teeth in a twisted snarl. 'The shades got Selavhir,' he growled. 'They came in here and took him, right under our noses. The Dark Mother alone knows what they've done to him.' He glared at Malus. 'You won't be seeing the houses of the dead now, highborn. We're breaking camp and getting out of here while we still can.'

Malus eyed the man coldly. 'I did not pay you to turn and run at the first sign of danger, Hathan Vor. We will continue to the crypt of Eleuril as planned.'

The guide laughed again, but this time there was a tone of desperation in the sound. 'You're mad, highborn! We're heading back for the Slavers' Road as fast as we can run – you can either saddle that reptile and come with us or be hanging from a shade's meat hook by nightfall!'

Now Malus was fully awake. 'You listen to me, you half-witted lump of flesh,' he snarled, rising slowly to his feet. 'I have men awaiting my return at Karond Kar. If you show your face there without me – or don't show your face at all within a few weeks' time – I guarantee they will find you and make you suffer in ways that would make a shade pray for mercy, *after* they kill every living thing you've ever cared about. The only hope you have of surviving this expedition is to get me to the crypt of Eleuril and then guide me safely out of these woods.'

'Is it worth your life to reach this damned crypt?' Vor cried.

'That's not the point,' Malus said, his voice hard as stone. 'The point is that it's worth *your* life to get there and more besides. Now get your men moving.'

They set off from the ruins at a rapid pace. Malus kept Vor close, leaving three men to scout ahead and three more to bring up the rear. Vor ordered the men to keep in sight of one another at all times, but the dense undergrowth and the steady rain made it next to impossible. The guides travelled with weapons in hand and Malus walked with one hand against Spite's flank, trusting the nauglir's senses over his own. The sense of being watched was overpowering, seeming to come from every direction at once.

For hours the small column plunged through the dense forest, trudging up steadily steeper terrain. At mid morning, Vor called a brief halt.

The druchii grouped together under the dripping branches, drinking greedily from their waterskins and chewing strips of dried meat. Vor counted heads.

'Where's Uvar?' he asked, looking from one man to the next.

One of the men looked back the way they'd come. 'He was the last man in the line,' he said fearfully. 'I saw him just before we stopped. I swear it!'

'It doesn't matter,' Malus said darkly. 'He's gone now.' The highborn looked to Vor. 'How far to the outskirts of the necropolis?'

'Another four or five hours,' Vor said without thinking. 'What of it?'

'Out in these damnable trees the autarii have the upper hand,' Malus said quietly. 'Once we reach the streets and towers of the crypts we might be able to even the odds. The shades are like ghosts in the wilderness, but believe me, if you cut them they bleed like normal men. Now let's go!'

The men climbed to their feet and pressed on, setting a brutal pace. Malus's plan, such as it was, gave them at least a chance for survival and it kept them moving even as the terrain grew steeper and more treacherous. The rain never let up. More than once Malus considered drawing his crossbow from its oiled wrappings and loading it, but he knew that the damp conditions would damage the weapon in the long run – and besides, he had no targets to shoot at.

Two hours later Vor called another halt. When he counted heads another man was missing. Huril, a tall, stout druchii with a bare blade in each scarred hand had taken the lead at the last stop and had quickly disappeared from sight in the dense foliage. No one knew when the shades had taken him.

Fear gripped the survivors. Malus stood before them with sword in hand and said, 'Get up. You can either get moving and take your chances with the shades or stay here and die by my hand! Make your choice!'

The guides fixed Malus with looks of pure hate, but they struggled to their feet and set off. This time everyone stayed as close together as possible, no longer worried about Spite's dripping jaws or his lashing tail. Vor jogged along just behind Malus, his head swivelling back and forth as he tried to keep all his men in sight.

Even with only a yard or less between each man the dense under-growth still made it difficult to keep everyone in view at all times. Malus concentrated on putting one foot in front of the other, pressing on through the tangled brush as quickly as he could and hoping that beyond the next wall of hanging vines or thicket of dripping ferns he would stumble onto city streets of grey stone.

Almost three hours later the highborn's single-minded reverie was broken by relieved shouts from up ahead. He pressed forward through a thicket of tall bushes and found himself stumbling along the hard surface of cobblestones hidden within the thick grass at his feet. Ahead he could see that the undergrowth was all but gone and the trees them-selves were thinning out, giving way to tall, dark buildings and slender, dagger-like towers bordered by the iron-dark flanks of towering stone crags. Malus could see the two lead druchii just ahead, waving at him excitedly.

'That's it!' Malus said, baring his teeth in a feral grin. 'You see, Vor? The shades are not infallible. They tried their best to stop us and failed. If they follow us into the necropolis, I promise you we will make them pay.'

The scarred guide said nothing. Malus turned, a jibe forming on his lips, but when he looked back his voice died in his throat.

There was no one there. Hathan Vor was gone.

Chapter Seven
THE HOUSES OF THE DEAD

'BLESSED MOTHER OF Night,' Malus said breathlessly, staring into the depths of the forest as though Vor might appear from the undergrowth at any moment. Just then the banks of ferns and vines thrashed back and forth and one of the tail-end guides appeared, his eyes wide and fearful. The druchii pulled up short. 'Where's Vor?' he asked, his voice growing thin with panic.

'Run,' Malus said. In one swift movement he swung into Spite's saddle. The druchii guide simply stared at him, still getting to grips with Vor's disappearance. Malus clouted the man on the shoulder with the flat of his sword. 'Run, damn you!'

The man lurched into motion and Malus spurred his mount into a ground-eating trot. Spite wove easily among the thinning trees, his loping strides carrying him past the lead druchii guides and on into the outskirts of the necropolis. The cold one's feet slapped against tightly fitted black cobblestones as the highborn brought his mount around and counted the heads of the druchii scrambling in his wake. He saw three of Vor's men; the druchii charged with bringing up the rear of the column had yet to appear. Malus crouched low in the saddle, trying to make himself as small a target as possible as he scrutinised the tree line for signs of movement.

'Your master is gone,' the highborn told the frightened guides. 'The cursed shades plucked him right out of our midst.'

The men looked to one another, their expressions stricken with panic. 'What do we do?' one asked.

'What else? We make them pay,' Malus snapped. 'They've been toying with us since last night, thinking us easy prey. Now we have the chance to make them regret their arrogance.'

'No,' said another of the guides, an older man with a bald pate and a notch carved from his right nostril. 'This is madness. We can't fight the autarii!'

Malus fixed the man with a burning glare. 'What would you have us do, then? March like sheep into their stew pots? These savages *eat* city druchii, just like we would skin and eat a suckling pig. It's fight or die, fool!'

'It was your stubbornness that got us into this,' the man shot back. 'If we'd done as Vor said we'd be on the Slavers' Road by now.' He turned to his compatriots. 'I say we make a run for it and leave the highborn to his fate. It's him the shades want, not us!'

Malus's hand tightened on the hilt of his sword. He was ready to strike the man's insolent head from his shoulders when a thin scream echoed from the forest. The last of the guides stumbled through the trees, his face pale and his eyes wild. He saw Malus and his kin and stumbled towards them, his mouth working soundlessly. After a few steps he tripped on a root and tried to catch himself against the bole of a nearby tree, but his hand slipped on the wet bark and he went face down into the grass. Three crossbow bolts jutted from the man's back and his robes were black with blood. The man shuddered once, then went still.

The highborn turned back to the assembled guides. 'That is the fate that awaits you if you go back into those woods,' he said. 'If you want to live, stay close to me. Now move!'

Without waiting for a response he kicked Spite into a trot and headed deeper into the shadowy lanes of the necropolis.

Tall buildings of grey stone rose up around Malus, structures that would not have looked out of place in Hag Graef or any other prosperous druchii city. Tall, blade-like towers climbed into the leaden sky just beyond the square buildings, arrayed loosely on the left and right as the city of the dead worked its way along the twisting valley, climbing ever higher between mountains invisible behind clouds of mist and rain. For the first few moments Malus felt a sense of dislocation so powerful it crowded all other thoughts out of his mind. The sense of homecoming was so potent that he caught himself looking to the sky, expecting to see the clustered spires of the Hag.

He rode upon a main avenue of sorts, a road of black stone that followed the valley floor between the serried ranks of crypts and monuments. Side lanes ran off at irregular intervals from the main road, leading to specific tombs. Malus studied the layout keenly and formed a battle plan. The highborn twisted in the saddle to see the three surviving guides hot on his heels, then led Spite down a side lane shrouded in afternoon shadow.

About twenty yards down the lane another road branched away to the right, leading to what appeared to be a decorative stone garden. A large structure stood at the corner – possibly a representation of a flesh house or a house of sport. Strangely tall, square windows lined the building's facade on both street fronts, black gaps in the grin of a grey skull. It would do, Malus decided, baring his teeth.

He drew Spite to a stop and turned to the men. The highborn indicated two of them with his sword and pointed down the side road in the direction of the garden. 'You two keep heading that way,' he ordered. 'And make all the noise you can.'

The men nodded, breathing hard. The third man – the bald druchii who had argued for abandoning Malus – looked to the highborn and said, 'What about us?'

Malus gestured at the building with his chin. 'Inside. When the shades run past, we give them a taste of their own mischief.' He turned back to the two decoys. 'When you hear Spite roar, turn back and help us cut some throats.'

The men grinned evilly and headed off towards the garden, their boots splashing through the puddles scattered along the street.

Malus slipped from the saddle and led the nauglir to the closest window. The warbeast sniffed at the darkness beyond the portal and leapt through the opening with surprising agility. The highborn waved the bald druchii inside and then followed right on his heels.

The air inside was musty and dank. He could see nothing beyond the faint squares of weak grey light painted on the floor by the setting sun. Drifts of dust puffed from long cracks that ran in wild patterns across the stone floor and Malus heard an ominous groan echo from the rafters above. *Small wonder these old buildings haven't fallen to pieces in all this time,* he thought to himself. *It would be just my luck to come this far and die because I leaned against the wrong pillar and brought a ton of rock down on my head.*

There was the sound of ponderous flesh sliding over stone as Spite shifted about in the blackness. 'Stand,' Malus hissed and was rewarded with the shuffling thud of the nauglir settling onto the stone.

'What now?' the bald druchii whispered.

'Wait and watch,' Malus said, barely loud enough to be heard. 'Stand just beyond the light and watch the street outside. Move only when I do.'

The highborn heard a faint grunt in reply. It occurred to him that the bald guide would never have a better opportunity to cut his throat and make a run for it, but Malus pushed the thought from his mind. He counted on the druchii sensibility for vengeance outweighing craven cowardice and turned to watch the shadowy lane.

At once Malus saw a flaw in his plan. Rain made a grey haze in the air and much of both lanes held pools of deep shadow that he couldn't see into – only a narrow band of roadway running down the middle of both lanes was fully lit. The stealthy autarii could keep out of the dim light and slip right past Malus's ambush if he wasn't very careful. The highborn took a deep breath and tried to concentrate, careful to focus on the larger picture in front of him rather than narrow in on a specific area or set of details. When the moment came it would announce itself with subtle shifts in the view outside – motion that would register at the corners of Malus's vision rather than rushing past in plain sight.

For several long minutes nothing happened. Malus could distantly hear his decoys somewhere in or near the garden, calling out to one another. Nothing stirred in the shadows outside. Could the shades have already slipped past him? There was no way to know.

Spite shifted ever so slightly. Malus almost turned to silence the beast when his eye caught the barest hint of movement, a subtle change in the depth of the shadows opposite the building they were in. It could have been a trick of the light – or his weary mind – but then he saw it again. The shades were creeping down the road, stealing silently up to the men in the garden.

Malus grinned in the darkness. 'Up, Spite,' he hissed and as the nauglir rose to its feet he raised his sword. 'Now!' he cried and raced for the window.

The highborn leapt into the street with a piercing war scream, his blade held high. Half a dozen crossbows *thumped* in response, but the shades had been taken by surprise and the bolts went wide of their mark, shattering against the side of the building in a storm of razor-sharp fragments.

Malus counted at least ten autarii in the shadows outside the building. Six of them worked the reloading levers of their crossbows while the rest leapt at the highborn with short swords glinting wickedly in their hands. A year ago the sight might have filled him with dread, now his heart sang with savage exultation as the battle was joined.

The shades' weapons were almost a foot shorter than Malus's lean, curved blade and the highborn took full advantage of it. He rushed at the foremost autarii, feinting at the man's head with a flurry of blows. The shade was as quick as a snake, blocking left and right with short, ringing strokes – then Malus swept his sword in a wide, downward arc and struck the man's leg just above the knee. The master-forged blade sliced through layered robes and into the flesh beneath, severing the leg in a shower of dark blood. The shade collapsed with an anguished scream but Malus was already gone, rushing forward to meet the next pair of foes.

They came at him from both sides at once; Malus leapt at the man on his right, driving the shade backwards with a lightning thrust at his eyes. The highborn stepped forward, opening his right side to the second autarii. The shade, seeing his opportunity, lunged forwards, his short blade stabbing for Malus's throat. The autarii never reached his target; the highborn waited until the man had committed himself to his attack, then spun on his heel with a backhanded slash that struck the shade's head from his shoulders. Malus spun back to face his second foe – and was surprised when the headless body of the man he'd just killed continued to stagger forward and crashed into him, knocking both of them to the ground.

Hot, salty blood splashed across Malus's face as he landed on the rain-slicked cobblestones beneath the twitching corpse. There was the unmistakeable ringing sound of steel thudding into flesh – the other shade had rushed in and stabbed the wrong target in his haste. Malus writhed beneath the body, trying to push it aside and swing at the autarii at the same time. The shade leapt nimbly out of reach, which was all Malus could have asked for. He kicked the body off himself in the direction of his opponent and rolled in the opposite direction, getting as much distance as he could so that he could scramble to his feet.

The ground shook and a scaled foot the size of a large shield crashed down mere inches from Malus's head. Spite let loose a thunderous roar as he charged into the melee, his dripping jaws snapping at the sword-wielding autarii. The shade screamed in fear and turned to run, but didn't reckon on the nauglir's surprising speed. Spite lunged, catching the autarii by the shoulder and shaking him like a rat in a terrier's jaws. Ribs and collarbones snapped in a staccato series of pops and the shade went limp.

Malus changed direction, rolling away from the rampaging nauglir and staggering to his feet. He heard the sound of crossbows firing and more bolts hummed through the air. One glanced off the highborn's left pauldron and then struck the building opposite. Other bolts struck Spite in the shoulder and flank, eliciting a roar of pure rage from the angry beast. The highborn watched the cold one spin in place, his blunt snout snapping at the shaft of a bolt jutting from his shoulder. Whether by accident or design, his lashing tail smashed into one of the crossbowmen, flinging the shade down the street in a welter of crimson and splintered wood. The highborn caught sight of the bald druchii grappling with another of the shades, the points of their short blades quivering before one another's throats.

There was a grunt and a metallic clicking sound to Malus's right. He turned to see another of the autarii intent on reloading his crossbow. The highborn leapt at him with a maddened howl.

Time slowed as he raced across the street, closing the distance with the crossbowman as swiftly as he could. Malus continued to howl like one of the damned, hoping to unnerve the man enough so that he couldn't ready his crossbow in time. It was a deadly race – one Malus lost.

The autarii levelled the crossbow and fired while Malus was still a few yards out of reach. He tried to twist out of the way, but the bolt flashed across the intervening space like lightning. There was a sharp impact against his shoulder, then a white-hot blast of pain that drove the air from his lungs.

Malus stumbled, struggling to breathe, but caught himself and leapt forward. The shade's fierce grin turned to a rictus of agony as the highborn drove the point of his sword into the autarii's groin. The man collapsed, writhing in a spreading pool of blood as the highborn crashed headlong into the stone wall on the far side of the street. He leaned there for a moment, panting for breath and watching heavy drops of red run down the shaft of the crossbow bolt jutting from his left shoulder. They splashed like raindrops at his feet, the sharp pain pulsing in time with his labouring heart.

A shadow loomed on his left side. Malus lunged at it with a feral snarl, his bloody sword raised. At the last minute he recognised the bald-headed guide, who fell back from him with a frightened cry.

'We did it!' the druchii said, holding up his dripping knife. 'They're running for their lives!'

Malus stood on unsteady feet and tried to focus past the pain. He could hear panicked cries over the clashing of Spite's bony jaws – the nauglir was sating his hunger on one of the dead shades – and after a moment the highborn discerned that the autarii were retreating in the direction of the stone garden. He frowned, shaking his head. That made no sense.

Then he heard the sounds of battle within the garden itself and realised what had happened.

'The damned shades laid a trap of their own,' he growled. 'They saw where we were going and sent most of their men down the main road to head us off.' There hadn't been time to check during the fight, but he could see that neither of the twin shades were among the dead littering the street.

The bald guide's face went from triumphant to fearful in the space of a heartbeat. 'What now?' he asked, his voice tinged with despair.

'First, grab hold of this bolt and pull the cursed thing out,' Malus grated, leaning back against the wall.

The guide gingerly grabbed the bolt's bloody shaft. 'All right,' he said, steeling himself. 'On the count of three–'

'Just *pull*, damn your eyes!' Malus roared and the guide tore the bolt free.

The world seemed to spin. Deep inside his chest, Malus could feel the daemon writhing in ecstasy, floating on a sea of delicious pain.

'Spite!' Malus cried and the nauglir trotted obediently to the high-born's side. Dark ichor flowed freely from four crossbow bolts jutting from the cold one's side, but the warbeast's strength and speed appeared unaffected. Malus stumbled against his mount and quickly pulled the bolts free, then pulled himself painfully into the saddle. Already the sounds of battle in the garden had fallen silent. They were running out of time.

The highborn kicked the cold one into a trot, heading back onto the first side road. 'Hurry!' he said to the guide and turned right, heading away from the main avenue.

They passed more ancient, empty buildings in varying states of disre-pair. Malus studied each one in turn, looking for something two men could easily defend. For several grim moments it looked as though Malus's luck had run out – but then, at the end of the lane, he spied a square, windowless building, its four sides carved with elaborate bas reliefs showing a procession of dancing druchii nobles. A single, narrow doorway stood out starkly amid the splendour. Malus kicked Spite into a gallop just as a chorus of howls echoed down the lane behind them. The highborn turned and spied a large band of autarii, possibly as many as thirty or more, standing in a loose pack around two distinctive figures. The twin shades had pulled back their hoods and howled at the weeping sky like a pair of wolves. Even at so great a distance, it seemed to Malus as though their tattoos glowed with a ghostly light.

Spite reached the end of the lane in moments and the last surviving guide was right behind the nauglir as Malus dropped from the saddle and led his mount into the imposing building. Inside, the chamber was a single open space, with a ceiling that soared fifteen feet overhead. Shafts of weak light and streams of rainwater cascaded down in places where the ancient ceiling had given way over the centuries, giving barely enough light to see by. There was a dais at the far end of the chamber and what looked like a weathered altar of dark green stone. Malus led Spite across the rubbish-strewn space and found that there was a ramp behind the dais that descended into cave-like darkness.

Malus ordered Spite to stand, then reached back and pulled his cov-ered crossbow and quiver from his saddle. He tossed them to the guide. 'Get up on the dais and shoot any man that gets past me,' he said.

The man caught the bundles with a confused look on his face. 'What are you going to do?'

Malus dropped to the ground and drew his second sword. 'I'm going to kill every goddess-cursed shade that comes through that door,' he said grimly and walked back the way he'd come.

To the bald man's credit, he didn't waste his breath arguing the matter; Malus heard the reassuring click of the crossbow's cocking lever being worked as he headed to the door. He avoided the shafts of rain and light, sticking solely to the deep shadows. Once he thought he'd gone far enough he whispered to Tz'arkan. 'All right, daemon. I know you've been waiting for this. Lend me your strength.'

'Of course,' the daemon purred. 'For your sake, I hope it will be enough.'

The words sent a thrill of fear coursing down the highborn's spine. 'What does that mean?' he asked, but the question was drowned beneath the cold weight of Tz'arkan's power. Blood turned to ice; flesh and skin knitted together, leaving a black, star-shaped scar on Malus's shoulder. He was whole once more. In fact, for the first time in days he felt truly alive.

Shadows played across the doorway. With a joyous smile Malus went to greet them.

The autarii came in a black wave, filling the air with ululating howls. To Malus, they moved as slowly and ponderously as cattle to the slaughter. His twin swords wove a tapestry of death just beyond the door, severing limbs, spilling guts and slashing throats with every sweep of his blades. He laughed like a madman at the red harvest he wrought; many of the shades were dead before they hit the floor, struck down too swiftly to even cry out in terror or pain.

Malus stopped counting how many men lay piled in the doorway. In fact, after the tenth man was struck down the killing became almost mechanical. His laughter faded. He started to become *bored*.

That was when one of the twin shades nearly killed him.

Dead men were falling lazily to the ground, their wounds just beginning to bleed, when the boy leapt at Malus with a pair of bloody swords in his hands. He struck like an adder, stabbing for the highborn's face and throat and it was only by purest luck that Malus turned his head at the last moment and had his cheek slashed open instead of his neck. The highborn stumbled backwards, parrying wildly and the autarii slapped aside his swords as he launched another whirlwind attack. Twin blades pummelled his breastplate and pauldrons; joints creaked and pins snapped under the blows. A moment before he'd been a god of death; now Malus found himself fighting for his life.

The shades, it appeared, were not without sorcery of their own.

Up close, Malus could see the dragon tattoo glowing and writhing across the autarii boy's face. His face was serene, his violet eyes soulless and blank as he hurled a constant stream of blows at Malus. The highborn recovered quickly, parrying each stroke with skill and speed, but the boy was relentless, slipping past Malus's guard again and again to strike ringing blows against his armour.

Malus gave ground, falling back deeper into the room as he tried to find some weakness in the boy's defence. He wielded a pair of short blades like the other autarii, but his raw strength and speed more than made up for their short length. Each time Malus pressed forward with an attack, the boy responded with a counterstroke that nearly killed him. Even with the daemon's power, he was almost outmatched.

The highborn leapt farther backward, gaining a short breathing space. There was the thump of a crossbow over his shoulder and Malus watched the boy swat the bolt aside with one of his swords. In the space of a dozen moments the shade had backed him all the way across the large chamber.

Malus edged to the right. The shade shifted to the left. They circled one another slowly, looking for an opportunity to strike. Malus noted that the autarii wasn't even breathing hard. 'Even now you're playing with me,' the highborn growled. The boy smiled faintly in reply.

The highborn's back was to the distant doorway. Malus rocked back, then leapt at the autarii. Swords clashed and Malus continued to drive forward, but the boy stood his ground and the two locked swords. The highborn ground to a halt, his face just inches from the boy's own. 'You can't win,' Malus said through clenched teeth. 'Where does your power come from? Tell me and I'll let you live.'

The boy laughed. 'Empty words, highborn,' he said. 'Your swords are no match for mine.'

Malus struggled, but the boy moved not an inch. 'True,' he admitted grudgingly. 'That's why I decided to turn this into a battle of wits.'

The boy frowned. 'I don't understand.'

Malus put his boot in the autarii's chest and shoved. Fuelled by the daemon's strength, the boy flew backwards through the air – and straight into Spite's snapping jaws. The shade's startled cry was cut short by a meaty *crunch*.

'I know,' Malus answered, swaying on his feet. 'Fools like you never do until it's too late.'

'Dread lord!' the guide shouted. 'The ceiling!'

Malus looked up. The shafts of sunlight were flickering as shapes flitted about their edges. Once again, he'd been outmanoeuvred. The assault at the doorway had just been a diversion while the rest of the shades scaled the walls and reached the roof.

The highborn looked back towards the doorway. More shadows were mustering there as well. 'Down the ramp!' he cried. 'Hurry!'

Malus grabbed Spite's reins, pulling the beast away from what was left of the dead twin. The guide scrambled off the dais and disappeared down the ramp and Malus was not far behind.

The guide got no farther than the base of the ramp and stopped in his tracks, his one free hand reaching blindly ahead of him as he edged into the darkness. Malus brushed the man aside, trusting that the nauglir's subterranean-bred senses would alert him to any danger.

He walked perhaps a dozen feet into the abyssal blackness when Spite brushed against something tall and made from stone. There was an ominous crack, Malus smelled dust in the air. The ceiling overhead let out a long, rumbling groan.

Malus froze. It appeared that the real danger had nothing to do with pitfalls or hidden wells. One wrong move and Spite could bring the entire building down on top of them.

The highborn took a deep breath, tasting dank, still air. In the room above, he heard the dead shade's twin sister let out a cry of mourning that quickly transformed into a bestial shriek of rage.

'That… that boy,' the guide said, his voice thick with fear. 'What was he? What are *you*?'

'Shut up,' Malus hissed. 'I'm trying to think of a way out of here.'

'There is one,' the daemon said, the voice seeming to reverberate out of the blackness. 'It's right under your nose, but I doubt you have the wit to see it.'

'This is no time for your damned riddles!' Malus shot back. 'Unless you can spirit me out of this hole, I don't want to hear from you!'

'I can't… but you can,' the daemon said. 'All you lack is the will.'

'The will?' Malus snapped. 'The will to do what?'

'The will to use all the tools at your disposal, fool.'

'What in the Dark Mother's name are you talking about?' Malus looked helplessly around him in the darkness. Glancing back over his shoulder, there was just enough light coming from the room above to see Spite's hindquarters and beyond that the guide staring fearfully up the ramp. 'He's of no use,' Malus said quietly, 'and Spite can't run fast enough to get me past a score of shades. And I'd have as much luck wielding the Idol of Kolkuth as I would of finding my way through this pit of a room–'

Malus stopped, his mouth hanging open. The idol.

He sheathed his swords and reached back to his saddle bags, fumbling through them in the dim light. After a moment his hand closed on a small, cold shape, wrapped in silk. He drew it out and uncovered it. The brass figure gleamed dully.

Legends said the Idol of Kolkuth had the power to bend space and time. He'd seen its power first hand back on the Isle of Morhaut. But how did it work? What did he know of sorcery?

Something his mother, herself a potent witch, once said echoed in his mind. Power is shaped by the wielder. It is made to serve, as a slave is bent to the master's will. And what was sorcery, if not power made manifest?

Malus took a deep breath. The daemon's power had left him and his body felt weak. His will remained undimmed however. It still burned bright, fed with hatred and desire.

He climbed into the saddle. The idol was a cold weight in his right hand. This was madness, he thought. He was no sorcerer! But if he didn't do something he was going to die, down here in a dank, empty tomb. He would give what was left of his soul to cheat death just a bit longer.

The guide turned. 'Mother of Night, I see them! That autarii girl and her kin! They're coming!'

'Let them,' Malus said. With a cry he tugged at Spite's reins, whipping the cold one in a tight circle. His thick tail struck the column nearby, smashing it apart with a tremendous crash.

There was another long groan that didn't fade, but instead grew in strength. Drifts of dust fell from above. Malus held up the idol and envisioned the lane outside the building. He bent all his will into a single, furious command. Take me there!

Malus put his boots to Spite's flanks, then there was a tremendous, rending crash and the world turned inside out.

Chapter Eight
THE REAPER OF SOULS

THERE WAS THE sound of wind rushing in his ears and for a sickening moment Malus felt himself suspended over an endless void. He heard himself cry out in terror, but it was too late to turn back. He had stepped from the precipice and realising that, he began to fall.

Destination, he heard a voice murmur in his head. You must walk a path, or be lost to the void forever. Choose!

Malus closed his eyes and mustered his will. He could feel nothing. Was the Idol of Kolkuth still clutched in his hand? He tried to forget the terror of his plunge and focus on the street outside the ancient building. This is my path, he thought. This is where I choose to go. Do as I command!

An invisible fist closed about his guts, squeezing them with merciless strength. Terrible, agonising cold radiated out from his bones and he was grateful for the sensation. Then came a crushing impact and he knew no more.

MALUS AWOKE TO the tickling of raindrops on his cheek. He opened his eyes and found himself face down on black cobblestones, his head resting in a pool of brackish water and bile.

With a groan he rolled onto his back, snarling savagely as a wave of painful convulsions wracked his body. For the first time in days the damnable rain felt like a blessing, their tiny impacts outlining the planes and edges of his face. His limbs were weak, his insides hollow and cold. This is what it feels like to lie among the dead, he thought suddenly. I have become a walking corpse.

The sensation of scales sliding against the inside of his ribs disturbed the highborn's thoughts. 'You just had your first taste of sorcery, Malus Darkblade. Was it to your liking?'

'It was terrible,' the highborn said wearily. 'But I should have expected no less. Damned sorcery,' he said with a grunt, trying to force himself upright. His limbs trembled and his guts churned at the strain, but after a moment he managed to lever himself onto his elbows. It was then that he noticed the idol still clutched in his right hand. He couldn't feel it. He couldn't feel much of anything.

He found that he was lying in the narrow lane some ten yards from the windowless temple where he'd made his stand. Two or three torn bodies lay outside the doorway and smears of blood made streaks on the lintel and the grey wall. Long, deep cracks ran along the walls of the building and many of the bas reliefs had broken into pieces, littering the street with debris. A thick pall of dust hung in the air over the structure, slowly sinking to the earth under the weight of the falling rain. From what he could see, not one of the shades had escaped.

'I would do it again, though,' he said with cold certainty. 'I will do whatever I must to be rid of you.'

'Of course you will,' the daemon chuckled knowingly. 'You will do a great many terrible things before you and I are done, Malus Darkblade. It is your fate.'

'Fate!' Malus spat. 'I make my fate, daemon.' Slowly, one finger at a time, he released the idol from his grasp and let it clatter to the cobblestones. 'For good or ill, the path I choose in this world is mine and mine alone.'

'Believe what you will,' Tz'arkan said. 'In the end, the result is the same.'

'Spare me your games,' the highborn growled. He looked around for Spite and saw the nauglir a few yards behind him. The cold one was lying on its side. That was a very bad sign. Summoning his strength, Malus climbed shakily to his feet.

'There are forces swirling around you, Malus. Even now they exert their pressures on you, shaping the trajectory of your fleeting existence. Blinding yourself to them will not make them go away.'

Angered, Malus drew a knife from his belt and placed the needle-sharp point at his throat. 'I could kill myself right now,' he said. 'There is no one to prevent it. If I can do that, what does it say about the illusion of fate?'

'An excellent question,' the daemon said. The infernal being sounded genuinely amused. 'Let's test your theory. Kill yourself.'

'What?'

'You heard me, highborn. Drive the dagger into your throat.'

'I…' Malus hesitated. 'I have no wish to die, daemon. That's not the point.'

'Yes it is,' Tz'arkan said. 'It is *precisely* the point. Nothing in the world could make you kill yourself, because it's not your fate to do so.'

'No, now you're twisting my argument,' Malus shot back. 'I don't want to kill myself because I wish to make my family suffer for the indignities they have done to me. I wish to claim the title of vaulkhar and more besides. I have ambitions, daemon, worldly ambitions.' He paused to catch his breath and managed a fleeting laugh. 'Dying now would be… inconvenient.'

'And so you live… as your fate requires,' the daemon agreed.

'I knew you were going to say something like that,' Malus snarled. He sank to his knees beside Spite, resting a hand on the beast's flank. The nauglir was breathing shallowly. The highborn crawled over next to the beast's head and gently pried open one great eyelid. The eye was rolled back, showing only white.

Suddenly the great reptile spasmed, thrashing with all four legs and long, cable-like tail. Malus hurled himself backwards, narrowly escaping a swipe from the nauglir's foreleg as the cold one leapt to its feet. The one-ton warbeast spun in place, snapping and snarling at thin air, then subsided. It sniffed the air warily, eyeing Malus and letting out a querulous grunt.

Malus shook his head. 'Stupid lizard,' he said affectionately. 'If I didn't know better, I'd say you fainted.'

The nauglir let out a long rumble, settling tentatively on its haunches. Malus couldn't say he blamed the beast.

MALUS RODE THROUGHOUT the long night, winding his way up the valley in the driving rain.

He had pulled the bolts from Spite's hide and cleaned them as best he could. The highborn knew from long experience that the cold one's constitution would heal the punctures within days, so long as the bolts hadn't been poisoned. With darkness drawing on he'd walked the cold one back to the main avenue and started his quest for Eleuril's crypt, switching to the saddle only after he became too weary to take another step. The nauglir plodded on tirelessly, scarcely affected by the armoured druchii on its back. Vor had told him that the prince's tomb was near the head of the valley, another full day's hike up the black road. With luck he would reach it by dawn and find some place to rest for a while.

Hours passed in silence, save for the steady drumming of the rain and the soft slap of the nauglir's feet. The numbness had finally ebbed to a kind of pervasive cold that chilled his flesh from head to toe. He craved a warm fire and better yet, a warm goblet of wine, but there was none to be had. More than once his thoughts drifted to the flask of wine in his pack, but each time he pushed the temptation aside. Who knew what other dangers lurked in the houses of the dead? And so he rode on, cold and sore and the daemon's words preyed upon his mind.

What he needed was a seer. The Witch King and his lieutenants could call upon their services to show them the possible outcomes of their efforts, the better to govern and confound the plans of their enemies. *When I return to the Hag, Eldire and I will have much to discuss,* he vowed.

Of course, given his suspicions, could he trust anything she said?

He was so lost in brooding that at first he didn't notice the change in Spite's gait. The nauglir sank lower to the ground and its gait became slower and more fluid. The cold one's nostrils dilated, drinking deeply of the wet air and its blunt snout lowered until its chin nearly touched the ground. It was only after the warbeast began a low, throaty rumbling that Malus snapped out of his reverie. He realised at once what was happening. The cold one had caught the scent of its favourite food: horseflesh.

The highborn hurriedly reined Spite in, leading him off the road and into the shadowy depths of a side lane. It was close to dawn, he noticed with a start; the grey sky was turning pearlescent with false dawn. Tendrils of fog curled around the foundations of the empty buildings and the looming towers. Malus studied his surroundings more closely – the buildings were made of finer materials and ornamented with graceful, sinuous carvings that seemed both familiar and alien at the same time. The towers stood in greater profusion, though many had been worn down by untold ages and some few were little more than toppled ruins. He had reached the abode of the Old Kings, the crypts of the last princes of Nagarythe.

'Stand,' Malus ordered and dropped stiffly to the cobblestones. Every sound seemed unnaturally loud in the fog-shrouded stillness, setting the highborn's nerves on end. Out of habit he reached for his crossbow, only to remember that he'd given it away during the battle with the shades.

Looking quickly about, Malus took stock of his surroundings and noticed a tall pile of rubble farther down the lane. The mass of bricks made a steep slope up the side of a partially fallen tower, the rough summit rising two or three storeys above the buildings in this part of the necropolis.

'Stay,' he told Spite, wishing he had a way of hobbling or otherwise corralling the hungry beast – if he was gone too long it was possible that the nauglir's appetite would override its self-control and it would go hunting for the source of all the tantalising equine smells. Glancing warily over his shoulder, the highborn moved swiftly and silently to the broken tower, then began to scale the heavy, rain-slicked blocks of stone.

The climb took far longer than he expected; the rubble was somewhat unstable and every time a hand or boot touched off a clatter of small stones he froze in place, listening for sounds of alarm. After almost an hour he reached the summit and pressed himself flat against the stones, peering out across the vista of close-set buildings and narrow lanes.

He saw the watch-fires at once: twin pyres set twenty yards apart that sent flames ten feet into the damp air. They had been lit in a small square several hundred yards distant, casting a flickering glow across rows of dark campaign tents and against the carved facade of a mortuary tower at the square's far end. The faint sounds of restless horses carried over the soft pattering of the rain.

Malus studied the tower more closely, a sick feeling of dread starting to churn in his gut. The stonework decorating the arch of the recessed entryway was a giant bas relief of a druchii prince clad in ornate armour. A clutch of severed heads hung by their hair from the prince's right fist, while his left hand reached upwards, closing about the curve of a crescent moon.

'Blessed Mother of Night,' he cursed softly. 'They're trying to break into Eleuril's tomb.'

HIS QUESTING HANDS found the Idol of Kolkuth first – the brass statue was colder than ice, despite being wrapped in layers of grimy rags. Malus set it hurriedly on the cobblestones and continued rummaging through his saddlebag. 'Of all the places in Naggaroth to come seeking adventure, they had to come here,' he muttered angrily. A quick glance at the sky showed that he had less than half an hour until dawn. The druchii in the camp could wake at any moment. He was going to have to move quickly if he was to have any chance at all.

'Do you imagine this to be mere coincidence, Darkblade?' The daemon sounded genuinely surprised.

Malus found a small object wrapped in cloth and drew it out, then realised at once it was his brother's skinned face, neatly salted and folded for safekeeping. He returned it to the bag and dug deeper. 'It's the campaigning season,' he said absently. 'Druchii lords take to the field in search of glory, or treasure, or both. I don't doubt that many of them take up grave-robbing if they think they can get away with it.'

'But at the head of so large a force?'

'The woods are full of shades, daemon. If I'd had my choice I'd have brought a small army myself.' His hand closed around a smooth, rounded shape. It sloshed gently as he pulled it free. Malus stared at the flask for a moment, started to put it away, then pulled the stopper free with his teeth and took a deep drink before dropping it back in the bag.

'How many lords could raise such a force, just to go hunting relics?'

'In all of Naggaroth? Dozens, I'm sure,' Malus snapped. 'You expect me to believe that this has anything to do with me?'

'Foolish druchii,' the daemon sneered. 'Of all the crypts in this valley, that warband just happens to be camped outside the tower you're looking for.'

'But that would mean that someone else knows I'm looking for the Dagger of Torxus and knows where the dagger might be found,' Malus said. 'And no one–'

The thought brought Malus up short. Urial would know, he realised. Could he have raised a force so quickly? Har Ganeth was only a few days' ride farther down the Slavers' Road.

Malus took a deep breath, set his jaw stubbornly and resumed his search. 'Perhaps you are right,' he said, 'but what does it matter? Whoever the lord might be, he hasn't got the dagger yet, or he wouldn't still be here. So I can still beat him to it.'

To the highborn's surprise, the daemon let out a long, rolling laugh. 'You are your own worst enemy, Darkblade,' the daemon said. 'So clever, so vicious, so deliciously hateful, but so single-minded. You think the world begins and ends with you.'

'And what is that supposed to mean?' Malus asked.

'Consequences, Malus, consequences. You have already disturbed the schemes of a great many people in your quest for power. Did you think they would forget you once you were done with them? Even now they lay snares for you, but you are too impetuous to avoid them.'

'And this, coming from a mighty daemon who allowed himself to be trapped in a crystal for thousands of years? I can do without your attempts at wisdom,' the highborn replied. Just then his hand closed on a flat, hard object wrapped in silk. 'That's the one,' he muttered and pulled it forth.

Malus reached into the folds of silk and uncovered an octagonal medallion worked from thick brass and etched with an eye-twisting array of strange runes. The Octagon of Praan was the first of the relics Malus had recovered at the daemon's behest. Where the Idol of Kolkuth could warp space and time around it, the Octagon protected its bearer from sorcery. Frowning in distaste, he slipped the medallion's chain around his neck, then picked up a small pack hanging from the cantle of his saddle and slung it over his shoulder. Then, reluctantly, he picked up the idol and returned it quickly to his saddlebag.

On impulse, Malus reached out and patted Spite's flank. 'If I'm not back in a day's time you have my permission to go over there and eat every living thing you can get your teeth around,' the highborn growled. 'In the meantime, *stay.*'

That done, Malus glanced at the dark sky, trying to gauge the hour. It would take quite a while to work out the positions of the sentries around the druchii camp and still more time to slip past them and reach the tomb. The last thing he wanted was to make it into the tower and then find himself trapped inside as the sun rose and the grave robbers returned to their labours.

'You could always use the idol again,' Tz'arkan whispered coyly. 'One step would take you from here to the front doors of the tomb. Imagine that.'

Malus grimaced. 'Oh, I can imagine it all too well, daemon,' he said. 'That's why I'll take my chances with the guards.'

THE TOMB'S ENTRYWAY was a short passage less than ten feet long that opened into a square chamber perhaps twenty feet across. Statues of manticores kept a silent vigil to either side of the crypt's vaulted doors opposite the entryway and the walls of the chamber were decorated with mosaics showing a tall, handsome druchii inflicting terrible tortures on a wide variety of noble-looking men and women.

Malus saw at once that the would-be grave robbers had already gone to work on the crypt's large doors. Hammers and chisels lay scattered about the threshold and there were deep divots carved out of the doors' surface. The highborn glanced the other way, out into the square and saw that there was still no one moving among the dark campaign tents. It had taken less time than he'd thought to find his way past the guards. Between the constant rain and the late hour the sentries had taken shelter inside the ruined buildings surrounding the square, leaving him an easy path into camp.

The highborn turned back and crept carefully into the entry chamber, scrutinising the tall doors and the damage the druchii warriors had done to them. 'It's like they're digging into stone,' he muttered, stepping closer – then he noticed the dark splotches staining the floor in front of the threshold.

So, he thought. Eleuril's crypt was not without its traps for the unwary.

Malus stepped closer still, careful not to pass between the two manticores. He crouched on his heels, studying the floor for hidden switches or plates. 'Wish Arleth Vann was here,' he muttered. 'He could probably do this blindfolded. I have no idea what I'm looking for.'

He searched the floor for several long minutes, knowing that he had few of them to spare, but found nothing out of the ordinary. Perhaps they set something off when they tried to get through the doors, he thought, studying their iron rings, hinges and fittings.

The highborn stared carefully at the divots carved into the doors. The wood was so dark and ancient it looked like stone.

Malus frowned. He scanned the floor, looking for fragments scattered by the workers' chisels. After a moment he saw a piece matching the hue of the doors and picked it up. The edges were razor sharp and the fragment had no discernible grain.

The door wasn't wood hardened to stone. It *was* stone.

'That's not the way in,' he realised. 'It's a decoy to distract looters. So… where is the real door?'

The highborn retreated to the centre of the chamber and began to study each wall in turn. He pored over each scene depicted on the walls, but nothing seemed out of the ordinary. Then he considered the scenes as part of a whole and began noticing differences in the appearance of Eleuril himself. There was a definite progression to the scenes, showing a chronology of his exploits as the Witch King's inquisitor. The last scene in the sequence showed him vivisecting a shrieking warlock with a strange-looking black dagger. Intrigued, Malus approached the mosaic. It was, curiously enough, set at the centre of the right-hand wall.

He reached out and ran his fingers over the smooth stones of the mosaic, testing their solidity. When his fingertips probed at the long, black stone of the dagger's blade, he felt it depress and heard a gritty *click*.

Suddenly a greenish blast of light enveloped Malus, sizzling as it coursed over his body like liquid fire. He felt the hot wind of its passage, but the energy itself rolled over him like water and vanished in a rattling boom.

The highborn staggered backwards, his eyes dazzled and his ears ringing from the blast. It took him a moment before he noticed the medallion around his neck glowing like brass hot from the forge and realised that the Octagon of Praan had saved him from the sorcerous trap.

As the ringing in his ears faded Malus heard surprised shouts coming from the square. Malus hesitated, then reached out and pressed against the wall with both hands. A section of the wall swung silently inwards, revealing a narrow stairway winding up and out of sight.

THE EYES OF the dead were upon Malus as he climbed the stair to the prince's tomb.

Grey stone gave way to polished black marble within the stairwell and globes of witchlight flickered to life as though awakened by the highborn's echoing footsteps. Every three feet Malus passed a narrow alcove set into the inner wall of the stairway, its archway chased in gold and carved with delicate runes. A mummified servant stood in each alcove, hands folded and head bowed to their chest in eternal supplication. Their eyes were open – perhaps they had been left that way intentionally, or perhaps their eyelids had receded over the centuries as their bodies slowly succumbed to the forces of time – and they seemed to stare at Malus as he hastened upwards in search of their master.

He could not say how long he climbed, nor how many silent, staring figures he passed before the staircase ended at an open doorway. Beyond lay a circular chamber of polished marble, bathed in sorcerous light.

A thin rug of dark silk ran from the doorway to the centre of the chamber, where a lectern held a massive book bound in dark leather. Beyond this lectern rose an octagonal dais and upon this dais, standing in an upright casket and clad in black enamelled armour, stood the withered corpse of Prince Eleuril.

Eight more caskets lay in a ring around the prince's dais and from where Malus stood he could see that each one held the body of a druchii knight, laid out in full panoply of war and bearing a long, gleaming sword upon his breast. The highborn hesitated in the doorway. The very air reeked of magic; he could not say why, but he could feel it, like a tingle across his skin.

Faint sounds echoed up the stairwell. To Malus's ears they sounded like voices. Was it Urial and his men, bursting through the hidden door and racing up the stairs?

Malus turned his eyes back to the prince's body. Eleuril's hands were clasped around something on his chest. It could be a dagger, he thought.

Moving cautiously, the highborn crept into the chamber. The air felt heavy with age; an arched ceiling curved thirty feet above and motes of dust danced in the green glow of the witchlights high overhead. He trod carefully along the silk carpet, watching it crumble to dust beneath his feet.

In ancient times the highborn of Naggaroth would come to pay respects to their ancestors in the houses of the dead. They would walk on rugs such as the one Malus now walked on and kneel before books such as the one before the prince's casket and read of the legendary feats of their forebears. They would be reminded of the glories that were lost when Nagarythe sank beneath the sea and they would swear powerful oaths of revenge in their ancestors' names. Once upon a time the warlords of the Witch King would make the long trek to the necropolis on the eve of war and invoke the spirits of the Old Kings, as the princes were sometimes called.

But those times were long gone, Malus thought. Ancient ways passed into obscurity. Tomes of great deeds went unread in sepulchral darkness and silk rugs crumbled to dust beneath the feet of a thief. Such was the way of things.

The highborn edged past the great tome and gingerly climbed onto the dais. There was little room on the platform, it being just wide enough to accommodate the prince's casket and Malus found himself grasping the marble rim to steady himself. Mere inches from the body of the dead prince, Malus could clearly see the long, black dagger clutched in Eleuril's gauntleted hands. Strange that he was laid to rest with the knife like that, he thought, reaching up to pry the hands apart. One would think he would have preferred a sword.

Malus's fingers touched the cold silver steel of the gauntlet – and Prince Eleuril screamed.

Terror raced along the highborn's spine as the prince's shrivelled eyes snapped open, revealing angry points of bluish light blazing in their black depths. The highborn recoiled and found himself fighting for balance on the edge of the dais, but before he could right himself the prince's body jerked to unnatural life and a gauntleted hand smashed against Malus's face.

The wight's strength was terrible, flinging Malus backward as though he were a child. He crashed through the lectern, knocking the great tome across the polished floor and landed with a crash between two of the knights' caskets. To Malus's horror, he saw that they, too, were rising from their silk beds, their eyes ablaze and jaws gaping with wordless cries of rage.

Malus got his feet underneath him and drew both of his swords as the undead knights leapt from their resting places with fearsome speed and attacked from both sides. Their long blades flashed like wands, faster than any living hand could wield them and the force of their blows almost drove Malus to his knees. Instead of giving ground, however, he counterattacked, feinting at the knight to his left and then spinning on one heel with a back-handed slash to the knight on his right. The highborn's sword caught the undead knight just above the hip; parchment skin and brittle bones snapped, tearing the tomb guardian in half.

Fierce and strong, but fragile, Malus noted with a savage grin as he turned his full attention to the remaining knight. He did so just in time to parry a crushing blow aimed at his chest. The highborn was pushed backwards by the force of the blow – and felt a cold hand close about his ankle. From where he lay on the floor the fallen knight smashed his sword into Malus's back, the blade biting into the highborn's armour and stunning him. Another blow from the second knight crashed into Malus's left arm, sending a jolt of burning pain running from wrist to shoulder and knocking the blade from his left hand.

With a feral snarl Malus stomped on the wrist clutching his ankle, shattering it beneath his heel, then brought back his foot and kicked the fallen knight's head from his shoulders. As the splintered body collapsed, the highborn threw himself against the second knight, unbalancing it and driving it back against its casket. Dust burst from the seams of its armour as Malus grabbed the knight's sword arm at the elbow and ripped it from its socket, then drove the hilt of his blade into the leering skull and sent it bouncing across the floor.

Two down, six to go, Malus thought, pushing himself off the crumbling body when a bony hand as hard as steel closed around the back of his neck. The highborn had just enough time to cry out in rage before Eleuril's wailing cry filled his ears and the Dagger of Torxus plunged into his side.

Chapter Nine
THE DAGGER'S PRICE

THE DAGGER OF Torxus bit deep and Malus Darkblade felt himself begin to die.

There was a horrible, wrenching pain that wracked him from head to toe and it felt as though a part of him had been torn loose, leaving him unmoored in his own skin. The highborn felt his heart stop and the blood begin to pool in his flesh. All strength left him – distantly he heard the ringing clatter of his sword falling to the stones – and then as darkness flowed like oil into his eyes it seemed like his body was shrivelling from within, the flesh turning black and hard like cured meat and his bones hardening to stone. It was as though the dagger was a shard of the Outer Darkness itself, drawing in every shred of heat and life he had left and leaving behind a misbegotten husk that was neither fully daemon nor fully man.

The last sound he heard was his own scream of pure, wordless horror.

HE AWOKE WITH a gasp, breathing in the dust of the grave.

Dry air rattled in his ravaged throat, provoking a spasm of coughing that sent dull pain throbbing from his side through his entire body. His eyes felt as hard as polished stones, brushed by leathery eyelids. Malus could not say if he was warm or cold; those sensations seemed foreign somehow, as though he were formed of wood or stone instead of pale flesh.

He lay on his back at the bottom of a high-walled casket, his head resting against satin cushions that crackled with age and stank faintly of corruption. His left leg was draped over the lip of the casket and felt heavy and numb. Malus wondered at the sensation, uncertain if the dead ever suffered the indignity of having a limb go to sleep. It seemed unlikely to his battered mind, so he was forced to accept the fact that he was somehow still alive. The damned prince had stabbed him with the dagger and then tossed him aside like a slaughtered rabbit.

It was silent and dark inside the tomb. The musty air was thick with the smell of spilt blood and entrails. Slowly, painfully, Malus raised his left hand. His muscles creaked like old leather as he closed his fingers on the lip of the casket's side and tried to pull himself upright. Even the faint caress of air against his face felt strange as his body struggled into a sitting position. With a start, it occurred to him that he couldn't feel the beating of his heart. Had the dagger transformed him into one of the unquiet dead, like the prince and his undead knights?

'But for me it would have, Malus,' the daemon said, the words rasping like saw teeth over Malus's bones. 'I saved you from an eternal prison even worse than my own.'

The highborn leaned against the wall of the casket and used both hands to pull his numb leg over and stretch it out beside the other. For a moment, the limb remained heavy and lifeless, but then little by little he felt a rash of pinpricks spread from knee to toes. Malus gritted his teeth at the pain, but was grateful that he could at least feel *something*. 'This is your fault, daemon,' the highborn grated. 'Were it not for you and your damnable quest I wouldn't even be here.'

'Were it not for you and your greed, you mean. No one made you put that ring on your finger, as I recall.'

Malus noticed that a greenish glow was slowly suffusing the chamber, as though the witchlights in the tomb were designed to wake in the presence of the living and he only grudgingly met their criteria. In the waxing light the highborn realised he lay in the middle of a battlefield: dozens of armoured corpses lay in twisted heaps around the marble caskets and the dais of the prince. Sightless eyes stared accusingly at Malus from pale, blood-flecked faces, their expressions contorted in grimaces of terror and pain.

It took several long moments for Malus to take it all in. As many as fifty men lay dead in the prince's tomb, hacked and torn by the swords of the undead knights, but in the end, victory lay on the side of the living. Not one of the prince's guardians could be seen and the prince himself was nothing more than a heap of tattered rags and splintered bones that some druchii had placed in an untidy pile at the foot of his upright casket.

'The dagger is gone,' Malus groaned. 'The survivors made off with it.' He didn't need to paw through the bodies to be sure. The men who'd pitched their tents in the square hadn't come to seek Eleuril's blessing, but to rob him. If they were gone it meant that the dagger had gone with them.

The highborn rubbed a hand over his face. His skin felt like boot leather. 'How long have I lain here?'

'A full day,' the daemon said. 'The dagger took every bit of life from you that wasn't already mine.'

'What does that mean?' Malus said.

'It means that you're the first mortal to survive the bite of the Reaper of Souls,' the daemon said. 'But only because you had no soul for it to take.'

'And for *that* I should be grateful to you?'

'The alternative was to become a tortured spirit, bound for all time to the spot where you were slain,' the daemon said. 'Compared to the cruel power of the dagger I am the most benign of tyrants.'

A hundred peevish comments bubbled to the surface of Malus's mind, but at that moment he felt too wretched to debate the issue. 'So Eleuril was indeed slain by the vengeful spirit of his wife?'

'Him and his knights as well?' Tz'arkan sneered. 'No, at the end of his life he allowed himself – and commanded his retainers – to be slain by the dagger in order to protect the druchii people from destruction. And he kept his vigil for millennia… until you came along, that is.'

'Vigil? What are you talking about?'

The daemon sighed. 'Eleuril took the dagger from a Slaaneshi warlock named Varcan, who had himself gone into the Wastes and claimed it from a Chaos warlord there. Varcan was seeking the blade because he'd uncovered a prophecy that warned of a soulless man, who would one day take up the dagger and consume the druchii in blood and fire. When Varcan was arrested by Eleuril's men, he swore to accept whatever punishments the prince deemed appropriate – so long as Eleuril would see to it that the dagger was kept safe. And the prince kept his word, even unto death. He was rather strange, as druchii went. Many thought him to be quite mad.'

'You knew this?' Malus cried. 'All along you knew I was walking into an ambush and you said nothing?'

'Why bother?' the daemon replied. 'It was just some old story about a prophecy. I thought you didn't believe in such things.'

The daemon's laughter was lost beneath a torrent of vicious curses as Malus climbed over the side of the casket and dropped onto the carpet of bodies littering the floor. The highborn was still invoking the wrath of every spirit he could name when he landed on his wounded side and passed out from the sudden explosion of fiery pain.

Some time later Malus's eyes fluttered open again. The first sensation he registered was the cold feeling of spilt blood staining his aching side. Slowly, gingerly he pulled himself upright. The laboured pulse in his temples was more of a thin tapping than the pounding of a drum. The highborn tried to inspect his wound, but could discern little with his armour on beyond the triangle-shaped hole the weapon had made in his breastplate. 'A vicious wound,' he hissed. 'Daemon, much as I hate it, you will have to heal this. It will not close on its own.'

'In time, Malus, in time,' Tz'arkan said. 'I have already been too generous with my gifts of late. I will replenish some of your strength, but you will have to wait for the rest.'

Malus felt the cold touch of the daemon spread through him and the pain lessened. His limbs regained some of their vigour and his heart ached as it laboured to greater life. The highborn took his mind off his wretched state by heaping still more curses on the daemon. Meanwhile, he began searching among the corpses for his swords.

It was only after turning over the eighth or ninth body that Malus realised something. He studied the face of the man he'd just moved, a chill racing down his spine. 'I know this wretch,' he said fearfully. 'His father is a member of the vaulkhar's personal retinue. These aren't Urial's men at all.'

The highborn knelt among the bodies, considering the implications. Who else could have raised so large a force *and* knew of Malus's interest in the dagger? After a moment, the answer was obvious. 'Isilvar,' he hissed, his voice full of dread.

'You suspect your other brother?' the daemon enquired.

'Of course,' Malus said. 'He has the money and the influence to raise such a warband and ample reason to oppose me.' The highborn nodded thoughtfully. He was also certain beyond any doubt that the hierophant of the Slaaneshi cult in Hag Graef was none other than Isilvar. Though he'd escaped the destruction of the cult, Malus had given Isilvar a terrible wound in his throat that would be a long time healing, if it ever did. 'He knew that I'd been to the temple in the north and that I was your… servant,' Malus admitted. 'It's possible he would also know about the relics and their power to free you.'

'Your logic is inescapable,' Tz'arkan said. Was there a hint of mockery in his voice? Malus couldn't be certain. 'The question is: what will you do about it?'

The highborn saw a familiar sword hilt glinting on the marble floor. He pulled the blade clear of the men lying upon it and used a fallen warrior's hair to wipe the sword clean. 'Clearly it would be a mistake to challenge Isilvar and his men on my own,' Malus said, sheathing his blade. 'I'll have to follow him back to the Hag and pay whatever price he asks in order to get the dagger from him.'

'A costly but prudent plan,' the daemon said approvingly. 'You are joking, of course.'

'Of course,' Malus said darkly. 'I'm going to run him down like a fox and hang his ears from my belt and if he gives me the dagger without too much trouble I might let him die with his manhood intact.'

'I expected no less,' Tz'arkan replied. 'If nothing else, Malus Darkblade, you can be counted on to react to adversity with as much violence as physically possible.'

IT WAS NEARLY dawn by the time Malus emerged from Eleuril's tomb. Every step to the base of the tower had been torture, pushing his ravaged body to the limit of endurance and beyond. By the time he staggered out into the empty square he was a haggard, shambling figure, his limbs working by virtue of sheer, burning hate and little else.

The tomb raiders had wasted no time breaking camp and had at least a day's ride head start. Malus assumed they would return to the Slavers' Road and head west, past the blood-soaked walls of Har Ganeth and onward to the safety of Hag Graef. He had no intention of letting Isilvar and his men make it that far.

More time was lost, however, before Malus could get Spite ready to travel. He found the cold one where he had left him, curled up within one of the empty buildings and noisily devouring a pair of horses. Judging by the saddles and tack that were still on the beasts, Malus deduced that the nauglir had succumbed to hunger and attacked the druchii column as it was leaving the necropolis. The cold one's hide was studded with more crossbow bolts, but the highborn knew better than to approach the warbeast until it had eaten its fill. When the nauglir had finally gorged itself, Malus was able to get to his pack and eat some of the dry rations he had left, washing the dried meat and bread down with two cups of bitter horse's blood. He still felt perilously weak and he reckoned there were days of hard riding ahead.

By mid-day Spite's wounds had been tended to and they started on the raiders' trail. The rain had finally slackened to a cold, clinging mist that distorted sounds and concealed distant objects behind a veil of thick fog. Malus drove the nauglir on in a steady, tireless lope; it was well into the night when the highborn was forced to call a halt. Though Spite could have kept going for many hours yet, Malus had felt his strength leaching away little by little as the day progressed, until he was no longer convinced he could stay in the saddle. He led the nauglir into the empty shell of a smithy and propped himself against Spite's scaly flank with both swords laid across his lap. Moments later he was asleep.

He awoke at dawn, only slightly more refreshed. His lap and the stone floor were stained with red. Somehow he'd opened the knife wound in his sleep and when he saw the congealing pool of blood Malus wondered how close he'd come to simply not waking up at all. It was all he could do to choke down another meal of dry rations before climbing back into the saddle and setting out again.

Malus spent the day delirious from blood loss and fatigue. Rain showers came and went, alternating with patches of weak grey sunlight that provided little warmth. The nauglir's rolling gait was hypnotic. All too often he would jerk himself from some blank reverie with a start and realise many miles had passed without him being any the wiser.

By the end of the day he had reached the far end of the valley. The entrance to the necropolis was a tall, free-standing gate, the pillars formed in the shape of two regal and forbidding dragons. The gate was carved in long, curving lines of those sinuous runes Malus remembered seeing in Eleuril's tomb; he wondered if there was a druchii alive anywhere in Naggaroth that could still read and write the dead language of Nagarythe.

Beyond the gate was a procession of statues, all worked in glossy black marble. They were carved in the image of tall, voluptuous druchii women, their naked bodies evoked in exquisite grace and detail. Long, curved talons grew from their fingertips and their sensuous mouths boasted terrible, leonine fangs. Malus supposed they represented guardian spirits from the forgotten myths of his people. They were forbidding figures and the highborn could not help but feel a sense of unease as he rode beneath their fearsome gaze.

The barrow road was made of the same black stone as the necropolis and was wide enough for two riders to travel abreast. Of the raiders there was no sign.

Malus pressed on after nightfall, determined to make up lost time, but as darkness gathered beneath the trees he found himself struggling to stay awake. He thought to try and swallow a little more dried meat, but after fumbling helplessly at the pack for several minutes he gave up. Before long he was leaning against the cantle, his head bobbing on his chest. The next thing Malus knew, he was lying on the grass beside the road. He hadn't felt it when he'd hit the ground. The highborn looked around for Spite, but the nauglir was gone. Part of his brain warned that he needed to get up and find the cold one, but instead he curled up in a ball and fell asleep.

He awoke hours later to the sound of crunching bones. Sunlight was streaming through the trees and Spite was resting on his haunches nearby, feasting on a boar he'd caught in the forest. When the warbeast was done with the carcass Malus crawled over and buried his face in the warm flesh, eating every scrap of meat he could reach. When he finally staggered to his feet his pointed chin was stained red and his chalk-white cheeks were streaked with black gore.

As the day wore on Malus felt more of his strength return, until by the evening he was alert enough to notice the abandoned lodge at the base of the mountain. It lay just to the side of the barrow road, with a view of both it and the Slavers' Road, less than fifty yards further south.

The highborn slid wearily from the saddle and inspected the ancient structure. There were signs it had been used only the day before: there was an intact fireplace sheltered by a large square of solid roof and even a pile of dry wood laid nearby.

The prospect of a warm fire and a roof to keep the rain away practically made Malus giddy with desire, but at the same time he knew that somewhere, farther down the road, the tomb raiders were settling into camp as well. If he didn't keep moving while they rested, he would never catch them. Shaking his head wearily, the highborn returned to Spite and headed west.

This time he was lucid enough to know when he'd gone as far as he was able and managed to find a crude traveller's shelter to huddle under out of the rain. He even took a chance on peeling away his breastplate and kheitan to get a good look at the wound Eleuril had given him. To his relief, the triangular puncture had squeezed shut, leaving behind an ugly, star-shaped scar. The daemon had managed to heal the ghastly wound, but it had evidently taken considerable time and effort. Even Tz'arkan's power had its limits, Malus noted, which elated him almost as much as the scar did.

As his strength gradually returned Malus increased his pace, riding on for hours after sunset until he was too weary to sit upright. He and Spite settled into a routine of sorts: when the highborn could go no further he would lead the nauglir into the tree line bordering the north side of the road and find a black oak or a pine to shelter beneath. With the last of his strength he would unsaddle Spite and turn him loose to hunt and by morning he would have a meal of fresh, bloody meat awaiting him. It was just enough to keep him going, drawing ever closer to the raiders and their plunder.

By the end of the third day on the Slavers' Road, Spite caught the scent of horses. The change in the cold one's manner brought Malus from his weary reverie and he reined the warbeast in as he studied the course of the road ahead. In the far distance along the curve of the coast, Malus could see the square towers of Har Ganeth, the City of Executioners. Even leagues away, the sight sent a chill down the highborn's spine. Much closer, perhaps only a few miles away on the other side of a series of rolling hills, Malus saw the very top of a single, narrow tower – Vaelgor Keep, one of the dozens of despatch-forts that lined the Slavers' Road. Tendrils of smoke rose in twisting plumes around the spire – camp fires, the highborn reasoned, enough for a large band of druchii.

Night was drawing on. The rain had stopped for the time being and even the heavy grey overcast had broken into scudding clouds, driven by a mild wind from the west. The slate-coloured hills were tinged with deep orange by the setting sun and the Sea of Malice was dark as raw iron. Weak and hollow as he felt, Malus's heartbeat quickened at the thought that his prey was finally within reach. The highborn slid from the saddle and began to formulate his plan.

A SINGLE FULL moon shone heavy and golden just above the eastern horizon, gleaming against a backdrop of tattered cloud. The wind continued to whisper out of the west, hissing over the sharp edges of the slate hills. Sounds from the encampment carried clearly to Malus from where he hid in the thick trees on the north side of the Slavers' Road: men talked and cursed over games of dice, or hissed quiet laughter over cups of wine as they sat around one of the many watch-fires. Horses whickered nervously in the despatch-fort's corral and hammers rang against steel as craftsmen at the fort went to work patching armour and weapons for the visiting warband.

As near as Malus could tell, there were at least a hundred men camped outside the tower – low-ranking warriors and the staff of the fort itself, ejected from their tower to make room for their highborn guests. There were no standards flying within the camp, announcing the identity of the warband, an unusual practice, but not unheard of. Malus suspected that Isilvar had no desire to advertise his movements, possibly hoping to return to the Hag before anyone even suspected he was gone.

The daemon chuckled coldly. 'You stand upon the threshold, Malus. Will you take the fateful step?'

Malus paused, his face twisting into a scowl. 'What are you talking about, daemon?'

For a moment Tz'arkan lay silent, then: 'You were angered when I did not tell you of Eleuril and his prophecy. There is a prophecy at work here as well. Do you wish to hear it?'

Malus's fists clenched. 'You know what will happen when I enter the tower?'

'Oh, yes. The threads were woven centuries ago, Darkblade. Many, many twists and turns of fate have brought you to this point.' Malus could sense a slow revealing of pointed teeth as the daemon smiled, savouring his discomfort. 'Shall I tell you?'

'It matters not,' Malus snapped. 'I will go into the tower regardless of what you say – if I don't have the dagger, my soul is forfeit! So amuse me. What waits for me there?'

The daemon's reply was a whisper, like the intimate voice of a lover. 'Ruin,' it said into his ear. 'It is here that all your plans will be undone.'

A chill raced along Malus's spine. For a long moment he was too stunned to speak. 'You're lying,' he finally managed to say.

'Why would I do that?' the daemon said. 'Have I lied to you yet, Darkblade? I'm giving you a gift, warning you of the precipice ahead. You can turn aside and save yourself if you choose.'

'You know I cannot!' the highborn raged, snarling under his breath. 'If I wait any longer the tomb raiders will be under the protection of Har Ganeth and then later Naggorond itself! I must strike tonight!'

'Then you must accept your fate – as it was foretold long ago,' the daemon said. 'The stage is set, Darkblade. Go and play your role.'

Tz'arkan's laughter echoed in Malus's head as he broke from the trees and crept through the shadows towards the tower. With every step it felt as though a noose was tightening around his throat, but still he continued, determined to succeed.

AT THE EDGE of the encampment, just beyond the light of the watch-fires, Malus crouched on his heels and studied the route he would take through the camp to the doors of the tower. There were few druchii milling about; many were settled down eating, drinking or gambling after another long day's march.

Malus eyed the moon overhead. Its glow waxed and waned as streamers of cloud blew across its face. After a few moments another tattered shroud of grey fell over the shining orb and the camp was plunged into deep shadow. The highborn closed a hand on the hilt of his sword. It was time. Malus pulled his hood over his face and drew his dark cloak tight around his shoulders, then crept forward.

He passed like a ghost through the camp, his steps so light that they were lost in the rustling of the wind. Most of the men in camp took no notice of him at all. A few caught a glimpse of a dark shape moving at the edge of their vision, but when they looked up from their meals or their dice they saw only darkness.

Malus was across the camp in the space of a few minutes, nestled deep in the shadow of the tower itself. The keep was a tall, square-topped structure, dominated by a round, stained-glass window near the top. Clearly the fort was popular among warlords as a stopover during raids into the mountains to the north.

Moving quietly and swiftly, Malus edged up to the keep's thick black oak doors. Beyond, he could dimly hear the sounds of revelry. The highborn laid a grimy hand against the dark wood and pushed. It was clearly bolted against the night. Very well, he thought grimly, casting his eyes upwards once more.

By the time he'd climbed the three storeys to reach the great window, his limbs were trembling with exertion. Summoning the last dregs of his bitter hate he drew his blades and pressed himself against the panes of red and cobalt glass. He could see the keep's main hall below, dominated by the dim outline of the master's table. There were figures seated there, eating or sipping wine. At the head of the table, a figure rose from his chair, holding an object aloft. The warlord's voice filled the hall, rising blurrily to Malus's ears.

'The fabled Dagger of Torxus is ours! Our names will be inscribed in the roll of honour in Khaine's own temple upon our return!'

The cheers of the men filled Malus with a fiery rage and he threw himself against the window. The window panes shattered and the highborn leapt like a lion into the hall. 'No, they will be inscribed on mortuary urns!' he declared as he landed in a shower of coloured glass.

Shouts of alarm and the crashing of chairs filled the hall as half a dozen highborn retainers leapt to their feet. Swords hissed from their scabbards. Then the man at the head of the table turned to face Malus, his regal expression one of shock and anger entwined.

The warlord met Malus's eyes and the highborn felt the icy knife of recognition punch into his heart.

The warlord fixed Malus with a furious glare. 'Who dares intrude here?'

'I do,' Malus heard himself say. The words came out in a tortured growl as the highborn choked back his dismay. He wanted nothing more than to flee the firelit hall, but it was too late for that now. The die was cast.

The warlord's eyes widened as he studied the sword-wielding figure before him. 'You... you are druchii! One of us! What has happened to you?'

Malus paused, his brow furrowing. Then he realised how he must look – a gaunt, haggard figure, covered in layers of dried blood and grime. 'Who cares?' He pointed to the dagger in the warlord's hand. *'That* is all I am interested in. The Dagger of Torxus – I spent weeks searching for it, only to find that your warband had already looted it.' Malus sheathed his sword and took a step forward, extending his hand. 'Give it to me.'

The warlord looked at the dagger, then considered Malus's out-stretched hand. His eyes widened as he saw the thick, black veins pulsing beneath the highborn's skin, then a look of shock passed over his face as his gaze fell upon the ruby cabochon gleaming dully from Malus's index finger.

'Wait... I know you now,' he said suddenly. The warlord looked more closely at Malus's face – and his expression dissolved into a look of blackest rage. 'Malus. *Malus!*' he cried. 'What are you doing here?'

It was all slipping from his hands. All his careful plans and secret ambitions; he could feel them tumbling from his grasp. Malus drew his second sword and rushed at the warlord with a howl of rage.

The warlord's face went pale. 'Stop him! In the name of Khaine, stop him!' he commanded and his retainers leapt to obey.

The warriors were flush with wine and overconfident in their numbers. They expected Malus to give ground at their approach, but he threw himself at them like a wounded wolf. The first man barely got his blade up in time to parry a savage cut to his face – Malus knocked the warrior's blade aside and thrust his other sword into the retainer's neck. Bright blood sprayed from the wound and the man fell, choking on his own fluids.

Blows rained upon Malus from every direction. A sword crashed against his back and rebounded from his armour, another bit a notch from his left ear. The highborn blocked a thrust to his shoulder and brought his other blade down on the attacker's wrist. The master-forged blade sheared through the jointed wrist and sent the retainer's hand spinning across the chamber. Sensing an opening, another warrior leapt in from Malus's left, stabbing for his arm. The blade struck between two armour plates and scored a deep wound across the highborn's bicep. Without thinking, Malus slashed his blade across the man's eyes with a backhanded stroke. 'Aghhh! My face! My face!' the man screamed, reeling away from the fight.

A sword crashed into Malus's right shoulder, knocking him sideways – saving him from the second man's blade, which tore a ragged gash in the highborn's scalp instead of splitting his skull. Malus felt hot blood spill down the side of his face as he threw himself against the warrior to his right. The retainer tried to forestall the highborn with a cut to Malus's neck, but the highborn blocked it with his left-hand blade and crashed headlong into the man, knocking him to the floor. Before the warrior could recover the highborn stomped on the retainer's groin and then cut the man's agonised scream short with a thrust through his right eye.

Malus jerked his blade free and spun in time to meet the charge of the last warrior. The retainer aimed a flurry of blows at the highborn's head and neck, driving him backwards across the hall. Malus blocked each stroke with swift slashes of his right-hand blade, holding back his left-hand sword like a viper poised to strike. The warrior steadily beat his way through the highborn's guard, scoring a cut on Malus's cheek – and then his foot came down on a spilled goblet and he stumbled. The highborn checked his retreat and thrust with his left-hand sword, taking the retainer in the throat. Two feet of red steel jutted from the back of the man's neck, severing the spine, and the retainer collapsed lifelessly to the floor.

The highborn's sword rang on bone as he tore it free from the warrior's neck. A sudden movement at the corner of his eye made Malus turn, raising his blade just in time as the warlord swung his broad blade at Malus's chest. 'May the inferno take you, you scum!' the warlord cried. The point of the warlord's blade struck the highborn in the right arm and found an unprotected gap between vambrace and pauldron. Malus scarcely felt the blade slice through his flesh.

The warlord redoubled his attack, slashing furiously at Malus's chest. The highborn leapt backwards out of the sword's reach. The sword flashed at Malus's face and this time he was able to strike the flat of the heavy blade and knock it aside. As it was, he was being driven steadily backwards, towards the far end of the hall. The druchii hammered at Malus without pause, berserk with rage.

The warlord let out an anguished roar and leapt at Malus, his sword held in a two-handed grip above his head. The movement drew the man's breastplate up and away, opening a narrow gap in his overlapping armour. Without thinking, Malus dropped to one knee and thrust forward with all his strength. The point of the sword hit the mail covering the warlord's abdomen and split the rings neatly apart. The weight of the druchii's charge did the rest. He drove himself full onto Malus's sword, sinking down its razor-edged length almost to the hilt. The warlord groaned, falling to his knees.

Numb with despair, Malus put his boot against the warlord's chest and pulled his sword free. Dark blood poured from the wound in a torrent. The druchii stared dumbly at the gore staining his palms, then looked up at the highborn.

'Why, Malus, why?' he asked, his mind already succumbing to shock.

The highborn's hand tightened on the hilt of his sword. 'I do what I must,' he replied. 'Goodbye, father,' he said bitterly, then struck the warlord's head from his shoulders.

Lurhan's body toppled to the stone floor. Malus stared at the corpse and tasted ashes in his mouth. How many times had he longed for such a moment? In his dreams the scene had always played out as a triumph, not a tragedy.

Malus bent down and pulled the dagger from Lurhan's belt. He'd gained the relic, but at the cost of his own life. He was an outlaw now.

The highborn felt the daemon stir within him. 'Father?' Tz'arkan said, his voice thick with feigned shock. 'Malus, did you just kill your own father?'

'I got the relic you wanted, didn't I?' he snarled, half-sick with rage and dismay.

I had no choice, he thought fiercely. *I had no choice!*

Chapter Ten
THE WOUNDED WOLF

MALUS FELT THE floor beneath him tremble as a heavy weight crashed to the ground several floors below the main hall and faint cries of alarm began echoing up the keep's central staircase. The highborn whirled, catching sight of a trail of bright crimson leading across the hall and down the tower stair. A quick count showed that one of the vaulkhar's retainers was missing – the man whose hand Malus had severed early in the fight. The warrior had summoned his courage and staggered downstairs to throw open the doors and warn the camp that their lord had been killed.

The highborn let out a feral snarl as reason warred with animal desperation. The only way out was back the way he'd come. He glanced back at the shattered window. 'Daemon!' he cried. 'Lend me your strength. Hurry!'

'You are too greedy, little druchii!' Tz'arkan replied. 'Your veins are already black with my touch and you would have still more?'

'Enough of your mockery!' The highborn got a running start and leapt to the window sill. He barely reached it, his muscles weak from the bite of druchii swords. A cool wind blew against his face, its touch deceptively warm compared to the chill that emanated from his bones. Black night yawned beneath him. Three storeys below, figures with naked steel in their hands charged across the fort's open square and disappeared into the keep. Malus leaned out into that perilous gulf, his weak fingers straining to keep purchase on the narrow window frame. 'Will you give me what I desire, daemon, or shall I simply flap my wings and hope to fly?'

'It matters not to me–' the daemon began.

'Liar!' Malus snapped. 'I hold three of the five relics in my hand, you damnable fiend! If I die here this mob will claim them and they will be scattered once again! This is not just my life you toy with, but your own freedom as well. So help me – or resign yourself to another millennium of captivity!'

An enraged cry reverberated in Malus's head – but at the same time a trickle of icy vigour spread painfully through his limbs. Strength returned and the world snapped back into crystalline focus. Just as the first of Lurhan's men lumbered clumsily into the hall, Malus swung from the window frame and leapt lightly to a narrow ledge several feet away. Like a spider he descended down the walls of the keep as the retainers searched the hall above in a vain attempt to avenge their lord.

LURHAN'S SURVIVING RETAINERS were all virtuous men – or perhaps they feared the consequences of returning to the Hag without the head of the vaulkhar's killer. By the time Malus had made his way back to Spite, the air shivered with the cries of hunting horns as the warband set itself upon his trail.

After running the three miles back to his mount, Malus was in no shape to be stealthy. He crashed through the underbrush, slapping aside branches and lumbering through vines as he raced for the nauglir's hiding place. It was only the slow, rumbling hiss emanating from the small clearing up ahead that brought the highborn up short. In the darkness beneath the trees Malus could just see the shape of the cold one, its shoulders hunched and its head low to the ground. He'd startled the nauglir with his sudden approach, the highborn realised. Another step and he might have been bitten in half.

'It's me, Spite,' Malus said. He folded his arms and tucked in his head, making himself appear smaller and less threatening. 'Calm yourself. We have some hard riding ahead of us tonight.'

He took a step forward. Spite hissed again, louder this time. Malus's eyes widened. Something's wrong, he thought. The beast doesn't recognise me.

Nauglir were famously stupid creatures, but Spite was a rare exception – being a runt compared to other cold ones, the warbeast had survived in the caverns by being cleverer and more vicious than his kin. It's the daemon, Malus thought. He smells the cursed spirit's corruption on me.

Moving slowly and carefully, Malus reached back to a small pouch on his belt and drew out a tiny bottle of dark blue glass. Pulling the stopper free, he poured a dollop of clear, acrid liquid onto his palm and wiped the thick fluid over his face and hands. The vrahsha stung where it touched his skin, then within moments the highborn's exposed flesh was cold and numb. Cold without as within, the highborn thought bitterly.

Malus replaced the vial. Spite had not moved a muscle, still regarding him threateningly. The highborn took another step forward. Spite hissed again, then sniffed the air experimentally. The highborn saw the nauglir's posture relax slightly. 'That's it,' he said, taking another step forward. 'It's *me*, you great fool. Now can we go?'

The beast sidled closer to Malus, extending his drooling muzzle. Malus held out his hand and the nauglir sniffed at it with one huge nostril. After a moment, the cold one straightened, but Malus could tell that Spite wasn't entirely convinced. One day no amount of vrahsha in the world will disguise the daemon's stink, Malus thought grimly. What will I do then?

A hunting horn wailed off to the west – less than a mile away, to Malus's ear. He knew that they would have to have senses like an autarii to find his trail, even in the moonlight, but if their horses caught the scent of the nauglir and panicked, that would give him away just as readily. The problem was, he couldn't go back east, towards Karond Kar, not after the mess he'd left there. Heading due north, into the mountains, meant risking another encounter with the shades. To the west lay Hag Graef and his men, plus a fortune in gold. But he had to slip past Lurhan's men first.

Malus bit back a curse and considered his options. None of them were very good. The road was out of the question, for the moment. The only choice he had was to work his way through the forest, leading Spite by the reins and paralleling the road. Once he was past the despatch-fort, he could risk returning to the road and riding like a madman for the Hag. If he could arrive in the city ahead of the news of Lurhan's death, he could gather men and gold and…

The highborn's thoughts ground to a halt. 'And then what?' he said to himself. 'Where will I go? Once the drachau – and the Witch King – learn of what I've done, there will be no city in Naggaroth that will harbour me.'

Life was cheap in the Land of Chill and any man could die by another's hand except for the chosen servants of Malekith himself. That included each of the drachau of the six cities and their vaulkhar; they lived and died at the pleasure of the Witch King and no one else. To spill their blood was to invite a blood feud with Malekith himself and by extension the entire druchii people.

The highborn's lips twisted in a bitter smile. 'Perhaps I'll let Tz'arkan and Malekith fight for the privilege of tormenting me,' he said to Spite as he took the beast's reins and led the nauglir deeper into the forest. 'Who knows? Maybe they'll destroy one another and I'll claim Naggorond for my own.'

It grew steadily darker as the night wore on; the scudding clouds thickened, swallowing the bright moon and the air turned cold. For hours Malus led Spite through the dense forest, attempting to stay parallel to the coast road. From time to time he had to stop and leave the warbeast while he attempted to locate the tree line and regain his bearings.

The clamour around the fort never lapsed; horns and shouted orders echoed up and down the road all through the night as Lurhan's vengeful retainers tried to find his trail. Malus led the way past the despatch fort well after midnight. By dawn he reckoned he'd covered only a few more miles to the west, but the cold air had brought a thick wall of fog rolling in from the sea, muffling sounds and shrouding the keep in a mantle of grey. Weariness and pain made the decision easier for Malus. He could barely put one foot in front of another after spending almost the entire night struggling through the dense wood, so the risks of the open road seemed almost welcoming by comparison.

Spite was eager to be out of the confusing environs of the forest and set off at a rapid trot down the Slavers' Road. Malus clung tightly to the reins and fought to stay awake. He'd lash himself to the saddle if that's what it took. Lurhan's men had been searching all night; they and their horses had to be almost as tired as he was. Every hour the nauglir spent on the road meant another league or more between them and the keep.

The white fog made it difficult to hear anything, much less see beyond twenty yards or so. At first the change of pace lent Malus an extra burst of energy and alertness, but after half an hour his eyelids grew heavy. He shook his head fiercely, trying to keep awake. Every hour is another league, he reminded himself again and again, like a temple prayer.

Malus was so lost in his fight against the pull of sleep that he did not hear the horses' hooves until it was far too late.

The horsemen materialised out of the fog directly in Malus's path, moving along the road at a weary trot; three riders travelling abreast, their spears laid back against their shoulders and their horses' heads drooping from weariness. Lurhan's men were no fools. They had hedged their bets by sending search parties in either direction down the Slavers' Road and Malus had ridden full onto the western search party.

Malus and the retainers saw one another at the same instant. Mouths dropped and eyes widened in shock, but for a moment not a word was spoken. They stared at one another in a kind of fearful wonder, as though they'd crossed paths with a ghost in the morning fog. Then the wind stiffened and Spite caught the scent of horseflesh and the nauglir shattered the stillness with a thunderous roar.

The horses reared and pawed at the air at the sound of the nauglir's bellow, but they did not panic – these were well-trained warhorses, conditioned to the presence of the fearsome cold ones. It was all the advantage Malus would get and he seized upon it, drawing his sword and putting his heels to Spite's flanks with a savage war scream.

Spite responded at once, leaping at the closest horse and rider, who saw his doom approaching and raised his spear to stab for the cold one's eye. The horseman's thrust was strong, but his rearing horse threw off his aim and the point of the spear raked along the cold one's snout instead. The retainer cursed and drew back for another strike, but by then the nauglir was upon them, closing its powerful jaws on horse and rider both. Man and animal shrieked as one as dagger-like teeth sheared through flesh and bone. The horse collapsed, its spine broken, and the rider tried to drag himself clear of the thrashing animal, leaving a trail of torn intestines in his wake.

Horsemen rushed at Malus from left and right. Having recovered from their initial shock, Lurhan's chosen warriors reacted with speed, skill and ferocity. Malus twisted in his saddle, knocking aside a spear thrust on his left side with a sweep of his blade, then parrying the spear on his right with a lightning-fast backhand stroke. The horseman on Malus's left continued past the highborn, angling for a spear thrust to his back, while the horseman on the right pressed his attack, jabbing his spear at the highborn's face.

Thinking quickly, Malus jerked on the reins and jabbed his right heel hard into the nauglir's ribs. On command, the warbeast whipped to the right – slamming its powerful tail into the horse on its left flank. The animal went end-over-end, its front legs snapped like kindling and the horseman went down beneath his crippled steed. Meanwhile Spite lunged for the horse to his right, closing his jaws on the animal's neck.

The bitten horse went mad with pain and fear, its eyes showing nothing but white as the animal tried to escape the reptile's jaws. The horseman snarled a furious oath and drove his spear deep into the cold one's neck. A jolt of fear went through Malus, but he saw at once that the spear had missed the cold one's vitals – it was a dreadful wound but not a fatal one. He leaned forward as far as he could and hacked at the shaft of the spear, breaking it with two swift strokes.

The retainer threw the splintered shaft at Malus's head and reached for his own sword – but at that moment Spite's muscular body gave a single, convulsive wrench and tore the horse's head from its neck. The animal toppled, spraying Malus with hot, bitter blood. The highborn

let out a triumphant yell and kicked Spite into a gallop, leaning down
to take a passing swipe at the unhorsed retainer as they leapt over him
and raced west down the Slavers' Road. Malus spared a single glance
backwards to see that he'd failed to do the last retainer any serious
harm, then turned back to inspect Spite's spear wound.

Dark shapes materialised out of the fog just ahead. Malus had just
enough time to notice the five druchii standing in a rough line across
the road before their leader shouted 'Fire!' and the crossbow bolts
struck home.

At such close range it was impossible for skilled crossbowmen to
miss. Spite let out an angry roar and stumbled as a bolt thudded into
his muscular chest. The bellow masked the sounds of the three bolts
that slammed into Malus – one pierced his left pauldron, penetrating
shoulder plate and breastplate alike just below his collar bone, while
another struck his left side, just below his ribs. The third bolt smashed
into his right calf, just below the knee. By a cruel turn of fate the point
hit a small dent and found enough purchase to penetrate the armour
plate instead of hitting a more rounded portion and glancing away.

There was no pain. Partly due to the vrahsha, partly due to the shock
of so many blows, for a few heartbeats he felt nothing and his mind
was eerily clear. He saw the men scatter out of Spite's path, already
reloading their weapons. Beyond them, standing in a protective knot
on the north side of the road, waited the retainer's horses. Malus
pulled on the reins, angling Spite for the animals and the battle-
frenzied cold one eagerly obeyed. Without riders to steady them, the
horses went wild at the nauglir's charge, scattering in every direction
before the reptile's gaping jaws.

Malus used a combination of knee and rein to aim his mount at a
horse fleeing west, noticing with a curious detachment that the bolt in
his shoulder had locked the armour plates together, effectively pinning
his arm. Ahead, the horse was in full flight, ears back and tongue hanging out as it galloped for its life ahead of the hissing warbeast. Slowly
but surely the distance between the animals lengthened; nauglir were
tireless and tough as stones, but they were not very swift. Not that
Malus cared, all that mattered was plunging as far into the concealing
fog as possible before the crossbowmen could shoot again.

A hasty shot from one of the crossbowmen buzzed through the air
to Malus's right. He bent low in the saddle, breathless from the mounting pain. His eyes focused on a steel ring set on a swivel on the cantle
of his saddle – in battle the cold one's reins were fed through the ring
to keep them laid close to the reptile's neck and thus harder to grab or
cut.

Malus fumbled for the sword belt, numbly grasping the slack portion and began feeding it through the ring. With an effort of will he

took the threaded end and tucked it through the tightened portion of his belt, making a loop.

He heard Spite hiss in frustration as the horse was swallowed by the fog ahead of them. Malus took a deep breath and pulled the belt loop taut, then lost consciousness in an explosion of fiery pain.

MALUS AWOKE TO the cold touch of rain on his cheek.

He opened his eyes and saw the pewter surface of the Sea of Malice off in the distance, veiled by shifting curtains of rainfall. They were no longer moving, he realised after a moment and a surge of alarm sharpened his senses and lent a fleeting burst of strength to his limbs. Slowly, cautiously, he pushed himself upright, noticing belatedly that he had been slumped almost the entire way out of the saddle, held tenuously in place by less than six inches of belt leather.

The pain hit, starting with his leg. Malus let out an involuntary moan as he continued to push himself back into the saddle. Streaks of dark, dried blood covered the entire left side of his armour, from shoulder to knee. He'd been out for some time. Malus looked to the sky, trying to gauge the position of the sun in the middle of a rainstorm. It felt like the afternoon, but in his state he couldn't be certain.

First things first, he thought, steeling his resolve. At least the bolts had armour-piercing heads, meaning they were tapered instead of broad and barbed.

He reached down to the bolt jutting from his calf, gripping it carefully. Malus took a deep breath, gritted his teeth and pulled.

The bolt came free in a spurt of fresh blood and breathtaking agony. Malus's vision swam, but he closed his eyes and breathed deeply until the moment passed. Then he turned his attention to the bolts in his side.

Once he'd drawn the bolts free, he stopped to try and take stock. Neither of the bolts that had hit his torso had penetrated deeply, particularly the shot that had hit his shoulder. The wound in the calf, however, was another matter. It had gone deep into the muscle and hurt more than the other two wounds put together.

'Tz'arkan,' Malus said through gritted teeth. 'Aid me.'

The daemon did not reply.

Malus cursed bitterly, calling upon Tz'arkan again and again, but the daemon would not answer him. Had he drawn too much from the daemon's well of power? For a few, fleeting moments he dared hope that Tz'arkan was gone entirely, unable to maintain his grip on Malus's soul. One glance at the ring around his finger and the black veins pulsing like worms along the back of his hand quickly dashed any such hopes. In the end the highborn was forced to fall back on a desperate measure that cold one knights had used for centuries. He drew out his bottle of vrahsha and poured a tiny amount of the toxin into each wound. The injuries were numbed in an instant and the highborn breathed a shaky sigh of relief. Using the nauglir slime to treat wounds was fraught with risk – infections, madness and death were real possibilities each and every time he used the toxin on an open wound – but at the moment the benefits actually outweighed the risks. If he wasn't on the move soon he was dead anyway.

Moving carefully, Malus lowered himself from the saddle and hobbled on his good leg as he checked Spite's wounds. The stab wound to the nauglir's throat was deep but would heal in time. The crossbow bolt had been torn free at some point – Malus suspected that the cold one had clawed the aggravating thing loose – and had left a ragged wound that could cause problems if it wasn't tended. At the highborn's urging the cold one rose easily to its feet, which was an encouraging sign. If a cold one could stand, it could also run.

The highborn pulled a water skin from his saddle bags and took a long drink, then tried to find his bearings. They were much closer to Har Ganeth now. Malus had a full view of the ominous city and its blood-streaked walls. Looking back, the despatch fort was nowhere to be seen, lost in the rain and the rolling hills.

Lurhan's men were out there, drawing nearer. He was certain that the survivors of the search party would have raced back to the fort and roused the tired camp. But the winded horses wouldn't make good time today, especially with the rain, so he had at least a few hours' lead to decide what to do next.

Har Ganeth offered no safe haven. No sane man set foot in the City of Executioners if he valued his life. And if his suspicions were right and Urial had fled there with Yasmir, he would only be trading one noose for another.

After four more days' ride west the Slavers' Road met the Spear Road in the shadow of Naggorond, seat of Malekith himself. Malus suppressed a shudder. Better to try his luck in Har Ganeth than shelter behind the Witch King's walls!

What did that leave? Hag Graef lay three days south along the Spear Road. Silar waited there with Hauclir and the rest of his men and enough gold to flee Naggaroth if he wished. But that would be where Lurhan's men would expect him to go; worse still, seven days on the road would give them a good chance of overtaking him with their faster mounts. Malus had no illusions as to what would happen then. He was in no shape to stand, much less fight. And he would sooner cut his own throat and be damned than be marched to the Hag in chains.

That left the desolate, icy north. If he could reach the Spear Road ahead of Lurhan's men he could throw them off his trail by heading for the Wastes. But what then? There was nothing between Naggorond and the border watchtowers except… Malus straightened, his brow furrowing in thought.

'Do I dare?' he asked aloud. 'They have no love for Lurhan or Hag Graef, that's for certain, but no love for me, either. Still, I can claim ties of blood, which may be enough…'

A plan began to take shape in Malus's mind. The chances of success were slim, but far better than the other options at hand.

It took him three tries, but after several agonising minutes Malus was able to climb back into the saddle. He gathered up Spite's reins in his good hand. 'Up, Spite!' he ordered and the nauglir obeyed. 'We've a long ride ahead, but there will be a stable and good, warm horse meat at the end! We ride north, where Lurhan's men won't dare to follow. Malekith himself has seen to that. It is high time I met my uncle; with Lurhan dead I expect he and I will have quite a bit to talk about.'

With a tug of the reins and a touch of Malus's heels Spite lurched into motion, his long, tireless stride carrying them swiftly west. The highborn set his jaw and decided to press on through the night, pushing the nauglir to the limit of its endurance in order to reach the crossroads ahead of his pursuers. Once he was on the road north, Lurhan's men were welcome to follow him – in fact, their presence would be most helpful.

Lost in his schemes, Malus raced down the Slavers' Road, heading for the icy wastes and the Black Ark of Naggor, the realm of Balneth Bale.

Chapter Eleven
THE HATEFUL ROAD

AYS PASSED; HOW many days Malus could no longer say for certain. There were times when he couldn't even say for sure whether it was day or night.

There was no rest, no pause in his flight from Lurhan's men. The vaulkhar's vengeful retainers were faster on their horses, so Malus simply never stopped for more than a few minutes at a time. Spite loped along tirelessly, the cold one's broad, flat feet slapping along the black stones of the Slavers' Road and Malus slipped in and out of consciousness, delirious from blood loss and fatigue.

They passed Har Ganeth in the night, close enough to hear the wails of the sacrificial mobs within the city walls. The scent of blood was so strong in the air, even more than a mile distant, that Malus had to fight to keep the nauglir on the roadway. The highborn had to fight a three-mile contest of wills with the one-ton warbeast until they were finally upwind of the charnel city.

Things became blurry not long after the food ran out. Spite, Malus knew, could run for a week on the meat it had killed and eaten on the road, but the highborn wasn't so fortunate. Nor could he afford to let the cold one spend an entire night hunting in the wood. Each morning and evening Malus would study the road back the way they'd come and measure the pall of dust kicked up by his pursuers and by the end of the day it was clear that the swifter hunters had all but erased any gains the highborn had made during the night before. It was all he could do just to stay out of the jaws of the vaulkhar's hounds.

During the long hours in the saddle he would invoke Tz'arkan's name and call upon the daemon's power to heal him. There was never any reply. The highborn cursed the daemon, calling it a coward and a weakling, but the serpents never so much as stirred around Malus's labouring heart.

Three days and two nights past Har Ganeth Malus was jerked from dreamless oblivion by Spite's threatening growl. The highborn reeled in the saddle, thinking irrationally that the nauglir had stopped by the side of the road to sleep and Lurhan's men had caught him, until he heard the faint sounds of wailing hanging in the night air.

Malus gripped the reins with white-knuckled hands, realising as soon as he saw the tall black stakes rising into the night sky ahead that he'd reached the great crossroads where the Spear and Slavers' Roads met. Bodies in varying states of decomposition were lashed to the forty-foot stakes, their limbs stretched and bones broken as they were wrapped around the unforgiving poles and held there with metal wire. Nearly all of them were limned with a guttering, greenish fire that pooled in sightless eye sockets and gaping mouths.

Some of the bodies had hung on the stakes for days; others had endured for years, worn away by slow inches by the ravages of wind and ice. Each of them had been highborn once, many of them more prominent and powerful than Malus had ever been. Each one had broken one of the Witch King's laws and now their spirits glimmered in agony as their bodies were consumed by the merciless Land of Chill.

Even Spite sensed the pall of undying pain hanging over the crossroads, snapping irritably at the chill air. There waits my own fate, Malus suddenly realised. The things Lurhan's men will do to me would be a kindness compared to Malekith's judgement.

Then he remembered the daemon and his delirious mind once again conjured the image of the Witch King and Tz'arkan wrestling for possession of an outcast's soul. Laughing wildly, Malus put his heels to Spite's flanks and trotted among the forest of wailing figures. In the distance off to the west the highborn could see the fortress city of Naggorond, its black spires painted with cold witchlight. A white ribbon of roadway gleamed under the moonlight, winding a sinuous path to the dread city from the western side of the crossroads. Made from the skulls of Aenarion's cursed kin, the Hateful Road ran to Naggorond alone and many druchii who were called upon to walk that path never came back. On impulse, Malus drew his sword and raised it to the distant fortress in mocking salute, then spurred his mount northwards. Let them come for me now if they dare, he thought wildly. They'll have to deal with the black ark first.

TWO DAYS NORTH of the crossroads Malus saw the first signs of ice. His breath made great plumes of mist in the cold air and the wind felt like a blessing against his feverish skin.

He'd been applying the vrahsha daily to his wounds since the fight near Vaelgor Keep. Without the toxin's numbing effects he doubted he could have stayed conscious for even one day of hard riding, let alone nearly a week. The toxic slime was even fairly effective at killing mortified flesh, but there had been no time to keep the wounds clean while travelling and at some point they had become infected.

There was no way to know for certain how close he was to the black ark, but there was no point in stopping – he had neither the knowledge nor the materials to treat the wounds properly. All he could do was ride on and hope that rot didn't take hold. If that happened, Spite would turn on him as soon as he became too weak to assert himself. He was in a race not only against Lurhan's men, but against his own failing body as well.

He reeled drunkenly in the saddle and bellowed curses at the daemon for hours on end, but Tz'arkan had forsaken him.

Worse, it seemed that the vaulkhar's retainers were closing the distance. For a while Malus discounted the evidence of his own senses, blaming it on his fever. Every morning the highborn forced himself to turn in the saddle and stare southward, looking for signs of camp fires and since turning north the thin tendrils of smoke seemed a little closer each day.

It was only after Malus passed the third despatch fort on the road that he realised what was happening; the retainers had become desperate enough to begin buying or commandeering fresh mounts at each fort they passed. That would allow them to ride much longer and faster than before, though at enormous cost. The men must have concluded that it was better to risk torture for misusing state resources than lose their honour by returning to the Hag empty-handed. It was a fateful decision, he realised. If he did not reach the limits of Bale's territory in the next few days, Lurhan's men would catch him. Time was no longer on his side.

At some point, in desperation, he left the road altogether, hoping that his pursuers wouldn't spot his trail. He couldn't recall what made him angle north and east. The terrain was steeper and more forbidding and perhaps, he thought perversely, it was simply par for the course that the only way to his destination was over the most difficult ground possible. Regardless, Lurhan's men were undaunted. Malus reckoned he gained a few hours before his pursuers realised he was no longer on the road and backtracked far enough to find his trail.

Spite gamely tackled the steep, forested hills, but even Malus could sense that the great beast was growing tired. In this rough terrain the odds between hunter and hunted became roughly even, boiling down to which side was willing to ride harder for their goal.

The night after he left the Spear Road the torturous hills gave way to a rolling, glacial plain that shone pale blue beneath the moonlight. Mountains loomed white and unforgiving on the northern horizon; for hours Malus stared at their irregular lines, hoping to catch a glimpse of the black ark.

Time lost all meaning as he rode over the endless plain. His body burned and trembled and his mind drifted. Dreams came and went. Once he found himself riding among a company of druchii riding their nauglir across the frozen plain. He could not see the faces of the riders, but the voices that echoed in his ears seemed eerily familiar – they laughed and called to one another, sharing jibes and wagers.

Malus tried to speak to them, but they paid him no mind, as though he were a ghost riding among them. After a time, one of the riders sidled alongside, close enough to touch. The knight's armour was covered in dried gore, as though he were a corpse left on a battlefield. Malus reached out to touch the mounted warrior with a trembling hand and the knight turned to look at him. Eyes glowing with grave mould shone from the helmet's eye slits, burning with hate. Malus recoiled, fumbling for his sword with a curse. By the time he'd drawn his weapon the vision was gone.

Another time it felt as though someone sat behind him in the saddle. It was a woman – he knew that in the strange omniscience that dreams sometimes granted – and she pressed against him, her hands sliding around his waist and up across his armoured chest. He could feel the passage of her fingers even through the silvered steel; they left a trail of ice along his bones like the passage of a bitter frost. Malus felt a head against his shoulder and smelled fresh earth mixed with grave rot just as the icy hands closed about his throat.

Malus thrashed and twisted, reaching back to wrest the wight from the saddle, but his hands closed on empty air. Suddenly he felt a breath of cool air against his cheek and then came a wrenching impact as his falling body slammed into the glacial ice.

He awoke with a monster looming over him. Spite's toothy snout nudged his right leg, as though trying to prod some life back into its pack-mate. The head drooped to the highborn's calf, sniffing at the crusted wound there and Malus watched the nauglir's lips draw back, revealing yellowed fangs. Malus let out a startled shout and kicked the cold one in the nose. Startled, the beast sidled a few feet away and settled on its haunches, studying Malus with one red eye.

* * *

MALUS AWOKE TO painful sunlight and the wailing of horns.

The ground trembled as Spite roared out a challenge. Malus raised an arm that felt heavy as lead and tried to shield his eyes from the painful glare. He saw the nauglir on its feet, snarling back the way they'd come. A horse whinnied fearfully in response and Malus realised that the long race had come to an end.

With a cry of effort Malus rolled onto his side and got his feet underneath him. Lurhan's men sat on their mounts a hundred yards away, watching their prey from a low ridgeline. Black streamers – the colour of vengeance and the blood feud – snapped in the cold wind from the ends of their long spears. Their horses trembled with exhaustion, but the riders' faces were stoic, set in frozen masks of unquenchable hate.

As Malus watched, their leader pulled an object from his saddlebag and held it aloft for the highborn to see. It was Lurhan's severed head, its black hair streaming raggedly in the wind. It was the badge of the feud. When the retainers marched him through the gates of the Hag he would be forced to carry his father's head in his hands so that the entire city could behold the awful nature of his crime.

Without a word spoken the warriors lowered their spears and began to advance. Spite let out a hungry hiss; ice crunched beneath the warbeast's feet as it moved between Malus and the horsemen. The highborn fumbled for his sword; it seemed to take forever to pull it free and when he did it was all he could do not to drop it onto the ice.

The retainers advanced warily; there were at least a dozen of them, possibly as many as a score – to Malus's wavering eyes their dark forms were like a flock of ravens picking their way across the ice. Their spears were reinforced with steel and the heads were broad and razor-sharp; weapons ideal for fighting cold ones from horseback. Through his delirium Malus could see how the battle would unfold. They would surround Spite first, distracting the hungry cold one with tempting horseflesh while other riders drove in from both flanks and stabbed their spears into the nauglir's vitals. Then once Spite was dead they would come for him. The best he could hope for was to take one or two of the bastards down before they took his sword away.

Malus's cracked lips worked. His voice came out in a ragged whisper. 'Tz'arkan,' he croaked. 'Help me. Help me or I'll tell these men everything. I'll tell them to give the relics to Eldire. I swear it! You won't be free until the stars are cinders in the night sky!'

It was the worst threat Malus could think of on the spur of the moment, but it evoked no response. 'Curse you,' Malus said. 'When they drag me before the drachau and vivisect me before the court you can have the bitter leavings and may you choke on them!'

The highborn closed his eyes and summoned the last of his strength. He would go down fighting, charging at the oncoming men and shedding hot blood – when a roll of thunder echoed from the north and the ground shook beneath Malus's feet. He spun, staggering from the sudden motion and saw a party of ten cold one knights charging down the slope of the hill to the north, their lances levelled at Lurhan's men.

The warriors of Hag Graef hesitated but a moment. Given the situation, there was only one possible response. The leader of the hunters turned to his band. '*Charge!*' he cried over the rumble of the cold ones' advance and the warriors responded with a fierce cry, hurling themselves at the knights of the black ark.

The retainers swept down the ridge in a wall of galloping horses and glittering spear points. They veered slightly to the right, shying away from the highborn and his hissing mount, but Spite was not to be thwarted so easily. The nauglir's talons sent shards of ice and frozen dirt in the air as it threw itself at the right flank of the horsemen.

Two men and their mounts went down in a sickening *crunch* as the one-ton warbeast pounced on them like a hunting cat. Spite rolled across the ice with its huge jaws locked around the shoulder and neck of one of the horses; the second one lay in a twisted heap, its back broken by the nauglir's impact. The armoured horsemen had fared little better than their mounts: one lay motionless some feet away, his neck clearly broken, while the other struggled to regain his feet while clutching a limp and broken arm. A cold clarity settled over Malus at the sight of the wounded man – hefting his sword he staggered across the ice towards the retainer, coming up on him from behind.

The two mounted forces came together in a rending crash of steel and flesh. Horses, men and cold ones roared and screamed in anger and pain as spears and talons sank into living flesh. Wood splintered as spear hafts shattered against armour or were broken off in their targets.

The sound caught Malus's attention; the impact was so earth-shaking it brought his head around in spite of himself. He saw warhorses thrown backwards by the collision – one of Lurhan's warriors was hurled ten feet into the air, still clutching the splintered haft of his weapon. A cold one crashed through the wall of horses, rolling snout-over-tail in a spray of scales, blood and torn earth; the beast had died instantly when a broad-bladed spear had driven deep into its brain. Another nauglir snapped and thrashed like a hound, scattering pieces of mangled armour as it tore a screaming warrior apart. The sturdier cold ones plunged like catapult stones through the line of horsemen, their broad feet clawing for purchase as they tried to slow down and make another pass. Many of the surviving horsemen had already turned their more nimble mounts and were even now bearing down on the cold ones, touching off a swirling melee.

The injured horseman charged Malus with a hateful scream, brandishing his sword in his left hand – had the warrior not given in to his pain and rage he could likely have taken the highborn completely unawares. As it was, Malus got his sword up in a weak block that was barely enough to keep the warrior from splitting his skull with a downward cut. The force of the impact drove Malus backwards, even as the icy thrill of imminent death drove the delirium from his mind.

Still screaming, the warrior aimed a series of clumsy blows against Malus's head and arms. What the man lacked in dexterity he made up for in vigour. Each blow used up a little more of the highborn's reserves of strength, making each successive parry a little slower and a little weaker. One of the retainer's blows left a long, shallow cut on Malus's right cheek; another smashed into his left pauldron, sending bright streaks of pain shooting along the highborn's shoulder. A third blow rang against Malus's right vambrace, nearly knocking the sword from his grasp. Reacting instinctively, the highborn planted his right heel and stopped in his tracks, causing Lurhan's man to crash against him. The warrior let out an agonised cry as his broken arm hit Malus's chest, only to scream even louder as the highborn grabbed the injured limb with his free hand and twisted it as hard as he could. Malus watched the man's face turn the colour of chalk; the retainer's eyes rolled up and he fainted from the unbearable pain a split-second before the highborn's sword tore into his throat. It was all the highborn could do to stagger out of the way as the warrior collapsed to the ground. Malus fell to his knees beside the dead man, his own limbs trembling with exertion.

The sound of thundering hooves broke over him like a wave. Malus looked up to see the surviving horsemen fleeing back the way they'd come, their swords and armour stained red. Their leader still survived, clutching the head of his dead lord close to his chest. As he passed Malus some ten yards away he threw the highborn a look of bitterest hate. You've won but a small reprieve, those dark eyes told Malus. There will be another reckoning. We do not forgive and we do not forget.

By the time Malus rose unsteadily to his feet the horsemen were gone. The ground shook with the loping strides of the cold ones – only six now – as they moved among the dead. A tall highborn in black and gold armour walked his mount over to Malus, his aristocratic features twisted in a furious scowl.

Malus bent and wiped the blood from his sword with the hair of the man he'd slain. 'Well fought, men of the black ark,' he said, sheathing his blade. 'I am Malus, formerly of Hag Graef.' He looked up at the knight. 'Your lord, Balneth Bale–'

The knight's boot took him right between the eyes. One moment he was talking and the next he was falling into blackness.

Visions came and went after that, ebbing and flowing like the tide. He saw strange faces peering down at him, their expressions distorted as though reflected in a pool of water. Their mouths moved, but their voices were blurry and vague as well. Only the hatred burning in their eyes was clear and unequivocal. That much at least he understood.

MALUS TASTED BITTER liquid on his tongue. His body felt swollen and burned, like meat left to char in a fire. The sensation stirred memories like rotting leaves. 'Father?' he whispered fearfully.

He lay draped on his stomach across a hard, rolling surface. When he opened his eyes he saw nothing but a blur of white. Malus felt his guts heave and he vomited noisily.

There was a creak of saddle leather. Somewhere above him, a disgusted voice, thick with a rustic northern accent, said, 'Damn it, there he goes again. Next time we stop, someone else gets to carry him.'

Hissing laughter echoed around him. Malus screwed his eyes shut against the terrible whiteness and lost consciousness once more.

HE WAS SHIVERING, lying naked on the icy ground. Strong hands closed on his ankles and his wrists.

Malus smelled smoke. When his eyes fluttered open he could see a black sky shot through with countless stars. The hands holding him tightened; a circle of silhouetted heads crowded his vision.

Someone grunted. 'A bad time to wake up,' a voice said. 'This should be fun.'

Just then a tall figure appeared, outlined against the sky. There was a flare of orange light as the figure held the glowing end of a red-hot dagger over Malus. In the reflected light he recognised the man as the knight who'd kicked him.

'Don't kill me with the dagger,' he heard himself say. 'Anything else, but not the dagger.'

'Shut up,' the knight said, crouching beside his men and pressing the glowing steel against Malus's leg.

He was still screaming and cursing every foul oath he knew when the man pulled the knife free and then put it to the wound in Malus's arm. The smell of burned flesh hung heavy and sweet in the air. The highborn soiled himself. Someone let out a curse of his own and cuffed Malus in the side of the head.

The knight pulled the dagger away and paused to inspect his work. Apparently satisfied, he rose to his feet, his pale face seeming to recede all the way into the night sky.

'You're going to a lot of trouble for nothing,' someone said. 'Look at his veins, my lord, they're black with corruption. He won't last beyond a couple more days, if that.'

'He just has to make it to the auctioneer's block tomorrow,' the knight growled. 'After that the Outer Darkness can take the bastard.'

Malus was already sinking back into darkness when the full import of the man's words sent a jolt of pure terror coursing up his spine. They meant to sell him in the slave market!

He thrashed violently, managing to pull an arm and a leg free before the warriors surrounding him regained their hold and pinned him to the frozen earth. One of the men bent close and took his jaw in one calloused hand. Iron-hard fingers squeezed, prying open his mouth like he was a new-born calf.

'Give him another taste of the hushalta,' the druchii holding his jaw said gruffly. The warrior was handed an open bottle of milky fluid as he studied the highborn critically. 'Who'd pay good coin for this lout?' he muttered. 'I wouldn't cut him up and feed him to my nauglir.' Appreciative laughter hissed in the darkness as the man poured the bitter liquid down Malus's throat. When he was done, the druchii handed the bottle back and bent to peer closely into the highborn's eyes.

'Of course, there's no lack of fools in this world,' the warrior said as darkness swallowed Malus's sight. 'This one here is living proof of that.'

Chapter Twelve
THE BLACK ARK

'AWAKEN DARKBLADE,' A scornful voice echoed in his head. '*Awaken*, or spend the rest of your brief life in chains!'

The words reverberated through the darkness like a tolling bell. Malus stirred slightly, touching off waves of fiery pain from the burns in his leg and arm. The agony banished the lingering effects of the hushalta and within moments he was awake. He was lying on his stomach, draped once again across the back of a moving nauglir and his hands and feet were bound with rope. The highborn's stomach felt like a clutched fist, hard and empty and the burnt copper aftertaste of the hushalta left him with a raging thirst. A sudden gust of wind raked icy claws along his back and neck, leaving him shivering but also grateful with the realisation that his fever had finally broken. The crude cauterisations performed by the druchii lord had managed to burn away the infections festering in his wounds.

Malus heard a dry chuckle some distance behind him. 'I just saw him shiver, Hathair,' an amused voice said. 'Looks like he's lived long enough to reach the ark after all. That's a bottle of Vinan you owe me, if memory serves.'

The highborn heard a creak of saddle leather close to his ear. A gloved fist grabbed a handful of Malus's hair and yanked his head painfully back. The movement took Malus by surprise. On instinct he fought to keep his body relaxed and limp.

'Those are death throes,' a gruff voice said, close enough that Malus could smell the druchii's foul breath. 'It's a long climb up the southern stair. He'll be cold and stiff by the time we reach the top.'

Malus heard the first knight laugh and the fist abruptly let go. The highborn's cheek slapped back against the nauglir's scaly hide and another wave of fierce pain reverberated across his chest and arm. Again, he steeled himself to show no reaction. The two knights lapsed back into silence and after a few moments the highborn could discern the rhythmic slap of nauglir feet on paved stones. Somewhere ahead came other faint noises: the creak of wagon wheels and the sounds of livestock and the murmur of rustic druchii voices. Slowly, carefully, the highborn opened his gummy eyes a hair's width and tried to see where he was.

They were on a road, that was clear enough – Malus saw ice-rimed black paving stones, laid wide enough for at least two riders to travel abreast. The cold ones were travelling up a long, gentle slope towards what looked like a steep cliff of rock and ice rising several hundred feet in the air. The highborn opened his eyes a bit more and followed the cliff's rough face to its summit. There, sure enough, he saw black, forbidding fortress walls and a profusion of circular towers interspersed with the splintered remnants of giant oak masts, like the kind found on a sailing ship. The cliff was the side of an enormous shard of rock, topped by nothing less than a small city dominated by an overlord's fortress. It was the infamous ice-locked ark: the Black Ark of Naggor, seat of the self-styled Witch Lord Balneth Bale.

Ahead of the advancing column Malus saw a commotion as tradesmen and lesser highborns tried to calm their skittish mounts and move to the side of the road to allow the knights to pass. Some distance further on the highborn saw an arch of dark grey stone at the base of the ark, guarded by a company of spearmen. Traffic came and went through this arch like the gates in any other druchii city, but this one led into the tunnels honeycombing the ark itself.

Much of the city was hidden deep within the rock, Malus knew, hollowed out by druchii hands – and later refined by dwarf slaves – after the ark came to rest in the far north. Only the wealthiest and most influential citizens of the ark had the privilege of living in the ancient towers, while the rest lived like cold ones in the warrens below.

It was the first time Malus had ever seen one of the famous arks up close – it was shards of stone such as these that had saved the druchii when Nagarythe had been lost beneath the waves, thousands of years ago. The shard was in fact a piece of lost Nagarythe itself – when the great cataclysm struck the northern part of Ulthuan there were a number of cities and fortresses protected by such powerful sorceries that they survived the onslaught of the waves when the rest of the land around them was washed away. They floated on the angry waves like unmoored islands, holding all that remained of the elves of the north. The arks themselves transformed the people of Nagarythe into the druchii, or so the legends said.

Faced with the loss of everything they'd known, the people on the arks were faced with a choice: abandon their drifting havens and throw themselves on the mercy of the rest of Ulthuan, or harden their hearts and survive on their own. The druchii chose the path of defiance, raising tremendous masts and bending their sorceries to transform the shards into ocean-going fortresses and the black arks were born.

When the druchii reached Naggaroth many of the arks were beached along the eastern coast, becoming outposts for conquering the mainland. Of the remainder, most remained at sea as mobile fiefdoms, terrorising the Old World with small fleets of corsairs. Not so the Black Ark of Naggor. When the druchii reached their new home, Malekith wished to make a display of power that illustrated his dominance of the new land – and the druchii people as a whole. So it was said that he turned to the sorcerers of Naggor, once a famous centre of arcane knowledge in Nagarythe and commanded them to create a spell that would transport his own ark onto the mainland and create a literal and symbolic seat of power he could rule from.

The sorcerers of Naggor complied and at enormous cost they moved Malekith's ark hundreds of leagues inland, creating the foundation for the great fortress-city of Naggorond. But the sorcerers were not done yet. Not long afterwards they moved their own ark, sending it even farther northward than Malekith's seat of power. Some legends claimed that the sorcerers simply wished to be able to continue their studies in private, removed from the petty intrigues of the kingdom, while other, more cynical tales suggested that the Naggorites meant to send a message to Malekith, reminding the Witch King that their power had helped cement his pre-eminence.

Not long afterwards Malekith outlawed the male practice of sorcery, sending the Naggorites a message of his own.

The column walked its mounts up the road towards the gate until Malus heard an officious-sounding voice command the knights to halt. 'Who goes there?' called the commander of the guard company.

'Lord Tennucyr and his warband, with a prisoner and a nauglir for the flesh market,' one of the warriors replied, making no effort to disguise his annoyance. Malus thought of Hauclir and his brazen attempts at extortion back when he was a guard captain at Hag Graef and wondered if such things were common at fortress gates all across the Land of Chill.

If so, Lord Tennucyr was in no mood for games. 'Stand aside, you worm!' he bellowed, drowning out both his retainer and the guard captain. There was the hurried shuffle of feet and the column jerked back into motion. Within moments Malus saw the arch of the great gate and its huge, iron-banded doors slide past and then the knights were plunged into the riotous, stinking gloom of the inner part of the city.

Just past the great gate there was a low-ceilinged cavern full of noise and bustle, much like any small market square anywhere in Naggaroth. Servants, soldiers, slaves and citizens mingled with one another as they went about their daily business. Huge witchlight lamps burned from stone pillars set at intervals across the square; the cold light did little to banish the darkness in the huge space, wreathing the city dwellers and the market stalls in eerie shadows.

Pale faces moved past Malus like disembodied ghosts, studying him and the knights with emotionless faces. The press of the bustling crowd seemed to press against the highborn with invisible hands, squeezing him in their grasp. It was like living in a tomb, he thought, suddenly eager for a breath of fresh wind and the gleam of faint northern sunlight.

The riders turned left in the square and worked their way through the crowds until they reached a broad ramp that wound upwards into shadow. Another group of guardsmen stood at the base of the ramp, taking coin from druchii moving both up and down the curving lane. Servants and highborn on foot paid a toll to the guardsmen to use the tunnel road, which Malus suspected was another tool to keep the masses in their place throughout the city. The soldiers took one look at Lord Tennucyr and his men and quickly shoved the toll lines out of the way, allowing the column to pass unhindered.

Riding along the curving road was not unlike climbing the spiral stair of a druchii spire, only each level took nearly half an hour to reach. Malus counted each level. He made it as far as six before the riders suddenly halted and a set of commands was passed back down the line from Tennucyr. The highborn heard the knight in the saddle beside him grunt an acknowledgement, then nudge his mount out of the column.

Malus watched through slitted eyes as they rode across a small, deserted square and then into a dimly-lit side passage that ran deeper into the rock. Broad feet slapped along the stone in their wake, accompanied by the rhythmic jingle of a heavy chain. Malus risked a quick look backwards and saw Spite being led along in the knight's wake. The nauglir had been stripped of saddle, tack and bags and for the first time the highborn realised with a shock that Tennucyr had not only his sword and armour, but also the three relics he'd fought so hard to obtain. He fought down a surge of panic. I know who has them, he told himself. And I'll get them back, preferably over Tennucyr's dead body.

The passage was flat and smooth as a road and smelled of horse and nauglir. Narrow, inset doorways and shuttered windows slid past at regular intervals; to Malus, it wasn't unlike travelling down a narrow city street late at night. Familiar sounds carried through the air: the crack of whips and the rustle of chains, screams and angry shouts and the brassy clash of cages slamming closed. He was in the Slavers' Quarter of the ice-bound ark, where tradesmen bought and sold living goods for highborn towers and flesh houses alike.

They rode on for several minutes and as they went deeper into the quarter Malus noted that the individual 'buildings' were separated by narrow, filth-strewn alleys and the structures themselves took on the shape of blocky, thick-walled forts. These were the compounds of the most successful slave dealers in the city, built to hold hundreds of slaves as well as provide training grounds for those meant for the fighting pits of the city's flesh houses. The nauglir strode past three of these imposing structures before lurching to a halt in front of a fourth. Malus noted that the facade of the slave traders' compound was worked with bas reliefs of pit fighting scenes, presumably advertising famous pit warriors that came from the owner's stock.

There was a sudden lurch backwards as the nauglir settled onto its haunches; with a rattle of chains Spite did the same. There was a creak of saddle leather as the knight dismounted, then Malus felt the man grab the back of his kheitan and drag him off the back of the cold one like a bag of grain. He hit the ground hard enough to knock the wind from his lungs. Try as he might he couldn't help curling into a ball on the road and groaning for breath.

The retainer cursed softly at Malus's weak signs of life. 'That's a bottle of good wine you've cost me,' he said, aiming a kick at the highborn's back. The man approached the compound's double doors and banged against them with the pommel of his sword.

It was several long minutes before a spy-hole in one of the doors slid open. 'Master Noros isn't here,' a man's voice said. 'Come back later.'

'Open the door,' the knight growled. 'I've got a prisoner and a nauglir to sell, compliments of Lord Tennucyr.'

'The Witch Lord's cousin?'

'The very same.'

There was a loud *clack* as the spy door slid shut, then a rattle of bolts being drawn back. One of the large doors swung noisily open and a slight, stooped druchii stepped tentatively outside. He wore stained robes and a faded brown kheitan and carried a cudgel and a coiled whip at his belt. The servant sketched a cursory bow to the retainer and stared down his long, crooked nose at Malus. 'Him? He looks half dead.'

The retainer turned his head and spat. 'Bastard ought to be entirely dead, but he's either too mean or too stupid to know it. He's tough for a city-born.'

'That's not saying much,' the servant said, crouching on his heels and prying back one of Malus's eyelids. 'He ought to be lying on a bier somewhere,' he muttered disdainfully. 'What about this nauglir, then?'

'It's right over there, fool.'

'*That* runt? What do you take me for? If Master Noros were here he'd be threatening a blood feud over this. It's an insult!'

'Do I look like a baker's apprentice to you, dung worm? I'm not here to haggle with you. Lord Tennucyr said to take this lot to the House of Noros and sell them, so here I am.'

'All right, all right. No need for all the shouting,' the servant said querulously. The man shuffled back to the doorway and let out a sharp whistle. 'Cut him loose,' he said to the retainer.

'Why?'

'I want to see if he's strong enough to stand. If he can't, he's not good for anything but nauglir fodder.'

Malus lay perfectly still as the retainer drew his knife and bent to cut the ropes binding the highborn's wrists and ankles. For a moment he thought his opportunity had arrived, but by the time his bonds had been cut away two large, muscular human slaves had emerged from the compound. They took him by the arms and set him on his feet as though he were a doll. Malus gave them a weak groan and let the two slaves bear much of his weight while the servant studied him critically.

Master Noros's man was clearly not impressed, but after a moment he sighed. 'All right,' he said, 'but only as a favour to your lord. Come inside and we'll settle on a figure.' He turned to the slaves and jerked his head at the doorway. 'Take him in and have him branded, then throw him in with the rest of the runts.'

The humans grunted a response and dragged Malus through the doorway into the slaver's compound. He was taken through a large room furnished with gleaming marble pillars, each one fitted with pol- ished silver steel manacles for displaying the owner's wares. Malus was surprised to note that the pillars themselves were entirely decorative; in fact, there wasn't even a ceiling for them to support. Looking up, he saw that the walls of the chamber were uncommonly high, but beyond them there was nothing but shadows and a dim hint of a cavern roof some fifteen feet above.

Beyond the display room was a long, narrow gallery that offered views of a series of training rooms. Each room displayed one or more pairs of slaves being taught the various techniques of pit fighting by scowling druchii instructors. As they passed one of the rooms Malus heard a wretched scream; one of the instructors was demonstrating the different ways to cripple an opponent by cutting the tendons of an emaciated human slave. That's what they do with their runts, Malus thought grimly.

At the end of the gallery was an imposing iron door. One of the slaves pulled a ring of keys from his belt, unlocked the door and pushed the heavy thing open. Beyond the doorway lay another passageway, this time flanked by the iron bars of a number of large cages. Hundreds of pairs of eyes followed Malus as the slaves dragged him down the passage towards a small room at the far end. The highborn's heart began to race as he smelled burning coals and the stink of hot iron.

Inside the room a heavily scarred druchii sat at a small table poring over ledgers and scribbling notes on a sheet of thick parchment. Whips and cudgels hung from pegs on the walls of the room and a small brazier with a single iron stood in one corner. The man scowled at Malus as the slaves hauled him over to the desk. 'What's this?' he asked scornfully.

'New runt, master,' one of the slaves mumbled. 'Master Lohar wants him branded.'

The druchii's ravaged face twisted in an expression of disbelief. 'He paid coin for *this*? Noros will have his hide,' he said. The man pushed away from the table and limped over to the brazier. 'Stretch him over the table,' the man said absently, 'just be careful of the ledgers.'

Before Malus knew it the men bent both of his arms behind his back and pushed him face-down across the desk. One of the slaves laid a broad hand between Malus's shoulders and pinned him in place, while the other grabbed a handful of the highborn's hair and turned his head so his left cheek was exposed. He felt dry parchment against his face and smelled the bitter tang of fresh ink. A small knife, used for trimming quills, rested inches from Malus's face, though it might have been on the other side of the Sea of Ice for all the good it did him.

Malus tensed, trying to push away from the table, but he couldn't move an inch. For a fleeting moment, Malus thought of calling to Tz'arkan for help, but he angrily pushed the thought aside. If the cursed daemon hadn't helped him when he was near to dying on the Spear Road, why would he share his strength now?

There was a hiss as the druchii pulled the iron free from the coals. A thin wisp of smoke rose from the glowing symbol of a crescent moon – evidently the mark of the House of Noros. The druchii studied the brand carefully, then nodded to himself. 'Now don't let him flinch like the last one,' the man admonished, limping over to the table. 'If his eyeball bursts it'll ruin my papers.'

The brand descended towards Malus's face, the orange glow beating against his skin like an angry sun. At the last moment Malus closed his eyes and cried out – then picked up his left foot and smashed his heel into the knee of the slave next to him. The human let out a shout of surprise and pain as his leg gave way beneath him and pitched him forward into the path of the brand. The red-hot metal struck his shoulder and the slave's cry turned to a scream of agony as his woollen robes caught fire. Roaring in pain, the man panicked, letting go of Malus and beating at the fire with his hands. The highborn snatched the quill-knife from the desk and rolled onto his side, stabbing backwards and burying the blade to the hilt in the side of the other slave's throat. Bright blood sprayed across Malus and the startled druchii slaver as the wounded man collapsed.

Malus pushed away from the table and reversed his grip on the bloody knife. The blade was less than four inches long – hardly a fearsome weapon in the best of circumstances. The slaver recovered from his shock and advanced on the highborn, holding the branding iron ahead of him like a sword. The metal was still glowing a dull cherry-red, more than hot enough to char flesh with a touch.

The slaver crept closer, jabbing at Malus's face and chest with the hot iron. The highborn retreated, feinting left and right, but every time he tried to get past the man the searing brand was there, reaching for his face. The slaver gave him a lopsided sneer – and Malus flipped his knife end-over-end, caught the tip between two fingers and threw the weapon at the man's face. The man ducked the thrown knife easily, but it gave Malus time to turn and dash for the nearest wall. With a startled shout the slaver was right on his heels – but not fast enough to prevent Malus from snatching a heavy oak cudgel from its peg. He spun on one heel and lashed out with a vicious swing, connecting solidly with the slaver's temple. There was a crunch of bone and the scarred man groaned, toppling to the floor.

By this time bedlam reigned among the cages outside the room. Slaves of every race crowded at the bars and shouted for blood. They shook the doors of their cages and caused a thunderous racket. That's certain to attract unwelcome attention, Malus thought. Sure enough, the highborn glanced down the passage and saw a group of overseers racing towards him, brandishing their cudgels.

Thinking quickly, Malus checked the belt of the dead slaver and found a ring of thick iron keys. He went to the still-twitching slave he'd stabbed and grabbed the second key ring, then tossed them through the bars of the two nearest cages. 'Open the doors and pass the keys to the next cages in line!' he bellowed in a commanding voice. 'Then arm yourselves as best you can. Now is your chance for revenge!'

The slaves answered Malus with a feral roar that brought a merciless grin to his face. He turned to the overseers, still several yards away and saw at once that they'd seen what he'd done. The highborn took a step towards them, brandishing his cudgel and they turned and ran. Howling like a wolf he set off after them. Behind him the first of the cage doors slammed open and the passageway resounded with the thunder of pent-up feet.

The overseers reached the iron door and left it gaping wide in their hurry to escape. Malus gained on the fleeing men rapidly, listening to their cries of alarm. As the highborn swept down the gallery the druchii instructor who'd been crippling runts minutes before clambered into the hallway ahead of Malus with a confused look on his face. Malus slashed downwards with the cudgel, shattering the man's knee in passing and left him writhing on the floor for the other slaves to find.

In the display room beyond, Malus found Lohar the slaver standing next to Tennucyr's retainer. The slaver was shouting frantic commands at the panicked overseers, trying to get them to explain what had happened. When Lohar saw Malus dash into the room with his bloodstained cudgel his face went deathly white. Tennucyr's man let out a startled shout, as if he'd seen a ghost. Malus bared his teeth hungrily. 'Care to make another wager, little man?'

Lohar let out a yell and rushed at Malus, uncoiling his scourge with a swift, fluid motion and aiming a flesh-tearing stroke at the highborn's face. A slave would have quailed from such a blow, but not a battle-hardened warrior. Malus ducked the blow and rushed at Lohar, swinging the cudgel in a two-handed grip and striking the man in the groin. The slaver doubled over with a choked scream that ended when Malus struck the back of the man's head with a backhanded blow that dropped him to the floor.

Malus spun to face Tennucyr's man – and caught a glimpse of the retainer's back as he dashed through the compound's open door.

The retainer was running for his mount as fast as he could, not bothering to look back. Malus stepped outside, took careful aim and flung the cudgel at the man as hard as he could. The heavy club spun end-over-end and struck the retainer in the head, sending him tumbling to the ground.

Screams and the sounds of fighting echoed from Master Noros's house as Malus reached Tennucyr's retainer and rolled him onto his back. The man was just regaining consciousness as the highborn plucked the man's dagger from his belt.

Malus knelt on the druchii's armoured chest and rested the tip of the blade beneath the man's chin.

'A bad time to wake up,' Malus said coldly. 'But I must say your luck has finally turned here at the end.'

The retainer blinked. 'My luck? What do you mean?'

The highborn bent close, peering into the man's eyes. 'Because I can't afford to get any blood on your armour or it will ruin the disguise,' he said and drove the dagger upwards into the man's brain.

Chapter Thirteen
DARK ALLIANCE

ALUS PUT HIS heels to Spite's flanks and thundered down the narrow road through the Slavers' Quarter. Fire and ruin followed in his wake.

The retainer's armour fitted Malus poorly, shifting and rattling across his chest and shoulders with every one of the nauglir's heavy steps. The vambraces and greaves felt dangerously loose, threatening to slide from his limbs – there had been little time to tighten all the straps and ensure every buckle was set while a mob of angry slaves rampaged through Master Noros's house. By the time he'd put the dead man's hadrilkar and armour on the compound was burning fiercely and armed slaves were spilling into the street, eager to spill more slavers' blood.

Druchii slavers and their men were stepping into the street at the far end of the lane, listening to the distant commotion and eyeing the rising column of smoke from Noros's compound with increasing alarm. 'Noros's slaves have escaped!' Malus roared at the men in his path. 'They're burning everything they can reach. Barricade your doors and arm your men!'

The slavers scattered out of the highborn's way and began shouting orders to their men. Malus galloped on, trusting that none of the druchii would think to question the business of one of Lord Tennucyr's men.

Within minutes Malus reached the curving passage that connected the many levels of the black ark. The guardsmen collecting tolls from passing druchii frowned at the onrushing highborn, but Malus only spurred his mount harder, scattering soldiers and citizens alike out of his way as he turned right and headed for the highest levels of the ice-locked fortress. 'Sound the alarm!' he cried to everyone he passed. 'The Slavers' Quarter is on fire!'

Figures appeared and then receded in the gloom as Malus ascended the long ramp, their pale faces marked by anger or fear. The highborn thought he could smell smoke and imagined the consequences of a major fire in the enclosed vaults of the ark. Just then Malus felt the sensation of dry scales brushing against the insides of his ribs and T'zarkan murmured in his head. 'You are going the wrong way, little druchii,' the daemon said coldly. 'As ever, you rush headlong into your enemies' arms.'

Malus shook his head sharply, gritting his teeth at the sudden return of the hated daemon's presence. When he'd first put on the dead retainer's armour and collar he'd considered simply riding Spite down the long ramp and barrelling out into the icy wastes. But just as quickly he realised that escaping the ark brought only the illusion of safety. Beyond the walls of the ark he would be a hunted man, dogged by warriors from the Hag and assassins. His only hope was to throw in his lot with Balneth Bale and trust that the Witch Lord's enmity with Hag Graef – and mysterious détente with Malekith – would be enough to stymie his foes long enough that he could at least free himself from Tz'arkan's damnable grip. 'Such timely concern,' the highborn sneered. 'Especially after so much silence when I was being hunted like a wolf after the fight at Vaelgor Keep.'

'Fool,' the daemon spat. 'I kept you alive after you blundered into Lurhan's men and got yourself riddled with bolts. Were it not for me that infection would have taken your leg at the very least, if not killed you after days of pain and delirium. I am your staunchest ally, Dark-blade, but you are too stupid to see it.'

Malus was incredulous. 'Ally? You did not tell me it was Lurhan who took the dagger, did you? No, you mocked me with riddles. For all I know this is another one of your cursed games.'

'Have I ever lied to you, Malus?' the daemon hissed. 'No. Not once.'

'But when have you ever told me the complete truth?' Malus shot back. 'Answer that if you can. I *know* Bale is my enemy. *Everyone* in Naggaroth is my foe, you damned spirit. Tell me something useful for once and explain to me *why* I shouldn't throw in my lot with him.'

'He will use you against Hag Graef,' Tz'arkan replied. 'You will be a weapon that he will aim at the city's heart.'

The warning was so absurd the highborn could not help but laugh. 'Are you so simple as that, daemon? Of course he would do such a thing – did you honestly imagine this wouldn't have occurred to me? The sword cuts both ways, daemon. He will seek to bend me to his purposes and I will do the same to him. That is how the game is played.' Malus grinned savagely. 'No country lord will get the better of a druchii of Hag Graef!'

Spite rounded another corner in the long climb just as a deep, resonant boom resounded through the very stone of the ark itself. The sound rolled like thunder, reverberating through the highborn's bones and no sooner had its echoes faded than a second beat followed in its wake. It was the beat of a great and terrible drum, spreading a portentous alarm through the tunnels and caverns of the enormous fortress. The sound sharpened Malus's calculating grin. Chaos and panic were his real allies at the moment; the longer the alarm was raised, the greater his chances of reaching Bale's fortress and gaining an audience with the Witch Lord himself. Part of his mind was already hard at work formulating a proposal to Bale that he hoped the Witch Lord would be unable to refuse.

The drum was still tolling its alarm when Malus reached the next level above the Slavers' Quarter. One moment he was speeding through the gloom of the curving passage and the next he was galloping past a group of startled toll-guards and up the side of an enormous cavern. Vast, dank space stretched away to Malus's right and for a moment the highborn felt a wave of dizziness at the sudden change of surroundings. The chamber was so huge that the far side was lost in the diffuse haze of witchlights, their glow limning the gleaming sides of scores of marble pillars rising almost a hundred feet to the arched ceiling overhead. Among the pillars Malus glimpsed small buildings and more narrow lanes bustling with armed, purposeful druchii. Then the ramp reached the top of the great chamber and the narrow walls of a subterranean passage closed about Malus once more.

Minutes later the highborn smelled fresh, cold air and sensed he was nearing the top of the ark. Then around the corner came the measured tramp of marching feet and the highborn led Spite up against the inner wall of the passageway just in time to avoid the rushing mass of a regiment of Naggorite spearmen marching double-quick to reach the fighting below. Lamplight gleamed on the curved surfaces of their breastplates and glittered like frost on their fine skirts of heavy mail and their faces were lit with anticipation as they rushed past Malus with nary a curious glance. A small detachment of crossbowmen followed in the spearmen's wake, then a large troop of knights mounted on cold ones, their lances tipped with pennons of black and red. It was a swift and fearsome response, the highborn noted with some admiration. Not even the warriors of Hag Graef could have reacted so swiftly.

Once the troops were past the highborn spurred his mount to extra speed, conscious of the fact that the uprising wouldn't last for long once the ark's warriors arrived. He was so intent on speed that he didn't recognise that the passageway was gradually levelling out and the air was becoming fresher until he rounded a final corner and found himself rushing headlong at a tall gate of iron bars wrought with sharpened, thorn-like spikes.

'Whoa!' Malus cried, dragging at the reins, his eyes widening as Spite slowly recognised the command and started to back-pedal, his broad feet skidding along the smooth stone ramp as they hurtled towards the thicket of sharp iron. Closer and closer the spikes came, until the highborn fought the urge to hurl himself from the saddle. At the last minute the nauglir's claws found purchase, scoring deep grooves in the stone as the one-ton warbeast skidded to a halt. The gate loomed like a wall to Malus's right, close enough to touch. A spike glinted less than five inches from his exposed neck; another poked threateningly against his right greave.

A contingent of spearmen stood watchfully on the other side of the gate, their dark eyes wide with shock at the highborn's sudden and perilous arrival. Malus quickly singled out the leader of the detachment and fixed him with a hard stare. 'Open the gate, damn your eyes!' he snapped. 'The slaves are in full revolt and I have an urgent message for the Witch Lord!'

The sharp tone of command in Malus's voice sent the guards scrambling for the winch that controlled the gate. Within moments a sally port creaked open and the highborn guided his cold one through the narrow gap. The guard captain shouted something at Malus, but the highborn ignored him and kicked Spite back into a gallop.

Beyond the gate a broad, arched tunnel ran for almost ten yards. Pale sunlight shone on dark grey walls at the far end. 'Almost there,' Malus said to himself and within moments he burst from the tunnel into a wide city square bordered by the citadels of the city elite.

The highborn expected to find market stalls and citizens going about their daily business, instead he rode into the midst of an armed camp. Companies of spearmen stood in black-armoured ranks, arrayed by regiment in huge formations to either side of the tunnel. Across the square light cavalry waited nervously, the warhorses skittish in the presence of a large company of cold one knights in full panoply some distance away. Malus felt a thousand pairs of eyes turn his way as he barrelled from the darkness of the tunnel and he fought to keep his expression neutral as he realised he had no idea where he was going.

Thinking quickly, he scanned the towers looming all around him and picked out the one that rose above all the rest, standing out against a forest of weathered masts off to the northeast. Without slowing,

Malus crossed the square in that direction and plunged down the first street he found. To the highborn's relief, there were no shouts of alarm or sounds of pursuit. He was just one more knight among scores of others, hard about his master's business.

The streets of the upper city were deserted, the doors of the citadels shut tight at the sound of the tolling drum. Malus made his way through the maze of streets as quickly as he could, keeping one eye on the tall tower at all times. Slowly but surely his haphazard path drew him closer and closer to his goal, until without warning he found himself riding across another large square that stretched at the foot of Bale's citadel. This open area was also packed with formations of alert troops, many wearing newly polished armour and weapons untouched by the grit and grime of the battlefield. Again, hundreds of eyes followed Malus as he entered the square and on instinct he checked his furious pace, slowing Spite to a brisk lope. These weren't citizen militia called to action by the riot in the Slavers' Quarter, Malus realised. They were regular troops, many of them freshly equipped from the Witch Lord's arsenals. Bale was in the process of raising an army. The black ark was marching to war.

Malus barely had time to consider the implications of such a move as he rode up to a tall, imposing gate of polished iron set at the base of Bale's citadel. A phalanx of armoured spearmen stood before the portal and lowered their weapons at the highborn's approach. On either flank of the spear phalanx half a dozen crossbowmen took careful aim at Malus, reminding him of his wounds.

The captain of the guard company stepped forward, his sword pointed – for the moment – at the ground. 'Halt!' he ordered. 'State your business.'

'I serve Lord Tennucyr,' Malus answered, reining Spite in a dozen yards short of the captain. 'I have an urgent message for the Witch Lord.' The highborn resisted the urge to try and order the man aside. This wasn't some toll-collector who lived in fear of earning a highborn's ire. Threatening the captain would only garner Malus more attention than he really wanted.

Despite the highborn's businesslike tone, the captain frowned. 'Tennucyr, you say?'

Malus paused, hearing the suspicion in the captain's voice. He considered his response carefully. 'I was sent into the Slavers' Quarter by my lord to ascertain the situation there and now I must make my report to the Witch Lord.' On impulse, he added: 'Several compounds are already ablaze, captain. Time is of the essence.'

At that, the captain nodded. 'Very well,' he said and waved to his spearmen to stand aside, then turned to face the battlements above the gate. 'A messenger for the Witch Lord!' the captain declared in a powerful voice. 'Open the gate!'

There was a pair of dull thuds as bolts were drawn aside and the fifteen-foot iron gates swung open with scarcely a sound. Malus nodded curtly to the captain and kept his face carefully neutral as he spurred his mount forward and entered Balneth Bale's citadel. As he entered a short tunnel that ran from the gate and through the thick citadel wall, the daemon whispered, 'I warned you, Darkblade. When the trap springs shut, remember that.'

'Speak plainly or shut up, daemon,' Malus snarled. 'So far you've told me nothing I didn't already know.'

The tunnel opened into a small courtyard bordered by stables, a nauglir pen and a smithy. A tall, forbidding statue of a druchii in stately robes and bearing a rune-carved staff stood imperiously in the centre of the space. A beast handler was waiting as Malus reined in and slid from the saddle and the highborn handed Spite off to him. 'Keep him saddled until you hear otherwise,' he told the handler, then strode briskly to the citadel's entrance.

Malus fought the urge to fidget and rearrange his ill-fitting armour as he approached the citadel's arched wooden door. It opened silently at his approach and a liveried servant waited upon the threshold. 'Where is the Witch Lord?' he demanded of the servant.

The servant bowed and stepped aside to allow Malus to enter the citadel's entry hall. 'My lord holds council in his private chambers,' he said with downcast eyes. 'He is not to be disturbed, dread lord.'

'I shall be the judge of that,' the highborn snapped. 'I have an urgent message for him from the men fighting in the Slavers' Quarter. Take me to him.'

The servant did not hesitate. 'At once, dread lord,' the man said quietly, then turned and led Malus through the small entry hall and into the great chamber beyond.

The main hall of the citadel was a large, circular space made of seamless, dark grey stone and hung with archaic tapestries depicting the deeds of warlocks long dead. The vaulted ceiling soared more than thirty feet over Malus's head and when he looked up he was shocked to see a gleaming moon and a scattering of stars glowing in a black velvet sky. Illumination from the illusory moon was the only source of light in the chamber, limning the dais and the iron throne in the centre of the room with a patina of burnished pewter. Statues of warlocks and witches stood in alcoves around the perimeter of the room, their marble faces astonishingly vibrant in the sorcerous light. Beyond the dais, the statue of a wingless dragon rose in a spiralling pillar of stone up into the darkness. Illusory moonlight shone on iridescent dragon scales formed from crushed pearl.

The grandeur of the room stopped Malus in his tracks. The air was heavy with age and solemnity, and for the first time the highborn realised he was in a tower that had once stood in Nagarythe, thousands of years before. It was a remnant of glories past and Malus was surprised at the sudden sense of loss he felt beneath the unblinking light of forgotten stars.

I will not forgive and I will not forget, he swore to himself. Death and ruin to the sons of Aenarion for all that they have taken from us.

The servant was moving swiftly across the gleaming marble floor, oblivious to the wonders surrounding him. Malus shook himself from his reverie and hurried after the retreating form. As he drew near the towering stone dragon he saw that the statue was in fact a cunningly constructed staircase, rising to the tower floors above. The risers were steep and narrow and there was nothing to grip during the climb, but the servant climbed the stairs with quick and nimble steps. The highborn climbed doggedly after the man, focusing his attention on the servant's feet just a few steps above his eye level.

They climbed into the ghostly night sky. Malus felt no heat from the gleaming points of starlight, but the smell of sorcery was thick in the air. When he reached out his hand to touch the gleaming moon his fingers passed effortlessly through it; skin tingling from the touch of sorcerous energies.

Up into the false twilight they rose, until their steps were all but lost in shadow. They left the main hall behind and after a time Malus dimly glimpsed vague outlines of other tower floors that they passed in the gloom. More sorcery played across his skin, he suspected that some protective spell kept him separate from parts of the tower that Bale did not wish strangers to see.

At length the servant stopped his nimble climb and stepped sideways off the stair. Malus moved quickly after the man, part of him fearing that if he could not keep up with his guide the dragon would keep him in its clutches forever. Leaving the staircase was like emerging from night into false dawn – one moment Malus was peering into twilit gloom and the next he was standing in a room lit with a soft glow, as from nascent sunlight. The chamber was smaller but no less lavishly appointed than the main hall below. Ancient tapestries hung at intervals along the circular wall, interspersed with statuary of arcane creatures like hydras, basilisks and griffons. The air was hushed and sombre, perfumed with the faint scent of incense. Across the chamber stood an arched doorway of dark oak banded with polished iron. Decorative iron bands on the surface of the door depicted a pair of wyverns locked in a mating flight above a range of narrow mountains.

The servant crossed soundlessly to the door and from the surroundings Malus sensed that he'd reached Bale's private chambers. The highborn took a deep breath and composed himself, tugging impatiently at the hadrilkar that hung loosely around his neck. He would toss the cursed thing aside the moment he found his way into the Witch Lord's presence; wearing the collar had been galling enough on the way to the tower, much less in the presence of other highborn.

Malus was considering the wording of his offer to the Witch Lord when the servant laid a hand on the iron-bound door and then stepped deferentially aside. The door swung open slowly and silently – just as an armoured highborn came barging through from the other side, flanked by his retainers.

Lord Tennucyr checked his stride just in time to avoid walking into the opening door and scowled fiercely at the man waiting on the other side. His brow furrowed in confusion as he recognised the collar around Malus's neck as his own – then his eyes went wide when he realised who was wearing it.

'You!' Tennucyr cried. 'But how?'

Malus masked his shock with careless grin. 'That would be a rather long story, I'm afraid. Let us just say I have a talent for trouble and leave it at that.'

The Naggorite lord went pale with rage. He drew his sword and levelled it at Malus's throat. 'Assassin!' he roared. 'Kill him!'

Tennucyr's men slipped like eels past their lord, their blades glittering in their hands. Malus raised his hand in protest. 'My lord, you're making a mistake!' he said quickly, but then the two retainers were upon him, their swords flickering like adders' tongues.

Malus retreated from the two men and groped frantically for his own blade. The two men advanced on either side of the highborn, pressing their advantage and slashing at his elbows and knees. The joints of the plate harness were among the armour's weaker points and the men were well-versed in the art of bringing down fully armoured knights. One sword glanced off Malus's right elbow joint, knocking the loosely-fitting armature askew and momentarily locking the joint. The second man's stroke chopped downward and caught the highborn's left knee joint, snapping pins and popping the metal armature apart. Malus felt a flare of pain from his battered knee and just managed to get his sword drawn in time to block a vicious cut to his throat from the man to his right.

The highborn bit back a savage curse. A fight was the last thing he needed at the moment. If Balneth Bale was in the chamber beyond it would only be a matter of moments before his personal guardsmen became involved, effectively ending any chance to make his case before the Witch Lord. Desperation fuelled his thoughts. 'Daemon...' he whispered under his breath.

'Do not ask, fool,' Tz'arkan snapped. 'I have given you all that I intend to give. What happens now must be of your own making.'

Malus roared in rage and hurled himself at the two retainers, slashing furiously at their faces and regaining some of the ground he'd lost.

The warriors were thrown off-balance only for a moment, then began to circle around Malus from opposite sides. The highborn fought the urge to turn along with them – if he moved to keep them in sight he would be turning his back on Tennucyr, who stood some ways off with sword in hand, waiting for the moment to strike.

Pain throbbed in Malus's shoulder, leg and arm and he could feel his limbs burning as he reached the limits of his meagre strength. He had to do something, or all was lost.

Malus locked eyes with Tennucyr just as his two retainers rushed at the highborn from either side. The Naggorite lord grinned mirthlessly and on impulse Malus hurled his sword at the man's face and charged at him.

Tennucyr's grin vanished as Malus's sword spun end-over-end at his face, but the highborn was skilled and swift, ducking and bringing up his own sword to knock the flung weapon aside. Before he could recover, however, Malus crashed into the man and knocked him off his feet. The two nobles crashed to the floor and skidded across the polished tiles and through the doorway.

The room beyond the door was dimly lit and redolent with burning spices. Lit braziers cast a ruddy glow against the eddying smoke and outlined heavy tapestries that hung from the unseen ceiling. The tapestries were set in an archaic style that further subdivided the chamber into smaller spaces, concealing the efforts of servants and retainers as they waited upon the highborn gathered in the centre of the chamber.

Malus took all this in with a single glance as he closed a hand around Tennucyr's sword wrist and pinned the weapon to the floor. His other hand closed around the Naggorite lord's throat. Tennucyr's eyes bulged and his free hand pummelled Malus's arm and head. Malus heard running feet behind him and knew that his time had almost run out. He raised his head to the silhouetted figures sitting in the room's central chamber and cried out, 'Balneth Bale! Witch Lord of the black ark! I am your kinsman and I have come to offer you a gift.'

The highborn heard the snarled curses of Tennucyr's men as they raced into the room. Malus tensed, expecting to feel a sword bite into the back of his neck, but one of the dark figures before him straightened slightly and held up a forbidding hand. 'That is enough,' the figure said in a cold, commanding voice and Malus heard the men behind him stop in mid-stride. The forbidding hand then beckoned. 'Release my cousin and come forward, Malus of Hag Graef,' the figure said. 'I would hear of this gift you would give me.'

Relief washed over Malus. With effort, he released Tennucyr and rose unsteadily to his feet, then reached up and unclasped the hadrilkar hanging around his neck. Malus dropped the torc onto Tennucyr's chest and calmly approached the Witch Lord.

The haze parted like fog as Malus approached the assembled Naggorites. Balneth Bale reclined in a massive throne formed of thorned ebony and wrought with carvings of wyverns on the hunt. The Witch Lord wore finely crafted armour chased with silver and gold and his black hair fell loose about his narrow shoulders. Bale was a handsome man, with an uncharacteristically square chin and high, flat cheekbones; Malus was immediately reminded of his mother Eldire, Bale's sister and former seer. The Witch Lord's new oracle, a surprisingly youthful-looking woman, sat just behind and to the left of Bale, clutching a glowing green orb in her slim hands. She was a voluptuous, white-haired figure with piercing black eyes and her sharp features bore an expression of secret mirth as she watched Malus approach.

What does that damned crone know, the highborn wondered?

Three other nobles sat in a rough semicircle before Bale, reclining in ebony chairs of their own and watching Malus with hooded eyes. They, too, wore full armour and sat around a low table set with a parchment map of northern Naggaroth. The part of the map in the centre of the table focussed on the Spear Road between the black ark and Hag Graef.

Now Malus knew where Bale and his army were headed. He smiled, inclining his head in a gesture of respect. 'I see you've heard the news,' he said.

Bale regarded Malus intently, though his expression betrayed nothing of his thoughts. 'Is it true?' he asked. 'Is Lurhan dead?'

Malus nodded. 'Your bitterest foe is no more, dread lord. I slew him with my own hand. And now I come to offer you my allegiance as a kinsman and an enemy of Hag Graef.'

'Allegiance. Indeed?' Bale smiled, but the mirth did not reach the obsidian flecks of his eyes. 'And what would you ask for in return?'

'Only what is any highborn's right – property and position within your realm and a place in your army.' Malus turned back to Tennucyr, who was being helped to his feet by one of his men. 'You could grant me his possessions, for example.'

'Mine?' Tennucyr gasped. 'I am the Witch Lord's cousin!'

'But *I* am his nephew,' Malus countered. 'Who you captured, tortured and attempted to sell into slavery at the house of Master Noros.' The highborn glanced enquiringly at Bale. 'If I am not mistaken, even by the laws of the black ark that could be considered treason. You could be stripped naked and impaled on the wall of the ark, my lord. Merely stripping you of your possessions is being *generous*, to my mind.'

Now the Witch Lord's smile broadened. 'I begin to see the family resemblance,' he said. 'Tell me: are there any particular possessions you wish to take from my cousin?'

Malus frowned. He had been thinking specifically of regaining the daemon's relics, but had no intention of revealing their importance to Bale or anyone else. 'I… I'm not certain what you mean, dread liege.'

Bale raised an armoured gauntlet and made a small gesture. Immediately a retainer glided soundlessly from behind a nearby hanging and knelt beside her lord. She held a polished wooden box in her hands, which she held up for the Witch Lord to inspect. Bale reached down and lifted the lid of the box with one steel-clad finger. Within, nestled in red velvet, lay the Octagon of Praan, the Idol of Kolkuth and the Dagger of Torxus.

'Perhaps you take my meaning now, Malus of Hag Graef?'

Tz'arkan shifted uneasily in Malus's chest, constricting tightly around his heart. The highborn fought to keep his voice calm. 'I don't understand.'

Bale laughed – a hollow, heartless sound. 'Your coming was not unexpected, Malus. In fact, it was *foreseen*.' The Witch Lord reached for the seer's hand, taking it in his own and a brief smile played across the oracle's cruel features.

Malus started to speak, but words failed him. His mind reeled at the implications of Bale's words and the room seemed to spin. Bale laughed and his men joined in – along with a thin, cackling voice from the shadows that sounded eerily familiar.

The highborn turned and bolted for the door, reaching for a sword he no longer possessed. Tennucyr's retainers moved to block the exit, but then Malus heard a sibilant hiss and the air around him seethed with power. The highborn felt as if a net of invisible fire had drawn tight around him, freezing him in place. Lines of searing heat glowed across the surface of his armour and somehow burned the skin beneath. Malus let out a furious groan, but the sorcery held him fast.

Malus watched the fierce expressions of Tennucyr and his men turn into looks of atavistic terror; without a word to the Witch Lord they retreated from the room. The highborn heard another hiss and the lines of fire around him twisted and contracted, forcing his limbs to obey the will of another mind. Slowly, haltingly, he turned back to face the Witch Lord, his expression a mask of fear and loathing. The cackling laughter continued, growing steadily closer.

Balneth Bale still reclined, his black eyes alight with triumph. Two figures stepped from the darkness behind the chair – one a hunched, trembling shape that laughed like a madman, the other a cloaked and hooded figure of medium height who supported the cackling wretch with an outstretched hand.

'You *will* serve us Malus Darkblade,' Balneth Bale said. 'Be assured of that. Already you have done our bidding and slain the Vaulkhar of Hag Graef. Soon you will become the instrument of the Hag's utter defeat.'

The cackling figure stepped into the red-lit haze. Lank black hair hung loosely around a youthful face that was crisscrossed with a pattern of deep and poorly healed scars. Two silver earrings glinted from the chewed nub of his right ear and a patchy grey goatee was the only hair left on the man's ravaged head.

Malus knew the man at once.

Fuerlan, Balneth Bale's son and formerly the black ark's hostage to Hag Graef, looked up at Malus with dark eyes devoid of mercy or reason. When he spoke his voice rasped like broken glass, shattered beneath the weight of hours of agonising screams.

'And when we take that cursed city you will have the honour of placing the drachau's crown upon my head,' Fuerlan whispered hatefully.

Malus trembled in the sorcerous trap, helpless in the grip of his enemies. Tz'arkan was right, he thought. Mother of Night protect me, the fiend was right.

Perhaps seeing the horror in Malus's eyes, Fuerlan threw back his head and cackled like a madman. Then the figure at Fuerlan's side withdrew her hand from the Naggorite's arm and extended a pale finger at Malus's forehead. As she did so, the light of the braziers reached inside the depths of her hood and Malus saw a familiar pair of dark, hateful eyes burning into his own.

Nagaira! Malus thought – then the finger rested lightly against his forehead and the world dissolved in an explosion of white light.

Chapter Fourteen
COUNCILS OF WAR

MALUS AWOKE WITH sunlight on his face, lying on a wide bed beneath piles of heavy blankets and furs.

He opened his eyes tentatively, squinting against the glare. His mouth felt as though it had been filled with paste and left to set overnight. With a groan he rolled onto his side – there was a faint sense of soreness in his left shoulder and arm and his limbs were weak, as if he'd lain in the grip of a powerful fever. A few feet across the bed-chamber stood a small table and upon the table sat a pitcher and a polished metal goblet. Malus took a deep breath, summoning his strength and slid his bare legs out from beneath the blankets. The air in the room was cool and the stone floor was colder still as he shrugged off the covers and slowly rose to his feet. Naked, he padded quickly to the pitcher and poured himself a cup full of dark red wine. He gulped the first cup down greedily, then poured another and sipped it steadily as he surveyed his surroundings.

It was a large room, fit for a well-to-do highborn. The bed, table and chairs were expertly carved from blooded oak and thick hangings covered the smooth stone walls to help keep out the chill. A tall chest of ebony wood stood against one wall. When he opened it, Malus found rich woollen robes and an indigo-dyed kheitan, along with a pair of fine black boots. Next to the chest stood an empty armour stand, which led him to wonder where his plate harness and weapons were.

Stranger still was the fact that the question didn't trouble him in the least. He felt entirely at ease, despite the fact that he didn't recognise the room and hadn't the faintest idea where he was.

Malus finished off his second goblet of wine, savouring the warmth filling his belly and reluctantly set the cup back on the table. The only illumination in the room was the shaft of grey sunlight streaming through the tall window opposite the bed; thin curtains shifted restlessly in the breeze streaming in from outside. The highborn walked to the window and pulled back the curtains enough to peer outside. He looked out on a profusion of tall, slate-roofed towers – and a trio of worn, blackened masts rising more than a hundred and fifty feet into the air.

He was at the Black Ark of Naggor, Malus realised with a start. Then he noticed that the hand holding back the curtains was covered in lines of fine, black script. Bemused, Malus inspected his scarred body and found it covered in line after line of arcane script.

'Some of my best work, if I do say so myself,' said a voice from behind Malus. 'It took hours upon hours to get it right, but the end result was quite satisfactory.'

The voice sent a chill down Malus's spine. It was familiar, seductive – and yet alien, somehow. Something about the timbre of the voice, or the tone… he couldn't quite say what, but it filled him with unease. He turned, clumsily and saw her sitting in a low chair in a dark corner of the room. She wore heavy, woollen robes dyed a deep red and a kheitan of blackened dwarf hide. Nagaira's strong fingers were steepled contemplatively as she studied him. He could feel her eyes upon him like a blade against his skin, though her face was masked in deep shadow. 'Tell me, dear brother, how do you feel?'

A dozen intemperate responses tumbled through Malus's mind. He struggled to maintain his composure. 'Right now, I feel like having another drink,' he managed to say. 'Would you care to join me, sister?'

Nagaira smiled – Malus couldn't see her expression, but he could *feel* her amusement – and she shook her head slightly. 'I would have a care with this country wine if I were you,' she said. 'It's potent stuff and you've been ill for a long time.'

Malus returned to the table and poured another drink while he tried to dredge his memory for clues to his situation. Everything was hazy and indistinct and the more he concentrated, the hazier his recollections became. 'How long?' he asked.

'Just over a week. The corruption in your wounds ran very deep – without my sorcery, I doubt you would have survived.'

Malus frowned, taking another sip of wine. Already his head felt light, but he welcomed the feeling. He glanced down at his left shoulder and arm and saw a pink scar on his bicep. 'Wounded, you say?'

For a moment, Nagaira was silent. 'How much do you remember, brother?'

Malus took a deep breath, grasping mentally at wisps of fog. Fragmentary images came and went, tumbling through his grasp like bits of broken glass.

Glass. An image of a hall in some far-off keep. Dead men lying in pools of blood and a head leaving a trail of steaming blood as it rolled across the stone floor.

The highborn glanced at Nagaira. 'Father is dead,' he said simply. 'I killed him.'

'Yes. Do you remember why?'

'I needed a reason?' Malus asked with a half-hearted smile. Just as quickly his expression changed to a worried frown. 'Honestly, I don't know for certain. We were in a tower somewhere–'

'Vaelgor Keep,' Nagaira said. 'It's a despatch-fort on the Slavers' Road near Har Ganeth, or so I'm told. Lurhan had concluded some secret campaign up in the hills and was headed home when you appeared out of nowhere and confronted him.'

'I? Confronted him about what?'

Nagaira spread her hands. 'Only you can answer that, brother. No one else survived to tell the tale. You slew Lurhan *and* his chief retainers single-handedly and fled into the night.'

Malus nodded thoughtfully, reaching for more shards of memory. 'There was a fight on the road...'

'More than one, I should think. You'd been shot several times and the wounds were festering by the time you arrived here. You were raving like a madman by the time you encountered a Naggorite patrol. Fortunately for you, the lord in charge was one of the Witch Lord's cousins and he must have recognised the family resemblance. They chased off Lurhan's men and brought you here, where I've been trying to save you ever since.' She folded her arms and inclined her head thoughtfully. 'Loss of memory is common after a long fever, though it should return over time.'

Malus eyed Nagaira warily as he finished his wine. 'I must say I'm surprised at your efforts on my behalf.'

Nagaira chuckled. 'I see there are some things you have no trouble recalling.'

He could remember her hanging in the air above her ruined tower, surrounded by a swirling vortex of unearthly power. She had tried to lure him into the forbidden Cult of Slaanesh and he'd betrayed her to the Temple of Khaine because... Well, he couldn't remember exactly why. 'I was certain you'd died in that explosion, sister.'

'That's because you're no sorcerer,' Nagaira said smugly. 'It suited my purposes for Lurhan and the drachau to believe me dead, though.'

'And so you came here.'

'What better refuge for an outlawed witch? Balneth Bale was sympathetic to my plight for a number of reasons,' she said. 'I daresay you thought much the same thing or you wouldn't have come here yourself.'

Malus shrugged, conceding the point. 'You still haven't explained why you went to such lengths to heal me.'

'Instead of weaving a robe out of your living nerves, you mean?'

The highborn suppressed a chill. 'The thought had occurred, yes.'

Nagaira sighed, like a cold wind whistling over broken stone. 'I was tempted, of course,' she said, a hint of steel slipping into her tone. 'You will never appreciate how much knowledge was lost when my library was destroyed. For that alone you deserved to be unwound from your bones an inch at a time. And it may happen yet, dear brother. Do keep that in mind. For now, though, Balneth Bale expects great things from you and I am of course obligated to aid my host in any way I can.'

'Ah,' Malus replied. Things were becoming a bit clearer, even if his memories remained jumbled and vague. 'And what exactly does the Witch Lord expect of me?'

'You will have to ask him yourself,' she said. 'He has summoned you to attend a war council with the rest of his banner lords.'

'Banner lords?' Malus raised a questioning eyebrow. 'I've sworn myself to his service?'

'As I said, you were delirious for some time,' Nagaira replied. 'When Lurhan's men entered Bale's territory to try and catch you they technically violated the terms of the truce between the black ark and Hag Graef. And now that our father is dead the Witch Lord sees an opportunity for a swift campaign against the Hag.'

'A resumption of the feud? To what purpose? It was Lurhan who defeated Bale's army in the field and conquered the ark all those years ago.'

'That's so,' Nagaira agreed, 'but he did it upon the orders of the drachau, Uthlan Tyr, who got them in turn from the Witch King himself. If Lurhan had simply done as he was ordered and killed Eldire for her crimes Bale's feud would have been with Malekith alone. Instead the vaulkhar took her as his concubine and the two cities have been fighting ever since. Now, I think Bale intends to seize Hag Graef and install Fuerlan as the drachau and by the laws of blood feud Malekith will have no choice but to sit by and watch.'

Malus gave a snort of disgust. 'Bale and his men defeat the army of the Hag? They don't stand a chance.'

'That, I expect, is where you come in, dear brother.' Nagaira rose smoothly to her feet. There was something in the motion that was vaguely unsettling, but Malus couldn't put his finger on what. 'The council is underway even now, so best not to tarry,' she continued. 'Although I would suggest putting some clothes on before we go.'

Malus bit back an angry retort. He wasn't some hound to be dragged about on a leash and paraded before some country lords! When had he agreed to serve Balneth Bale and why? What had he been thinking?

Conversely, what other choice did he have? After killing Lurhan he obviously thought that Bale would offer him sanctuary – and he'd been right, though at a steep price. He had no stomach for waging war against a city he'd one day hoped to rule himself – but war had a way of creating opportunities for the ambitious, he told himself. Before he knew it he was standing before the chest of clothes and pulling on a robe and boots. 'What of my armour and swords?' he asked.

'The armour is being mended. I confess we don't know what happened to your swords, which is a pity since they cost me a fortune,' Nagaira said.

Malus turned to his sister, a jibe rising to his lips – and the words died in his throat. She had stepped from the shadows of the corner and was pouring herself a cup of wine – but her face was still hidden in deep shadow. It was as though darkness hung about her like a cloak, concealing her features behind a shifting veil of night. Her pale hands almost glowed against the backdrop of sorcerous shadow as she lifted the polished goblet to her lips. She took a drink and noticed Malus's stare. Nagaira turned, setting the cup deliberately on the surface of the table. He could feel her eyes upon him again like a bared blade.

'My apologies, brother,' she said coldly. 'Were you not finished with the wine?'

TWO GUARDS IN full armour stood with bared blades before the iron-bound door. When Nagaira approached they bowed their heads respectfully and stepped aside – a little too quickly, Malus noted as he followed in his sister's wake. Not that he much blamed them. If the woman garbed herself in woven darkness, what else might she be capable of? But it was more than just the cloak of shadow – she had changed profoundly since that fateful night in the tower. A price had been paid for calling up the Chaos storm, he surmised, but he couldn't bring himself to ask what that might have been. In truth, he wasn't certain he would like the answer.

The witch reached out and laid a fingertip against the entwined necks of the wyverns and the door swung silently open. A rush of sound flooded out into the anteroom: men arguing, bottles clinking against cups, raucous laughter and bitter curses. But for the surroundings, Malus could have sworn he was about to step into a brewhouse rather than a council of war.

Nagaira glided like a ghost across the threshold and the clamour was snuffed like a candle. Malus heard his sister address Balneth Bale. 'If it please you, my lord, Malus of Hag Graef has come in answer to your summons and stands ready to assist you in your council of war.'

The highborn stifled a growl at Nagaira's announcement. Who was she to speak for him so freely? Yet he held his tongue as he entered the presence of the Witch Lord and his lieutenants.

Half a dozen armoured highborn sat in low chairs arranged in a rough circle before a tall chair of thorned ebony. Servants moved among the men, pouring wine or offering trays of food and retreating behind screens of heavy tapestries. A table sat in the centre of the circle, laid out with a large map of northern Naggaroth. On it, someone had drawn an arrow in red ink that ran from the black ark south and east along the Spear Road to Hag Graef.

Balneth Bale sat straight as a banner-pole on his ornate chair, his hands clasped together thoughtfully. On his left sat the ark's seer, who was peering into the glowing green depths of a crystal orb in her lap and whispering softly to herself.

The Witch Lord nodded gravely as Malus entered the room. 'Well met, slayer of Lurhan,' he said formally.

'My lord,' Malus answered, bowing to Bale. The smells of food and wine assailed him, making him dizzy with hunger, but he summoned up his willpower and refused to show any sign of weakness. 'How may I serve you?' he said carefully.

The assembled lords eyed Malus with barely concealed disdain. They were all older men, scarred by the kiss of sharpened steel and weathered by years of campaigning. All but one – a young highborn sat at Bale's right, wearing ornate, rune-marked plate armour. His bald head bore more scars than all the other men in the room combined.

'You could start by throwing yourself on the first enemy lance you find,' Fuerlan muttered into his cup of wine and the rest of the lieutenants laughed along with the young prince.

'Now that our new ally joined us, I will call the war council to order,' Bale said severely, as though Fuerlan hadn't spoken. He turned to the servants waiting in the shadows. 'Bring a chair for Lord Malus.'

Malus smiled. Lord Malus, he thought. I like the sound of that. Two servants rushed from behind a tapestry bearing another low-backed wooden chair and the highborn took his seat in the circle opposite Bale. Nagaira glided soundlessly around the perimeter of the men and took a place just behind and to the left of Fuerlan. The scarred young prince watched her movements and smiled possessively at the witch as she settled into her chosen spot.

What have we here, Malus wondered? Did Bale demand a marriage in return for giving Nagaira sanctuary? Or had she allied herself with Fuerlan as a way to set father and son against one another?

Once Malus was seated, Bale leaned back in his chair and spoke. 'All of you here are well aware of the crime committed against us by the men of Hag Graef years ago.' Grizzled heads nodded and growls of assent rose from the assembled lords. 'Many of you have lost sons and daughters to the feud and shed blood of your own to win back our lost honour. Time and again we have failed. The forces of Hag Graef were always too numerous and their damned general was a veritable daemon on the field of war. Yet we did not relent. We did not forgive and we did not forget.'

More nods and seething murmurs. Hot glares were turned upon Malus and the highborn met the stares with a cold look of his own.

'The ill winds of war have finally turned in our favour. Lurhan the vaulkhar lies dead at the hands of Eldire's son and many of Hag Graef's most powerful lords are on campaign with their warbands or at sea harvesting flesh from the Old World.' The Witch Lord gave his lieutenants a smug grin. 'Now you know why I've kept you all here at the ark this last month and commanded the marshalling of our allies, besides. Our foes are scattered and reeling from their loss, creating an opening for us to strike at their beating heart.'

The restless murmurs subsided. Wood and leather creaked as men shifted in their chairs and set their goblets aside. Bale had the lords' complete attention now. Malus studied the scene carefully, considering the implications. Vague memories of city squares full of armed men came and went before his mind's eye. It was no small thing to call upon ancient agreements and summon one's allies to war, Malus knew, nor was it wise to confine one's lords at home at a time when they could be seeking fortune and glory abroad. Bale foresaw all this, Malus concluded and a strange tickle of memory teased at the back of his brain. Had he seen something else when he'd been brought to the ark? The more he concentrated on the thought, the harder it was to resolve.

'The key is to attack swiftly, while the lords of the Hag are still in disarray,' Bale continued, bending over the map set before the council. 'Since Lurhan's intended successor Bruglir has died on campaign in the North Sea, the title of vaulkhar has – for now at least – passed to Isilvar Darkmoon, Lurhan's second son. By all reports, Isilvar is a libertine and a wastrel, unsuited to the field of war.' Bale glanced across the table. 'Do you agree, Lord Malus?'

'He is all that and more,' Malus said, galled to the core at the news. 'The man would have a difficult time running a flesh house, much less leading an army to battle.' The assembled lords laughed eagerly at the jibe. Malus stole a glance at Nagaira; her shadowy form was still as death itself, yet he thought he could sense a kind of predatory satisfaction there. She and Isilvar had been conspirators in the Cult of Slaanesh back at Hag Graef. Were they still allies? Was it possible that her presence at the ark was part of some still larger scheme? Malus reached up and rubbed at his forehead, feeling the beginnings of a headache.

Bale nodded at Malus's assessment. 'The acting vaulkhar has of course accused us of harbouring Lurhan's assassin and gone to Uthlan Tyr demanding a resumption of the old feud. This has served to complicate the drachau's plans to name another, more experienced highborn as the city's war leader, thus sowing more confusion in our enemy's ranks. The city's nobles will still be scheming against one another to claim the title when our message arrives at the drachau's court tomorrow.'

The Witch Lord eyed his lieutenants in turn and smiled wolfishly. 'An envoy bearing the severed heads of Lurhan's retainers will be dropped at Tyr's feet at midday. Thanks to the sorcerous skills of my son's betrothed–' Bale indicated Nagaira with a sweep of his hand– 'Those heads will proclaim to all assembled how Lurhan's men invaded our territory and slew our knights in a deliberate raid to seize our new ally Malus. That will give us ample proof to declare Hag Graef in violation of the Witch King's truce and resume the feud.' Bale chuckled coldly. 'By that time, of course, our army will have been six hours on the march.'

Bale leaned forward and ran an armoured finger across the frozen plains from the ark to the Spear Road, then south. 'We will make a forced march for the first few days until we've passed the Hateful Road and Naggorond. That will place us within three days' march of Hag Graef.'

'That will leave the men exhausted before they even meet the enemy in battle,' one of the older lieutenants growled.

To Malus's surprise the Witch Lord accepted the criticism with equanimity. 'The point, Lord Ruhrven, is to act so swiftly that there will be few enemies to face along the way. If the Dark Mother is with us, we shouldn't encounter any resistance at all until we reach Blackwater Ford.'

'And then?' Malus asked, growing intrigued with Bale's plan.

'By that time Hag Graef will have assembled their own force and taken to the field,' Bale said. 'Lurhan's men remain hungry for vengeance and his retainers are powerful men. Isilvar will have to take action to avoid looking weak, so he will have to raise as potent a force as he can manage in a short amount of time and send them north. The only uncertainty at this stage is whether Isilvar will lead this force himself or delegate it to another general.'

'He will not go himself,' Malus declared. Despite himself, he found that he saw great potential in Bale's strategy. 'He has no reputation as a war leader and his power base at home would still be too tenuous. He would remain at home to keep his rivals at bay and claim credit for any victory won against the forces of the ark.'

'Excellent,' Bale said, nodding approvingly. 'Then while Isilvar is still at the Hag stirring up political strife with his rivals, a large portion of his available forces will be heading into the jaws of our army – a force many times larger than the vaulkhar or his general will expect.' The Witch Lord's fist came down on the dark line of the Blackwater River. 'We will crush the enemy force decisively and then drive on to Hag Graef. By the time Isilvar learns of the destruction of his force we will be at the gates of the city and while the drachau and Isilvar's rivals turn on their titular warlord in the wake of his first defeat, we will take the city by storm.'

The assembled lords looked to one another with a mixture of apprehension and battle-lust. If it worked, the plan would bring them glory and riches beyond imagining. If it failed, however, their severed heads would be feeding the crows on the battlements of Hag Graef. One of the older lords put their doubts into words. 'Your plan is swift and daring,' the druchii said, 'but ends in a siege of one of the most powerful of the six cities. Every day we stay camped outside its walls is another day for the Hag's scattered nobles to gather into an army to come to the city's relief.'

At that, Bale reclined in his thorned ebony seat and gave the man a feline smile. 'There will be no siege, Lord Dyrval. The witch Nagaira will see to that.'

Eyes turned to the shadowy figure standing at Fuerlan's shoulder. Bale's son took a sip of wine, giggling into his cup.

It was Malus who broke the resulting silence. 'And how will my esteemed sister bring down the city gates?' he asked.

The Witch Lord replied. 'All things in their time, Lord Malus. All things in their time.' Bale raised his empty goblet and surveyed his men as a slave poured fresh wine. 'Let us concern ourselves now with who will lead our banners to war.'

Every other question Bale's lieutenants may have had vanished as the Witch Lord prepared to name the men who would command the divisions of the black ark's army in the field. It was longstanding tradition for a city's warlord to assign positions of rank within an army to whomever he deemed most worthy and capable. Typically, this meant that the army was led by allies and political favourites whose fortunes were already closely tied to the warlord himself. Such persons were guaranteed to reap a substantial share of wealth and glory if the army was successful, so competition for these positions was naturally fierce.

Since the black ark was too small to have a vaulkhar of its own, the privilege of assigning rank rested in the hands of Bale himself. Malus steepled his fingers thoughtfully and prepared to take note of whom he would need to curry favour with – and whom he would need to watch out for – in the coming days and weeks.

'According to our heralds, our mustered strength now stands at seven banners of foot and four banners of horse, plus one banner of household knights and a troop of autarii scouts,' The Witch Lord began. 'The infantry will be formed into three divisions of two banners each, with one banner held in reserve. The horse will be formed into a single division, as will the household knights.'

Malus nodded to himself. It was a fairly standard organisation of forces. Along with the obligatory captain in charge of the baggage train and the artillery, that would mean six positions of rank in the army forming the general's field council. A quick count of heads in the room revealed that there would be three highborn besides himself who would be thrown in among the rank and file – providing none of Bale's choices 'fell ill' before the army marched on the morrow.

'The command of the artillery and baggage train will go to Lord Esrahel,' Bale declared and the oldest of the assembled lords set his jaw and bowed his head respectfully, offering no complaint. 'Command of the three infantry divisions will go to Lords Ruhven, Kethair and Jeharren.' Ruhven accepted his assignment gravely, while Kethari and Jeharren – both much younger highborn – smiled fiercely and bowed deeply to their lord.

'Command of the cavalry will go to Lord Dyrval,' Bale said and the highborn almost jumped from his seat, his eyes widening in surprise. Many of the other assembled lords stole questioning glances at one another, but held their tongues. For his part, Bale kept his voice level, but there was a hint of a warning in his eyes as he regarded Dyrval. Malus considered the reactions. It appears Bale is giving Dyrval the chance to redeem himself for some past error, he thought. The man must be highly esteemed in the Witch Lord's eyes to be given such a coveted post, Malus concluded. That's something to keep in mind.

That left the command of the household knights, a position that promised even less in the way of plunder than the captain of the baggage train, who could at least expect to skim a healthy portion of gold from the army's own treasury. What the position lacked in profits it made up for in prestige, however, for the captain of knights was the army's second-in-command and could form alliances with many high-ranking nobles during the course of the campaign.

Malus eyed Fuerlan across the table and tried to hide his disgust. There was little doubt who Bale would assign the position to – and who would likely be his immediate superior in the army. He was lost in thought, contemplating various ways to quietly assassinate the man when Bale made his announcement and was jolted from his idle schemes when several of the lords leapt to their feet in outrage.

'This is an insult!' one of the older highborn shouted. 'My household has served the ark with honour for centuries.'

'And mine as well!' cried another noble, his face scarred from years of campaigning. 'You cannot do this, my lord!'

'I cannot? I *cannot*?' Bale said, his voice rising in anger. 'It is my right as Witch Lord to assign rank to whomever I please – and slay those who oppose me!' There was a rustle of steel as armoured warriors appeared from the shadows, hands on the hilts of their swords and the angry lords sank back into their seats before the forbidding presence of Bale's Witch Guard. 'He is an expert rider and breeder of nauglir and a fierce warrior in his own right. I have no doubt he will serve well as captain of the knights,' Bale growled at his lords. He turned to Malus. 'What say you? Will you take the position?'

Malus paused only for an instant. 'It is a great honour, my lord,' he said, rising to his feet and bowing deeply. 'I will not fail you or the army, my lord.'

'Naturally not,' Bale replied. 'Your life depends on it, after all.' The Witch Lord's smile did nothing to lessen the weight of his warning. 'In addition, you will command the army's scouts. Have you any trouble working with the autarii?'

'None at all, my lord,' he replied. Will they have trouble working with me? That's another question entirely. Was that why I was given this role?

'Then there is but one position left to assign,' Bale said.

The lords – including Malus – shared looks of bemusement. Lord Ruhven spoke up. 'If I am not mistaken, all divisions have been assigned.'

'That is so, but the commander of the army has not been named,' the Witch Lord said. 'Overall command will fall to my son, Fuerlan.'

The stunned silence that followed Bale's declaration told Malus all he needed to know about Fuerlan's reputation at the ark. Several of the lords turned pale at the thought. Bale's son took note of their discomfort and laughed uproariously, sloshing wine from his cup.

Lord Esrahel, the captain of the baggage, looked from son to father. 'Surely my lord would wish to command the army himself on the eve of so great a victory?' he began.

The Witch Lord shook his head. 'It is enough that I have laid the foundation for Uthlan Tyr's humiliation,' he said. 'My son will rule over the Hag in my name, so it is only fitting that he leads the army that will conquer it.'

It was a clever stroke, Malus had to admit. Having Bale's idiot son seize the city would only deepen Uthlan Tyr's humiliation – and by extension Malekith's as well. And I have been put in a position to ensure his success, the highborn thought grimly, or likely become the scapegoat if he fails.

Bale turned to his son. 'Have you anything to say to your men, general?'

Fuerlan brought his goblet to his lips and drained it in two noisy gulps, then threw the cup to the floor. A thin rivulet of wine ran along the ridge of a fine scar that pulled at the corner of his lower lip. He wiped his mouth with the back of an armoured hand and grinned mirthlessly at the lords. 'I have no way with words, my lord,' he said with a thin laugh. 'Deeds will have to suffice.'

He eyed Malus with a look of black-eyed hate. 'We march at dawn, Lord Malus,' he hissed. 'One minute later and I'll have you flogged in front of the rest of the army. Do you understand?'

Malus inclined his head. 'Perfectly, lord general,' he said with a wintry smile of his own. Then and there he realised that one of them would die before the campaign was over.

'Then all of you had best get to work,' Fuerlan declared. 'Assemble the army at the Great Gate an hour before sunrise for inspection. I will see you then.'

The lords shifted uncomfortably, grappling mentally with the epic task set before them. Esrahel turned to Bale. The captain of baggage already looked haggard and worn. 'Do we have leave to depart?'

Bale nodded. 'The council is adjourned. May the Dark Mother ride with you and reward your hatred with vengeance and victory.'

The highborn rose from their seats without a sound. Malus followed suit, moving as if in a dream. Hundreds of questions weighed on his mind. How was he going to get an army of thousands ready to march in twelve hours when he didn't even know where all the companies were camped, much less who commanded them? He could feel Fuerlan's eyes on him as he strode woodenly from the chamber.

The thought of being flogged in front of thousands of men filled him with rage, but he knew that there was no point dwelling on it. Fuerlan was going to find ways to torment and humiliate him no matter what he did – that much was clear. Better by far to focus on the campaign at hand and watch for opportunities to engineer the young general's demise.

The antechamber outside the council room was surprisingly crowded. Junior officers in the army had gathered like crows, waiting for word from their lords. As Malus began working his way through the crowd, he heard his sister's voice behind him.

'A moment, dear brother,' Nagaira said. 'I have a gift for you.'

Malus turned to find his sister standing just to the side of the council chamber's door, attended by a trio of armoured lords and two hooded druchii. Suppressing his irritation, he smiled. 'Poisoned wine, perhaps, or an adder stuffed in a bag? Something to abbreviate my misery?'

Once again, he sensed the witch's smile. 'Perhaps,' she said. 'A lord, particularly one of your position, needs skilled retainers to fulfil his duties.' Nagaira indicated the assembled group with a pale hand. 'So I present to you these warriors, all of them hungry for glory and eager to serve.'

And to spy for you, no doubt, Malus thought. Or stab me in my sleep if you so desire.

'Nothing could please me more,' he said tersely.

Nagaira gestured to the first lord. 'Lord Eluthir is a young knight from an old family. He is a fine rider and promises to be a terrible fighter in your service.' The young lord, wearing an old suit of battered armour and a heavy cloak of bearskin, bowed deeply to Malus. His long black hair was wound in a braid and fastened with a pair of gilded finger bones and his features were sharp and inquisitive like a fox's.

The second lord was an older man, balding and scarred, with a crude false eye made from red glass gleaming dully from his right eye socket. He bowed curtly when Nagaira indicated him. 'Lord Gaelthen is a well-respected and knowledgeable warrior who knows the ark's many household knights by name. He has fought in many battles against Hag Graef and is famous for his hatred of our former home.'

The third lord wore armour of black chased with fine gold scroll-work, his youthful features haughty and aristocratic and his eyes dark with simmering rage. When Nagaira turned to him the lord gave Malus a flat, almost accusatory stare.

'Lord Tennucyr is a rich knight and a fine rider, who has fought many battles with Hag Graef's men,' Nagaira said. Her voice sounded faintly amused, but Malus couldn't say for sure if she was mocking himself or Tennucyr. 'When he heard that you were entering the Witch Lord's service he was the first to volunteer to join your household.'

Malus surveyed the men. A young fool, an old fool and a knight with murder in his eyes, he thought with dismay.

The witch turned and beckoned to the hooded figures, who approached Malus on silent feet. 'I confess I've known the Witch Lord's intentions for some days,' she told her brother, 'and I knew you would also be required to command the army's scouts. So I searched far and wide in hopes of finding men who could aid in your work with the shades and help translate their slippery tongue. As luck would have it, these autarii had just arrived in the ark and were looking to sign on with the army and were honoured to accept a role in your household.'

The two figures drew back their hoods. One was a young autarii man with few tattoos, his face marred by fading bruises and a still-healing cut over one eye. He bowed his head deeply to Malus, but his body seemed tense and expectant.

The second autarii was but a girl, but her violet eyes were deep with knowledge of terrible deeds. Her black hair was pulled back in a number of tight braids and the tattoo of a coiling dragon worked its way from her slender throat up the side of her aristocratic face.

Another strange tickle of memory plucked at Malus's mind. A chill ran down his spine. 'Have… have we met before?' he asked the girl.

When the autarii spoke, her voice was musical but devoid of warmth. 'We have shared neither meat nor salt,' she said gravely.

'No, I suppose not,' Malus said. 'No doubt we will have such an opportunity soon.'

The ghost of a smile passed across the shade's face. 'Who can say what the future will bring?'

Chapter Fifteen
BEARER OF SACRED BLOOD

MALUS HAD BEEN in the saddle three hours before dawn, riding from barracks to barracks across the black ark and readying the army for war. It had been a long, sleepless night, filled with a hectic procession of introductions, assessments and orders, many of which had to be delivered forcefully and in person in order to actually get the companies moving in the right direction. There had been little time for the news of Bale's new appointments to filter through the rest of the ranks in the wake of the council and few captains were prepared to believe that he, of all people, had the authority he claimed. One particular fool had even gone so far as to call him a liar and laugh in his face. Fortunately his lieutenant had proved to be much more circumspect and sensible after Malus fed the captain to Spite.

Dawn was paling the sky and it looked to be a clear, cold day as Malus sat in his saddle beside the household knights in the sprawling square of the Great Gate. Of all the divisions in the army, the knights had been the easiest to organise and the hardest to command; with their own small army of retainers the knights could pack and be ready to move at a moment's notice, but convincing them of the need to do so was a tricky business.

After almost an hour of bickering over pride of place in the ranks Malus had lost patience and simply delegated the task to Lord Tennucyr, who was far more familiar with the peccadilloes of the ark's nobility. He hadn't seen Tennucyr for the rest of the night, but shortly before false dawn the first knights began filtering into the square and within half an hour the entire division was arrayed in columns before the gate, the pennons on their gleaming lances snapping in the brisk wind.

The first division of foot followed shortly thereafter, marching by company into the square and halting in columns a safe distance from the sluggish and sullen nauglir. The rest of the army was well out of sight, stretching along more than two miles of roadway that wound like a snake among the towers of the ark. Malus had ridden from one end of the line to the other and back again, checking with the other captains to ensure that the divisions were formed and ready for inspection according to Fuerlan's orders and by some miracle they had done it.

The highborn leaned back in his saddle and studied the sky. As near as he could reckon, Fuerlan was an hour late.

A heavy tread across the cobblestones of the square brought Malus's head around. Lord Gaelthen trotted down the rank of knights towards Malus, riding a huge cold one almost as old and scarred as he was. Spite growled in warning at the giant nauglir and Malus jerked Spite's reins with a warning of his own. Gaelthen reined in at a respectful distance and raised his hand in salute. 'Lord Esrahel sends his greetings, my lord, and says that there's no way the baggage train will be ready to move before mid-afternoon at the earliest.'

'Blessed Mother of Night,' Malus cursed wearily. The fighting divisions of the army wouldn't be clear of the city until mid-morning as it was, but that would still leave the artillery and supplies as many as six hours behind the rest of the force. 'What's the problem?'

The old knight leaned over and spat on the cobblestones. 'The leaders of the draughtsmen's guild decided to hold out for more coin. Said they couldn't provide enough wagons and oxen on such short notice.'

'And he didn't make an example out of the thieving wretches?' Malus snarled.

'Of course, but it takes time to crucify twenty men. Once Esrahel had everything sorted it was well into the night. They're just trying to catch up at this point.'

'Damnation,' Malus growled, his sword hand clenching into a fist. 'Do you think Esrahel truly has things in hand, or does he need to be replaced?'

Gaelthen gave Malus a sidelong glance with his one good eye. 'Not wise to replace one of the Witch Lord's appointments, especially before the army's even marched.'

'I couldn't care less about politics,' Malus snapped. 'Victory is what I'm after. So, does Esrahel know what he's doing?'

Gaelthen gave the highborn a searching look, then grinned. 'Aye, my lord, he does. He's had a bad throw of the bones and is trying to make the best of it, but he'll come through.'

Malus let out a loud sigh. 'Then mid-afternoon it is,' he said. 'It's not as though we'll be making camp in the next three days.' Suddenly it occurred to him that he hadn't checked to be sure each of the companies was carrying enough food and water on their backs to last them through the march. He grimaced. 'Gaelthen, I've got a job for you.'

Before he could continue Malus heard someone else calling his name across the square. The highborn looked over to see Lord Eluthir riding towards him with a cloth-wrapped bundle across his lap. Malus gathered up his reins and turned back to the scarred knight. 'Check with the company captains and make certain they've enough rations for the next three days. They carry what they will eat or they'll go without. Understood?'

A weary look passed across the knight's face, but he answered without hesitation. 'Understood, my lord,' he said and heeled his mount around on yet another errand for his master.

Eluthir arrived as Gaelthen rode off. The younger knight's mount was smaller than the older retainer's but it was still a third again as large as Spite. The smaller nauglir tried to sidle away from the newcomer, but Malus checked the motion with a touch of his spurs. 'What have you got for me?' the highborn asked.

'Hot bread, cheese and some sausage,' Eluthir said triumphantly, passing the bundle to his lord, then reached back and pulled an earthenware jar from a saddlebag and carefully unclasped the lid. When he pulled the lid away a spiral of steam curled up from the dark liquid within. 'And I had one of my men boil a pot of ythrum,' he said triumphantly.

'Ythrum?'

'It's a drink made from boiled courva root,' Eluthir explained. 'Don't they have it in Hag Graef?'

Malus frowned. 'Certainly not. It sounds disgusting.'

'Oh, it tastes truly vile, I'll give you that,' Eluthir said with a grin. 'But it will banish sleep and keep your wits sharp for hours.' He offered Malus the jar. 'I thought you might find it useful.'

The highborn eyed the jar suspiciously. 'For all I know, this could be poison.'

To his surprise, Eluthir laughed. 'Oh, it's poison, all right,' Eluthir said. '*Necessary* poison, but poison all the same.'

Just then Malus felt a jaw-cracking yawn come on and reached for the jar. He took a tentative sip, jerking back as the scalding liquid hit his lips. 'Gods Below,' he said with a pained expression. 'Bitter as a temple maiden's heart.' After a moment he took a real sip. The taste was

just as vile, but he was grateful for the warmth that filled his belly.
Malus unfolded the bundle in his lap and began wolfing down the
food, realising he hadn't eaten a bite all day. 'Any sign of Fuerlan?' he
asked between mouthfuls.

Eluthir took a long drink from the jar. Malus wasn't sure if the man's
grimace was from the drink or his opinion of the army's commander.
'Word is that he did a tour of the flesh houses last night and wound up
sprawled on the steps of the local temple sometime past midnight.
He's been inside ever since.'

Malus finished the quick meal and wiped away the crumbs from the
front of his kheitan – then his weary mind registered the fact that he
wasn't wearing armour. He didn't even have a sword to call his own.
'May the Outer Darkness take me,' he growled. 'Everyone's ready for
war but me!' He turned to Eluthir. 'Have you any idea where Lady
Nagaira is?'

'Your sister?'

'Of course, my sister! Who else?'

Eluthir blinked at his lord. 'Isn't that her over there?' he asked, indicating a knot of riders entering the far side of the square.

Malus followed the man's gesturing hand and saw a hooded figure
astride a powerful black warhorse, accompanied by a pair of armoured
cavalrymen and what appeared to be a small retinue of mounted servants. He couldn't tell if the figure was Nagaira or not, but he certainly
had no idea who else it could be. He kicked Spite into a loping trot and
moved to intercept the small party.

The horses in the group turned skittish when they caught the scent of
the assembled cold ones – all except for the black destrier in the lead. Its
coal-black eyes glared a challenge at Malus and Spite both as they
approached, and the highborn couldn't shake the sensation of sorcery
about the animal as he drew near. Up close, the hooded figure was indeed
a woman; when she turned her head to regard him, Malus saw the gleam
of silver steel beneath the shadow of the voluminous hood.

'Well met, brother,' Nagaira said, her voice muffled slightly behind
an ornately-worked mask made in the shape of a leering daemon. 'The
army is arrayed in fearsome order. You have done your work well.'

'Yet I look like a poor knight's squire the day before battle,' he said
sourly. 'Where are my swords and armour? You said they were being
tended to.'

Nagaira raised her hand and two retainers slid from their mounts
without a word and began pulling wooden boxes from the backs of
their horses. 'I had not forgotten,' she said, sounding amused. 'The
armourer said the plate was of inferior quality, so I commissioned him
to take another harness and alter it to suit. A good thing I know your
measurements so well, is it not?'

Malus didn't know whether to be grateful – a galling thought all by itself – or outraged. 'Such generous gifts, sister,' he said. 'Won't your betrothed grow jealous?'

'Oh, I'm not paying for these, brother,' she said. 'I told the armourer that you had been appointed as the army's captain of knights and he was more than happy to extend you credit.'

'Credit!' Malus cried. 'Now you've put me into debt–'

'Be still,' Nagaira snapped. 'Climb down off that stinking beast and put your armour on. Fuerlan will be here any moment.'

Malus was halfway out of the saddle before his half-sister's words even registered on his sleep-deprived brain. He saw the witch's body-guards share a surprised glance at his unquestioning reaction and swallowed an angry rebuke. A confrontation with Nagaira at this juncture would just make things worse and if Fuerlan was indeed on the way he didn't have much time. He stepped away from his mount and the two servants set the boxes containing his armour down beside him. The pair went to work smoothly and skilfully, quickly buckling and lacing the overlapping plates onto his kheitan. He glared angrily at his sister. 'You have grown presumptuous since you left the Hag,' he said coldly. 'A trait you picked up from your betrothed, no doubt.'

'Don't be stupid, Malus,' Nagaira said. 'I haven't the time for it. There's enough to be done without your foolish ego getting in the way.'

The outrage was so extravagant it made Malus's jaw drop. His face went white with rage, so much so that the men arming him took a worried step back and were careful not to get between the two siblings.

Yet he did not move. No words of rebuke rose to his lips. Nagaira met his stare unflinchingly and after a moment the servants resumed their work.

What's the matter with me? Malus thought, galled to the core at his inability to lash out at his sister. Did the fever sap my courage instead of my health? He felt another dull ache building in his head and gritted his teeth against the pain.

The servants were done in moments and one of their number presented Malus with a dragon-winged helmet and a fine pair of swords in matched ebony scabbards. He'd just buckled them on when he heard a curious wailing echoing down the street from the north. 'What in the Dark Mother's name is that?'

'That would be Fuerlan,' Nagaira said. 'Prepare yourself, brother. He's probably still drunk.'

Cursing under his breath, Malus climbed back onto Spite's back and returned to his place beside the knights Lord Eluthir took his place at Malus's side, but Gaelthen was still not back from his latest errand.

'Sa'an'ishar!' Malus bellowed, standing in his stirrups. 'The warlord approaches!'

The cry echoed down the line as the company captains called their footmen to attention. A ripple ran through the thicket of spears as the men dressed their lines. The wailing was much louder now; Malus could make out women's voices, crying out a shrill chant, then he caught sight of an ornately armoured figure riding an enormous cold one striding into the square.

Fuerlan swayed slightly in the saddle as the huge nauglir tromped over the cobblestones. His bald head glistened with streaks of fresh, steaming blood and he held in his hands a goblet of burnished brass. Behind the warbeast danced a procession of naked, blood-streaked women, chanting fiercely at the sky and slicing their flesh with curved daggers made of brass.

'Mother of Night,' Malus whispered, appalled at the ostentatious scene. 'Who does he think he is?'

'The spoiled son of Balneth Bale and the conqueror of Hag Graef,' Eluthir replied, just as quietly. 'And mad as a cockatrice these days. He was bad enough before, but his time at Hag Graef changed him for the worse.' Eluthir glanced at Malus. 'You're from Hag Graef, my lord. Do you know how he came to get all those scars?'

Malus shot the young knight a hard glare. 'He was overly familiar with his betters,' the highborn said tersely, then kicked Spite into a trot.

Fuerlan's procession was still streaming into the square when Malus met the general mid-way across the open space. Besides the temple maidens Malus saw that he had brought a troop of retainers, a multitude of servants and at least a dozen pack animals laden with everything from wine casks to furniture. Biting back his annoyance, he halted his mount and sat to attention, ready to report.

The young general glared evilly at Malus and hauled on the reins of his mount, but the old beast tossed its head and snapped at the bridle rings, bellowing in anger. Its tail lashed, whistling through the air like a giant's club, until even the temple maidens had to stop their chant abruptly and give ground. Fuerlan cursed the animal, spilling thick red liquid from his cup as he alternately kicked and lashed the beast with his reins. Finally the nauglir subsided and Fuerlan glared at Malus as if somehow he was to blame.

Malus took a deep breath. 'The army stands ready to march, dread general,' he said in a loud, clear voice. 'We await your order.'

'Did I order you to have them ready to march, you idiot?' Fuerlan sneered. 'I said have them ready for inspection.'

'And so they were, dread general,' Malus replied stiffly. 'An hour before sunrise, as ordered.'

A shiver of rage wracked the blood-soaked prince. 'Such impertinence!' he seethed. 'You dare mock me?'

'I am merely repeating the orders you gave to me,' Malus replied. 'No impertinence was intended.' For just a moment Malus heard Hauclir's voice in his head, repeating the same words with a carefully neutral expression on his face. Now I understand the man's infuriating tone, he realised.

'Liar!' Fuerlan snapped. 'I'll have you flogged!'

'As you wish, dread general,' Malus said past clenched teeth. 'But may I remind you that your father urged the army to make haste and a proper scourging will cost us several hours' delay.'

'More impertinence!' the general hissed. 'Rest assured, I see through your clumsy artifice! When we make camp I'll have you stripped naked and flayed down to your bones!'

'Very well,' Malus replied, knowing that they wouldn't be making camp for at least three days. 'Do you wish to address the troops before we march?'

'We will not march yet, you mutinous wretch!' Fuerlan shouted, leaning forward in his saddle. Malus could smell the wine on the man's breath from fifteen feet away. 'I said I wanted to inspect the army and that is what I will do!'

Mother of Night preserve me, Malus thought, struggling with his anger. 'Dread general, an inspection will cost us at least an hour of daylight, likely more. Your father–'

'Do not speak to me of my father, you damned kinslayer!' Fuerlan sneered. 'I know full well what he expects of me. Just as I know what is expected of *you*.'

Malus frowned. What does that mean, he thought?

'I will begin by inspecting the scout detachment,' Fuerlan declared imperiously.

'You can't,' Malus blurted, taken aback by the statement. Traditionally scouts weren't even considered part of the proper army. 'They left the ark at midnight.'

Fuerlan's eyes went wide. 'They *left*? For what purpose?'

'To *scout*, what else?' Malus snapped, finally losing his patience. 'They can't be out hunting for the enemy if they're here kissing your arse!'

'You… you…' Fuerlan stammered, his expression livid. 'You mutineer! I'll have you skinned alive! I'll have your bones broken! I'll tear off your privates and stuff them down your throat!'

Malus smiled at the scarred highborn. 'The dread general is welcome to try,' he said. 'But he would do well to remember what happened the last time he laid a hand upon me.'

The words struck Fuerlan like a physical blow. He trembled with animal rage, the goblet shaking in his hand. He snarled like a maddened wolf, reaching for his sword, until a cold voice stopped him in his tracks.

'My lord is being wasteful with the Lord of Murder's blessing,' Nagaira said from behind Malus. 'You spill his sacred blood upon the stones. It is an ill omen on the eve of war.'

Fuerlan paused, his eyes going to the goblet tilted precariously in his grasp. With an effort he righted it and attempted to regain some of his composure. 'This… this treacherous wretch provoked me,' he said, his voice a plaintive whine. 'He seeks to sabotage my campaign before it is even begun! Slay him! Slay him now!'

Malus stiffened. Fuerlan was one thing, but Nagaira was another matter entirely. His right hand twitched, creeping for his sword, but his sister's voice turned stern as she spoke to the general. 'I will do nothing of the sort,' she snapped. 'Compose yourself, my lord and remember all that we have discussed. Now is not the time for rash action.'

Fuerlan started to make a heated reply, then caught himself as he met Nagaira's gaze. Malus clenched his fist, fighting the urge to look over his shoulder at his sister and see what passed between them. The general locked stares with the witch for a moment, then lowered his gaze. 'You are right, of course,' he grumbled. 'Now is not the time.'

'My lord is very wise,' Nagaira replied, like a mother speaking to her child. 'Your army awaits, general. Show them Khaine's blessing and let us begin the journey to Hag Graef, where your crown awaits.'

'Yes. Yes of course,' Fuerlan said, gathering up the reins of his querulous mount. The old nauglir growled and began to walk forward. Malus nudged Spite backwards, out of the general's path, when the scarred Naggorite kicked his mount savagely and it leapt at Spite.

The older cold one bellowed in rage and charged at its smaller kin, but Spite was not one to back down from a challenge. Malus's nauglir roared in response and snapped its massive jaws in the cold one's face. Malus cursed savagely, hauling at the reins and Fuerlan did likewise, turning the old warbeast's head aside and bringing the two cold ones almost flank-to-flank for a brief moment. When they did, the general glared down at Malus, his face twisted with hate.

'I've dreamt of this for months,' he said, a deranged giggle escaping his lips. 'Look around you. I have an *army* waiting on my every command. I don't need to lay a hand on you in order to destroy you. By the time this campaign is over you will deliver your precious city into my hands. I'll have you skinned alive and marched through the Court of Thorns to place the drachau's crown upon my head and after you are dead I'll have your skull made into a chamber pot. Think on that with the few days left to you.'

Before Malus could reply Spite snapped at the old nauglir's flanks and the huge beast leapt away, bellowing in rage. Fuerlan cursed and kicked, spilling still more of Khaine's sacred blood upon the stones. An angry hiss went up from the temple maidens, causing Malus to smile. Nagaira's mount ducked out of the old nauglir's path, the fierce warhorse taking a nip of its own at the warbeast's shoulder.

It was several moments before Fuerlan got the animal under control; when he did he turned the nauglir to face the household knights as though nothing had happened. The highborn warriors watched Fuerlan stonily as he stood in his stirrups and cried out in a thin voice.

'Warriors of the black ark! It is I, the bearer of sacred blood, anointed in Khaine's cauldron!' Fuerlan held aloft the goblet continuing the ritual benediction. 'Before you I drink of the Lord of Murder's blessing, promising glory and plunder for all those who march beneath my banner!'

Fuerlan raised the goblet to his lips and a ragged cheer went up from the knights and the first division of foot. Malus watched the general tilt the cup farther and farther back, until its base pointed into the air. When Fuerlan straightened and raised the cup in triumph, Malus noted that there wasn't even a thin stain of red on his lips.

You spilled every drop of holy blood with your stupidity, the highborn thought bitterly. An ill omen indeed.

Malus listened as the young general began barking orders to set the army on the march. Bale's plan was audacious, but like all daring plans, it was a dangerous gamble. If the army of Hag Graef didn't do as the Witch Lord predicted in every particular, they could be heading into disaster.

THE AUTARII GIRL studied him with the dispassionate malevolence of a hunting hawk. Malus ran a gauntleted hand over his face and tried to wipe the dirt of the road and the weight of exhaustion from his eyes. 'What do you mean there are enemy troops north of the Blackwater Ford?'

'Horses and spears,' the girl said in her sweet, dead voice. 'Many scores of them.' She turned and pointed south along the road, beyond the hill in the distance. 'They gather wood and wait among the broken towers to either side of the road.'

Malus straightened in the saddle and tried in vain to work the stiffness from his aching back. The household knights were stretched along a quarter mile of the Spear Road, resting their weary mounts in the late afternoon sun. They were a half day past Naggorond; the black spires of Malekith's fortress city could still be seen, far to the northwest. Blackwater Ford lay another five miles south, nestled among a line of low hills and pine forests running east to west along the line of the rushing river.

The past few days had stretched into a blur of cold food and constant travel. The household knights had been ordered to march in the vanguard of the army, along with the first division of foot – Malus suspected this was so he would be the first to encounter any trouble along the way. The column paused for fifteen minutes every four hours; men learned to doze fitfully in their saddles and steal quick meals of hard biscuit washed down with brackish water. The highborn couldn't imagine how the spearmen were keeping up. Even the iron stamina of the nauglir was wearing thin.

They were only a few miles from their intended camp site. According to the plan the army was to make camp just short of the ford and rest for a day and a half while the scouts and dark riders crossed the river in search of the enemy. Unfortunately it seemed that the warriors of Hag Graef had other plans.

'Stand,' Malus ordered and Spite sank eagerly onto the surface of the road. The highborn slid stiffly from the saddle. His face and hands were caked with dust and grime and his lank hair was pulled back with a simple rawhide strap. Curiously, the runes Nagaira had painted on his skin remained as clear and vivid as ever – no amount of rubbing seemed to blur their sharp, black lines. The realisation left him uneasy.

Malus beckoned to the autarii and her companions. He'd sent her ahead with the scouts more to keep her out of his hair than anything else – when she was around she lurked like a vengeful ghost, watching him when she thought he wasn't looking. Nearby, Eluthir and Gaelthen dismounted as well, joining their lord. Tennucyr remained in the saddle, keeping an eye on the division.

'Show me,' the highborn said, kneeling in the dirt by the side of the road. 'Draw me a map.'

The girl sank gracefully into a crouch, drawing a long knife. She gave him a strange look over the point of the blade, then began scratching lines in the soil. 'Over the hill yonder the road passes through fields bordered with woods,' she said as she worked. 'Half a mile ahead there are ruins to either side of the road – broken towers and fallen statues. The men from the Hag wait there, cutting firewood and driving rails into the earth.'

'Rails,' Malus echoed, studying the autarii's map. 'Likely setting picket lines for the horses. Did you see any nauglir?'

'Dragon kin?' the girl said. 'No. Just horses and spears.'

The highborn nodded thoughtfully. Eluthir drank deeply from a water flask and eyed his lord. 'What does it mean?' he asked.

'An advance party,' Malus said. 'Cavalry scouts and foragers sent ahead to establish a camp for the main force, which means the Hag's army is crossing the ford as we speak.'

The highborn studied the map, trying to ignore the dull headache throbbing between his temples. There would be no way to approach the ruins down the road without being seen and he was sure the advance party would have at least some crossbowmen standing watch. He considered the rough outlines of the forests. 'Are there decent trails in these woods?'

'Hunting paths,' the girl said with a shrug. 'We have little need for them.'

'But could nauglir use them?'

The girl paused. 'Yes,' she said.

Malus studied the map for another few moments, trying to see if there was anything he was missing. If they could strike the enemy army while they were crossing the river they could wreak a terrible slaughter. But they would have to move quickly and the advance force would have to be defeated first.

He checked the map one last time and nodded sharply. 'All right,' he said, rising to his feet. 'Eluthir, mount up and ride back down the road as fast as you can. Fuerlan and the rest of the army should be only a mile or so behind us. Tell him that the army of the Hag is crossing the Blackwater right now and he is to come with all speed.'

'At once, my lord,' Eluthir said and ran for his mount.

Gaelthen watched the boy go and turned to Malus. 'What are we going to do in the meantime?'

Malus shrugged. 'The men have been marching non-stop for days and they've had nothing to eat but hard biscuits and water. We've two banners of foot and a single banner of cold ones; the enemy likely outnumbers us and has a strong defensive position.' He turned to the old knight. 'What else? We attack.'

Chapter Sixteen
A TERRIBLE COMPULSION

THE NAUGLIR WERE not stealthy creatures. Though too tired to do more than grunt irritably at their handlers, the long procession of cold ones along the narrow game trail touched off a near-constant chorus of snapping limbs and rustling brush. Each noise sounded as loud as a thunderclap in Malus's ears as the household knights worked their way through the dense forest. Like the rest of the division the highborn walked along beside his cold one, his hand tightly gripping Spite's reins. From his position near the head of the column all he could see were trees and dense brush all around him. For all he knew, the enemy force could be only yards away, but he clung to the thin hope that if he couldn't hear the activities of the enemy camp they likely couldn't hear the passage of the knights.

Ahead of Malus, Gaelthen's cold one abruptly stopped and sank to its haunches. Malus gave Spite's reins a slight jerk. 'Stand,' he said quietly and the nauglir stopped. Behind Malus, the next knight in line repeated the command to his mount and so on down the line. They had been working their way through the forest for almost three hours and the shadows beneath the trees were lengthening. He imagined the main body of Fuerlan's army bearing down the road as quickly as it would go, eager to come to grips with the enemy. If the knights didn't get out of the woods and deal with the advance party soon, the army would have to commit to a frontal assault against the camp that would stall their advance on the ford.

A trio of cloaked figures glided down the path towards Malus, cross-bows in hand. The autarii paid no heed to the volatile cold ones; the nauglir in fact didn't seem to notice the shades at all. Malus knew the figure in the lead to be his erstwhile retainer, the autarii girl with the dead voice and disturbing eyes. He reached up and pulled off his dragon-winged helmet as the scouts approached.

The shades reached Malus and settled into a crouch; that was the closest thing to a respectful salute the hill-clans seemed to be capable of. The autarii girl pulled back her hood and Malus was surprised to see her pale face was flushed and her violet eyes were gleaming with excitement. She leaned forward, resting her arms on her knees and Malus noticed that her slender hands were stained with fresh blood.

'We are past the enemy camp,' she said, a little breathless.

'Do they know we're here?' Malus asked.

The girl shrugged. 'They have heard the noise, but don't know what to make of it. City-bred fools,' she sneered. 'Your spears have appeared on the ridge and that is all they worry about.'

Malus nodded. He'd told Lord Ruhven to give him two hours to get the knights into position, then march the first division just over the ridge into plain sight. He'd told Ruhven in no uncertain terms that he was not to attack, just hold the enemy's attention. Hopefully he wouldn't get any strange notions when he realised that the knights were running behind schedule. 'Does the enemy have any scouts in the woods?'

To the highborn's surprise, the girl actually smiled. 'No longer,' she said, reaching beneath her cloak to hold up a cluster of freshly-cut scalps. 'Autarii from the rock adder clan. Almost as blind and deaf as the city folk.' The other two shades hissed in quiet amusement.

'How much farther until we can return to the road?'

'Not far,' the girl replied. 'A hundred yards or so. There is a field hidden by a bend in the road.'

Malus nodded, replacing his helmet. 'Good. Let's get moving.'

The shades rose as one and headed back up the line. In moments Gaelthen's cold one rose to its feet and the column was moving again.

Ten minutes later the woods began to thin just ahead and Malus could glimpse a grassy meadow between the trees. Moments later Spite was trotting eagerly through trampled brown grasses. True to the scout's word, the field was hidden from the ruins to the north by a spur of woodland that would allow them to form up unnoticed.

Malus pulled Spite to a halt and climbed into the saddle. 'Form into columns,' he said quietly to each of the knights as they emerged from the trees. 'No horns, no banners, no lances.'

The cloudy sky to the west was already iron-grey, shading into purple. Minutes passed as the household knights trotted their mounts across the field and formed into companies by column. Malus strained his ears, dreading the faint sound of trumpets to the north as Fuerlan's troops appeared on the scene ten minutes too early.

After what seemed like an eternity, the division was formed up and ready to march. Malus kicked Spite into a trot, heading for the front of the column. The autarii waited there on their haunches, showing off their scalps to one another. They straightened as he approached.

Malus drew his sword – a heavy, straight, double-edged blade, forged in the archaic style of the hinterlands – and pointed to the tree line on the other side of the road. 'Take position there with the full troop,' he said. 'Shoot down any foes who try to flee back down the road.'

The girl gave Malus one of her enigmatic stares. 'They won't escape us,' she said, then trotted into the shadows beneath the trees with her men in tow.

Malus watched her leave, still unable to explain why she discomfited him so. He'd find reasons to keep her well forward with the scout troop until they reached Hag Graef, at least. Once they were gone, Malus wheeled Spite about and addressed the knights. 'No one draws steel until I command it. Once the fight begins, kill every man you find.'

A feral mutter went through the assembled force. For just a moment, Malus was struck by the sheer power of the armoured force assembled in the field awaiting his orders. It was almost enough to forget that he was about to make war on his own city. Are you turning sentimental and weak, all of a sudden, he asked himself – Who in this whole land is truly your kinsman? You have slain Hag Graef's vaulkhar and every hand is turned against you. Your only choice is to run… or fight.

Malus raised his sword. 'Sa'an'ishar! Advance in column!'

A ripple went through the ranks as the long column of riders started to move. Malus rode in the forefront, leading the knights to the road and turning right, approaching the ruins from the south. As soon as the front of the column had turned onto the road Malus turned in the saddle. 'Household knights!' he called. 'Advance at the canter!'

As one, the armoured riders put their spurs to the cold ones' flanks and the huge animals leapt forward, picking up speed. Malus and the front rank of knights were around the bend of the road in moments and the highborn took in the scene that stretched before him.

The ruins might once have been a village, or a way station for soldiers travelling north – now they were nothing more than tumbled piles of stone and vague square foundations lines. The remnants stretched for fifty yards or more along either side of the road at a point where the forest fell away on either flank and gave a commanding view of the road north and the terrain to east and west. From Malus's perspective, the white and grey ruins were teeming with black-armoured men, all arrayed in a thin line of spear companies facing north. A reinforced company of spears stood athwart the road in close formation, presenting a thicket of gleaming steel points directed at the dense formation of troops stretching along the ridgeline to the north. The troops of the black ark were formed up for battle, well out of crossbow range, but were ready to sweep down the gentle slope into the ruins at a moment's notice. Lord Ruhven had chosen discretion over recklessness and looked prepared to hold his men in place until nightfall if necessary.

To the south of the ruins a sizeable force of enemy cavalry waited in loose formation, held in reserve to counter-charge any attack on the camp. The nauglir caught wind of the mass of horseflesh and quickened their steps. To some extent, the hungry warbeasts decided Malus's tactics for him – better to smash the fast-moving cavalry first and trap the enemy spear companies in the ruins. He could order Ruhven's men to attack from the opposite side if necessary and grind the enemy between them.

Less than a hundred yards ahead, many of the horsemen turned at the sound of heavy footfalls on the road. A ragged cheer went up from the cavalry, believing that the first units of their main force had finally arrived. Malus grinned mercilessly and let his force draw ever closer. The longer they could approach unchallenged the greater the impact of their charge.

Sixty yards. Fifty. Up ahead, Malus saw a group of riders peel off from the formation and begin trotting towards the oncoming knights. It was likely the cavalry commander – possibly even the overall commander of the advance party himself – heading over to appraise the arriving knights of the situation. The rider in the lead was a tall, aristocratic highborn with ornate armour and a flowing cloak of dragonhide. Malus tightened his grip on his sword and picked him out as his first target.

Forty yards. Thirty. Malus could clearly see the man's features. He looked familiar. Was he one of his father's former retainers?

Twenty yards. The expression on the man's face changed from one of smug viciousness to a blank look of shock. His eyes met Malus's and the highborn suddenly recognised the man as one of the cabal of nobles who'd invested their coin in his slaving raid the previous summer. The noble let out a shriek of surprise and anger and Malus answered it with a bloodthirsty laugh. He raised his sword high, its edge catching the fading light. *'Charge!'* he cried and a thousand knights took up the call, shaking the air with their battle-cries.

Spite leapt eagerly into a run, snarling hungrily at the enemy horses. The cavalry mounts snorted and screamed as the onrushing beasts bore down on them and chaos ran like wildfire through the enemy ranks.

The nobleman, seeing death rushing down upon him, grabbed for his sword and put his spurs to his horse's flanks, charging into the teeth of the Naggorite attack.

Had the noble been better prepared and his horse had more room to run, he might have gained enough speed to strike hard and present a more difficult target, but to Malus the lumbering fool might as well have been standing still. Spite raced past the squealing horse, jaws gaping for another and Malus brought his sword around in a short, precise arc, letting the weight of nauglir and rider provide most of the force behind the blow. The stroke knocked the noble's weak parry aside and the edge of the heavier sword took the top of the man's head off in a burst of blood and brain matter.

At once Malus pulled the blade free and aimed an overhand stroke at the rider passing him on the left, striking a glancing blow on the cavalryman's left pauldron and taking a sword stroke against his own left arm in return. Then Spite crashed headlong into a shrieking warhorse dead ahead and it was all Malus could do to stay in the saddle as the nauglir tore open its thickly muscled neck.

A flung spear came from nowhere, smashing against Malus's right pauldron and glancing away. Spite's prey collapsed to the ground in a welter of hot blood and the rider tried to roll away, screaming in fury. The nauglir snapped at the man, catching him by the hip with a crunch of bone and tossing his bleeding form high into the air. 'Go, Spite! Go!' Malus cried, kicking at the nauglir's flanks and sending the beast deeper into the melee.

The knight's charge had struck home like a hammer against glass, scattering the enemy cavalry in all directions. Panicked mounts stampeded through the ruins, trampling shocked spearmen who were trying to reorient their formation against the sudden threat from their rear. Crossbow bolts buzzed angrily through the air, finding their marks in friend and foe alike. The stink of blood and ruptured organs was thick in the air and Malus's ears were battered with a surf-like roar of shouts and screams and the clash of steel.

An enemy cavalryman charged at Malus from the right, his spear levelled at the highborn's chest. With a yell he brought up his sword and parried the sharp, steel spearhead, letting the man's thrust carry the weapon past him on his right. The druchii rider cursed sharply and drew on his reins, wheeling his mount away – but Malus brought his left heel into Spite's flank and the nauglir whipped its powerful tail across the horse's path. The animal pitched over head first, its forelegs snapped and the rider was caught beneath the weight of the wounded beast.

Spite crouched and reared, roaring its bloodlust and Malus bent low against the warbeast's neck, trying to gauge the course of the battle swirling around him. The bodies of horses and men littered the ground and all he could see immediately around him were blood-stained knights driving their nauglir deeper into the ruins in search of more foes. As near as he could tell the enemy cavalry had been entirely overrun and the knights had carried on into the ranks of the spearmen hiding among the stones. There were screams and the clash of arms among the rocks, as well as the sharp twang of crossbow strings.

Malus found himself wishing he'd kept a trumpeter close by to keep control of his men, but it was too late for that now. The battle was joined and would run its course and he would have to hope that he still had a division left to command when all was said and done.

Malus kicked Spite into motion, following after the red tide of the household knights. The heavily armoured warriors had cut a swath through the disordered ranks of the enemy spearmen, focusing on the company caught in the open in the middle of the road. Nothing but broken spears and shattered bodies remained of the force, their lifeblood soaking into the cinders of the road. Beyond, he could see the knights fighting isolated groups of infantry in the fields north of the ruins and further battles were going on amid the broken foundations themselves. Malus looked left and right, seeking the enemy and spotted a small knot of footmen running down a rock-strewn lane with crossbows in their hands. They saw Malus at the same instant, their faces twisting with rage.

The highborn felt his guts turn to ice and the searing image of a line of crossbowmen silhouetted against a wall of fog brought a near-panicked cry from his throat. 'At them, Spite!' he shouted, kicking hard with his spurs. The nauglir spun on its heels and leapt at the four men just as they levelled their weapons and fired. One bolt struck Malus a glancing blow in the chest and bounced away in pieces, while another broke against Spite's bony skull. The other shots missed, hissing past Malus and the crossbowmen threw down their weapons and ran, screaming in terror. Spite trampled one and Malus smashed the skull of another with a single stroke of his sword, then the cold one lunged forward and caught a third with a clash of its terrible jaws. The fourth man leapt over the remnants of a retaining wall and disappeared from sight.

Malus reined in Spite and realised that the sounds of battle had ceased, replaced by savage cheers. The highborn turned Spite around and returned to the main road, where he saw knights filtering through the ruins singly and in pairs. Freshly severed heads bounced on trophy hooks attached to their saddles. When they saw Malus they raised their swords in salute and he knew then that they had won a crushing victory.

Spurring his mount into a canter, Malus headed for the fields north of the ruins. Many of the knights had collected there, taking trophies from the dead. By the number of bodies on the field it looked as though the enemy spearmen had retreated from the ruins and tried to reform in the open, but the knights had simply run them down. Malus stood in his stirrups. 'Gaelthen!' he cried. 'Lord Gaelthen!'

'Here, my lord!' came a hoarse response. Across the field, Gaelthen spurred his mount and trotted over to Malus. The older knight was covered in gore, but none of it looked to be his own.

'Assemble the division here in the field,' Malus ordered. 'Have them ready for rapid movement.' He gauged the height of the sun. 'Fuerlan should be here at any moment and we have just enough time to strike south for the ford.'

'Yes, my lord,' Gaelthen said, then nodding towards the ridgeline. 'That might be Eluthir now.'

Malus turned to see a lone nauglir trotting down the slope towards the ruins. He nodded to Gaelthen, who turned away and began shouting instructions to the jubilant knights, then reached up and pulled off his helmet. The cool air felt good against his face and neck and he suddenly realised how bone-weary he truly was. No time to rest now, he thought grimly. We've miles to go and more men to slay before the day is done.

Eluthir reined in before Malus, surveying the carnage with an envious grin. 'Congratulations on your victory, my lord. I pray that the next time I'll be along to share in the slaughter.'

Malus chuckled tiredly. 'You'll get your wish before the hour's done, I'll warrant. How far is Fuerlan and the main force?'

The young knight's face fell. Malus frowned. 'What has happened?'

Eluthir took a deep breath. 'My lord, I delivered your report, but the general has decided to encamp for the night. He orders you to fall back with the vanguard and prepare for an attack on the enemy at dawn.'

Malus couldn't believe what he'd just heard. 'An attack at *dawn*? Is he mad? Did you tell him that the enemy force is crossing the Blackwater Ford right now? We could reach them in an hour and slaughter them piecemeal! By dawn they will be in good defensive positions – right *here*, most like – and will be ready and waiting for us.'

The young knight gave Malus a pained look. 'I explained the situation as clearly as I could, but he said the men needed rest and time to prepare. He… He said he needed time to consider his strategy.'

'Time to tap another cask of wine is more like,' Malus spat. For a moment he was sorely tempted to disregard Fuerlan's orders and march on the ford with just the household knights and Ruhven's spears, but without any word as to the size and disposition of the enemy he could easily find himself outnumbered and outmatched. He couldn't very well stay where he was, either. The enemy could reach the ruins within the next few hours and he would then be facing the entire army with just two divisions of troops. He ground his teeth in frustration. That damned wretch had left him with no other choice.

Just then, Gaelthen returned. 'My lord, the division is formed up and awaiting your command,' the scarred old warrior declared. 'What shall we do?'

Malus straightened in the saddle, taking one last look at the scene of his first battlefield victory. 'We retreat,' he said bitterly.

THE TENTS FOR the general and his retainers had been erected first, even before the camp's perimeter had been set. They stood out incongruously in the centre of an exhausted army; some companies were making half-hearted attempts at erecting their own shelters, while other units simply stopped in their tracks, curled up on the ground and went to sleep. Picket lines had gone up for the horses and weary cavalrymen held their own fatigue at bay long enough to see that their mounts were cared for, while men from the baggage trail unpacked provisions and began lighting camp fires for a cursory evening meal.

Weary heads turned as the household knights and Ruhven's spears made their way into camp. The mounted warriors were a fearsome sight, caked with blood and grime and sporting grisly trophies from the battle at the ruins. Malus dropped out of the procession and reviewed the division as it went past, taking stock of their condition. Casualties had been very light, owing to the knights' heavy armour and the element of surprise. He doubted they would be so lucky on the morrow and the thought galled him to the core.

Once in the camp, the knights dispersed in search of their tents. Malus headed for the general's pavilion.

The guards outside Fuerlan's large campaign tent paled at Malus's forbidding, bloodstained figure and neither dared challenge him as he stalked like a hungry wolf into the raucous atmosphere within.

He followed the sounds of laughter, passing through small 'rooms' created with cloth partitions to allow the general's servants to do their work without intruding upon his leisure. Malus passed through an antechamber where scribes were busy compiling orders for the following day and emerged into a large space in the centre of the tent where Fuerlan held court amid his retainers and sycophants.

Incense filled the space with a faint blue fog, rising wispily from three small braziers. The chamber was laid with piles of thick rugs and low tables had been set with platters of meat and cheese for the general's guests. Almost a dozen young highborn sat around the room, drinking wine and talking or playing games of dice in the shifting fire-light. Fuerlan sat in the centre of it all like a strange spider, his lanky limbs sprawled over the arms of a high-backed chair of blooded oak as he gulped wine from a gilded skull. When he saw Malus his eyes gleamed with hateful mirth.

'It is about time you arrived,' Fuerlan sneered, his voice slurred by wine. 'And looking like you've rolled in a midden heap. I suppose I shouldn't be surprised.'

'Not surprised that I'd choose to fight instead of hiding in a tent with a bunch of toadies?' Malus hissed. 'You had a great victory in your grasp and you let it slip away, you scarred, simpering wretch!'

Fuerlan's eyes went wide. His hands trembled as he went white with rage. 'Seize him!' He roared. 'Tie him to a pole and skin him alive!'

Two of the lordlings leapt to their feet and rushed at Malus. Without thinking, Malus drew his gore-stained blade. 'Come ahead, then, if you dare! I'll hang your narrow skulls from my saddle!'

'Enough!' Nagaira's cry cut through the din like a thunderclap.

The lordlings froze. Malus turned to face the source of the witch's voice. A stir passed through the deep shadows at the far end of the room and she stepped up to the edge of the firelight. Her eyes smouldered like hot coals from the silver edged sockets of the daemon mask, stopping Malus in his tracks.

Of them all, only Fuerlan was bold enough – or foolish enough – to take umbrage at Nagaira's appearance. 'Go back to your tent,' he snapped. 'This is no concern of yours.'

'Is it not?' She hissed and Malus saw the light from the braziers go dim. 'Think, you twisted fool! Think of the plan and all that remains for Malus to do! Would you kill him now and see all our work undone?'

Malus's eyes went wide. What is she talking about? Unbidden, his eyes strayed to his sword hand and the lines of precise runes painted there. 'What do you mean for me to do?' he said without thinking.

Nagaira turned her gaze on him again and he felt his rage snuffed out like a candle flame. 'For now, you will go to your tent and rest. There will be hard fighting tomorrow and you must lead our army to victory.'

It was no true answer, but Malus found he couldn't bring himself to defy her. He watched, helplessly, as he sheathed his sword and turned on his heel without a word. As he left Fuerlan's tent he heard Nagaira say something vicious to her betrothed, but he couldn't make out quite what she said.

A spike of savage pain stabbed through Malus's head as he stumbled from the general's tent. The pain made his stomach lurch and his knees weak, but his body kept moving all the same, driven by Nagaira's powerful compulsion. It was only after he'd walked more than a dozen yards from the tent that he could finally drop to his knees, gasping at the blinding pain.

What has that witch done to me, he thought? And how can it be undone?

Chapter Seventeen
SHIELDS AND SPEARS

THE RIDGELINE WAS dark with armoured men. Hours before dawn the army of the black ark had been shaken from their bedrolls and fed a cold meal of meat and cheese. Then they'd formed up in column and marched south, where the army of Hag Graef waited. In the pale glow of false dawn they had left the road and formed into line on the reverse slope of the ridge. Dark riders had busied themselves chasing off small parties of scouts and keeping enemy skirmish parties well away from the Naggorite force. The banners of foot were ready and the ground shook beneath the measured tread of twelve thousand men as they crested the ridge and levelled their spears at the enemy waiting for them in the ruins.

Malus sat in his saddle farther back upslope than the waiting infantry divisions, allowing him a clear vantage to glare hatefully down at the ruins a hundred yards south. The enemy general had made good use of the time Fuerlan had foolishly ceded to him. During the night huge blocks of stone had been dragged from the ruins and strewn carefully through the fields to the front of the army's position, creating fields of obstacles that would make a Naggorite cavalry charge a difficult proposition at best. Units of spearmen were arrayed in serried ranks behind the stone obstacles, ready to impale any foe that drew too near. Behind them, two large building foundations, one to either side of the road, had been built up enough to allow units of crossbowmen to stand and fire over the spearmen's heads at oncoming enemy troops.

The highborn glared bitterly at the enemy fortifications and once again counted the number of troops. Three banners of foot and possibly a full banner of horse somewhere back behind them. He kept getting glimpses of men on horseback moving south of the ruins, but never enough of a look to discern how many there were. There was something about the enemy dispositions that bothered him. Something wasn't right, but he couldn't say what. Malus glanced down at the autarii girl, who stood at his left stirrup. 'You say they have men watching the woods to either flank?'

She nodded. 'Crossbowmen and spears, waiting behind deep ditches to spoil a cavalry charge,' she said. 'Perhaps the enemy has a seer amongst them.'

The idea sent a strange tremor of foreboding through Malus, but he pushed it aside with a snarl. 'Not likely,' he said. 'The drachau won't call on the witches except in dire emergencies. Too much trouble to deal with otherwise.' He turned his head and spat over Spite's right side. 'No, I'll wager the enemy captain took a look at how the men and horses were killed and where they fell and pieced it together himself. If nothing else, the men of the Hag are wise in the ways of war.'

'And trickery,' the girl said coldly.

'Even so,' Malus nodded. 'It sounds as though you've had some experience with them.'

The girl gave Malus another one of her strange looks. 'Just once,' she said. 'But rest assured I will have my revenge.'

Malus winced as a jolt of pain throbbed behind his eyes. 'Is that why you joined the army?' he asked, absently, rubbing his forehead. 'You hope to find this man who wronged you?'

'I thought I had already,' the girl said quietly. 'But when I looked him in the eye he did not know me.'

Malus chuckled. 'Then it likely wasn't him. You're not the sort of person who is easily forgotten.'

The autarii gave him an enigmatic look. 'Perhaps,' she said. After a moment, she reached up and pointed a tentative finger at the upper part of his bare neck. 'How did you come by those markings, my lord?'

Malus's hand went to his neck. 'The runes? My sister put them on me when I was in the grip of a fever and now they won't come off. Why? Can you read them?'

She shook her head. 'I'm no witch, my lord, but it's clear that she's laid a spell on you.'

The highborn considered the scout. 'Have you any knowledge to remove spells?'

'No. As I said, I'm no witch,' she replied. 'But I've heard it said that witches carry books and scrolls marked with their spells. Perhaps there is something in her tent that might be of use.'

'Hmmm. Perhaps,' Malus said slowly. 'That might be worth pursuing, if an opportunity presents itself.' He leaned closer to the scout. 'I have a proposition for you.'

'Oh? What is that?'

'Help me find a way to undo this spell and I will do everything I can to help you find the man that wronged you.'

The girl gave one of her ghostly smiles. 'Very well, my lord.'

There was the sound of horns to Malus's right. He turned and saw Fuerlan climbing the reverse slope of the ridge, surrounded by a crowd of retainers and servants. Some distance behind the crowd Nagaira rode her black warhorse, attended by her own small group of hooded servants.

'First things first,' Malus growled. 'The general has finally deigned to join us and now we must find a way to survive the day.' He wheeled Spite around, throwing a parting glance at the scout. 'Stay where I can find you,' he ordered. 'I may have orders for the scouts depending on how the battle progresses.' Then he kicked Spite into a trot and made his way towards Fuerlan.

He never reached the general. Nagaira saw his approach and spurred her horse forward, blocking Malus's approach well short of his goal. Spite growled at the destrier, but the warhorse stood its ground and bared its square teeth with a challenge of its own.

'Out of the way, sister,' Malus said. 'Or is the great general no longer interested in reports from his own scouts?'

Morning sunlight gleamed on the snarling daemon's mask that Nagaira wore. The shadows that clung to her skin turned the mask's eye holes into pools of impenetrable night. 'The enemy is arrayed before us,' she said hollowly. 'What more need we know?'

The highborn gritted his teeth. 'The enemy has three banners of foot and possibly a full banner of horse,' he said tersely. 'Their flanks are protected and they are in well-fortified positions controlling the road.'

Nagaira's masked face regarded the enemy force to the south. 'Unless I am much mistaken, we still greatly outnumber them,' she said at length. 'They haven't the strength to defeat us.'

'But they have ample strength to *bleed* us,' Malus snapped. 'And to delay us. This isn't the only battle we will have to fight, sister. Whatever happens here, we must be able to carry on with enough of an army to still conquer the city. And right now I'll wager what's left of my soul that there is a messenger killing horses to get back to the Hag and warn the drachau we're coming.' The highborn glared at Fuerlan, who sat astride his nauglir some yards away, sipping wine offered by one of his servants. 'That fool has already squandered our greatest advantages: speed and surprise. From now on, the closer we draw to Hag Graef, the more we will play into the enemy's hands.'

Nagaira's laughter echoed faintly behind her mask. 'Have faith, brother. We have more at our disposal than mere soldiery.'

'Then best make use of it now,' Malus shot back. 'If you have the same sort of power over Fuerlan as you have over me, convince him to withdraw and lure the enemy into pursuit–'

'I do not know what you speak of,' Nagaira said, but Malus felt her piercing gaze like a wash of heat over his skin. 'Do not talk of such foolishness again, Malus. Not to anyone. Do you understand?'

The highborn's retort was snuffed like a candle flame. He felt his rage sputter and go out, no matter how hard he struggled to maintain it. 'I… I understand…' he heard himself say.

'Very good,' his sister said, as though he were some sort of trained beast. 'If you are so concerned about the Naggorite army, you will have to find a way to pull them from the fire. I have no great power over Fuerlan. Indeed, the more blood his army spills, the more he hungers to send them into battle. There – you hear? The trumpets have sounded. The battle has begun.'

Sure enough, Malus heard the skirling, wailing cry of trumpets echoing down from the ridge, signalling the army to advance. As one, three banners of infantry lowered their spears and began to march towards the ruins. At either flank, a banner of horse followed slowly in their wake, held back in anticipation of breaking through the enemy line. Down among the stones, the Naggorite trumpets were answered by Hag Graef's horns, readying the troops for battle.

'Is there no sorcery you can employ?' Malus asked. 'Bolts of fire or terrible apparitions? Something?'

His sister merely shook her head. 'I must preserve my power for the decisive strike,' she said. 'That time is not now.'

'If we don't triumph here you may not get another chance!'

The witch chuckled, pulling on her reins. 'All is going according to plan, brother. You shall see.' She kicked at her horse and set off at a canter towards Fuerlan and his retainers. Malus couldn't even bring himself to glare at his sister's back as she left.

Gritting his teeth in frustration, he returned his attention to the battle developing at the base of the slope. The Naggorite spearmen had almost reached the ruins and already the air between the forces was dark with the flitting shapes of crossbow bolts. The spearmen advanced with their shields before them, presenting a moving wall of wood and steel to the hail of bolts. Here and there men fell, clutching at short, feathered shafts that sprouted from chest, neck or leg. Wounded men staggered from the ranks, limping or stumbling back towards the ridgeline or crawling weakly in any direction that would take them away from the awful rain of steel. Highborn officers in the rear ranks bellowed at the spearmen, ordering fresh warriors to fill the gaps and the companies pushed onward.

From his vantage, it appeared to Malus that the initial advance was going well. Losses were minor, so far, but the closer the banners came to the enemy lines the more powerful the enemy crossbows would become and the Naggorites would have to worry about the foes in front of them as well as the bolts falling on them from above. He spied more movement to the south of the enemy's front line – more horses shifting position, it looked like. The cavalry commander was either an indecisive sort or he was trying to make it appear as though there were many more horsemen around the ruins than there really were.

Where was the general? He started at the far left flank of the enemy force and searched the ruins carefully. He would want to be in a spot with a good field of view, he thought, focusing on tall piles of stone or lanes that afforded a broad view of the battle line.

He caught sight of a nauglir loping slowly down the Spear Road, right in the centre of the enemy position. An armoured highborn sat tall in the saddle, but his hands held neither weapon nor shield. Behind him followed a small retinue of knights mounted on cold ones – only five, too small to make much difference in a pitched battle. The general and his bodyguard, Malus thought. It could be no one else.

As Malus watched, the general reined in some ten yards from the line as the spear companies met with a keening of battle cries and a rattle of steel on wood. The Naggorite banners were arrayed four ranks deep; the front rank thrust their long weapons at neck level, holding their tall shields close to their bodies, while the second rank stabbed overhand, aiming over the heads of the men in the front rank and thrusting downwards at their enemies' heads. The men of Hag Graef were formed in two lines, allowing them to cover more ground. Ordinarily this would have made the formations less resilient, but their impro-vised fortifications lent them added protection and deploying only two ranks ensured that every man in the banner was able to fight.

The clatter of blows and the screams of the dying echoed back from the ruins. More and more wounded began streaming back from the Naggorite companies – for now, only a trickle, but each man was like a drop of blood, sapping the formation's strength. There was no way to tell how badly the enemy was suffering. If just one of Hag Graef's banners fell back, it would open the way for the horses to break through and wreak havoc. So far, however, the enemy stood firm.

We will grind them down, he knew. We have two banners to their one. Sooner or later they will break, but at what cost?

He studied the battle line from one end to the other, trying to see some weak spot where perhaps the horsemen or the household knights could make their presence felt. But the ground did not allow for it. The dense forests to either side of the road funnelled the Naggorite troops towards the ruins and the line of spear companies completely filled the fields in front of the enemy positions.

The general, Malus decided. The enemy general was the key. If he fell then resistance would swiftly unravel. But how to reach him?

A cheer up went from the battle line. The Naggorite banner in the centre of the line had pushed hard against the Hag Graef spearmen covering the main road, driving them almost ten yards south. The enemy line was bending. When would it reach the breaking point?

Malus looked to his left and caught sight of the autarii girl crouched on her haunches, studying him with dispassionate malevolence. He beckoned to her and she ran like a deer to his side. The highborn gestured over his shoulder. 'Find Lord Gaelthen and tell him to bring up the household knights.'

As the scout ran off, more trumpets sounded. When Malus looked back downslope he saw that the Naggorite banner on the right flank was falling back! The relentless hail of crossbow bolts had taken a fearful toll of its companies – from their ragged numbers Malus estimated that the banner had lost at least half of its strength. The spearmen were falling back in good order, facing the enemy and still fighting as much as they could, but the nerve of the division's leaders had broken. The division's second banner – led by its captain, Lord Kethair – was already charging down the slope to prevent the flank's collapse and salvage the division's honour.

In the centre, the spearmen of Hag Graef continued to give ground. Malus caught sight of the enemy general again, close to the rear rank of the retreating companies. He wasn't panicking, the highborn realised, and he wasn't calling for reinforcements.

Just as the Naggorites pushed past the first line of ruins, the reason for the retreat became apparent. Black bolts flashed into the spear companies from either flank as concealed groups of crossbowmen caught the Naggorite troops in a withering crossfire. Malus watched in horror as the huge block of troops seemed to shrivel before his eyes.

The ground shook beneath Malus as the household knights trotted up the road. A quick glance behind him showed that the division was drawn up in good order and ready for battle. The centre of the Naggorite line couldn't hold for much longer. The highborn reached a quick decision. Drawing his sword, he stood in the stirrups and cried in a carrying voice. 'Sa'an'ishar! The household knights will advance to battle!'

There was the icy rasp of a thousand swords leaping from their scabbards and a lusty roar from a thousand throats hungry for slaughter. Malus roared along with them. 'Forward!' he shouted, lowering his heavy blade and kicking Spite into a trot.

Fuerlan's trumpeter was already blowing urgent notes, but the general had seen the danger a few moments too late. The centre banner would collapse within moments and Lord Ruhven's remaining troops would not be able to reach them in time. The column of armoured knights crested the ridge and Malus spurred his mount into a canter. Lord Gaelthen, in the front rank, shouted a command and the column picked up speed. Ahead, the spear companies of Ruhven's second banner parted with hurried shouts of encouragement as the mounted warriors rolled down the Spear Road like a thunderbolt.

With the long slope working in their favour the nauglir covered the hundred yards in the space of just a few seconds, the heavy warbeasts knocking aside or jumping over rocks that would have broken a horse's leg. Thirty yards from the ruins the first enemy crossbow bolts began to whir angrily through the ranks, cracking against shields and ringing off heavy armour.

Pressed hard from the front and sides and in the path of an impending cavalry charge, the centre Naggorite banner fell apart. Soldiers threw discipline to the winds and ran, dropping their spears and racing for their lives. The enemy spearmen let out a triumphant shout and pressed forward, killing all they could – and realising, too late, that the tables had abruptly turned.

At twenty yards from the enemy line Malus raised his sword once again and brought it down in a sweeping cut. 'Charge!' he ordered and the household knights responded with a furious shout, giving their mounts their head. Spite roared and dug in with his clawed feet, leaping for the enemy troops with jaws gaping wide.

The enemy spear line faltered in the face of the Naggorite charge. The front rank recoiled with frightened shouts, bunching up against the men behind them. The thicket of spears that would normally have given a cavalry formation pause became tangled, forcing the deadly points out of alignment. Malus raced at the wall of armoured men and glittering spear points and howled like one of the damned.

Nauglir crashed into the disordered line with a rending crash and a chorus of screams. Spear hafts snapped, sending steel spear points whirling and ricocheting among the ranks. Huge jaws snapped shut on armour, flesh and bone. Somewhere, a nauglir bellowed in mortal pain. Blood sprayed and burst all around Malus as men went down beneath massive cold ones and were torn apart.

He hit the spearmen expecting to be struck in return, but none of the enemy spears found their mark. One of the warriors tried to turn and run but disappeared beneath Spite's claws. Another had his head bitten clean off and simply collapsed where he stood. Malus brought his sword down on a spearman to his right, finding the gap between the bottom edge of his helmet and his backplate and breaking the man's neck. He pulled the blade free and held its dripping length over his head. 'Forward, knights! *Forward!*' he cried, spurring his mount ahead.

Spite leapt forward, catching a running man in its jaws in passing and dragging him along as though he were a doll. The man shrieked and gurgled as the nauglir galloped on, driven hard by Malus as the knights shattered the banner of spears and fell like wolves upon the general and his bodyguard.

The sound of horns screamed wildly in the air around Malus as the enemy was hurled back by the fury of the charge. Ahead, he saw the enemy general pull a heavy, long-handled mace from a hook on his saddle. His armour was expertly made and warded with numerous sigils of protection. His face was hidden behind an ornate helmet worked in the shape of a dragon's skull, but Malus was certain he was one of Lurhan's chief retainers and a powerful highborn in his own right. His bodyguards were surging forward, trying to get between the Naggorites and their lord, but Spite was smaller and swifter than the larger beasts and Malus was upon the general in the blink of an eye.

Spite leapt for the throat of the general's cold one, raking the side of the nauglir's face with its talons and grinding dagger-like fangs against the warbeast's scaly hide. Malus lunged forward, chopping downwards with his sword, but the blow fell short and glanced from the general's armoured leg. He heard the lord bellowing behind his dragon-faced helm as he let Malus's sword slide past and then lashed out with his mace. The blow landed on the highborn's right pauldron and to Malus it felt as though he'd been hit by a boulder. There was a flare of intense pain at his shoulder joint and his arm went numb to his fingertips. It was only through sheer force of will that he managed to keep a grip on his sword.

Enraged, Malus swung again, but his shorter sword was still almost a foot out of reach. He hauled at the reins and pummelled Spite's flanks with his spurs, but the nauglir was locked in a life-or-death struggle with the general's mount and was oblivious to all else. There were shouts and screams all around him as the household knights threw themselves at the general's bodyguard. Men on foot were running past, cursing and shouting in fear. The highborn glanced to his left and saw Lord Gaelthen just a few feet away, splitting the helm of one of the general's bodyguards with a vicious stroke of his sword.

Malus caught a flash of movement to his right and turned just as another of the bodyguards charged at him. The man's nauglir snapped at Spite's flanks and got a tail in its snout for its trouble; the beast recoiled slightly, spoiling the bodyguard's aim. The man's blow fell short and struck Malus hard on the right knee. The armour turned the blow, but the shock of the impact caused his knee to explode in pain. Malus cursed at the man and threw all his strength into a vicious thrust at the bodyguard's head. He expected to stun the man with a ringing blow to his helm, but by the Dark Mother's fortune the point of the sword caught in the helmet's eye slit and drove through into the warrior's skull. Blood and fluids ran in rivulets down the length of the broad blade as the man screamed and convulsed, then pitched forward out of the saddle with Malus's sword still lodged in his helmet.

The weight of the armoured man pulled Malus downward as well – and then something struck the back of his helmet with a rending crash and everything went black.

Chapter Eighteen
INTO THE TRAP

MALUS RODE THROUGH a warm, red haze that swallowed sound and blurred his vision. He couldn't feel his arms – in fact, he couldn't feel much at all – but he could tell he was riding in the saddle behind an armoured knight. Each swaying step of the nauglir caused him to brush against the cold steel of the knight's backplate; he smelled metal and oil, blood and raw earth and old leather. He tried to speak, but his mouth refused to work. Instead, all that escaped his lips was a low groan.

The knight's head turned ever so slightly. Malus heard the creaking of hide and smelled something like damp mould.

'Do not speak,' the knight said. The voice was deep and sepulchral, as if it echoed from the bottom of a tomb. 'Your head has been split and your brains scooped out.'

The knight turned and showed Malus his hand. Clotted clumps of wrinkled brain matter rested in his palm, oozing blood and clear fluids between the knight's fingers. 'You must put them back in before it's too late.'

Malus screamed in terror, recoiling from the knight and his gruesome gift. The wind of his passing felt strange against the back of his head, touching icily on jagged shards of bone and drying blood. He tried to move his arms but could not and was grateful for it. If he could, he would have reached up to the back of his head, and he dreaded what awful ruin his fingertips would find there.

He heard a strange, muffled shout and invisible hands seized him. The world spun crazily and he screamed again, closing his eyes tightly against the red mist.

Malus felt himself falling like a leaf on a winter breeze, settling gently to the ground. There was a murmur above him, a buzzing of voices that he couldn't quite make out. Summoning up his will, he forced himself to be calm and slowly opened his eyes.

The fog was receding. He was lying on his back near one of the fires of the Naggorite camp, staring up at the clouds and the mid-morning sun. Two men stood over him; it took a moment to recognise one of them as Lord Eluthir. The young knight's face was streaked with gore and fresh blood oozed from a deep cut along the side of his right cheek. The other man wore heavy, stained black robes worked with runes in silver thread and his long face was old and seamed. The two men were arguing fiercely, but at first Malus couldn't make out what they were saying. He tried to raise his head but only managed a few inches before a wave of pain and nausea almost overwhelmed him. The highborn fell back, closing his eyes and tried to take stock of his rebellious limbs.

'Why did you bring him here?' the older druchii said angrily. 'He's a highborn, take him to his tent and let his people care for him. We've too much to do as it is.'

'If he had his own healer do you think I'd be wasting my time with the likes of you?' Eluthir answered haughtily. 'And he's no mere highborn, either – he's Malus of Hag Graef, second-in-command of the army!'

'Mother of Night,' the chirurgeon cursed. 'All right,' he said querulously and knelt beside the highborn. 'What happened to him?'

'We were in battle, you old fool,' the young knight snapped. 'The enemy general struck him in the head with a mace. It was just a glancing blow–'

'Obviously, or else you wouldn't be here troubling me,' the chirurgeon grumbled. He reached down and grabbed Malus by the jaw with one rough hand, then bent over and peered into the highborn's eyes. 'Can you hear me?' he asked, speaking slowly. Malus grunted an affirmative. The chirurgeon nodded and waggled his fingers in front of the highborn's eyes. 'Well enough,' the older man said, then took his hands and ran them carefully around Malus's scalp from around the eyes all the way to the back of the skull. Sharp pain blossomed on the left side of his head and Malus hissed warningly at the healer. The chirurgeon nodded and pulled away, his left hand wet with blood.

'There are two sizeable punctures, probably from bits of his broken helmet,' the older druchii said. 'His skull seems intact, but I don't doubt it's been cracked like a boiled egg. Take him to his tent and get him some hushalta. He should rest for several days and you should have someone watch him closely the entire time. If his health holds up through tonight, he should be all right.'

Eluthir was incredulous. 'That's all? Give him mother's milk and let him sleep it off like he's had too much wine?'

The chirurgeon was about to give the young knight a blistering reply when Malus cut in. 'Get me up,' he said weakly. 'I don't need a chirurgeon. Let him go about his business, Eluthir.'

The older druchii looked down at Malus and bowed his head respectfully, then hurried off. Malus tried to lever himself into a sitting position and Eluthir took his arm and pulled him clumsily upright. At once the highborn felt a wave of dizziness and nausea sweep over him, but he closed his eyes and bit his lip until it passed. 'What happened?' he finally managed to ask. When he opened his eyes, Eluthir was still supporting him. Nearby, Spite and Eluthir's cold one sat on their haunches, their snouts, forelimbs and chests brown with dried blood. The two highborn were, if anything, even filthier.

'You stabbed one of the general's men and then he hit you–' Eluthir began.

'I *know* that part,' Malus snapped. He caught himself reaching back to probe at the back of his skull and forced himself to lower his hand. The vision – or was it a hallucination? – was still strong in his mind. 'How goes the battle?'

'Ah, of course!' Eluthir's face brightened. 'We've won, my lord. Our charge carried the day – when we broke through the spear companies covering the road, the enemy called up their reserves, but Lord Kethair's fresh troops hit the enemy's flank and the enemy spear line broke. The fight in the centre stayed hot for a few minutes more, because the general seemed to realise who he'd hit and ordered his men to seize you. The household knights put a stop to that, though. Lord Gaelthen killed the last of the general's bodyguards and would have gone after the general himself except that the enemy's reserves arrived and covered his escape.' The young knight's face was alight with triumph. 'I slew one of the general's bodyguards myself. Took his fine sword and hung his head from my saddle. He was a quick one, but I–'

'Where is the army now, Eluthir?' Malus prodded.

'The army? Strung out halfway between the ruins and Blackwater Ford by now. Lord Fuerlan ordered a general pursuit with the cavalry and the household knights to hunt down and finish off the enemy banners. The infantry is re-forming at the ruins – from what I could tell, they took a bad beating. Some of the spearmen were saying Lord Kethair himself had been killed, but there's no way to tell just yet.'

'And the scouts?'

'Well, you can ask them yourself if you want.' Eluthir pointed to a group of shades crouching some distance away. 'Fuerlan had no orders for them and your autarii girl took some of her men and followed me back when she heard you'd been wounded.' The young knight eyed Malus and gave him a roguish wink. 'That one would make a feisty concubine, wouldn't she?'

Malus stopped the conversation with a sharp look. His mind was working furiously, trying to take stock of the situation. He eyed the shades and one of the things the autarii girl had told him sprang to mind. The highborn glanced at Eluthir. 'One last question: where is Nagaira?'

Eluthir frowned. 'Last I saw, she was still with Lord Fuerlan, but that was before he took off with the cavalry. I expect she's still at the ruins, or on her way back here.'

The highborn nodded. It was the best chance he was likely to get. He looked about the camp, getting his bearings, then beckoned to the shades. They rose to their feet and glided soundlessly to him. The autarii girl pulled back her hood and regarded him closely. 'Is my lord well?' she asked.

'Well enough,' Malus answered. 'Tell me: do you know where my sister's tent lies?'

After a moment she nodded. 'It is near the general's tent. Black sides and small runes over the doorframe. It stinks of magic.'

Malus nodded. 'Leave one man behind to guide us, then take the rest and scout it out. See if there is anyone inside.'

A knowing look came into the scout's eye and she nodded, hissing curt orders to her companions in an impenetrable autarii dialect. The shades slipped gracefully among the clustered tents, leaving a young man behind who beckoned to Malus and started off after his mates. The highborn pushed away from Eluthir and followed on unsteady legs.

'My lord?' the young knight said. 'My lord? What are we doing?'

Malus looked back at Eluthir and smiled. 'Why, we're going to ransack my sister's tent, of course,' he said. 'There's something of mine I'm looking for and I think she has it.'

'Oh. I see,' he said, though the bemused look on his face suggested otherwise. 'I'll go and get the nauglir.'

THE TENT'S DOORFRAME was narrow and formed of some polished, black wood, making the carved runes nearly invisible to the naked eye. Malus peered closely at them, careful not to cross the threshold and tried to make out their meanings, but it was an exercise in futility. 'I doubt they are charms to keep the dust and the flies out,' he muttered. He glanced at the autarii girl beside him. 'You are certain there is no one inside?'

She nodded. 'I counted all her retainers with her on the field this morning and none have returned.' As she spoke, her eyes wandered up and down the lane running past the tent's entrance. The rest of the shades had disappeared, on the lookout for Nagaira or her men.

Malus scratched at clots of dried blood caking his narrow chin. 'I suppose the tent walls are warded as well.'

'Most like, but that is of little consequence.'

'Oh?'

The girl took another look around, then went around to the back of the tent. 'A ward on a tent wall only awakens when the fabric is cut,' she said, studying the shelter's exterior. 'So the challenge is to slip past without cutting it.' The autarii's gaze settled on two tent stakes, about four feet apart. She pointed at one and knelt by the other. 'Take hold of that rope and unwind it. Keep it taut, lest the side of the tent collapse.'

The highborn unwrapped the guy rope, digging in his heels at the surprising weight pulling at the line. The side of the tent started to fold, but he took the rope in both hands and pulled it taut again. The scout had undone her own rope and beckoned to Malus with her free hand. 'Good. Now pass your rope to me.'

Carefully, Malus worked his way over and guided his rope into her small hand. She wound the line around her wrist and palm and held it effortlessly. 'All right,' she said absently and slowly inched forward. The side of the tent started to fold inward, losing tension. Abruptly she stopped. 'There. Now you should be able to slide underneath.'

Concealing his surprise at the girl's strength, Malus edged forward and got down on his belly. There was just enough of a gap for him to wriggle under. Once he was past the tent wall he straightened again and found himself in a narrow compartment where one or more slaves were meant to sleep. He stepped over the neatly stacked bedrolls and pushed aside the inner flap to enter the tent's main chamber.

The air was close and thick with incense and the black roof let in little light to see by. Three banked braziers cast a dull, red glow over the rug-lined floor. Once he had let his eyes adjust, Malus could make out a low, narrow bed in one corner, then a table with two chairs near one of the braziers. Two large sub-chambers were partitioned off from the main chamber, each on opposite sides of the tent. Both were enclosed by walls of tanned hide and accessed by a heavy leather entry flap. One of the sub-chambers reeked of spilled blood and magic, causing his skin to crawl.

There was nothing of interest in the main room, Malus quickly realised. After a moment, he took a wary step towards the sub-chamber that smelled of fresh blood.

'You are the arrow, Malus.'

Malus whirled. The voice had come from the second sub-chamber, on the other side of the room.

It was the voice from his vision.

'What do you mean?' Malus asked. 'Who are you?'

There was no answer. The highborn rushed across the room and drew back the leather entry flap. There was no one there. Instead, Malus saw a chair and a travelling table covered in parchment sheets and heavy, leather-bound books. Another small table was stacked with arcane objects – goblets, bottles of coloured glass, sheathed daggers and a small wooden chest carved with sorcerous glyphs.

'I'm hallucinating,' he muttered to himself. 'There's no other explanation.' But what did the voice mean, he wondered?

He went to the desk and began leafing through the pages. They were all very old, the parchment dry and brittle to the touch. Nearly all of the pages seemed to map the sprawling tunnels of an enormous labyrinth, with notes written in faded black ink. The writing appeared to be druchast, but he couldn't make out a single word. Malus grimaced in annoyance. 'Some damned sorcerer's code.'

Malus studied the curving paths for several moments, trying to divine what they were. They looked familiar somehow, but he couldn't quite place them.

Outside Malus heard muffled hoof beats. He froze, listening intently, but the riders passed on by the tent. Nagaira could be here any minute, he thought. Keep looking!

He turned his attention to the books piled on Nagaira's table and picked up the one on top. It was a large, heavy volume, with faded yellow pages and heavy iron clasps binding the cover.

After several moments of fumbling with the clasps, the book fell open to a spot marked with a flat braid of black hair. The pages contained an elaborate drawing of the front and back of a naked druchii male. The body was covered in line after line of elaborate script.

Malus set the open book down and pulled off his left gauntlet. His bare hand trembled slightly as he held it over the book and compared the runes on his hand to the ones on the page. They matched in every particular.

There were lengthy sections of text describing the ritual involved, all written in a language Malus had never seen before. Page after page of writing, evidently detailing a powerful and complex spell. 'So you cured me of a fever, dear sister?' Malus hissed.

He was just about to close the book when he noticed a notation in the margin of one of the pages. The ink was fresh and the writing was obviously Nagaira's: *If memories can be walled away, can thoughts be channelled to suit the sorcerer?'*

The knight's voice spoke behind Malus. 'Does an arrow choose where it is shot, or who it strikes down?'

When the highborn turned, no one was there. 'Speak plainly, spirit!' Malus snapped in frustration. 'What does Nagaira intend for me?'

There was no reply, but Malus heard a faint scratching against the side of the tent. 'What is it?' he asked in a low voice.

'Horses on the Spear Road,' the autarii girl hissed. 'Nagaira has entered the camp.'

'Mother of Night,' Malus cursed. Acting quickly, he closed the book and returned it to its place. He gave the second table a quick once-over, looking for anything of interest. None of the bottles were labelled and he wasn't about to start tasting them. 'Would it be too much to ask for one to have the word "antidote" written on it?' he grumbled.

Lastly he examined the wooden box. The clasps were simple enough and didn't look to have hidden needles in them. He undid them and opened the lid. Inside he found three strange objects: an octagonal medallion etched with runes, a small brass idol and a long, narrow black dagger. 'Now what are these?' he muttered.

The scratching came again. 'Hurry, my lord! She is almost here!'

For a moment he was tempted to take the relics, thinking he might use them to force Nagaira to release her hold over him – but then realised that all she had to do was command him to hand them over and he would have no choice but to comply. He snapped the box shut with a snarl and rushed from the chamber, heading for the tent's entry flap. He gambled that the wards laid upon the entryway weren't meant to keep people inside from getting out, so he pushed the heavy leather hanging aside and dashed out into the bright sunlight. Only then did he realise that his head was pounding fiercely and his legs would barely support his weight. He took a deep breath and managed to compose himself just as Nagaira and her retinue appeared, trotting their lathered horses down one of the camp's main avenues.

The witch noticed Malus in an instant and turned towards him. He watched her approach, suddenly aware that the autarii girl had disappeared. Damned useful skill, he thought enviously.

Nagaira reined in her horse a few feet from Malus, close enough that the highborn could feel the destrier's hot breath on his cheek. The witch's retainers dismounted, seeing to their own horses and Malus noticed a sheepish-looking Lord Eluthir bringing up the rear with Spite in tow.

'Your retainer says you were looking for me,' Nagaira said forbiddingly.

'I was,' he said, thinking quickly. He held up his bare hand. 'I was wondering how I could remove these tiresome marks. It's been almost a week. Surely you don't expect my fever to return at this point, do you?'

To Malus's eyes, Nagaira seemed to relax slightly. 'The magic makes the ink difficult to erase,' she said smoothly. 'Have patience. You won't have to worry about it much longer.'

Malus forced himself to smile. 'That's a relief,' he said. 'What news of the battle, sister?'

Nagaira slipped from the saddle and passed the reins to one of her men. 'Our noble general has chased the enemy nearly all the way back to Blackwater Ford,' she said absently. 'The last we heard, he'd sent a messenger back to summon the infantry to join him at the ford. Something about a rearguard of enemy spears guarding the river crossing.'

The highborn frowned. 'A rearguard? But that makes no sense. The enemy general had taken pains to ensure we couldn't slip past him through the woods and cut him off. If he'd had those spears with him at the ruins he could have done us much more harm.' His eyes widened. 'Unless…'

'Unless what?'

Suddenly Malus realised why the enemy force at the ruins troubled him. 'Unless they never meant to stop us at the ruins in the first place,' he said, his pulse quickening. 'The bulk of the enemy army is waiting at the ford. Fuerlan has been lured into a trap!'

IN RETROSPECT, THE clues had been there all along, Malus thought angrily as he and Eluthir raced south along the Spear Road. Shadows raced in the highborn's wake as the army's scouts ran along behind the galloping nauglir.

They hadn't seen a large detachment of knights at the ruins. What army of Hag Graef would march without a large force of knights, especially where the honour of the city was concerned? Also, the advance party Malus and his knights had ambushed the day before had been too large for the relatively small force that had been waiting for them this morning. If he had to guess, Malus figured that the full army had originally intended to camp at the ruins, but the general had changed his plans once he'd learned that his advance party had been destroyed by a large Naggorite force. So he'd laid an ambush at the ford and had gone ahead to present himself as bait. Now the Naggorites had taken the lure and had rushed forward into the trap's steel jaws.

Malus bit back his rage as he and Eluthir rode up on the last column of spearmen to leave the ruins in response to Fuerlan's message. The highborn nudged Spite off the road and raced past the tired-looking warriors. He tried to force his aching mind to calculate distances and times. If they were only three miles or so from the ford and all the infantry were on the road in column, then the lead banner of spearmen was at least halfway there. There might still be time to salvage the situation if they moved quickly.

Nearly ten minutes later they reached the head of the long, snaking line of spearmen. Lord Ruhven's banner was in the lead, the old warrior marching alongside his men as tradition demanded. He glanced over as Malus drew alongside. 'I heard you'd had your head knocked off back there in the ruins,' he said in a rough but cheerful voice.

'Wishful thinking I'm afraid,' Malus answered. 'But the enemy will have another chance, I think. We've been tricked.'

'What?'

'The main enemy force is laying in wait at the ford,' Malus declared. 'The battle at the ruins was just to draw us in. Fuerlan and our cavalry are likely fighting for their lives right now. Pass the word down the column: double-time march and prepare to form a line of battle just short of the river crossing. I'm going ahead to try and pull the cavalry out of the trap, but we'll need a wall of spears to break up the enemy pursuit.'

Lord Ruhven nodded gravely. 'We'll be there, dread lord. Count upon it.' Then he turned and snapped orders to his retainers and trumpets began to wail.

Malus waved the scouts on and kicked Spite back up to a gallop. His heart was racing as the infantry picked up the pace behind him. In his mind he saw the elements of his plan coming together and despite the desperate situation, he thrilled at the power at his command. Blessed Mother of Night, this is what I was born to do, he thought, suppressing a wave of bitterness at the realisation that he would never command a true druchii army in battle. That dream had died along with his father.

The cruelty of the gods never ceased to amaze him. So many lost opportunities: the slave raid, then the expedition to the north that had turned out to be a fool's errand. Why hadn't he accepted Nagaira's invitation to join the cult? What had he been thinking? The pain in his head began to throb again. Malus ground his palm into his forehead as though he could wipe it away by brute force.

'The mind is a mirror,' Malus heard the knight whisper in his ear. It was so real that he could feel the man's breath against his skin. 'It reflects what it is shown.'

Malus didn't bother looking back. He knew there wasn't any point. All that mattered was the battle that lay ahead and how he planned to win it.

Chapter Nineteen
DEATH ON THE BLACKWATER

MALUS AND ELUTHIR had gone another half mile when they came upon the first fleeing horsemen.

The Naggorite cavalrymen were racing down the road as fast as their mounts would carry them. Their armour was battered and bloody and their faces were white with exhaustion and fear. Malus gritted his teeth and drew his blade. The rout at the ford had already begun.

'Stand fast!' he roared at the oncoming riders. When they didn't slow he pulled on the reins and put Spite directly in their path. 'Stand fast or your lives are forfeit!' he said again and this time the riders drew rein and came to a shuddering stop. 'Who is the ranking man among you?' Malus snapped.

The riders looked to one another. One man bowed his head. 'I am, dread lord,' he stammered. 'You must flee – the enemy is right behind us! They laid a trap at the ford–'

Malus spurred his mount forward and ended the man's panicked protest with a swift stroke of his sword. The rider's head bounced along the road. '*Now* who is the ranking man among you?' he asked.

The surviving men watched with stricken faces as the headless body of their comrade slid from the saddle and hit the ground with a wet thud. Finally, one of the men drew a deep breath and said, 'I am, dread lord. What are your orders?'

'You will follow along behind me and collect any more riders retreating from the battle,' he said. 'Kill any who refuse to obey. The infantry is just up the road and will be here in minutes. We're going to turn the tables on the men from Hag Graef. Do you understand?'

The man met the highborn's eyes and struggled to find his courage. 'I... yes, dread lord. I understand.'

'Very good.' Malus turned to Eluthir. 'Stay with them. When you've got a credible force assembled, advance to the ford and join the battle. Use your best discretion, Eluthir and don't fail me.'

'You can count on me, my lord,' Eluthir said gravely.

Malus nodded. More riders appeared on the road and the young knight began bellowing at them to halt. Leaving the cavalrymen to their task, the highborn resumed his race to the ford with the silent scouts in tow.

Even at a full gallop, the last mile seemed to last forever. The farther he went, the more fleeing men Malus passed. Many were wounded and struggling to remain in the saddle. They shouted incoherent warnings at him as he rushed past, but he spared them not so much as a glance.

At last he crested a low hill and saw the dark ribbon of the Blackwater only a few hundred yards away. The view was obscured by a seething pall of dust that swirled over the melee raging just short of the river and Malus saw at once that his worst fears had been realised.

Fuerlan, the household knights and what was left of the cavalry were making a last stand on the Spear Road, fighting a pitched battle with horsemen and knights from the Hag within a virtual cordon of spear companies. The trap had been well-sprung and the Naggorites were completely encircled, but those that remained were fighting to the death. As Malus watched, a company of enemy cavalry staggered away, nursing wounded horses back to the safety of their own lines. Two other ragged companies of enemy horse were limping south across the ford, clearly spent and unable to continue the fight. The Naggorites were taking a fearful toll of Hag Graef's fighting men, but it would not be enough. If they didn't break out of the encirclement, they were doomed.

There was a banner of enemy spearmen between the trapped Naggorites and the road north, formed in line and waiting to catch any cavalrymen who tried to escape the trap. They were the first obstacle Malus would have to deal with. He turned to the scouts. 'Advance and begin firing on those spearmen,' he said, indicating the enemy banner with his sword. 'Keep killing them until they advance on you, then retreat back up the road. Lead them back to Eluthir and his riders.'

'What about you?' the autarii girl said.

The answer was obvious to Malus, absurd as it sounded. 'Where else? Into the thick of things,' he said with a fierce laugh and charged off down the slope.

Tireless as ever, Spite raced downhill towards the enemy spearmen. Malus angled his charge to pass down the narrow gap between two of the banner's spear companies, counting on the din of battle to cover his approach until the last moment. As he approached, the first of the enemy spearmen began to fall to the autarii's crossbow bolts. The scouts were singling out anyone that looked like an officer or a trumpeter, he noted with grim approval.

Ten yards from the rear ranks the spearmen began to realise the threat that had appeared behind them. Heads turned and fingers pointed at the scouts – and the lone rider charging their way. Confusion reigned as the soldiers noticed that their leaders were dead and the spear companies began to react independently of one another. Some of the men broke ranks and tried to block Malus's path, but it was too little, too late. Spite knocked two of the men flying back into their fellows and bit the arm off another, further adding to the bedlam in the ranks. Malus roared a fierce oath as he raced through the surprised enemy force. Then he was past them and facing the rear of an enemy cavalry unit fighting with the household knights just a few yards away.

The enemy horsemen never heard him coming. Spite fell in among their packed ranks like a wolf among sheep, slashing and snapping with tooth and claw. One horse was borne over by the force of the nauglir's charge and the rider was crushed beneath Spite's feet. A horseman to Malus's right tried to turn and face the new threat and the highborn brought his sword down on the rider's helmet, splitting it and the head beneath almost completely in two. Without pause Malus pulled his blade free and hacked at the rider on his left, catching the man's right wrist and chopping off the thumb and first three fingers of his sword hand.

A roar went up from the embattled knights as shock reverberated through their enemy's ranks and they tore into the cavalrymen with renewed fury. The horsemen in the rear rank were so tightly packed that they couldn't turn around to face Malus's unexpected attack. The riders began to fight clear of the press so they could better defend themselves. The unit's cohesion collapsed as the men scattered and someone panicked and shouted for a retreat. Within moments the horsemen were falling back and the beleaguered knights saw them off with a weary cheer. Several raised their swords in salute to Malus as he entered their ranks.

'Keep fighting!' he called to his men. 'Help is on the way!'

The battle continued all around them, with the Naggorite forces having been pushed back into a single loose mass of troops and assailed from all sides. 'Where is Fuerlan?' he shouted, but the few men who heard him shook their heads wearily. 'Gaelthen then? Where is Gaelthen?'

Helmeted heads turned in every direction, trying to make sense of the chaos around them. Without his own helm, Malus could make out a bit more of the battle, but it was hard to tell one man from another amid the dust and the confusion. Then, a few yards further south, Malus saw nauglir fighting nauglir as the knights of both cities struggled near the river's edge. Amid the crush of men and cold ones Malus saw the enemy warlord battering away at two Naggorite knights and he realised that if Fuerlan were still alive he was certain to be directly in the warlord's path.

Not that it mattered, the highborn thought with a fierce grin. He now had another plan. 'Keep a lane open to our rear,' he commanded the knights around him. 'Watch for our infantry to the north. When they appear we're going to break out and join them!' Without waiting for a response he kicked Spite's flanks and dived into the press, working his way inexorably towards the enemy general. Weary knights parted to let him pass as he cut through the centre of the struggling force and joined the fight farther south.

Spite's clawed feet slapped on crimson-stained sand as Malus reached the river's edge. Here the battle had become a series of individual fights as the knights grappled with one another at close quarters, neither side willing to give ground to the other. Nauglir tore at one another as their riders traded blows with sword, axe and mace. Armoured bodies littered the ground, some still locked together in bitter struggle even as the last of their lifeblood was spent.

Malus got to within ten yards of the enemy warlord before his path was blocked by knots of struggling men. Had he a crossbow he could have shot the bastard in the head and left the enemy army reeling; as it was he had to watch helplessly as the warlord smashed the skull of one of his opponents and threw himself upon the other.

Right in front of Malus, another Naggorite reeled in the saddle, his hand pressed to a mortal wound in his throat. His foe reached over and grasped the knight's crested helmet, pulling him forward and hacking off his head with a savage downward stroke. The dead knight's cold one was still locked in a fight to the death with the victor's nauglir and neither one gave an inch.

Malus's frustration reached a boiling point. 'If I can't go through, then by the Dark Mother I'll go over!' He put his spurs to Spite's flanks. 'Up, Spite! Up!'

Spite gathered himself and jumped, landing on the riderless nauglir's back. The smaller cold one scrabbled for purchase, digging its claws in. Malus continued to apply the spurs. 'That's it!' he cried. 'Forward, beast of the deep earth!'

The nauglir hooked a claw in the dead knight's saddle and leapt forward again, this time landing squarely on the back of an enemy knight's mount and smashing its rider from the saddle. The larger nauglir thrashed and roared, snapping at the cold one on its back. The enemy warlord was just a few more yards away, still focused on the opponent in front of him. 'Once more!' he shouted. 'Forward!'

Spite again tried to gain a claw hold, but this time the cold one beneath them rolled onto its side, taking Spite with it. Huge, drooling jaws snapped shut mere inches from Malus's leg as he was hurled forward. Instinct took hold and the highborn threw himself from the saddle lest he be crushed beneath the weight of the struggling warbeasts.

Malus hit the sandy ground hard enough to knock the wind from his chest. He rolled for more than a yard and crashed into the side of the warlord's mount, just as the general finished off his second foe and began looking for someone else to kill.

The highborn gasped for breath as a clawed foot the size of his chest loomed over him. Malus threw himself forward, rolling underneath the cold one and coming up on the beast's other side.

The warlord struggled with his mount's reins and tried to turn to face Malus, shouting with surprise and fury. The highborn howled like a fiend and swung his sword in a two-handed grip at the back of the general's knee. Flesh, bone and jointed steel burst asunder in a spray of gore and the warlord's shout turned to a howl of agony as he lost balance and pitched sideways out of the saddle. He disappeared from sight on the other side of his mount and without thinking Malus pulled the man's severed leg from its stirrup, put his foot in the leather loop and vaulted onto the cold one's back.

The general was trying to crawl across the sand, leaving a bright trail of blood from his ravaged limb. The nauglir tried to snap at Malus, turning in place as it tried to catch him in its jaws, but the highborn paid no heed, launching himself through the air at his retreating foe.

Malus landed a few feet short of the general on the hard-packed sand. Pain spread in fiery waves from his hips and knees but he forced himself forward, scrabbling on all fours like a wolf. The warlord saw him coming and lashed out with his fearsome mace, but Malus anticipated the blow and ducked beneath it. The force of the swing flipped the general onto his back and the highborn clambered onto him, his sword held high. 'Congratulations, general,' he hissed. 'You came north with an army to find me and here I am.'

The sword flashed down, shearing through the general's neck and the dragon helm rolled heavily across the sand. Malus crawled after it, picking up the helmet and prying loose the dripping trophy within. He staggered to his feet on the blood-stained sand and held the general's head aloft. A fierce wave of déjà vu inexplicably struck him, quickly transforming into a rush of triumph.

'Naggor!' he roared and he heard a cry of despair go up from the closest of Hag Graef's knights. At that moment it was the sweetest sound he'd ever heard.

Malus tucked the general's head beneath his arm and snatched up his sword, looking wildly about for Spite. He spotted the nauglir limping towards him several yards away and he ran to meet the wounded beast before some enemy knight decided to try and run him down. Another nauglir would have forgotten its rider and thrown itself into the fight, but Spite was smarter than the typical cold one. 'Well done,' Malus said as he clambered into the saddle. 'Well done, terrible beast!'

He took the general's head and impaled it on the tip of his sword, then held it high for friend and foe to see. The enemy knights nearby were already in full retreat, shocked and dismayed at their warlord's death. Household knights saluted Malus with raised swords, shouting his name to the sound of skirling trumpets.

Trumpets! Malus looked to the north. A mass of horsemen were charging down the hill with Eluthir in the lead and a wall of glittering spears following in their wake. The banner of enemy spearmen to the north had held its ground and suffered the murderous fire of the scouts, but now they lost their nerve and retreated from the onrushing cavalry. The jaws of the trap had been broken open and the trapped Naggorites could escape.

A cheer went up from the cavalrymen and just then Malus caught sight of Fuerlan near the centre of the largest mass of knights. The Naggorite general had lost his helmet in the fighting and his face was mad with fear and rage. The highborn turned Spite around and worked his way through the cheering mass to Fuerlan's side.

'My lord!' Malus cried as he drew near. 'The infantry has arrived and Eluthir has opened a path for us to withdraw. We must be swift before the enemy recover from their surprise–'

'Withdraw?' Fuerlan's dark eyes narrowed hatefully. 'The army of the black ark does not retreat! We will press forward and when the battle is done I'll have you beheaded for cowardice!'

'Press forward?' Malus said incredulously. 'Our cavalry is scattered and their strength is spent! We must fall back and regroup – the trap could close again at any moment and we won't get another chance to break away!'

'Silence!' Fuerlan shrieked, fairly trembling with rage. He held out a gauntleted hand; Malus realised at that moment that the general didn't even have his sword drawn. 'That man's head belongs in the hands of a true warrior, not a darkblade and a traitor like you. Give it here and get out of my sight. I'll deal with you when the battle's done.'

Malus turned away from Fuerlan and searched the eyes of the weary Naggorite horsemen and knights. They watched the scene unfold with

barely concealed shock, but none dared gainsay the son of Balneth
Bale. The highborn plucked the trophy from the tip of his blade and
handed it to Fuerlan without a word, then turned away.

Fuerlan raised the general's head. 'Victory for the black ark!' he cried,
as though he'd just hacked the head from the warlord's body himself.
As he did Malus turned back and struck the Naggorite general in the
head with the flat of his sword. The Witch Lord's son let out a groan
and toppled from the saddle.

For a moment silence reigned among the Naggorites. Malus waited,
eyeing each of the men without a word.

Finally, one of the household knights spoke. 'The lord general has
been wounded,' he said pointedly to the rest of the men. 'That leaves
you in command, Lord Malus. What are your orders?'

Malus nodded and carried on as though he hadn't just committed an
act of gross mutiny. He caught sight of Fuerlan's trumpeter and fixed
the man with a commanding stare. 'Sound the call for the horse to
withdraw,' he said. 'The household knights will form up and act as rearguard to cover their retreat. With luck we'll drag the enemy's
counterattack onto our spears.'

'Aye, my lord,' the trumpeter said hoarsely, then put the trumpet
to his lips and played a complicated series of notes. At once, the
household knights sprang into motion, spreading the word to their
scattered mates. Around them the dust was starting to settle and
order asserting itself out of chaos. Their cordon of steel broken, the
enemy spearmen had pulled back a dozen yards to the east and west
and their cavalry had retreated in the direction of the river. The Naggorite horse was already streaming back towards their lines in
ragged groups of three or four. The highborn shook his head grimly.
They would be lucky if a single whole company of horsemen
remained after the day was done.

The household knights were in equally battered shape. Less than half
of the ark's elite warriors remained, an appalling loss by any standard.
And the battle was far from done.

Trumpets sounded among the forces of the Hag. Conflicting signals
from different leaders, but Malus reckoned that wouldn't last long.
Most of the horsemen had already reached the Naggorite lines or were
nearly there. The highborn raised his sword. 'Household knights!
Advance at the gallop!'

The haggard formation of knights lurched into motion, picking up
speed as the nauglir found their legs and started to run. Almost at once
a roar went up from the enemy lines. Malus looked back to see the
curving arms of the spear companies surging forward again. The sight
of their most hated foes fleeing from their grasp had given them a clear
course of action where their commanders could not.

Normally the race would not have been in doubt, but the nauglir had been in a long day of battle and pursuit and even their legendary stamina was nearly spent. Howling spearmen closed in on either side of the retreating formation. Crossbow bolts whirred through the air – but this time they came from the autarii on the hill, firing into the mass of enemy infantry. A hurled spear passed close enough that Malus could have reached out and caught it if he'd been so inclined. To the rear of the formation, he heard the clash of arms; when he looked back he saw that the enemy spearmen had caught up with the rearmost rank of knights and were trading blows with the mounted men.

Ahead, a trumpet sounded and two companies of spearmen shifted left and right, opening a lane for the knights to pass through. A cheer went up as the first of the nauglir thundered through the gap and Malus raised his sword in salute as he went past.

The enemy spearmen crashed into the waiting Naggorites with a rolling thunderclap of steel. Captains bellowed orders to their men; the banners recoiled a step from the impact, then the Naggorites dug in their heels and pushed back. Men in the front ranks were pierced through again and again by the frenzied storm of spear points; the wounded staggered out of the ranks and streamed to the rear, limping or clutching at bloody holes in their chest and arms. The two sides ground at one another like tumbled stones, shedding a red grit of savaged corpses as they wore one another down.

Once safely behind their lines, the knights' short sprint ground to a halt. Men reeled in the saddle, drunk with exhaustion and bled white from dozens of minor wounds. Malus turned away from the formation and trotted back to the line. The Naggorite spear companies were holding their own against an even number of enemy troops. On the far right flank the autarii continued to send a lethal rain of crossbow bolts into the ranks of the enemy spearmen and Malus noted that the enemy forces had no crossbowmen of their own, so they held a slim advantage there.

Malus's eyes were drawn to the dark mass of horsemen and nauglir still standing on the north side of the ford, some seventy yards away. Would they enter the battle, or were they too spent to continue fighting? There was no way to tell. It was clear to Malus that unless someone among the Hag nobility asserted himself as the new general, the spear companies weren't going to retreat. The inertia of their pursuit had carried them into battle with the Naggorite line and they would continue to fight it out until one side or the other lost their nerve and broke.

The battle was his to win or lose, Malus realised. The thought thrilled him to the core.

Within moments he reached his decision. He turned and led Spite back to the exhausted knights, arriving at the same time as Eluthir. The young knight's face was alight with savage joy. Half a dozen fresh heads hung from his trophy hooks.

Malus surveyed the group. 'Where is Lord Gaelthen?' he asked.

One of the knights cleared his throat and spoke in a rasping voice. 'I saw him fall by the river, my lord, during the third or fourth enemy charge.'

'I see,' Malus said gravely, surprised to feel a real sense of loss at the news. 'Very well. That's one more blood debt those bastards owe us,' he said. 'And we're going to collect. Right now.'

The men straightened in their saddles, their expressions blank with exhaustion. Malus met their gaze squarely. 'The enemy infantry is fully committed, but their cavalry is wavering. If we hit their foot troops with a charge in the right place, they'll break. I know it. You've seen a lot of hard fighting today and you've lost many kinsmen to the hated foe. Their shades are watching you. Will you deny them vengeance?'

A stir went through the weary knights. After a moment one of them spoke. 'If you'll lead us, dread lord, we'll ride into the Outer Darkness and back!'

Malus grinned like a wolf. 'Then follow me,' he said.

The highborn led the knights down the line to the right flank, where Lord Jeharren's division was punishing the enemy spearmen under cover of the autarii's crossbow fire. The young captain saluted as Malus and the knights approached. 'A good day for fighting, dread lord,' Jeharren said, as though he were discussing the weather or a public execution. The broken stub of a crossbow bolt jutted from his left shoulder, but the Naggorite lord paid it no heed whatsoever.

'My compliments, Lord Jeharren,' Malus said. 'The household knights will pass your lines and charge the enemy. When I give the signal you will order your companies to give us a lane into the centre of the enemy formation.'

Jeharren bowed. 'Your will be done, dread lord.'

Malus rode back to his men. 'Form columns!' he ordered. 'Prepare to charge!'

The knights shook themselves into columns quickly and smoothly, despite their exhausted state. When they were ready, he raised his bloodstained sword and saluted Lord Jeharren. The captain nodded and turned to his trumpeter. 'Make ready!' Malus shouted, his hand tightening on the hilt of his blade.

The trumpet pealed. Ahead, two companies split left and right, opening a gap in the line. Enemy spearmen poured through, shouting exultantly. Malus swept his arm down in a glittering arc. '*Charge!*'

The household knights leapt forward with a terrible shout, racing at the enemy line. The spearmen pushing into the gap saw their doom approaching and tried to push their way back out of the narrow lane. Many dropped their spears in panic, pushing and beating at the men behind them to give way.

The knights of the black ark struck the enemy line like a spear, crushing the men in their path and plunging deep into the heart of the formation. Malus hacked down at the heads and necks of the tightly packed troops around him, inflicting terrible wounds to upraised faces and exposed throats. He snapped spear hafts and cracked helms, while Spite tossed crushed bodies in the air like a hound among rats. The air reverberated with screams and the sounds of clashing steel and Malus exulted in it, laughing like a madman.

Just as suddenly as it had begun, the press of troops receded from the knights like a swift-flowing tide. The spearmen, overwhelmed at the ferocity of the Naggorite charge, broke and ran for the ford. The enemy's left flank had completely collapsed and now the Naggorites pressed hard on the Hag's centre and right.

Malus reined in and raised his sword. 'Halt! Halt!' he cried to his men. The battle still hung in the balance, depending on what the enemy cavalry did. If they counter-charged, the Naggorites might quickly find themselves fighting for their lives.

He looked for the enemy horsemen farther down the hill – and saw them halfway across the wide river, fleeing south. The enemy knights were riding hard behind them. They'd lost their warlord and with him their will to continue the fight.

Moments later the centre of the enemy line broke and the retreat turned into a rout. Spearmen threw down their weapons and stumbled back down the hill, fleeing for their lives. A trumpet sounded and the Naggorite divisions advanced after them at a measured pace, killing every warrior they could catch. Even the battered cavalry joined in the pursuit, taking their own revenge for the bloody beating they'd taken an hour before.

A cheer went up from the household knights. '*Malus! Malus!*' they cried and he laughed and cheered along with them, drunk with the red wine of victory.

Eluthir moved his nauglir among the piles of enemy dead and joined him. 'Where now, my lord?' he asked.

'Where else? Onward,' Malus said, pointing south with his blood-stained sword. 'To Hag Graef!'

Chapter Twenty
THE VALLEY OF SHADOW

COLD RAIN WHISPERED through the pine boughs over Malus's head, heavy drops soaking his hair and running beneath the collar of his breastplate into his robes. Rivulets coursed their way down his filthy armour, turning bright pink as they washed away layers of dried gore. He and the other captains of the army stood in a tight ring beneath the sheltering pines, peering at a large oilskin map of the valley ahead. By the time they were done the ground beneath them would be as red as a battlefield, the highborn thought wearily.

It was late in the day and darkness promised to fall early due to the overcast sky. They had marched almost without pause since the battle on the Blackwater; now the army sat by the side of the Spear Road in the driving rain, too tired to do more than pull their cloaks about them as they tried to get some desperately needed rest.

They were less than a mile from the mouth of the Valley of Shadow. Had the sky not turned grey and misty with rain they could have seen the tips of the dark towers of Hag Graef from where they stood, but Malus welcomed the miserable weather and the concealment it gave. During the long march the cavalry and the scouts had been sent far ahead with word to kill any fleeing soldiers heading south or any travellers going north. Malus reasoned that the Drachau of Hag Graef knew of the disaster at Blackwater Ford, but would not guess how close the army of the black ark was to the walls of his city. It was a slim advantage, the highborn knew, but at the moment he would take whatever he could get.

The battle at the ruins and the subsequent fight at the river crossing had badly mauled the Naggorite army. Less than a quarter of their cavalry remained fit for duty, as well as only a third of the household knights. Between the losses at the ruins and the battle at the ford an entire division of infantry had been lost; Malus had ordered the second division reconstituted with the reserve infantry banner and a half-banner of survivors from the original unit. Lord Kethair had died storming the enemy's left flank at the ruins and Lord Dyrval had died with many of his fellow cavalrymen during the ambush at the ford. Their replacements were both young highborn with little field experience, but the wounds on their faces and the hard look in their eyes showed that they were no strangers to hard fighting and they were willing to do whatever was necessary to claim victory in the war against the Hag.

The problem, Malus thought bitterly, was that he hadn't the faintest idea how to give it to them.

Heavy raindrops made audible thumps against the dark, wrinkled oilskin. The map looked as though it had been drawn up during the first days of the feud with Hag Graef, many decades ago. Details of the valley and the terrain around Hag Graef were drawn with thick, black brushstrokes. The highborn traced the sinuous line of the Spear Road as it descended into the valley and wound among the thick forests that led to the north gate of the great druchii city. He knew its every turn and twist by heart, just like he knew the walls and heavy gates of the city in every particular. This was his home, the prize he'd longed to claim for his own since the first day he'd been presented to the Court of Thorns many years ago.

He also knew that three divisions of exhausted footmen and a handful of knights and cavalry weren't nearly enough to take the city by storm, even if they could get past the city gates. During the long afternoon he'd considered the problem from every angle, trying to imagine how Nagaira planned to capture the Hag for her betrothed and he still couldn't see a way to do it. Even sorcery wouldn't work, because the drachau could call upon the witches of the convent to counteract Nagaira's spells. And since the element of surprise had surely been lost, he couldn't think of any trick that would get an entire army into the city unchallenged.

The only people who knew the full plan were the Witch Lord, Fuerlan and Nagaira. Balneth Bale was more than a hundred leagues away and Malus wasn't even sure Fuerlan was still alive. He presumed someone in the division would have seen to it that the general had been carried out when the household knights retreated at the ford, but he never saw Bale's son afterwards and Malus hadn't the time or energy to

bother finding out what had happened to him. For now, he commanded the army and with Hag Graef almost in sight he couldn't help
but be tempted by the thought that he could use Nagaira's secret plan
for his own ends. If she knew a way to put Fuerlan on the throne with
the tools at hand, then why not him?

Unless there was no plan at all and this was an elaborate betrayal to
cement the power of her ally Isilvar, the new vaulkhar. A great victory
over Naggor would give Isilvar much-needed legitimacy among the
nobles of the Hag. But if that were the case, what did Nagaira need
with him? Why go to all the effort to place him under her control?

You are the arrow, the knight had said. What did that mean? Where
did the visions come from?

His head ached. The skin around the punctures in his scalp was hot
and painful to the touch and waves of dizziness had come and gone
while he sat in the saddle during the march. Every bone in his body
cried out for rest. Was he just exhausted, or was he hallucinating from
his wounds – or was there something else?

Malus suddenly realised that the captains were staring at him. He
shook himself from his fugue, scattering red-tinged droplets from his
face. 'Yes?'

Lord Esrahel cleared his throat and spoke in a quiet voice. 'We were
discussing placement of the camp, my lord.'

'Ah, yes,' Malus said, rubbing absently at his forehead. The headaches
had grown increasingly worse over the course of the day, pounding
inside his skull like a temple drum. He focused his attention on the
map once more. 'The terrain in the valley is ill-suited to a large
encampment and I'm loath to pause in our advance in any event.
Speed is of the essence. We must strike while our enemy is reeling.'

'Respectfully, my lord, we're near to reeling as well,' Lord Ruhven
said. The old druchii's face bore a line of rough stitching that high-
lighted an ugly spear wound in his cheek. The lord's face was flushed
and his eyes sunken, but his voice remained strong. 'The men have
fought two hard battles and made a forced march in a single day.
They'll fight if you order them to, but they won't last long against fresh
troops.'

Lord Eluthir nodded. In the wake of Gaelthen's death and his successful charge at the battle of the ford, Malus had made him his chief
aide-de-camp and given him control of the household knights so he
could focus on commanding the overall army. 'The nauglir are worn
out,' he said. 'Many of them are wounded and they haven't been fed for
hours. If we push them much harder they'll die just marching to the
fight.'

Malus took a deep breath and wiped the rain from his face. He hated
the thought of stopping just short of their goal, but he saw no other

choice. 'You're right,' he reluctantly agreed. 'There's no point pressing on in the state we're in.' He studied the map and referenced the notes made by the Witch Lord detailing the march. 'The plan has us making camp here,' he said, pointing to a spot within the valley less than two miles from the city, 'but the location is perilous. There's no room to manoeuvre if the city sends troops against us. We'd be trapped between the forests and the valley walls and smashed to bits by sheer numbers if nothing else.'

Reluctantly he reached a decision, tapping another spot on the map farther north and not far from where they stood. 'Lord Esrahel, pitch your tents here,' he said. 'The area is abandoned farmland with good fields and plenty of room to move about. We'll rest the night while I consult with my sister as to our next move. Be prepared for action at first light. If we don't make our move by then it will be too late.'

'It is already too late,' whispered a cold, dead voice. Malus froze, thinking for a moment that the knight was speaking in his ear – until he noticed the other lords heard the voice as well. He turned and saw the slender form of the autarii girl standing in the shadows of the pine trees at his back.

The highborn felt a chill run down his spine as he met the girl's dark, empty eyes. 'What have you to report?' he asked dully.

'The vaulkhar has taken to the field,' she said simply. 'The banner of chains waits outside the city with many spears and dragon kin.'

'Blood of the Dark Mother,' he cursed. 'Show me. I want to see this for myself.'

THEY CROUCHED IN the rain with night coming on, huddled in the shadows of a pine wood within half a mile of the city. The autarii girl was tense, holding a bared blade in either hand and searching the darkness beneath the trees with a penetrating stare. The rest of the army's scouts were out there somewhere, Malus knew, providing a defensive cordon for him. There were enemy scouts stalking the valley as well, the girl said, and from her wary demeanour it was clear that it wasn't hapless rock adders this time.

Malus lay flat on the rain-soaked ground, staring in dismay at the force assembled in the fields before the city. He could see the vaulkhar's banner clearly, with its circle of linked silver chains on a red field. Eight banners of spearmen – sixteen thousand men – waited in rough field camps that filled the barren meadows almost to overflowing. Worse, the highborn counted three banners of knights encamped close by the city walls, their nauglir kept close to their dark tents and ready for immediate action.

'Blessed Mother,' the highborn muttered, pointing out another sodden banner of black and red posted close by the vaulkhar's. 'He's even called out the temple executioners.' He couldn't even hazard a guess at the number of warriors the temple of Khaine could muster in the city. A thousand? Ten thousand? Who knew? 'Isilvar has called up the city militia and somehow marshalled every minor noble in the Hag. Where did he get such influence so quickly?'

'You gave it to him,' the girl said.

Malus glared at her. 'What do you mean?'

'We've been following their patrols most of the afternoon,' the autarii said. 'All they talk about is you. A few survivors reached the city ahead of us and told wild tales of your prowess. You are like a daemon and with the old vaulkhar dead and so many powerful lords away on campaign the city trembles at your approach.'

'It seems I've developed a reputation at last,' Malus said bitterly. Frustration burned a searing hole in his heart. 'And it has proven our undoing.' His fists clenched. 'A messenger must have been sent back to the Hag the day I destroyed that advance party at the ruins. If we hadn't made camp that day we could have caught the enemy unawares at the ford and made it here before Isilvar could have raised his army.'

'And now?'

'Now we have no choice but to withdraw. Even at our full strength we could not have stood against a force this size.' The highborn turned a calculating eye on the enemy dispositions. 'If they have scouts in the woods as you say, then the vaulkhar is likely waiting to hear we've entered the valley, where we'll be hemmed in like cattle. That way he can just throw troops at us until we're too worn down to keep fighting and then he'll send in the knights to finish us.' Slowly, cautiously, Malus rose to a crouch. 'The plan was a gamble from the start and it failed. Now we have to try and survive the consequences,' he said. 'I fear we won't find the highborn you're seeking.'

'Perhaps,' the girl said. 'Did you learn anything in Nagaira's tent?'

Malus grimaced. 'She has placed some kind of compulsion on me,' he said hesitantly.

'Compulsion? For what?'

'I don't know,' he growled. 'She and Fuerlan have some purpose in mind for me. There were also some maps of a labyrinth of some kind–'

Malus froze, his eyes going wide. Slowly he turned and regarded the dark walls of the city. 'Mother of Night,' he hissed. 'I'm such a fool. The plan was right there in front of me and I just didn't see it.' He turned to the girl. 'We have to get back to the camp. This whole campaign has been a trick from the very beginning!'

MALUS WAS PREPARED to run the entire way out of the valley to reach the new campsite. In the event, he and the autarii girl had gone less than two and a half miles before he heard the clatter of hammers and the shouted orders of an army making camp well within the Valley of Shadow.

The highborn stopped dead in his tracks. 'What in the Dark Mother's name is this?' The girl paused, her expression worried, and started to move to the edge of the forest where it ran alongside the Spear Road, but Malus brushed past her, running headlong towards the sound. He didn't need the oilskin map to know where in the valley they were. Esrahel and the others had disobeyed his orders and gone on to make camp in the spot determined by the Witch Lord – placing them directly in the path of Isilvar's waiting force.

It was dark on the roadway. The men of the baggage train were hard at work, raising tents and breaking out rations for the evening meal. The Naggorite army staggered like drunkards amid the hustle and bustle of the camp builders; many warriors had simply lain down on the wet ground and fallen instantly asleep. Malus watched the mutiny unfold before him and trembled with frustration and anger. What were they thinking?

'Go find Eluthir,' he told the girl. 'Tell him to report to me at Lord Esrahel's wagon at once!'

The girl slipped away like a fleeting shadow and Malus stalked into the campsite with murder in mind.

He found his bearings quickly enough; all druchii army camps operated along a common plan. The highborn and knights were in the centre, well-protected by rings of spear companies, while the cavalry encamped in two groups to east and west, where they could picket their horses and come and go on patrol with minimal difficulty. The baggage train and artillery camped just north of centre, far enough in to protect the army's valuable supplies and siege weapons and close enough to provide the highborn with everything they desired.

Malus cut through the narrow alleys between the highborn tents and found himself among a veritable city of enclosed wagons that belonged to the baggage train. Within moments he worked his way among the wagons and the hectic work of their owners and reached Esrahel's huge conveyance. Witchlight gleamed from the wagon's narrow windows and the highborn could hear Esrahel inside, snapping orders to his underlings.

Malus drew his blade and rounded the back of the wagon. 'What is the meaning of this?' he snapped, his voice as sharp as the sword in his hand.

The highborn pulled up short at the sight of eight armoured men standing at the rear of the open wagon with bared blades in their hands. Malus didn't recognise them at first, but when they saw him they smiled wolfishly at one another and then looked to a figure standing in the wagon's open doorway. Malus followed their gaze to the

aristocratic-looking highborn glaring haughtily from the narrow doorway. He recognised the man at once.

'Tennucyr?' he said with a frown. 'What are you doing?'

'Restoring order,' the highborn snapped. 'The *rightful* order of things,
you murderous bastard.'

The highborn's hand tightened on the hilt of his sword and he took
a step towards Tennucyr, fully intending to kill the man where he
stood, but the retainers moved as one man and tackled him in a silent
rush. Malus managed a single, outraged shout before an armoured fist
crashed into the back of his skull and the world went dark.

MALUS AWOKE WITH a scream as the point of a knife traced a ragged path
across his cheek.

He was stripped naked and hanging by his hands from a thick tent
pole and Fuerlan's leering face was inches from his own. The tent was
lit by a pair of large braziers, giving the general's ravaged face a daemonic cast in the ruddy light. Malus could smell the stink of cheap
wine on Fuerlan's breath and saw the fires of madness dancing in his
dark eyes.

The general giggled like a malevolent child. 'There, you see? I knew
I could bring him around.'

Blood ran down the side of Malus's face as he looked about the tent.
Tennucyr was there, reclining in a camp chair and sipping wine with
an expression of hateful disdain. Fuerlan's retainers and sycophants
crowded the main room of the tent, standing silently as though bearing witness to an execution. The highborn wondered if that wasn't
about to be the case.

He didn't recognise the tent. Malus reckoned it was Tennucyr's.
Clearly he'd rescued Fuerlan back at the ford and sheltered him during
the afternoon until the general had regained some of his strength. The
highborn shook his head. 'I was such a fool,' he seethed.

'For striking me?' Fuerlan asked.

'No – for not finishing the job when I had the chance.'

Searing pain exploded across Malus's forehead as the general let out
a furious cry and struck the highborn with a backhanded slash of his
knife. The highborn growled and hung his head low, trying to keep the
dripping blood from his eyes.

Fuerlan leaned closer. 'It's a mistake you will soon come to regret, I
assure you. I've already given the household knights to Lord Tennucyr
in reward for his loyalty and courage. You no longer have a place in this
army. As a mutineer you can be summarily executed – but I'm going to
spend the night skinning you alive instead.' The general raised the
knife, watching the firelight play along its stained edge. 'I only regret
that I have so little time to spare. You don't know how much I've

wished for this opportunity, Malus. I've dreamed of spending *days* slowly vivisecting you. I've spent a fortune building a special room in my tower where I could have torn you apart, rebuilt you and torn you down again, day after day after day. It would have been glorious.'

Fuerlan grabbed Malus by the chin and inserted the point of his knife into the skin above Malus's right eye. Slowly, deliberately, he began to cut through the skin, tracing almost a full circle around the socket. The highborn gritted his teeth and trembled at the pain and a nervous smile lit the general's face. 'Have you ever drunk wine from a highborn's skull, cousin? The vintage soaks into the bones, subtly altering the flavour. By morning I'll be sitting on the drachau's throne in Hag Graef and drinking sweet red wine from your brain pan and I cannot wait to see how it tastes.'

Malus gasped at the pain, blinking hot blood from his eye. Dull agony pounded in his skull. Then he heard a voice.

'You are the arrow, Malus,' he heard the knight whisper in his ear.

The highborn started to laugh – a silent heaving of his shoulders at first, swelling in strength and volume as he saw the fear glimmer in Fuerlan's eyes. 'If you kill me, you fool, who will do your assassin's work then?'

The general recoiled. 'What are you talking about?'

'I see your plan now, *cousin,*' Malus spat. 'This whole campaign has been a diversion to draw out the armies of the Hag. I've been thinking of every trick and tactic I know to take the city with the forces at your disposal but I haven't been able to think of a single way to do it – and that's because you never intended to capture the city in the first place. I'm supposed to sneak into the city through the burrows and assassinate the drachau for you – then you'll step from the shadows and claim the crown for your own. That's the compulsion Nagaira put in my head, twisting my memories to make me forget, isn't it?'

Fuerlan took a step back, his eyes widening in surprise. 'She... She said you wouldn't remember.'

Malus saw a figure moving through the shadows of the tent. The tall knight was lit in silhouette, hiding his features. 'The arrow does not choose where it is shot, or who it strikes down,' the apparition warned in its sepulchral voice.

'I needed no memories. The clues were right in front of me,' Malus snapped. 'Once you've got the crown, no one can take it from you except by force of arms or the declaration of the Witch King. That is the law and you can call upon the powers of temple and convent to enforce it. A young and inexperienced vaulkhar and an army of conscripts will think twice before tempting the wrath of the city's witches, so I expect that after some initial resistance Isilvar will accept the status quo. By the time the more powerful lords return from campaign your power base will be solidified and they will have no choice but to accept it.' The highborn smiled bitterly. 'Being the assassin my life is forfeit of course, but if I manage to survive the attempt you can hand me over to Malekith for execution and gain tacit support for your rule. It's actually a brilliant plan, which makes me suspect my sister was the one who devised it.'

'Such flattery,' Nagaira sneered. 'It would be charming, were you not such a cold-hearted, treacherous bastard.'

The witch swept into the tent like a cold wind, coming up behind Malus and looming over Fuerlan like a vengeful ghost. She had dispensed with her silver mask and thrown back the hood of her sodden cloak and the shadows veiling her head seemed to writhe like billowing smoke. Only her eyes could be seen clearly and they blazed with sorcerous fire. The general quailed at her approach and started to speak, but the witch struck him across the face with a ringing slap that nearly drove him to his knees.

One of Fuerlan's retainers let out an angry shout and leapt at Nagaira with a dagger in his hand. The witch spoke a word that curdled the air in the tent and caused the braziers to flare and the man fell dead at her feet.

'Get up you wretch,' she snapped at Fuerlan. 'Have you taken leave of what's left of your senses?'

'He committed an act of mutiny on the field of battle!' Fuerlan said querulously. 'I couldn't let that go unanswered.'

'Of course you could!' she hissed. 'You can do anything you want, you stupid little man. Do you think this is how a drachau behaves, giving in to his petty desires when there are greater things at stake? Are you worthy of the Court of Thorns or not, son of the Witch Lord?'

'How dare you address me in that way,' Fuerlan shot back. 'When I'm drachau, I'll–'

'Ah, but you aren't the drachau yet, are you? Nor will you be without *him*,' Nagaira said, pointing a finger at Malus. 'Cut him down and get him dressed. Time is short.'

Glaring hatefully at the witch, Fuerlan gestured sharply to his retainers, who cut Malus free and brought him his clothes. The highborn shook his head ruefully, wincing in pain as he slipped on his robes. 'Why the hurry, sister?'

Before the witch could answer there was the thunder of heavy footfalls outside the tent. Nagaira's luminous eyes narrowed warily and she stepped back towards the far wall of the tent, all but disappearing into the shadows. As she did, she stepped unknowingly past the shadowy knight, who seemed to stare impatiently at Malus.

'What a witch gives, only a witch can take away,' the figure said. The knight leaned close and Malus saw his face for the first time. It was not the sharp features of a druchii, but the malevolent face of a daemon. 'And they tell no truths but their own.'

The tent's entry flap was yanked unceremoniously aside and Malus turned to see Lord Eluthir and a dozen grim-looking knights crowd their way into the tent. The young knight took in the scene with a sweeping glance and bowed to Fuerlan. 'My apologies for the intrusion, my lord,' Eluthir said smoothly. 'I was looking for Lord Malus.' He turned to the highborn, pointedly ignoring the cuts on his face. 'The household knights are formed up and ready for inspection as ordered,' he said.

'Lord Malus is no longer your captain,' Fuerlan interjected.

To the general's surprise, the young knight laughed. 'A fine jest, my lord,' Eluthir said. 'Lord Malus led us to victory at Blackwater Ford and slew the Hag's general in personal combat. Remove a hero from his command? How absurd! Think of the dissent it would cause in the ranks, to say nothing of the insult it would mean to your father, who gave him the command in the first place.' The knight smiled appreciatively. 'I had no idea my lord general had such a refined sense of humour.'

Fuerlan could only stare at the man, his jaw working in frustration. Eluthir turned back to Malus. 'The men are waiting, my lord. Shall I carry your armour?'

'I'll put it on as we go,' the highborn said, slipping the kheitan over his shoulders and picking up the pieces of his plate harness. He gave Fuerlan a pointed look. 'A captain's work is never done,' he said with a grin. 'You will excuse me, my lord. The men are tired and hungry and apt to become… unruly… if they are kept waiting too long.'

ONCE OUTSIDE, ELUTHIR leaned close to Malus. 'My apologies for taking so long, my lord. We searched nearly every tent in the camp before we found you.'

The rain stung in his open wounds, but the highborn turned his face to the sky and savoured the pain. It was like a benediction from the goddess, a reprieve from the bonds of slavery. 'Apologise for nothing, Eluthir. You did well. Now we must hurry, if we are to avoid disaster.' He took a deep breath, focusing his thoughts as he put on his armour. 'Gather all the captains and have them come to my tent at once. We have to get out of here.'

Eluthir frowned. 'We're retreating?'

'We have no choice,' the highborn said. 'The campaign was never meant to succeed. It was just a diversion for a grander scheme. It was meant to draw the warriors of Hag Graef out of the city and it succeeded. If we aren't clear of the valley by first light the army will be destroyed.'

'You're talking about mutiny. Real mutiny,' Eluthir said gravely. 'Fuer-lan intends to stay and fight, doesn't he?'

'No, he intends to sneak away while you are getting killed,' Malus said. 'You can either stay here and die or return to the ark and take your chances with the Witch Lord. I'll wager he abhors wasting good troops as much as I do.'

Eluthir thought it over a moment, then made his decision. 'I'll go and get the captains,' he said.

Malus nodded. A line of tired-looking nauglir waited in the road outside the tent, including Spite. The highborn ran his hand along the back of the cold one's scaly neck and climbed wearily into the saddle. 'Get to my tent as quickly as you can, then get the knights ready to move. We may need them to overcome any resistance to the plan.'

Eluthir nodded and led the knights away. Malus headed in the oppo-site direction, following the methodical layout of the camp until he reached the spot where he knew his tent would be. His mind was whirling as he tried to formulate a plan to withdraw the army in the dead of night, right under Isilvar's nose. We'll see how Nagaira and Fuerlan plan to compel me with an army at my back, he thought grimly.

He'd hoped to find one or more of the scouts waiting at the tent. Without servants of his own there was no one to light the braziers in the tent or fetch food from the kitchens. Malus pushed the tent flap aside and darted in, surprised to find the two braziers already lit and filling the tent with a warm, red glow.

They would probably have to leave all the baggage behind, Malus thought. Less noise, less weight and less time to get ready to leave. That decision made, he headed for the nearest fire, reaching out to dry his wet hands and the four hooded men standing to either side of the door closed in behind him, their swords gleaming in the firelight.

Chapter Twenty-One
DARKNESS AND RUIN

JUST AS MALUS reached the brazier the daemon-faced knight spoke. 'Beware! Your enemies are upon you!'

He whirled, his hand reaching for his sword and the four men moved as one, hemming him in with a sudden, silent rush. They wore black-dyed leather armour and short, woollen cloaks with deep hoods that hid their faces in shadow, but Malus knew they were men from the Hag. 'Assassins!' he shouted, just as the lead attacker leapt upon him.

The two men crashed together, knocking Malus back against the brazier and toppling it over in a shower of angry sparks. Moisture in his sodden cloak hissed into steam as Malus landed amid the hot iron and coals. His sword arm was trapped beneath the assassin's knee and the hooded man closed his left hand about the highborn's throat. A short, broad-bladed sword rose above the highborn's head.

Malus let out a choking cry and threw a handful of burning coals into his attacker's gaping hood. The assassin recoiled with a pained shout and the highborn shoved him away. Immediately, the three other men swept in, but the highborn tore his sword from its scabbard and swept it in a vicious arc at their knees. The smell of burning wool and canvas was heavy in the air as the scattered coals smouldered hungrily against the tent's fabric walls.

The highborn's swing drove the men back for an instant and he took the chance to roll away from the pile of cinders and struggle to his feet.

He rose to a crouch just as one of the men rushed him, stabbing at his throat with a long-bladed knife. Malus parried the thrust, then snarled in pain as the attacker smashed his wrist with a heavy, knotted cudgel. The blow knocked the sword from his hand and before Malus could grab for it he had to hurl himself back to avoid a deadly slash aimed at his throat.

Malus felt waves of heat against the back of his neck. The inside of the tent was burning and the attackers were skilfully hemming him in against the flames. Another swordsman darted in from the right – Malus drew his second sword and narrowly bloked a powerful cut to his shoulder. As he did, the second attacker's cudgel came at him from the left and struck him just behind the temple, dashing him to the ground.

It felt as though he lay on the steaming ground for a long time, blinking flashes of white pain from his eyes. Everything seemed to be happening in slow motion – he saw his hand groping numbly for the sword he'd dropped, only to see a leather boot slowly kick it aside. A gloved hand closed around a handful of his hair, pulling his face back until he could see tongues of flame licking across the tent's canvas ceiling. He opened his mouth, trying to speak, but all that came out was a tortured groan.

Two of the assassins stood over him, staring inscrutably at him from the depths of their cloaks. A third man stood nearby, standing upright like a judge about to pass sentence.

'Finish it,' the third man said gravely. Malus blinked, trying to remember where he'd heard the voice before.

The fourth assassin staggered to his feet, shaking his hooded head. Smoke curled from the fabric where the coals had found their mark. He moved through a nimbus of flame, his sword red with reflected fire. When he reached Malus, he placed the sword's razor edge to the highborn's throat and pulled back his hood. The man's pale face was blotched with angry red burns and his long, white hair was singed. Eyes the colour of hot brass regarded Malus with a mixture of burning anguish and hate.

Malus looked into that face and felt his heart freeze. 'Arleth Vann?'

'Well met, my lord,' the former assassin said in a dead voice. 'But I fear it is for the last time. You have broken the Witch King's law and betrayed your city to its foes and as your sworn men we have all been tainted by your infamy.'

The man at the front of the tent pulled back his hood. Silar Thornblood's handsome face was twisted with rage. 'You have ruined us, Malus. Every hand in Hag Graef is set against us because of your crime. We are less than slaves now!'

Arleth Vann's sword sank a fraction of an inch into Malus's throat. 'If we are to reclaim our honour, you must die,' he said. 'There is no other way.'

The two men at Malus's side drew back their own hoods. Dolthaic the Ruthless spat in Malus's face. 'Do it,' he snarled.

Hauclir's expression was bleak. There was no anger in his eyes, nor any hint of surprise. He looked at Malus searchingly. 'Tell me this is part of some plan,' he said. 'Tell me you meant for all this to happen and there's a point to everything we've suffered since we returned to Hag Graef. Tell me you have a way to make things right again.'

Malus met his retainer's pleading stare. 'Can you give me a moment to think?' he asked, attempting to smile.

'Kill him,' Dolthaic said. 'Get it over with.'

Distantly the sound of horns echoed in the night air. Arleth Vann shuddered, then sank to his knees before Malus, his eyes wide with surprise. The assassin let out a groan and fell against him and the highborn saw the three crossbow bolts that jutted from his back.

The shades rushed into the tent from three sides, charging through the entryway and from two rents torn in the side of the burning tent. Silar let out a yell and was immediately thrown back by the fierce attacks of two autarii scouts, his sword flashing as he parried their short, stabbing blades. Dolthaic let out a curse and made to strike off Malus's head, but staggered back with a shout of pain as another crossbow bolt sprouted from his shoulder.

An autarii with twin swords rushed at Hauclir, his blades dancing like vipers. The former guard captain let Malus go and drew his knife, feinting a stroke at the shade's face. The autarii ducked the blow and Hauclir's cudgel smashed into his forehead. As the scout fell, Hauclir grabbed Arleth Vann's arm and pulled him off the ground with surprising strength. 'Run!' he said to Dolthaic and dragged the unconscious assassin towards the rear of the tent. Weaponless, Dolthaic gave Malus a passing glare of hate and ran at the wall of flames, plunging through the weakened fabric and out into the rain.

As the wall burst apart, the tent began to collapse. Malus felt hands grip his arms and drag him from the fire. He caught one last glimpse of Hauclir and Dolthaic dragging Arleth Vann around the corner of a nearby tent and then they were lost from sight.

The night air trembled with horns and the sound of fighting. A slender form knelt in front of the highborn, setting Malus's swords by his side. The autarii girl peered searchingly in his eyes, then slipped a small piece of bark between his lips. The taste was painfully bitter. He gagged and bent over, retching into the grass.

'Are you well, my lord?' she asked. 'You must gather your wits at once – the camp is under attack!'

Malus paused, tasting bile in his mouth and gasping for breath. The sounds echoing among the tents suddenly gained a dreadful meaning: Isilvar had found the camp and decided not to wait for dawn,

Dan Abnett & Mike Lee

launching a surprise attack on the exhausted and disorganised Naggorite troops.

The highborn clenched his fists and squeezed his eyes shut until his entire body trembled from the effort. He forced himself to clear his mind of distractions, pushing the sight of Hauclir's pleading face into the dark depths of his brain. 'Find Eluthir,' he said. 'The captains are with him.' As he considered the situation and their options the seeds of a plan started to fall into place. 'Tell Eluthir to counter-attack with all the knights he can find, then tell Esrahel to set fire to the baggage to cover the infantry's retreat.' Slowly, he gathered up his swords and rose to his feet, forcing himself to focus solely on the situation at hand. 'Tell the infantry commanders to gather their companies and make a fighting retreat north.'

'Retreat to where?' the girl asked.

'Anywhere but here!' Malus snapped. 'Let's get the army moving and we'll worry about the rest later.' The highborn sheathed his swords and forced his legs to move, making his way to Spite.

The girl snapped orders in her thick autarii dialect and most of the shades scattered like crows. She nodded to the three that remained and they stole quietly into the shadows nearby. Malus frowned. 'What are you doing?'

'Watching over you,' she said quietly, her eyes searching the shadows. 'I believe we are approaching the end of things,' she said, her voice distant. 'Your campaign is at an end and your enemies circle like wolves.'

'It was never my campaign,' Malus said, surprised at the bitterness in his voice.

She turned to him. 'And the witch's curse?'

He shook his head. The daemon knight's words came back to him. 'What a witch gives, only a witch can take away,' he said, reaching Spite and quickly checking his saddle and reins.

'So be it,' the girl said gravely. She slipped up behind him, laying a hand on his shoulder. 'Turn around, my lord. There is something I must say to you.'

Malus started to turn – but Nagaira's voice stopped him in his tracks.

'Night has fallen, brother,' the witch said as she stepped from the darkness into the guttering light thrown by the blazing tent. 'It is time.'

He paused, reaching stealthily for the dagger at his belt then remembered he'd lost it in the fight. 'Time to flee, sister,' he said, stalling for time. 'The army is in grave danger.'

'The army? The army's purpose is to die,' the witch said. 'I have another task in mind for you. Turn around.'

He turned, his eyes seeking the autarii by his side, only to find that the girl had vanished.

Nagaira stood some distance away, flanked by a dozen black-garbed retainers. Fuerlan stood close by with a naked blade in his hand. The former general's expression was twisted with rage and fear.

The witch's glowing eyes narrowed and Malus could feel the cold weight of her smile. 'You will do exactly as I say,' she commanded. 'Follow me.'

Pain faded as Nagaira exerted her hold over him. A terrible vigour swelled in his chest, writhing like a bundle of snakes around his heart. His feet began to move of their own accord.

Malus looked wildly about. Where were the shades? Why weren't they doing anything? In desperation, he turned to Spite as he walked towards his sister. 'Up, Spite! Hunt!' he commanded. He would be damned if the beast died because it waited in vain for him to come and claim it.

The nauglir was still sitting on its haunches as Nagaira led Malus and her companions into the darkness.

Isilvar's knights and cavalry had attacked up the Spear Road from the south. Nagaira led Malus and her companions west, out of the camp and into one of the dense woods that dotted the valley floor. Malus followed in his sister's wake like a trained dog, listening helplessly to the shouts and screams of the army – his army – as it died. He prayed to the Mother of Night that Eluthir and the household knights escaped, or at least received warriors' deaths. If Tennucyr was leading them, neither possibility was assured.

He couldn't stop moving, no matter how hard he tried. No amount of will, or rage, or fear could stop his limbs from carrying him wherever Nagaira went. However, he found that he could slow down, dropping back through the ranks of the group only as far as he could without losing sight of his sister. He could move off the path if he wished, so long as his sister stayed in sight and could increase his pace. It appeared that he was compelled to follow Nagaira's commands to the letter, if not necessarily abiding by them in spirit. That left him more freedom than he expected and his mind worked furiously as they picked their way through the dark woods, looking for a way to capitalise on his discovery.

They travelled into the forest for half a mile before they came to a huge, granite boulder rising out of the earth. The rock was the size of a small cottage and created a small clearing for itself in the middle of the tangled wood. Rain fell steadily, gleaming off the clear patches of the stone. At once, Nagaira's retainers spread out around the rock, half-assuming a posture of prayer and the other half taking up sentry positions around the clearing as Nagaira summoned a globe of witch-fire and began to examine the rock.

More than once during the trek Malus thought he detected signs of stealthy movement in the trees. The shades were following them, of that he was certain. But why hadn't they acted? Were they biding their time, waiting for an opportune moment far away from Isilvar's men? Standing at the edge of the clearing, he eyed Nagaira and the two Naggorite highborn warily. The witch was oblivious to her surroundings, immersed in the study of the stone, but Fuerlan was almost on the point of panic.

'I've been thinking, sister,' Malus ventured. 'How did our illustrious brother manage to assemble a punitive force to attack Naggor so swiftly? Bale had every reason to believe that we wouldn't see any serious resistance until we were past the Blackwater and I daresay he knows the Hag and its leaders as well as anyone.'

'It would appear that Isilvar is a much more effective leader than anyone imagined,' the witch said absently.

'Or you and he were working together this entire time. Did you warn him of the ark's plans?'

Fuerlan turned to Nagaira, his eyes widening. 'Is that true?'

'Why would I do such a thing, you little fool?'

Malus wasn't certain who she was referring to, but Fuerlan took offence. 'None of this has gone according to plan!' he shouted. 'You never said my army would be destroyed! How am I supposed to control the city without loyal troops?'

An idea suddenly occurred to Malus. Suddenly a number of pieces fit neatly into place. 'You aren't,' he declared, his brows furrowing as he contemplated his theory. 'I do believe you've been betrayed.'

Fuerlan slowly turned to regard Malus. A nervous tic began to pull at his right eye. 'Shut up,' he said. 'You're just trying to turn us against one another!'

Malus laughed in the man's face. 'She and Isilvar have been allies for years, you little wretch! They're both Slaaneshi cultists!' He took a savage pleasure at the look of horror that dawned on the man's face. 'Did she not tell you? But I thought the two of you were betrothed!' He chuckled. 'Don't you Naggorites ever talk to your potential wives?'

Fuerlan turned to Nagaira, his face pale. 'Is this true?'

'Oh, yes,' Nagaira said absently, tracing a finger across an indentation in the stone.

'She means for me to kill the drachau, but who else would benefit from his assassination? Isilvar, of course.' Malus said. 'After he destroys your army he will be lauded as a hero. Then when he returns to the Hag and learns of the drachau's death who will gainsay him if he assumes the throne?' He grinned at the Naggorite. 'I assume you'll be handed over so Isilvar can parade you through the streets during the victory celebration.'

'Shut up! *Shut up!*' Fuerlan was trembling with rage. 'Nagaira, tell him he's wrong. You could never rule beside Isilvar. Only I could make you a queen!'

The witch straightened and turned to face the two men. 'Malus,' she said peremptorily. 'Come here.'

He grimaced as his body lurched into motion, quickly increasing his step to assuage his pride and make it look less like he was his sister's plaything.

Nagaira beckoned to one of her retainers. The hooded figure came forward and presented a familiar wooden box. 'Open it,' the witch said.

He did. Within were the same three relics he'd seen before.

'Do you see the dagger there?' Nagaira said.

'Yes.'

'Excellent. Pick it up and kill Fuerlan with it.'

Malus took the black dagger in his hand. Fuerlan screamed in terror. 'You lying whore!' he cried. The Naggorite raised his sword. 'You think to kill me, son of the Hag? Come ahead, then! I've trained with the finest duellists in the ark–'

His words were cut short by the flat sound of steel striking steel. The Naggorite's mouth still hung open, his eyes locked on Malus several feet away. Slowly, slowly, his gaze fell to the hilt of the dagger jutting from his breastplate. Fuerlan's last breath spilled from his lips in a startled sigh as he sank to one knee and then toppled onto his face.

'An impressive throw,' Nagaira observed.

'Anything to shut him up,' Malus replied sourly.

The highborn watched as a retainer rolled Fuerlan over and used two hands to pull the black dagger from the Naggorite's chest. Malus was struck by the look of utter terror on the man's face. What had he felt in the last moment of his life that had been so awful? Whatever it was, he thought it wasn't half of what the fool deserved.

But where were the shades? He looked anxiously into the woods. Why hadn't they made their move?

Nearby, Nagaira chanted softly and there was a flash of blue light. When Malus looked back at her, she was standing before a hole in the massive rock that seemed to curve downwards into the earth.

The witch turned to him, her eyes gleaming with unnatural light. 'Let us go home, brother,' she said.

FOR A WHILE, Malus began to think Nagaira was lost.

Not that it would have been difficult to lose oneself in the twisting labyrinth known as the burrows. The tunnels ran for miles, twisting and turning back on themselves again and again in a pattern no logical mind could fathom. According to legend, the burrows were centred on Hag Graef, and no one knew how deep into the earth they went.

They were made one winter, several hundred years after the city was built and close to the surface the passageways cut through cellars and sewers alike. The tunnels were home to a fearsome number of vicious predators, from nauglir to cave spiders, but a clever – or desperate – soul could use them to come and go throughout the city without being seen.

Nagaira was well-versed on the layout of the tunnels, or at least those close to the Hag itself. Now, however, she held the sheets of parchment Malus had first seen in her tent, consulting them closely as she led the group on a circuitous path through the burrows. He had long since lost track of time, following her orb of witchfire through the endless tunnels. It could have been hours or days since they left the surface world behind.

The witch appeared to be looking for something, but Malus couldn't fathom what. Every now and again when they reached an intersection she would pause, bow her head and utter an incantation in a language that he couldn't understand yet set his teeth on edge just the same.

Finally, their path led them to a dead end of sorts – a huge pit whose bottom was lost in abyssal darkness. Noxious fumes rose from the blackness, making Malus cough. The air above the pit was still and cold and no sound echoed up from below.

Nagaira stepped to the edge of the pit and peered into the emptiness. Apparently satisfied, she turned and beckoned to one of her retainers. The man stepped forward and drew back his hood, looking at the witch with an expression of serene adoration. She reached up, holding what looked like a glittering ruby in her hand and slipped it between the retainer's lips. 'My gift to you,' she said.

The retainer smiled. 'I sleep in darkness so the dreamer may awake,' he said and stepped into the pit. He fell without a sound.

Nagaira turned from the pit and headed back the way they'd come.

They returned to the twisting tunnels and Nagaira consulted her maps. Some time later they came upon another pit and another of her worshipful followers took her gift and stepped into oblivion.

Malus watched with growing horror as the ritual continued. After the third retainer went to sleep in darkness, he began to feel a charge building in the air. Were these sacrifices Nagaira was making and if so, to what or whom? What did it have to do with her plan to kill the drachau?

In the end, six retainers were given to the darkness. The dank air in the tunnels seethed with built-up power – Malus could feel it shifting and pulsing against his skin like a living thing. It felt as though they had been wandering the labyrinth for an eternity and finally the highborn could take no more. 'Will we walk these accursed tunnels until the fall of Eternal Night?' Malus exclaimed, angry at himself at the unease that was plain in his voice. 'Bad enough you've turned me into your assassin's arrow, sister. Loose me on the drachau or throw me down one of your bottomless pits. I really don't care which any more.'

Nagaira slowly turned to face him. 'Very well,' she said, her tone icy and amused.

She extended her hand at a pile of rubble that covered the side of a nearby wall and spoke a word of power. The air rippled like water at the sound and the pile of stones blew outward, away from the witch's hand. When the dust cleared, Malus saw a ragged hole in the burrow wall and some kind of chamber beyond.

'We have arrived,' Nagaira said.

The witch pointed to the hole and Malus stepped through it as though moving in a dream. Backlit by Nagaira's witchfire, he could tell that he stood in a small, rough-hewn chamber. Pairs of manacles were evenly spaced around the walls, their cuffs hanging open. Near the centre of the room he saw a mound of dusty skeletons, piled between two overturned braziers. On the other side of the chamber another opening hinted at an even larger space beyond.

A chill ran down Malus's spine. He knew where he was.

Nagaira stepped into the room, her light flooding the space with pale green light. She crossed the room, pausing to touch the piled bones and then continued into the revel chamber beyond.

The huge cavern was empty. The holes in the walls where the executioners of Khaine had unleashed their deadly ambush were bricked over and the many bodies had long since been taken away and burned. Malus followed his sister as she walked to the spiral staircase that soared up to the chamber's vaulted ceiling.

'It took me a decade to carve out this place,' Nagaira said. 'I smuggled a score of dwarf slaves from Karond Kar to do the work. A *score*. Imagine the expense.' She laid a hand on the curved balustrade of the stair. 'And that was just the construction. I spent twice that much time and sacrifices unnumbered to build the cult here in the city.' The witch turned to face him. 'All of that undone in a single night.'

Malus stared into her gleaming eyes. 'Shall I pity you, sister?'

'There is no sorcery in the world strong enough to wring pity from your cold heart,' Nagaira snarled. 'And neither will you have any from me.' She raised her hand, pointing to his forehead. 'I know of your ambitions, Malus. I have watched you in the Court of Thorns and seen how you yearned to place the crown of the drachau upon your brow. Now you will destroy those dreams with your own hand. My compulsion is upon you, Malus Darkblade,' she intoned. 'It is written into your flesh and carved into your brain. Go to the drachau's fortress and fulfil it.'

Chapter Twenty-Two
VICTIMS OF FATE

BLOODLUST FLOWED LIKE black ice in Malus's veins.

The hunger to kill caused his muscles to twitch, propelling him ever upward, climbing the curving staircase in Nagaira's wrecked tower and through its ruined entry chamber. Collapsed, partially melted rubble filled the once-grand room and the heavy double doors hung from broken hinges, each propping the other upright by virtue of its massive weight. Malus half-stumbled, half-crawled across the debris-strewn chamber, his body trembling with barely contained power. His limbs felt swollen with unnatural strength, his heart hammering with sorcerous vigour. The highborn's skin burned in thin, razor-edged lines of script as the spell Nagaira etched into his flesh drove him onwards, into the jaws of death.

He threw himself at the tower's double doors with a bestial snarl, sending them crashing to the cobblestones in the courtyard beyond.

Malus staggered into the night air, his chest heaving. He no longer felt his wounds, or the fatigue of days marching and fighting on the road to the Hag. There was nothing but the gnawing hunger to find and kill his prey. If he stood still too long he could feel the urge burning like a coal in his guts, growing fiercer by the moment. Steam curled from his lips as he bared his teeth to the starry sky. It was all he could do not to howl like a blood-starved wolf.

Instead, he tried to harness the fury he felt, turning it back upon itself in order to resist Nagaira's compulsion. The coal searing his insides grew hotter and hotter. He staggered across the rubble-strewn courtyard, past a makeshift bier where scores of Slaaneshi worshippers were taken from the tower and burned only a few months before. The air still hung heavy with the smell of burnt flesh and spilled blood.

The centre of the courtyard contained a broken fountain, its decorative stonework pitted and melted. He fell against the curved lip of the pool and buried his face in the brackish water that remained there.

When Malus pulled his head from the polluted water he disturbed enough of the rubbish floating on its surface that he caught a glimpse of his reflection in the pool's oily surface. His black hair was lank with grime and dried blood, his pale face stained with a layer of mud and gore that transformed him into a leering daemon. He looked back at the twisted visage of the knight from his visions and heard his words once more: *What a witch gives, only a witch can take away.*

Malus ground his teeth in frustration, staring at the knife-like spires of the drachau's tower rising into the night sky. His doom called to him, pulling at every fibre of his body. He could no more turn back and retrace his steps to his sister than he could breathe the turgid fountain water rippling beneath his chin. His stomach roiled at the sensation of snakes writhing within his chest. What terrible seed had his sister planted within him and what horrible fruit would it soon bear?

His mind churned, desperate for a way to escape the witch's compulsion. 'What do I know of damned sorcery?' he seethed. 'I am no witch like my mother!'

The thought struck Malus like a blow between the eyes. Thunderstruck, he slid from the edge of the fountain and sprawled upon the cobblestones. The angry coal of his sister's compulsion burned still hotter, spreading waves of pain through his gut, but for a brief moment the possibility of freedom gave him the strength to endure its pain.

Eldire, he thought. Of course.

He struggled to his feet and studied the drachau's tower once more. The convent was part of the fortress's inner complex of towers, accessible only through a single passage within the central keep itself.

The first challenge was to make it inside the keep. Malus grinned mirthlessly. For a time at least he could make the power of Nagaira's compulsion work in his favour.

THE FORTRESS OF the drachau was almost a city unto itself. Surrounding the central spires of the ruler's keep were a host of subordinate towers that were the residences of the city's highest-ranking nobles and their children. Many of these spires were interconnected by narrow, delicate-seeming walkways, built by dwarf slaves hundreds of years in the past. Few of the subordinate towers connected directly to the drachau's keep, but one exception to the rule was the tower of the city's vaulkhar.

The inner courtyards and the passages of the great fortress were deserted and dark; it appeared as though every able-bodied druchii who could bear arms had been conscripted by Isilvar to swell the ranks of the army in the face of the Naggorite threat. Malus could not help but admire the foresight and thoroughness of his sister's scheme as he stole swiftly and easily though the dark byways of the outer courtyards until he came to the doors of the vaulkhar's tower itself.

There were no guards standing watch before the tall double doors. Malus pressed his hands against the old wood, bound by iron and ensorcelled to be stronger than steel. The highborn smiled cruelly. 'Let me in,' he whispered to the power that boiled beneath his skin. He planted his feet, bent his head and *pushed*.

The fire in his belly dimmed, hardening to a solid knot of unbreakable will. At first the doors did not budge; Malus growled beneath his breath and pushed all the harder. He willed the black ice in his veins to flow outward, into the planks of hardened oak and the iron bolts beyond.

There was a faint creak. Blood leaked from Malus's nose and his limbs trembled from the strain. Somewhere distant, thunder grumbled across the sky.

Malus heard a single, splintering crack. Then another. Beyond the door, Malus heard a faint, muffled shout. He rejoiced in the despairing sound and pushed with all his might, his voice rising into a feral roar. Then, with a rending crash, the bars securing the great doors warped and burst from their moorings and the great portal swung wide with a groan of tortured iron.

A handful of servants cowered in the vaulkhar's grand entry hall, covered in stone dust. They screamed in terror as he stalked across the broken threshold and fled at the sound of his maddened laughter. Malus crossed the great chamber, with its soaring roof and pillars worked in the shape of watchful dragons and climbed the main stairway. He had never seen the vaulkhar's personal apartments, but he knew enough of the tower to be able to find them.

The tower had the feel of a deserted town; hallways and landings were silent and echoing as he climbed the long, twisting staircase. Lurhan's men were gone and Isilvar had yet to create his own large retinue, so there was no one to stand in Malus's way as he smashed open the double doors to the warlord's personal quarters and crossed the modest antechamber to a single, unassuming door.

Malus twisted the iron handle from its fittings and pushed the door open into blackness and rushing wind. Thunder rolled again, apparently nearer this time, though he could see the cold points of stars glimmering in the sky overhead. Knees crouched and head bent against the treacherously shifting wind, Malus trod implacably along the narrow walkway towards the dark bulk of the drachau's keep.

He took the two guards for statues at first; within the sheltered alcove surrounding the drachau's door the wind did not even pluck at the sentries' heavy cloaks. As it was, he was caught by surprise when one of the armoured men took a half-step forward and extended his spear to bar passage into the alcove. The sentry's voice sounded uncertain. Who was this black-cloaked stranger crossing from the tower of the vaulkhar? 'You may not enter, dread lord,' he shouted, trying to be heard over the angry wind. 'The drachau does not wish–'

Malus grabbed a handful of the guard's thick cloak and pitched him off the bridge as though he were no more than a child's doll. His terrified scream was swallowed by the keening wind and another rumbling groan of thunder.

The second sentry froze. Malus reached the man with two swift steps, grabbed the front of the guard's helmet, and smashed him against the iron-bound door at his back. The door shook on its hinges but did not give, so Malus struck it twice more in quick succession. Wood cracked and metal crumpled; the guard in Malus's grip writhed and twitched in his death throes. After a fourth blow the door swing open and Malus tossed his bloodstained ram aside. The guard room beyond was empty. He stood there for a few moments, listening for the sound of an alarm over the torrent of blood thundering in his temples.

All was silent. The coal in his gut seethed, driving him onward. Taking his bearings, he found a narrow set of stairs leading down into the lower floors and headed for the witches' convent.

The drachau's keep was just as deserted as the rest of the fortress. Malus wondered how many druchii servants and men at arms were out in the forests beyond the city, slitting throats and looting the bodies of the Naggorite dead.

THERE WERE ARMED men waiting outside the black door of the witches' convent.

By tradition, the guardsmen standing watch outside the Brides' Door did so with bared steel in their hands: long, two-handed draichs, wrought with sorcery to give their edges supernatural keenness and power. The two guards stood at their customary posts, but were reinforced by four more men carrying the heavy axes of the drachau's personal troops.

Malus fell upon them without a word, drawing his sword and stepping from the shadows in one graceful, silent motion. The first of the axe-wielders fell, blood pouring from a slashed throat; the highborn

plucked the axe from the man's hand and hurled it into the face of one
of the swordsmen near the door.

As the swordsman's brains spilled out on the floor Malus dropped to
one knee and swung his sword two-handed at another axeman's legs.
Knee joints popped and metal tore as he severed both legs in a single,
powerful stroke. Again, the highborn snatched the axe from the dying
man's hand just in time to block a furious downward stroke from the
third guardsman's axe. Fuelled by sorcerous strength, Malus stopped
the blow with ease, swept the man's weapon aside and stabbed his
sword into the man's screaming mouth. Vertebrae popped wetly as the
guardsman collapsed, his spine shorn through.

The last axe-wielder swung wide of Malus, swinging a vicious blow
at the back of the highborn's head. He ducked, feeling the wind of the
keen blade's passing, then slashed at the man with a powerful backhanded blow that caught the guardsman behind his right knee.
Leather, flesh and muscle parted in a fan of bright blood and the warrior collapsed as his leg gave way beneath him. Before the man could
recover Malus continued to turn and severed the guardsman's head
with a sweep of his axe.

A thin whistling of shorn wind was the only warning Malus got as
the last warrior's draich flashed down at his head. He brought sword
and axe into an X above his head and caught the downward blow, staggering slightly at the power of the man's swing. With a roar Malus
surged to his feet, sweeping the draich away with his axe and spinning
on his heel to strike the warrior's head from his shoulders.

He was at the black door before the last body had fallen to the
ground. Unlike all the others, the entry to the convent swung open at
the slightest touch.

The door was bare, flat black marble, unpolished and cold. At his
touch, its stone surface flared with the magic runes laid into its surface
and a portentous shiver trembled through the air. As he crossed the
threshold from the drachau's keep into the sacrosanct tower, he felt the
fire in his belly flare into agonising fury. The black snakes in his chest
squeezed tightly around his heart, making it nearly impossible to
breathe. With all his will, he forced his body to move forward.

Let my skin blacken and my bones crack, he thought, teeth grinding
at the pain. Better by far to suffer and die than become the killing hand
of another!

Beyond the doorway was a short, dimly-lit passage, alcoves to either
side held tall, forbidding statues of crones from ancient times. Pale
light, like moonlight, gleamed faintly at the end of the corridor.

Malus staggered down the passage, biting back his screams as Nagaira's
compulsion ravaged him from within. He all but fell across the threshold
at the far end, into a huge, cathedral-like chamber lit by dozens of glowing

witchfire globes. Huge pillars soared to the arched ceiling high overhead, supporting tier upon tier of galleries that looked out onto the devotional space below. At the far end of the space rose a statue of Malekith himself, the cold husband to the brides of the convent.

Before the statue, surrounded by a small group of novice witches, stood Eldire, the eldest and most potent of the seers of Hag Graef. Her cold beauty and forbidding stare made the majestic statue behind her seem small and ill-formed by comparison. The seer's eyes narrowed at Malus's approach.

A man stood before Eldire, his hands open in supplication. At the sound of Malus's approach he turned, his thin, boyish face taut with apprehension and fatigue.

Uthlan Tyr's face went white with shock as he recognised the tortured face before him and Malus let out a terrible groan as Nagaira's compulsion bore its final, bitter fruit.

Pain and rage exploded inside Malus's chest, spreading through his entire body like searing fire. He felt his veins shrivel and his muscles writhe like serpents – and then they swelled with vigour, pressing against the insides of his armour. It felt as though some rough beast crouched within his skin, freshly awakened and hungry for hot blood. When Malus threw back his head and howled, the voice bore no resemblance to his own.

'Mother!' he cried hungrily, his face transported with murderous ecstasy as he looked upon the object of his sister's compulsion and craved nothing more than to hold her beating heart in his hands. Thunder groaned, reverberating through the stone and earth and the floor shook with the awakened fury of a titan.

He threw himself at his mother, stained blades flashing in the pale light. Uthlan Tyr fell back with a terrified cry, reaching for his sword. The novices raised their hands and spat words of power and black flames arced like lightning into Malus's chest. The bolts traced molten lines across the highborn's breastplate, burning like blades deep into his chest, but the beast within scarcely felt the pain. Women screamed as the highborn plied axe and sword in a deadly dance; blood flew and torn bodies crumpled to the floor. A figure rushed at Malus from the corner of his eye. With a contemptuous flick of the wrist he sent the drachau reeling backwards, clasping his hands to his ruined face and screaming like a child.

The last of the novices leapt at Malus, her fingers transformed into iron knives shimmering with molten heat. He cut her in half with a swipe of his heavy sword and leapt through the shower of blood and organs, hurling himself at his mother.

Eldire was already fleeing beyond his grasp, receding like a shadow before the moon. He roared in fury as she simply dwindled from sight, flowing like smoke across the devotional chamber and receding up a long, narrow staircase at the far end of the room.

The whole tower seemed to shake as Malus took to the stairs, chasing after his mother like a starving wolf. Thunder roared and rumbled as he ran on, blind to everything else but his mother's pale face. Lost to compulsion and battle lust, he was oblivious to bolts of sorcerous fire and flashes of green lightning that lashed and scored his body as witches emerged from their cells and unleashed their power upon the intruder. He could feel his skin melt and his muscles fray, but the beast inside him would not yield. It knit his body together with skeins of black ice and he laughed as pale figures were caught in his path and were cut down by his gore-stained blades. Malus ran through the stark, grey galleries, climbing ever higher and leaving red ruin in his wake.

She was always just out of reach, receding like a distant dream. It seemed as though he would run forever, loping across a black landscape and whetting his bloodlust with the slender bodies of novices and witches alike. His armour was falling away in pieces, the straps burnt through and the joints split by savage spells and a haze of smoke from his own burnt flesh wrapped him like a shroud.

His feet fell upon another stair, this one steeper and narrower than the rest. He climbed in a tight spiral, shrouded by darkness, reaching for the haunting vision of Eldire. Without warning, he emerged from the darkness into roaring wind and rumbles of thunder. Then the blackness surrounding him fell away like a curtain and he found himself on top of the square tower of the convent. Eldire stood less than a dozen feet away, settling like a raven into a spot among a circle of chanting crones.

All at once, Malus realised he was surrounded by witches and stood within a sprawling sigil that covered much of the tower's roof. Without hesitation he leapt for Eldire – just as she spoke a word of fearsome power and he found himself wrapped in chains of fire.

The beast within Malus roared with madness and hate. He writhed and thrashed in the grip of the sorcerous bonds, but the magic of the crones held him fast. The highborn crashed to the stone roof, feeling as though his skin would burst from the fury of the spirit within him.

A shadow fell over him. Eldire rose above Malus, her arms outstretched. She chanted words that froze the air around the highborn and unseen, icy fingers plunged into his chest. He doubled over, screaming in agony as the sorceress bent her will against the furious spirit. For a moment the two wills contested and neither could gainsay the other, but Eldire had the power of the convent to draw upon and slowly but surely the beast's strength began to wane. Shrinking like a flame starved of oil, the beast grew weaker and weaker beneath Eldire's power and Malus felt more of his sanity return. He lay, trembling and insensate, as the fire of the murderous spirit dwindled beyond his ability to ken.

Then Eldire pointed a long finger at Malus's face and spoke another command and his body began to burn.

Lines of transcendent pain burned bright against his skin. He lay rigid, frozen into motionlessness by the sheer power of his suffering. His staring eyes watched tendrils of twisting fire rise from his skin and he realised how they took the shape of symbols.

Eldire was burning Nagaira's compulsion from his body and as it was consumed, Malus's buried memories rose once more to the surface. Illusions faded. No more was he a highborn of Naggor or Hag Graef. No more a general, no more a hero or a leader of men. He was an outlaw, forsaken of his oaths and honour. He was a spent arrow, lying broken on unyielding stone and he wept tears of rage beneath the howling wind.

Malus looked up at his mother. 'You… knew I would come…? '

Eldire fixed her son with a cold, black stare. The ghost of a smile passed across her perfect lips. 'It was foreseen,' she said.

'But why? Why you and not the drachau?'

'Because cities and crowns mean nothing to one such as her, not any more,' Eldire replied. 'She cared nothing for Isilvar's aims, or Fuerlan's, or your own,' the seer explained. 'Nagaira returned to the Hag for the purest of all motives: revenge.'

It was then that Malus noticed the red glow staining the sky. The wind was warm and carried with it the scent of smoke. Thunder rumbled and he felt the great tower shudder beneath him. Slowly, painfully, he rose to his feet. The sigil was dark – indeed, its quicksilver traceries had been burned black in the monumental test of wills. The circle of witches glared at Malus with implacable hate, but no one moved to stop him as he made his way to the tower's edge.

Hag Graef was burning.

From where he stood, Malus could see collapsed buildings and pillars of fire rising high into the night sky. Great arcs of glowing destruction cut through the narrow streets and districts. Steam rose from terrible rents in the earth and the edges glowed with molten stone.

The rumble of thunder came again and this time Malus saw a gleam of pure yellow-white as a ribbon of fire broke the surface of the ground and slid like a ruinous worm through the Blacksmiths' Quarter. Where the ribbon touched, stone melted and split and houses burst into flame. Sparks scattered beneath the worm's writhing course; it took but a moment for Malus to realise the sparks were the burning bodies of people.

'Mother of Night,' Malus gasped. 'What has she done?'

'She has called up the Dreaming Ones,' Eldire said. 'Nagaira has found a spell to disturb them from their sleep and now they vent their rage on the city.'

'Dreaming Ones?' Malus replied. A memory flowed across his mind's eye of Nagaira's acolytes stepping soundlessly into darkness.

'This is an old world,' Eldire said. 'For all that we laugh at the foolishness of humans, we are little older than they compared to the span of this world's existence. Countless races have come and gone; empires rose and fell aeons past that never knew the light of day. An empire of worms, some legends say, that burrowed up from the burning heart of the world.' She joined Malus, looking out at the devastation. 'Some of their children – mere infants – still linger, slumbering in the deep places of the earth.'

'The burrows,' Malus said, suddenly realising how the tunnels beneath the city had been made. 'Will they destroy the city?'

Eldire nodded. 'No stone will remain, which is why you must return to Nagaira and stop her.'

'Stop her?' one of the sorceresses cried. At the witch's outburst the sisters of the coven stepped forward, their expressions twisted with rage.

'If anyone will stop that child it will be us, Eldire,' the witch continued, 'and then you will face a reckoning of your own for the meddling you've done.'

Eldire turned to the witches and her alabaster face twisted with black rage. 'Be still, you worthless hags,' she said and the air suddenly bristled with power. The circle of sorceresses was flung backwards by an invisible wind, the energy so intense their bodies burst into ravening flame upon contact. Their screams were lost in the howling wind and naught but blackened bones remained by the time they were cast off the tower's edge.

Malus watched the display of power with wide-eyed awe. When Eldire turned back to him her face was tight with strain but her voice was calm and even. 'Nagaira sought to slay me because she believed I was the only power within the city strong enough to stop her. She used her power to mould you into her weapon, fuelling the compulsion with the daemon's own energies but erasing the memories of Tz'arkan's possession from your mind so you would suspect nothing – until it was too late.'

The highborn's face twisted into a grimace as he thought of the daemon – he could still feel Tz'arkan inside him, weak but ever-present. Then the import of Eldire's words struck him like a physical blow. 'Tz'arkan!' he exclaimed. 'You knew?'

'Of course,' she said tartly. 'It was my machinations that sent you north in the first place.'

For a moment Malus couldn't speak. Fire bloomed as the city died behind him, but all he could hear were his mother's words, over and over in his mind. 'Nagaira was doing your bidding all along?' he asked.

'I'm certain she thought otherwise at first, but yes,' Eldire replied. Suddenly she reached out and laid a hand on his cheek. His skin stung at even that faint touch, but he did not flinch. Her hand was cold as marble. 'She was just another pawn in a game I have played for a great many years,' she said proudly. 'You are the culmination of all my labour, child. From becoming the Witch Lord's concubine to returning to the Hag with Lurhan, from poisoning Lurhan's wife and youngest child to becoming Nagaira's secret patron – all of these acts and more I have done to make you who you are tonight.'

Malus tried to imagine the tangled skein of manipulations that Eldire described and the sheer magnitude of it took his breath away. 'But why?' he asked. Then he remembered Urial's accusations back on that fateful night aboard the *Harrier*. 'Does it have to do with that damnable prophecy? With my *fate*?'

'You make your own fate, child, much good may it do you,' Eldire snapped. 'Everything in this world is defined by action and reaction. With causes and effects. If you stab a man, he dies, does he not? When a man reacts to the forces of the world around him, he becomes one link in a chain of events stretching back to the beginning of the world. When he is stabbed, he dies. It is his fate. Do you see?'

Malus frowned. 'When a man's actions are shaped by events around him, he is acting according to fate.'

'Exactly,' Eldire said. 'Divination has nothing to do with sorcery, Malus, though it is a talent that few possess. Seers intuitively read the tapestry of cause and effect and discern how future events will unfold. A prophecy is a likely outcome – a consequence of a sequence of events that could occur a year, or ten years, or a thousand years from now. They can happen of their own accord – or be fulfilled by design, if one has the foresight to orchestrate them.'

The highborn's mind whirled, struggling to grasp the implications. 'And you deliberately set this prophecy into motion? You forced this future upon me?'

'Yes.'

Malus reeled, his eyes wide with horror. 'You sent me into Tz'arkan's clutches for the sake of some goddess-forsaken scheme?'

'You are my child, Malus,' Eldire said coldly. 'It is my right to do with you as I wish.'

He struggled with a new spark of rage. 'If you know so much then – if my every step has been charted out by you before I was even born – then tell me, do you see my future?'

Eldire looked out at the burning city. 'Your fate, you mean? Yes.'

'And where does it lead?'

'To your destruction. To fire and misery and enslavement.'

'Mother of Night,' Malus breathed. He fought against a rising tide of despair. 'No. You're wrong, mother. I won't allow it!'

To the highborn's surprise, the seer smiled enigmatically. 'So you reject your fate?'

'Of course!' Malus snarled.

'Good,' Eldire said, nodding to herself. 'It is a simple thing to say, but far harder to achieve. For too long you have let yourself be shaped by the actions of others. You have lived from moment to moment, thinking yourself too swift or too clever to be caught up in the consequences of your actions.' Again, she smiled. 'But all along you have placed yourself at the mercy of fate and look where it has brought you.' She turned, looking out over the burning cityscape. '*She* has learned the lesson, child. And it has made her dangerous indeed.'

Malus considered Eldire's words. 'And if I reject my fate and choose my own path... what then?'

Eldire looked at him, her eyes alight. 'That will be for you to decide,' she said. 'In time, you will see that what has happened to you up to this point has been a gift. You have been given the potential for great power and with the death of Lurhan you have lost everything you have ever valued or desired.' She grasped his hand, holding it up to his face. Malus saw the thick, ropy black veins and the dark, corrupted skin. 'Fate can no longer touch you unless you permit it. Choose your path, lest it be chosen for you,' she said. 'Glories undreamt of lie within your grasp.'

Malus studied his mother for a moment, trying in vain to fathom the purpose behind her black eyes. Slowly, he clenched his fist. 'Very well,' he said at last. 'First, the daemon.'

Eldire nodded. 'First the daemon. Nagaira has the three relics – she is using them as the key instruments of her spell.'

The highborn raised an eyebrow. 'They can be used to cast spells?'

'Not precisely. Their abilities can be used as tools to make certain spells possible,' Eldire explained. 'The relics were more than just possessions wielded by the five sorcerers who bound Tz'arkan – they were integral to the process that bound him to the physical realm. That is why he must have them if he is to undo the binding laid upon him.'

She reached into the sleeve of her robe and produced a slim band of silver. 'Take this,' she said, placing the ring upon his finger. 'After tonight you will not be able to return to Hag Graef. With this ring we can speak to one another whenever the moon is bright. Now you must go,' she said, gently pushing him away. 'Once you have dealt with Nagaira and regained the relics, you must seek the Warpsword of Khaine in the city of Har Ganeth. Step carefully in the City of

Executioners – your brother Urial awaits you there, scheming to make the sword his own.'

'Along with my lovely bride,' Malus said grimly. 'I look forward to the reunion.'

He stepped to the tower's edge, clutching his weapons tightly. The dark courtyard lay thirty feet below. 'By now the drachau has called out the guard. I expect they're searching the convent.'

'Yes,' Eldire said. 'They will be here in a few moments.'

Malus glanced at Eldire and smiled mirthlessly. 'Give him my regards,' he said and leapt into the red-tinged night. His cape billowed like a dragon's wings as he plummeted into darkness.

ELDIRE'S SORCERY ENFOLDED Malus as he fell, slowing his descent until his landing was no harder than stepping off a staircase. He landed without losing a beat and began to run, heading for Nagaira's tower.

On the ground, the rampage of the worms was much more apparent. Waves of heat rose from the paving stones and the ground roiled without warning. Poisonous steam burst from rents in the ground, forcing Malus to cover his face with his cloak and alter his course more than once. Above the groaning of the tortured earth there was a howling sound in the air, as though a cyclone was building overhead. The sky was a deep, bloody red from horizon to horizon as more and more buildings caught fire. From what Malus could see, the damage was still confined to just a few portions of the city, but unless something was done soon Hag Graef would be destroyed.

Once, just short of the witch's tower the entire courtyard heaved up before him and a furnace-like blast of heat drove him back as though he'd run into a stone wall. As he watched in horror an incandescent hump of flesh, larger than a nauglir, rose and fell before him like a sea serpent in a rocky ocean. It sank almost as quickly as it appeared, disappearing in a cloud of poisonous vapour. He saw neither head nor tail and thanked the Dark Mother for small blessings.

It felt as if he spent half the night running through the ruined courtyards of the fortress, until at last he reached his sister's ravaged tower. With all the destruction at work around him he was amazed the half-melted structure still stood – but then he realised that if Nagaira was inside she would have taken precautions to ensure her own survival. The dead savour nothing, as the old proverb went. Revenge was a pleasure for the living.

He reached the open doorway and halted, feeling waves of magic rippling across his skin. Tz'arkan lay almost dormant in his chest – the daemon had been leeched of much of its vitality by Nagaira's compulsion and then Eldire's spell – so he knew that he could not count upon its strength. His armour was wrecked, hanging loosely from his ravaged kheitan. After a few moments' consideration he stripped off the remaining pieces, as they were more likely to hinder his movements than provide real protection from Nagaira's spells. He was only now beginning to feel the pain from his injuries and fatigue was rolling over him in a slow, black tide. If he did not act soon, he wouldn't be able to act at all.

Not that he had the slightest idea how he was going to stop her. The memory of his sister killing one of Fuerlan's men with a single word stood out starkly in his mind. How was he going to deal with that kind of power?

The earth trembled and groaned and a hiss of molten stone filled the air as one of the worms broke the surface again. Malus listened to the terrible sound and the beginnings of a plan took shape. Gripping the hafts of his weapons tightly, he entered the ruined tower.

The entry chamber was deserted, as he expected it to be. Malus crossed to the staircase and descended into darkness.

He hadn't gone more than a few steps before he heard the chanting – six voices working in frenzied chorus, braiding words of power together into an ongoing spell. As Malus crept down the spiral staircase the darkness became tinged with a faint blue luminescence. After a few more turns the light grew brighter, until finally he emerged into the open air high above the cavern floor and saw Nagaira's magical power unveiled in all its terrible glory.

She stood in the centre of a huge sigil carved into the cavern floor. Silver bubbled and boiled along the arcane markings, glowing blue with sorcerous power. In her hand was the Dagger of Torxus and at her feet lay the Octagon of Praan and the Idol of Kolkuth. How they figured into her workings Malus could not guess and didn't care to understand.

Beyond the ring of magic lay yet another, broader circle, attended by Nagaira's six surviving acolytes. It was their chanting he heard as they faced away from his sister and raised their hands forbiddingly against the cavern's shadows.

The highborn nodded, his suspicions confirmed. They were her protection. She raised the worms and her followers kept them from intruding upon her. He bared his teeth and descended the staircase, taking the steps two at a time. By the time he reached the cavern floor he was at a full run, charging for the nearest acolyte. The chanting druchii was almost lost in a trance, concentrating on maintaining his part of the complex chant. At the last moment his eyes widened as he realised his peril and his chanting voice turned to a momentary scream before Malus brought down his axe and split the man's skull.

The chanting stopped and Malus thought he felt their ward collapse, washing over his skin in jagged little sparks of power. Before the first man fell he was charging at the next, howling like one of the damned. The druchii screamed and drew a broad-bladed knife and Malus laughed at the man's helplessness as he severed the acolyte's knife hand with a sweep of his axe and then plunged his sword into the acolyte's chest. He collapsed with a bubbling scream, pink froth gathering on his lips from a punctured lung.

Then the world exploded in pain as an arc of green lightning lashed across Malus's back. He staggered, half-turning to see an acolyte on the other side of the circle drawing back his hand and chanting furiously, preparing another bolt. With a roar the highborn hurled his axe and the acolyte's fierce expression turned to one of shock as the weapon buried itself in his abdomen.

Malus staggered as invisible hands closed about his chest and legs. He struggled out of reflex, as though he could wrestle free of the sorcerous bonds, but only succeeded in toppling to the stone floor. Then a lash of bright green fire ripped across his left hip and leg, tearing a scream of agony from his tortured throat. On the far end of the circle, the surviving acolytes approached him, their hands glowing with malevolent force.

Through a haze of pain, Malus saw Nagaira notice what her acolytes were doing. She turned to see who they were focussing their energies upon. Surrounded by a corona of power, the tone of her chanting voice changed from anger to shock as she saw Malus lying within her protective circle.

'Hello, sister,' he gasped, as the sound of thunder swelled in the chamber. 'There's someone I'd like you to meet.'

Nagaira's voice grew thick with rage – then the wall five yards behind her dissolved in a wave of heat and caustic steam as one of the great worms burst into the chamber. The three remaining acolytes screamed in agony as their bodies burst into flame and Nagaira herself staggered backwards, raising her free hand as if to block the wave of blistering air that swept through the cavern.

With the acolytes' death, the lines of force enclosing Malus vanished. His throat burned at the touch of the poisonous vapour, but he forced his ravaged body to work, lurching to his feet and charging at Nagaira with the last of his strength. He tackled her and they fell together in the centre of the magical circle. She writhed like a snake in his grasp, turning beneath him and spitting words of power. In desperation he closed a hand around his sister's throat, choking off her incantation, then ripped the knife from her clutches and plunged it into her chest.

Nagaira's body lurched and the witch screamed in agony – then she placed her hands against his chest and hurled him into the air with a thunderous blast of power.

Malus landed in a smoking heap several yards away, pain shooting through his body from burns and bruised ribs. He still held the Dagger of Torxus in his hand – the fingers of which were stained with dark ichor instead of blood. The highborn looked to the centre of the magical circle and saw to his horror that Nagaira was climbing slowly to her feet. Black ooze bubbled and spilled from the triangular hole in her kheitan.

The witch howled in rage and pain as she extended her hand and hurled a ghostly black dart at Malus's head. Before it had crossed half the distance to its intended target the spell failed, dissolving into nothingness. Nagaira sank back to one knee and as the highborn watched, the shadows wreathing her face disappeared. He found himself looking into eyes that were orbs of unrelieved blackness. Her face, angular and fierce like her father's, was now a pallid grey. A network of thick, pulsing black veins covered her cheek and throat. Malus's heart went cold with fear. His sister was no longer a mere druchii. She had become a daemonhost!

Nagaira attempted a laugh, a thin stream of ichor running down her chin. 'The dagger cannot take what is no longer there,' she said, laughing mirthlessly. 'I have you to thank, dear brother. Had you not driven me to take shelter in the storms of Chaos I would have never looked upon the Dark Ones in all their terrible glory. And they found me worthy, Malus,' she said, a terrible echo reverberating in her voice that hinted at the unnatural power singing in her veins. 'They have blessed me with power you cannot dream of and they have given me this world to burn in their names.'

Malus stared at his half-sister, suppressing a shudder of dread. 'You do not frighten me, witch,' he said, managing to sound scornful despite his fear. 'For all your power, your scheme has failed. Eldire still lives and the city will be rebuilt. I'm no warlock, but even I know that the Ruinous Powers do not tolerate failure.'

To Malus's surprise, Nagaira laughed. 'You little fool,' she said, her black eyes glittering with hate. 'All goes according to plan, Malus. The only failure here is your own.' The daemon-ridden witch straightened, glaring haughtily at him. 'You have earned yourself a small reprieve, brother. Hide in this pile of stones or flee to the far ends of the earth, if you wish. When the time comes I will find you. Tz'arkan will bow before me and the world will end.' Nagaira smiled, her teeth stained black with curdled blood. 'It has been forseen.'

She placed an ichor-stained hand over her wound and spoke a single, terrible word. Shadows congealed from the air itself, enveloping Nagaira. When they faded, she was gone.

HE WAS ONE more battered, bloody figure making his painful way through the chaos of Hag Graef's rubble-strewn streets. Soldiers and citizens raced past Malus, struggling to put out the many fires burning across the city. No one paid any attention to him as Malus stumbled through the city's northern gate and disappeared into the darkness. Tz'arkan's relics lay like lumps of ice in a bag at Malus's hip.

Two hours later he reached the ruins of the Naggorite camp. The dead lay heaped in great piles and fires still burned where wagons had been tipped over and set alight. Somehow, the devastation amid the charred tents struck him more powerfully than all the broken buildings in Hag Graef. The city would be rebuilt in short order, but the proud army Malus had led from the black ark would never march again.

Malus found Spite at the western outskirts of the camp, not too far from where his tent had stood. The nauglir was feasting on dead flesh, his thick hide marked with half a dozen minor wounds, but he rose from his haunches and trotted immediately over to the highborn when Malus called.

They headed into the woods, retracing Nagaira's steps from earlier in the night. The clearing with the stone outcropping seemed as good a place as any to make camp for a few hours' rest.

After another half an hour's searching he managed to find enough dry wood for a fire. By the time he'd returned to the camp Spite had found more carrion to eat. Fuerlan's body was gone from the waist down, the crumpled plates of his armour spat out into a neat pile nearby. While the nauglir ate, the highborn got the fire going, then sat down on the wet ground and stared into the flames.

He never heard the autarii girl settle down on the other side of the fire. One moment he was alone and the next his gaze was following a dancing tongue of flame and he found himself looking into a pair of violet eyes.

They stared at one another for several moments. A look of mutual recognition passed between them.

The autarii girl leaned forward slightly, her hands on her knees. 'I am Ahashra Rhiel, of the hill dragon clan,' she said gravely. 'My brother was Nimheira.'

Malus let out a sigh. 'I know you well, Ahashra,' he said wearily. He affected a grin. 'Will you share meat and salt with me?'

'You know I will not,' she replied in her dead voice. 'There is a blood feud between us. My brother's shade cries out for revenge.'

'Yes. Of course,' Malus said. 'It's a pity. I would have enjoyed your company under other circumstances.'

Ahashra watched him with cold, catlike eyes. 'No. From this night forward you walk alone, Malus of Hag Graef. I see now how much has been taken from you. You have lost your name and your honour. Your dreams lie in the dust. There is nothing left for you in this life but loneliness, fear and pain.'

Malus frowned. 'So you will not kill me after all?'

The shade studied him silently for several moments. 'No,' she said at last. 'You deserve no such mercy.' Then she rose to her feet and stepped back into the darkness, seeming to vanish before Malus's eyes.

He stared long and hard into the small fire for some time afterwards, lost in thought. Try as he might, he found it difficult to argue with the autarii's logic.

'Blessed Mother, I need a drink,' he croaked, shambling weakly to his feet. Spite had stopped eating and watched him incuriously as he walked over and began rummaging through his saddlebags until his hand closed on his half-empty flask. On his way back to the fire his foot struck a soft lump that bounced away across the rough ground. Fuerlan's head rolled to a stop within the circle of firelight, the look of terror still plastered on his scarred face.

Malus sat down by his cousin's head. The black hair was starting to singe in the heat and he drew the grisly trophy towards him. Ahashra was right. Death meant an end to suffering, but also an end to ambition. He picked up the skull and stared into Fuerlan's sightless eyes. 'We've both lost everything,' Malus said. 'But unlike you, I can build again.'

First, he thought, there was Har Ganeth and the Warpsword of Khaine to consider. Once word spread of the disaster at Hag Graef, Urial might very well think him dead. He smiled. It was an advantage he would make good use of.

Malus set Fuerlan's head on the ground and drew his sword. A single, careful stroke clipped off the top of his cousin's skull. Setting the sword aside, he scooped out what little he found within and tossed it into the flames, then sat back down on his haunches. Grasping the flask's stopper in his teeth, he opened it with a quick pull and poured himself a good dollop into Fuerlan's brain pan.

'To fate,' Malus said, raising the skull in a toast to the darkness and drinking deep.

Glossary

Ancri Dam

Literally 'Heart of the Stag', an arcane talisman worn as a symbol of rule by one of the larger Autarii clans. Thought to possess potent magical powers.

Autarii

Translated either 'Shades' or 'Spectres', it is the name adopted by the druchii mountain clans north of Hag Graef. Superlative woodsmen and hunters, the Autarii are considered cruel and pitiless even by druchii standards.

Caedlin

A mask, usually of silver or gold, worn by highborn citizens of Hag Graef to protect their faces from the fog that sweeps over the city each night. Sometimes called a nightmask.

Courva

Root extract from a plant found in the jungles of Lustria. When chewed, it acts as a stimulant, sharpening the senses. It is believed to increase reflexes. Favoured by duellists and assassins. Mildly addictive.

Drachau

Literally 'Hand of Night', the title held by the six rulers of the great druchii cities as appointed by the Witch King Malekith. The drachau serve as the Witch King's lieutenants and his inner council, each fulfilling a specific function in that capacity. Traditionally the drachau of Hag Graef serves as the general of the Witch King's armies in times of war.

Druhir

The spoken language of the druchii.

Hadrilkar

Literally 'collar of service'. A torc worn by members of a highborn's retinue or followers of certain religious cults or professional guilds. The torc is typically made of gold or silver and etched with the highborn's family sigil.

Hakseer

The 'proving cruise' made by every druchii highborn upon reaching adulthood. Every highborn is expected to lead a yearlong raiding cruise to demonstrate his skill and ruthlessness and establish his reputation in highborn society. Oftentimes, success on the cruise depends on how much the family spends to outfit it. It is not uncommon, for example, for a drachau's son to take to the sea with a small fleet of ships at his command. The commander of the cruise keeps the lion's share of the plunder, as is customary on all raiding cruises.

Hanil Khar

The 'Bearing of Chains', an annual ceremony held in all six of the great druchii cities, where highborn families restate their oaths of allegiance to their drachau and present some form of tribute as a symbol of their fear and respect for him. The Hanil Khar marks the end of the raiding season and the beginning of the long winter of Naggaroth.

Hithuan

The druchii, with their passionate and murderous nature, have evolved a rigid etiquette of social space that allows the highborn to function socially without the near constant risk of bloodshed. Distance is measured in sword lengths; lowborn may not approach closer than three sword lengths (approximately twelve feet) without being summoned, while retainers may stand as close as two sword lengths from their masters. Valued retainers, lieutenants and lower-ranking highborn stand just out of sword reach. The closest, most intimate space is reserved for lovers, playthings and mortal foes. Hithuan does not apply to slaves, as they are expected to shed their blood at a druchii's whim.

Hushalta

A thick, acrid liquid also called 'Mother's Milk', made from plant extracts taken from Tilea and alkaloid substances found in the mountains of Naggaroth. The drink induces a deep sleep, characterized by vivid nightmares and lingering hallucinations after waking, though it also speeds the healing process for the druchii. High doses can result in memory loss and even dementia over a prolonged period of use.

Kheitan

A thick gambeson of leather and cloth worn over a dark elf's layered robes, covering his upper and lower torso. Typically worn beneath a coat of fine mail (in social situations), or an articulated breastplate (in wartime), the kheitan provides both added protection and insulation from the elements.

Maelith

Malevolent spirits, supposedly the ghosts of druchii who offended the Dark Mother and were consigned to haunt the earth until the end of days. They feed on the blood of the living and cannot be harmed save by the touch of cold iron. Occasionally used by powerful sorcerers as familiars and guardians.

Nauglir

Literally 'cold one', the druchii name for the huge, lizard-like predators found in the caverns beneath Hag Graef. Mistaken as large reptiles by humans, the nauglir are in fact a distant relative of the dragon, and are used by the highborn as cavalry and hunting mounts.

Raksha

One of the Autarii's many names for the restless dead. In this case, the name specifically refers to a vengeful ghost that preys upon the living.

Sa'an'ishar

A shorthand of the command 'Shields and spears!' – the standard druchii order for a formation to ready itself for action. Druchii lords often use the phrase as a general command for attention.

Urhan

Literally 'High One', the title of an Autarii clan leader.

Vaulkhar

Literally 'Maker of Chains', a title held by the warlord of a drachau's army. The title comes from the warlord's right of indenture – rather than killing or ransoming prisoners of war, he can enslave them if he so desires.

Vauvalka

Literally 'Shadow-casters', illegal users of the dark arts who can raise angry spirits and inflict them on a druchii's rivals – for a price.

ABOUT THE AUTHORS

Dan Abnett lives and works in Maidstone, Kent, in England. Well known for his comic work, he has written everything from Mr Men to the X-Men. His work for the Black Library includes the best-selling Gaunt's Ghosts novels, the Inquisitor Eisenhorn and Ravenor trilogies, and the Horus Heresy novels, *Horus Rising* and *Legion*.

Mike Lee was the principal creator and developer for White Wolf Game Studio's *Demon: The Fallen*. Over the last eight years he has contributed to almost two dozen role-playing games and supplements. An avid wargamer and devoted fan of pulp adventure, Mike lives in the United States.

THE STORY CONTINUES...

ISBN 978-1-84416-194-2

buy these books
or read
free extracts at
www.blacklibrary.com

ISBN 978-1-84416-195-9